THE COLD COLD SEA

LINDA HUBER

Legend Press Ltd, The Old Fire Station,
140 Tabernacle Street, London, EC2A 4SD
info@legend-paperbooks.co.uk | www.legendpress.co.uk

Print ISBN 978-1-9098785-9-4
Ebook ISBN 978-1-9098786-0-0
Set in Times. Printed in the United Kingdom by TJ International.
Cover design by Gudrun Jobst www.yotedesign.com

Linda Huber grew up in Glasgow, Scotland, where she trained as a physiotherapist. She spent ten years working with neurological patients, firstly in Glasgow and then in Switzerland. During this time she learned that different people have different ways of dealing with stressful events in their lives, and this knowledge still helps her today, in her writing.

Linda now lives in Arbon, Switzerland, where she works as a language teacher in a medieval castle on the banks of beautiful Lake Constance.

Her debut novel *The Paradise Trees* was published in 2013 and she has also had over 50 short stories and articles published in magazines. *The Cold Cold Sea* is her second novel.

Visit Linda at
www.lindahuber.net
Follow her on Twitter
@LindaHuber19

Acknowledgements

The Cold Cold Sea has developed over more than a decade. I can't even count the people who have encouraged me along the way, but thank you all so much.

Thanks also to the team at Legend Press for their help, patience and general hard work.

Thanks again to my sons, Matthias and Pascal, for their IT help; and to Pascal for setting up my website.

Special thanks firstly to Olivia Azoughe, whose four-year-old self was the inspiration for my Olivia in this book; and also to Christine Grant for her invaluable help with police procedure.

And to those in Cornwall who, many, many years ago, gave a Glasgow child unforgettable holidays in the most beautiful place she had ever seen. Writing *The Cold Cold Sea* brought it all back to me: the sights, sounds and smells of Cornwall.

And last but not least, to my army of 'card-people' - keep up the good work!

*To the Mathieson family,
especially my father, Forsyth,
and my brother, Gordon*

Prologue

A glint in the sand caught her eye and she crouched down. It was a beautiful pink shell, exactly like the one she'd found yesterday. She eased it out from under a thick strand of brown seaweed and brushed it gently with one finger. It was covered in sand, it wasn't nice to hold like the other one. She looked round for someone to help, but her dad was right along the beach with his back to her, staring at something up towards the hotel. She hesitated for a moment. The sea was just nearby. She would wash the shell herself and then she would take it home and give it to her Granny. Her eyes shone at the idea.

The sun was hot on her shoulders as she turned towards the water. It was difficult to rush along the loose sand; coarse grains were rubbing the skin between her toes. Nearer the ocean the beach firmed up and she stopped to empty her sandals. It was the only thing she didn't enjoy about the beach, the way sand got everywhere.

What she liked best, of course, was the sea. It was like magic, the way the colour changed all the time. Today it was shining blue in the sunshine, sparkling like the jewels in her mother's ring. She giggled as her toes met the first of the baby waves fizzing up the beach.

The water was cold but it was silvery-clear, rushing up round her ankles and pulling her in to play. She bent over and swished the shell in the sea. Immersed in her task she rubbed and rinsed and rubbed again, oblivious to the cold water creeping up her legs. The shell was cleaning up nicely. It would look so pretty on her Granny's windowsill, lined up with all the other shells they'd collected last year.

Satisfied with her work, she stood up straight, jerking in surprise when she saw that the water was up over her knees now. She could feel the waves swirling round her legs, pulling her this way and that. It felt as if she was wobbling on a trampoline. It would be easier if there was someone to hold her hand. She looked back at the beach.

Both her parents were tiny figures in the distance now, much too far away to hear her if she called. The sea was right here, teasing her. She giggled again as the wash from a distant motorboat slapped and tickled against her thighs. This was better, it was fun again now.

Further out the waves were white-tipped and rolling towards her, and she remembered the picture book she and Daddy had read just before coming here. A fairy tale princess had caught a beautiful white horse on a wave, and rode away to the place where the sea joined up with the sky. If only she could do that too. She stood on tiptoe and walked a few paces to see if there were any white horses nearby.

Quite suddenly the water was deeper, and it was freezing cold too; it was splashing right up over her tummy. A larger wave almost lifted her off her feet and she cried out in panic, sobbing when she realised that she had dropped Granny's beautiful shell. Tears hot on her cheeks and teeth chattering, she struggled to regain her balance then waded a few steps in the direction of where the shell had vanished.

But the shell was nowhere to be seen. The water took hold of her again, pulling at her and pulling and all at once it was right up to her chin and there were no white horses at all, just cold cold water. It got in her eyes and nose and in her mouth, too, when she tried to shout for help.

Salty water was burning in her nose and pulling her down;

the sea was filling her up and washing her away and she couldn't stop it. The whole world was getting smaller... It was so cold. She was floating in cold, white water now, just floating, and then suddenly everything was gone.

Part One
The Beach

Chapter One
August 22nd

Maggie stood in the doorway and stared into Olivia's bedroom. It was tiny, like all the rooms in the cottage, but this one was still. Toys, games... everything in here had been motionless for a week now. Baby dolls vied with Barbies on the shelf, an assortment of soft toys lay strewn across the bed, and Olivia's darling Old Bear was sitting on a wooden chair by the window.

Maggie could hear the sea battering against the cliffs. High tide. The beach would be covered in water now; surging, white-tipped waves beneath a flawless blue sky. How beautiful Cornwall was, and how lucky they were to have a holiday cottage here. That's what they'd thought until last week, anyway. If this had been a normal day they'd have been picnicking on the clifftop, or shopping in Newquay. Or just relaxing around the cottage, laughing and squabbling and eating too much. All the usual holiday stuff.

But nothing was normal any more, and Maggie knew that tomorrow was going to be the worst day yet. The twenty-third of August. Olivia's birthday. Right now Maggie and her daughter should have been making the cake Olivia had planned so happily, the raspberry jam sponge with pink icing and four pink and white candles.

No need for any of that now. Maggie stepped into the room, grabbed the pillow from the bed and buried her face in it, inhaling deeply, searching for one final whiff of Olivia, one last particle of her child. But the only smells left were those of an unused room: stale air, and dust.

'Livvy, come back to me, baby,' she whispered, replacing the pillow and cradling Old Bear instead, tears burning in her eyes as she remembered holding Olivia like this, when Joe had whacked her with a plastic golf club on the second day of their holiday. She'd had two children then. She hadn't known how lucky she was.

'I didn't mean it, I didn't.'

Her voice cracked, and she fell forwards, her kneecaps thudding painfully on the wooden floor. How could she live on, in a world without Olivia?

'I'm sorry, Livvy, I'm sorry!'

She had barely spoken aloud all week, and the words came out in an unrecognisable high-pitched whimper. Bent over Old Bear on the floor, Maggie began to weep. Her voice echoed round the empty cottage as she rocked back and forth, crying out her distress.

But no-one was there to hear.

Chapter Two
August 15th

Phillip Marshall drove as swiftly as he dared to the top of the hospital complex, and then slowed down for the often futile crawl round the oncology car park. Spaces here were like gold dust and he was late; he'd fallen asleep after lunch. The heat of the Californian summer wasn't conducive to staying awake when you were blobbing on the sofa digesting a hamburger.

But thank God, there was a space just by the side entrance. So one small thing had gone right today. Phillip reversed in for a quick getaway after his visit, and then jogged towards the building. Gran didn't deserve to be kept waiting, and it was ten minutes into visiting time already.

'Hi Phillip. Edwina's having a scan, but she won't be long.' Joe the charge nurse clapped Phillip's back as he entered the ward. 'And a single's available now so we moved her this morning. Room Thirty-Five.'

Phillip winced. 'Available' on an oncology ward probably meant that someone had died in the night. He grinned his thanks and continued down the corridor. Gran's new room was right at the far end, that was a good sign, wasn't it? If she had been critically ill surely they'd have kept her nearer the nurses' station. Phillip pushed the door open and found himself staring into a small room with a huge window. The

Pacific stretched out before him. God he hated the sea. Today of all days he could have done without being so brutally confronted by it. He slumped into a hard chair and stared at the empty bed.

It was Hailey's birthday. On the fifteenth of August, five years ago today, he and Jennifer had become parents. It had been the best day of Phillip's life. He had promised a tiny little bundle cradled in his arms that he would give her all the fatherly love and attention he'd never had himself. For a while it had worked out like that, too.

'Phillip, darling!'

He leapt to his feet as the nurse pushed Gran's wheelchair up to the bed. She was paler today but her eyes were bright. Phillip hugged her carefully, feeling the fragile ribs though the towelling robe and realising with a jolt that he was going to lose her soon. She patted his back and held on a few seconds longer than she normally did. She was remembering Hailey's birthday of course, she might have cancer of God knows where but there was nothing wrong with her mind.

He helped the nurse settle her back into bed and then pulled up a chair.

'Phillip, are you okay, darling? Have you called Jennifer?'

Gran took his hand and Phillip squeezed back. How brave she was, not a word about the illness or the pain she'd been in. He shrugged.

'I called a few times, but her mobile is switched off and she's not answering the landline. I left messages. Don't worry, she's fine now. She'll be out with Thea, or maybe Bea's made up with her and taken her down to Torquay.'

Gran nodded.

'I hope so. She shouldn't be alone today.'

Phillip closed his eyes briefly. Life was cruel. No, Jennifer shouldn't be alone today, she should have been organising a birthday party for an overexcited five-year-old. That wasn't happening, and he should be with her. His planned couple of weeks in the States had been stretched when Gran had twisted

13

her ankle, and then yesterday she'd been admitted here with terrible stomach cramps. Phillip wasn't hopeful that he'd be able to return to England at the weekend as he'd intended. He couldn't leave his Gran now, not when she looked so frail. He owed her so much. She had been there for him when his parents had died, she had given up her life here to look after him in England. Now she was home again and it was his turn to help her.

'I'll catch her tomorrow. It's too late to phone again today, it's nearly midnight in England now,' he said, managing a smile to show her that he was alright too.

Gran dozed off and Phillip sat watching her breathe. Was she going to get over this? Go into remission and have a bit more time to enjoy life? And what the hell was he going to do? He couldn't stay in LA indefinitely with his home and business in England, not to mention Jennifer who was maybe 'fine' but it wasn't a stable fineness. God knows he should be with her today and not sitting here in sunny California. He'd felt bad about leaving her for the two weeks he'd originally planned and now he'd been gone twice as long. Guilt cramped his stomach and the taste of his lunchtime hamburger rose into his throat.

The door opened and Jeff Powell, the head oncologist, beckoned Phillip out to the corridor.

'It's bad news, Phillip,' he said. 'Two tumours, one on the stomach and one attached to the large bowel. And I'm afraid both are inoperable. We'll give her radiotherapy to try and shrink them, try and buy her more time. I'm really sorry.'

Phillip swallowed. It wasn't unexpected, but it was still tough.

'What about chemo?' he said, but the doctor shook his head.

'It's too advanced for mild chemo, and the strong drugs are an enormous strain on the elderly. She's eighty-five, we have to think of quality of life. We want her last few months to be comfortable.'

14

Phillip went back into the room and lowered himself into the chair in the corner. So now Jennifer needed him in England and Gran needed him here, and he couldn't possibly jump back and forth between them. He would have to persuade Jennifer to overcome her fear of flying and come out here for a few months. It was the only way.

A helicopter swooped down towards the landing spot by the Emergency Room and Phillip went to the window to watch as it landed. Just fifty yards beyond it was the beach. Golden sands. Happy holidaymakers. Summer at Winchester Beach.

Hailey would have been five today and Gran was going to die.

Phillip leaned his head on the cool glass. He made no move to wipe away the tears that were dripping from his jawbone and merging into a salty pool on the window ledge.

Chapter Three

She would never forget the moment they'd first realised Olivia was missing. Blind panic had taken possession of her head, her vision blurred and the taste of bile rose into her mouth. It was every parent's worst nightmare come true.

They were into the second week of their holiday; the children were suntanned and happy, Colin spent his time tanking up fresh Cornish air, and Maggie herself was in her element. Wall to wall sunshine and nothing to do but enjoy it.

They'd been on the beach. It was a real picture postcard place of dark cliffs and golden sands. The sea – beautiful surges of blue and green and white – was creeping over the rocks where the headland jutted into the ocean. It would wash into the two deep caves there and then slowly eat its way up the beach until it was battering against the cliff beneath the cottage. Dozing on her towel within the ring of rocks keeping the stiff breeze at bay, Maggie could hear Joe's high-pitched little voice getting nearer, chattering non-stop, and Colin's deep tones answering him. She grinned drowsily - family approaching at speed. Well, that was the peace and quiet over for a bit. Better get ready for the onslaught.

'Mum! Did we bring the biscuits?'

Joe ran into the ring and flopped down.

'When did I ever come to the beach with all you vultures and no biscuits?' said Maggie, smiling and handing him the packet. 'How were your rock pools?'

Joe bit into a ginger snap, kneeling beside her.

'We saw *eight* crabs! And we rescued two baby jellyfish that'd got stuck on the sand. We carried them down to the water on my spade and they just swam away.'

Maggie listened, nodding seriously and loving him for his enthusiasm. He was such a good boy, he cared so much about his pools and the creatures that lived there.

She poured coffee from the flask and handed a beaker to Colin. The beach was deserted. Now that the hotel further along was closed, the only people who used this beach were those staying in the five cottages on the clifftop. Today, they were the only ones down here. Maggie looked across to the sea, now lapping into Smuggler's Cave, and saw that Borrower's was almost completely under water too. How long had she been asleep?

'Where's Livvy?' said Colin, looking around.

Maggie stared. For a split second she froze, then relaxed. It was a joke, of course.

'Gone to visit the Leprechauns, maybe?' she suggested in a loud voice. 'Come on, Livvy-lovey! Come and get a biscuit!'

There was silence for a moment, apart from the gulls and the waves crashing on the rocks further down the beach. Maggie sipped her coffee, then glanced up to see Colin gaping at her. He jumped to his feet and looked around the rocks.

'She's not here,' he said, his voice urgent.

'Well, she was with *you*,' said Maggie. 'Where did she go when you came back?'

Colin was glaring at her now and Maggie saw that his lips had gone white round the edges. That was the moment, the split in time when she'd realised that something was terribly wrong. In less than half a second her life changed into something more like a crappy sensationalist TV film on a channel with more ads than programmes.

'What are you *talking* about? You know she wasn't with

17

us, she hates the rock pools,' said Colin, his voice rising. 'She was with *you*.'

Maggie's stomach lurched painfully.

'But she went across to you about twenty minutes ago, maybe. Or less, I don't know. We built a sandcastle and then she didn't want to play here anymore, and I said she could go and join you! Oh my God!'

She struggled to her feet, staring around wildly, legs buckling after sitting so long. The beach was still devoid of people. There was nobody here to distract Olivia or take her to play behind some rock. Nothing was moving over at the rock pools; no pink and white t-shirt was running around between the rocks.

'You let her go by herself?'

Colin's tone was accusing, and Maggie snapped back.

'Well the beach was bloody deserted, wasn't it? She couldn't have got lost… '

'Mum?'

Joe's voice was small and afraid, and Maggie hugged him to her side. Colin leapt out of the ring.

'She must have gone back to the cottage. I'll go up. You search down here.'

He raced off towards the cliff path and Maggie stood still for a moment, forcing back the panic. This was her fault. What had she been thinking, sending Livvy across the beach by herself? She'd been annoyed, that was what, miffed because a three-year-old had wanted to join her father and brother instead of making sand pies with her mum. Christ, how pathetic.

Maggie pressed her lips together. There would be time to worry about her own inadequacies later, right now they had to find Livvy. *Had* she gone back up the cliff path? It didn't sound likely, but there was nowhere else…

Except… Livvy *wouldn't* have gone into the water, they could be sure of that. She wasn't a fan of the breakers that crashed up the beach. But the waves weren't big today, the sea looked relatively calm. Yet back up the path seemed equally unlikely. The steps zigzagging steeply through a crevice in the cliff face were hard work for three-year-old legs. What on earth could have tempted Livvy to go back up all by herself?

Frantically, Maggie looked from left to right along the beach, horror swirling into her head when she saw that both caves were filled with water now. If Olivia had gone into one of them…

Swallowing her panic, Maggie tried to focus her thoughts, forcing herself to think clearly. When Olivia left she had been sitting in the ring drinking coffee, facing in that direction. She *would* have seen her if she'd run down to the caves. So she *must* have gone the other way, towards the cliff path and the rock pools. Or had she gone further along the beach? Maggie stood on tiptoe. The rocks and their pools were the remains of what had once been another headland, a couple of centuries ago. Beyond was another beach, part of it belonging to the old hotel, the rest stretching back towards town.

Grabbing Joe's hand, Maggie ran as fast as she could in the irritating, sliding sand. Past the cliff path, around the rocks. More than half of them were under water now, and Maggie shaded her eyes, straining to see anything that might be a pink and white t-shirt amongst the waves.

Nothing. Thank God.

Keeping a tight hold of Joe, she ran on, searching round crevices in the cliff.

Nothing. The beach was shrinking rapidly, waves licking round the sandcastle she and Olivia had built.

'Look, Mummy! Isn't it beautiful? We'll put shells round the top and that can be the princess' tower. I'm the princess and you're my servant girl. Joe can be boot boy and Daddy's the king, of course.'

Maggie swallowed painfully. At the time she'd been hurt. It was one of those ridiculous little knife-thrusts that kids attack their parents with so expertly. Daddy was the king and she herself was a servant girl. It had taken a moment before

19

she'd been able to smile; she could remember thinking that it might have been worse, she could have been the wicked witch. And now Olivia could be lying unconscious among the rocks. She could have fallen and banged her head. And the tide was creeping up and up...

Quickly, Maggie climbed up a rock and gazed over to the hotel beach, where a row of brightly painted beach huts stood at the edge of the sands. Was it even remotely possible that her daughter had clambered all the way over there?

But if Livvy had been there Colin would have noticed her as he went back up. It was only the section of beach right underneath the cliff that you couldn't see from the path and she'd just run all the way along it. So Livvy *must* have gone up to the cottage.

Still dragging Joe behind her, Maggie ran back towards the cliff path, her heart thumping painfully at the unaccustomed exertion.

'My legs won't go any more,' said Joe, tears tracking through sand on his face.

Maggie stopped. There was no use rushing, Colin was up there already. And there was simply no other place that Livvy could be. She made herself slow down and helped Joe along the path, her mind screaming in frustration that he couldn't go faster.

Back on the clifftop she saw immediately that no-one was there. The car was gone.

Her breath ragged, Maggie ran down Cliff Road. Some of the neighbours would help them search. Three of the other cottages were occupied this week, but today no-one was at home. Maggie stood still for a moment, her legs shaking helplessly. What could she do? What was there left to do?

Maybe Colin had tried to phone her. Maggie ran inside and grabbed her mobile, charging in the kitchen. No new messages. So their daughter was lost and Colin was driving around searching for her. Her darling, infuriating, wonderful Olivia was missing.

At that moment their pale green Opel bounced along the uneven track and into the parking space beside the cottage. Maggie ran out to meet it.

Colin almost fell out, hope illuminating his face when he saw her, then disappearing to make way for blank fear when he realised that she and Joe were alone.

'She's not on the beach,' whispered Maggie. 'The tide's coming in… '

'I went as far as the crossroads,' said Colin. 'She wouldn't have got any further.'

They stared at each other, and Maggie felt the tightness in her middle expand as it shifted, burning its way up. She turned behind a nearby hydrangea bush and vomited.

'Mummy, Mummy!'

Joe was crying now, but all Maggie could do was hold her middle and retch. Painful sobs rose from her throat as Colin, his face expressionless now, reached for his mobile and dialled 999.

Chapter Four

At the time it seemed as if the police took forever to get to Cove Cottage, but in reality they arrived just ten minutes after Colin's call, blue lights flashing as they turned into Cliff Road. Two uniformed officers got out and walked towards them. Maggie stared. Only two policemen?

She had spent the last ten minutes hunched on a rock at the top of the cliff path, staring down at the waves rushing up the beach. Colin had binoculars trained round the cove, the sands, the cliffs. Maggie shivered. Livvy wouldn't go into the sea, she couldn't swim, she didn't even enjoy the cold, salty water.

A terrible train of thought started in Maggie's head. Maybe Livvy *had* gone down to the water. Maybe she'd wanted to wash the scratchy sand from her feet before joining Colin. One of those Cornish breakers might have wrapped itself round Livvy's three foot one inch frame and swept her out to sea. A picture flashed into Maggie's head, Olivia sprawled on anonymous rocks; waterlogged, sightless eyes empty and staring. This normal, happy-family day had turned into the biggest nightmare imaginable, the kind you tried so hard to wake up from but somehow you never could. For the first time since Livvy had existed, Maggie didn't know where her daughter was.

And Colin had ignored her completely since making the

emergency call. Maggie felt loose inside; the sour taste of sick was still in her mouth and although she could feel the sun on her neck, her arms and legs, she was cold.

Another ghastly thought crashed into Maggie's head and she almost fell off the rock. It was the most appalling thought of all and yet so logical that she didn't know why she hadn't thought it right at the start.

'Col, you don't think she's been… she's been taken, do you?'

It was the worst thought of all. She hadn't watched Olivia this morning and in those few moments… Olivia could be in the clutches of some pervert right now and it would all be her fault.

'Fuck,' said Colin, staring along the road to the hotel about three hundred metres away.

Maggie raised clasped hands to her mouth. Today was Sunday, so none of the usual crew of construction workers were banging around there. The hotel was empty.

'Mr and Mrs Granger? I'm Sergeant Craig Wilson and this is Constable Tim Davidson. Your little girl hasn't turned up?'

'No. We don't know if she's lost or taken, please, you must do something quickly, please!'

Maggie couldn't hold her tears back. The two men glanced at each other and the younger one took Joe's hand and spoke to Maggie.

'I'll just take your boy over here while you talk to Sergeant Wilson. What's your name, son? Would you like to see inside the police car?'

Maggie nodded to Joe and Tim Davidson led him away.

'I won't say "Don't Worry," but nine times out of ten lost kids are exactly that, and we soon find them,' said the sergeant.

He rattled off a few quick questions and Colin answered. Maggie relaxed slightly. This was obviously routine to the policeman, he had all the right questions at his fingertips. Surely they would soon find Livvy.

The sergeant stared at them for a few seconds and then cleared his throat.

'Right. I'll report all this back to the station. We're going to need assistance. If you'll just wait here in the meantime.'

He strode across to the car. Maggie stood motionless as Colin raised his binoculars again. Joe was sent back and he pressed himself against Maggie's side, his face blank.

A few minutes later another car swung into Cliff Road. This time the occupants were plain-clothed: a middle-aged man with a tired, weather-beaten face and wearing a grey suit, and a younger woman clad in black.

'Mr and Mrs Granger? I'm Detective Chief Inspector Howard Moir and this is Detective Sergeant Amanda Donnelly. A helicopter is on its way to help search for your daughter and the coastguards are out now too - look, there's the boat coming round the headland. A land search party's being organised as well.'

He walked a few steps to the side and spoke tersely to his uniformed colleagues, then turned back to Maggie and Colin.

'You understand it's most important to get the sea search going as quickly as possible.'

Maggie pressed her hands to her chest. It was a relief that something was being done, but - the sea? She watched as the coastguard boat began to move round the edge of the cove, as near to the cliffs as it could get.

A helicopter appeared further down the coast, flying towards them and then quite suddenly sweeping down low over the water, right along the beach beyond the hotel and then back out to sea again.

Maggie's knees began to tremble and she could hardly stand up. She pressed both hands down on Joe's small shoulders, aware that she was hyperventilating. Colin was staring at the helicopter too. He made no effort to touch her.

'Mr Granger, I think your wife…' started Howard Moir.

Maggie stumbled the two steps towards Colin and he hugged her to his chest. All she could hear now was Colin's heartbeat and the thuka-thuka-thuka throb of that helicopter engine; she could feel it all the way inside her. She moved to get a tissue from her bag and Colin immediately let her go.

The next question was unexpected.

'Have you been inside since Olivia went missing?'

'Only to check she wasn't there,' said Colin, and Maggie nodded.

'I went in for my bag. For my phone.'

'And apart from yourselves, who saw Olivia this morning?'

Maggie froze. It sounded like something from a murder mystery.

Colin's voice cracked with fury.

'You cannot seriously think… '

'I'm sorry,' said Howard Moir steadily. 'I have to ask. Let's just get it over with and go on.'

'Colin and Livvy went into Newquay for croissants this morning,' said Maggie dully. 'The woman in the shop gave Livvy a biscuit.'

'And the neighbours saw her later, when we were setting off for the beach,' said Colin. 'They were in their garden and we chatted for a moment.'

'Good,' said Howard. 'So what happened on the beach?'

Maggie moved towards Colin but he moved away, and she folded her arms to stop her hands trembling.

Howard was looking at her, his face neutral.

'Colin and Joe were looking round the rock pools and Livvy and I were over at the other side,' she said, trying to keep her voice steady. 'We played in the sand and then we went back to the rocky ring for biscuits, and Livvy wanted to go to her dad and I - I said she could… '

It sounded so polite when she said it like that. But the guilt of those few moments was still niggling away inside her. She hadn't been kind to Olivia.

'I want to go to Daddy.'

The same whine for the hundredth time, and Maggie felt her patience desert her. This was her holiday too, and there

25

was nothing in the marriage contract that said she had to be the one looking after crabby daughters all the time. Colin could do his bit now.

'Oh, for goodness sake, on you go,' she said, spreading her towel inside the ring. 'But they might not be very pleased to see you, you know.'

Olivia had dashed off across the beach without a backward glance. Maggie shivered.

'And then?'

They were looking at her, these police officers, what were they thinking? Had they noticed her guilt, seen how much she regretted what had happened?

Maggie took a deep breath.

'I watched her start across the beach and I could see Col and Joe at the rocks, they weren't far away. But I… '

Her voice trembled and broke, sobs welling up in her throat.

'I didn't watch her all the way round. I - I sat down and had a cup of coffee!'

Sheer terror doubled her up, and she tore at her hair, hearing her own voice moaning. *Was* Livvy in the sea? This time Colin did take her in his arms, and she clutched the front of his t-shirt, fighting for composure.

Howard bent towards them.

'I know how difficult this must be,' he said quietly. 'But we need an accurate picture of what happened. That way, we can conduct the search more efficiently.'

One of the uniformed officers approached and murmured in Amanda Donnelly's ear.

'We can go inside now,' she said to Howard, and Maggie flinched.

They had been searching inside the cottage. Looking for signs that Olivia had been hurt in some way. She led the way into the tiny living room and sank down on the sofa beside Colin. Howard sat opposite, looking expectantly at them.

Maggie forced herself upright and scrabbled in her bag for another tissue. She had to talk to this man, help him find Olivia.

'I was looking out to sea at first,' she said, wiping her eyes. 'I was in the rocky ring but I could see the caves. The water was just up past Borrower's. So I know Livvy didn't go in there.'

'Good,' said Howard. 'But you couldn't see the whole sea line from where you were sitting?'

Maggie shook her head, trying to breathe calmly. It was impossible.

'I'd have noticed if she'd run down to the sea,' said Colin. 'Joe and I were wandering from pool to pool. I did see her at one point, dancing about with Maggie, and I'm *sure* I'd have noticed if she'd clambered over the rocks to get further along the beach. So she *must* have come back up here.'

'Mmm, yes,' said Howard, and Maggie could hear the doubt. Sadness, pity and professional police manners were mingling in his face.

'How much time passed between you noticing Olivia on the beach, and realising that she was gone?' Amanda Donnelly asked Colin.

Colin shrugged. His mouth was still white round the edges, and Maggie saw a nerve twitch repeatedly at the corner of one eye.

'Fifteen, twenty minutes?'

Howard nodded.

'Do you have a recent photo of Olivia?'

Maggie reached for her handbag and gave him the snap she carried in her purse. Olivia, tousle-haired and happy, beamed out at them all. A birthday girl with her cake, a 'sea' cake with green and blue marzipan waves and three candles. It wasn't very recent but it was the only one she had here.

'Thanks. What was Olivia wearing today?'

'A pink and white t-shirt, pink shorts and blue plastic sandals. And her hair's longer now.'

'There are recent photos in here,' said Colin, handing over his phone.

Maggie felt a kind of numbness start inside her. She sat

back, grateful as it worked its way up her body, taking over from the pain.

The sound of cars and voices came from the end of the lane. The search party had arrived.

'I want to go with them,' said Colin. 'If they find Livvy I want to be there too.'

Howard glanced at him and then at Maggie, his face expressionless. 'You should stay here, Mrs Granger,' he said. 'In case she's found elsewhere. Detective Sergeant Donnelly will stay with you.'

A grim-faced crowd had gathered, some policemen and others in ordinary clothes. Most were armed with long sticks, and stood waiting quietly for instructions. The lane was full of cars. Maggie stood in the doorway and watched as Colin strode off with the first group of searchers, hands deep in his pockets.

There was nothing to do but wait. Policemen were searching along the lane, peering into the other cottages and opening garden sheds. They had dogs and Maggie had given them Olivia's pyjamas for the animals to sniff.

She perched on the front garden wall, massaging her middle, where the muscles were aching as if she'd done a hundred sit-ups. After a moment Joe joined her, and she hugged him close.

'Oh, Joe, love. My poor sweet boy.'

He burst into noisy tears and Maggie held on to her remaining child as tightly as she could.

The numbness inside her spread out again. It was as if her body knew that she couldn't cope with so much fear. She stared down the road towards town, willing a small pink and white t-shirt to appear. This was the kind of thing that happened to other people and then you read about it in the newspaper. *Child (3) missing from beach - Search for Olivia, (3), missing since... - Where is Olivia (3)?*

What might be happening to Olivia right now? Maggie leapt to her feet, and lukewarm coffee splashed over her legs as the half-empty mug she'd been holding shattered on the stony ground. Clutching her middle, she retched violently. Joe began to cry again.

Amanda patted her back. 'Try to keep calm. The search parties might find her quite quickly, you know.'

Maggie nodded, forcing herself to breathe, in and out. *The search parties might find her quite quickly.* That was something to hold on to.

The hours passed slowly. Maggie sat watching Joe push his cars up and down the garden path. Amanda was still with them, playing with Joe, and Maggie wondered suddenly if the younger woman was actually there to make sure no harm came to her son.

It was late afternoon when Colin came home.

'Nothing,' he said heavily. 'We went right along the cliff as far as the river and back up the gorge. Another party's going out again now. I - oh God, Maggie, where is she?'

Maggie took him in her arms, and for a few moments they stood there, hugging silently. But there was no comfort that either of them could give the other.

At six, Howard returned.

'Nothing yet,' he said. 'There's no sign of Olivia, not in the sea or on the clifftop or any of the other places we've searched. No-one we've spoken to has seen her today and no-one has noticed anything unusual. The dogs were taken through the hotel but found nothing. The search will continue, of course, but at the moment there's just no trace of her. An officer from the Special Investigations Unit is here now to interview your son; a social worker will be present at the interview too. You'll both have to come to the police station with me to make an official statement now. We'll bring you back afterwards.'

Numbly, Maggie stood up. So now her son was to be interviewed by the police while she had to report her daughter missing. She caught sight of herself in the hall mirror as she passed. She looked twenty years older at least.

Chapter Five

This is *not* happening, thought Maggie, sitting limply on a plastic chair in the cheerlessly furnished interview room. It was all so grey and cold, and the strong smell of bleach was making her eyes water. Left alone with a policewoman, Maggie sat staring at her hands. She had picked her nails right down to the quick. Nothing in her life up until today had prepared her for this; there was no past experience she could draw on now to help her.

She became aware of her clothes - crumpled t-shirt and old denim shorts, stained now with sand and sweat and vomit. What a state she was in. But that wasn't important.

Was Olivia still alive? Or in the sea? Washed up on some rock, being picked at by gulls? Or was she locked up somewhere, terrified?

Footsteps sounded in the corridor, and she heard a man's low voice.

'A hundred to one she's in the water.'

The answering murmur was clearer.

'Well, if she's not, something a whole lot worse has happened to her.'

It was impossible for Maggie to feel more frozen. She sat stiffly on her plastic chair until Howard came back in with a woman. He introduced her, but the woman's name didn't register in her mind. The first WPC closed the door with a bang that echoed down the corridor.

Maggie told her story again. There were more questions this time.

Exactly what happened that morning?

'I don't want to go to the beach, I don't like rock pools. Why can't we go to the funfair?'

Maggie tried to sound positive, after all, she fully sympathised with her daughter's dislike of creepy-crawly crabs and limpets.

'I know darling, and we'll go to the funfair this afternoon, I promise. But the tide will be too far in later for the pools.'

'Joe always gets to do more things with Daddy.'

Olivia's voice couldn't possibly have been more petulant and Maggie felt her patience wane.

'Oh Livvy, that's nonsense, sweetie. You know Daddy enjoys doing things with you both,' she said, forcing herself to sound upbeat. 'Anyway, don't you like being with me, too?'

'But that's not special,' said Olivia, with her almost-four-year-old's brutal logic. 'You're always there.'

The fate of the stay-at-home mother, thought Maggie, wryly acknowledging the little twist of pain inside her. She had always felt that she was lucky, not everyone could afford to stay at home with their children. But somehow, by devoting herself to Joe and Olivia, she had become 'not special'.

Leading Olivia down the cliff path, Maggie deliberately tried to look on the bright side. Wait until she gets to puberty, she told herself. Then you'll learn all about foul moods. And Livvy was a happy little soul most of the time, look how she was chattering away again now. 'Being with Daddy' was forgotten for the moment.

'Off you go and do your pools, you boys,' she said, when they were all standing on the fine yellow sand. 'We'll camp in the ring.'

Joe dashed off towards his favourite rock pools beneath the cliffs, followed by Colin. Looking down at Olivia, Maggie saw that her bottom lip was trembling again.

31

'So you and Olivia were left alone?'

Maggie hesitated. There was a definite edge to the other woman's voice.

'Yes. We made a sandcastle and then… '

'And then Olivia "went to join her father" - but she apparently ran off instead. Has she ever run away before, Mrs Granger?'

God, no, of course not. She's not even four yet, she's not at the running away stage. Maggie heard the words in her head as clearly as if she'd actually spoken them, but all she said was 'No.' Even in her own ears she didn't sound convincing.

'Why didn't Olivia choose to stay with you, if she didn't like the rock pools?'

Maggie bit her lip. 'She wanted to be with her daddy. You know what kids are like. She was cross because Col and Joe enjoyed the rock pools and she didn't. That's all.'

The detective didn't look as if she knew in the slightest what kids were like. She stared at Maggie, and Maggie flinched both at the tone of the other woman's voice and at the question.

'And were you cross too, Mrs Granger?'

Maggie picked at her nails again, determined not to break down in front of this woman. 'No. Well, I was a bit annoyed because she wouldn't stay with me. She's such a Daddy's girl just now. She said I was not special.'

'Ah,' said the detective, and Maggie winced again.

Oh, God, she shouldn't have said that, she loved having a little girl. And they had started trying for number three. How Livvy would enjoy helping with a baby. It would be a real mother-daughter thing for them. Dear God they just had to find her Livvy safe. Why wasn't Howard asking the questions anymore? And what the fuck had all this to do with finding her daughter? Shouldn't they all be out searching, not sitting about here asking misleading questions?

'And when Olivia went to join her father you didn't go with her? And you didn't watch her all the way?'

The insinuation was clear - she was a God-awful mother. Which of course was absolutely correct. She was to blame for whatever had happened to Olivia. Should she ask for a lawyer? Would she end up in a prison cell tonight? And Christ almighty *where was her daughter?*

Fear for Livvy made it difficult to breathe, and Maggie's mouth filled with saliva, which she swallowed down, knowing it would soon make her sick. Weakness spread through her, but she forced herself to reply.

'No. But, the beach was empty. I - '

'Mrs Granger, are you sure Olivia *did* go across the beach to her father and brother? I can't help feeling they would have noticed her running across the sands towards them. What really happened this morning, Mrs Granger?'

The question knocked the wind out of her. Oh my God, thought Maggie, feeling the acid in her stomach shift. They think *I* harmed Olivia.

Chapter Six

'Don't worry about me, Phillip. I know you have to go back to Jennifer.'

Phillip jumped. He hadn't realised that Gran was awake. She had slept on and off all afternoon, giving him plenty of opportunity to plan. The different time zones meant he still hadn't been able to talk to Jennifer, but he had made the decision for her, and hopefully she'd agree.

'I'm going to fly home and bring her back here,' he said, leaning over to give his Gran's hand a quick squeeze. 'Yes, I know it'll probably take a general anaesthetic to get her on the plane but we'll manage, don't worry. Then we'll both be here to cheer you on.'

And he needed to be there to cheer her on, he realised. She had been his parent, really. He didn't feel he'd missed out on anything.

She nodded, her eyes sliding towards the locker on the other side of the bed.

'There's a candle in my handbag, I saw it in one of the tourist shops before I conked out the other day and I thought it would be just the thing for Hailey's birthday. Let's light it, darling.'

Phillip gave her the handbag and she produced one of those seaside candles, mass-produced for holiday-makers wanting something pretty to take home with them. A couple of sea-horses and some green aquatic plants were drawn on sea-blue wax and Gran was right, Hailey would have loved it. They sat watching it burn until one of the nurses came in and pointed out apologetically that candles weren't allowed.

Phillip snuffed it out and rose to leave. Gran was half-asleep again and visiting was nearly over anyway. He would go back to the apartment and wait until it was midnight. Surely Jennifer would be home at seven in the morning to answer the landline, even if her mobile was still switched off? It was a pity she'd never gotten into skyping. She really was the world's worst technophobe.

Gran's apartment was on the ninth floor, five good-sized rooms and two balconies, one overlooking the park and the other with a splendid view of the ocean. Of course he never sat there now, the park was all the view he wanted. Phillip cracked open a can of beer and flopped into the lounger. Christ, he was dead on his feet, how on earth was he going to stay awake for another four hours to phone Jennifer? But he had to talk to her, there were plans to be made, and more importantly he had to reassure himself that she really was as 'fine' as he'd assured Gran.

Hailey. It seemed like yesterday. The memories played round his head, he couldn't switch them off and the pain was as sharp tonight as it had been two years ago. Back then he had hardly been able to believe that such a dreadful thing was happening to them, a completely normal family who had done nothing to deserve such anguish.

For days afterwards, Jennifer had sat on a corner of the sofa, moaning softly to herself. It was the start of what she still referred to as 'the Black Patch', like some innocuous frozen puddle on the pavement. She hadn't spoken, hadn't eaten, hadn't even gone to bed, and in the end the doctor had sent her to a psychiatric hospital. While she was there, Phillip sold the house in Torquay and bought a new place in Truro, well away from the sea and with no agonising memories to contend with. His buy had been a success, because just a couple of weeks after coming home from hospital, Jennifer had woken up one morning and been right back to her old self. Confident and energetic, as if nothing had ever happened.

Except… Phillip forced himself to remember the truth.

It hadn't really been her old self; the post-Black Patch Jennifer had been subtly different. The woman he'd fallen in love with had been clever, witty, confident, an able woman and a beautiful one, in command of a chain of estate agents. This new Jennifer was harder. Brittle. She never talked about their old life, it was as if she'd erased the memories from her mind. But then, it was only natural that she wasn't the same person as before. He had changed too.

In the end he didn't have to wait up late to talk to his wife. Just half an hour later he was determinedly doing the crossword and nibbling garlic bread when his mobile rang in the kitchen.

It was Jennifer, he saw in disbelief, lifting his phone. She was calling him at half past four in the morning, her time. Was she still taking her meds?

'Jennifer, honey - how are you?'

He was careful to keep his voice normal, friendly. Overly-concerned people always infuriated Jennifer.

'Phillip! I couldn't sleep so I thought I'd call you. I saw you'd phoned earlier, thank you, darling. It's a bad day to be apart, isn't it?'

She was alright. Phillip breathed out slowly, only now realising just how worried he'd been.

'It is. Gran and I lit a candle. Were you okay, honey?'

'I was out with Thea, and I'm staying at hers for the moment, so you don't need to worry at all,' she said.

Phillip closed his eyes in relief. Thea had known Jennifer since they were teenagers at school; he could depend on her to keep an eye on things.

Jennifer wasn't finished yet.

'You remember that house in Polpayne that we talked about last spring? Well it was still on the market so I put an offer in. And you'll never guess what darling, it's been accepted! I'm having it done up so it'll be perfect for us, you'll see. You're going to love it.'

Warning bells rang in Phillip's head. Their house in Truro wasn't ideal and they'd been talking about another move for a while. But this was all very sudden. And once Jennifer had a new house project underway, she wouldn't be keen on leaving the UK. He tried to explain, carefully.

Jennifer listened to the story of his Gran's cancer and his proposal that he should come and get her.

'Heavens, no, darling! You stay as long as you have to with darling Gran, it's you she needs near her at a time like this. I'll have plenty to do getting the house ready. And now I have to go, get some more beauty sleep before the new day starts. Take care, darling!'

The line went dead. Phillip stared at his phone. Well, Jennifer was okay, so much was clear. In fact she had sounded a lot brighter than most people would so early in the morning. And maybe it *was* better if it was just him and Gran for a bit. The doctor had scheduled her in for radiotherapy, and if this worked he could go back to England in a couple of weeks and persuade Jennifer to come here for a while.

He showered and lay down on his bed, thinking sad, idle thoughts and listening to the sounds of Winchester Beach settling down for the night. Thank God Thea was there in England for Jennifer. Now he could be here in the States for Gran with a clear conscience.

If only someone had been there for Hailey.

Chapter Seven

She would have said they had a good marriage. They talked to each other, and they made a point of having a 'date night' every few weeks. They went away together for short breaks, leaving Joe and Livvy with the grandparents. Everyone thought they were rock solid.

But apparently they weren't. Colin was sitting on the arm of her chair in the police station, his hand on her shoulder, but he wasn't looking at her and he wasn't talking to her and if there hadn't been a policewoman in with them he might not have sat down anywhere near her. But for the moment his presence alone was almost enough for her. Almost.

They'd brought her to this larger, more comfortable room after she'd been sick on the interview room floor, and for the first time since Olivia had gone missing, Maggie had shed quiet, helpless tears. The police doctor came and gave her two pills to swallow with the tea that arrived with him. She could hardly hold the mug, her hands were trembling so much, and she was so cold, her feet were freezing. The shaking subsided as the pills took effect, and Maggie felt her body relax. Everything was going fuzzy round the edges. It was comforting, if anything could be comforting today. When Howard arrived with Colin she was able to speak again.

'Where's Joe?'

'At your cottage playing with Amanda,' said Howard.

'They interviewed him. He said he noticed Olivia, probably after she'd been dancing round her sandcastle. She was looking at something in the sand. But then he turned back to the pools and he didn't see her again.'

Maggie shivered. Livvy must have been on her way to the pools - or the cliff path. Minutes passed. The police had left them alone. Colin didn't say anything more and neither did she at first. There was nothing to say. But she had to explain why she'd been so sick. Maggie blew her nose.

'I - I thought they thought I'd harmed her,' she said. 'And maybe they did and they were right, weren't they? It was all my fault, I didn't look after her properly.'

'Let's just wait for now,' said Colin. 'Just believe they'll find her safe.'

Maggie clasped cold hands as if she were praying, though she really couldn't remember the last time she'd prayed. She knew she couldn't even hope any longer that Livvy was safe. The harrowing thoughts that were banging around in her head were hers alone. She couldn't share them with Colin. If he still had hope, she couldn't take it from him. She would be condemning him to the same hell she was in herself.

Howard came back in. 'The search groups have reported back,' he said. 'There's nothing yet, even the dogs haven't picked up a scent more than a few feet from your cottage.'

He looked at them with his sad eyes and went on gently. 'I'm sorry this was such an ordeal for you, Mrs Granger. Your statements are ready to sign, and there's a car waiting to take you both home. I'll be round first thing.'

Back at Cove Cottage, Joe and Amanda were playing Memory. Joe ran to Maggie, and she held him close, feeling his sturdy little body warm against her own.

'Mummy, where's Livvy?'

'They haven't found her yet, sweetheart. Let's get you to bed. Maybe, maybe when you wake up in the morning… '

But Maggie couldn't go on. How could she encourage Joe

to hope for something she knew herself wouldn't happen? He finished for her, though.

'Maybe Livvy'll be home!'

But of course she wasn't. Maggie, forced into drugged sleep by another of the doctor's pills, went to bed straight after Joe, leaving Colin sitting outside listening to the helicopter still droning overhead.

And the helicopter was the first sound Maggie heard the next morning.

For a fraction of a second when she woke, her world was as usual. Then the realisation of the previous day's events swept through her and she moaned aloud.

Colin was lying on top of the duvet with his back towards her, still wearing the clothes he'd had on yesterday. Maggie could tell he was awake.

'Col?'

She touched his shoulder. He rose to his feet and staggered towards the door, not even looking at her.

'They haven't found her,' he said, his voice expressionless. 'If they don't find her today...'

He went through to the kitchen and Maggie listened to him crashing around among the mugs. The radio crackled for a moment and was then abruptly silent. Maggie heard Colin's voice talking to Joe, and then the front door slammed. She rolled into a ball. She knew that Colin had turned away from her, and she knew why. He blamed her.

He was right, too. This whole horrible situation was her fault and no-one else's. She had allowed a fit of pique at a small child's thoughtlessness to colour her actions, and now Olivia was gone.

'Mummy? Are you up yet?'

Her son's voice in the kitchen drove Maggie out of bed. Joe needed her to be strong. She couldn't fail him too, she had to be a mother to her little boy, at least.

He was sitting at the table spooning up yoghurt, his usually bright little face clouded.

'Mummy,' he said, and Maggie blinked back tears, he looked so worried. 'Mummy, when will they find Livvy?'

Maggie sat down beside him, struggling to find words. Colin strode into the room in time to hear Joe's question.

'It might take a long time,' he said. 'If Livvy's badly lost it might take days to find her. I think the best thing would be if I took you to Grandma and Gramps, Joe. You can stay with them until… in the meantime.'

Maggie shivered. It was a good idea, but since when hadn't they discussed decisions like that? Colin's parents lived in Looe on the south coast, not exactly next door, but her own mother was on holiday in Tuscany. And whatever happened today it would be better if Joe wasn't around.

'We'll wait until Howard comes, then we'll go,' said Colin. 'You'd better pack, Joe.'

Without a word, Joe went into the living room and began gathering toys together.

Maggie stared at Colin. He was angry, she could see that little pulse beating near his hairline and his jaw was tight.

Quite suddenly he turned to her and she shrank back at the expression on his face. 'Don't put the radio on until we've gone,' he said, his voice low and furious. 'She's on the news. And there's a policeman outside making sure a herd of reporters don't cross the tape they've put up at the start of Cliff Road. They all want horror pictures for their news sites. "Drowned girl's parents in grief." Fucking shit.'

For a brief moment, Maggie closed her eyes. Then she stood up and slowly stepped towards Colin, but he evaded her and opened the back door.

'You should have bloody watched her,' he said viciously, going out and banging the door behind him.

There was nothing to say. Alone in Joe's room, Maggie opened drawers, unable to keep her tears in check. Joe's belongings only half-filled the blue canvas bag. Last week, she'd packed Livvy's things in here too. How happy they had been, Olivia most of all. Packing was a wonderful game now

41

that she was old enough to remember the cottage. Pink t-shirts and Old Bear. Looking forward to making sandcastles and eating ice cream every day. Then the next minute stomping around in disgust because the cat wasn't going with them. Typical Livvy.

Howard arrived at half past eight.

'No news,' he said briefly, glancing at Joe.

'Joe, run out to the garden for a moment while we talk to Mr Moir,' said Maggie, hearing her voice shake. Joe gave her a stricken look and left.

'I'm taking him to my parents at Looe,' said Colin, and Maggie clasped her hands beneath her chin when Howard nodded, looking from her to Colin.

'I have to tell you that while we feel the most likely thing by far is that Olivia went into the sea, the investigations on land will continue intensively in the meantime. It's being reported on both radio and TV news so we're waiting for a response. Someone may have seen her.'

He paused, and Maggie stared at him. His voice was downbeat. He didn't think they would find Livvy alive, she could tell. But in spite of this her child's photo was on TV and it would be all over the Internet too.

'I understand,' said Colin, and Maggie heard a new, weary tone in his voice. So now Colin didn't believe Olivia would be found safe either. And like he'd said, Livvy was gone because she, Maggie, 'hadn't bloody watched her'.

Howard grimaced.

'I'm sorry I can't do more. You'll have seen the reporters down the lane. I hope they'll leave you alone, I'll have a word on my way back.'

Maggie felt his eyes on her, saw that he wanted to help her and didn't know how. He really did think that Livvy was dead, and would probably tell that to the reporters. And of course a dead child was of limited interest to these media people, they would want something a lot more sensational. But at least the search was continuing, because they simply

42

had to find Livvy. Life wouldn't be life with no Livvy.

Colin opened the door and called Joe. 'I want to know straightaway if there's any news,' he said to Howard.

Joe rushed up to Maggie and she carried him out to the car.

'I'll talk to you later, and I'll see you as soon as we can manage. I love you, Joe.'

'Will you and Livvy come to Grandma's too?' asked Joe, and Maggie cringed.

'We'll see,' she said. 'Bye, love.'

She stood aside as Colin deposited his bag on the back seat. He looked at her. Anger, grief and pain mixed in with disgust were plain to see on his face, and it was all directed at her. He got into the car and revved the engine. For a moment, Maggie thought he was going to drive off without speaking to her. Then he rolled the window down.

'I'll be back later. Probably. Phone me if there's any news.'

He pushed the car into gear and reversed into Cliff Road.

Maggie managed to wave to Joe as the car lurched down the road and disappeared round the bend after the row of holiday cottages. Both her children were gone. And in ten seconds time dozens of cameras would be clicking away, trying to get a good shot of Joe. She covered her face with her hands, feeling the shaking start inside her again.

Howard patted her shoulder.

'Just hang on for now. It isn't time to give up hope yet,' he said, and Maggie felt ridiculously grateful. At last someone had said something almost positive.

'I haven't, not really. But - my little girl. It's so unbearable that this is happening.'

'I know,' he said. 'I'll come by early this afternoon, or before, if we find her, of course. Try - to stay calm.'

Grateful that he hadn't said 'Try not to worry', Maggie watched as his car, too, went down the road, leaving her quite alone at Cove Cottage.

And what should she do now? Phone Mum in Tuscany,

for one thing, and ruin her holiday. And Sue, and Jess, her friends back home. If only they were here to help her right now.

Maggie had never felt so alone. Waiting, trying to hold it together, then crying, then waiting again. And then Howard's car was speeding back up the lane towards the cottage. She ran to the front door and he rolled down his window.

'Maggie,' he said, his voice completely neutral. 'You need to come and look at some CCTV footage. Cameras at Exeter picked up a child similar to Olivia at ten o'clock last night.'

Chapter Eight

They took her to a different part of the police station this time. This room was busy, full of computers and people either working at their own stations or standing looking over their colleagues' shoulders, all talking in low voices and sounding urgent. Were they all looking for Olivia? Maggie clutched her bag and forced herself to breathe calmly. This sudden new hope was even more difficult to cope with than the uncertainty; she could feel her heart thudding away in her chest. The fact that she was being active now helped, but every few minutes the reality of what was happening to her family would diminish any vestige of hope still inside her.

Howard took her to a table and sat her in front of a blank screen. She could feel the eyes on her back, but whatever they were thinking, it would be impossible for them to think as badly of her as she did herself.

'Have you phoned Colin?' she asked, and Howard nodded.

'Amanda was doing that when I left to get you.'

He rolled a chair over beside her and began to manipulate the mouse. The screen in front of them lit up.

'Okay. Now like I told you, this is far from a clear image. I've gone through all the photos Colin took here and I have no idea if this is Olivia. And Maggie… ' He looked at her, and she felt how very much he wanted to find Livvy for them. '… You should try to stay calm.'

She blinked at him, and he went on.

'See if you notice any little detail that could identify this girl as Olivia - the way she walks, maybe, or holds her head. Look at the child's posture, look at her body proportions, the length of her hair. Ignore the clothes. And look at the woman, too, you might have seen her somewhere.'

He double-clicked and a grainy, black and white image appeared on the screen. Maggie could see a brick building with shop windows and doorways, and cars parked diagonally beside the pavement. Howard had told her it was the main train station at Exeter. A man with a black Labrador was disappearing out of the picture.

'Here they come,' said Howard, and Maggie leaned forward. Moving jerkily, a woman and a small girl came into view. The woman was holding the child's right hand and they were hurrying, the little girl almost running to keep up with the woman's longer strides. The child was wearing shorts and a baggy jumper, and her hair was long. Neither face was turned towards the camera. The woman was dressed in a mid-calf skirt and a lighter coloured cardigan. The two hurried along by the building and vanished through a doorway.

Maggie looked at Howard in dismay. She'd thought she would know straightaway if this was Olivia, but she didn't.

'They've gone into the station,' said Howard. 'Unfortunately two of the cameras in there weren't operating last night, and the others didn't pick them up. We have people there making inquiries right now, and our CCTV expert is on his way in. He should be able to improve the picture, but I thought it was worth getting you here straightaway. Have another look, Maggie.'

He rewound the sequence and they watched again. On the third run through Maggie still didn't know. The expert arrived and took Howard's place beside her. He blew up some still images of the child without, however, significantly improving the quality. Frustration filled Maggie as she gazed at the indistinct pictures on the screen. If only the child's face was clearer. The hair fit. The size fit. There was nothing about the way this child was moving that was different to any other child trotting along beside an adult. But there was nothing special to say that it was Olivia. The pictures just weren't good enough to tell.

'Is Colin coming here to see this or are you sending it to Looe?' she asked. She knew she should phone Colin too, but horrible as it felt she was afraid to. He'd been so angry, and she would have to tell him that she had failed again because she couldn't tell if the child on this film was Olivia or not.

'I think he's on his way now,' said the man beside her. 'Let's look at the child's legs, maybe there are some bruises or something that would give us a negative identification. Look at the knees in particular, knees are pretty distinctive, you know.'

He blew up another image and Maggie leaned forwards again.

'The first reports from Exeter are all negative,' said Howard, returning and leaning over the back of Maggie's chair. 'Nobody remembers them at the ticket office or the kiosk. We're pulling in pictures from other cameras in Exeter now in case we find them somewhere else.'

'Howie, have a look here,' said the officer beside Maggie. He zoomed in on the child's left leg. At the top of the thigh the little girl's arm came into view, the long sleeve hanging over the child's wrist.

'Here.'

He froze the picture and blew up the child's hand. Maggie strained her eyes. Now that it was pointed out, she could see there was something unusual there, something bulky just peeking out beneath the over-long cuff of the jumper. The child's fingers were curled in an unnatural-looking grip.

'Shit. That's a plaster,' said Howard. 'She's broken that arm.' He shouted back into the room. 'Sam, Amanda, get onto the hospitals right away. Newquay, Exeter and everywhere in between first. We're looking for a girl plastered yesterday and one plastered at any time within however long they keep these things on for.'

Stunned by the new development, Maggie followed Howard back to the room with comfortable chairs. He went off to order tea, and she buried her face in her hands. This waiting and hoping was unbearable, and yet something was telling her loud and clear that there was no hope here, this child wasn't Olivia. And if it wasn't Olivia, they would still have no idea what had happened…

She sat there sipping stewed tea and making crumbs with a digestive biscuit. It was half an hour before Howard returned, and she saw immediately that the news wasn't good.

'A four-year-old girl was treated for a broken arm at the Royal Cornwall Hospital in Truro on the twelfth,' he said, sitting down opposite and looking straight at her. 'We've spoken to the doctor who saw her and he remembers she had long brown hair. Amanda's trying to contact the family now, so we'll soon know for sure.'

Maggie nodded, grateful when he left her alone again. It wasn't Livvy, she could feel that.

Howard returned a few minutes later.

'Maggie, Colin's here. He wasn't happy when I told him we hadn't been able to identify the kid from the film so he's having a look for himself now.'

'You mean he was mad at me because I couldn't identify her,' she said, startled to hear the bitterness in her own voice.

'He's hurting too,' said Howard. 'I'll bring him through when he's seen it.'

Maggie could hear Colin before she saw him, ranting about the miserable quality of CCTV films. She shrank back in her chair. His anger was even more apparent now than it had been earlier.

He strode into the room, his face pale.

'Maggie,' was all he said, barely making eye contact. She nodded, a lump rising in her throat. Before she could say anything, Howard appeared in the doorway.

'It's a girl called Meredith O'Brian. The family were on their way home from a day out when Meredith had to go to the loo. Exeter station was nearest. I'm sorry.'

Maggie's tenuous hope vanished abruptly, and hopelessness returned full force. Olivia was still missing. Believed drowned.

Colin stood up.

'We'll leave you to do your work. Come on, Maggie.'

Back at the cottage, the helicopter had gone. Howard had told them it would only be searching at low tide today, and the thought that it would be looking for a dead child felt unreal to Maggie. Yesterday's agony was gone, along with today's brief hope, and in their place the new heaviness was making every movement so difficult she didn't know how she was managing to stay upright. She was moving into uncharted waters now. Whatever happened, her life would never be the same again. And with every second that passed, the already miniscule likelihood of getting Livvy back alive was growing smaller, and the dread of what was almost certainly coming was quite unbearable.

Colin strode into the bedroom and yanked the case out from under the bed. He pulled clothes from the wardrobe, squashing t-shirts, jeans, everything in any old way. There was no expression on his face now but Maggie could tell by the set of his jaw that he was at the limit of his endurance.

'Col, we can't leave now,' she said, standing in the doorway. 'We have to be here in case… when… '

He stared at her, his lips pressed together. He was furious, she could tell, but when he spoke his voice was quiet. Not a gentle kind of quiet, though, but guarded, as if he was afraid of saying too much.

'Maggie, I just can't look at you and think of what happened. I have to get away. I'm going to Looe, I promised Joe I'd be back before bedtime. You stay on here if you want, or go back to Carlton Bridge. You know they won't find her alive now.'

'No,' she said, reaching out to him, but he pushed past her to get his things from the bathroom. 'Colin. Please. We have to get through this together. Joe needs us to be his… '

'Livvy needed us too,' he said, and his use of the past tense hurt her even more than the news that it had been a girl called Meredith she'd spent so long staring at today, not Livvy. She watched as he finished packing and then followed him out to the car. He was going to leave again, and this time he wasn't going to come back.

'Please, Colin, please don't go.'

'No, Maggie. I just - I can't.'

He flung himself into the driving seat and stabbed the key into the ignition.

This time she didn't wave as the car bumped away from the cottage.

Chapter Nine
End of August

Maggie stood at the kitchen window. She couldn't see the ocean from here, but she could hear the waves crashing up the beach at the front of the cottage. The tide was going out and it was raining softly, more like mist really. September rain. Or it would be, tomorrow. Shivering, she turned and put the kettle on. The fifteenth of August seemed like a lifetime ago now.

Maggie dropped a tea bag into the clown mug that Olivia had won at the hoopla last summer. Livvy's mug, for hot chocolate and bedtime stories. She poured the water in and cradled the mug in both hands. The warmth was comforting, if anything could be comforting now. Drearily, Maggie went through to the living room, and the whole scene at the beach began in her mind yet again, like a never-ending film going round and round, not letting her switch it off. She could smell the seaweed, hear the still distant breakers and the gulls circling and crying above them. She stood at the front room window and stared out over the ocean. The cold, grey sea.

Waiting for Livvy was all she could do now. Hot tears streaked down her face as she held the mug against her heart, because of course it wasn't the only thing here to remind her that she'd once had a daughter. Olivia's blue hair slides were still on the window ledge, and the picture book she'd been leafing through that last morning was lying on a chair that no-one had sat on for two weeks. Maggie turned from the greyness outside and wandered round the cottage.

Livvy's beach ball was lying deflated in the corner beside the bookcase. They'd forgotten it on the fifteenth. And her trainers were under the sofa where she'd kicked them off the night before. The fifteenth, of course, had been sandals-for-the-beach weather.

The bathroom was the worst place of all.

Livvy's stripy peppermint toothpaste. The lotion Maggie had smoothed into her daughter's skin every evening; the strawberry shower gel. The smells of lost Olivia.

Maggie lay awake for hours each night, struggling with the less than five minutes on the beach when Olivia must have disappeared. She hadn't seen where her daughter had gone and neither had Colin or Joe. Howard and his colleagues had reconstructed the entire beach scene and were satisfied that they had drawn the right conclusions, but Maggie knew that one day she would have to go down there and establish for herself just what she and Colin could and couldn't see. If she checked for herself, then she might believe that Livvy had drowned. Col was so adamant he'd have noticed if Livvy had gone into the water, but Maggie wasn't so sure and neither was Howard. Colin and Joe hadn't seen her, but then they hadn't been watching out for her either.

Trembling, Maggie went for her jacket. The rain had almost stopped; there was no excuse not to go. In the two weeks since Olivia had vanished, this would be the first time she'd been back on the beach.

Of course now there were only two possibilities. Either Livvy had drowned, or someone had taken her away. If she'd simply wandered off by herself she would have been found by now.

Hands deep in her jacket pockets, Maggie walked across to the rock pools. How much of the beach *could* Col and Joe have seen? They'd been moving about all the time, standing up and crouching down, digging round jellyfish and talking.

Maggie stood for a moment watching a swarm of tiny fish flit around amongst some seaweed and stones, the odd raindrop shivering the surface of the water. Joe would have had them in jars as quick as anything. Tears stung her eyes at the thought of her son, but she blinked them away and looked back across the beach to the rocky ring.

She knew that from inside the ring, she'd been able to see about a third of the shoreline. What could Colin see? She would check now and then call him tonight.

The frostiness between them was thawing, albeit slowly. He had phoned twice now, and they'd talked like strangers, but it was something. A start, maybe.

Maggie crouched in the middle of the rock pools area, facing the rocky ring but still staring into the nearest pool. From here she *would* have noticed a little girl running towards her. And if she faced the sea, she *would* have seen Livvy going into the water. Even if she wasn't actually looking, the movement would have attracted her attention. But the other direction, facing away from the ring…

Maggie squatted for a moment, then stood up slowly, massaging her thighs. None of the waves that were rushing up the sand had been within her line of vision just now. If both Colin and Joe had been facing this way, engrossed in the pool-life in front of them, they might well not have seen Olivia go down to the sea. From the very beginning, Colin had refused point-blank to even consider that Livvy could have gone into the water without him noticing her, but he was wrong and she'd just proved it.

Maggie trudged back across the sand. She'd known all along really that the sea was the most likely option. That was probably why she'd avoided the beach so determinedly. It hadn't been as painful as she'd expected, though she knew that the pills she had from the doctor were taking the edge off a lot of the pain.

Halfway up the cliff path she turned and looked back at

the beach. This end was deserted. On the other side of the rock pools area two dog walkers were sitting on the steps of one of the beach huts, throwing sticks for their dogs.

Her mobile buzzed in her pocket, and she jumped. It was Howard.

'Maggie, I'm at the cottage.'

She hurried on up the steep path. Howard or Amanda came by most days to report the lack of progress in the search for Olivia. She didn't know if this was what would routinely have happened or if they were doing it because they felt sorry for her. Poor Maggie, her daughter drowned and her husband and son gone.

Occasionally they did have something to report. There had been several 'sightings' of Olivia, all of them negative. The police had been round all the hotels, petrol stations, shops, hospitals and restaurants in the area, but Livvy hadn't been seen in any of them. She had vanished off the face of the earth. The news reports all said 'missing, believed drowned'. But there was still no proof, and dear God, as Livvy's mother, she just needed proof.

He was waiting by the door, a green plastic bag in one hand, and she hurried across the lane. There had been a lot of green plastic bags; the coastguards had found nearly everything Maggie had left on the beach that day. Except, of course, the one thing that was irreplaceable.

'Nothing,' said Howard, following her inside. It was a kind of code they'd developed. 'Nothing' meant 'we haven't found a body'. Wilting, Maggie waved him to the sofa and sank into the single armchair opposite, staring at him. He looked different today, his face was set in resignation.

'Maggie. We found this. It's a size ten.'

He opened the green bag and produced a blue plastic sandal. It was exactly like the ones Livvy had, except this one was faded and scarred. Maggie bit her lip, surprised that she wasn't falling to pieces here. But then maybe there was a limit to the number of times you could do that.

'Can I hold it?'

He handed it over. 'It was found yesterday at Warders Bay.'

Maggie held it in both hands. This one was harder, stiffer than she remembered Livvy's being, but then maybe that was the salt water. And of course there was nothing, just absolutely nothing to say if this particular sandal had ever belonged to Olivia.

'It's the same as hers, but…'

Howard returned the sandal to the bag. 'I know. Okay.'

He looked at the floor, and suddenly she knew what was coming. The helicopter had stopped searching days ago, of course, but the coastguards still went out. As did the searchers along the clifftops and in the towns. But apart from the contents of the beach bag and now this anonymous blue sandal, nothing had ever been found. She looked at him, feeling the apprehension grow.

'Maggie, I am so, so sorry. You know we've gone over the whole area thoroughly, so many times. There's no sign that Olivia came back up here. We're going to call off the active search. We'll keep the file open, we'll investigate anything that comes in that might even possibly be a lead, but you know yourself that the most likely thing by far is that Livvy went into the sea. And was lost. But if that did happen, she's at peace now, Maggie.'

She stared at him. In a way she'd been expecting this, it was the logical next step, but it was still brutal. He was telling her that they were so sure Livvy was dead that nobody would be out there looking for her.

'We've drawn a blank everywhere,' he said, his voice heavy. 'The team has shown her photo for miles around, but no-one has seen her. There are hundreds of posters up all over the place and we've had dozens of calls, but, just nothing. And every single person on the sex offenders register that could have been anywhere near here has been checked. I'm sorry, Maggie. I really am.'

For a moment Maggie stopped breathing. She couldn't say anything, she couldn't even cry. There was nothing more that anyone could possibly have done to find Olivia.

She nodded at Howard, and he stood up.

'Amanda or I will come by again tonight. Maggie - you shouldn't be alone now.'

'My mother's coming again tomorrow.'

The relief on his face was obvious.

'Good. That's great. Maybe you should go home with her for a while.'

Maggie shook her head. Her mother had been here three days last week too, but it had been difficult for them both. Mum loved her, but she had loved Livvy too, and every word the older woman spoke was tinged with reproach.

'I want my little girl back,' she told Howard. 'I'll stay here and wait.'

'It could take weeks. It might not happen at all,' he said helplessly. 'When people are lost at sea… we don't always get them back.'

Maggie knew there was no way she could leave Cove Cottage without Olivia. She would stay here until she was an old woman if necessary. Because if Howard was right, then Livvy was just a few yards away outside. In the sea.

'I'm waiting for her,' she said, and he nodded.

'I'll see myself out.'

Maggie remained slumped in the armchair. There was nothing more to do now.

Chapter Ten
Mid September

Phillip pushed the wheelchair through the hospital park, where tall palm trees were providing welcome shade to those patients well enough to be outdoors. Even halfway through September it was still hot. It was great that Gran was well enough now to come down here again; he loved to see her with more colour in her face. The radiotherapy had made her tired and sick, but the course was over now and she had been for a scan that morning.

'Let's sit by the bandstand for a bit, have an ice cream,' he suggested, pleased when she smiled and nodded. If the radiotherapy gave her a few more 'quality' months he would definitely bring Jennifer over. A long holiday would do them both good, well away from home and all the unhappy memories.

He parked the wheelchair under a tree and went for the usual strawberry cornets. They sat in companiable silence, the old lady eating her ice cream with a dreamy, far-away expression in her eyes. Phillip glanced at her uneasily. She had always been such a chatterbox and these new silences were unnerving. It was almost as if she was slipping away from him already. She was better in that the side effects of the radiotherapy had gone now, but somehow she didn't seem to be the same person. Or maybe he was expecting too much too soon. Maybe she simply needed more peace and quiet and time to do normal things. Exactly what you didn't get in a hospital.

His thoughts turned to Jennifer. How could he best persuade her to come out to California? She had always hated long haul flights, her aversion almost amounted to a phobia and God knows he didn't want to stress her. But she had to come, she had already been alone since the beginning of July, and now that she'd moved to Polpayne, Thea wouldn't be around every day to keep an eye on things.

At least the new house was giving Jennifer something constructive to do, but it was difficult to know exactly what was going on. It *was* strange that Jennifer hadn't waited for his return before tackling such a big project. Was she coping? She hadn't spoken to her mother for months so he couldn't ask Bea how things were, and none of their old friends lived anywhere near Polpayne to check up on Jennifer. She must be feeling pretty isolated. Phillip came to a sudden decision: if Gran's scan results were good, he would go over for her at the weekend.

It *would* be alright. Jennifer always sounded busy when they phoned, she was organising the house and settling into the village… she was talking and laughing, telling him stories about the new front door and the garden. Surely she wouldn't be doing that if she wasn't alright.

Tears rushed into Phillip's eyes as he remembered her terrible silence at the start of the Black Patch, and he blinked them away before Gran noticed. All this time, and he still couldn't face the awful thing that had happened to them.

They'd been in Turkey, in a beautiful hotel complex near Side. It was the first holiday abroad they'd had for a couple of years, since Hailey had been born, in fact. Jennifer had booked it, and as usual her judgement had been spot-on. The beach, private to the hotel, was perfect, sloping gradually into the water. And the hotel itself had been out of this world. It should have been a wonderful holiday. Even the weather was almost guaranteed.

And for the first nine days their holiday *had* been wonderful. They had long lie-ins and leisurely breakfasts. Afterwards, Jennifer generally went off to do whatever was on the keep-fit schedule that morning, while Phillip and Hailey spent their time by the pool. How he'd loved those mornings alone with his daughter. They would meet Jennifer for a lunchtime sandwich in the gardens, and then in the afternoons they had done something different almost every day.

They'd visited Side, with its quaint shopping alleys. They'd gone on a boat trip to see basking turtles, which Hailey had loved. They'd driven to Antalya once, to see the market. And several times they had spent the afternoon on the beach, because that was what Hailey liked best.

There was a children's playground where the hotel garden met the beach. Hailey had always gone there first, while he and Jennifer swam in the sea. Then he would fetch Hailey back and the two of them would go for a ride on the banana-boat. It had been such a joy, watching his little girl having fun, laughing with her, building sandcastles, looking for shells. Phillip had truly felt that this was the best time of his life.

Then came the tenth day.

'Phillip, darling, do you have any tissues?'

Consumed with memories and grief, Phillip tossed his half-eaten cornet into a nearby bin and pulled out a wipe for Gran's chin.

'Here you are. Enjoy that?'

She took the wipe and applied it to her mouth, and he noticed that her fingers were shaking. She was tired, it was time to go back to the ward and let her rest. He pushed the chair back towards the oncology unit, taking deep breaths, forcing the memories to the back of his mind. This was

Gran's time now, not his, not Jennifer's and not Hailey's. He should remember that.

'Thank you, Phillip darling. It was wonderful to be outside and hear the ocean and smell the wind,' she said as they approached the building.

'We'll do it again very soon,' said Phillip, unwaveringly cheerful, pushing her inside and realising just how very antiseptic the smell here was.

She was silent in the lift and Phillip couldn't think of anything to say either. Perhaps she was worried about the scan. They would have the result very soon. But she was in less pain now so surely the tumours must have shrunk.

He was abruptly less sure about this when he wheeled Gran out of the lift and into the ward. Dr Powell was standing at the nurses' station, clutching one of these portable screens they showed scans on. His eyes met Phillip's, and the expression on his face was grim.

Chapter Eleven

Maggie sat on her rock at the top of the cliff path. Out here, with the wind whistling past her ears it felt as if she was sitting on the edge of the world. If she concentrated hard enough she could imagine that there was no world at her back, just the never-ending ocean before her and the heavens above - and somewhere out there in the enormity of it all was Olivia. The rock had turned into the only place where she still felt connected to her daughter, and so here she would sit, from morning until night when the weather was fine, and sometimes even when it wasn't. Livvy was gone, summer was dying, and the smell on the wind was autumn.

Today there was greyness everywhere. The sea was grey and swollen, and thick grey clouds were sweeping across a grey sky. Foamy grey waves rushed up the sands then back again. The tide was going out, and Maggie could see the rocky ring and the sand where Olivia's last castle had stood so briefly. In the distance the beach huts were providing the only splash of colour: blue, green and yellow against the grey sky.

The rock was cold, but Maggie knew she would stay here until she barely had the strength to move away. Sitting here she could watch over the entire sweep of the bay, from Borrower's cave on the right, all the way along to Joe and Colin's rock pools on the left, filled with cold, fresh seawater now that the tide was retreating. The wet sand looked dull and uninviting, and no kids were playing down there today.

If only the sea would give them Olivia back. Until it did there would always be one thought hidden at the back of Maggie's mind, an unbearable hope that she didn't dare put into words because no-one believed it. She didn't believe it herself any more, but if only they knew what had happened on that day. On the fifteenth of August.

She heard footsteps behind her, and turned to see Mary Barnes, shopping bag clutched under her arm while her husband reversed their Nissan into the lane. The elderly couple had the cottage two along from Maggie, and they had known Livvy since she was a baby.

'We're going to the supermarket,' said Mary, and Maggie struggled to concentrate on the words. 'Would you like to come too, Maggie? Or can I bring you anything?'

Maggie shivered. She hated going into town. Posters of Olivia were still everywhere; torn, battered affairs now, destroyed by the wind and rain.

And the stares that followed her everywhere, faces full of pity and horror and 'thank God my kids are safe'. Eyes that never quite met her own, and she didn't want them to, either. All she wanted was to be left alone and wait for Olivia.

But she had to eat, and Mary and Charlie were both over eighty. It wasn't fair to let them lug bags of groceries around for her.

'Could you maybe bring me a loaf and some eggs, please?' said Maggie, reaching a guilty compromise. 'That would be very kind.'

'It's quite alright, dear,' said Mary, and Maggie could hear the concern in her voice. 'Why don't you go back inside and warm up? You've been sitting out here far too long.'

'I will,' said Maggie, standing up. Just go, she wanted to scream. Leave me alone, I'm waiting for my daughter.

'Alright then, goodbye now,' said Mary, patting Maggie's shoulder anxiously.

Maggie forced herself to smile at the old woman. Poor

Mary, poor Charlie. She had ruined this holiday for them, and who knew if they'd be able to return next year to enjoy another.

'We'll be back in an hour, and I'll make us all a nice pot of tea. I'll come and get you, dear.'

She turned away, and Maggie waved dutifully as their car lurched out of sight. They hadn't deserved this. But what else could she do? She wasn't even coping with the basic things in life, like shopping. Sitting here watching the sea was always more important. She was the last of the summer family, and it was up to her to wait for Olivia.

When the search was called off, Colin had gone back to Carlton Bridge with Joe and his parents. He phoned and texted her often now; the coldness between them was over and he was trying to rebuild the relationship. So was she. He'd come down to see her, but nothing could persuade Maggie to give up her vigil. It had turned into a sort of pact - if she watched long enough, the sea would give them Olivia back again. And then what?

Then she could go home and bury her daughter and be a mother to her little boy and never, ever go anywhere near Cove Cottage again.

Crossing her arms for warmth, Maggie sat back down and stared out to sea. After weeks of keeping watch, she knew the tides intimately. She knew exactly how the sea crept up the sand into Borrower's and over rock pools, into Smuggler's and up and up the beach, until the whole thing went into reverse and the water crept away again leaving the sands wet and clean.

It was windier than usual on the clifftop today and Maggie hugged herself, shivering. The Barnes would soon be back and Mary would fuss if Maggie was still outside. She would rush around heating soup and making motherly noises. She was a good, kind neighbour, and had actually helped Maggie more than her own mother had. Mum was stuck, trapped in her own grief, and of course it was less than a year since Dad had died.

Maggie stood up and took a long, hard look round the cove. One day, here or at another cove, there would be something, she knew. One day, a little body... Maggie felt the scream begin inside her, the one that left her weak and shaking, and she was helpless to stop it.

'*O - liv - i - a!*' The wind carried the name from her lips. '*Li - vv - y!*'

The scream was still echoing round the cove when something caught Maggie's eye. Something at the edge of the water, just at the entrance to Smuggler's Cave. Something pink.

Maggie ran. Down the cliff path, sliding on loose stones, grabbing rocks to steady herself, going over on her ankle at the first bend but rushing on in spite of the pain, down and down and down to the sand, the sliding sand, over the beach, there *was* something there. She was up to her knees in freezing cold water now, where *was* it, that pink thing...

It was gone. Perhaps it was in the cave. Maggie waded into darkness, frantically searching. She couldn't see a thing, it was too dark. And what was she looking for anyway, what did a little girl in a pink and white t-shirt look like after so many weeks in the sea? The mental image was horrifying. Maggie retched and vomited, and the waves swirled the sick against the cave wall and then back to her. It was dark and cold and Olivia wasn't here. Maggie turned and waded back to the entrance. Icy water splashed up her thighs, she could hardly feel her feet now. The pink thing, where was it? She *had* seen it...

And there it was. Just a few feet from the beach, bobbing underwater. Maggie fell to her knees, unheeding of the waves rushing over her legs and up her back, soaking her hair and stinging inside her nose. Dry sobs closed her throat as she knelt there and gathered a child's torn rubber ring to her chest.

Strong hands grasped her and lifted her to her feet.

'Come on, Maggie. Let's get you inside.'

She dropped the rubber ring and allowed Howard to lead her out of the water.

'On you come, that's it. Mary Barnes saw you running

64

down here and phoned us. Come on, Maggie. We'll soon have you back in the warm.'

Maggie felt completely numb. It wasn't Livvy she'd seen. Nothing of the sort. Just a piece of torn plastic that someone had thrown away.

Amanda Donnelly was waiting on the beach with a blanket that Maggie recognised as belonging in Howard's car. There were tears on the other woman's face. She and Howard wrapped the blanket round Maggie's shoulders, pushing her towards the path.

'Up we go, Maggie. That's it.'

Mary and Charlie were hovering at the top of the cliff and ushered everyone into their own cottage. Maggie couldn't speak.

'She needs dry clothes,' said Mary firmly, and Maggie saw a pair of her own jeans, and a jumper warming in front of the electric fire. Of course, she hadn't locked her door. She had been stupid, she knew, and she was so tired…

The doctor arrived when she was sitting wrapped in a blanket with a hot water bottle, being fed lentil soup by Mary. It was as if she were at the theatre, and all the people here were putting on a performance especially for her. They were acting out a story, speaking their lines and gesticulating, but none of it was real.

'It was lucky I suppose that I had forgotten my purse and we came back for it,' said Mary. 'Thank you for coming right away, Chief Inspector.'

'We were just heading back from a case,' said Howard. 'You'll be alright, Maggie.'

He looked at her sadly, but she was grateful that someone had spoken directly to her.

The doctor gave her two pills, and she knew that in half an hour's time she wouldn't be hurting half as much as she was now. Maggie took a deep breath. She had never behaved like that before. Like a crazy woman. She didn't know what had got into her, she could easily have drowned. She and

Livvy both could have been lost. And she had a little boy who needed his mother; she should be helping him, not sitting in an empty cottage endlessly waiting. Maggie took a deep breath and leaned back in her chair. A drugged sense of peace seeped slowly into her bones.

'I'm sorry,' she said to Howard, who was standing in front of the electric fire, his trousers steaming. 'I thought it was Olivia.'

'I know,' he said. 'Maggie, I phoned Colin. He's coming to get you. Go home, Maggie. I'll watch out for Olivia for you, I promise.'

Colin arrived later that afternoon and hugged her tightly. He was thinner now. So was she, of course. And he was calmer, much calmer than she was these days. He was grieving, but he had accepted that Olivia was gone.

'Col, I - I can feel her. I can still feel her inside me.'

She sat on the bed, watching as he packed her clothes. He sat down beside her and she leaned against him gratefully. Whatever else had happened, the rift between them was healing. She knew that their relationship would never be the same again, but they were still together, and for the moment that was enough. She knew he didn't blame her any more, but that didn't stop her blaming herself. She had, after all, killed her daughter.

'Maggie, keep her there inside you. I know it's hard, but for Joe's sake, we have to go on.'

He was right, she thought. It was the only way forwards. She would go back to Carlton Bridge and Joe, take her pills, and wait for the pain to lessen. And she would keep her Livvy safe inside her forever.

'I spoke to Mum and Dad,' said Colin, clearing the few contents of the fridge into a cardboard box. 'We thought we'd sell this place. It's the wrong time of year, of course, but come the spring we'll put it on the market. We could buy another cottage somewhere… '

'Don't,' said Maggie. 'I can't think about that.'

Drearily, she pulled Livvy's clothes from the wardrobe and laid them in another box. The toys went on top, first the dolls, and a couple of rainy-day jigsaws. And Old Bear. He'd been a third birthday present, Livvy had chosen him herself.

In spite of everything, Maggie found herself smiling at the memory. What a golden, glorious third birthday Livvy'd had. They'd baked a cake, of course, Olivia had wanted 'a seaside cake'. So they'd constructed waves with green and blue marzipan, and even made a little marzipan boat. Olivia loved marzipan. The grandparents all visited for the weekend, a squash in the little cottage but fun, too. They'd had a party on the beach, with cake and scones and cream, and Old Bear tucked under Olivia's arm all day. It was the last time all the family had been together.

Colin taped the box shut.

'We'll put it in the attic with the rest of her stuff,' he said, and Maggie knew then that Olivia didn't have a bedroom at Carlton Bridge any more.

When there was nothing left to pack she helped Colin carry everything out to the car. Howard had returned to say goodbye. He had been so kind, he and Amanda both, and Maggie knew that in a different situation they would have become friends. But kindness hadn't found Olivia, and Maggie could never think about Howard without feeling the agony of losing her child.

She gazed at the cottage. So many memories were here, happy memories originally but now they were too painful to think about. And this would be her last time at Cove Cottage, maybe the last time at Newquay, too, unless by some miracle the sea did give Olivia back to them and they could come down to collect her. For the last time, she would say goodbye.

Howard gripped both her shoulders when she tried to say thank you.

'I'll watch every day, Maggie. I promise.'

She got into the car and they drove away. And she didn't look back.

Part Two
The Wait

Chapter One
16th August

A brief whimper crackled through the baby monitor. Jennifer grabbed the remote and silenced the evening film, holding her breath as she listened. The last thing she needed was Hailey up again. The wretched child had woken every hour on the hour all through the previous night - another session like that would be the end of them both. And Jennifer hadn't even been able to nap while Hailey was sleeping after lunch because there was too much to do, and the babies had spent all afternoon using her bladder as a trampoline. She was exhausted.

Just thinking about the babies seemed to activate them again; a sudden surge from the inside made tiny circular waves tremble across the surface of the tea she was balancing on her bump. Tiredness forgotten, Jennifer massaged her swollen belly, pleasure warming through her as the answering knock came from within.

It was amazing. Even now she could hardly believe it, especially after everything that had happened. She was pregnant again. With twins. By the end of November she would have two darling babies to love and treasure and dress in beautiful new baby clothes. Phillip would be so surprised.

She had been four and a half months pregnant when he left, but she had kept the news to herself. He would only have made a silly fuss if she'd told him, and there was no need for him to worry - they were all just fine.

The fact that it was twins seemed to make up for everything. Twice the amount of luck and twice the amount of love. Jennifer laughed aloud. And darling Hailey was right here with her too, and in a funny way that was even more wonderful.

The monitor remained silent, and Jennifer relaxed back on the sofa. Of course staying at Thea's ex-farm cottage wasn't the usual thing for Hailey, and children of that age were creatures of habit when it came to bedtime routines, weren't they? But this was better than going home to Truro. Long Farm Cottage was miles away from everywhere; they'd have peace and quiet here. Jennifer was only too glad she'd had the key to this place, so even with Thea in Canada she'd been able to bring Hailey straight here yesterday morning. The seclusion was perfect.

Jennifer smiled happily. It was marvellous having friends when you needed them. She'd phoned Thea earlier that evening when it was mid-afternoon in Toronto, and her friend had believed every word when Jennifer said that she was going to join Phillip in the States and needed a stopping-off place on the way to Heathrow. Just for one night, of course. Phillip and Thea didn't know each other well enough to start comparing notes on Jennifer's whereabouts, so she could stay right here at the farmhouse for as long as she needed to.

The monitor crackled again, and Jennifer rose to her feet. She could *not* go through another night like the last one. Another magic pill was needed. That had worked beautifully yesterday, the child had slept all afternoon while Jennifer collected a carful of necessities from home. So if she gave Hailey the same dose now they should both have a good night.

She stared at the packet of blue pills. They were indeed magic. They'd helped her through the Black Patch but of course she had stopped taking them as soon as she'd realised she was pregnant again. Now they would help Hailey with... but she didn't know what was wrong with Hailey.

It wasn't just that the child wasn't sleeping well, she'd been crying, too. Was she feverish? Jennifer could remember her own mother coming to her bedroom at night when she'd had a high temperature saying, 'Time for the magic medicine.' Back then it had been a crushed junior aspirin. These weren't aspirin, but drugs had evolved a lot since her own childhood. You didn't even need to crush these ones, they were small and easy to swallow.

Carefully, Jennifer extracted the other half of yesterday's tablet and took it upstairs with a glass of water. Half a pill was surely alright for a small child. She'd read the leaflet but the dosages were confusingly varied. Hailey was quiet again, lying on her side with one arm dangling over the edge of the bed. Jennifer stood for a moment gazing down at the sleeping child.

Such a miracle. For a moment Jennifer felt exactly like she had when the midwife laid baby Hailey in her arms. She crouched beside the bed and pushed the half pill to the back of the sleeping child's tongue, following it up with a mouthful of water. Hailey opened her eyes and choked, and Jennifer smiled encouragingly.

'Time for your medicine, Hailey darling. Swallow it down and have a lovely sleep,' she said, and the little girl closed her eyes again.

Jennifer sat on the edge of the bed, stroking the suntanned little face. She'd done this for nearly all of the previous night too; Hailey had been restless and weepy for some reason, and Jennifer hadn't dared give her more medication so soon after the first dose.

The half pill worked its magic as she had known it would, and Hailey was soon in a deep sleep. Jennifer wiped a little trickle of saliva from the little girl's chin. Medication had its uses, but those doctors had given her far too much of it during the Black Patch. It had muddled her thoughts; she no longer remembered everything that had happened back then. Something had happened to Hailey, but here she was asleep in bed, so she wasn't hurt. Something had changed, though, but Jennifer couldn't remember what.

Thinking about it was unsettling, and Jennifer stood up, tucking the duvet round Hailey's neck. Sound asleep. And thank goodness there were plenty more pills.

Downstairs, she made fresh tea and put the television on again. The babies started kicking as soon as she sat down and Jennifer smiled happily. Life was going to be so good now. In a few weeks' time the new house in Polpayne would be ready and the two of them would go there to wait for Phillip... and when he came home they would all be together again.

Her mobile buzzed in her handbag and Jennifer hesitated. It was Phillip again; he often called at this time but she really didn't have the energy to talk to him tonight. Quickly, she rejected the call and switched her mobile off. She would call him tomorrow and say she'd been at the theatre; a good night's sleep before she spoke to him was an absolute necessity or she'd ruin the surprise.

The news was starting and Jennifer watched idly as the usual mixture of politics, suicide bombings and knife crime in London flashed in front of her. The fourth report jolted her awake, however, and she stared in horror as a child's face filled the screen, followed by a view of a deserted beach beneath high, threatening cliffs. The newsreader's voice was grave.

'There is still no sign of the three-year-old girl who vanished from a Newquay beach yesterday morning, and it appears increasingly likely that she has drowned. Police have - '

Jennifer stumbled back upstairs and fell to her knees by the bed. Thank God, thank God, her baby was right here, breathing beautifully and looking so peaceful. Jennifer covered the child's face with kisses and then leaned back, still trembling, her heart beating frantically in her throat.

It was as if a distant memory was fighting its way to the surface, but remaining tantalisingly out of reach. What had happened? Was it something to do with the beach? Had Hailey been lost? Yes she had, hadn't she, but here she was back in bed again. Everything was alright.

Jennifer watched the child for a few more minutes and then crept to the other side of the bed and slid under the duvet. The best way to keep Hailey safe was to stay right here with her.

Chapter Two
Mid August

Long Farm Cottage was centuries old. Battleship grey stone walls supported a darker roof of slate, and the whole building was dwarfed by three enormous oak trees whose roots were making the old stone floors even more uneven. Inside, solid wooden beams traversed low ceilings and the whitewashed internal walls were at least a foot thick. Thea was an Aga-user, so the kitchen had a quaint, old-fashioned look to it. The entire atmosphere was one of age and tranquillity. And silence.

Jennifer stared out of the window. She could see why Thea loved her home. Long Farm Wood started just the other side of the lane; trees stretched for miles down towards the ocean, oaks and sycamores as far as the eye could see. They weren't quite in the sticks because if you stood out in the lane and looked downhill you could see the last few houses of Trevaren in the distance. But few people except the occupants of this cottage and its distant neighbour ever came up here, so it was ideal for her and Hailey. They'd been here four days now and Jennifer was beginning to get used to country life with her daughter.

And that was the important thing. They were together. The fact that the child was behaving so strangely could be put right. It was possibly just nerves, or drowsiness from the pills, but Hailey hadn't given the correct answer to a single one of the questions Jennifer had put to her so far. It was infuriating.

Jennifer took a deep breath. Sometimes she didn't know what was happening to herself, never mind Hailey, and the feeling of helplessness frightened her. She needed more order in her life, that would be it. The doctor in that place had said that a set routine was important. Well, when they moved to Polpayne she would make sure her days had all the structure she needed. Everything would be fine as soon as they got there. Jennifer hugged herself. She would cope. She was a mother.

Mind you, children came with their own problems, as Hailey's behaviour proved more and more every day. Getting her to eat was incredibly difficult. Jennifer sighed. It was a pity she had to drug Hailey during the day too, but she couldn't stay here babysitting all the time. She had to talk to the workmen about the house in Polpayne, and yesterday she'd gone to the supermarket to get supplies. But then Hailey hadn't touched the soup Jennifer had bought for her, even though minestrone had always been her favourite. In fact the only thing the child had eaten these past few days was yoghurt, and that was only because Jennifer had spooned it into her mouth when she was half asleep.

They couldn't go on like this, and there was no reason for Hailey to be so moody and uncooperative. Maybe a little plain speaking would do some good. It was time things returned to normal. Jennifer ran upstairs, cradling her bump.

The child's eyes were half open, and Jennifer bent over the bed.

'Hailey? It's time for your shower.'

She pulled Hailey's arm as she spoke, and to her relief the little girl allowed herself to be led along to the bathroom. Jennifer pushed the unresisting little body under the shower and lathered it generously. Goodness, she'd never noticed that little mole on Hailey's shoulder, when had that come?

She rinsed the last of the soap from Hailey's hair and turned the water off.

Smiling happily, Jennifer wrapped one of Thea's bath towels round Hailey and hugged the child fiercely. She had her three children close to her heart and *at last* Hailey smelled like their own girl again.

Now for that hair, it was far too long now. Hailey had looked much prettier with shoulder-length hair and it was easier to keep, too. So shoulder-length it would be. Jennifer sat the child on the bathroom stool, combed out the section of hair closest to Hailey's scalp, and lifted the scissors.

The little girl was slouched on the stool, a blank expression on her face, but the first snip made her jerk upright, eyes wide open.

Jennifer inhaled sharply and prodded Hailey's shoulder with the pointed end of the scissors.

'I'll cut your ear off if you do that again,' she said. 'Here, you can hold the plastic bag.'

It didn't take long, the soft brown hair was easy to cut. Lock after lock landed in the bag and Jennifer frowned. It looked very brown today, dirty, almost. They would need to do something about that. Hailey had to look her usual pretty little self when they went to live in Polpayne. Jennifer tied the bag shut and thrust it into the bin.

'Excellent. Now for some breakfast,' she said, propelling the child into the kitchen. 'You sit there and Mummy will sit right beside you. Look, toast and honey. You like that, don't you, Hailey?'

The little girl looked at her bleakly and began to eat. Jennifer relaxed, watching as a piece of toast and a glass of milk disappeared down Hailey's throat. Well, that was one thing sorted.

And yet - Jennifer frowned as the child finished her milk. Why was Hailey's hair more brown now? Before the Black Patch her hair had been a lovely mid-brown colour with golden reflections. Now it was a muddy dark brown, and the gold lights were missing entirely. Maybe a different shampoo would help, she could go to the chemist today.

Jennifer stared at Hailey. She had to go to Polpayne this morning, to check the new kitchen with the head of the interior design company that was renovating the house for her. Should she take Hailey with her? Show her the new house? That would be fun, wouldn't it? Hailey would like that. But on the other hand, the child was so silent. It was almost as if she'd forgotten how to speak. How embarrassing it would be if someone spoke to Hailey and she didn't reply, or gave the wrong reply. It might be better to practise a whole lot of questions and answers before she took Hailey out among people again.

Jennifer reached for the pills.

Chapter Three
End of August

Jennifer watched as the child sat at the table, head bent over her drawing book. She was making heavy weather of it and Jennifer bit her lip. Surely Hailey used to be better at colouring in? Still, at least the hair situation was improving. That spray she'd bought at the chemist was working at last, the highlights it was producing looked just like Hailey's hair had always looked. Sun-kissed. She was using lemon juice too on the days in between, that made the hair very dry but it smelled better than the spray.

Jennifer clasped her hands under her chin and stared at Hailey. The tiny worm of doubt that had plagued her at the start of their stay here was almost – but not quite – gone. That lost girl had drowned, they'd said so on the news last night. The search was over. So this was her Hailey, but the very fact that she'd had doubts at all was unsettling. Was she going mad? She certainly felt *different*, here with her daughter, but it didn't feel like madness. Still, the Black Patch had frightened her. Was she ill again?

A new idea slid into Jennifer's mind like warm, bright sunshine: Of course, how silly she was not to have realised - she was *better* now that she was here with Hailey. She was back to normal again, so much so that Phillip had stayed in the States to be with Gran, and she was even pregnant so that just proved she was completely alright. Jennifer smiled in relief.

Hailey lifted sombre eyes and stared at her. Dear Lord. Had the child's eyes always been so dark?

Jennifer swallowed painfully. She was thinking thoughts that couldn't ever be put into words. This *was* her daughter, but she wasn't going to find confirmation in her own head, that was clear. But maybe there was another way to make sure. She would take Hailey to the doctor. They needed a medical certificate for school, and the doctor would know if this was Hailey. And of course it would be, she was being silly here. It was just after the Black Patch and the medication and - she needed a little reassurance, that was all.

Jennifer leaned forward, feeling the babies squirm inside her.

'Who am I, Hailey?'

The child stared, then quickly smiled, just as they'd practised.

'Hailey, what have we said about replying immediately when people speak to you? Again, please. Who am I, Hailey?'

'You're my mum?'

Happiness spread through Jennifer and she kissed the child's head.

'Very good. But say 'Mummy', Hailey, it's so much nicer. One more time. Who am I?'

'My mummy.'

The child ducked her head and reached for a red felt tip.

'Excellent. Now, Hailey, pack your things away for today. We'll have lunch now and this afternoon we're going out in the car. That'll be nice, won't it? We're going to Polpayne to see the house, then we'll pop into the doctor's, and if you're good I'll show you your new school too. You start in two weeks.'

The child rose to her feet immediately and began to stuff felt-tips into their box. Jennifer nodded, satisfied. Actually, Hailey had made real progress this past week or so. They had developed a nice little routine. Breakfast, then lessons.

Hailey knew all about answering questions with a happy smile now, and she knew her name, her date of birth, and what her favourite food and activities were. After the lessons came lunch and a magic pill for Hailey who then slept while Jennifer was out doing whatever needed doing that day. Then it was dinner, more lessons or a nice game, another magic pill and off to bed.

Jennifer placed a slice of quiche in front of Hailey and smiled as the little girl started to eat. Knife and fork skills were coming along very nicely too. Yes, she was completely satisfied with Hailey. And of course the doctor would be too.

What a lovely home she had created, thought Jennifer, gazing complacently round the elegant blue and white living room. The designers had done an excellent job, and their own possessions had arrived from Truro yesterday so the house was ready for occupation. It would be a real haven for them all. A family home.

'We'll move in here tomorrow,' she said, and Hailey nodded, smiling happily as usual.

Jennifer beamed triumphantly. With a whole new wardrobe to fill, she could buy lots of beautiful clothes for Hailey. She'd bought the child a few necessities already, of course, but now that Hailey could come too and try things on they would have much more fun. There was a children's boutique in Bodmin, they would go in on the way back to Thea's. What a lovely afternoon they were having, she and her daughter. Jennifer lifted the school prospectus from the coffee table and handed it to Hailey.

'Look, your new school. We'll drive past later, but first we'll go and see about your medical. Then if you're good we'll buy you a beautiful dress, maybe even two or three. And if you're not good, you know what'll happen.'

Hailey blanched, then smiled up at her, and Jennifer raised her eyebrows.

'Thank you Mummy.'

It would do. Hailey had to know how to behave amongst strangers, of course, but it was the child's first outing, and she was being very cooperative. So of *course* this was Hailey.

The medical centre was quiet, and Jennifer led Hailey up to the desk, where a middle-aged woman was tapping away at a keyboard.

'Good afternoon. We've just moved to the area. I want to register and make an appointment for my daughter to have a medical. She needs a certificate for starting school.'

'No problem,' said the receptionist, sliding a form across to Jennifer. 'If you'd just fill this in. Hello, lovey. What school are you going to?'

The answer came promptly with a beautiful smile. 'Polpayne Castle Primary.'

'Lovely. I hear they have a super new gym hall now. Right, Mrs ah, Marshall… '

Jennifer held her breath as the woman skimmed over what she'd written.

'That seems fine. Oh, you've missed this one. Who was Hailey's GP at your last place?'

Hot confusion swept over Jennifer. Who *was* Hailey's doctor?

'Goodness, it's such a long time since she's been to the doctor. I don't think she was even registered with one in Truro and before that it was Torquay… yes, it was Dr McKenna in Torquay. I think.'

The woman stared. 'Right. I'll just get in touch with them for her records. Excuse me.'

She went into a room and closed the door, and Jennifer felt sweat gather on her brow. She glared at Hailey, who was jiggling around beside her.

'Do you need to go to the bathroom? Over there, look. Be quick, please.'

What was the woman doing? Why had she gone away like that?

Forcing herself to breathe calmly, Jennifer waited. Hailey

80

returned before the woman and stood motionless beside Jennifer, who was beginning to feel sick. She massaged her bump, feeling the babies kick.

'Right, Mrs Marshall. I've just called Dr McKenna's practise and Hailey *is* still registered there. Are you quite sure she hasn't seen a doctor since the last time she was there? She should have had a couple of jabs since then.'

Jennifer relaxed. She'd been right. 'We've been travelling a lot,' she said loftily. 'I thought before starting school would be time enough.'

The woman shrugged, then turned to the screen and manipulated the mouse. 'When would you like to bring Hailey in?'

The world had never seemed so bright when Jennifer ushered Hailey out of the medical centre. Everything, just everything was alright now. She beamed round the car park. Bright sunshine was positively bouncing off the cars and even the blackbirds were shining. For a moment it was quite dazzling.

Hailey stumbled as they crossed the car park and Jennifer caught her, hugging the child tightly. This was all she needed, right here. Her little girl and her babies. What a dreadful pity Phillip wasn't with them on this wonderful day. Eyes shut tightly against the brightness, Jennifer rocked back and forth with Hailey in her arms.

When she opened her eyes again the world had gone back to normal hues and Hailey was pale.

'Goodness, darling, you look as if you need a treat. Let's go and look at your new school and then go shopping.'

The beautiful feeling of elation lasted all the way along the coast road and up the private road to show Hailey the school buildings. It was lucky there had been a vacancy, even at such short notice. A prolonged shopping spree in 'Bambinos' in Bodmin further increased Jennifer's sense of well-being, and back at Long Farm Cottage she made spaghetti for dinner as a treat. Hailey ate hungrily, her normally pale little cheeks

81

now rosy. What a darling she was.

Jennifer leaned across the table. It was time for Hailey to be a proper daughter. The pills made her so sleepy, they really couldn't have that when school started.

'Now Hailey, you know you've been ill. You had an allergy, I think. Yes. But you're better now. You don't need pills to sleep at night any more. Is that clear?'

The child smiled promptly.

'Yes Mummy.'

Jennifer smiled back. Everything was going perfectly.

Chapter Four
Mid September

Katie McLure extracted fifteen brightly-coloured cardboard folders from the staffroom cupboard and took a deep breath. New term, new class, and after four years of teaching primary five and six she had realised her life's ambition to be infant mistress. Here at Polpayne Castle Primary, this meant five-year-olds. The 'pre-school' section of the school was at the other end of the village, the philosophy being that five years old was time enough to sit at a desk. Katie agreed completely; after all, in most other European countries children didn't start formal schooling until they were six. Folders under her arm, she strode along the corridor to her new classroom.

In less than an hour's time the children would be here, fifteen eager little faces. And today all the elegant yummy mummies would be there for the start too. Heart sinking, Katie stacked the folders on her desk and looked wryly down at her own outfit, which could hardly be described as elegant. She expected to spend quite a lot of the day blowing noses, mopping tears and kneeling on the floor - not the kind of things you wanted to do in a posh frock.

The first day at school was a big occasion in everyone's life. As yet the children were only names on a list to Katie. Graeme. Hailey. Julia. Norman. Rich kids. Something she'd never been herself.

Katie knew that the moment she stepped into the classroom and started to teach, she would forget the nerves and cope with whatever her new class chose to throw at her, but right now, immediately before the event, it was just a little scary. She had wanted this for so long.

She looked round appreciatively as she started organising chairs for the children's arrival. Here at Polpayne Castle Primary they had all the private school benefits. The classroom was brilliant - a large L-shaped room with windows all the way down the back. In the middle of the room the 'school' area had fifteen desks and chairs set out in three curves before the whiteboard. The craft table by the door was ideal for handwork; one long, low table they could all sit round. Round the corner was a generous play area, with a large selection of cushions, stools and toys. It was by far the most luxurious classroom Katie had ever taught in, and she knew she was going to enjoy the novelty.

Chairs organised, she straightened up. A strong coffee was what she needed now and there was plenty of time before the children arrived.

Jeanette McCallum, the head teacher, was in the staffroom with a tall, blond man.

'Oh Katie, come and meet Mark Gibson. He's taking over Year Four now that Caroline's definitely leaving us.'

Katie shook hands, conscious that Mark Gibson was looking at her. She smiled briefly. After the disaster with Stuart, the last thing she needed right now was an appreciative man ogling her every time she went into the staffroom.

'Welcome,' she said. 'It's a great place to work, isn't it, Jeanette?'

'It is,' said the Head. 'Katie, you'll have seen there's another little girl joining your class. Hailey Marshall. Her mother brought her in last week to register. I swear school-beginners get smaller every year. I must be getting old.'

Katie laughed. She poured coffee and stood chatting to Mark about the school, glad when some of the other teachers arrived. Polite conversation wasn't easy when your insides were as nervous as hers were. She gave Mark a quick smile and left him with Phyllis, who was talking enthusiastically about the new gym hall. At the moment, all Katie wanted to think about was her new pupils. Would they all get along? Would there be any problems she might not be able to solve? And most importantly, would the children be happy here? She would soon find out.

Chapter Five

'Breakfast, Hailey! Come along, you don't want to be late on your first day!'

Jennifer shouted up the stairs of her new home, then turned back into the kitchen, smiling as she drew her hand over the gleaming work surfaces. She was exactly where she wanted to be in life. A beautiful house, a darling daughter, two lovely babies to look forward to and Phillip coming home. Soon now surely.

Her good mood disappeared as she glanced at the kitchen clock and called to Hailey again. The child had been up since seven and she was still pottering around upstairs.

A twinge under her ribs made Jennifer's breath catch. She was getting bulkier by the week, and standing around like this was uncomfortable. She stood rubbing her back with both hands, forcing herself to relax. There was still plenty of time.

Hailey wandered into the kitchen as Jennifer was pouring boiling water into a mug. Wisps of hair behind the child's ears were still damp, and the blue and white of the uniform skirt and blouse seemed to swamp her. Jennifer pressed her lips together hard.

No matter how much she tried, there was always something to do with Hailey that wasn't quite right. Jennifer found herself fighting frustration at some point every day and it wasn't good for her, or the babies. It was so important that Hailey made a good impression on her teacher today, but here she was looking as if she'd thrown her uniform on. And her appearance would become even messier as the day progressed; Jennifer was under no illusions about that. She mulled over the fact that she would have no control whatsoever over the child all the time Hailey was at school. The realisation was unsettling. She wouldn't be able to tweak Hailey's blouse into place. And the hair… it was just all wrong.

Pulling the child into the downstairs bathroom, Jennifer wielded a hairbrush, tutting as Hailey whimpered. The length was fine and the colour was good now too, the spray had seen to that. Recently Jennifer had been trying camomile tea in combination with the lemon juice, because the smell of the spray was much too chemical for school. Hailey's hair truly was golden brown like it had always been, but the dryness was worrying. In spite of all the conditioner Jennifer lathered the child's hair with, it just didn't look good, and today it was so important that Hailey looked her best.

'You can wear the hairband,' said Jennifer, sliding the uniform blue band over Hailey's head and settling it over the child's scalp. That would do very nicely. It was hiding the thin parts and pushing the bulk of Hailey's hair to the back of her head, nicely out of sight when anyone was face to face with the child. It had been a good idea to get the broader band meant for older girls and then shorten it. The only problem was that Hailey hated the band; they'd tried it out on Saturday and the stupid girl had pushed and pulled at her head until she looked like some kind of ragamuffin. That wouldn't do today.

'You are not to touch this band, do you hear?' said Jennifer sternly. 'I'll notice if you do and you'll be punished severely. Now come and have some breakfast.'

'Yes Mummy.'

Jennifer glanced heavenwards. Hailey had forgotten her smile yet again.

'I wish there wasn't a uniform,' she said, sliding a piece

of toast onto the child's plate. 'You'd look much prettier in a nice dress. Hurry now. We'll leave at half past.'

Silently, Hailey began to eat, and Jennifer sat down with her tea.

'Please can I have some apple juice?'

Jennifer closed her eyes for a moment. Was she to have no peace at all this morning?

'Of course not. You don't want to have to go to the bathroom every ten minutes on your first day, do you? And for heaven's sake remember to go at break time. You can have a very little milk.'

Jennifer set a small glass in front of Hailey and tucked a few hairs back into her elegant chignon. She needed to relax here, everything was going to be alright. Mothers were always nervous when their children started school. It was a pity she'd had to give Hailey a pill to make her sleep last night; they made her so dopey the next morning too. Still, the teacher would surely make allowances on the first day.

'It's time to get ready,' she said, plucking the remainder of the toast from Hailey's fingers and pulling her away from the table. 'Go and do your teeth, and remember to leave that hair alone.'

At exactly half past eight, Jennifer reversed her BMW out of the garage. Her mood swung upwards again as she drove down through the village. Polpayne was lovely - a charming little fishing village nestling on and between sturdy North Cornwall cliffs. Their new home was near the top of the cliff and the view was magnificent. A steep lane wound down to sea level, where the area round the noisy fishing harbour was the heart of the village.

Jennifer smiled happily. Phillip was going to love it here. It was such an ideal place to bring up their family. Surely Gran couldn't last much longer, the cancer seemed to be everywhere now. They would soon be a wonderful little family of five.

A baby kicked, and Jennifer patted her bump. Such a *lot* of surprises for Phillip. The downside was it was getting more and more difficult to keep all her lovely secrets. Phillip did know about the house, of course, so she had at least been able to talk about how the work was progressing. But that was finished now, and she couldn't tell Phillip that she was spending her days teaching Hailey to smile politely and print her name ready for school. That would ruin everything.

The signpost for St Mary's Castle loomed up in front and Jennifer jammed on the brakes. The BMW swerved across the road, which was fortunately deserted. She'd driven right past the lane up to Polpayne Castle Primary. Frustration filled her yet again and she struggled to control herself, glaring down at the child beside her.

'Why didn't you *say* we'd gone past?' hissed Jennifer between her teeth, her anger fuelled by the fact that Hailey was now cowering in her booster seat. 'You can be absolutely hopeless sometimes, you really can.'

Her jaw tight, Jennifer pulled the car around, forcing herself to breathe calmly. It was just nerves, this was such an important day. She glanced down at Hailey's trembling lips and over-shiny eyes.

'Oh for heaven's sake, it's alright. We're in plenty of time. Let's practise talking to your teacher again. I'll be Miss McLure.'

She switched to a haughty, Oxford English accent.

'Good morning, and what's your name?'

Hailey's voice was thick with tears, but she replied clearly enough, even remembering the smile.

'I'm Hailey Marshall.'

'And your address?'

'Four Castle Gardens, Polpayne.'

'And what's your date of birth?'

'The fifteenth of August. And I'm - five.'

Jennifer smiled brightly. The fifteenth of August, such a special day.

89

'Good,' she said in her own voice. 'Just remember not to mumble and you'll be fine. Now blow your nose, we're here.'

The sun was shining hazily now, and Jennifer looked up at the school - beautiful red sandstone with two hideous concrete extensions. Three tall ash trees were waving in the wind at the side of the main building, two coaches parked beneath them. The air rang with shouts and high-pitched laughter as blue-uniformed children ran round them and into the building. Hailey, standing beside the car with her schoolbag, looked very small and very young and very frightened. Jennifer pulled out a tissue and scrubbed the little girl's face.

'Come on now,' she said, giving the child's arm an impatient shake. 'And remember your manners, please.'

She pushed Hailey towards a door where a middle-aged woman was standing with a clipboard.

'Hello. And you are?'

'Hailey Marshall.'

Hailey's voice was clear and the smile was gorgeous. Jennifer beamed proudly. The woman ticked her list.

'Excellent. My name's Mrs Wilson and I'm the Juniors' matron,' she said. 'You and Mummy can go down the corridor to the first room on the right. Alison the classroom assistant is there, and Miss McLure will be along in a few minutes. See you later!'

Jennifer poked Hailey's back.

'Thank you,' said Hailey obediently, and Mrs Wilson smiled and nodded.

'There! You see? You'll be fine,' said Jennifer, striding along the corridor.

She turned back to Hailey, her pleasure vanishing as she looked at the child trudging along with her schoolbag. Hailey looked so young and lost, and her lips were trembling again. Maybe school hadn't been such a good idea. Maybe she should have waited with that, after all, they'd only just moved to the area.

But it was much too late to go back now. And Hailey was

five years old for heaven's sake, she *had* to go to school. She would get used to things. The other children in her class were all new too. Yes, everything would be fine in a week or two. Of course it would.

Her confidence returned, Jennifer put a hand on Hailey's neck and propelled her briskly into the classroom.

Chapter Six

Katie grabbed her handbag and hurried towards the staff loo, pulling out her comb. The school buses were arriving, and today a good number of children had come in private cars too. Nora and Alison were busy greeting her own class right now.

'You'll be fine. You look great!'

Jeanette McCallum passed by, and Katie grinned. The other teachers had laughed at her, going to do her face and hair for the infant class, but Cornish winds and weather had wreaked havoc with both and the kids definitely didn't need to start their school lives with a teacher who looked like Snow White's wicked stepmother.

Katie stared at her reflection. Her long dark hair hung loose and her make-up wasn't quite hiding the anxious expression. She was a teacher, though - she could act.

There was a murmur of voices coming from inside her classroom and Katie hesitated at the door. Fifteen five-year-olds were waiting for her to appear, plus however many parents had decided to come along. She pushed herself through the door.

Instant silence fell as soon as she stepped inside. About forty people were sitting round the big crafts table near the door, parents behind the children, and they were all staring at her with expressions ranging from interested and welcoming to just plain scared. Most of the parents were mothers, and Katie felt her eyebrows rise as she looked round the assembled women. Every single one of these women might have stepped out of a glossy magazine. The dads looked a little more neutral, and the children seemed all sizes, from a big, burly boy head and shoulders above the rest, to a frightened-looking waif of a child wearing a large school headband. This must be the newest addition the Head had talked about.

'Good morning, everyone!' In spite of her nerves Katie's voice rang out confidently. 'Welcome to Polpayne Castle Primary. And now… let's get started!'

She fetched the pile of folders from her desk and sat down at the table, smiling round the group.

'My name's Miss McLure, and I'm your teacher,' she said, deliberately addressing the children only. 'And this is Alison, our classroom assistant.' She nodded towards the student who was completing a work placement at the school.

'Now, I have a folder here for each of you. I'd like to know your name and where you live, and maybe if you know any of the other children. Who wants to tell me first?'

There was a second's pause, then to Katie's relief, the child sitting beside her waved a hand in the air and said, 'I'm Julia and I live at St Mary's Castle and I'm five and I know Ian and Martin and Amy and Melanie and Aiden.'

The mentioned pupils giggled self-consciously and the adults all laughed, including Katie. These were the children who'd come from the pre-school section, and thank goodness, a little light relief to start them off.

'Well done, Julia,' said Katie, handing over the folder. 'Let's just go round the table, shall we?'

The next child was the slight little girl with the headband. Her mother, heavily pregnant and looking very uncomfortable perched on the miniature chair, leaned towards her daughter.

'Hailey Marshall 4 Castle Gardens Polpayne and I'm five and my birthday's on the fifteenth of August,' the child said in one breath, smiling shakily, her eyes sliding up to her mother's face. To Katie's surprise, the woman frowned at her daughter.

'Very good indeed, Hailey,' she said quickly, pulling out the child's folder. 'Do you know any of the others?'

Hailey shook her head.

'We only recently moved to Polpayne,' said Mrs Marshall, looking more relaxed, and Katie nodded.

When they had been round the entire table, Katie took the children to their desks and left Alison to help them put stickers on the folders while she went back to the parents. The fifteen mothers and seven fathers had reassembled round the big table, and Katie grinned at the group.

'This first term is very much a settling-in time for the children,' she said. 'We want them to be happy here, and learn to work in a relaxed atmosphere. They'll have homework in their folders most days, but please don't let them spend more than fifteen minutes on it. Messages from the school will be in the folders too so it's a good idea to check them each day. Now, I know you've all seen the school's prospectus, but are there any questions?'

She spent the next ten minutes answering the usual questions about sport, computers, lunches and so on. The children were in her line of vision, and Katie noticed that both talkative Julia and the biggest boy had problems sitting still. Little Hailey sat with huge, unblinking eyes fixed on her mother most of the time. We'll have tears there when it's time to say goodbye, thought Katie wryly. Good job she had plenty of tissues and a couple of good games at the ready.

To Katie's surprise, however, it was Derek Cameron, the biggest boy, who howled when the parents left, not Hailey. The little girl didn't speak for the rest of the morning, but she seemed quite happy to sit matching fish cards with three other girls.

At lunchtime, Katie watched as Alison took the children to the dining room, then headed towards the staffroom.

Mark was sitting at the table with a packet of sandwiches.

'How was it?' he asked.

Katie poured herself a large mug of coffee.

'Intensive. We have Julia who never stops talking, Hailey who opened her mouth exactly once, and Derek who was inconsolable when his mum left and has spent the rest of the morning shoving people out of his way. And a few others too. How about you?'

He grinned. 'I gather I'm the first male teacher they've ever had. No-one uttered a squeak uninvited.'

Katie laughed. 'That'll soon change!'

She opened her own lunch and sat chewing silently, thinking about her new class. First impressions could tell you a lot, and her first impression of this class was that in Derek and Hailey she had already identified two children who might need more than the 'normal' amount of attention. Mind you, nervousness might well be the reason for both Derek's aggression and his terrible stutter, and Hailey's shyness.

That afternoon she read *The Rainbow Fish* to the children before letting them choose if they wanted to play or draw. Only three children chose to draw, quiet little Hailey and two boys who were soon giggling away over the same sheet of paper. Even after less than a day, Katie could see that Hailey wasn't a child who made friends quickly, but she couldn't let her smallest pupil draw all by herself for the next half hour. In the end she sent Alison to sit with Hailey and went to oversee the others in the play area.

Ten minutes later the assistant was back at her side.

'Hailey's fallen asleep.'

Katie looked over to the craft table and grinned. Hailey was sprawled over her drawing, out for the count.

'Tiring business, starting school. We'll give her half an hour.'

At half past three she called the children together. Hailey was awake now, looking more than a little rumpled. Quickly, Katie straightened the child's headband, a whiff of lemon reaching her nose. She smiled round the group.

'Well done, everyone. That was a very good first day at school. We'll finish with a song now, and then the bus people can go with Alison, and Graeme and Hailey, you stay with me until your mums or dads pick you up.'

Most of the children knew 'I'm a Little Fish', which fitted in well with the first term's theme of The Ocean. Katie led them through it twice, noticing in amusement that Julia sang the loudest and Hailey didn't open her mouth. Trends had been set already. The children gathered round to say goodbye, and Katie realised that exhausted or not, this was definitely what she wanted to do in life. Teach little kids. She waved the bus people off before taking Graeme and Hailey out to the car park, where Graeme's dad was already waiting.

Hailey's face was bleak as she watched Graeme running to his father, and Katie patted the little girl's shoulder.

'Don't worry, your mum'll soon be here too.'

The little girl looked up with startled eyes. 'My *mum'll* soon be here,' she echoed slowly, and stood staring expectantly down the drive. Katie smiled to herself. Hailey looked as if she was waiting for a bus that should have arrived hours ago.

The Marshalls' BMW appeared at the bottom of the driveway, and Hailey turned to Katie, tragedy written right across her face.

'It's Mummy,' she said, her voice trembling.

Katie hid another smile. You didn't often see a child look so completely gutted to be going home from school. She certainly hadn't expected it of this child.

'It is indeed,' she said. 'Don't worry, Hailey, you'll be coming back to school tomorrow. We'll have lots of time to play and learn things, you'll see.'

She hurried Hailey across to the BMW and bundled her in before her poor pregnant mother could struggle out.

Katie stood waving as the big car set off down the drive. Well, her first day as infant mistress had gone pretty well, all things considered. She grinned at Nora and Alison, who were waiting inside.

'It's nice when they don't want to go home, isn't it?'

Nora laughed.

'Definitely one of the perks of having a class of fresh new five-year-olds. It won't last.'

Katie grabbed her jacket, aware that all she wanted now was to cuddle the cat on her sofa and watch something unchallenging on television.

'Tell me about it. Alison, well done, and I'll see you tomorrow at half eight. Thanks ladies.'

She stood for a moment at the door, looking round her classroom with some satisfaction. There would be a lot of tomorrows in here, just like she'd told Hailey. And what a very good feeling that was.

Chapter Seven

Jennifer turned into the coastal road and glanced across at Hailey. The little girl hadn't spoken since saying goodbye to Miss McLure, and Jennifer gave a sigh of impatience. All she wanted was to have a happy, loving time with her child, and here she was frustrated already and Hailey hadn't been in the car two minutes. Jennifer had been eagerly waiting to hear all about her first day at school, but now the wretched child was sitting there looking like a wet weekend. She didn't appear at all glad to be on her way home and she certainly wasn't bubbling over to tell her mother about her day. It was infuriating, pure and simple, and Jennifer hated feeling like this. It would be the pregnancy hormones of course but her moods were swinging all over the place. It wasn't what she wanted from motherhood.

'Well? What did you do this afternoon? And what did you have for lunch?'

Hailey's voice sounded as if tears weren't far off but her reply was prompt and the smile was back on her face when she spoke.

'Miss McLure read us a story and then I did a drawing. It was spaghetti and meatballs for lunch.'

Jennifer nodded. 'Very nice. I hope you managed to eat without making a mess,' she said, turning left at the lights. 'Did Miss McLure like your drawing? Whose was the best?'

Hailey shook her head. 'It was just me drawing and two boys, but they were playing really. Alison was with me.'

'Oh? What were the other children doing?' said Jennifer, pulling into the driveway and turning to give Hailey her full attention. She didn't much like the sound of this. Why had Hailey been working with the assistant? Wasn't she able to keep up with her classmates? It didn't seem like a very positive start.

'They were playing shops,' said Hailey. 'I wanted to draw.'

Jennifer pursed her lips. The child had been awkward at school already. 'Go inside. You can change into your pink dress and we'll talk about this later.'

Hailey heaved her schoolbag out of the car and went upstairs without speaking.

Jennifer put the kettle on, wishing with all her heart that she could have something stronger. Dealing with Hailey took every bit of patience she had. And she was tired too, even though she'd been able to lie down this afternoon. She'd been constantly worrying about Hailey at school.

Teacup in one hand and the other supporting her belly, Jennifer lowered herself into the sofa. A framed photo on the bookshelf at her side caught her eye and she lifted it, smiling. There they were, the three of them, in Yorkshire. Phillip with a big proud smile on his face, Hailey aged two looking adorable in a yellow sundress, and herself in that blue silk suit they'd bought in Paris. Jennifer sipped her tea, content again. Such happy memories. She would sit here in her lovely new house with her lovely new schoolgirl and enjoy them.

Apart from the tiredness, the only downside about her life right now was that Phillip was still away, but at least when he did come home he wouldn't need to start work straight away. He'd been a partner in a successful antiques business in Devon, and with the money he'd inherit from his grandmother he'd be able to start his own place. There would be a lot of money, and of course Phillip had already inherited a very sizable fortune from his parents. Jennifer stroked the deep blue softness of the velvet sofa cushion and smiled again. Life was going to be so good. She couldn't wait to see Phillip's face when he saw that she was pregnant.

Hailey slunk into the room and Jennifer sighed, replacing the photo frame on the shelf. Two-year-olds were a lot more adorable than five-year-olds, somehow. She pulled Hailey towards her and adjusted the pink dress before motioning the child to sit beside her.

'Now, Hailey. Tell me all about you drawing while the other children were playing,' she said, forcing herself to sound casual.

'Miss McLure said we could choose. I wanted to draw,' said Hailey, picking at the hem of her dress.

'Stop fidgeting. And listen to me. You must *not* go off doing things by yourself,' said Jennifer, hearing the sharp tone in her voice.

'I wasn't by myself. Two boys were drawing too and Alison was with me,' said Hailey sheepishly.

Jennifer took a deep breath and made herself sound pleasant. 'Listen very carefully, Hailey. Two things are important. One, you should join in with whatever the other children are doing. It doesn't matter whether you want to or not, the important thing is that you don't make yourself noticeable.'

The little girl nodded, blinking back tears, and Jennifer leaned forwards, taking hold of Hailey's wrist. The child pressed herself back into the cushions.

'And two, even more important, Hailey, and we've said this before, you must be very, very good. If you do anything silly, Miss McLure will punish you in exactly the same way as I would. Is that clear?'

Hailey nodded, her face white.

'Good. I'm glad we understand each other,' Jennifer said, loosening her grip on the small wrist. 'Daddy and I want you to learn your lessons and show everyone what a nice, clever little girl you are. Now bring me your school folder and we'll see what the homework is.'

The homework was to copy three fish and colour them in. Jennifer watched as Hailey drew unsteady lines on the worksheet, but the end result was more or less satisfactory.

'There! Just make sure you always do as well as this,' said Jennifer, sending the little girl upstairs with her folder. 'Now bring me down your hairbrush.'

She relaxed back into the sofa. It was going to be more work than she'd thought, having a daughter at school. In a way things had been easier back at the farmhouse, where life had consisted of eating and learning how to behave properly. And of course the child had spent a lot of her time there asleep, too. But then, that had been down to Hailey's magic pills. They had tamed her, she had behaved just like... well - just like Hailey.

Jennifer drummed her fingers on the arm of the sofa. Forget the bad times. They had never happened. Hailey had been there all along. The Bad Patch had made her doubt her own capabilities, but everything was fine. No-one had ever been lost.

Chapter Eight

Katie glanced at the clock above the classroom door. Ten past twelve. It was nearly time to clear up for lunch.

'Five more minutes!' she called, and the children groaned, bending over their paintings with frantic last minute enthusiasm.

Katie smiled, watching them. It was still only the first week, but her classroom was looking more homey by the day. Those paintings would look great on the 'theme wall' by the door. She had bought some plants to scatter around, and she was planning to start a fish tank as well. Amazingly, only four of her fifteen pupils had a pet at home.

'Time to stop!' she called, and the children groaned again.

Katie walked round the table. 'Well done, everyone. Leave your pictures where they are to dry, please, put the water beakers on the rack, then wash your hands for lunch.'

Chairs scraped across the floor as the children carried out these tasks, chattering loudly. Katie stood in the doorway to make sure that no-one was knocked down in the rush for the cloakroom - another bonus to working here, each class had their own private cloakroom with two loos and a long, low sink. When everyone was busy washing hands or struggling out of their overalls, she turned back into the classroom.

Hailey Marshall was sitting hunched up in front of her painting, her eyes brimming with tears. Startled, Katie went back to the craft table and sat down beside her. Up until now, Hailey had done everything she'd been told on the dot, though both Katie and Nora Wilson had noticed that not only did the child rarely speak, she didn't often make eye contact either. It was only the first week of term, of course, and some kids needed longer than others to settle down to school life, but still, Hailey was by far the most introverted child Katie had ever taught.

'What's the matter Hailey? Haven't you finished your painting?' she asked, putting her hand on Hailey's head, where thin strands of dull brown hair had escaped the confines of the band. To her dismay the child immediately flinched away before shaking her head, her gaze still fixed on the table.

'You can carry on with it this afternoon, Hailey. Lots of the others aren't finished either. Come along and get changed now.' She stood up and held out a hand. Hailey glanced at her, blinking the tears away. Katie saw anxiety in the child's eyes. Anxiety, and what looked like fear. It wasn't the sort of expression that anyone would want to see on a five-year-old face.

'I'm wet,' whispered Hailey.

For a brief second, Katie didn't understand what she meant, then realisation dawned and she grimaced in sympathy.

'Did you have an accident? Never mind, sweetie, these things happen and it's easily put right. Let me see.'

Shivering now, Hailey stood up and displayed a large damp patch at the back of her skirt. Katie smiled reassuringly.

'Okay, Hailey. Sit down again until I see the others off to Mrs Wilson, then I'll give you a hand.'

She strode through to the cloakroom, where the rest of the class was almost ready. Alison was still on her lunch break, but the children would manage to take themselves along to the dining room.

Katie clapped for silence. 'Off you go, and remember not to run in the corridor today. Julia, will you tell Mrs Wilson that Hailey will be along in a minute, please? Her skirt got wet while she was painting and I'm just going to dry her off.'

It was the truth, too, she thought. No point embarrassing poor little Hailey.

She hunted through the spare clothes box until she found a pair of knickers and a skirt that looked as if they might fit, and sent the child into the cloakroom to change.

'It's alright, the others think you just spilled some water,' said Katie gently, when Hailey came back with her wet clothes in one hand. 'Hailey, is it a problem for you, getting to the loo on time?'

Hailey stood there, her head low.

'I know we said that you should always ask before going to the cloakroom,' Katie said, making her voice as understanding as she could. 'But if that's difficult for you, then you can go without asking. Alright?'

A brief smile flickered over Hailey's face and Katie nodded. Hailey was going to need lots of support during these first few weeks, but she'd be running around with the other kids within no time, Katie was sure. Although she reasoned it might be an idea to see what Mrs Marshall felt about her daughter's introverted behaviour. And where had Hailey been to pre-school? Maybe she could speak to a previous teacher. She would need to have another look at the school files.

'I'll put your clothes in a plastic bag for you to take home,' she said. 'Off you go for lunch.'

Hailey's face fell a mile and a half at the mention of plastic bags, but she turned and trotted off towards the dining room. Katie stared after her.

She turned into the school office on her way to the staffroom. The children's files were here; she had seen them all before term started, but now that she could put names and faces together it might be a good idea to look at some of them again. It wasn't only Hailey's introversion that needed an explanation, there was Derek and his stutter - perhaps there had been a speech therapy report about that.

The secretary, Beverley, produced both files, and Katie

flicked through them. There was all the information she could possibly want about the five years of Derek's life, including a speech report, but Hailey's file seemed on the thin side.

'Can I take them with me?' she said, and Beverley nodded.

'Sure. Just don't take them home.'

After school that afternoon, Katie went out to have a quick word with Hailey's mother about the wet clothes episode. Mrs Marshall was standing by her car with Graeme's mum, who was chatting away in a deep, posh voice. When Katie approached with the plastic bag and Hailey in an over-large skirt, the other mother very obviously grasped the significance of what had happened, grimaced sympathetically at Mrs Marshall and melted away with her son.

Katie smiled at Hailey's mother, whose face had turned slightly pink. She seemed to accept Katie's assurances that this wasn't at all uncommon at the start of the school year and Hailey was in no way to blame. With a thin smile and a 'Thank you, that's very kind', Mrs Marshall opened the car door for Hailey.

Katie watched the BMW drive off. The more she saw of Hailey's mother the more intimidating the woman seemed, which might well explain Hailey's reaction.

Back at her desk, Katie opened Hailey's file. The child had been given a cancellation place just three weeks before term started. Hailey didn't appear to have attended pre-school or nursery education anywhere, in fact apart from the registration form, the only other documents were a copy of her birth certificate, and a doctor's certificate signed just last week. Katie saw that it was noted Hailey's father was away, and so all contact would be through the child's mother. It all looked rather rushed. What with Mrs Marshall being pregnant, and an absent father, Katie could see that Hailey had a lot to cope with at the moment.

'Katie! How's things?'

Mark was standing in the doorway, and Katie grinned at him. According to his lunchtime report, his class of nine-year-olds was rapidly losing their awe of their first male teacher. Mark looked more tired every time she saw him.

'We're fine,' she said cheerfully. 'Spent a long time painting today, so the walls are looking less bare.'

Mark came in and wandered over to where Katie and the children had pinned up fifteen child-like works of art that afternoon.

'Seascapes,' he said, gazing at the blue and green waves and splashes.

'This term's theme is The Ocean. I'm taking them beachcombing on Monday, if the weather is okay.'

'Sounds good,' said Mark. 'I've got a sea life poster, if that would help.'

'Thanks, I'll have a look at it tomorrow. I'm planning to start a fish tank, too - not that that has much to do with our sea project.'

'I have a better idea if you want something oceanic,' he said, looking at her. 'There's a brilliant seafood restaurant just this side of Polpayne. Let's go there for a meal sometime. My treat.'

Katie hesitated. She definitely wasn't looking for any kind of romantic involvement with a colleague. On the other hand, three days' experience of Mark in the staffroom had taught her that he was both funny and friendly. One meal couldn't hurt.

'Great idea, but we go Dutch,' she said firmly. 'And as colleagues.'

'Colleagues and friends,' he said, equally firmly. 'I'll book a table for tomorrow night, how's that?'

Katie agreed, and Mark gave her a quick grin before leaving the classroom. She packed her things and jogged across the car park, looking at the space where Mrs Marshall usually parked.

Smiling at the contrast between her own little Clio and the Marshalls' BMW, Katie drove towards Polpayne. She could hear breakers crashing up the beach below, and sniffed appreciatively as a fresh, tangy smell floated into the car. It had turned into a real wild weather day, the sea was going mad down there.

Stopping for the lights at the harbour, she sat watching as a gangly youth pasted a new poster in the bus shelter. The image he was covering was tattered and ripped, a little girl laughing into the camera. Katie recognised her as the child who'd drowned near Newquay that summer, a beautiful little girl with tangled dark hair. *Have you seen Olivia Granger?* was printed in thick black lettering above the photo. The boy smoothed an advertisement for an insurance company into place, and the little girl vanished.

Soberly, Katie put the car into gear as the lights changed. No child deserved to die like that.

And now she was off to the pet shop to find out about fish tanks. The day's work wasn't done yet.

Chapter Nine

Jennifer lay in bed as the dimness outside gave way to early-morning sunshine. The delicate flowery pattern on the curtains that matched the bedspread grew lighter, and she gazed around her. It was a beautiful room, but she should really have been asleep at this time of the morning. It was only half past six and here she was, awake for the day. The babies she was carrying were early risers - or one of them was, anyway.

Jennifer stroked her extended tummy. Not long to go now. She'd been to the antenatal clinic yesterday and Dr Rosen had assured her that everything was going well. Both babies were well-developed, and all they needed to do now was grow. Jennifer turned on her other side, feeling the babies roll and squirm before settling down again.

There was no reason to get up yet. She had set Hailey's alarm to go off at seven, and after oversleeping just once since school started, her daughter had become a good riser. Jennifer relaxed into her favourite daydream.

Mother of three, in spite of the Black Patch. The world had looked like a black and white film then, colourless, jerky, the sound distorted. But that was all over now.

If only she wasn't so alone here. Of course Phillip was close to his Gran so it was only natural that he'd want to be with her in the last weeks of her life. What they hadn't known was that the old lady would linger so long, and LA was too far away for him to pop back and forth. It was a no-win situation for Jennifer. If she told Phillip about the babies he'd be on the first plane home, but then her beautiful surprise would be ruined. She wanted to see for herself the expression on his face when he realised that he was to be a father again. She would just have to wait. He'd only been away ten weeks, which was nothing really. The surprises would be a comfort to Phillip when Gran died, and a little extra time to improve Hailey's behaviour would only be an advantage.

A frown creased Jennifer's brow. That stupid child had brought wet clothes home from school two days running now.

It was embarrassing. Miss McLure had been very pleasant about the whole thing, but what must she have thought? And the silly girl still needed pull-ons at night. Jennifer had blamed that on the pills when they were at the farm, but Hailey only had the very occasional pill now and she was still wet every blessed morning. Lugging sheets in and out of the washing machine was no fun at all when you were seven months pregnant with twins, so any kind of training, with the risk of relapses, would have to wait. It was infuriating. A cleaning lady was out of the question, too, they couldn't possibly have a stranger nosing around the house. Jennifer knew she would just have to battle on with Hailey. But wetting during the day - that was quite inexcusable.

Jennifer shivered angrily, then made herself relax. If it happened again, she would have to take matters into her own hands. Hailey was spoiling their perfect family life. There was always something to worry about. The latest was the permission slip that Miss McLure had sent home yesterday.

Hailey's class was going to a beach on Monday. When Jennifer had first read the slip she'd had to sit down. Were schools allowed to take the children to dangerous places like that? One teacher couldn't possibly watch fifteen children all at once. And Hailey didn't like beaches.

A second look at the note had reassured her slightly; it

said specifically that they weren't going anywhere near the water and there would be three adults with the children. But Jennifer knew she wouldn't be able to relax until Hailey was safely back home again.

One of the babies shifted, as if the uncomfortable thoughts had disturbed it. Jennifer breathed out shakily. Everything would be alright.

Hailey only needed time, Miss McLure had even said so. If only Phillip could come home soon, he'd straighten his daughter out in no time. A smile tugged at Jennifer's mouth as she pictured her husband. How worried he had been during her Black Patch, and how relieved when the blackness had departed and colour came back into her life.

In the meantime she would just have to deal with Hailey by herself.

A baby inside her kicked again, and Jennifer smiled lovingly. 'It's alright, sweetie-pies. Mummy's right here.'

Chapter Ten

The morning air was cool and damp, a subtle reminder that September was more than half over and summer was making way for autumn. Katie whistled as she drove towards Polpayne Castle Primary, then chuckled aloud as she realised that she was looking forward to this morning's outing as if she were one of the children herself. It was her first school trip with the class, a two-hour expedition to the beach to collect shells and seaweed for their ocean theme. Her pupils were all highly enthusiastic about it - or most of them were.

Katie frowned, thinking about her two 'problem' children.

Derek Cameron had more going wrong for him than a mere stutter. He was rude and boisterous with the other children, and Katie wondered which had come out first, the aggression or the stutter. She hadn't yet found a way to get through to Derek, which worried her.

And Hailey Marshall seemed to be plain backward, to use a non-professional description. It wasn't only the poor bladder control; both her speech and her drawing were those of a considerably younger child. Much of the time she just sat there in her own little world, brown eyes vacant and strands of thin hair straggling from the headband she obviously hated wearing.

Katie didn't understand the child, and as Hailey rarely talked in more than monosyllables it was difficult to know where to start. She needed help, so much was clear, but Katie didn't know if she was the right person to provide that help. An expert might do better. On the other hand the child had only been at school for a week, it was a bit early to start dragging psychologists into the picture.

Driving past, Katie glanced at the restaurant she'd been to with Mark. It had been a surprising evening in more ways than one. Mark had outed himself as a fish-eating vegetarian, and away from school he was altogether more serious, talking intelligently about his life and plans for the future. The time had flown by and it was nearly midnight when he drove her home. So the one thing Katie had worried about hadn't come into the equation - whether or not to invite him in.

'I won't ask you up for more coffee, if you don't mind. It's a school night, and I need my beauty sleep,' she'd said as he pulled up under the streetlight by her flat.

'Now you know yourself that's not true,' he said, getting out to open the car door for her.

Katie stood in the front doorway, watching as he drove off down the road.

She knew it wasn't a good idea to get involved with someone at work, but couldn't ignore the smile that was spreading across her face.

Katie pulled up in her usual space in the teachers' car park, where Jeanette McCallum was emerging from her car.

'Morning, Katie. You've got a good day for your trip!'

'Thankfully,' said Katie, looking towards the distant ocean. She lifted the plastic bag containing her expedition clothes and grinned at the Head. 'I wonder how many of the kids have remembered jeans and jumpers - I told them they were old enough to take a message like that home without me writing letters. Everyone who does remember gets an extra sticker for their fish poster.'

Jeanette laughed. 'Bribery and corruption, works every time!'

The children were buzzing round the cloakroom, hanging up blazers and changing shoes for slippers. When Katie arrived they all hurtled into the classroom and crowded round her.

'We're going, aren't we, Miss McLure?'

'It's warm enough, isn't it?'

Katie smiled round the circle of excited faces.

'It's the perfect day for a beach outing,' she said gaily. 'Not too hot, not too cold, and not too windy. Now, who remembered to bring old jeans?'

'Me!'

'I did!'

Katie looked round the hands waving in the air. Unsurprisingly, two children had forgotten: Derek Cameron and Hailey Marshall.

'Derek? Hailey?'

'F-f-forgot.'

Derek looked so miserable Katie almost laughed.

'Oh, well - we'll find you something in the clothes box. Did you forget too, Hailey?'

Hailey, however, shook her head. Katie and the other children looked at her.

'Didn't tell Mummy. Haven't got any trousers now,' said Hailey, staring at the floor.

The other children giggled.

Katie blinked in surprise. 'You don't have *any* trousers? Just skirts and dresses?'

Hailey nodded, and a few children sniggered again. Katie frowned, regretting her impulsive question. She didn't want to turn Hailey of all people into a laughing stock.

'No problem, Hailey. I prefer skirts too,' she said quickly, pulling out the spare clothes box. 'Time to get changed, everyone, and then we'll be off.'

They were going to a cove three miles from Polpayne, where it was possible for the school minibus to drive right down to the bottom of the cliff. Katie didn't want to start any

113

mountaineering expeditions with the class, even if Nora and Alison were there to help her.

The minibus was parked by the side door. The children, noisy and looking quite different out of school uniform, rushed out eagerly. Nora took the wheel, while Katie checked everyone's seatbelt then sat at the front as the minibus rolled along the coast road, back into Polpayne and out the other side. She gazed out along dark, rugged cliffs providing a stark contrast to the soft blues and greens of sky and sea. The tide was well out, breakers crashing far in the distance, so the sands would be perfect to explore.

Slowly, Nora guided the minibus down a steep track. The children oohed and aahed, but finally the bus jerked to a stop at the bottom. Katie stood up and faced the class.

'Okay, you each have a plastic bag. Collect anything you like, but remember, nothing enormous, nothing too smelly, and no dead animals or fish. No live ones, either. And if anyone even goes near the sea we all go straight back to school. If you're not sure about anything, ask one of us.' She turned to Nora and Alison. 'You and I can mingle and answer questions, Nora, and Alison, you stand seawards of the mob and watch out that no-one separates too far from the group. Okay, everyone, let's go!'

She stood by and watched as the children leapt out of the bus, most of them splitting into chattering groups of three or four. Hailey, however, jumped down on the sand, looked wildly about her and then turned left and sprinted along the beach.

'Whoa, Hailey!' called Katie. 'Don't go off by yourself, sweetie.' She ran after the child and led her back to the others. 'Look, you join up with Aiden and Melanie and see what you can find together.'

Hailey stared mutely, and Katie was taken aback to see tears on the little girl's face. There was no pleasure in Hailey's expression, she just looked dazed. Katie watched as the child trudged after Melanie and Aiden, but to her relief the three of them were soon digging away in the sand.

Katie grinned at Nora. 'Right, that's us started!'

The children were shouting to each other across the length of the beach and collecting shells, driftwood and seaweed with appealing enthusiasm. Katie and Nora moved among them, admiring and advising.

'Look what I've found! What is it, Miss McLure?' Derek rushed up waving something green.

Katie examined it. 'Looks like a piece of fishing net. Some poor fisherman had a big hole to mend, didn't he?'

The children nearby giggled. Proudly, Derek stuffed the net into his bag and moved on.

'No stutters this time,' murmured Nora, and Katie looked at her. It was true. Derek *hadn't* stuttered anything like as much as usual. He was obviously having fun, too, running around and laughing with the other children.

'You know, I think he'll be fine in the end,' said Katie, and Nora nodded in agreement. Katie watched Derek for a moment, then turned to see where Hailey was.

The little girl was standing by herself, staring into her plastic bag. Katie crouched beside her.

'What have you collected? Oh, shells, how lovely. What are you going to do with them?'

For once the child looked straight into Katie's eyes. 'I want to make a sandcastle for a princess and put shells on the tower like me and my mum did.'

It was the longest speech Hailey had made so far, and Katie smiled warmly.

'That sounds wonderful, but we've no time for sandcastles this morning, sweetheart. But I'm sure Mummy'll take you to the beach at Polpayne soon. You could make your castle there.'

Hailey's face closed immediately. She shook her head. Katie thought quickly. She didn't want to block off Hailey's new communicative mood.

'Or your daddy, when he comes home?'

Hailey nodded, fierce hope blazing in her eyes. 'I wanted to go to my daddy,' she said, her voice trembling.

Katie hugged her, glancing round to see if Nora and Alison were coping with the rest of the class before turning back to Hailey.

'It hasn't been easy for you, has it? There have been lots of changes going on, but don't worry, Hailey. Things'll be better soon. I had to move house too when I was little, so I know what it's like.'

Hailey stared up at Katie with huge, amazed eyes. 'You did?'

'I did. Twice, even. It was difficult at first both times, but I was soon happy again in my new homes and my new schools. You will be too. When exactly is Daddy coming home, do you know?'

Hailey took a deep breath, her face full of hope again. 'Mummy says he's coming soon.'

'Bet you can't wait to see him,' said Katie.

The little girl's lips were trembling, and Katie hugged her again.

'I hope he's home very soon. Now, you go back to Melanie and see if you can find some other bits and pieces for your bag.'

Hailey rejoined Melanie and Aiden, and another half hour passed before Katie blew her whistle.

'Elevenses!' she called, and the children cheered.

Back in the staffroom, Katie told Nora about her chat with Hailey.

'Thank goodness she's opening up a little,' Nora said. 'It would be interesting to see her in her own home, mind you. She might be more talkative there.'

'I've wondered about that too,' said Katie. 'And wasn't that odd right at the start today when she dashed off along the beach like that - what on earth was she thinking? Maybe I should do a home visit to the Marshalls. My plan was to wait

116

until after the October holiday before starting my visits, but Hailey *is* a problem, and Mrs Marshall might prefer a visit now, rather than later.'

'Yes. And Hailey's problems might get worse when the baby comes, too,' said Nora. 'We should be prepared for that.'

'It's twins,' Katie told her.

'Then I'd definitely go on your visit soon. Twins often come early.'

'Good trip?' Jeanette McCallum said as she walked into the staffroom with two of the other teachers. Katie took her lunch from the fridge and joined them at the table.

'Very. They gathered loads of stuff, I don't know where I'm going to put it all. And my prize stutterer almost stopped stuttering, and my non-talker was really quite chatty, once we'd persuaded her not to run away. In fact when I think about it, we had a brilliant morning!'

The others laughed, and Katie joined in. A teacher's life is full of moments like this, she thought with satisfaction. Small successes that make all your efforts seem worthwhile.

Chapter Eleven
Late September

Jennifer slammed the phone down and strode back into the kitchen.

Pacing the floor, she recalled the conversation.

'It's a routine visit, to have an informal chat about Hailey's progress and let you know a little more about the work we'll be doing throughout the year,' Miss McLure had said. 'We do one for each child before Christmas.'

Jennifer sniffed, reaching for the kettle. A cup of tea would calm her down. Her tummy was tight, and she massaged it gently. Practice contractions, Dr Rosen called them. She remembered them from her first pregnancy, but they were stronger this time.

She took her tea through to the front room and lowered herself into the sofa. Hailey must have made herself conspicuous again at school. Such an ungrateful child - not every little girl was lucky enough to go to such a nice school. The least Hailey could do was buckle down to her lessons and not disrupt the class with infantile behaviour. The more Jennifer thought about it the angrier she became. It was impossible to understand why Hailey was behaving like this. She used to be such a happy little girl.

A worrying thought struck her. Did Miss McLure want this home visit because Hailey had said something? About her hair, maybe? All the chemicals and lemon juice had made the child's hair dull and brittle, and Jennifer was beginning to think that a haircut was the only solution. But Hailey's hair was so pretty that little bit longer. It always had been. She'd have one last attempt at using camomile before making any difficult decisions.

A mixture of confusion and anger swept through Jennifer and her large tummy tightened painfully. She had to calm down. All she needed to do was be nice and pleasant to Miss McLure, and everything would be alright.

She and Hailey had better start practising. Just to make sure they were word perfect when Miss McLure came.

Chapter Twelve

'Katie? Not having any lunch?'

Katie looked up from her perch on the wall surrounding the school's rose garden. It was a dull day, in fact the odd spot of rain was already falling from a sky that had been darkening all morning. September was almost gone; there was a definite autumn chill in the air now. Cut stems and yellowing leaves had replaced the pink and white blooms in the rose bed, and Katie's mood mirrored the desolate state of the garden.

'Hi, Mark. I had a bit of a headache, so I came out for some fresh air. I was going to come in for a bite in a minute.'

'You'd better. Afternoon school on an empty stomach is not to be recommended.'

He sat down beside her, slightly closer than Katie found comfortable. She inched further along. The last thing she felt like today was a tête-à-tête in the rose garden, especially after Saturday morning. She and Mark had gone for coffee after bumping into each other in the supermarket, but the conversation had been stilted this time. Katie couldn't help feeling that Mark was looking for more than a 'colleague' relationship, and it just wasn't what she wanted right now.

'I know. And my head's much better now so I'll get myself inside for some gourmet pasta salad.'

'Why don't we do something after school?' said Mark, as they went back into the building. 'You name it – coffee shop, restaurant, casino, zoo – I'm up for anything.'

Katie frowned. 'Oh, I don't know, Mark, I'm going on my first home visit with Hailey Marshall after school. It might not be easy and I'm half dead on my feet already. I didn't sleep well last night.'

'The Marshalls live in Polpayne too, don't they?'

Katie nodded, and he gave her elbow a little shake. 'Listen. I can see you don't want to get involved with anyone at the moment, and I respect that. But we're friends, and you have to eat. Why don't you call me when you're home from Hailey's? I'll pick you up and we'll go for fish and chips in Newquay, there's a brilliant chippie in a backstreet there, you'll love it. You can be fast asleep in bed by eight o'clock, if you like.'

Katie thought for a moment. What he said was true, and he had said it kindly. And the home visit might well throw something up she'd be glad to discuss with Mark.

'Alright,' she said eventually. 'On two conditions: one, you don't complain if we talk about work all the time… '

'We won't,' said Mark confidently. 'And two?'

Katie smiled up at him. 'It's to be my treat,' she said, going into the staffroom where a few of the other teachers were having lunch.

Mark gave a little salute and strode off towards his classroom.

That afternoon, Katie and the children finished making the cardboard seagulls they had started the week before. They had turned out splendid little creatures, with beady eyes, woolly yellow feet and wings that flapped when their tails were pulled. Each had a string on its back so it could easily be hung up. The children were loud in their enthusiasm.

'You can pin them to your bedroom ceilings, or hang them in a window,' said Katie, standing on a chair to pin her own gull above the crafts table, and pulling his tail to set his wings flapping. The children cheered, and Katie looked round the fifteen bright little faces with pride and satisfaction. Even Hailey looked happy for once, and Derek had only bashed someone twice all day. The children were coming together as a group. It was a good feeling.

'Right, Hailey,' she said, when the second bus-load of children had disappeared down the school drive. 'Let's get going to your place. You can tell me the way.'

She settled the little girl into the back of her car and drove off. Hailey apparently knew exactly where she lived, giving precise directions along the way. Katie nodded to herself. The child might not speak much, but she was receptive to what went on around her.

At the traffic lights, Katie turned in her seat to grin at Hailey, who was sitting still, limply clutching her gull. There was a different – perfume, for want of a better word – coming from the child today and Katie sniffed thoughtfully.

'That's a new shampoo you've been using, isn't it? Something herby?'

Hailey's voice was dreary. 'It's the stuff Mummy has to make my hair better. Cam-cama… '

'Camomile,' said Katie. 'It'll be conditioner. I use that too.'

Hailey stared and the lights changed before Katie could say more. She drove past the harbour and continued up the hill on the other side of the village. Hailey's hair certainly needed something, it was dry as a stick, but did such young children usually use conditioner? Frowning, Katie drove into Castle Gardens.

The houses here were large, and well-kept garden bordered on well-kept garden. It was rather an affluent little district, which did nothing to calm the nervous churning in Katie's middle. She grimaced ruefully. Theoretically, she was the one in charge here, but somehow it never felt like that when she was dealing with Hailey's mother.

They stopped at the near end of a wide, tree-lined street that reminded Katie of an old American movie. Like the other properties on this street, Hailey's home was detached, a generously-sized white building with enormous windows on the ground floor and a well-established wisteria climbing up the side.

'What a lovely big house,' said Katie, helping Hailey out with her schoolbag and gull.

'It's got four loos,' said Hailey glumly, and Katie couldn't help laughing at the resigned expression on the child's face.

'Four! Well, you'll have no problems here, then,' she said teasingly, and a thrill of achievement rushed through her when Hailey actually giggled.

The front door was arch-shaped with two valuable-looking stained glass panels. Katie pressed the bell, and Mrs Marshall answered very promptly.

'Miss McLure, come in. Hello, Hailey darling. Oh my goodness, what *have* you brought home today?'

Her words were pleasant, but the tone was brittle, and Katie wondered if the other woman was nervous too.

'Hello, Mrs Marshall,' she said warmly. 'Thank you for agreeing to a visit at such short notice. How are you?'

'Quite well, thank you. But I do get tired. Hailey darling, run upstairs and change, and then join us in the sitting room.'

The child's giggling mood was gone now, Katie noticed, though she had smiled brightly when her mother spoke to her. They didn't get cheesy grins like that at school, thought Katie, looking on in puzzlement as Hailey switched the smile off and walked on upstairs without speaking. The little face was closed again. It was Hailey's usual expression, devoid of passion, only now it was more so. And this was her home. Dismayed, Katie allowed herself to be led into one of the front rooms.

It was a beautiful, luxurious room. White leather armchairs and a sofa with blue velvet scatter cushions were grouped round a glass-topped coffee table where a tea tray was waiting. Blue-toned oriental rugs contrasted with the gleaming parquet floor, and two display cabinets showed off glassware that was obviously valuable.

'What a lovely room,' said Katie, wishing with all her

heart that she had thought to wear something else. Her school 'uniform' of a sensible grey skirt and checked blouse looked distinctly out of place among all this splendour. It was difficult not to feel like a poor relation.

'Thank you,' said Jennifer Marshall. 'I had people in to do it all, of course. My husband is still away, and I couldn't do any lifting and carrying myself.'

'Of course not. And you'd want to have everything finished before the babies come,' said Katie, sinking into the sofa and trying to look relaxed and in control.

Hailey entered the room silently, now dressed in a blue and white dress, a white band pulled lopsidedly over her wispy hair. Her mother straightened the band and tied the sash, and was rewarded with another bright smile. Katie blinked. That smile didn't seem natural at all. The child's face now, in repose, was so solemn it was almost sullen. Katie took a deep breath. This was a good opportunity to bring up her first point.

'Hailey, you look gorgeous. Mrs Marshall, before I forget, something that would help Hailey when we're doing outside projects is some casual clothes to change into, like a pair of jeans and a jumper. The children can concentrate better if they don't have to worry about getting their uniforms dirty.'

Jennifer Marshall inclined her immaculate head. 'I'll see to it. Thank you. I'll just make the tea now. Hailey, why don't you show Miss McLure your album?'

Hailey fetched a white leather-bound album from a small bookshelf and joined Katie on the sofa. Katie opened the album curiously, and found herself looking at a selection of baby photos.

'What a pretty baby you were,' she said, and Hailey stared silently. Katie turned the pages, trying to encourage the child to talk about the photos, but the responses were limited. Hailey as a tiny baby, Hailey's christening, her first Christmas, Easter and birthday were all catalogued by the usual kind of family snapshot. The album ended just after the birthday photos.

'Thank you, Hailey. They're super photos. And now I know what your daddy looks like,' said Katie, smiling sympathetically when the little girl stared at her again, tears shining in her eyes.

The phone on a table by the door started to ring, and Katie looked expectantly out to the hallway. All was silent, though. Mrs Marshall must have gone to one of the four loos.

'Should you maybe get that?' said Katie, and Hailey lifted the phone to her ear. Katie could hear a man's voice, but Hailey just stood there with no expression on her pale little face. Fortunately, Mrs Marshall sailed back into the room with the teapot and took charge of the phone.

'Cut off,' she said, replacing the handset. 'It was my husband, the connection is often poor. I'll call him back later.'

Katie accepted a cup of tea and a piece of shortbread, and began to talk about school, feeling more and more awkward all the while. Jennifer Marshall sat there looking polite and unemotional, her perfectly made-up lips pursed slightly while Katie described the aims of the first school year. Hailey was nibbling a digestive, her face still blank. Katie began to wonder if the child was even less talkative at home than at school.

When they had finished tea she turned to Hailey.

'Hailey, I'd like a quick word alone with Mummy now, so maybe you could go and play in your room for a little while? Afterwards I'll come and help you hang up your gull, I'm sure Mummy's not keen on climbing on chairs just now.'

Jennifer Marshall nodded at Hailey, who trailed out, turning back at the door to give Katie a look that was quite incomprehensible. Katie hesitated, wondering how best to start. The atmosphere in this house just wasn't conducive to frank, constructive conversation.

Hailey's mother began for her.

'I know you must think Hailey rather peculiar,' she said. 'She has reacted very badly to the move, poor darling, and of course she misses her father terribly. Thank goodness he should be back very soon now. Hailey was always such a happy child - before.'

'Moving house can be very disorientating for a child,' agreed Katie. 'I know that from my own experience. Is Hailey able to talk about it? Has she said what she - '

'No,' said Jennifer Marshall, her voice cold. 'And I'm quite sure the best way is simply to carry on as normal. Hailey will recover, and everything will be alright.'

'I'm sure it will, but I do think it might help Hailey if she was able to talk through her feelings about the removal, and how much she has missed her father. I've only spoken to her about it once, but if she - '

Jennifer Marshall stood up.

'No,' she said emphatically. 'I must ask you most particularly, indeed I must insist that you do *not* engage Hailey in that kind of conversation. She lives here now, and will soon be happy again. Now do you need a hammer and nail for that bird, or will a drawing pin do?'

The other woman's expression was absolutely determined, and Katie realised she would get no further here today. More than a little dismayed by Mrs Marshall's reaction, she accepted a packet of drawing pins and went upstairs. Quiet elegance was the theme up here too. The generous upstairs landing was covered in thick carpeting and housed two mahogany occasional tables and a small oriental chest. Katie thought wryly of the hallway in her own little flat, cluttered with three overflowing bookcases.

Hailey's bedroom was predictably luxurious, with pink and white furniture and enough toys to keep the entire class happy all week. The little girl was sitting on the bed holding a baby doll, and Katie sank down beside her. Right now, she felt as glum as Hailey looked. She had failed miserably here today; she had only succeeded in antagonising Mrs Marshall and that was going to be no help at all to Hailey.

'Where would you like your gull? By the window?' she asked, and Hailey nodded.

Katie pinned up the gull and returned to the bed, struggling to think of something she could say in two minutes which might help the child.

'I like your dolly. What's her name?' she said at last.

Hailey hugged the doll fiercely. 'Mummy says she's called Amelia but I call her Maggie.'

'Is she your favourite? What else do you like playing with?'

Hailey considered this, then heaved a deep, shaky sigh. 'I like my Heidi book and my dolls' tea set. But I wish my bear was here too.'

'Where is he, then?' asked Katie, glad that Hailey was speaking openly. It was just a pity that this would have to be a quick conversation, or Mrs Marshall would be coming to see what was taking her so long.

'At the last house. He didn't move here with me,' said the child, tears in her voice.

Katie winced. 'Oh sweetheart. What rotten luck. Things do get lost sometimes when you move house, but what a pity it was your bear.'

'Is everything alright?'

Mrs Marshall's voice came from the landing, and Katie stood up.

'Perfect. We've hung the gull in the window,' she said, leaving Hailey in her room.

Exactly five minutes later, Katie found herself driving back to the less posh side of Polpayne, having achieved exactly nothing more in the way of frank conversation with Mrs Marshall. She gripped the steering wheel tightly, still stunned by the display of non-emotion she had just witnessed.

No wonder Hailey was so withdrawn. Her mother allowed her no feelings at all at home, and why that should be was anyone's guess. Hailey needed help, that was clear now, but Mrs Marshall was hardly likely to agree to therapy or counselling. Katie pulled into her parking space and switched the engine off. All she could hope was that Hailey's dad would put in an appearance soon.

Chapter Thirteen

Jennifer was fuming. She couldn't remember the last time she'd been so angry. It was all she could do to contain her wrath for the time it took Miss McLure to hang up that pathetic, battered-looking bird Hailey had made, say goodbye, and go.

How *dare* she come here and calmly state that Hailey needed *help* to be happy. Hailey had *everything* she could wish for. There couldn't be one single other little girl in this village with as many toys, as beautiful a bedroom – not to mention a place in a private school – and that interfering, do-gooding teacher was saying that Hailey needed more than Jennifer had given her. And as for the suggestion about jeans... Jennifer shuddered. What kind of teacher dressed the children in jeans for their lessons? What a terrible advertisement for the school.

Furious, she paced up and down the immaculate sitting room. Her swollen tummy tightened, and she stood holding it, trembling. She shouldn't get upset like this, she knew it wasn't good for the babies.

Jennifer sat down, waiting for the spasm to pass. When it did she went through to the kitchen and filled a glass with water. She *deserved* a good life now, she had experienced enough of the bad life before. But that was over and done with now, all over. Hailey was right here, and Phillip would soon be home too. And in a few weeks the babies would be born and the family would be complete.

Calmer, Jennifer finished her water then checked her hair and face in the downstairs lavatory. She was in control again now. And the conversation Hailey and Miss McLure had apparently had about moving house needed clarification.

'Hailey!' she called up the stairs. 'Come down here at once, please. I want to talk to you.'

Hailey came immediately, holding a life-size baby doll in both arms. Jennifer smiled. Hailey was playing with her new baby doll. And that dress was so sweet. But the hairband was all over the place again, and as for the hair...

Hailey perched on the edge of the sofa, in exactly the same place Miss McLure had occupied an hour ago. Jennifer bent down until her eyes were level with Hailey's. The expression on Hailey's face changed from dull to wide awake in an instant.

'Hailey, we've practised this, a smile alone is not enough. Always say 'Hello Mummy' or 'Thank you' or whatever might be suitable, as well. Especially with strangers. Is that clear?'

Hailey nodded, and Jennifer raised her eyebrows.

'Yes Mummy.'

The smile was shaky to say the least, but Jennifer let it pass.

'And even more important, Hailey. I want you to tell me everything your teacher has ever said to you about moving house. Every last detail, please.'

Hailey sat there, staring at the doll. For a moment Jennifer thought she wasn't going to answer, but then she spoke, her voice trembling.

'I don't remember.'

It was little more than a whisper. She ducked her head down and pressed the doll to her chest.

White-hot rage filled Jennifer and she snatched the doll, flinging it into a corner where it thudded against the wall. Hailey gave a little whimper. Jennifer bent down again.

'Don't. You. Dare… ' she said, poking Hailey's chest with stiff, vicious fingers. The little girl cringed back against the cushions. 'Don't you *dare* lie to me. Tell me at once what she said.'

Hailey started to cry, and then to Jennifer's fury she clutched her middle, rolled off the sofa and ran from the room. Jennifer heard the upstairs bathroom door bang shut. She strode up the stairs, her feet thudding against the floor with each step.

Hailey was cowering in the corner of the bathroom, her scrawny arms wrapped around her knees. As soon as Jennifer appeared, she moved towards the toilet bowl and clutched the rim.

'Don't you dare be sick,' said Jennifer. 'Here.'

She held a cloth under the cold tap and then wiped the child's face. Hailey stood there trembling, then burped loudly and spat into the bowl. Revulsion filled Jennifer and she yanked the band from Hailey's head, seized the plastic bottle of lemon juice still on the window ledge and emptied the contents over the dull brown hair.

'Will you *please* act like a proper daughter?' she hissed. 'And for heaven's sake do something about this hair!'

Hailey was crying loudly now, rubbing lemon juice from her face, her eyes tightly shut.

'Go to your room,' said Jennifer coldly, and the child stumbled from the bathroom.

Jennifer returned downstairs, feeling satisfied. She would make herself a sandwich now and watch TV, there was a documentary about twins on soon, that would be interesting. Hailey could just wait for an hour or two, then she might be ready to answer important questions.

It was well after nine when she called Hailey downstairs again. The little girl's eyes were red-rimmed and she was in her nightie, but she obviously hadn't done anything about her hair. Jennifer pointed wordlessly at the sofa, struggling to quell the rage that was starting up again.

'Now Hailey - tell me everything your teacher said to you about moving house. Her exact words, please.'

Hailey, her face set in that annoying blankness, answered promptly now in a nice clear voice. She must have used her time upstairs to think about the question, thought Jennifer. Good.

'She said it was hard when you moved house. All the new people and new schools and things. She said she moved house when she was little too. She said everything was alright, afterwards. And she said sometimes things get lost and that's bad luck.'

Jennifer sat unmoving as a wave of fresh, cool relief washed over her. That would do, that would do very well indeed. Maybe Miss McLure wasn't so bad after all. She had apparently said exactly what Hailey needed to hear.

'What else?'

'That's all,' Hailey mumbled, her head bowed low.

'Miss McLure is quite right. I've told you the same things myself. And you're a very lucky girl, you know, to have such a beautiful new home and so many toys. You should be very grateful.'

Hailey didn't look at all grateful. She sat there, rocking mutely like some stupid imbecile, and frustration welled up in Jennifer again. Hailey was ruining everything. Jennifer gripped the child's thin arm, squeezing as hard as she could. Hailey's face crumpled and she gave a little cry. Jennifer shook her.

'Listen to me, Hailey. Miss McLure told me she doesn't like the way you behave at school. Not at all. She wants you to talk more. Laugh. Be like all the other children. And Hailey - '

She squeezed the child's arm again, feeling muscles give way beneath her fingers, and Hailey screamed. Furious now, Jennifer entwined her other hand in the thin hair and twisted, pulling Hailey to her feet.

'Don't be such a stupid baby! Listen. This is very

important. You know I don't want you talking about anything before we moved here. Do you understand? Talk about this house, and school, but *nothing else*. I'll act immediately if you talk about the wrong things, you know, and you won't like it. Not one bit.'

Hailey rolled tear-filled eyes towards Jennifer.

'Tell me what you have to do. I want to be sure you understand.'

The voice came out in a whisper, and Jennifer strained to hear.

'Laugh and play at school and not talk about the last house.'

'Perfect,' said Jennifer, giving the child's arm another vicious squeeze before releasing her. 'Off you go to bed, now, it's high time you were asleep. Oh, and another thing Hailey, this idiotic running to the bathroom every five minutes must stop. Immediately. Is that quite clear? You know what will happen if you disobey me.'

Hailey stared at her, unmoving, and then to Jennifer's fury she gave a sudden gulp and then retched.

Jennifer seized Hailey's shoulders with both hands and pushed her towards the door. The little girl's head collided with the door frame, and she dropped like a stone and lay still.

It was Jennifer's turn to stare.

'Come on, Hailey. Stop being stupid. Get up this minute.'

But Hailey lay motionless. Jennifer bent over her. The child was unconscious.

Chapter Fourteen

'Bad, was it?' said Mark, when they had ordered wine to go with their meal.

'Oh, it was just such a cold house. Hailey has everything she could wish for, except jeans, but there was no warmth at all between her and her mother. I was there for nearly an hour, and in all that time Hailey didn't utter a single word to her mum. Not one single word. And they didn't touch each other, either, except when Mrs Marshall was arranging Hailey's clothes. I mean, can you believe it?'

Katie went on to tell him what Jennifer Marshall had said about Hailey's problems.

'I couldn't make her change her mind. And I couldn't even begin to talk about how Hailey ran off at the beach the other morning and came back crying. So I went upstairs and hung the gull from the ceiling. Her bedroom's wonderful, but she told me that they'd lost her favourite old teddy when they moved. She just sounded so sad.'

'Strange,' said Mark. 'Favourite teddies are usually right at the top of most parents' list of "things that absolutely mustn't get lost while moving". Mrs Marshall doesn't seem to be a very nurturing kind of parent, does she?'

'Yet it's "Hailey darling" all the time,' said Katie. 'I'll need to think about what to do next.'

'Carry on what you are doing,' said Mark. 'Hailey spends

seven hours a day, five days a week at school. Use that time, help her. She's obviously one of those poor little rich kids - swimming in possessions and emotionally deprived.'

'You're right. And what will happen when those babies arrive is anyone's guess. It makes me glad I grew up in a two bedroom terrace in Leeds.'

Their food arrived then, and Katie realised that she was hungry. Mark's 'chippie' was really a tiny restaurant, just seven or eight tables squeezed into a narrow room between the Christian Bookshop and a laundrette. There were people here too, real people talking to each other and laughing. Katie looked down at her plate and took a deep breath of wholesome, fish-scented air.

'Good, isn't it?' said Mark, and Katie nodded, grateful when he went on to chat about food while they were eating. But in spite of – or maybe because of – the warmth and sheer normality of the restaurant, her mind returned to Hailey in that comfortable, cold house.

'I think I'll do Families instead of Farming as my next theme,' she said suddenly. 'I could start after the October holiday.'

'Don't rush into anything,' said Mark. 'Remember, Mrs Marshall gave you a very definite "hands-off" warning.'

'Oh, you have no idea how subtle I can be,' said Katie grimly. 'And I have to help that child, Mark. There's something going badly wrong for her, she's crying out for help.'

'Just don't help her so much that her mother removes her from school,' said Mark, signalling for the waiter.

'My treat,' said Katie. 'Remember? Shall we have coffee at my place? A *quick* coffee?'

He went home well before ten o'clock, but Katie's mind was churning much too hard to think about sleep. This had been her worst day by far since taking over the infant class, and she knew she should tell the Head, Jeanette, what had happened, in case Mrs Marshall complained.

Katie's cat, Mr Chips, jumped up for a cuddle, and she was glad of his warm heaviness on her lap. Idly stroking his soft fur, Katie thought about the situation. She knew she shouldn't get too close, and she was aware that she had done nothing but worry about Hailey all evening. That wasn't good; she had to keep things professional.

Tomorrow she would book a talk with Jeanette and see what she thought. But right this minute tomorrow was hours away; her pupils would certainly all be asleep by this time and she should be too. Time for bed.

Chapter Fifteen

She would phone that nice Doctor Evans. He'd given Hailey her certificate for school, surely he would come and help them now.

Her knees shaking, Jennifer stepped over Hailey's still form and grasped the phone. Dark, terrifying thoughts were swirling in the back of her mind. She couldn't lose her darling Hailey, not now. Not again.

It wasn't Doctor Evans but his answering machine that took her call, calmly informing her that at this time of night she had the choice of calling 999, or the NHS number for non-emergencies. Jennifer broke the connection and went to look at Hailey again. The child hadn't moved, and Jennifer felt a practice contraction pull at her belly. She lifted the phone again and heard her own distraught voice describe her daughter's fall. After a short conversation the NHS service promised to send a doctor within the next few minutes.

Jennifer replaced the phone and rubbed her middle. She glanced at the child on the floor. Hailey had come downstairs for something… the doll?… and then she had tripped and fallen, hadn't she… yes… of course it was all Hailey's fault. Jennifer had been so angry, she couldn't remember exactly what *had* happened, but she was sure this was the case. What a silly little girl.

Hailey's eyelids were fluttering, she was moving her head.

Jennifer knelt beside her.

'Hailey darling? Wake up, that's a good girl. Wake up now.'

Hailey gave a hiccup and rolled to her side. Relief washed over Jennifer.

'You silly little thing. You fell and banged your head. Do you remember?'

'No,' said Hailey hoarsely, and Jennifer nodded.

'You tripped. I think you tripped over your doll.'

She pulled herself to her feet and fetched the doll from the corner. Hailey sat up, her face pale, and Jennifer examined the child's head. No blood, thank goodness, but a very respectable bump had appeared on the left side.

The doctor arrived and was sympathetic.

'All part and parcel of childhood,' he said, flashing his torch into Hailey's eyes. 'Kids dash about the place and sometimes they fall over, it's a fact of life. Don't beat yourself up about it, Mrs Marshall. Right, young lady, watch my finger... good. How do you feel?'

'I bumped my head,' whispered Hailey.

'We'll get Mummy to put a nice cold cloth on it in a moment,' said the doctor. 'Or one of those cold-packs, if you have one. No medicine needed.'

He smiled at Hailey, then to Jennifer's relief he began to pack his things into his bag.

'She seems to have got away with it. Kids are tough, don't worry. If she feels sick in the night, if her headache worsens, or if she complains of blurred vision - don't waste any time, call an ambulance. You should wake her every two hours and make sure she's orientated. Again, if she's not, call an ambulance. And take her to your own doctor tomorrow morning and get her checked again.'

Jennifer saw him out, conversing graciously, her panic now gone. She fetched a cold washcloth from the bathroom and placed it on Hailey's head. The child looked up at her without speaking.

'You'll be better tomorrow,' said Jennifer. 'On you go up to bed now. Look at the time!'

Hailey, pressing the washcloth to her head, doll under the other arm, stumbled out to the hallway without a backward glance. Jennifer sat back. She knew she had overreacted about Miss McLure. As Hailey's teacher, of course she was concerned. But Hailey hadn't talked about what she shouldn't, so everything would be just fine. She would make a point of being extremely pleasant to Hailey's teacher next time they spoke. Just to show that everything was normal.

The phone rang, and Jennifer struggled up to answer it. This would be Phillip again - she had forgotten to call him back. The time difference sometimes made it tricky to organise calls but this was a good time, afternoon in sunny California and evening here in England.

It *was* Phillip, and Jennifer forced herself into her role of a non-pregnant wife missing her husband.

'Hi, Jennifer honey, how are things with you?'

'Phillip, darling! I was just about to call you back. Everything's fine, but tell me how *you* are. And darling Gran, of course.'

'Well, good and bad. She's still lucid and the pain's more or less under control. They say she'll have another six weeks or so, but she wants me to come home, Jennifer. She wants to say goodbye now while things aren't too bad. She's proud, you know, and I think she feels guilty about me being away from work so long too. So I'm planning to wait until next week for her birthday, and then catch a flight to Heathrow on the Friday. Why don't you come to town and meet me? We could spend a couple of days in London, treat ourselves a bit, and then drive back down to Cornwall at the beginning of the week. How about it?'

Jennifer thought swiftly. A weekend in London would have been marvellous before her pregnancy, but the babies...

'Jennifer?'

Jennifer made her voice warm and loving.

'Darling, I'd much rather spend the weekend right here in our new home. I can't wait for you to see it all. Just come straight on down to Newquay and get a taxi home. I'll be waiting here, and oh, darling, I've got *such* a surprise for you!'

For a brief moment there was silence at the other end of the phone. When Phillip spoke again Jennifer could hear the tension in his voice.

'Sure, of course I can do that. Jennifer, are you alright? You sounded a bit odd there.'

Jennifer laughed. 'Now I know you're coming home I am so alright you wouldn't believe it. Phillip, you're going to love the house... and the surprise.'

'And you're quite okay? No bad dreams, nothing like that? Are you still taking the pills?'

'Everything is absolutely fine, I promise. But I *have* missed you, darling. I'm so glad you're coming home. It's been a long time.'

To her relief, the tension left his voice. 'I know. I'll see about flights and talk to you soon. Take care.'

'You too. Love to Gran.'

Smiling, Jennifer put the phone down. How wonderful. Phillip was coming home.

She sat on the sofa, watching as the living room turned bright with happiness. It was like one of those snowstorm ornaments children sometimes had, where you shook a little plastic ball with a winter scene inside, and sparkling snow swirled round. It was dazzling.

But... something had been dark too, something bad had happened... Jennifer found she couldn't remember exactly, and it was boring trying to think about bad things when everything was so bright and lovely. She focussed on the brightness: Phillip would soon be here. He and Hailey and the babies were all that mattered. Her own little perfect world.

She rose to check that Hailey was asleep. The child was huddled in the corner of her bed, baby doll clutched in her

139

arms. Jennifer removed the doll in case it woke Hailey in the night and stood looking down at her daughter. A bright halo was shining round Hailey in the dimness of the bedroom. She looked just like an angel.

Back in the kitchen, Jennifer made tea to take upstairs. She would sleep well tonight, she was sure. A packet of pills on the shelf beside the sink caught her eye and she lifted it. These were Hailey's pills, they should be in Hailey's bathroom.

Humming, she took the pills upstairs along with her tea and dropped them into the shell box Hailey had made at school last week. A lovely box made by her beautiful daughter.

What a splendid day it had been.

Chapter Sixteen

Katie knocked on the door of Jeanette McCallum's office. It was time to confess about yesterday's disastrous home visit, and she wasn't looking forward to it.

The Head listened without speaking as Katie detailed Hailey's problems and then as much as she could remember of the unsuccessful visit to the little girl's home.

'Hailey looked like a sulky teenager most of the time, except for this really weird smile she kept flashing. And Mrs Marshall wants to deal with the whole thing by pretending everything's fine. She practically threw me out. I should have realised that the direct approach wasn't the best option there.'

'Well, it's easy to be wise after the event,' said Jeanette. 'And we should remember too that Mrs Marshall probably isn't her normal self at the moment. Pregnancy does that to you. I was in floods of tears from start to finish; I must have kept several tissue manufacturers going all by myself. They probably wondered what had happened when Maxine was born and I stopped buying fifteen boxes of the things every week.'

She sighed reminiscently, and Katie laughed. 'She must get tired, and of course she's on her own at the moment. Maybe we should offer them a place on the school bus for Hailey. The Newquay bus goes right past the end of their road. That would give Mrs Marshall more time to rest.'

'Good idea, and Katie, don't be too hard on yourself. Mrs Marshall is obviously a difficult parent. Let's wait and see what happens when Hailey's dad gets back. If things haven't improved in a few weeks then we can think about getting a psychological assessment done, but from what you've said, that wouldn't go down well with Mrs Marshall and it's early days for Hailey still.'

Cheered by the support, Katie walked along to the school office to phone Hailey's mother before she left to pick her daughter up. She still felt guilty about her handling of the home visit, but it was good to know that her boss was on her side.

The secretary tactfully left the room while Katie punched out the number and listened as the phone started to ring.

'Yes?'

As usual, Mrs Marshall sounded distant and haughty, and Katie struggled to make her own voice warm and pleasant.

'Hello, Mrs Marshall, this is Katie McLure at Polpayne Castle Primary. I was wondering if you'd like Hailey to come to school by bus for a while? There's room on the Newquay bus, and it would give you more time to rest.'

The other woman's voice was surprisingly gracious.

'What a kind thought, thank you so much. But I would be a little afraid that the other children on the bus would tease Hailey. As you know yourself she might not cope with that.'

'So you'd prefer just to bring her yourself as usual?'

'Yes. My husband should be home by next weekend, and things will be easier then.'

They exchanged a few closing pleasantries before Katie put the phone down thankfully.

That had gone alright, she thought. In fact it had gone very well, maybe she had caught the other woman on an off-day yesterday.

Katie returned to the classroom where Nora and Alison were overseeing the children at play. Hailey was sitting by herself in the baby-corner, a doll clutched in her arms. How

142

pale she is today, thought Katie, clapping for silence.

Derek was having a bad day, which meant that several other children were over-excited too. Katie had her hands full, and heaved a sigh of relief when Nora and Alison eventually took the still-squabbling mob outside to wait for buses and parents. She straightened the chairs round the craft table and then went round the corner to the play area. It was the cleaner's job to tidy up, but it wasn't fair to leave the place in a state like this. She would just...

Voices were coming from the corridor.

'... not good enough, Hailey. You really are careless. If anything like this happens again we'll have to see what... '

It was Mrs Marshall. Katie hurried round to the classroom area to see Hailey and her mother entering the room. Hailey was even paler than before, and her mother's face was grim.

'Miss McLure, I'm so sorry. This silly child has lost her hairband, have you seen it?'

Katie smiled as pleasantly as she could. The graciousness shown by Mrs Marshall on the phone just half an hour ago was now entirely missing.

'Let's have a look. I'm not surprised she took it off, it was very warm in here this afternoon, wasn't it, Hailey?'

The child stared, then glanced up at her mother and said, 'Yes, Miss McLure' with the same big smile she'd used the day before.

Troubled, Katie smiled back then started to search around. She soon found the hairband in the baby corner and gave it to Mrs Marshall, who immediately pulled it over Hailey's head.

'Thank you. I'm afraid we must rush off now.'

'Of course. Hailey worked very hard today, Mrs Marshall, that's probably why she was tired and forgot the band.'

The other woman's face relaxed somewhat. 'Thank you. She didn't sleep well, actually. I took her to the doctor before school to check that everything was alright, and it is.'

'Excellent,' said Katie. 'Then you should both go home and rest. See you tomorrow, Hailey.'

Alone again, she finished tidying the play area, thinking sadly about Hailey and her pushy mother. The woman's words on entering the classroom seemed more than a little harsh for a forgotten hairband. Thank goodness Mr Marshall would be home soon. Hopefully he'd be able to help his daughter. Although it was puzzling that Hailey hadn't spoken to him when he'd called yesterday afternoon. The connection had been okay at first.

Chapter Seventeen
Early October

Katie stood in the school gym, stopwatch in one hand and whistle poised as the two teams of children threw tennis balls into crates.

'Ten seconds!' she called. '... Five seconds! And... '

She blew, and an ear-piercing blast echoed round the gym. The blue team, who had very obviously won the game, jumped up and down cheering while the greens kicked their feet and groaned.

Katie laughed and clapped for silence.

'Well done blue team! And greens, that was a good effort considering you were one man short. Let's clear the equipment away now and have a few rounds of Beetle Tig before playtime.'

The children didn't need to be told twice. Beetle Tig was a big favourite. In two minutes they were ready to start the game.

'David, you can be catcher first,' said Katie, presenting David with the catcher's cap, which he put on back to front. 'Now, remember everyone, if David taps you, lie down on your back and wave your arms and legs in the air like an upside down beetle, until someone comes and rolls you over. Then you can run around again. We'll count beetles after two minutes. Ready - go!'

Shrieking, the children ran around the gym, a few of them allowing themselves to be caught, just for the fun of scrabbling like beetles on the floor. Several of the children were an easy mark for the catcher. Graeme and Julia both had two left feet, and although Hailey could be quick enough when she felt like it, today was obviously one of her dreamy days. She was trotting round the edge of the gym, a vacant expression on her face.

Katie blew her whistle and the children stood still, apart from those on the floor.

'Well done, David, you caught four beetles. Let's see how you get on, Amy.'

David passed the cap to Amy, and the game started anew. Katie glanced at the clock. We'll have one more round after this, she decided, walking up the side of the gym. She happened to pass Hailey, who was lying on her back waving arms and legs with no great enthusiasm. Katie gave her a grin, then stopped short.

The loose sleeves of Hailey's blue t-shirt had fallen back towards her shoulders, revealing a long, nasty-looking bruise on the inside of the little girl's left arm. Katie only just managed not to gasp. Blue, green, purple, yellow - this was the worst bruise she had seen in all her five years as a teacher. She was still staring at it when Sheila ran up and rolled Hailey over and they both trotted off.

Katie frowned, lifting the whistle to her mouth.

When the final round of Beetle Tig started, she made sure she was in a position to see the bruise again when Hailey was on the floor. It seemed a very strange place to have such an awful bruise. What on earth had happened? When the game was over, Katie sent the other children to get changed and called Hailey over.

'That's a nasty bruise, Hailey love,' she said, taking the little girl's arm and examining the discolouration. It wasn't wide, just long and thin and in places very deep. Katie put her arm round Hailey's thin shoulders and gave her a hug.

'What happened?

Hailey peered at her arm, then shrugged. 'I don't remember,' she said, her voice sinking to a whisper.

'Did you bang yourself in the last week or so? Or fall, or something?' asked Katie, rubbing the arm gently. It was difficult to believe that the child had injured herself to this extent without noticing.

'I don't remember,' whispered Hailey, staring at the door to the changing room with panic in her eyes. Katie decided to let it go for the moment. Hailey obviously didn't want to talk about it.

'Okay,' she said. 'I'll ask Mrs Wilson if she has some special cream for you. Does Mummy put anything on it?'

Hailey shook her head and ran to the door, moving a lot faster than she had during the entire gym lesson. Katie grinned wryly. Leaving the children with Alison she went back to the classroom, where Nora was setting out juice beakers.

'Have a look at the bruise on Hailey's left arm, would you?' said Katie, helping herself to a swig of vitamin-enriched orange and mango. 'It's not new but it looks sore, maybe you have some magic cream or something. Just for the feel-good factor, you know.'

Nora slapped Katie's fingers away from the juice bottle.

'Can do. Go and get your coffee, Miss. Depriving these poor children of their vitamins. Shame on you!'

When Katie returned to her classroom after break, Nora ushered her straight back into the corridor. The matron's usually pleasant expression was troubled.

'Katie, that's one terrible bruise. And there's another on her head, almost as bad. You can see it easily if you push her band back a little. She says she doesn't know what happened, but do you know what I think? I think the one on her arm has been made by a hand - like this.'

She grasped Katie's arm and squeezed.

Katie stared. What was going on? Who had squeezed Hailey's arm like that? Mrs Marshall? If so, why? And where

147

did the bruise on Hailey's head fit in?

'What do you think we should do?' she asked, and Nora grimaced.

'It's an awkward one. Play it very low key to start with, anyway. There may well be a completely innocent explanation; you know how kids do pick up bruises. But we'll have to ask about it. Do you want to do that or shall I?'

Katie pushed her fingers through her hair. She knew she would have to do this herself, tempting as it was to pass the buck to Nora.

'I'll do it. I can do it less officially than you could as matron. I'll just say exactly what happened - that I saw the bruise when Hailey had her gym kit on. But Nora, Hailey says she doesn't *remember* what happened. But she must, and if this is a squeeze mark… '

Nora patted Katie's shoulder. 'Don't get worked up until we know what's going on. Five-year-olds often can't categorise what's happened to them, and I must say Mrs Marshall doesn't seem to be the kind of person to go about hurting small children. She's always so correct and in control. You ask her casually, and see what she says, then we'll take it from there.'

That afternoon, Katie helped Hailey into the BMW, and then took a deep breath, her insides churning nervously.

'Mrs Marshall, can I have a quick word, please?'

She opened the driver's door, indicating that the other woman should get out. Immediately, a haughty expression appeared on Hailey's mother's face, and Katie had to concentrate to prevent herself from stammering. The woman had the unique ability to make her feel like a five-year-old schoolgirl herself.

'I wanted to ask about Hailey's arm,' she began, doing her best to sound helpful. 'We had gym this morning and I noticed a bruise. I wondered if you were putting anything on it? Our matron has some very good cream for that kind of thing.'

There was a perceptible pause, and Katie saw that Mrs Marshall's face was flushed. She felt her heart begin to beat faster. When the other woman spoke her voice was hesitant.

'I'm not, no. I'm sure there's no need to go to such lengths, it's only a bruise.'

'Yes, of course, but it's a bad one. What happened? Hailey doesn't seem to remember.'

There was another pause before Mrs Marshall gave an embarrassed laugh.

'Oh, she would say that. The silly child almost ran into the main road last week. I only just managed to reach her and grasp her arm before she went under a van. When I pulled her back on the pavement again she fell. I may have been a little rough, poor darling, but it all happened so quickly.'

'Gosh, well, better a bruise than being run over,' said Katie, relieved. 'Is it alright if we cream Hailey's arm at school?'

'Of course,' said Mrs Marshall graciously, getting back into the car. Katie waved goodbye as they drove off.

'Yes, that sounds plausible,' said Nora, when Katie reported back. 'We know what a dreamer Hailey can be. It explains the bruise on her head, too, she must have banged it when she fell on the pavement. You see? An innocent explanation. I'll bring you the magic cream.'

Katie agreed, but her doubts returned the following day when she was smoothing the lavender scented lotion into Hailey's arm, creating an interesting contrast to the child's camomile shampoo. Would one quick yank really produce such an awful bruise?

She told Mark about it after school, and he nodded.

'I can buy that, because it was Hailey's mother who pulled her back. If you or I had done it there probably wouldn't have been such a bruise. But when it's your own flesh and blood you often react more forcibly than you actually have to in a situation like that.'

Katie frowned. 'But why did Hailey say she couldn't

149

remember what happened? She must.'

Mark shrugged, grinning. 'She wanted to avoid a lecture on the sins of dreaming while she was crossing the road? Or maybe she got such a fright she's blocked it out. Search me.'

It all sounded reasonable. Katie knew she should make an effort to be more objective about Hailey. But try as she might, she couldn't put aside the feeling that there was something here she just wasn't getting.

Mark looked at her hopefully. 'That extra piece of advice will cost you one coffee. Let's go to the harbour caff and watch the fishing boats unload.'

Katie gathered her things together, grateful for the company but more than a little distracted by her thoughts.

Chapter Eighteen

Phillip slammed his laptop shut and the casing split at the corner, but that really didn't matter because the goddamn machine was dead anyway. He'd wanted to check his flights.

He stood by the window of Gran's hospital room and gazed at the scene below, blue-green water with white-tipped waves rolling up the long, golden beach. Happy Californians were out there having a good time, just as he'd done as a boy, when he and Gran had spent every summer here with Great-aunt Mary. He'd always dreamt of coming back with his own family one day, but soon now his last tie with this place would be broken. How strange it would be, no 'home base' at Winchester Beach. No Gran.

There was a tap at the door and Jeff Powell put his head round, beckoning Phillip out to the corridor when he saw that his patient was asleep.

'Anything new?' said Phillip, knowing that nothing now could be new. The cancer was everywhere and the doctors' aim was simply to keep the old woman comfortable.

'I wanted you to show you this,' said Jeff, leading Phillip into his office. Phillip watched apprehensively as the doctor accessed Gran's scans and pointed to the stomach tumour on the latest image. 'And this.'

He clicked on another set of pictures and indicated an area on Gran's spinal column.

'It's spread very quickly this week, Phillip. I know the two of you have arranged to say goodbye on Thursday, but we're looking at days here. A week, maybe. I don't know if that could change your plans.'

Phillip was silent. Only last Wednesday the doctors had thought that Gran could linger into November. So this really would be his last chance to be with her, but - there was Jennifer too. He just had to go home and see if she was coping as well as she said she was. If he was honest she'd sounded a bit odd the last several times he'd phoned. All this stuff about a surprise. And what the hell was he supposed to do now?

'How sure is that?' he said at last, and the doctor grimaced.

'Well, there's never an exact prognosis, and the fact that the lung tumour hasn't grown makes it even more difficult. If I was a betting man I'd say a week or less, though.'

'Right. I - I'd better stay, then.'

The doctor patted his shoulder and left him on a bench in the corridor. Phillip leaned his arms on his knees, trying to get his head round the decision he had just made.

It was a horrible situation to be in. He was waiting for his Gran to die, and no way did he want that wait to be over, and yet… he had a duty to Jennifer too. She'd had such a bad time before. Still, that was in the past now. He was just nervous because he couldn't see with his own eyes that she was okay.

He would have to phone and tell her about his delay coming home. If only she'd agreed to come over. She had repeatedly refused though, and now he thought about it, even that was a bit strange. Her fear of flying wasn't really a good enough reason to say no to his request that they spend a few weeks with his dying grandmother.

Apprehension settled even more firmly in Phillip's middle, and he sat straighter, thinking back to his last telephone conversation with his wife. What on earth could this surprise be?

A little shiver ran through Phillip as he remembered

Jennifer's voice on the phone. She was definitely hiding something big. If only he could contact Thea, but he had no phone number for her and he hadn't been able to find her on the web. Maybe he should phone Bea. But the last time he'd done that, Jennifer had made it very clear that she didn't want him to have anything more to do with her mother.

Maybe he was worrying about nothing. An over-bright voice on the phone and a mysterious surprise. That was all.

Chapter Nineteen
Mid October

'Last day of the holidays, Hailey darling, we're going to have such a lovely time!'

Jennifer watched as Hailey took her place at the breakfast table. Thank goodness the child had a little more colour this past week or two. The hair was still all wrong, but they were going to address that today and then she would look like a proper daughter and not some waif from the local orphanage. And the bruises were almost gone.

Jennifer spooned up her muesli. She was feeling surprisingly good these days. She'd expected the last few weeks of her pregnancy to be exhausting, but life was so bright and – exuberant, yes, that was the word – she really couldn't remember when she'd last felt so energetic.

Of course Hailey still had her moments of being sulky, and she could be a real scaredy-cat too, which was infuriating when Jennifer was in such a good mood all the time. But all in all, the child was settling in very well. There had been no more wet clothes brought home from school - it was amazing what setting clear boundaries could do. So all they needed was to fix the hair.

A rush of affection almost overwhelmed Jennifer as she looked at Hailey, who was drinking her milk exactly as a good child should. The little girl caught her eye and smiled promptly. Oh, it was *wonderful* to have a daughter. And in no time at all Phillip would be home to share her joy. The wait was nearly over now.

Jennifer massaged her belly, rejoicing when a baby moved beneath her hands, but her happy mood slipped when she glanced at Hailey again. What was the child thinking, scowling into her cereal like that?

Jennifer sipped her tea, deliberately looking away from the little girl. She was going to enjoy today, even if Hailey insisted on being miserable. It was marvellous, feeling strong and positive all the time. Jennifer laughed aloud.

'We have a busy day in front of us, darling. First, we're going to get our hair cut. Then after lunch we're going to the clinic and Dr Rosen will check that the babies are alright. That'll be fun, won't it?'

Hailey stared mutely, touching her straggling brown hair. Jennifer got up and walked round the table.

'Big smile, darling, Mummy wants you to be happy!'

The smile appeared immediately and Jennifer hugged Hailey tightly.

'Answer the lady nicely when she speaks to you,' said Jennifer, swinging into the last parking space outside the hairdressing salon near Polpayne harbour. 'And don't forget to smile. You know what will happen if you aren't good, don't you?'

Her face blanching, Hailey nodded.

It probably wasn't necessary to repeat warnings like that anymore, thought Jennifer, pushing the child into the salon. Hailey knew what was expected of her, look how nicely she was greeting the two hairdressers waiting for them. Jennifer's explanation of too much tropical sunshine, and shampoo that had done more harm than good was accepted, and the younger assistant started to wash Hailey's hair.

Jennifer leaned back, enjoying the soothing fingers massaging her scalp. There was nothing like a relaxing visit to the hairdresser. And she needn't have worried about Hailey because both hairdressers were interested in nothing but Jennifer's pregnancy.

When was the baby due? Twins! Did she know what sex they were? Was it to be a Caesarean? *Twins!!* Didn't she get awfully tired?

Jennifer enjoyed herself thoroughly. They left the salon an hour later, Jennifer newly washed and blow-dried, and Hailey shorn within an inch of her scalp.

As usual, the practice contractions started after lunch. Jennifer lay on the sofa, glancing through Hailey's baby album, still on the coffee table after Miss McLure's visit. What a special time babyhood was. Hailey had changed, look at the dimples in those first birthday photos. Did dimples just come and go like that?

Uneasily, Jennifer rubbed the tightness away from her bump, glad to see that it was time to go to the clinic. She had booked herself into the Rosen Clinic, a private hospital on the Bodmin Road. The NHS maternity unit at Newquay was nearer, of course, but the Rosen Clinic was quieter and she was guaranteed a single room there.

'Come along, Hailey,' she called up the stairs, and the child ran down quickly, a scared expression on her face until she remembered the smile.

Irritation flashed through Jennifer yet again. Hailey had rushed into the kitchen for her jacket without even looking at her mother - now a normal little girl would have given her mummy a hug on the way past, wouldn't she? But Hailey never showed any affection. They would start work on that later.

Jennifer eased the car out of the driveway. Driving was the one thing in her life now that wasn't effortless, in fact she knew she probably shouldn't be doing it at all. Her bulk made it difficult to turn properly, and the frequent surges and kicks from the babies were starting to make her jumpy.

'Afternoon, Mrs Marshall,' said Dr Rosen, and Jennifer gave

him her best smile. He looked like one of those perfect family doctors in an American TV series - glossy, greying hair and dimpled chin.

He glanced at her folder, where the nurse had printed out the various tests she'd just run.

'This is looking pretty good. Blood and urine are fine, only slightly swollen ankles, not much weight gain. Hm.'

He glanced over to Hailey, who was sitting near the door of the examination room.

'Hailey, you're the boss now. Tell Mummy she has to put her feet up and eat more peanut butter,' he said jokingly.

Jennifer laughed, and stared hard at Hailey to tell her she should laugh too. But of course Hailey didn't understand, she just sat there gawping up at Dr Rosen. It had been a mistake to bring her here.

'And quite a few of these practice contractions I see. Well, on paper you've another six or seven weeks to go, but I don't think the babies will wait that long. Two more weeks would be good, though, longer if possible. We'll just monitor your uterus activity for half an hour and see what's happening there.'

The nurse wheeled the monitor across the room, and to Jennifer's dismay, Dr Rosen sat down beside Hailey and started to chat.

'And how old are you, Miss Marshall?' he asked, leaning forward and grinning at her.

'Five,' said Hailey, and Jennifer pressed her lips together. One word answers really weren't appropriate for a child of Hailey's age. She had forgotten the smile, too.

'And are you looking forward to having two babies at home?'

Hailey took her time thinking about this, then to Jennifer's relief she said, 'Yes.'

Dr Rosen laughed, clapping Hailey's shoulder. 'I do like a woman who thinks things through and then speaks her mind clearly. Where do you go to school?'

'Polpayne Castle Primary,' said Hailey promptly.

'And is your teacher nice?'

'Oh *yes!*' said Hailey, beaming suddenly.

What a stupid girl, thought Jennifer. Why couldn't she have said 'oh yes' like that when he asked about the babies?

'Want some juice, Hailey?' asked the nurse.

Hailey nodded, then glanced at Jennifer and said, 'Yes please.'

'On you come with me then. We'll leave Mummy to relax for a while.'

Jennifer's tummy tightened immediately. But of course Hailey would be good.

'Hailey's small for her age, isn't she?' said Dr Rosen, peering at the printer.

'She was born six weeks early,' said Jennifer. 'She's never really caught up with her age group. Of course, both my parents are small too.'

'Yes,' said Dr Rosen, and she could tell by the tone of his voice that he wasn't thinking about Hailey any longer.

Home again, Jennifer heaved a sigh of relief. Driving was definitely too tiring now. She really should send Hailey to school in a taxi next week.

'I'm going to phone Daddy,' she said, easing herself down on the sofa. 'Go to your room and don't make a sound, please.'

She punched in the number, hugging her bump in anticipation while it connected.

'Phillip, darling! How are things?'

His voice sounded far away, and she strained to hear him.

'Oh Jennifer honey, I was about to call you. Gran's gone, she just drifted away. It's so – you know – a relief after the long wait, but it's been so hard. I'm having her cremated tomorrow and I'll bring the ashes home with me. We'll find a beautiful place and scatter them together. That's what she wanted.'

Jennifer closed her eyes and felt warmth flood through

her. It was over. Phillip was coming home.

'Oh Phillip, I'm so glad she's at rest. I wish I was there with you. Is there much to do before you come home?

'No. I'll get a lawyer to see to everything here. I should be home by the beginning of the week. Oh darling, I can't wait to see you.'

Jennifer said goodbye and smiled. The sun was shining brilliantly and so was the whole room, in fact she could feel warm sunshine fizzing away inside her.

In just a few days' time, her husband was going to get the biggest surprise of his life.

Chapter Twenty
Late October

Whistling, Katie set out a circle of chairs in the play area, then looked round in satisfaction. Just a couple of months had made an amazing difference to the place. Her classroom now reflected the personalities of the children who came here each day. The walls were covered with seascapes, and gaudily decorated cardboard fish hung in the windows. Four orange and two black goldfish were swimming in a tank near the door, and the 'show' table, where the children could lay out interesting finds from outside, was full to overflowing. It was a happy, lively room.

The children started to arrive, all keen to tell Katie about the half-term holidays. She listened to stories of Ian's week at the Red Sea and Janine's trip to New York. Her own break had been positively boring in comparison; a visit to her mother in Manchester where Katie had done some thinking about her almost-relationship with Mark. She had come to the conclusion that she was being silly - lots of people worked with their partners. They were both obviously attracted and if she didn't act on it she'd probably always regret it. So a meal out and a candid talk were high on her agenda for this week.

But now it was the half-term leading up to Christmas, and her new theme of Families led rather well into the Christmas story. She had decided not to use the word 'families' too much, though, in case this antagonised Mrs Marshall.

Katie glanced round the little circle of faces. Most of the children looked pleased to be back again. All, in fact, apart from Hailey Marshall. The little girl seemed very down, slumped in her chair looking as if she had no energy left at all. Katie stared at her in dismay. The child seemed to have shrunk in the holidays – or maybe it was the punkish haircut. Had it really been necessary to cut her hair so very short? Was Mrs Marshall afraid Hailey would catch head lice at school? Surely not. And shouldn't her father have returned by now? Another chat with Mrs Marshall was looming, Katie could feel it.

Pushing her uneasiness to the back of her mind, she smiled round the circle.

'This term, we're going to talk about important people. Who is your most important person, Julia?'

Julia thought, head to one side. 'The Prime Minister?'

Katie concealed a smile. 'Yes, he's very important, but you don't actually *know* him, do you? I meant who is your very own most important person?'

'Mummy,' said Julia promptly. 'And Daddy.'

'Good,' said Katie warmly. 'Ian? Do you have any other important people?'

'Granny and Grandpa,' said Ian.

'Right,' said Katie. 'Hands up everyone who has a Granny or a Grandpa.'

The children all raised their hands immediately, and Katie smiled to herself. This theme was certainly interesting the class; even Hailey and Derek were gazing at her with rapt attention.

She knew from the school files that all the children had both parents living, and all but Sheila and Jamie lived in intact families. The class should be able to put together a whole list of 'important people'.

'My sister!' called out Rebecca.

'Excellent,' said Katie. 'How many people have a sister?'

161

Eight children waved their hands around wildly.

'And who has a brother?'

Hailey was still following the conversation intently, and to Katie's surprise, she raised her arm promptly. Katie looked at her, and Hailey caught her breath and snatched her hand back down again.

Katie frowned. Hailey didn't have a brother. She quickly asked Martin about his brother, and the class went on to discuss their way through cousins, aunts and uncles, godparents and friends.

'Right,' said Katie when there was a little pause. 'You can all go and draw a picture of your most important people. They can be anyone at all. Draw maybe two or three of your own VIP's - that means very important persons.'

The children gathered paper and crayons and went to their desks. Katie sat watching as childish figures started to appear on drawing paper. Only Hailey was inactive, sitting staring into space. Katie looked at her in concern. She waited a few minutes and then went over and crouched beside Hailey's chair.

'Have you decided who you want to draw, Hailey?' she said in a low voice.

Hailey looked at her, and Katie was struck, horribly, by the misery on the little girl's face. She would have to find out what was making her look like this.

Hailey gave a sniff. 'They're not here anymore,' she said, and Katie winced. How stupid. She hadn't even considered that anyone might want to draw a deceased grandparent or the like. She patted Hailey's shoulder.

'That doesn't matter at all, sweetheart,' she said reassuringly. 'You can draw anyone important, whether they're still here or not.'

Slowly, Hailey bent over her paper. Katie went back to her desk, wondering if she should say something to the whole class. No-one else seemed to be having problems, though, and she decided to wait for the moment. There would be plenty of time to talk about death when they were further into the theme.

The children were working steadily and mostly silently when the classroom door opened. Katie looked up. One of the older girls came in and presented her with a note.

'Mrs McCallum wants all the teachers to read this.'

Katie glanced at the piece of paper. The staff meeting about the school Halloween Party had been shifted from four o'clock to lunchtime. Good.

'That's fine,' she said, accompanying the girl back to the door. 'Thanks, Olivia.'

There was a crash, and Katie looked round to see Hailey's crayon box on the floor. Hailey herself had gone as white as a sheet.

'Hailey! What is it?'

Katie rushed over to the little girl, who was staring straight in front of her, eyes wide, looking as if she had seen a ghost. Martin and Rebecca were picking up the spilt crayons, and Katie bent over Hailey's chair, hugging her and rubbing her back. The child was trembling. Dry sobs mixed with shivers shook her entire body. All at once Hailey gave a gulp and vomited on the floor beside her chair, splattering Katie's shoes with half-digested cornflakes. The other children cried out and Hailey retched again, then leaned back in her chair, pale and shaking.

Katie stepped out of her shoes and went to the other side of Hailey's chair, looking round the group with as reassuring an expression as she could manage. The children were silent now, staring unhappily at their stricken classmate.

'It's alright,' said Katie, trying to sound calm. 'Alison, would you go and find Nora Wilson, and tell her we need her here right now, please?'

The assistant ran, and Katie lifted Hailey's small body and carried her over to the craft table, away from the other children. She sat the little girl on her lap and hugged her, trying to ignore the sour, sick smell on Hailey's breath.

'Don't worry, sweetheart. You'll be okay soon,' she said, squeezing Hailey's cold hands and hoping that it was true.

Alison came back with Nora, who took Hailey's pulse and felt her forehead.

'Hailey, do you have a pain anywhere? Your tummy?'

Hailey shook her head.

'Looks more like shock,' said Nora in a low voice. 'What was she doing?'

'Drawing,' said Katie. 'Nothing that would set off something like this.'

'Hm, well, whatever's wrong, I think the best thing is for Hailey to come with me and rest till break-time. Then we'll see.'

Katie closed the door after Nora and Hailey, then turned to the other children.

'Hailey will be fine, don't worry. Back to work now.'

She lifted Hailey's drawing and examined it curiously. There were three figures here, all drawn in Hailey's usual childish style. The two larger ones were man and woman, though as the woman in the drawing had short brown curls it couldn't be Mrs Marshall. Maybe this was someone who 'wasn't here anymore'. The male figure was tall and thin and could have been anyone. The third, smaller figure was unfinished, but wasn't wearing a skirt so Katie assumed it was a boy. There was no sign at all of a pregnant mother or two babies.

Katie put the drawing into her desk drawer. She would ask Hailey to explain it later. And now she'd better clean up that sick mess, she thought dismally. *Not* one of the perks of being a teacher.

The children watched as she wielded the floor cloth, trying to keep her face neutral in spite of the cloying sick-smell. Of her own accord, Melanie opened a window to let in some air, and Amy ran for the can of air-freshener from the cloakroom. Katie was touched.

When the bell rang for break, she hurried along to Nora's

sick room, where Hailey was sitting on the bed, looking more like her usual self.

'Feeling better?' asked Katie, sitting down beside her.

'Yes thank you,' said Hailey politely.

Katie put an arm round the child's shoulders. 'Hailey lovey, what happened?' she said, but Hailey shook her head.

'I just went all shaky. And then I was sick.'

Nora came in with a damp cloth and wiped Hailey's face and hands.

'She's much better now,' she said to Katie. 'I'm wondering if we should send her home. What do you think, Hailey? Want to go home for a sleep? That might make you feel better.'

'I had a pill to make me better last night. I want to stay here,' said Hailey firmly, standing up and pulling her skirt straight.

'Right then,' said Nora. 'We'll go back to the others now, Hailey. It's break-time.'

The child nodded solemnly, and Katie, still puzzled, went along to the staffroom.

After break, she gave the children arithmetic worksheets and went round the room correcting their efforts in turn. Hailey seemed back to her own kind of normal now, finishing her first sheet with only two mistakes.

'Well done you,' said Katie, gesturing for Hailey to come up to her desk. She pulled the 'VIP' drawing from her drawer. 'Tell me about your drawing, Hailey.'

Hailey remained dumb, twisting one foot round the other leg and staring bleakly at the paper.

'This lady here doesn't have babies in her tummy,' said Katie carefully. 'This isn't Mummy, is it?'

Hailey shook her head.

'Do you want to tell me who your important people are?'

Katie made her voice as gentle and persuasive as possible, but Hailey shook her head again, looking scared.

Katie patted her shoulder. 'That's alright, lovey, they're *your* people. But Hailey, was it this drawing that made you sick this morning?'

Hailey stood with her head on one side. 'No,' she said at last. 'It was because – that girl – came in with the letter to show you.'

There was nothing Katie could think of to reply to this, so she sent Hailey back to her seat and went on with her corrections.

Before the staff meeting Katie cornered Mark, who was Olivia's teacher.

'I need a favour,' she said. 'Can you ask Olivia Bennet if she knows Hailey Marshall from somewhere? Hailey had an awful go of the shakes this morning and she said it started when Olivia came in.'

'I'll ask her,' said Mark, sounding surprised. 'But I honestly can't think of any child less likely to give another the shakes than Olivia.'

Katie settled down as the discussion about the Halloween party started, but her thoughts kept wandering back to Hailey. She still felt as though they were missing something important. It was frustrating that Mrs Marshall wouldn't volunteer any important information; they could only hope that Mr Marshall was more forthcoming.

Unfortunately, she was given no chance to talk to Hailey's mother that afternoon. Mrs Marshall bundled the child into the car as soon as Katie mentioned that Hailey had been sick, and Graeme's mum was waiting to ask about something, so all Katie could do was wave goodbye as the BMW exited the car park.

Back in her classroom, Katie lifted Hailey's drawing and stood staring at it. Who were these people? And what was the connection between Mark's pupil and Hailey's shakes?

Mark was waiting in the staffroom when she went to collect her things. 'Olivia barely knows of Hailey's existence,' he said.

'Thanks,' said Katie thoughtfully. 'Maybe she reminded Hailey of someone from the past. If it was some painful, submerged memory I suppose it could have given her the shakes without her knowing exactly what was going on. She's only five.'

'Yeah.' Mark stood up to go. 'She doesn't look it, does she? Okay, see you tomorrow.'

Katie took a deep breath and hurried after him. 'How about trying the new Chinese place behind the golf club sometime soon?' she said as they crossed the car park. 'My treat.'

Mark's face lit up. 'You're on. I've heard they do brilliant shrimps. Tomorrow night?'

Well, that hadn't been so difficult, thought Katie as his car disappeared down the road. Maybe this was the start of something exciting in her life. She needed to stop worrying about her students so much, and this, whatever it turned into, might be the very thing to help her do just that.

Part Three
The Baby

Chapter One
Late October

'Sir? Can you put your seat upright, please? We're almost at Heathrow.'

The flight attendant swayed elegantly down the aisle, checking that the passengers were ready to land. Phillip groaned inwardly. The jet lag was always worse flying west to east. The flight from LA to New York had been bumpy, one adrenalin kick after another, and on this flight he'd had an aisle seat and both his neighbours had been up and down like yoyos. On the plus side he was almost back in England and his life was his own again. Guilt stabbed into him. He knew it hadn't been the best thing, leaving Jennifer for so long, especially when she still wasn't talking to her mother.

Green was visible below them now, and Phillip heaved a sigh of relief. That was England, and somewhere down there was his wife. If only Jennifer had agreed to come out to LA. Not that he regretted his decision to stay; it had been the right one for Gran. Those last few days with her had been unforgettable. She'd been alert, almost pain-free, and they'd sat together holding hands, looking at photos and pulling out memories. In a strange way, Phillip had almost enjoyed it. But she was gone now, and there would be no need for him to return to California in the foreseeable future. He could get his life back on track.

But the thought that his journey to Cornwall hadn't even begun yet wasn't a great start. There were no suitable flights to Newquay so he was planning to hire a car and drive down, but really he was too tired for such a long drive. It would be more sensible to crash out at a hotel now and continue his journey tomorrow. Then at least he'd be fresh for his reunion with Jennifer - and for the mysterious surprise.

He would phone Jennifer from the airport, and if she sounded alright, he would wait in London. Otherwise he would just take his time driving down. It was Tuesday, the roads shouldn't be busy.

He still didn't know what he was going to find when he got to his new home. And whatever this wretched surprise was, it was big, he could tell. Jennifer had dragged it up in every conversation they'd had over the past weeks, but she'd refused to go into details. She was definitely different; something about her had changed and he couldn't put a finger on what it was. Apprehension as well as guilt gnawed away in Phillip's gut, and he rubbed his face. Maybe he should just drive straight down, exhausted or not. Jennifer would be impatient to see him again.

Maybe she'd just been lonely. After all, he'd been away for a lot longer than they'd anticipated, and Jennifer had moved to a new town where she didn't know anyone. Loneliness sounded quite feasible, actually. Not a Black Patch. Just lonely.

Please be okay, Jennifer, he thought as the plane taxied towards the terminal building. Surely she was, she'd told him that the doctors had been very pleased with her that last appointment. Her meds were balanced, she was in therapy, and even now she was obviously out and about, doing things. So why did he feel that something was just very wrong?

The terminal building was packed. A hotel was out of the question, Phillip realised, he would never manage to sleep.

He had to see for himself what was going on, and even driving quite fast it was going to take him almost four hours to get to Polpayne.

He collected his luggage from the carousel then steered the rickety trolley through customs. In the arrivals hall he arranged to hire a car, then looked round for the public telephones. His mobile phone battery was low and he didn't want his conversation with Jennifer cutting out. Fingers trembling, he punched out the number.

Come on, Jennifer, honey. Come to the phone and convince me everything's okay.

The phone rang on, and on. Phillip was just about to give up when there was a click and Jennifer's voice answered, sounding ragged and almost weepy.

'He - hello?'

'Jennifer!' he shouted, aware that people were looking round at him. 'Jennifer, what's wrong?'

Chapter Two

'Bye, sweetheart! You have a good day and I'll be waiting here for you at four.'

Maggie stood beside the car and watched as Joe ran across the playground and joined a group of children near the door. Several other mothers were chatting by the gate, but she didn't join them, didn't even look at them. She just waited until the bell rang and Joe's dark head disappeared inside the building. Now he was safe. He was someone else's responsibility until four o'clock, and for the first time since returning to Carlton Bridge over a month ago, Maggie was facing a whole day alone. Isa, her mother-in-law, had gone home yesterday, Colin was at work, and now Joe was at school.

She felt absolutely empty. The terrible hope, all the waiting and watching for Olivia that had kept her buoyed up at Newquay was long gone now, and no new feelings had awakened inside her to fill the gap. It was as if she were a robot - moving, going through the motions of living, but not alive.

Maggie flopped into the driver's seat and sat still. She had shopping to do, but straight after the school run wasn't a good time. The eyes following her round Newquay had been nothing compared to the eyes in Carlton Bridge. All those other mothers would be going to the supermarket now, with little kids tagging along behind, or being pushed in buggies, and she couldn't face the thought of meeting them all. The contrast to her old life was just too cruel. Before, she'd have enjoyed chatting with the other mums, and maybe going for a walk round the park with the little ones. But she knew if she met those mothers today they would look at her with embarrassed expressions on their faces. As if she were somehow inhuman because she was upright and walking about. As if she had any *choice* in the matter. If she went to the supermarket now, some of these mothers would slide round into another aisle to avoid speaking to her. She could understand this completely, after all, what could anyone say? She would do her shopping at twelve o'clock when those other mothers would be at home, preparing lunch for their younger children.

It would have been egg mayonnaise sandwiches for Olivia. Her favourite. A twist of pain stabbed through Maggie. That was how it went these days. Most of the time she felt dead, as dead as her daughter surely was, and then a sudden memory would slice into her mind; a mental image of her previous life, and although they belonged to the past now, these pictures still had the power to bring her to her knees.

Maggie closed her eyes. For a moment she could see her daughter, tangled dark waves running riot over her head, nibbling at her lunch, and saying 'Mm-mm!' in that funny way she used to. It was a beautiful picture.

Maggie turned the key in the ignition and forced herself to concentrate on the road.

Carlton Bridge had everything a young family could wish for: good schools, little traffic, and it was well within reach of both countryside and the coast. Plymouth was within easy driving distance too. It was a brilliant place to bring up your kids, but today the advantages just sat there mocking her as Maggie drove past.

There was the park where Livvy had swung on the swings. And the library, with the story group every Tuesday afternoon. Livvy had loved that. And the Postman Pat car

172

outside the supermarket. Maggie had rationed her daughter to three goes a week; she thought now how petty that was. Today she would empty her bank account to pay for rides if only Livvy could come home.

But the worst thing of all was the pre-school. It was at the beginning of their street, which was a cul-de-sac, so Maggie was forced to go right past the door every time she went anywhere at all. Livvy would have started there at the beginning of September.

Today, Maggie very determinedly didn't look at the building as she drove past. She didn't often do this; occasionally some of the children were at the windows and she would slow right down and look at them, wondering what they were doing. Olivia should have been in there doing it with them, and sometimes Maggie could almost hear her daughter's voice among the shouts and laughter in the building.

Staring straight ahead, she accelerated up the hill and parked in front of an empty house. Her fingers shook as she unlocked the front door. She'd lived here for years and never known how happy – and lucky – she'd been. She had never realised how different everything would feel when they lost… a child. Nobody ever could realise, unless it happened to them.

It was as though they had lost their entire family life, because all the little rituals, the family games and habits that had structured their days, had vanished with Olivia.

The whole house was different now. It even smelled different. Isa's choice of soap powder, perhaps. New smells replacing old ones.

Isa had been a tower of strength. She had told Joe firmly and compassionately that Livvy had drowned in the sea and was gone. She got up in the night, helping Colin when Joe awoke crying from a nightmare. When Maggie came home, Isa stayed on to help, running the house with loving efficiency, holding them all together.

'I understand,' she said, taking Maggie into her arms on her arrival. 'It's alright, Maggie. You did what you had to do.'

Thanks to Isa, Joe was coping. Once a week he had a session with a counsellor at school, and he was learning to live without his sister. He was coping better than she was, Maggie knew. She went upstairs into what had been Olivia's bedroom. Isa had dealt with that too. Olivia's parrot mobile still hung above the bed, and her beloved animal posters still decorated the walls. But there were no toys now, no clothes, no duvet or pillows.

Maggie touched the mobile and set the parrots swinging. At the cottage, she had agonised over the little things. Hair slides lying around, abandoned books and games. Here at home, the little reminders had all been tidied away, and in a way it felt like her daughter had been dead for years. It was all just so achingly sad.

And the worst thing of all was that Olivia, who had brought them so much joy, was now at the centre of all these painful, negative emotions. Maggie blinked back tears. Would she ever think of her daughter again and laugh? Would she ever be able to watch these happy-family videos, watch Olivia dancing, playing, posing…

The phone rang, and Maggie trailed through to answer it, wiping the tears from her cheeks. It would be Isa, wanting to know how Maggie was coping on her own. It wouldn't be Howard; she phoned him every evening to hear there was still no sign of Olivia's body, and really she had given up hope long ago that the sea would give them Olivia back.

It was Ronald Keyes, the vicar.

'Maggie,' he said. 'I was just wondering if you and Colin had decided about a service for Olivia?'

Maggie breathed in sharply. She knew she couldn't cope with a church funeral. There was *no way* she was going to accept Olivia's death as the will of any God - and she wasn't going to give thanks for the almost four years they'd had with Olivia, either.

'No,' said Maggie. 'Not until… later.'

If Olivia was found it would be different, of course. But with no body, Maggie knew it would be a long, long time before she was ready for a funeral. That really would be admitting all hope was gone, and she just couldn't do that yet.

'Right,' he went on, and Maggie stood willing him to hang up. Leave me alone, she thought, blinking hard to keep the tears in.

'Maggie, they're looking for helpers in the Geriatric Unit at Crow Road. They need people to help with the lunches and sit with the old folk for a while in the afternoons. Sort of elevenish until two. Would you be interested at all?'

She hesitated. It was an idea. It would be something to do. Something different to occupy her mind for a small part of each day.

'I might be,' she said cautiously. 'Can I think about it and call you back?'

'Of course,' he said. 'Bless you, Maggie.'

She put the phone down and went to make coffee. She would do it, she knew. She would go to the Geriatric Unit and spoon minced beef and mashed potatoes into old, toothless mouths, and listen to stories about life before she was born.

Another twist racked her body, and she dropped to her knees on the kitchen floor. Slinky the cat came up and sniffed at her face. Did he miss Livvy too? Had he noticed that his chief playmate and tormentor was gone now?

'I love you Livvy.'

She spoke aloud, the cat squeezed against her chest.

It was the most horrible, impossible thing, to let go and get on with life without Olivia. But there was nothing else she could do.

Chapter Three

'Phillip! Darling, how lovely!'

Pulling herself upright, Jennifer struggled to sound happy and excited. She'd lain down on the sofa after lunch, and deep sleep overcame her before she'd had time to think. She didn't sleep well at night now, the babies were restless and so was she. Last night had been a succession of naps, and when the sound of Hailey running along to the bathroom had woken Jennifer at half past seven, she felt as if she'd run a marathon backwards.

She heard the concern – the fear – in Phillip's voice, and swiftly forced herself to sound cheerful.

'Heavens, darling, what on earth could be wrong? I closed my eyes for ten minutes after lunch and the phone woke me. Where are you now?'

His voice was still uneasy. 'Heathrow. I'm driving off now, I'll be with you late this afternoon. Jennifer, are you sure you're okay?'

'Sure as sure,' she said sweetly. 'You'll understand when you get here. Drive carefully, darling! See you soon!'

'Yes,' he said.

She could tell he wasn't convinced.

Jennifer put the phone down and lay back again, smiling happily. In just a few hours Phillip would be right here on the sofa. And how very fitting it was that on this day the whole world was sparkling even more brightly than usual.

It was time to make her final plans. She would have a quick tidy round before she collected Hailey, and then she'd make sure that the child was quiet in her room when Phillip arrived. The surprise of learning about the babies would be enough for the first few minutes, then she would take him upstairs to see his beautiful daughter again and they would all be together at last. Just the five of them. Her own little family.

Humming, she stacked her lunch dishes in the dishwasher, dusted the already immaculate sitting room, looked into the as yet unused dining room, and was on her way upstairs to tidy round there when the first contraction hit her.

There was no doubt at all, this was the real thing. She had given birth before, she knew what real contractions felt like. Jennifer stood, leaning against the bannister until the pain eased off, then looked at her watch. Quarter past one.

She needed to keep calm. There would be plenty of time for Phillip to get here before she had to go to the clinic. She would do the bedrooms now and wait for the next contraction.

There wasn't much to do upstairs. Jennifer flicked a duster over the dressing table, and cleaned round the basin in the en-suite. She closed the doors of Hailey's room and the bathroom the little girl used, and stood for a moment thinking.

She would have to phone the school, she couldn't possibly collect Hailey if the babies had started. If only she had sent the child to school in a taxi after the holidays like she'd planned to, but it was such a short drive, and she simply hadn't been able to bring herself to hand Hailey over to a stranger. Jennifer lifted the phone.

The school secretary answered and was pleasant but curious.

'Hello, Mrs Marshall, how are you?'

'Fine, thank you,' said Jennifer. 'I wonder if I could speak to Miss McLure for a moment?'

A minute or two later Miss McLure's voice, rather breathless, spoke in her ear.

'Mrs Marshall? Everything alright?'

Jennifer shuddered. The woman was supposed to be a teacher, for heaven's sake, and she didn't even speak in proper sentences. She forced herself to sound pleasant.

'Thank you, everything's fine, but I'm rather tired. I don't feel quite up to collecting Hailey this afternoon. I'll send a taxi to pick her up.'

'No need for that, Mrs Marshall, I can bring her home myself. I'm going shopping after school so I can easily drive past your place. I'll drop her off around twenty past four. Is that alright?'

Jennifer opened her mouth to say that she would much prefer it if Hailey was just sent home in a taxi, but she felt the next contraction start, pulling at her womb, intensifying swiftly.

'Thank you very much,' she said crisply, and hung up.

The second contraction was powerful too, but this time she managed her breathing better. Jennifer checked her watch. Five past two, good, things were moving nice and slowly. How amazing it was to think that tomorrow at the latest she'd be able to hold her entire family in her arms. This happy thought carried her effortlessly up the stairs to pack a bag for the clinic.

Chapter Four

Katie put the phone down and grinned at the secretary.

'Short and sweet,' she said. 'I'm taking Hailey home after school. Her mum's a bit tired.'

'Oh?' said Beverly. 'When are those babies due?'

'Not for another four or five weeks, I think. Why?'

'Be careful,' said Beverly. 'You don't want to end up playing chauffeur for five weeks.'

'It's no problem. Hailey said yesterday that her dad's due back any day now.'

Katie hurried back to her classroom, where Alison and the children were making a collage with animal pictures. After Hailey's upset the day before, Katie wanted to be sure that everything ran smoothly today, and animal families seemed like a nice non-controversial subject. She stopped beside Hailey, who was cutting out a group of elephants.

'They're sweet, aren't they? Look at those big ears. You're cutting them out very nicely, I must say. Hailey, Mummy phoned. She's feeling tired so I said I would take you home in my car after school. Is that okay?'

'Uh-huh,' said Hailey, barely glancing up from her elephants.

Amused, Katie walked round the craft table, which looked like a miniature zoo at the moment. Hailey certainly wasn't worried about her mother, anyway. An older child might have started asking questions, but Hailey just went right on cutting out elephants. It was almost as if she didn't care.

Suddenly uneasy, Katie glanced back at Hailey. What would happen when the babies *did* come? That could actually happen any time now, Nora had said that twins often came early. Even after their relatively short acquaintance, Katie could tell that Mrs Marshall wasn't the kind of parent to have the sensitivity to prepare a child like Hailey for such an upheaval – another upheaval – in her life. Katie stood for a moment, thinking.

There was nothing she could do about Mrs Marshall, but new babies fitted into the Families theme very nicely. They could do quite a lot right here at school to help Hailey cope. Katie grinned to herself.

'Right, Mrs Babar,' she said, when the other children had gone, and was rewarded with one of Hailey's rare giggles. 'Let's get going. We'll stop off at my flat first, I want to change into something more comfy and collect my shopping bags.'

Katie parked at the side of her building and led Hailey up to her first floor flat. Mr Chips shot past when they were halfway up, and stood with his nose pressed against the flat door.

'He's probably hungry,' said Katie. 'He didn't have much breakfast.'

Hailey bent to stroke Mr Chips, who purred obligingly and pressed himself against her legs. To Katie's surprise she lifted him right up and buried her face in his back. Katie opened the door and ushered Hailey inside.

'I see you like cats - and he likes you too, I can tell.'

Hailey put Mr Chips down and watched while Katie opened a tin of cat food.

'I had a cat once too. He was called Slinky and he was a Siamese cat.'

'Oh, how lovely. Mr Chips is just plain cat. I've only had him since last April, he was a stray and he kind of adopted

180

me. What happened to Slinky?'

Hailey looked up and spoke drearily. 'Oh, he didn't move house with me.'

First a teddy bear that hadn't moved house with Hailey, and now an obviously much-loved cat. Katie smiled sympathetically.

'Maybe Mummy didn't want a cat now there are going to be babies very soon,' she said. 'Cats and babies don't always go well together, you know.'

'No, he was at the house before that,' said Hailey, and Katie racked her brains. The Marshalls had moved from somewhere in Devon, hadn't they?

'At Truro?' she said.

Hailey frowned. 'Not the last house, where I was sick and I had to take the pills and we were only there a little while,' she said. 'The one before that.'

Suddenly she looked frightened and closed her mouth tightly.

'Maybe you can have another pet someday,' said Katie, eyeing Hailey thoughtfully. She gave her a glass of juice and went through to the bedroom to change. The past few minutes had shown her clearly that the child was perfectly capable of having a normal conversation. She hadn't seemed introverted at all and the eye contact had been effortless. The only strange thing had been the way she'd suddenly looked scared at the admission of another previous house.

Hailey was silent during the short drive to her home, a wistful, far-away expression on her face.

Katie pulled up in the Marshalls' driveway and went to ring the bell.

Jennifer Marshall yanked the front door open, and Katie gasped. The woman was flushed, and her make-up was shiny and patchy. Ignoring Katie, she grabbed Hailey and pulled her indoors.

'Quick quick quick!' she cried. 'Upstairs and get ready. Daddy'll be here in less than half an hour!'

Her voice was high. Hailey glanced at Katie and then

went upstairs without a word.

'Mrs Marshall, can I help at all?' asked Katie. The other woman looked as if she'd just run to Land's End and back, and she seemed half hysterical too.

'No, thank you very much. Everything is perfect.' And with that, she shut the front door in Katie's face.

Chapter Five

Phillip gripped the steering wheel with both hands and forced himself to breathe calmly. Just a few minutes more. He was past Bodmin now and driving towards the coast. Soon he would come to the turn-off for St Mary's Castle and Polpayne, and in twenty minutes he'd be arriving at his new home.

He had made good time, considering how tired he was. His assumption that traffic would be light had fortunately proved correct, and the weather was dry and cloudy, ideal for driving long distances. He'd stopped in a lay-by after Salisbury, eaten the sandwiches he'd bought at Heathrow, and he tried to phone Jennifer again, but there had been no answer at home and her mobile was switched off.

In a funny way this reassured him. She would be out in the village, shopping for his favourite lamb chops - or maybe she'd do the salmon with pepper sauce recipe he liked. Or she might be getting her hair done. It was comforting to think of Jennifer keeping busy. And of course she'd be getting the house ready for him to see for the first time. They had noticed it in a brochure that spring, but they'd looked at details of so many houses he really couldn't remember what this particular one had been like. It did sound fantastic - two big reception rooms, a state of the art kitchen, four fully-fitted bathrooms. Phillip smiled suddenly. How very Jennifer. What on earth did they want with four bathrooms?

It wasn't as if they often had visitors.

Everything was going to be alright.

Here was the turn-off. The road ran along the coast now, near the edge of a high cliff. Phillip caught the odd glimpse of the ocean thundering up golden beaches far below. The tide was halfway in, and as always he marvelled at the force of the Cornish breakers. On another day, he and Jennifer would drive along here more slowly. They would admire the scenery and enjoy being together again, and they could look for a good place to scatter Gran's ashes. A remote little bay, perhaps, somewhere secluded where he could sit and watch the ocean and remember. Remember the good times, keep the happy memories, forget the bad ones.

He had never imagined that Jennifer would choose a house near the sea. It was probably a positive step forwards, but it must mean difficult days too. Phillip edged his foot down, seeing the road straight and empty for two hundred yards ahead.

A few minutes later he found himself driving into a quaint little fishing village with an impressive natural harbour. He pulled into a space outside a café and programmed the sat nav.

'At the next junction, turn left,' said the anonymous female voice. Phillip complied.

'Turn left. Take the third road on the right.'

Phillip drove uphill, looking round curiously. These houses were quite different to the Edwardian elegance of their last place, and that was another positive thing, surely. Jennifer wasn't living in the past here.

'In one hundred yards, turn right.'

So this was Castle Gardens, no castle in sight but there were plenty of beech trees lining the road. This seemed like a very pleasant place to live.

Heart pounding, Phillip inched the hire car along the street, looking for number four.

'You have arrived at your destination.'

Here it was, a good-sized house with lovely big windows. There must be a fantastic view over the ocean from upstairs. He would buy himself a really good telescope - or maybe that was the surprise? Cheered by this happy thought, Phillip pulled into the driveway beside the BMW and sounded the horn.

Nothing stirred in the house. His hands damp with sweat, Phillip strode to the front door. It was locked. Forcing himself to breathe quietly, he rang the bell.

Silence.

'Jennifer!' he called, hearing his voice shake. 'Are you there, honey?'

But then the door opened, and Jennifer was laughing up at him. Phillip stood rooted to the spot.

'Jennifer! You… you… my *God*!'

She laughed again. Her face was flushed, and her hair was tied back in a simple ponytail. And she was… how was it possible… but she definitely was…

'Oh Phillip!' she said, gripping his arm so tightly that it hurt. 'Yes, I'm pregnant! Isn't it a wonderful surprise? I knew before you left, of course, but I managed to hide it, I wanted it to be a surprise for you coming home, something good after losing darling Gran. Are you pleased?'

For a moment it was impossible to speak. Hot, tired tears welled up in Phillip's eyes as he looked at his wife. She was so lovely, her eyes were so bright and happy. Pleased? He was astounded. More than that, he was gobsmacked. He was pleased, yes, of course he was pleased, but – after everything they'd been through – another baby?

He put both arms round her and hugged her as tightly as he dared.

'Oh darling! It's… I just… it's a lot to take in. For heaven's sake let's go inside and you can tell me about it. How are you? And when's the baby due?'

She led him into the sitting room. 'I'm fine,' she said softly, her eyes shining up at him. Something about her just wasn't right. He didn't quite like to see it. This wasn't the woman he'd left behind this summer, something had happened, she was different now.

Why hadn't she told him about the baby? A tired surge of resentment flushed through him. He'd have cut his stay short, he'd have come home to support her. Gran would have understood, she'd have been thrilled for them. But instead of sharing it all, his wife had let him stay away for nearly four goddamn months and flung herself into an orgy of house-buying.

Jennifer was still smiling her new smile.

'I'm not due for another five or six weeks,' she said softly. 'And oh, darling, it's two! It's twins! And oh, Phillip… '

She laid a hand on his knee and he could feel her fingers start to shake.

'Actually they'll be here very soon, darling. I'm in labour…!'

And with that, she started to breathe deeply, leaning forward to grip the edge of the coffee table. Her face went red and he could tell she was trying hard not to moan, for his sake. When the contraction was over she lifted his hand and placed it on her enormous belly.

'My God, Jennifer!' shouted Phillip, hearing panic in his voice now. 'How long… where's the hospital… how far apart are the contractions?'

'Fifteen minutes this time,' said Jennifer. 'We should go. Don't worry darling, soon we'll have our babies. I didn't mean to greet you like this, but oh, isn't it a wonderful surprise?'

Phillip felt something begin to throb behind his left eye. This wasn't a surprise, this was a shock. A huge, enormous shock. And he was so tired, God help him, he was exhausted.

'Jennifer,' he said quietly. 'Tell me *now* where the hospital is, and get your jacket. We're going.'

'It's the Rosen Clinic, just a few minutes past St Mary's Castle on the Bodmin Road,' she said, and he relaxed slightly. At least she had arranged to go somewhere local.

'Where's your case?' he said, striding out to the hallway table and lifting the key for the BMW.

'Upstairs on the left,' said Jennifer. 'And darling, you must have a quick look in the small room at the top of the stairs too. There's another surprise for you in there.'

Phillip charged upstairs. God, oh God, he thought. This was all his fault, he should never have left her for so long. But she'd seemed so much better this year. Why the fuck had nobody noticed what was happening? She must have stopped going to the therapy. If he'd been delayed just half an hour on the way home... those babies, his babies... were they alright? Jennifer had been on strong medication, what was happening with that?

He pushed the bedroom door open. All he had to do was get her to the clinic, then they could take it from there.

Phillip grabbed Jennifer's case and turned to the small bedroom like she'd said. He opened the door and looked in quickly.

For a moment he was looking at a ghost. He actually staggered backwards as his mind struggled to take it in. But it wasn't a ghost, it was a child. A little girl was sitting on the bed, a baby doll in her arms. That little face. Hailey's face.

For a moment neither of them spoke.

'Who - who are you?' Phillip asked, his voice sounding like a stranger's.

The child was looking at him with big dark eyes.

'Hailey Marshall,' she said sadly.

Phillip's senses reeled.

'Oh my God,' he whispered, then heard Jennifer moaning downstairs.

'And the lady here is - ?' His voice broke on the last word.

'Mummy,' said the child. 'Are you Daddy?'

Horror filled Phillip and once again he could hardly breathe. He found himself shivering uncontrollably. Hailey. Another moan from Jennifer forced him back to the present.

'We'll talk properly later,' he said, trying to sound kind.

'Come on, kiddy. The babies are coming. I have to get - Mummy - to the clinic straightaway.'

He ran downstairs again. Jennifer was leaning on the hall table, clutching her middle.

'Jennifer,' he began, then realised that this was no time at all for questions or explanations. They had to go. Right now.

'Can - Hailey - stay with a neighbour?' he asked, helping Jennifer into her jacket. She took his arm and walked slowly to the car.

'Goodness, no, she can come with us, can't you, Hailey darling? She'll want to see the babies as soon as they're born, our own two darling babies, Phillip. We'll be a proper little family. You and me, and three lovely children.'

He helped her into the car and tossed her case into the back beside the child.

Sobs welled up in his throat, but he forced them down and drove as fast as he dared towards the Bodmin Road.

Three lovely children, he thought weakly. Then the full horror of the situation hit him, and an aghast, disbelieving shriek rang through his head.

But Hailey is *dead,* Jennifer. Had she forgotten? The tears, the helplessness, the unbearable grief, months and months of it, how could she have forgotten that? She must remember… Hailey was *dead*…

Chapter Six
Before the Black Patch

It was the last day he'd truly been able to say that he was happy. Holidays in Turkey, normal family seaside stuff. Until the tenth day.

The morning had passed as usual, with Jennifer at Keep Fit and the hotel beautician, and Hailey and Phillip by the pool. Hailey had gone to the mini-disco at twelve and Phillip watched indulgently as the children's entertainer led the group of small dancers through various disco hits under the palm trees. Every so often, Hailey would look across at him and smile, a happy, look-at-me-Daddy smile.

They all had chicken salad instead of sandwiches for lunch that last day, with a glass of white wine for himself and Jennifer. A rest in the garden, then they'd wandered down to the beach. Hailey ran off into the children's playground, and he and Jennifer had gone to their loungers under the blue sunshade.

The dreadful, ironic thing was, he hadn't even gone for a swim after lunch that day. They didn't usually have wine at lunchtime, and the heat was making him sleepy. He had dozed, half-listening to the waves splashing up the beach and the happy-tourist voices around him. Jennifer sat doing her nails and tossing him the odd remark. Sleepy, relaxing, holidays.

Would it have made any difference if he'd been sitting up watching what was going on around him? Probably not, with all those beach umbrellas obscuring the view. And even if he'd had his swim as usual, he still might not have noticed anything. It was a family resort; there were always children splashing in the sea, running around calling to each other. It was impossible to tell which child belonged to which family, or if any child was in the wrong place. And nobody had been watching for a little girl all by herself.

They would never know exactly what happened. Phillip had gone up to the playground to collect Hailey and discovered she wasn't there. It wasn't the kind of place you had to clock your kids in and out, and the hotel employee who kept an eye on the children hadn't noticed her at all that day. So she must have run out of the playground almost as soon as she'd run in.

Never to his dying day would Phillip forget the feeling in the pit of his stomach when he realised that his daughter had been missing for nearly an hour. He'd yelled for Jennifer, the hotel employee had phoned up to the reception for help, and they had searched the beach, running between the loungers shouting, calling her name. The hotel produced two beach buggies, and he and Jennifer were driven off, right and left, far along the beach, still shouting for Hailey. But there was no sign of her.

When they got back, the police and coastguards were there in cars and boats, and the search continued officially.

Two hours later they found her. He and Jennifer spent that time in the hotel, talking to policemen whose command of English just wasn't enough to inspire confidence. Jennifer had looked grey and shaky, and Phillip had felt the weight in his stomach grow heavier every minute.

Then shouting. Outraged, tearful voices. A white-faced young policeman and a doctor who'd appeared from somewhere. And a pathetic little sundress-clad figure in the hotel's medical room. She was soaked, seaweed in her hair, lips blue and skin white. Phillip had taken her in his arms and held her. She was so white… and so cold and he had never known pain like it. His Hailey. His own special girl. She was gone.

Chapter Seven

The evening wasn't turning out quite as she'd anticipated.

Katie looked across the table at Mark, who was ordering the meal for two they'd chosen. The restaurant was beautiful and the food sounded fantastic, but all Katie could think about was the expression on Hailey's face when her mother had pulled her into the house.

The waiter stepped away from the table and Mark lifted his eyebrows at her.

'Okay, out with it. What's making you look like you've lost the winning lottery ticket?'

Katie bit her lip. She'd wanted this date to be about the two of them. Now the conversation was going back to her inability to deal with a pupil.

Quickly, she outlined what had happened, grateful that he listened without interrupting.

'And it didn't strike me until I was in the supermarket, but, should I have left Hailey there? Mrs Marshall was obviously out of control, and Hailey looked like a deer caught in the headlights.'

Mark grimaced. 'If Mrs Marshall shut the door on you she wouldn't have reacted well if you'd barged straight back in armed with tea and sympathy. But her husband should have arrived home by now, shouldn't he?'

'Yes,' said Katie thoughtfully. 'And Hailey's been missing

him, they obviously have a good relationship.'

'Why don't you try phoning? Just say you were worried because she looked a bit stressed and can you do anything. She won't say yes, but you'd be able to judge how she sounds.'

Katie pulled out her phone. She made the connection and listened as the Marshalls' phone rang in her ear.

'There's no-one in,' she said at last.

'Which means that Mr Marshall has arrived and either taken them out for a meal, or is dealing with whatever's wrong,' said Mark. 'Either way, Hailey'll be fine. You're worrying too much.'

Katie looked at him miserably, and he reached across and squeezed her hand.

'Tell you what,' he said. 'You give me your one hundred per cent attention for the next hour and a half, and then on the way home we'll drive past the Marshalls' place and see what's happening. They won't be out late with Hailey on a school night.'

'Done.' Katie smiled, feeling better immediately. As Mark said, Mr Marshall would deal with anything wrong. She was being silly here.

'Good. So let's talk about something completely different now. Like shrimps.'

The waiter had appeared with their food. Katie grinned at Mark across the steaming plates.

Chapter Eight

Jennifer moaned, writhing in the passenger seat, and Phillip slowed down. The road was pretty uneven here, and he didn't want to drive fast over bumps with Jennifer in this state.

'Oh, honey,' he said helplessly, when the contraction had passed and she was leaning back again, breathing heavily. 'Have you phoned the clinic? Do they know you're in labour?'

'No,' said Jennifer, looking at him with those over-bright eyes. 'I wanted so much to be at home when you arrived, and I knew Dr Rosen would insist I went straight in. And it's fine, really. We're in plenty of time.'

'Yes, but… ' Phillip stopped before he said something he'd regret. To accuse Jennifer of risking the lives of her unborn children would be pointless - cruel, even. But just what was going on in her head? The babies were going to be premature, and here she was, more worried about surprising him than about her children. She wasn't capable of thinking straight at the moment, so much was clear. How long had she been like this? And most of all, why? She'd been doing so well when he left. But he was home to stay now, and he would deal with this. Just one thing at a time. Babies first, and then…

'Alright back there, sweetheart?' he said, glancing in the mirror at the child on the back seat.

She was cowering in the corner, her face white. Phillip pursed his lips. Deep down he'd been afraid that Jennifer wasn't coping, but this was worse than even his darkest thoughts.

She'd said her name was Hailey Marshall.

Where had this child come from?

'Oh no, Phillip, I have to push!'

Phillip pressed his foot down.

'Don't push! Pant!' he shouted, memories of a distant antenatal class leaping to the front of his brain. 'Here's the clinic now. Just two more minutes!'

Panicking now, Phillip gunned the car up the long driveway to the main entrance and stopped with a screech of brakes. He raced inside. Two women were already coming towards him.

'My wife's having twins in the car!' he yelled, and in a moment there were people running past him, helping Jennifer into a wheelchair and rushing her along the corridor.

Phillip went back for the child.

'Come along, honey. We'll just see about the babies first, and then afterwards I promise you I'll get things fixed up for you. Everything. Properly. Okay?'

She looked up at him, gave him her hand, and walked beside him along the corridor. Memories of his own girl's hand in his made him feel quite dizzy for a moment, and he clenched his other fist tightly. A grey-haired doctor, name-tagged Consultant Obstetrician G. Rosen with a string of letters after his name, came towards him.

'Geoff Rosen,' he said, shaking hands. 'Hello, Hailey. Don't worry, Mummy's going to be just fine.'

A nurse led the child away, and Phillip dismissed her from his mind and struggled into a green hospital gown. First things first.

Jennifer was propped up on a narrow bed in the labour room. Her breath was coming in pants, and Phillip hurried to her side. He'd been present when Hailey was born too, but he had no idea any more what he should do to help.

They'd been so happy and excited at Hailey's birth. The

whole future was theirs. And for a little while they'd been able to live the dream.

Now here they were in another hospital and two more babies were about to be born. What would happen to them all? Phillip knew that all he had ever wanted was the chance to be a family again. But there was no way to put the clock back, Hailey was gone forever and Jennifer was different now. Hadn't the clinic staff noticed her irrational behaviour? But they had obviously accepted the new Hailey as Jennifer's daughter so apparently not.

A nurse was attaching a monitor cable to Jennifer's huge tummy, and Phillip stroked damp hair back from her face.

'Wouldn't a Caesarean be safer?'

He could hardly get the words out, these were his children, *his children*. He was to have another chance at being a father.

Dr Rosen shook his head.

'Jennifer wanted a normal birth, and so far everything's looking good. Strong heart sounds from both babies, and because it's not your first birth, Jennifer, it should go quite smoothly. We're five weeks early but we know that both babies are over two kilos.'

Phillip nodded, not at all reassured. He tried to work things out. Jennifer must have been at the end of her fourth month of pregnancy when he left for California. He hadn't had the slightest suspicion, sex wasn't a regular event in their lives anymore and the medication had put a few extra kilos on Jennifer anyway. So when had the new Hailey entered the equation? Now he knew why Jennifer had been so very vehement about not coming to the States, even under the circumstances he'd been in.

Another contraction started. Phillip gripped Jennifer's hands tightly, holding his breath.

'Is everything okay?' he asked.

'Everything is fine,' said Dr Rosen. 'We know one baby is in the breech position, so I want to have the other one out first.'

Phillip stood by Jennifer's bed, his mind reeling. There

was no way he could work out what his wife had been thinking.

'Pant for the head, Jennifer,' said Dr Rosen.

Jennifer moaned loudly, tossing her head from side to side. Phillip dabbed the sweat from her face and panted energetically along with her.

'Good, here we are - it's a boy!'

The baby cried, a thin newborn wail, and Phillip felt tears gush from his own eyes. He had a son.

Another doctor had taken the baby to the side and was examining him. Phillip walked towards him.

'Two point four kilos, everything working well.'

The nurse wrapped the baby in a towel and handed him over. Emotion was making Phillip's hands tremble. He was holding his son.

'Look, Jennifer,' he whispered, taking the baby to the bedside. 'Our little boy. We need a name for him now.'

'Daniel,' said Jennifer, kissing the baby's face. 'Daniel John.'

Phillip nodded. Hailey would have been Daniel John if she'd been a boy. Another contraction gripped Jennifer.

'Just a little push, please, Jennifer,' said Dr Rosen. 'Here we are again, almost there - and it's a girl!'

The second baby cried too, less heartily than her brother. The paediatrician took her to the side. Phillip held his breath.

'She's fine too, but she's tired. Have a quick cuddle then we'll pop them both in an incubator for a rest,' she said, bringing the baby across. Jennifer lay there cradling both babies, and Phillip stared at her eyes. They were so bright, so happy.

Then he remembered the little girl. This was all such a mess. If only Jennifer had let Hailey go. Let her be a sad, treasured memory. Then they could have started again, been happy now with their twins. As things were it was all going to get very complicated. Very soon now he was going to have to go out of this room and do something about the child upstairs.

Dr Rosen clapped his shoulder.

'Congratulations, both of you. Two lovely babies. Phillip, why don't you go up and show Hailey her new brother and sister while I finish here with Jennifer? You can stay the night, if you want to, there's a family room with everything you need.'

'I'll see,' said Phillip. 'I've been travelling all day, I think I would quite like to sleep in my own bed.'

He needed space to think, too, how best to get them all out of this mess. Maybe he should just take Dr Rosen aside right now and tell him the whole story, let the medical people take over. But they might send Jennifer back to the psychiatric hospital. And what would happen to the babies if they did? He had to think first. He could decide what best to do when he knew who the little girl was.

He stepped into the lift. The easiest way to find out her real name was simply to ask her.

Chapter Nine

The child was sitting at a table in the family room, colouring. She stopped when he went in, and he saw that she had drawn two balls and two teddy bears. Phillip braced himself. He'd have to pretend this was all normal. At least until he got home.

He sat down opposite the little girl. 'Well, ah, Hailey. The babies are here. A boy and a girl. Would you like to see them?'

She nodded, and he took her hand and led her to the nursery. Again, the sensation of her hand resting trustingly in his own was almost more than he could bear.

Hailey seemed fascinated by the babies, lying side by side in the incubators. The nurse explained everything, and Phillip nodded, though he really wasn't registering what she was saying. It was too much to take in. His children. Tired or not, he could have gazed at them for hours. Those perfect little faces, eyes closed in sleep.

'Alright, Hailey?' asked the nurse, and the child by his side nodded. Phillip patted her shoulder. Poor little thing. She must know that he wasn't Daddy and the babies weren't her siblings. Or maybe she believed it now. Phillip looked at his watch. He felt as if it should be midnight at least, but it was only half past eight.

'Are you hungry, sweetheart?' he asked, and the child nodded again. She didn't speak much, he noticed. But that was hardly surprising.

'Let's say goodnight to - Mummy now, and then we'll go home and come back in the morning.'

Tomorrow he would know more, and he could have a frank talk with Jennifer and bring some order into the chaos she had created.

'I've got school in the morning,' said Hailey, and Phillip rubbed his face. One complication after another. How had Jennifer got this child into a school as Hailey Marshall, didn't you need paperwork for that? But of course, they had Hailey's birth certificate…

'School. Okay. Where is it?' he said, walking with her down the corridor.

'It's Polpayne Castle Primary. Mummy takes me in the car. I start at quarter to nine.'

'And you want to go tomorrow?'

'Yes.'

She seemed quite definite about that, and Phillip nodded. It would give him time to get things sorted out.

'Right. You can visit the babies after school,' he said.

As soon as the words were said he could have bitten his tongue. If he told someone about her tomorrow, she would be collected from school and taken back to wherever she'd come from.

'Will they both have names then?'

'Yes. We'll find a name for our baby girl tomorrow,' said Phillip wearily, but glad to be able to promise something definite. His head felt heavy, his eyelids like weights, but finding a girl's name was at least something within his control.

Jennifer was asleep in her private room. Phillip stared at her white face, pity almost overwhelming him. She had been through so much. He kissed her forehead, then took the child back to the car, settling her booster seat into the front and taking his place beside her. He needed to talk to her. He just had to start at the beginning.

'Um, sweetheart,' he said, leaning towards her and trying

200

to sound both casual and reassuring. 'What was your name before you were Hailey? Can you remember?'

The child shrank away from him, horror shining from her eyes. She ducked her head. 'Hailey Marshall,' she said quickly in a low voice.

Phillip patted her leg. 'I meant *before* you were Hailey Marshall. Before you met Mummy, what was your name then?'

She raised both hands to her face. 'Hailey Marshall,' she said.

Dismayed, Phillip saw that she was terrified. Her little hands were actually shaking.

'Sweetheart - Hailey, it's okay. I'm so sorry, I didn't mean to frighten you. You're a very, very good girl,' he said, frantically trying to make good the distress he had caused her. For a long moment she stared at him, then she nodded slowly. Phillip blinked back tears. It really was as if his own Hailey was sitting there nodding at him.

Jennifer must have said or done something terrible to instil such fear in this little girl. This was more than just a moment's madness, he realised dully, but they simply had to put it right again.

'Okay, Hailey. Home, food, and bed,' he said, starting the engine. 'How does that sound?'

The child didn't answer. She was still hunched up in the seat and Phillip pressed his lips together. She was much too thin, all eyes. How long had she been with Jennifer? And why, why, why had no-one realised? Wasn't somebody, the police or anybody looking for this child? She must have a family somewhere. What must they be going through? They couldn't know what had happened to their daughter. And he of all people knew how it felt when you lost a daughter.

He made himself smile at the child. 'Bet you're the smartest girl in your class,' he said.

She stared at him, and to his relief she smiled briefly.

Thank Christ she had school tomorrow. It would give him

time to talk to Jennifer and get some answers. He was going to need a lot of answers before he could decide the best thing to do. And something was telling him that none of it was going to be easy.

Chapter Ten

'It's next right,' said Katie as Mark drove up the hill from Polpayne harbour. She leaned forward in her seat and stared as Hailey's home came into view in the almost darkness. Mark pulled up under a street lamp a few yards from the house.

'They're home now,' he observed.

The blind was down in what Katie knew was the living room, and a dim light shone round the edges, as if maybe a small lamp was on. And upstairs another muted glow came from behind Hailey's pink curtains. Two cars were parked in the driveway, the BMW and a grey VW.

Relief washed through Katie. Mr Marshall was back, and by the looks of things the occupants of the house were settling down for the night.

'If that's Hailey's room, I think a little girl's fast asleep in there with her night light on,' said Mark. 'I don't suppose you want to ring the bell and ask how her parents are doing, their first evening together for months?'

'You're right, I don't,' said Katie. 'Sorry, Mark. I guess I got a bit over-involved here.'

'We all do that at times,' said Mark.

He reached across and took her hand, and Katie squeezed back. She should say something now. The restaurant, with all the other diners around them and Hailey still niggling at the back of her mind, hadn't seemed the place to bring up their own relationship. Over the shrimp they'd put the world to rights the way they usually did, then talked books over dessert. Fun, but light. Katie took a deep breath.

'Mark, I want you to know that I think we could be really good together,' she said nervously. 'It's just I wasn't expecting to feel like this… '

He gave her hand a little shake.

'Katie, I know. It's alright. I don't care how long we spend getting to know each other. On the other hand, we'll eventually come to a point where we either both want commitment, or we don't. I thought - '

He twisted round in his seat until he was almost facing her, still gripping her hand.

'I'm going to Aberdeen for a few weeks soon,' he said. 'My sister's going in for an operation; she was badly burned last year and this is the last big plastic surgery op. She's divorced with four kids so someone has to go and be with them. Caroline who had my class last year is coming back while I'm away.'

Katie nodded. Perhaps a little space would be a good thing. They could still be in touch but she would have time to get her thoughts organised.

'We could Skype,' he said, giving her a rueful almost-smile in the yellow light from the street lamp. 'And we can have lots of long, communicative phone calls, get to know each other properly without the stress of staring at each other in a restaurant wondering if we should leap into bed afterwards. And then when I come back, we'll both know the answer.'

'Yes,' said Katie. She smiled back. 'Well, Hailey's fast asleep, and we're sorted until you come back. Let's go back to mine for a quick decaf. Chinese restaurant coffee doesn't really cut it.'

Mark pulled the car around. Katie sat in the darkness, feeling peace settle over her. There was nothing to worry about now.

Chapter Eleven

'I think he's off again now,' said Maggie, flopping into the sofa beside Colin and exhaling wearily. It was nearly midnight.

'Let's hope so,' said Colin, rubbing his face. 'It's been a bit of a marathon tonight, hasn't it? Poor little sod.'

Joe never had any trouble falling asleep at night, but recently he had taken to waking up an hour or so later, hot and crying after a nightmare. He was never able to tell them what he'd been dreaming about, and Maggie could only assume it was connected to Olivia's disappearance. She should have been here for him long ago; staying at the cottage had done nothing for Olivia and if she'd come home sooner she might have been able to help Joe. But then again, her return could even be the cause of poor Joe's nightmares. It was a no-win situation all round.

This evening, Joe had wakened no less than three times, and eventually Maggie had dosed him with Calpol. Joe had school tomorrow and he needed his sleep. Pity for her son brought the tears, never far away, to her eyes again. Poor Joe. Poor all of them.

'Ronald Keyes phoned today,' she said, and Colin looked at her. 'He mentioned that the Geriatric Unit is looking for lunchtime helpers. I thought maybe I should apply.'

'That's a good idea. You need something different now. Something to - '

Maggie pushed him away. Did no-one understand how she felt? She had lost a child, for God's sake. Just four years ago she had given birth, and now her child was gone.

'Don't you dare say "something to keep me busy",' she snapped. 'Or "to take my mind off things". Don't you dare.'

'I wasn't going to,' said Colin, and her anger evaporated at the exhaustion in his voice. 'Oh Lord, Mags, let's not fight. We should be helping each other.'

He reached out to her and Maggie immediately slid back across towards him. He was right, they'd spent enough time estranged because of Livvy's disappearance. She put her arms round him and quite suddenly they were both in tears, clutching each other and sobbing.

'I was so angry with you at first, you know,' said Colin, holding her in a painful grip. 'Angry because you hadn't watched Livvy every single second. It was days before I realised that it could just as easily have happened the other way around. Any moment, any second, can be the last time; we just don't know.'

'I still blame myself,' said Maggie bitterly. 'Sometimes I can almost live with it and then I think that I sent her to her death. And now I wake up in the night and I wonder, what was the last thing Livvy ever thought before she died, and did she know how much I loved her... '

He sat rubbing her back, and she felt her breathing slow down again.

'Maggie,' he said, leaning his forehead against hers. 'I don't know why Livvy had to die, but I do know for certain that she knew she was loved. She did, you know.'

Maggie nodded, too tired to reply. Bit by bit, she felt the sick, horror-feeling slide away, and she knew it would soon be replaced by the no-feeling, robot nothingness inside her.

'Ronald once told me there's a support group in Plymouth, for people who have lost a child,' said Colin. 'What do you think?'

Maggie bit her lip. Sit in a circle of people all grieving

Chapter Thirteen

found herself driving up the school road behind the
[M]alls' BMW, and by the looks of things it was Hailey'[s]
[ ] in the driving seat. Now this was going to be very
[intere]sting, she thought to herself. She drove further up the
[p]ark than usual and slid into the space beside the BMW.
[So]on as Hailey saw Katie she jumped out, her face alive
[with p]leasure.

['T]he babies came last night!' she said, in the most
[enthu]siastic tone Katie had heard from her so far. 'They're a
[boy a]nd a girl, and I've seen them! They're tiny!'

[K]atie laughed, amazed at the difference in Hailey's entire
[dem]anour. And there it was, the reason for Mrs Marshall's
[distr]ess yesterday.

['W]ow, how exciting!' She smiled down at the little girl,
[then t]urned to the tall, thin man now standing beside the car.
['Mr Marshall? I'm Katie McLure. Congratulations. Are
[Mrs] Marshall and the babies alright?'

['A]ll doing well,' he said in a deep voice, and Katie was
[imm]ediately struck by the nervousness of the man. Beads of
[swea]t had broken out on his brow, and he wiped them away
[with] one hand.

['Q]uite a homecoming you had, then,' said Katie, wondering
[if he] was just tired. He seemed quite normal apart from the
[nerve]s. And Hailey was certainly more relaxed around him

---

for dead children? Tell others her innermost thoughts? *Share
Olivia with strangers?*

'Let's talk about it tomorrow,' she said, struggling to her
feet. 'Oh no, Col - I forgot to phone Howard.'

In all the upset with Joe she had forgotten to phone Howard
and ask if they'd found Olivia. But of course they hadn't.

'Leave it, Maggie,' said Colin. 'Howard will be asleep in
bed and we should be too. I'm going up.'

He lurched to his feet and left her on the sofa. Maggie
buried her face in her hands. She felt at times that although
the grief she shared with Colin brought them closer now,
sometimes too it seemed to drive a huge wedge between
them. She never knew when the wedge was going to appear,
and it was always brutal.

Maggie rubbed her hot face and blinked fiercely. She
hadn't phoned Howard. This was the start. After this she
wouldn't phone him every evening, there would be longer
and longer gaps between her phone calls to ask if they'd
found her dead daughter, and then, one day, she would phone
for the last time.

Chapter Twelve

The child was up before him the next morning, splashing around in the bathroom – *now* he realised why those four bathrooms had been necessary – and padding about in her room. Did she shower and dress all by herself every morning? It seemed very mature behaviour from such a small child and only added to his unease. Phillip pulled on jeans and a sweatshirt. His clothes had been neatly arranged in one side of the new double wardrobe, everything fresh, ironed, and arranged according to colour. He wondered how on earth Jennifer had found the energy to get this house so perfectly organised.

Downstairs, he pushed a mug under the coffee machine, and rummaged around the immaculate kitchen for a child-friendly breakfast for the little girl. The whole place was like a show house, something out of an exhibition. They would have to make it a home now, for Daniel and his sister.

Coffee made, Phillip sipped appreciatively. It felt so wonderful not to be tired. And in spite of the worry it was wonderful to have a new son and daughter, too. Daniel and - Laura? Miriam? Lara? Lara sounded good to him, they had considered it for Hailey too. And right after breakfast he was going to do something about this child who wasn't Hailey. Yesterday he'd been too exhausted to do anything but roll into bed as soon as the child was in hers. Today he would get

things organised for her.

She came into the kitchen while he phone into the charger, already in her uni

'Wow, don't you look posh,' said Phill

The girl stared at him, her face unmov

'Okay,' said Phillip. 'Breakfast. You c and toast, or cornflakes, or toast. Or of cou toast and cornflakes if you'd prefer that.'

He raised one eyebrow, wanting to se relief her face brightened, though it wasn'

'Toast, please. Can I have honey?'

'You sure can,' said Phillip, abandonin

He sat down opposite her, sipping co indulgently as she worked her way throu toast spread thickly with honey. By the tim he had made her laugh twice, telling her a porridge and his efforts to avoid it when face looked different when she laughed, obvious then that she wasn't Hailey. H would take this child to school and then g and talk to Jennifer. By the time he collect he would know who she was, where she ca to do about it.

He wasn't going to go to the police for best thing would actually be if he could get involving the police... appeal to her pare They might take pity on Jennifer. It was w

A thought struck him and he turned to t have your hair cut recently?'

She nodded dumbly, her eyes afraid a nodded.

'Good girl. Let's phone the clinic and a are this morning,' he suggested. 'Then y teacher the latest news. What's her name, a

'Miss McLure. And her first name's K Then she smiled. 'And she's very, very nice

than with her mother. She was standing there smiling up at him, and it wasn't the flashy, unnatural smile she always gave her mother.

'You could say that,' he said wryly. 'Is she - um, Hailey, doing alright? Settling in and all that?'

'Yes, I'm very pleased with her,' said Katie, not wanting to say more in front of the child. 'Why don't you come for a visit soon, and see her progress for yourself?'

'Ahm - thank you, I will,' he said, then ruffled Hailey's hair and turned back to the car. 'I'll pick you up at quarter to four, then, honey.'

The little girl waved as he drove off and then ran up to the side door beside Katie. 'Two babies,' she said confidentially. 'The boy's called Daniel John and the girl doesn't have a name yet but he - Daddy - said they'd choose one today. I'm going to see them again after school.'

Wonders will never cease, thought Katie. Daddy, assisted by Daniel John and his sister, seemed to have done more in just twelve hours to help Hailey settle into Polpayne than all the professional and motherly efforts of the past several weeks. Look at the child. She was positively blooming.

'You can tell us all about it,' said Katie. 'And as soon as you have a photo of the babies you must bring it in to show us.'

'Yes,' said Hailey. A little frown creased her face, and she slowed down to a walk. 'Will the babies have to leave home, sometime? I don't want them to.'

Katie laughed. 'Not until they're grown up,' she said. 'Same as you. Don't worry, you'll all be together for years and years.'

Hailey nodded slowly, then ran off into the classroom. Katie heard her call her news to Melanie.

Well, that was one problem sorted. And now that she didn't have to worry about Hailey any more, there would be more time to think about Mark. Which was actually a very pleasant prospect. But right now fifteen Halloween masks were waiting to be painted by fifteen enthusiastic budding artists. It was going to be another busy day.

211

Chapter Fourteen

'Mum?'

Joe came into the kitchen and stood beside Maggie as she loaded cereal bowls into the dishwasher. She kissed the top of his head. According to his teacher, Joe was coping better at school these days, he was laughing more, and his interaction with the staff and the other children was improving all the time. It was just the family stuff here at home that still felt so horribly new and different, and that might not change any time soon. She couldn't imagine ever finding life without Olivia to be normal.

'Want a banana for playtime?'

He shook his head. 'Mum, Mrs Grey said that if you had a bad feeling about something, you should talk to someone because they might have the same feeling and then you can help each other.'

'And that's exactly right.'

Maggie reached for the hand towel. Mrs Grey was Joe's counsellor, and though he never said much about his sessions with her they were obviously helping. She and Colin were still considering counselling, but at the moment the hurt still felt too raw to share. But Joe always went willingly to his hour with Mrs Grey, who had instructed Maggie and Colin to be open if Joe wanted to talk, but never to force a confidence. Now it sounded as if her son wanted to discuss something further.

Maggie sat down at the table and Joe leaned against it, rearranging the apples in the fruit bowl.

'Some kids said their mums said it was all our own fault when Livvy got lost. Jay said it was even in the *Carlton Gazette* yesterday.'

Maggie stared for a moment before reaching out to squeeze Joe's arm.

'Heavens, sweetheart, that sounds like very nasty talk. It was just a horrible accident that Livvy got lost. Probably the mums thought that we should have watched Livvy better but your dad and I and Mr Moir have talked about this and agreed that you can't watch people every single second. So you can tell those kids that a Chief Detective Inspector said it wasn't our fault.'

And if only she could believe that herself. Because no matter what anyone said, Maggie knew she would always blame herself for Olivia's death. She would have to forgive herself one day, she knew - but that day was still a long way off.

'Oh. Why was it in the paper, then?'

Maggie forced herself to sound brisk. 'I didn't read the *Gazette* yesterday so I don't know exactly what it said, but I'll find out and then we can talk again. But Joe, don't worry about this. If we had done anything wrong Mr Moir would have said so and I think we can trust him, don't you?'

'Because he's a Chief Detective?'

'Chief Detective Inspector, even.'

'Cool!'

Joe ran to get his schoolbag, and Maggie went to look for yesterday's paper. She usually managed a quick skim through at morning coffee time, but yesterday she'd had a headache. And Colin never touched it.

It was a short, cheerless article about children who had drowned that year, prompted by a fifteen-year-old's collapse during a school swimming lesson the previous week. Twenty-one other kids up and down the country had drowned since January, which was apparently more than average. The opinion of the writer was that death by drowning was almost always preventable. The article was accompanied by photos of several children, including Olivia.

Tears instantly filled Maggie's eyes. Shouldn't they have been asked before Livvy's photo was splashed over the paper like this? But that photo was the one they'd used for the poster. It was all over the internet already, and that didn't just apply to the photo. Maggie knew she wouldn't have to search hard at all before finding online forums and discussion pages where she and Colin had been viciously pulled apart and blamed for Livvy's death. It was horrible and hurtful. Howard had warned them never to look, and to ignore anything that they found.

Maggie stood forcing herself to breathe regularly. If she'd seen this when she was alone at home she'd have howled, but Joe was upstairs so she had to hold it together. All this stress and it wasn't even nine o'clock yet.

Chapter Fifteen

Jennifer rolled over in her high hospital bed and stared out of the window. Dark rainclouds were hovering, but for the moment it was still dry, and although there was no sign of the sun, the very air was shimmering with beautiful silvery brightness, like the sparklers they used to have on Guy Fawkes night when she was a child. It was a special day, because soon she would see her babies.

'Morning, Mrs Marshall!'

A nurse came into the room with a rubber ring wrapped in a pillow case. She waved it at Jennifer and grinned.

'Here you are, your new sitting companion! Let's get you ready and I'll take you along to the nursery.'

She bustled around cheerfully as she spoke, and Jennifer found herself sitting at the washbasin – on the rubber ring – clad only in her skimpy hospital gown. Some of the shine had disappeared from her day.

'If you'd just give me the blue robe and leave me for a few minutes,' said Jennifer haughtily. 'I want to look nice for my babies.'

'Sure,' said the nurse, pulling Jennifer's robe from the cupboard.

Alone, Jennifer heaved a sigh of relief. She washed slowly, changing into her own nightdress and dabbing perfume behind her ears. A little face powder too, it was important to look pretty for her darlings. That was better, now she felt human again.

The nurse tucked Jennifer's arm through her own for their walk down the corridor. Jennifer flinched, but found she was glad of the support.

'The first walk always feels a bit wobbly,' said the nurse, grinning. 'Must be worse after twins, too. Here we are.'

The nursery was a long, bright room, with several little fish-tank cots at the far end and three incubators nearer the doorway. Another nurse led Jennifer over to the first two incubators. The babies were lying there, both fast asleep, and Jennifer's heart pounded in her chest.

'Such darlings,' she whispered. 'How are they? Can I hold them?'

The nurse settled her into an armchair. 'They're doing really well. They'll be in there keeping warm for a day or two, but you can have them out to hold whenever you like. A nice cosy cuddle with Mum will do them the world of good too.'

Jennifer accepted a baby, reading the name band with a proud smile. Daniel John Marshall. She had a son.

'Do you have a name for this young lady yet?' asked the nurse, giving Jennifer her daughter and propping them all up with pillows.

Jennifer suddenly remembered Phillip, and realised she hadn't spared him or Hailey a single thought today.

'I'm expecting my husband soon, we'll decide when he comes,' she said, relaxing into the chair and giving all her attention to the babies in her arms. Her son, and her daughter. Her little girl.

Warmth and happiness surged through her like a bright fire. This was quite the most wonderful moment of her life. It made up for everything. Two darling babies. And one was a girl.

The baby girl squirmed in her arms, and Jennifer held on tightly, humming under her breath, her eyes shining. Her life was complete again.

Chapter Sixteen

Phillip drove away from Polpayne Castle Primary, conscious of an enormous feeling of relief.

At last he was alone, with peace and quiet to plan what he should do. Not in a million years had he expected his first twenty-four hours at home to turn out anything like this. He'd been worried about Jennifer, sure, but he'd never seriously thought that it would be anything as bad as this.

Best case, he'd imagined a cosy evening, after which he would sleep for twelve hours at least and then have a lazy, intimate day with Jennifer, exploring the village and the countryside. Jennifer's pregnancy and the child who wasn't Hailey were the two of the biggest shocks he'd had in his life. And now he had to work out what to do.

The first thing was to see what Jennifer would tell him. There were so many answers he'd need to wheedle out of her. Then he should set two priorities - one, get this Hailey-child back to wherever she belonged, and two, get help for Jennifer. And the more low-key he could keep the entire Hailey situation the better. He did *not* want to endanger his new family, and yes, Jennifer had acted very strangely but that might just be down to hormones or stopping her medication or simply being pregnant.

He still hoped he could contact Hailey's real parents *before* getting the authorities involved, but that might not be realistic. He would go to Dr Rosen - or Jennifer's psychiatrist in Torquay might be better. He at least would know her history. The police could come in after that.

Home again, Phillip made coffee and stood sipping. The clinic didn't open for visitors until ten o'clock, so he would go on the internet to research about a missing girl. But a quick house-search revealed that the computer had been placed in the cupboard under the stairs. Phillip stared blankly at the mess of cables. He didn't have time to get this sorted out before going to the clinic. What on earth had Jennifer been thinking? It was so annoying his own laptop was dead.

He lifted his phone, still charging, and accessed the search engine. All he had to do was google two words, and see if the child came up. His fingers twitched, and then he thrust the phone back on the shelf. He'd do it later on the computer. For now he'd have a quick look amongst their papers and then he'd be off.

He strode into the dining room and opened the Spanish cabinet under the window. There were the folders - tax, insurance and so on. He pulled out the 'family' folder, his heart sinking when he saw that was different now. Hailey's birth certificate was there in its plastic pocket, but her death certificate was gone. Phillip stared, struggling to understand exactly what Jennifer was trying to do. Frantically, he searched around for the manila envelope that contained the paperwork on his daughter's funeral, but it too was gone.

Phillip slumped into an elegant dining chair and buried his face in his hands. For a few seconds he allowed despair to engulf him, then he shook it off determinedly and faced the memory of the worst funeral he'd ever attended.

It had been a horrific day, second only to the day of Hailey's death. Except the day of the funeral had seemed longer.

He had battled with the Turkish authorities before they were able to bring their daughter home. At least it had seemed like a battle. He'd felt as if he was stuck in the middle of a nightmare - which he was.

Jennifer had shivered almost non-stop. The doctor had given her medication and she was always either asleep, or blank-eyed and shivering. He couldn't reach her to help her, and of course he'd needed help too, help that no-one had given him.

He had chosen the coffin, plain white wood, and given the Turkish undertaker some clothes to dress Hailey in. A blue summer dress and white socks and sandals. Jennifer hadn't helped with that or any of the preparation for the journey home.

And then the day of the funeral itself. Brilliant sunshine had mocked them from dusk to dawn. The vicar had meant well, but he hadn't said anything that had touched Phillip. And Jennifer... It was the day before her retreat into herself. Her parents had come, tried to help, been viciously snubbed by Jennifer, and then gone home again, hurt and offended. Gran had come over as soon as they'd arrived home from Turkey, but she'd left again the day after the funeral, having arranged with Phillip to bring Jennifer to California the following week. Of course that hadn't happened. He'd seen Gran off at the airport and come home to find Jennifer in the corner of the sofa. Friends and neighbours had rung the bell, thrust food into his hands, assured him that if he ever needed anything... and then they'd all gone home again.

He had never felt so alone in all his life.

Phillip gave himself a shake and closed the cabinet. He *must* persuade Jennifer to talk to him. He had to find out what had happened.

And he really should call Jennifer's mother, and people like Thea, but then what would they tell him? To go to the police, to get it sorted. Exactly what he didn't want to hear. No, he would 'find' the child first, by himself.

Half an hour later he was back at the Rosen Clinic, with an enormous bunch of pink and white roses and a box of Jennifer's favourite Swiss pralines.

A nurse took the flowers and told him that Jennifer was in the nursery. Phillip ran up the stairs two at a time, then stood motionless in the doorway. Jennifer was holding both babies, happiness radiating from her like heat from the sun, and Phillip only just managed to stop himself sobbing out loud. This was his family. All three of them. This was all he'd ever really wanted - a loving wife and a couple of kids. It wasn't too much to ask, was it?

He tiptoed up and kissed the top of Jennifer's head.

'You look gorgeous,' he said. 'How are you this morning, darling?'

'Tired, but so happy,' said Jennifer, looking up from the babies.

He saw that her eyes were still shining, and they were glassy, distant now. Her voice had changed too, it was harder, flatter somehow, although the words themselves seemed quite normal. His heart sank even further.

'Would you like to hold them? I'm getting stiff, sitting like this.'

Phillip gowned up and changed places with Jennifer. And now he was holding his own two children. Yesterday at this time he hadn't known of their existence. He gazed at them, spellbound. Both had fair, downy fuzz on their heads, and both little faces were relaxed in sleep. Phillip looked over at Jennifer, who was leaning on an incubator massaging her back with one hand. For a brief moment he allowed himself to enjoy just being a father again.

'We need a girl's name,' he said. 'I thought maybe Miriam. Or Lara.'

'Lara would be perfect,' said Jennifer, beaming at him. 'Lara Mary. No, Lara Grace. Lara Grace Marshall.'

'Brilliant,' said Phillip. If only everything else could be settled so easily. 'Hi, baby Lara. Oh darling, we'll have fun with them, won't we?'

They would, he thought. He would protect his little family. Whatever Jennifer had done, he would fix things, put their lives back together. They couldn't fall apart now, he had to prevent that from happening, at all costs.

'Let's go along to your room and have a chat,' he suggested, when Lara and Daniel were back in the incubators. 'A lie down will do you good.'

Jennifer allowed him to escort her back to her room. She lay back on the bed, her face pale, and he noticed uneasily how exhausted she was. If he upset her, he'd get no information at all this morning. He would have to be subtle with his questions.

'Hailey was a big surprise too,' he remarked easily. 'Tell me about that, darling.'

Jennifer smiled again, but she didn't meet his eyes. 'Oh, she's a lucky, lucky girl,' she said, and he saw in dismay that her eyelids were drooping now. 'She was lost, once, do you remember? But I found her again, didn't I, Phillip?'

Phillip stroked her hair back from her face. After all they'd been through, how could she possibly believe that she'd found Hailey?

'Where was she, darling, when you found her?'

'On the beach,' said Jennifer, and Phillip caught his breath painfully. On the beach.

Jennifer gave a strange little laugh, her eyes closed. 'A poor lost Hailey. But I found her, Phillip, she's back.'

Phillip swallowed painfully. So it was abduction. But she was denying it, she had convinced herself that the new Hailey was their daughter.

'Do you know who Hailey's parents are, Jennifer?' said Phillip, abandoning subtlety.

She laughed at him, tired eyes still shining. 'Silly! We are, of course!'

She ended with a yawn, and Phillip knew he would have to wait with his questions. She wasn't going to lose it completely; this was different to last time, she was talking and moving about. He would see what he could find out about the child himself first, and then try again.

Leaving Jennifer asleep, Phillip drove back to Polpayne. There was a little convenience shop in the harbour area that seemed to sell everything, and he bought a steak and some salad bits, and a couple of pizzas for later. He would go home, eat, and start planning.

He ate hungrily, allowing himself a small glass of wine, then sat in Jennifer's elegant sitting room to think.

So as far as he could gather, Jennifer had found the child wandering round some beach, and taken her for their own Hailey. Even he could see the similarities. Both little girls had the same delicate features, both were slightly built, and their own girl's hair had been almost the same colour. He knew what losing Hailey had done to Jennifer. But to take a child like that. And then frighten her into being 'Hailey Marshall', cut off her hair, send her to school…

But he had to start at the beginning. The new Hailey was on the beach… This beach couldn't be terribly far away, because Jennifer wouldn't have made any lengthy trips in her condition. So a lot of people right here in the village might know about a little girl who had gone missing, but no-one had connected it to Jennifer and Hailey Marshall moving to Polpayne. And if a kid disappeared from a beach it wouldn't be unnatural if everyone'd reckoned she had drowned. That would explain the lack of media attention now. A dead child was old news, he knew that himself. The internet would provide him with the answer.

He lifted his phone and tapped briskly.

'Missi - '

It was impossible to continue. Phillip sat there, trying vainly to convince his fingers to finish the words.

What if he did 'find' the child here, and contacted her parents? Their first reaction would of course be to call the police, and then he would lose control of the whole situation. There would be policemen and psychiatrists all swarming around investigating them all. And if Jennifer was found mentally ill, would she be allowed to keep the babies? It

222

would wreck the whole new life that was opening up for them now.

The more he thought about it, the better Phillip grasped the fact that if he wanted to keep his new little family, he mustn't involve anyone else. He had lost his daughter, he had lost his grandmother, his parents… He had lost enough.

So he would do this all himself. He looked at his phone, then put it away again. He would set the computer up tonight and find out in comfort who the child was. Then he would drive her home and leave her there. No-one would know that Jennifer had taken her.

For a brief moment he relaxed, but then he remembered all the people here who knew Hailey as his and Jennifer's child: Miss McLure, Dr Rosen, the nurses. What could he tell them? God, what a mess. What a ghastly mess.

The wine had made him drowsy, and he knew that yesterday's long journey had caught up with him. A nap before he went for Hailey would do him good. He set the alarm on his phone for an hour, and lay back on the sofa.

The child was waiting at the side door when Phillip arrived back at Polpayne Castle Primary. A crowd of other kids was there too, saying goodbye to Miss McLure. Hailey was the smallest, he noticed miserably. And Miss McLure's prompt invitation that morning when he'd asked how Hailey was doing seemed to indicate that the poor kid's school life hadn't started well. And no wonder.

He strolled over and touched Hailey's shoulder.

'Hi there, toots,' he said, and was rewarded by a smile from Hailey.

Miss McLure turned from waving goodbye to the departing school buses, and walked over to the BMW beside him. Phillip felt his palms turn moist. Was there a problem? Had Hailey said something she shouldn't?

Apparently not, however. Miss McLure helped Hailey into the car, closed the door, and then spoke in a low voice.

'Hailey's been a different child today, Mr Marshall. *Much* happier, and a lot more talkative. She missed you so much when you were away. And of course she's excited about the babies too.'

Phillip felt a sudden lump in his throat. 'Yes,' he said, trying to sound casual. 'We're off to the hospital now.'

'I won't keep you, then. Give my regards to Mrs Marshall. We're making a big congratulations card from the whole class, but I'll let Hailey tell you all about that.'

'Bye,' managed Phillip, and escaped down the road with Hailey.

'Good day?' he asked, and she nodded.

'I made a scary witch mask for Halloween. Are we going straight to see the babies?'

'We are. We'll stop off on the way and you can choose some flowers to take. Mummy'll like that.'

Hailey was quite agreeable to this, and walked into the Rosen Clinic carrying a bunch of yellow chrysanthemums. Jennifer received her graciously, and they all walked along to the nursery.

'Daniel John and Lara Grace,' said Hailey, standing on tiptoe to see into the incubators. 'What's my other name?' she asked, turning to Phillip.

'You're Hailey Andrea,' he said quietly, aware of Jennifer beaming proudly beside him.

'Sit down, Hailey darling, and you can hold the babies,' said Jennifer, and Hailey obeyed with an almost reverent expression on her face. Phillip watched her hold Lara first, then Daniel, a little smile pulling at her mouth all the while.

Her face had lost the pinched look he'd seen on her yesterday. And Miss McLure had said she'd been a different child today. Was that just because he was looking after her now instead of Jennifer? Could he – a stranger – make that much difference to her? She must have been so afraid. But he was here now, he would help her for the time she'd still be with them. He *would* get her home, someday soon.

224

He stayed for an hour or so, chatting to Jennifer while Hailey watched the nurse settle the babies back into the incubators. Try as he might, though, Phillip couldn't prise any more information from her. She blocked his questions with a laugh and panic rose in his throat. She was ill and she wasn't getting any treatment. He had no idea how much longer they could go on like this.

Back home, he and Hailey ate pizza in front of the television, watching a wildlife programme about an animal reserve in Kenya. Hailey was enthralled by the elephants, giggling happily when they splashed water over each other. When the programme had finished Phillip switched the television off.

'Let's get you bathed, and then I'll read you a story,' he said.

'Oh yes!' She jumped up and ran to the door, then turned to look at him, her little face blank again. 'When's Mummy coming back?'

'In a day or two. Mummy hasn't been well recently. Sometimes it makes people ill and cross, having babies in their tummies and moving house. Hailey, everything *will* be alright soon. Don't you worry.'

Hailey allowed him to bath her, then ran to her room while Phillip cleared the bathroom. He blinked back tears, remembering the happy times they'd had with their own girl. Standing in Hailey's bedroom doorway, he watched as she pored over the pictures in her *Heidi* book.

Twenty minutes later he was looking down at a sleeping child. If only she *was* his Hailey. If only they hadn't gone to the beach that awful day, then he might be standing right here looking at his own girl. Phillip realised that all he wanted now was the impossible, to somehow transform this child into his daughter.

Abruptly, he turned and walked downstairs.

He opened the cupboard under the stairs and crouched down to get to the computer. He would set it up in the dining room for the moment.

Slowly, he stood up again and closed the cupboard door. He was tired, he really didn't feel like messing around with cables and monitors tonight. And once you started trawling the internet it was difficult to stop. He would wait until his jet lag was quite gone.

Tomorrow was another day.

Chapter Seventeen
Early November

Maggie turned the page of the calendar and hung it up again, staring indifferently at the picture of Culzean Castle. The first of November. All Saints' Day. And tomorrow was All Souls'.

They had lived for two and a half months now without Olivia, and it felt more like two and a half years. All those emotions, she'd been through more of them since the fifteenth of August than in the whole of her life beforehand. And life was going on now, relentlessly, remorselessly, without her little girl.

So many things were different – her job, the house, the daily routine – quite suddenly it seemed that they had come to a place where Olivia had never been. Her life was no longer tied up with theirs. And however much Maggie agonised and remembered, and then tried to stop remembering because it was just too bloody painful, however much she tried to connect the past with the present - Olivia was gone.

Maggie shivered. After the first agony had subsided, it was the *living* – simple, everyday things, even the thoughts in her head that made each day difficult. Maggie had never realised before how often her daughter had entered her mind as she went about her day. A nature programme on TV that she knew Livvy would like. Her favourite cereal in the supermarket. Jars of honey stocked up in the cupboard.

227

The miniature knife and fork in the cutlery drawer. Just little things, but they meant so much. *Had* meant so much.

It was the uncertainty that really got to her. They knew Olivia was gone, but what *had* happened in the last few minutes of her life? She must have been so afraid, she must have tried to scream for help, struggling against the cold Atlantic. Livvy had been drowning while Maggie was drinking coffee and Colin and Joe were poking about rock pools. And the biggest question of all was *why*. Maggie knew there would never be an answer.

She poured herself more coffee and sat down at the kitchen table. It was almost time to go to work. She had just started at the Geriatric Unit, working three sessions a week. So far it had been alright; the old people on her ward weren't compos mentis enough to ask personal questions. Maybe they'd put her in that ward on purpose. Maggie didn't care. It was something to do, and it was fine for the moment.

The sound of Colin's key in the lock roused her from her daydream. He strode through to the kitchen and opened the fridge.

'Hello, love. Want some juice?'

'No thanks,' said Maggie, staring. 'What are you doing home at this time?'

'I need the car this afternoon, I'm taking a client to see the factory at Corriemer. I'll drive you to the hospital now, though, and I can collect you again at three.'

'That's okay,' said Maggie. 'I'll come home on the bus. Give me an excuse to walk through town, have a look at the shops.'

'Okay,' said Colin, staring at the photo of Joe and Livvy, attached to the fridge by a cat-shaped magnet.

Maggie sighed. There had been something on his mind for days now, she could tell. He'd been hovering around her, obviously wanting to say something but never quite managing it. She reached out and put a hand on his arm.

'Colin, for Pete's sake just spit it out.'

Colin laid the photo on the table and sat down. 'I loved Olivia,' he said, his face pale and serious. 'I was awake for hours last night, thinking about her. I loved being her dad, watching her grow. She was part of our lives and it was wonderful, a miracle. But she's gone now, Mags, and I - I don't want to give up on that miracle.'

'You want us to have another baby,' said Maggie, hearing the flatness in her voice.

'I know it's still too soon for another baby. But we always said we wanted more than two kids one day. I know that we could ever replace Livvy, but I think our family would be more complete if we had another child. One day. I just want to plan something good for our future.'

Maggie took a deep breath.

'I do not - want - another - baby,' she said, hearing panic rise shrilly in her voice. Slinky leapt up to his window and disappeared into the garden. 'We've lost a *child*, Colin, I gave birth to her and now she's gone, and it hasn't even been three months yet for Christ's sake, how can you even think of another baby? But you're right, you're damned well right we can never replace Olivia, and I am *not* going to try.'

She could feel the scream in her voice again. Love and loss, the most unbearable feelings, and they had lost their daughter in the worst possible way. She could never risk loving another child.

Colin's face was white. 'I'm sorry. I'm not talking about now. But I do want us to be a real family, with a couple of kids at least. We're young, Mags. You might feel different in a year or two.'

Tears rushed into Maggie's eyes and she pulled a tissue from the box. 'So we'll talk about it then,' she said tightly. 'In a year or two when I feel different. And not before. Okay? Right now all I want is Livvy, and she's not coming back, is she?'

Colin shook his head and slumped over the table. Trembling, Maggie went upstairs to put on her make-up. She stared at her face in the bathroom mirror. It was thinner, and more lined than three short months ago. And nowadays there was a blank, hopeless expression in her eyes that had never been there before the fifteenth of August. But Colin was right about one thing. They were young enough to have six more babies if they wanted them.

She blinked back the tears to apply her mascara.

Chapter Eighteen

'Well done, you three, that was a good game. Now you can join the others for a little while before it's time to go home.'

Katie gathered up the cards spread over the craft table and grinned as Julia, Derek and Hailey ran across the room to the play area. Having an assistant was another advantage of teaching little ones. It meant that she could work more individually with the kids who needed it. Their game of 'Happy Families' had helped Derek to speak up clearly, Julia to say the few words necessary and no more, and Hailey to maintain eye contact, something that was often still difficult for the little girl.

I'll give them another ten minutes, then we'll have a song before home-time, she thought, wandering over to the play area and noticing with wry amusement that Julia had completely taken over Martin and Melanie's game of shops. Oh well, the child had been very self-controlled for twenty whole minutes, they couldn't expect miracles straightaway. And at least Hailey was improving by leaps and bounds now that her dad was home. She seemed to be sleeping better for one thing; the tiredness that had often plagued her in the mornings had vanished.

Katie looked round for Hailey and saw that the little girl was standing by herself at the window, looking out with the old blank expression on her face.

Famous last words, she thought, and joined her smallest pupil.

'Okay, Hailey? Your dad'll be here in half an hour, don't worry.'

Hailey looked up at her, her lips trembling.

'Mummy's coming home today,' she whispered.

Katie smiled encouragingly. 'Well, that's good, isn't it? Are you worried because the babies will still be in hospital? They'll be home too before you know it, Hailey. Your dad said yesterday they're doing really well.'

Hailey nodded slowly. She didn't look convinced, and Katie racked her brains. Hailey'd had her dad all to herself ever since his return, maybe she was worried that he wouldn't have as much time for her now. Which, when you thought about it, was actually spot-on.

'Daddy'll be very glad of your help, you know, when Mummy and the twins are all home again. You're big enough to do all sorts of things now. It's fun, being in a big family and helping each other.'

Hailey stared at her, and Katie frowned. There was something still not quite right here, the expression on Hailey's face was actually more like fear than jealousy. Suddenly Katie remembered the photos Hailey had brought in to show the class. Two tiny babies in incubators. Had Hailey been frightened by the sight of her siblings in hospital? All that technology might well look very scary to a child. And the babies were only a few days old, they probably looked very fragile and sick to their sister.

'Sweetheart, you don't need to worry at all about the babies being in hospital,' she said gently. 'It's only for a little while until they grow. Your daddy told me they really are doing well. And when they're home, we'll ask Daddy if they can visit us at school sometime. That would be fun, wouldn't it?'

Hailey nodded, heaved the biggest sigh that Katie had seen in a long time, and turned back into the classroom, her face still glum.

Katie clapped her hands for silence. 'Right, everyone, let's start tidying up now. It's nearly time to go home.'

The other children buzzed around excitedly, but the expression on Hailey's face reminded Katie of the first day of school when the little girl had looked so sullen when her mother arrived. Today, like that day, it was obvious that Hailey didn't want to go home.

Chapter Nineteen

Phillip sank into the depths of the sofa and closed his eyes. All this worry and running back and forth between the hospital and the school and home - it was incredibly tiring. He'd just made Hailey's dinner, and when Jennifer came down from her nap he'd need to cook something for her too. The only thing he could be glad about right this minute was that he didn't have to rush back to work. He could stay at home with his family, but what a mixed blessing that was turning out to be.

He still hadn't found out about Hailey's real identity. The very fact that nobody seemed to be looking for this child was making it all too easy just to let things slide until he had more energy and more time to plan. That afternoon he had eventually got the computer set up again, but then he'd had to collect first Hailey and then Jennifer, there hadn't been time for research as well. Or – to be completely honest – there had been time, he just hadn't done it.

Right this minute he had time, but he was so exhausted, he really didn't know how he'd cope with whatever the world wide web would tell him about the child who called him Daddy.

He opened his eyes as Hailey wandered in, her baby doll held upright against her chest. It was nearly bath time.

Phillip smiled. 'Hi, honey. Finished playing with your

doll's house?'

Hailey nodded, her expression bleak.

'Mummy's awake again.'

She sat down beside him, rocking the doll in her arms. Phillip swallowed hard. It was good to see her playing with her toys, but the guilt he felt each time he looked at her, it crushed him. He would have to do something soon. If he could only work out a foolproof plan, but the way his brain was functioning at the moment that just wasn't likely.

'Is that baby Lara you've got there?' he said, trying to sound as if no guilt was torturing him.

Hailey shook her head. 'No, this is my Maggie. She's my very best baby.' She sat there for a moment, stroking the doll's face, then looked up. 'When are the babies coming home?'

Phillip smiled. Baby Maggie would take a back seat when baby Lara was home, he would bet anything at all on that.

'Probably next Monday, like I told you.'

Hailey nodded, looking thoughtful. 'Miss McLure says I'm big enough to help with them. I want to give them their bottles and bath them, can I?'

Phillip's breath caught. She was looking forward to her future in his family. A future that couldn't... shouldn't... be.

Hailey was still waiting expectantly for the answer to what was obviously a very important question. He forced himself to sound happy and enthusiastic.

'That sounds great. I'll be really glad of your help.'

Satisfied, the child turned back to her doll, and Phillip leaned back again, closing his eyes. He could dream a little longer.

Chapter Twenty

The letter flap on the front door gave its usual clunk as it snapped shut, and Maggie glanced up from the sofa, where she was catching up with the news on teletext. The postman exited the garden, leaving the gate wide open as usual - this had always infuriated Maggie before, but now it was just so completely unimportant.

Last night, for the first time since losing Livvy, she and Colin had made love. The inevitable bittersweet milestone, and they had sobbed together afterwards. Maggie needed to feel joy. She needed to feel free from worry for just a moment, and she knew that if this didn't happen, their marriage was unlikely to survive in the long run. But in the whole series of terrible 'firsts' they'd gone through since the fifteenth of August, this one had been the most poignant.

Maggie's stomach heaved as she stared at the three envelopes lying in the hallway. The cream-coloured one was a card. Recently they'd had a couple of sympathy cards; couldn't people have the sensitivity to at least wait until - what? Until they had a funeral? Made some kind of 'my daughter is definitely dead' statement? She lifted the envelopes, forgetting about the card when she saw the plain white envelope beneath it.

It was another of those hideous anonymous letters. They'd had about six now, and actually some were signed with

Christian names so they weren't completely anonymous. They all had one thing in common, though: the writers all thought that she and Colin were the worst parents in the world. And maybe they were right, of course. Howard had told them to discard these letters unread, but Maggie couldn't do this. She read through every page of insults that came.

This one was mercifully short and contained nothing but vile abuse. Maggie took it to the kitchen sink to burn. This pain was hers alone. There was no point showing it to Colin; the news that it had come would be enough to ruin his evening. Resentment flared inside her as water speckled with black and grey swirled around the plughole.

Chapter Twenty-One
Mid November

Philip drove through Saturday afternoon rain, conscious of the relief he felt at the opportunity to spend a few blessed minutes by himself.

Life was intense now that the babies were home. Jennifer spent every available minute with the twins, feeding them, rocking them, changing their clothes if they got as much as a speck on their designer outfits. Everything else was up to him, which meant that not only was he doing all the housework, shopping, and looking after Hailey, he was also being denied the pleasure of bonding with his own two children. He was allowed to deal with Daniel now and then, true, but he wanted to do more than change the odd nappy. Yesterday, Jennifer had been so caught up in her own world that she had barely spoken to him all day, and he felt both left out and powerless to change things. And he was afraid to confront her in case he made things worse.

So the chance to go down to the harbour store and buy a couple of things he'd forgotten yesterday was a welcome one. This was what his life had come to, he was delighted to be going to the village to buy fish fingers and cream.

Inside the cramped little shop the first person he tangled baskets with was Hailey's teacher.

'Miss McLure! Sorry. I don't even need a basket, I'm only

238

here for a couple of things.'

She smiled at him. 'No problem. How's Hailey enjoying her first weekend with the babies? She was so excited about it yesterday.'

Phillip struggled to smile back, and sound like any other dad having new babies home.

'Oh, it's exciting alright. And tiring, I'd forgotten how it feels when you're up half the night. But of course it's wonderful too, they're doing so well.'

'That's great. You must bring them to school for a visit soon. The kids would love it.'

'Sure,' said Phillip, turning towards the check out. 'Sorry, I'll have to go now. Jennifer's, um, waiting for the cream. See you Monday.'

She stood to the side to let him pass. 'Say hello to Hailey from me.'

He nodded, and marched as quickly as the other shoppers would let him towards the checkout. Standing in the queue, he fumbled for his mobile when it rang.

It was Jennifer, her voice petulant.

'What on earth are you doing so long, darling? I need you here.'

Phillip felt his heart rate increase. So yesterday Jennifer had ignored him all day, and today he couldn't even go down to the shop without her phoning and hurrying him back.

'I'm next in line at the checkout. Is everything okay?' he said hoarsely, but she had already rung off.

Back at the car, he tossed his shopping onto the passenger seat before flopping down behind the wheel and jamming the key into the ignition. No chance of a walk round the harbour now. He should have left his phone at home. But he had to know if Jennifer was coping with the babies by herself. And there was Hailey, too. Nothing must happen to Hailey, and Jennifer seemed only bothered about the twins.

Another car was hovering, waiting for the space. Phillip pushed the car into gear and drove slowly up the hill towards home. He'd told Miss McLure that life was wonderful. It should be wonderful, and in a way it was. His children. Two new lives just beginning, and a cute little five-year-old too.

In a strange way he had almost forgotten that Hailey wasn't actually his child. It was wonderful how natural it felt, being Daddy to a five-year-old daughter. Just as he should have been, and the fact that her face in repose really was a mirror image of his own Hailey's helped him ignore the truth. The new Hailey had slotted exactly into a hole in his life, filling a space that had badly needed filling. Phillip sometimes went for hours now almost forgetting, but then suddenly the guilt would resurface, and it twisted inside him, this guilt; he really couldn't live with it.

Fortunately a kind of fog had appeared in his life. Although he was fully aware of his first daughter's death, and he knew that the new Hailey shouldn't be there, he kept the actual feelings associated with all this in the foggy part. The guilt was intolerable, and keeping it in the fog meant he wasn't confronted by it all the time. Only very occasionally did he allow himself to think about Hailey's real parents and what they must be going through. And that it was all his fault. He wasn't having a breakdown, he knew that Hailey wasn't his daughter, but he had chosen to ignore the fact that he was, in effect, hiding an abducted child within his family. It was his fault that the new Hailey's real parents would be going through the very same hell that he and Jennifer had suffered. Each day was as haunted as the one before.

He had never typed 'missing girl' into a search engine, he had stopped reading newspapers and watching the news, and all because he was too much of a coward to face the reality of who this child really was. If only he had managed to get her home right at the start. But he hadn't, and that was something he would have to live with now. This was why he needed the fog; there was enough to worry him without feeling guilty about people he didn't even know.

And Hailey wasn't even his biggest problem at the

moment - that was Jennifer. He was so afraid now, in fact he was terrified that Jennifer's strangeness would lose him his family. She was just so obsessed. Possessed. Frighteningly different. It was as if she was living on another planet, in a place where he simply couldn't reach her. He had no idea what to do.

Home again, Phillip deposited his shopping in the fridge before looking into the sitting room. Daniel was asleep in his carrycot, and as usual, Lara was in Jennifer's arms.

'Hi, love,' he said, forcing himself to sound pleasant. 'Where's Hailey?'

Jennifer's eyes glittered in anger as she looked up at him.

'Oh, Phillip, I wish you'd do something about that girl, she is *so* inconsiderate,' she muttered savagely, then clutched Lara to her breast. The baby whimpered, and Jennifer rocked her. 'There, my angel, Mummy's right here.' The eyes turned back to Phillip. 'She was making a dreadful noise playing with that doll. I sent her upstairs with a flea in her ear. It won't do, I can't have it.'

'I'll - see to her now,' said Phillip, and he escaped upstairs. Surely Jennifer wouldn't have hurt Hailey. He had a feeling that something had happened before his return from California. The way Hailey sometimes flinched away from Jennifer, and the look on the girl's face whenever Jennifer came into the room. And yet, Jennifer had adored her daughter, idolised her, even. But that had been before.

He pushed the little girl's door open. Hailey was sitting on her bed, the doll called Maggie cradled against her shoulder. Her face was tearstained and to Phillip's horror there was an ugly red welt on her cheek. He could see the outline of Jennifer's fingers. In two steps he was beside Hailey.

'Daddy,' she said, and Phillip took her in his arms.

He sat on the bed with her in his arms and rocked back and forth. This child might look like his own girl, but her character was different, and now Jennifer was turning against

241

her. She wasn't the same doting mother as she was to the twins.

Phillip took a shaky breath, trying desperately to hold back his tears. The fog had disappeared for the moment and the guilt came crushing in. Hailey being here was as much his fault now as Jennifer's. Quite deliberately he had done an unforgivable wrong to Hailey. Hailey who wasn't Hailey, and he didn't even know her name.

And the horrible, ironic thing was that Jennifer, who had taken the child in the first place, didn't want her any more. And it wasn't just Hailey who was unwanted, no, both he and Daniel were surplus to requirements as well. Jennifer had her baby daughter. Nothing else mattered.

And it was much too late to put it right.

Part Four
The Accident

Chapter One
Mid November

A buzz of chatter filled the air, and Katie looked round contentedly. November was such a cosy month in a classroom. The wind might blow and the rain might pour, but here inside they were like those well-known bugs in a rug. The room was bright and cheerful in spite of the greyness outside, and everyone was busy.

That afternoon the children were making birthday cakes with coloured dough.

'Make the best birthday cake you've ever had, if you can remember,' said Katie. 'If you can't remember, make the best cake you can imagine. Tomorrow we'll have a secret ballot – that's when everyone votes for their favourite – and the winner gets a prize!'

She held up a red and white striped pencil. The children set to work at the craft table, and Katie sat watching them. She was continuing her Families theme, ready to run it into a Christmas theme in a week or two. After birthdays they would talk about other family celebrations, and that would lead naturally into Christmas.

They've made so much progress since the summer, she thought, looking round the group of chattering children.

Derek didn't stutter half as much now, and he got through most days without bashing anyone or being ganged up on, and Hailey - Hailey was much better too.

Katie frowned. Hailey was much better, but... There was a distinctly odd 'but' about Hailey, yet it was difficult to put a finger on what it was exactly. The little girl had been much happier in the weeks since her father's return, and most days she was even quite talkative and certainly a lot livelier than before, but she still had moments of sitting staring into space and looking lost. She often talked about her father and the babies, but her mother might not have existed for all Hailey spoke of her. This was particularly noticeable at the moment, when they were discussing families every day. And while her reading and counting were fairly average, her writing, and most especially her drawing, were immature. If you could call a five-year-old immature. The child was a puzzle, even if she was getting on much better than Katie had expected at first.

Katie rose to her feet and wandered round the table. She found herself missing Mark more each day, and often thought about him up in chilly Aberdeen, looking after four children and running his sister's house. But at least she'd had no major problems to deal with since his departure, and the way things were going, Katie wasn't expecting any.

Most of the children had created cakes of the round-with-candles variety. Julia's, however, was a heart shape, and Aiden was attempting something in green. Katie stopped at his side.

'What is it, exactly?' she asked, and Aiden heaved a sigh.

'It's a frog. But I'm not doing it very well.'

'You had a frog birthday cake?'

'I always have an animal. Mummy makes them. Next birthday I'm having a dinosaur.'

'Gosh. What a clever mummy you have.'

Katie went on to Hailey, who was creating a more traditionally-shaped cake with a blue and green top. The little girl's face was pink with concentration, and Katie smiled.

'You're looking well, Hailey - bet you're enjoying having your dad home.'

Hailey nodded slowly. 'I don't need pills anymore,' she said suddenly.

'Well that's good. And what a lovely cake.'

'I had a sea cake with three candles,' said Hailey, lifting a chunk of brown dough. 'With marzipan waves and a marzipan boat on top. I love marzipan. This is going to be the boat.'

'Super,' said Katie. 'Did Mummy make it?'

Hailey's face clouded. She shrugged, and went on shaping her little brown boat. Katie didn't press her. It was just another instance of Hailey being distant.

When most of the children were finished, Katie clapped her hands for silence.

'Tomorrow,' she said, 'I want you to bring birthday photos. We're going to make posters. We'll enlarge the photos on the colour copier, stick them on poster paper and you can draw and write things in between. Bring a photo of your first birthday, your second birthday, your third birthday and so on. It doesn't have to be a cake photo, just a birthday photo. Does everyone understand?'

Everyone did, and Katie started them clearing up for going home.

The next morning Katie was greeted by a small crowd of children waving envelopes of various sizes.

'I remembered!'

'We printed mine out already!'

'And I brought one of me when I was just born!'

'What a good idea,' said Katie, laughing. 'Right, kids, let's get settled now, are we all here?'

'Hailey and Graeme!' called several children.

'We'll wait, then. Has everyone written their name on their photo envelope?'

Four or five heads bent to work, and Katie went to get the poster paper from the office cupboard. When she returned,

Mr Marshall and Hailey were standing beside her desk. Hailey was holding an envelope, an oddly defiant expression on her face.

'Morning, Mr Marshall. Hello, Hailey.'

Katie looked inquiringly at Hailey's father. He looked tired, but then he'd probably forgotten what a full night's sleep felt like, with baby twins at home. He cleared his throat, and she noticed a muscle jumping under one eye.

'We had a problem with Hailey's photos. I'm afraid a couple of albums seem to have been mislaid when my wife moved house, and my laptop where they are stored is out of order. Hailey only has photos of her first two birthdays.'

'That's quite all right, don't worry. Hailey can draw pictures of her other birthdays, can't you, Hailey?'

Mr Marshall seemed to be in a hurry, so Katie saw him to the door. Hailey remained standing by the desk, still looking unhappy.

'It's really alright, Hailey,' said Katie, putting her hand on the little girl's head. 'Things do get mislaid when people move house. Your albums will probably turn up when no-one's looking for them.'

'They won't,' said Hailey, blinking hard. 'My albums are all still at the old house. I didn't bring them. I didn't bring anything.'

'I'm sure Mummy packed your albums somewhere,' said Katie, patting the short hair, which was looking much better now that it was growing out. Strange how it looked darker though. 'Don't worry, Hailey. We'll manage with what you've got here.'

Hailey went to her desk, and Katie thought how the Marshalls did seem to be more than a little casual about their daughter's treasures. Lost albums now... The list was getting longer.

The class settled down to work on a writing worksheet. One at a time, Katie took the children who needed to photocopy through to the office, leaving Alison to oversee the rest of the class. Hailey was still looking unhappy when it was her turn.

'This is a super cake too, Hailey,' said Katie, holding up Hailey's first birthday photo. A chubby baby with a thick hatch of unruly hair beamed out from behind a teddy bear cake. Hailey sniffed.

'I don't remember it,' she said.

'Well, I don't suppose you do. Let's - '

'I don't remember any of them. I had a beautiful sea cake, I don't want those.'

Hailey banged the photos down on the table and stood there, her lip trembling. Her face was flushed, and a slight bruise on her left cheek flared angrily.

Katie was amazed. The child had never been anything other than fully cooperative.

'Hailey, are you alright?'

'I don't want those photos.'

Hailey was speaking through real tears now, and Katie thought quickly.

'Alright. We'll go back to the classroom and you can draw your birthday pictures.'

Hailey agreed to this and set to work, alone at the crafts table. Katie finished photocopying with the remaining children then sat down beside Hailey. The sea cake was there, carefully drawn and coloured, plus a round cake with two candles and another with just one.

'That's looking good,' said Katie encouragingly. 'What about your fourth birthday now? What kind of cake did you have then, can you remember?'

Hailey blinked up at her. 'I was going to have pink and white candles on a pink cake,' she whispered. 'My mum and me bought the candles and we were going to make it and I wanted a party on the beach like last year. I wanted that!'

To Katie's horror she went chalk white and sat there rigidly, staring at nothing and trembling. Two tears ran down her cheeks. Katie put her arms round the little girl and called to the assistant.

'Alison, go quickly for Nora Wilson. Tell her Hailey's ill again.'

The girl shot off, and returned a few minutes later with Nora.

'She was drawing a birthday cake,' said Katie helplessly, still cuddling Hailey.

'Come on, Hailey,' said Nora, feeling the little girl's forehead. 'Let's get you tucked up with a blanket and a hot water bottle, shall we?'

Katie watched unhappily as Nora led Hailey off, then turned back to the table and collected Hailey's drawings. Miserably, she went back to the rest of the class. There was still something going on with Hailey, something they just weren't getting.

Chapter Two

Phillip Marshall turned the car back towards Polpayne. Normally he enjoyed Hailey's company, but it was a relief to have left her at school this morning. A simple request for a couple of photos had turned into a major problem, and Hailey had been more distressed last night than he had ever seen her. There had been an almost wild look on her face when she'd told him about the photos, and desperation shone out of her eyes when he produced Hailey's – his Hailey's – baby albums. She must have been remembering the birthdays she'd had before, birthdays spent with her real family. Something like that could happen any time, any place.

He wasn't in control of his life now, he thought, biting his lip as he remembered the child's face when he told Miss McLure they had lost the photo albums. It wasn't a lie, the albums were nowhere to be found. Jennifer apparently *had* 'lost' the ones with photos of their daughter as an older child. It would have been plain to see in those photos that his own girl and the Hailey they had now were two different children.

Stopped at the lights, Phillip rubbed his eyes, wondering exactly how much Hailey remembered about her old life. She lived in their family and called them Mummy and Daddy, but she must know that they were living a lie. And unless she had blanked everything, which given her reaction now was unlikely, she must remember a whole lot. She definitely hadn't wanted to take these photos to school. What was stopping her from speaking up, telling Miss McLure who she was? Hailey was very fond of her teacher, he saw that every day, but how did she feel about her new family? It was obvious that she loved the babies, and he knew she liked him too, but - Jennifer?

That bruise on Hailey's face where Jennifer had hit her, what a shameful thing that was. There had been lies then too, to explain away the mark when Hailey went back to school. He'd kept her off for three days, until the finger marks had gone. Had there been other bruises too, before he came home? He'd looked as well as he could without finding anything when he'd bathed her the day Jennifer had struck her, but then bruises don't take forever to fade. What if Hailey told someone about the bruise, or about the photos, or about anything at all?

'She won't say anything,' he said aloud, pulling into the harbour car park. There was no need to go home yet, a walk would do him good.

No, Hailey wouldn't talk. Jennifer had obviously drummed it into her that she was Hailey Marshall now and never to say anything else. But why had she turned so queer and uncooperative about the photos? Was Jennifer's terrible hold over the child slipping now that he was home taking care of her? Or was it something to do with her birthday? When *was* her birthday? But she was Hailey Marshall now, her birthday was the fifteenth of August.

Phillip took a deep breath of fishy sea air. How many times had he sat in front of the computer, willing his fingers to type? How often had he ignored those uncomfortable thoughts? Thoughts of that other family, the family who had lost their child. God forgive him for his weakness, but he had taken their child into his heart and he didn't want to let her go. Worse than that, he couldn't let her go. If he did he would lose everything, and they would send him to prison.

This was one of the days when the fog in his brain just

didn't hide the horror, and the pain of knowing what he'd done was enough to make him feel physically sick.

He stood by the boatyard, staring out towards the open sea. It was a cold, clear day, and the wind was salty against his lips. He could see a long way down the coast, dark cliffs and blue ocean. It was beautiful; it would have been a perfect place to live. He could have been so happy - a family man, like he'd always wanted. Daniel and Lara, his children. But there was Hailey too.

Phillip turned back to the car, allowing the fog to descend once again. Slowly, his guilt disappeared into the mist. It was better like this.

Chapter Three
Late November

'Mum! I can't find my football stuff!'

Joe thundered downstairs and burst into the kitchen where Maggie was filling his snack box for school. She grinned at him.

'And for once that's not your fault,' she said, handing over the box. 'It's in the garage. Dad cleaned your boots for you last night, so remember to say thank you.'

'Um. There's Sue and Greg now. Bye, Mum!'

Maggie hugged him, and stood in the doorway waving as Sue's car disappeared down the road. The usual deathly silence descended on the house, and Maggie sighed. Thank God she had her work to go to. Even though today was a free day, her job gave the week a definite structure, and it was something fresh to think about too. At the Geriatric Unit she was with people who didn't know her except in her new role of helper. Being Maggie-who-feeds-Vi-Simpson felt reassuringly normal, in fact it was the one part of her life where she felt like the same person she had been before. And heaven knows she had plenty of time to do the work - she only had her son to care for now, and he was at school all day.

Joe's routine was completely back to normal. He went to football practice twice a week and beaver scouts every Monday. His weekends were a mixture of family stuff with

Maggie and Colin, and playing – usually football – with his friends, and last week he had gone on his first sleepover since the summer and had a ball. The nightmares had all but stopped, and he certainly looked happier again, almost his old self.

Slinky the cat rubbed against Maggie's legs and she bent to stroke him.

'Oh, Slinky. You remember Livvy, don't you? She loved you to bits.'

Surely he remembered. He had loved Olivia too. And right now he was the only other living creature in the house, the only creature she could talk out loud to, and she had to talk some of the time to cover the silence.

Sighing, Maggie spooned cat food into Slinky's bowl and then switched on the radio. She'd never been a background music kind of person before, but now the radio covered the silence more effectively than she and Slinky could. The nine o'clock news was on.

- still no sign of seven-year-old Carla Graham, who went missing during a family outing to Edinburgh Castle yesterday afternoon. The police have asked -

In a split second Maggie was back on the beach realising that Olivia was gone. Bent double, she retched violently before stumbling out to the bathroom. She vomited, then splashed water over her face and patted it dry, staring at her reflection. She was sheet-white and her eyes were wild.

Another little girl was missing. And this child too had disappeared from the middle of her family, just as Livvy had. Could there be a connection?

Had her daughter been taken? Abducted? And if she had, what had she suffered? How long had she been tortured, was she dead, how did she die, had she been raped, had she... Sometimes little girls were taken and abused for years...

A voice screamed inside her. Livvy had drowned, she had drowned...

Maggie struggled to order the thoughts crashing around

253

her head. Edinburgh was right at the other end of the country…

Nausea took hold of her again, but she fought it down and went for the phone. She had to phone Howard. He would know.

Howard was at work, and she was on hold for ages before she eventually heard his voice. Breathless now, Maggie asked her questions, barely able to keep the scream of panic from her voice.

Howard's voice was calm and reassuring, but he had nothing definite to tell her.

'We've been in touch, of course, and at the moment there's nothing to indicate a connection. Carla was with a big family group and she disappeared while the others were queuing for tickets or looking over the battlements or buying postcards. It took them about half an hour to realise that she really was gone, and it's not quite impossible that she ran off. Just before she disappeared she and her mother had an argument about something Carla wanted to buy, and apparently there's an absolute warren of streets and alleyways with shops around Edinburgh Castle. She still could be simply lost. Maggie, I realise this must be awful for you, but you have to believe that Olivia went into the sea that day. I'm still watching out for her, you know.'

'Yes,' said Maggie, closing her eyes. Of course he was right, he must be. 'Oh, Howard, I wish we had her back.'

'I wish you did too,' said Howard, and she could picture his sad, lined face.

The doorbell rang as she put the phone down, and she went to answer it, dabbing her eyes with a tissue.

It was Sue, back from dropping the kids off and complete with baby under one arm and two-year-old following on behind. She looked keenly at Maggie and then walked in, dropping a large bag on the hall floor.

'I see you heard the news. We've come to keep you company for a while,' she said, handing the baby to Maggie. 'No arguments, Mags. I know you're not working today, and

254

you shouldn't be alone.'

Maggie found that she was grateful. It was good to have a friend here, making coffee and chatting to her, filling the silence. It was comforting to sit holding Rosie and smell her warm baby smell, and watch little Liam run around. But all the while crazy, painful thoughts were spinning round her mind, thoughts about poor lost Carla and her own lost Olivia.

At ten past ten the phone rang. Maggie reached for it, somehow certain that it would be Howard.

'They've got Carla, she *had* run off,' he said briefly. 'She found her way into a back shop, got locked in and spent the night there. The owner opened it an hour ago and there she was. So it was nothing to do with Olivia.'

'Good,' said Maggie. 'Good for them and good for us, too. Oh God, Howard, all I wish is that we knew for sure that Livvy - '

She couldn't continue, she couldn't bring herself to say aloud that she wished she knew for sure that her daughter had drowned. What had Livvy ever done to deserve this, what had any of them done?

And why had the Grahams, who would be an ordinary family no different to her own, doing ordinary things like visiting a castle - why had they got their little girl back, and she and Colin hadn't? It just wasn't fair, and there would never be any answers.

Howard was speaking again.

'I know. I do know,' he said. 'Maggie, you *have* to accept, inside yourself, that Livvy drowned. This will happen again, you know, and sometimes the worst does happen. Little girls go missing, and sometimes they *are* abducted and abused. Maggie, Olivia drowned.'

'I know,' said Maggie. 'It's okay. Thanks, Howard, for everything. I'll phone you later in the week.'

She put the phone down and began to weep. Those Grahams just didn't know, they couldn't know how lucky they were. But she shouldn't be feeling all this resentment because a seven-year-old child had been found safe. Grief and guilt welled up all over again. Sue patted her back, not attempting to stop the flow of tears.

To Maggie's alarm she felt the scream rise inside her. Shaking on the sofa, she could hear herself moaning as it came closer, and there was nothing she could do to stop it.

'Livvy! Oh, God, *Li - ivvy - y -y!*'

Sobs shook her, then gradually subsided. She could see again now, Sue's concerned face and Liam's amazed little one.

'You're okay. Just sit quietly for a moment,' said Sue, her voice shaking too.

'I'm sorry,' was all Maggie could manage. Slowly, she leaned back into the sofa.

'Take your time,' said Sue, handing her a tissue.

After a while, Maggie sat straighter and wiped her face. She took a deep breath, feeling the air flow into her lungs, bringing unexpected peace. She sat there breathing, in and out, and suddenly she knew that this had been the last time. She wouldn't lose control and scream again, that part of the grief process was over. She would cry, the tears would come and they would never completely stop - but the uncontrollable, piercing agony was gone.

And of course, everything Howard had said was right, and she had to deal with that. She turned to Sue.

'We'll be having a memorial quite soon, for Livvy,' she said, smiling through tears. 'I want it to be as cheerful as possible. To show how much we loved Olivia.'

It was time. Colin would agree, she knew. A goodbye service, sometime after Christmas, because they would need to plan it all carefully and get it just right. It would be the last thing she could ever do for her daughter.

Chapter Four

At lunchtime, Katie saw her fourteen remaining pupils off in the direction of the dining room, and went to find Nora.

'Hailey's gone home,' said Nora, when Katie put her head round the sick room door. 'I phoned her dad and he came to collect her. She was getting better, but I thought a day at home wouldn't harm her.'

'Good,' said Katie. 'Nora, what on earth is it - some kind of fit? She looked so out of it. Did you see the mark on her face?'

Nora looked at her, frowning. 'I don't know, Katie. I don't think it was a fit this time either. I told Mr Marshall she should be given a thorough check-up. I only hope he sees to it.'

'Yes.' Katie turned to the door again. 'It's just funny, when her dad's back and she's so much happier. '

Nora shrugged. 'It could simply be a reaction to all those things that have happened in her life recently, plus the fact that until she came here, no-one was helping her to deal with them. I've never seen a child react like she does.'

'You and me both. I think I'll stop by her home after school. Just ring the bell and say I was passing and see how she is.'

'You do that,' said Nora. 'But Katie, don't forget that every child gets a bang now and then. Don't overreact.'

'I know,' said Katie. 'But I'll go anyway. It'll only take a few minutes.'

'Right. And now I'd better get along to the dining room before all your other little darlings start a war with their lunch. Don't worry, Katie, Hailey's dad is obviously helping her a lot. She'll be fine in the end, I'm sure.'

'I hope you're right,' said Katie, turning towards the staffroom and her own lunch.

After school Katie drove home quickly to change, and bought an African Violet for Hailey at the shop on the corner. By half past four she was ringing the Marshalls' front door bell.

Hailey opened the door, looking more like her normal self.

'I saw you get out of your car,' she said, standing back to let Katie into the hallway. 'Daddy says come through to the sitting room. Mummy's upstairs resting.'

'Thank you. Are you better now?'

Katie presented Hailey with the plant, kissing the little girl's forehead when she nodded and beamed, obviously delighted with her gift.

Katie followed her into the sitting room and stood still. Phillip Marshall was on the sofa, giving one of the babies a bottle. The other was lying in a carrycot beside him, gurgling placidly.

'Oh! What darlings!' Katie felt a lump form in her throat. She reached out with one finger and stroked a soft cheek.

Phillip Marshall smiled at her, and Katie noticed that he seemed much less nervous here in his own home. He deposited baby and bottle into the corner of the sofa, surrounded by cushions, and reached into the carrycot.

'If you take a seat, I'll pass you Daniel while Lara's finishing her bottle. She's a lazy thing - takes twice as long over her grub as Daniel.'

Katie accepted the baby and sat there, her eyes moist.

'Hailey's fine now, as you see,' said Phillip. 'I'll take her to the doctor, but I'm sure there's nothing wrong. She was just upset about the lost albums, but we bought her two lovely big new ones on the way home, didn't we, toots? And we've taken the first photos to fill them up fast.'

He grinned at Hailey and she smiled back.

'I gave Daniel his bottle at lunchtime,' said Hailey, leaning against Katie's arm and stroking the baby's head. 'They *are* nice babies, aren't they, Miss McLure?'

'They're just gorgeous. I've never seen such little charmers,' Katie told her, watching as Phillip patted Lara's back until the baby gave a loud burp. He's a good father, she thought. He's good with the babies and he's good with Hailey too.

Back in the car, she thought about the family scene she had just witnessed. She knew she wasn't supposed to get emotionally involved, but Hailey seemed different, somehow.

And if she ever had children herself, thought Katie, she would make very sure that neither important bears nor photo albums were mislaid anywhere along the way. And all family cats would stay around until they'd lost every one of their nine lives.

Chapter Five
The Last Day

A van driving past outside woke Jennifer, and she stretched luxuriously before turning to gaze into the two cribs, both on her side of the bed. The babies were still asleep, and Jennifer smiled fondly.

They were four weeks old now, and they were the most important things in the world. Not things, of course. They her own little people, to love and to hold and to cherish. She could lie here beside them forever, watching over them, protecting them.

Jennifer pulled the duvet around her, not taking her eyes off the babies. A mother - she was a mother of twins. She had given them life. No power was greater.

Phillip, still asleep beside her, turned on his back and began to snore. Jennifer's pleasure vanished instantly and she frowned. He could be so inconsiderate. He mustn't disturb the babies. She gave him a little push, then a bigger one when he snored on. At last she lifted her pillow, placed it on his face and pressed. Phillip grunted and pushed it away.

'Hey!' he protested, sitting up and glaring at her.

'Sh! Don't wake the babies!' hissed Jennifer.

'I won't, but the babies woke *me* twice last night,' said Phillip. 'And you didn't move a muscle. Didn't you hear them?'

'I was up with them too,' said Jennifer, chin in the air. 'But I need to rest, you know. Don't forget I was the one who gave birth to them.'

Phillip rolled out of bed. 'Oh, let's not fight about it,' he said, walking round the bed to look into the cribs. 'They're worth it all, aren't they?' He picked up his bathrobe and went out to the landing.

Jennifer got up more slowly, glad that he was going to shower in Hailey's bathroom rather than risk waking the babies by using the en-suite. She went downstairs and prepared two bottles, then took them up again when a cry from above told her that Daniel was awake.

Checking that Lara was still asleep, she changed Daniel's nappy and put a bottle into his crib with him, propping it up with a pillow.

'There you are, my darling. And now - my little princess.'

She lifted Lara, who was starting to whimper, and kissed her daughter's soft cheek. 'It's alright, my love, Mummy's here,' she crooned, humming as she changed the baby and carried her over to the rocking chair by the window.

This was the part she liked best - just her and her little girl. Her own little Lara Grace.

'Mummy's precious darling. My sweet little angel. You won't go away and leave Mummy, will you, Angel? You'll stay Mummy's own girl, always.'

Chapter Six

'Well, ladies. It's Saturday morning and the sun's shining. What would you like to do today?'

Phillip spread Hailey's toast with peanut butter – Jennifer was always so angry if Hailey messed her clothes or the table, it was easier if he just did things like this for her – and passed it to the little girl.

'There you are, honey. What do you think, Jennifer? It's mild out, how about a walk in the park? Or shopping? Or shall we just stay home and relax?'

Jennifer worried him more and more. She was so withdrawn. She rarely spoke, and often she didn't seem to hear him when he spoke to her. Or she didn't reply, anyway. And it had got worse over the last few days, too. She would sit smiling away to herself, sometimes she even laughed out loud. The only thing she was sure to react to was a cry from one of the babies.

But he'd noticed that she was strange with them too now. This morning he'd found her feeding Lara in the bedroom, holding her so tightly the poor little thing could hardly breathe, let alone drink her bottle, but Jennifer had noticed nothing. She'd been locked away in some daydream, rocking in the chair and singing some queer chant. He'd given her shoulder a quick tap, and she'd smiled down at Lara and relaxed. But what if he hadn't been there? And more worryingly, she hadn't reacted to *him* at all - just to Lara. Meanwhile, Daniel was lying there whimpering because his bottle of milk had spilt half its contents into the crib.

And then there was the way Jennifer had half smothered him with her pillow that morning. The expression in her eyes then had frightened him for a moment. This woman was supposed to be his wife, and he loved her. But there was almost nothing of the old Jennifer there now.

He was afraid. Terrified they were going to lose everything. The fog had disappeared completely; he knew exactly what he had done. He was passing an abducted child off as his own, and he wasn't getting help for his disturbed wife. But if he involved other people now he would go to prison, Jennifer would be sent to a psychiatric hospital, the babies would end up God knows where and Hailey wouldn't be his Hailey any longer. And it was all down to Jennifer.

He knew now that this was much worse than the Black Patch. God knows she'd had reason to be withdrawn and depressed back then, but now, now that she had her own babies, plus Hailey, she had somehow lost touch with reality. Her world wasn't the world around her, and he didn't know how to help her. But he had to try.

Determinedly, he tried to jolly her out of her preoccupation.

'Want to go shopping, Jennifer?'

This time she heard him, and turned over-bright eyes towards him.

'Oh yes,' she said, laughing across the table at him, and he cringed. 'We need lots and lots of baby clothes. The darlings are growing so quickly. We'll go to that big new baby shop in Newquay, you know the one.'

He didn't, but at least they were conversing now.

'Good idea. I expect Hailey needs some winter things too.'

Jennifer looked right through Hailey and Phillip's heart sank even further. The only people Jennifer cared about now were the babies. Lara in particular.

He still had no idea what to do. All he knew was he had

263

to keep things normal. That might force Jennifer into doing normal things too.

'I know,' he said aloud, grinning frantically at Hailey, who was staring with wide eyes. 'We'll all go for lunch at the Mill Hotel in Newquay. Then we'll go to the baby shop. And afterwards I'll drop you and the twins back here, darling, and Hailey and I'll go to Polpayne market for fruit.'

Hailey touched his sleeve. 'Miss McLure said again about the jeans,' she said. 'We're going out in the garden next week and the others all have jeans.'

'You have plenty of beautiful dresses,' snapped Jennifer, leaning across the table and thumping Hailey on the nose so suddenly that Phillip had no chance to stop her. 'No little girl needs jeans.' She rose and marched through to the babies in the living room.

'Jennifer!'

Hailey touched her face, where blood was streaming from her nose and smearing across her mouth, her eyes huge and terrified. But she made no sound and Phillip knew that this could only mean she was afraid to cry.

'It's okay, sweetheart. Let me see.'

He grabbed the tea towel and wiped Hailey's face before pinching her nose shut to stop the bleeding. Still silent, she allowed him to press firmly, which was reassuring in a way as it meant the nose couldn't be broken. After a few moments he looked. The bleeding had stopped, and he rose and filled a glass with cold water.

'Sip this, honey. You'll be fine in a minute.'

Hailey sipped, her teeth chattering against the glass. Phillip sat rubbing her back, looking through to the living room where Jennifer was rocking one of the babies.

He needed to take her to a doctor. This couldn't go on.

Jennifer walked back into the kitchen, Lara in her arms, and Hailey immediately ran upstairs.

Phillip found he couldn't look at his wife. He loaded the dishwasher and then went up to see what Hailey was doing.

He found her huddled right underneath her duvet, sobbing quietly, blood trickling from her nose again and staining the sheet.

'Come on, sweetheart. Let's hold this tight for a minute or two. Hailey, Mummy really isn't well. I'm going to take her to a new doctor on - on Monday, but for now we have to keep her happy. Okay? Nothing bad will happen if she's happy.'

Hailey nodded. Phillip waited until the bleeding had stopped, then washed her face in cold water, glad to see that apart from some slight swelling the nose looked alright.

Hailey held his hand tightly as they went downstairs. Phillip let her help wash the car, bringing a smile to her face again, then chivvied Jennifer into getting herself and the babies dressed to go out. She sang happily while she was dressing, and Phillip felt the tension inside him loosen slightly. His plan was working, they were doing normal family things and Jennifer was happy. It would be alright, it would.

The Mill Hotel was busy with lunchtime guests, but Phillip had reserved a table by the window. He settled Hailey beside him, with Jennifer and the twin buggy opposite. Hailey looked round the room, a faint smile pulling at her lips, and a lump came into Phillip's throat. I love her, he thought suddenly. I really do love her. We can get through this.

His positive moment was short-lived. Try as he might, Phillip couldn't get any kind of conversation started with Jennifer. She didn't answer, she simply didn't seem to understand that she should reply to his comments. He rubbed one hand over his face. She had hummed and sung most of the morning at home, and now she was refusing to utter a word. But the singing hadn't been normal either, he thought dully. Jennifer never used to sing about the house.

She was getting worse. He was watching her deteriorate. All her attention now was given to Lara, who she was cradling right here in the restaurant. The baby gave a little bleat, and

265

Jennifer reacted immediately, murmuring reassurance.

She's having a breakdown and there's nothing I can do to prevent it, thought Phillip, cutting up Hailey's pizza for her and talking determinedly on about school, holidays, restaurants in America - anything to maintain a semblance of normality. At least Hailey was here to provide the odd answer. He wasn't quite talking to himself.

Phillip was glad when the meal was over. He was aware of curious glances from other diners, and they weren't all because of the babies. Jennifer was noticeably abnormal today. He doubted whether he should go to the baby shop with her in this state. But she might make a scene if he refused, and whatever happened, he had to keep her happy.

'I want to go to the loo,' said Hailey, when he had paid the bill.

'It's over there behind the bar. Mummy'll go with you,' said Phillip, firmly taking over the buggy from Jennifer. 'I'll wait by the car.'

To his relief, Jennifer followed Hailey towards the ladies. She wouldn't do anything to the child here in the hotel, he knew. She would consider that undignified. Phillip pushed the buggy out across the car park. There were two different cars on either side of theirs now, both parked right up close. He would have to back out a bit before they could load the carrycots into the back.

Hailey suddenly popped up beside him. 'I like pizza,' she said, and Phillip smiled. Thank God for Hailey. She was the best thing in his life just now.

'I know you do,' he said, rubbing her thin shoulders. 'Where's Mummy?'

'Don't know.'

When a full five minutes had passed with no Jennifer appearing in the hotel doorway, Phillip's nerves had reached breaking point. He placed Hailey's hands on the buggy.

'Stay right here with the babies,' he said. 'I'll go and get Mummy.'

266

What was she doing? He couldn't cope any longer; he would have to take her to a doctor today, he saw that clearly now. He would find Jennifer, get her into the car and drive them all to the Rosen Clinic. Someone there would help them.

As soon as he opened the hotel door he saw her, walking towards him. She had been renewing her make up, and the full red lips made him shudder.

'Okay?' he asked, taking her arm. 'Hailey and the babies are just over there. We - '

She turned glittering eyes towards him.

'You've left my baby alone?' she hissed, and began to run across the car park, teetering on her high heels.

It was like a scene in a film. He saw Hailey turn and look at them, he saw Jennifer running towards the babies, and then he saw a high-backed van reverse abruptly out of its parking space.

'Jennifer!' he yelled, and ran, ran, ran and pushed her away from the van. But not quickly enough. The van ploughed into his side as he desperately tried to push Jennifer out of the way. Phillip felt himself rolling on the ground, Jennifer crushed beside him then abruptly pulled away by the van. He couldn't see where she had gone.

He heard one short, shrill scream from Hailey, and then there were people around him, above him, shouting for ambulances and pushing him down when he tried to get up. Everything was moving in circles, and the pain in his leg was excruciating. For a moment he couldn't hear properly. It was getting dark, too.

'Hailey!' he shouted, but it was less than a whisper.

'Lie down, mate, keep still. An ambulance is on its way.'

He still couldn't see Jennifer, or Hailey or the babies.

'Hailey!'

This time someone heard him.

'The lady's over there, someone's looking after her until the ambulance comes. Your children are fine. Keep still.'

He heard sirens, far away at first, then swooping right up

here beside him, and a green-clad figure was touching him.

'What's your name, sir?'

The green figure was waiting, but there was no way Phillip could manage even a whisper now. He could hear everything again but he couldn't speak. He couldn't see much, either. Waves of pain were washing through his entire body.

'He said "Hailey" a minute ago,' said the first voice. 'And there's three kiddies over there, but they're all okay.'

Phillip felt himself float away. It wasn't unpleasant, rather like lying half asleep on an air mattress on the sea. He felt himself being moved and then something was holding him down. The pain abated slightly. There was a lurch, and he realised that he was in an ambulance. Darkness was hovering right above him.

'Okay, sweetheart. You can come in this ambulance with Daddy, and the babies can go in the other one with your mum. Then there's room for everyone.'

It was the ambulance man's voice again. Phillip tried to say something to Hailey, but he couldn't. The ambulance jerked as it moved off, siren blaring.

'We'll be at the hospital in just five minutes,' said the voice reassuringly. 'What's your name, sweetheart?'

Phillip could hear Hailey breathing, but she didn't speak.

'What's your name, darling? My name's Davie.'

He heard Hailey's voice then, it had to be her voice, but it was almost unrecognisable.

'My name's Livvy.'

Her name was Livvy. And in the midst of his pain, Phillip knew he would never see her again. His Hailey. His Hailey was someone else's Livvy. And they would find that someone now and she leave him.

The paramedic was adjusting the oxygen mask over Phillip's nose and mouth. His fingers were warm.

'That's a nice name. Right, Libby, here's the hospital now. Someone will take care of you while the doctors are helping Mummy and Daddy.'

More bangs, and Phillip felt himself being lifted. The voice was speaking, telling other voices that according to his driving licence he was Phillip Marshall, that he had a leg fracture, possible fractured ribs and a head wound.

'And this is Libby. Not hurt but very frightened. Needs some TLC.'

Another voice, shocked and sympathetic.

'Oh, poor sweetie, don't worry, we'll find someone to come and help you. Have you got a Grandma nearby, or an auntie? Don't worry, Libby, the doctors will look after Daddy.'

Phillip tried to shout to Hailey. Tried to tell her he was sorry, tried to say he'd only done it because he cared for her. But no sound came when he opened his mouth, and the darkness was getting heavier, surrounding him, pulling him into nothing.

Chapter Seven

Maggie heaved her bags of groceries into the car boot and strode round to the driver's seat. She was late. She'd said she'd be home by half past twelve, and here it was, long gone one o'clock. The supermarket had been unusually crowded, even for midday Saturday, stressful, but entirely her own fault. She should have done the shopping yesterday.

The Christmas decorations had all been up for weeks now, and everyone was stocking up on food. Maggie blinked back hot tears as she waited for the lights to change.

It was going to be difficult. They only had one sock to fill this year. It sounded impossible but they had to get through it, they had to make a go of it for Joe's sake. But listening to cheery Christmas songs blaring from supermarket loudspeakers in November was already too much.

She knew it didn't matter that she was late. Joe was spending the day with a school friend, and Colin never noticed when he ate. It didn't make any difference if lunch was half an hour earlier or later.

The fifteenth of August seemed like half a lifetime ago. Maggie's arms still ached to hold her daughter, but somehow, in spite of the grief and the horror, she knew that her life was starting to come together again. Planning the memorial service was helping them say goodbye to Livvy in a positive way. They'd had two meetings with Ronald already, and a third was planned for just after the New Year, to finalise the arrangements. The service itself was to be on the first Friday afternoon in January. A children's service. Maggie wanted everyone who came to light a candle. Instead of a coffin they would have a table at the front, full of brightly burning coloured candles, to symbolise the light Olivia had brought into their lives. And she wanted flowers of all colours, everywhere. They would sing hymns and Ronald was going to read a story to the children, about how people live on in their loved ones' hearts forever. And she was making a list, the longest list in the world, of all the things Olivia had loved, from raspberry lollies to Slinky the cat, and she and Colin would read it out at the service. A description of a little girl's life and loves.

Having the service early in January was a good idea too. A New Year goodbye, a new beginning for them all.

But first there was Christmas to get through. After that, nothing would be so painful again. Life was moving on, and every day seemed a little more normal than the one before. She'd only phoned Howard three times last week, and sometimes now she even laughed aloud at something Joe said, or at a comedy on television. And she knew that one day next year they probably would start thinking about another baby.

She drove home quickly and started to fill the fridge. Colin was watching television, his eyes glued to yet another post-mortem of Wednesday's big game.

'Pizza okay for tea?' called Maggie, pushing Joe's – and Olivia's – favourite Hawaiian pizza into the fridge.

'Sure. Did you remember the batteries?'

'No, I didn't. Sorry. I'll get them on Monday. Col - '

She broke off, and Colin rose from his chair, staring.

Children's voices were coming from the garden next door, little girls playing in the late autumn sunshine, calling to each other and screaming with excitement. Just for a moment Maggie was convinced she had heard Olivia's voice out there too.

'Mags? What's wrong? Here, sit down.'

Colin gripped her shoulders and she blinked up at him.

'Oh Col. Livvy. I heard her voice just now, I swear I did.'

She looked at him helplessly, still holding the fridge door open, with the pizzas sitting there on the shelf.

'No, Maggie, no. She's gone, love, she's gone.'

The children outside were quiet now, and Maggie went to the window. It was Delia, Lucy and Maisie out there. Not Olivia.

Maggie pushed her hair back, heard her voice, dull and dreary again. 'I know. She's gone. I just felt as if I heard her calling. But you're right. I'm sorry.'

Chapter Eight

Something was wrong. She couldn't move, her head was buzzing, and she couldn't open her eyes. Someone was touching her hip.

People were speaking too; they sounded far away but something told her that these were the people touching her so intimately. The voices were all unfamiliar.

'BP's up again, 140 over 95.'

'Pulse is stable, John, she's back with us.'

'Good. Jennifer? Can you hear me? Open your eyes, Jennifer.'

She was trying so hard to do just that. She had to take control, get away from here.

'You had an accident, Jennifer, you're in hospital. Can you squeeze my hand?'

Yes. She could do that, but why should she? Who was this person? They were wrong, these voices – she hadn't had an accident, that had been – that had been Hailey, hadn't it? What had happened to Hailey?

The voices were discussing her again.

'She's given birth quite recently - have we found her notes yet?'

'Her family's here too. She's in the system but her last time at the hospital was with a twisted ankle four years ago.'

'Book her in for a scan, Viv. We'll need to fixate that

pelvis and I'm a bit worried about her spleen, too.'

Jennifer felt herself floating away. She was stuck in some kind of nightmare and she couldn't wake up. She'd been with Phillip and Hailey, and something had gone wrong... Hailey had vanished. Cold horror crashed down on Jennifer as realisation struck. They'd been at the beach and they had lost Hailey. Her angel was lost.

She opened her eyes but immediately closed them again, the light, why was it so light? With the light came pain, her hips, her stomach. She was lying on a hard, narrow bed and there were lights and machines and green-clad people all around her.

'That's better. Jennifer, my name's John, I'm your doctor. You have a broken pelvis. Shift that light, Viv, it's blinding her. Open your eyes, Jennifer.'

A blessed shadow fell over her face and Jennifer peered through her eyelashes. An older man wearing a blood-stained plastic apron was standing beside her.

'My baby.'

They didn't understand. She had to make them listen. Jennifer managed to raise her left arm and struck out at the doctor as hard as she could. He grasped her hand and held it down on the table, and she moaned. They needed to find Hailey.

'Keep as still as you can, Jennifer. We're sending you for a scan in a minute and then we'll have to fixate your pelvis. That means an operation but don't worry, we'll give you something for the pain.'

Jennifer struggled to get up, but it was as if she had lost all her strength. Her enormous effort was only producing a pitiful little movement and her head felt really strange.

Her voice came out in a whisper, 'I want my baby! Where's my little girl?'

'Calm down, Jennifer. As far as I know they're all fine. Viv, can you go and see what's happening with Jennifer's family, please?'

The relief was incredible. Obviously Hailey had been found, and Phillip must be alright too. Jennifer relaxed slightly then squeezed her eyes shut as a sharp pain stabbed through her lower belly.

'BP's down again, John, pulse is up.'

'Give her another five of morphine.'

Jennifer listened as a machine beeped away in the background. What had happened exactly? Hadn't Hailey been at school? Something had changed, what had changed? Hailey had been frightened, but Jennifer couldn't remember why. And there had been a funeral… She could remember the white casket, and the look on Phillip's face… But Hailey had been fast asleep at the farmhouse.

The voice called Viv was back.

'Jennifer? Your little girl's fine, they all are. We're just looking for someone to take care of them while you and your husband are here. His leg's broken and he'll need an op too.'

Hailey was fine? But hadn't it been Hailey's funeral? If only she could remember what had happened.

They'd been at the beach, no, they'd been at school, yes at school, and then Phillip had taken them to a restaurant. Had that all been today?

It took another monumental effort because her mind was going fuzzy round the edges, but she managed to speak quite clearly. 'Bring me my baby. Now.'

Nobody answered. Hadn't she spoken aloud? The beeping sound was closer now and Jennifer felt her bed shift, but the pain didn't come back and she was able to open her eyes again. The monitor was beside her on the trolley now and a man was pulling her towards the door. She tried to scream but no sound came.

The nurse bent over her, a dark blob against the light.

'Time for your scan, Jennifer. Don't worry about your family. They'll be fine.'

The ceiling was moving and Jennifer realised they were taking her away from the doctor called John. Another pain stabbed into her, a new one, on her left side this time and now she felt sick too. This pain stretched from her shoulder right through her middle and into her leg. But she had to see if Hailey was okay, and Phillip…

The beeping beside her head was faster now and the voices were further away. The trolley jerked and moved abruptly in the opposite direction.

'BP's way down! She's going to crash… Get her back in there, that's an internal bleed, her spleen - '

She was back under the lights again. Jennifer felt the fuzziness return.

'Lavage, Viv. And someone phone theatre.'

Jennifer felt herself retreat into her head. It was peaceful here and the pain was gone. Whatever they were doing it was helping the pain. Maybe they'd let her see Hailey afterwards. But Hailey was gone… in a little white casket… her baby had died… her baby…

What had she done?

For a moment sheer terror consumed her, and then a new kind of calmness swept over Jennifer and she found that she could no longer move. Everything was going to be alright, she felt that quite clearly. But it was cold now and the commotion of the hospital had disappeared. The world was getting smaller… It was so cold here. It was as if she was floating in white water, just floating, and then suddenly, everything was gone.

Chapter Nine

Katie deposited an armful of plastic bags on her sofa, and sank down beside them. An afternoon shopping for clothes was more tiring than a whole day's teaching, she thought ruefully. The shops in Newquay had been packed with early Christmas shoppers all fighting for bargains while Katie was searching for an outfit for tonight's celebration. Mark was coming home.

He was flying down late that afternoon, and she planned to meet him at the airport. They would come back here for dinner and it was all going to be perfect. Katie shook out her new clothes. Those black linen trousers were a terrific fit, and the cream silk top might have been made especially for her. She had wanted something special, and thankfully she had found it.

A smile pulled at her lips. She had missed Mark. Missed his company more than she thought she would, and she wanted to savour every minute of the evening ahead. She'd have a bath and a face pack, but first she needed a coffee.

The phone rang while she was waiting for the machine to produce an espresso, and she frowned. Hopefully this wasn't Mark to say his flight had been delayed.

But it was a woman's voice that greeted her.

'Oh Miss McLure, good. We've been trying to get hold of you. I'm Adele Morrison, senior social worker at Newquay

General Hospital. There's been an accident and I'm sorry to say a little girl from your school class was involved, Libby Marshall. She's not hurt but her parents are both badly injured and Libby's very shaken. Yours was the only name she could give us. Do you know if there are any relatives nearby we could contact? Or could you come down? Libby needs someone here for her.'

Katie's mind was reeling.

'Marshall? Do you mean Hailey Marshall? Small, thin, very short brown hair?'

'That's her. She told the paramedic her name was Libby.'

'No, it's Hailey, oh poor thing. I'll come straightaway. I don't think there are any relatives around here. And the babies?'

'They're fine too. Come straight to A&E, then.'

Katie ran for her jacket. If the Marshalls were badly injured it must have been a serious accident; Hailey would be terrified. The paramedic must have misheard the child's name, it was a wonder she had spoken at all under those circumstances.

Katie had never been to the hospital in Newquay, but it was easy enough to find, on the Polpayne side of town. Once there, however, finding a parking space proved more difficult. Saturday afternoon seemed to be a popular time to visit, and hot frustration filled Katie as she circled the complex for the third time. At last she spotted someone leaving behind the outpatients department, and backed in quickly.

The A&E department looked new, and it was very busy. Katie wouldn't have believed that there would be people drunk and belligerent on a Saturday afternoon in Newquay, but there were. She had to wait in a queue while three other people gave details to a single receptionist, and each one seemed to have a more complicated story than the last. There was no sign of either Hailey or the Marshalls, and Katie was almost dancing with impatience when she arrived at the head of the queue. The receptionist directed her to a room further up the corridor, and she ran along and pushed the door open.

Hailey was perched on the edge of a hard wooden chair, a very young nurse beside her holding her hand.

'Hailey, lovey!' Katie rushed over and took the little girl in her arms. 'Oh, you poor thing! What a fright you've had. Are you okay?'

Hailey's little body was trembling, and Katie held her close, relieved when the child snuggled up to her.

'What happened? And how are the Marshalls?' she murmured to the nurse.

'They were run over by a van. Mr Marshall's been taken up to orthopaedics. I'll just get someone to speak to you.'

The nurse left, and Katie took out a tissue and wiped Hailey's face.

'Hailey, love, can you just remind me about your grandparents? You have a Grandma, don't you? Or do you have any aunties and uncles who're nearer?'

Hailey looked at her with red-rimmed, bleary eyes. 'I don't know,' she whispered. 'Will Daddy be alright?'

Katie made her voice as reassuring as she could. 'I'm sure he will. Doctors are very clever nowadays, you know, but if Daddy's broken anything he might be in hospital for a day or two. Where are the babies?'

'They took them away to look after them.'

Hailey sniffed again, and Katie pulled out another tissue.

A small, middle-aged man in a stained scrub suit burst into the room almost at a run. Still holding Hailey in her arms, Katie stood up, conscious once more of the child's slightness.

'Miss McLure? I'm John Peters, A&E consultant. This young lady is going to need someone to look after her, and her brother and sister for a while. Mr Marshall's mobile was damaged in the accident and his wife wasn't carrying one so we've no information yet about friends or relatives. Do you know anyone we could contact?'

Katie shook her head. 'I don't know offhand, but I can look after Hailey for now. She has at least one grandparent, but I can't remember where. Maybe we could go and see if there's a phone number for them at her home, and collect some stuff for her? How are the Marshalls?'

'I can only tell you that neither will be going home immediately,' said Mr Peters, already on his way out. 'Someone from social services will come and arrange things with you. The babies can stay here until we see if you find relatives for them. If you've no joy, the social worker will find a foster home for them all.'

Twenty minutes later, Katie was leading Hailey out towards her car. It was raining now, and the wind was blowing wet leaves across the parked cars.

'Poor sweetie,' she said softly. 'We'll go back to your place first and look for phone numbers, okay?'

Hailey was silent for the entire journey back to Polpayne, though Katie kept up a stream of comforting remarks. An accident can turn people's lives upside-down in less than half a second, thought Katie. Now poor Hailey's life had been changed, yet again. Just as she was settling down, too.

'Well,' said Katie, when they were standing in the hallway. 'Here we are.'

The house was completely and eerily silent. There was no sound of traffic here, and no neighbours' voices or radios to be heard. Katie's heels echoed on the polished wooden floor of the hallway, and she looked round uneasily. It didn't feel right, being here.

Katie shook herself. They had better get on with the job in hand, then she could take Hailey back to her own flat to wait. She would have to phone Mark and tell him she couldn't collect him. She bent down and hugged the little girl.

'Right, Hailey, you can help with this. I expect Mummy and Daddy have all the important numbers saved in the phone, do they?'

Hailey only shrugged, so Katie lifted the handset of the landline and after a moment found the address book function. To her dismay the only numbers listed there were Phillip and

Jennifer Marshall's mobiles, the school, and a hairdresser's. The Marshalls must use their mobiles for normal phoning. Lots of people did that, of course, but it didn't make things any easier now. Was Mrs Marshall's mobile around? Katie tried the number, but it was switched off.

She smiled reassuringly at Hailey. 'Nothing useful here. Does Mummy have an address book, or a phone index, or anything like that?'

Hailey pointed to the hallway table. The drawer revealed an old-fashioned pop-up index, and Katie sat down on the stairs with it. Good, there were plenty of names and numbers in here. Surely one of them would be able to help.

'Bingo,' she said. 'Now, what's your Grandma's name, Hailey? Is it Marshall too?'

But Hailey didn't seem to know, and Katie wondered anew at the relationships within the Marshall family. She tried the 'M' section first, but no-one there was a Marshall, so she went back to the beginning and much to her relief soon found what she was looking for. Under 'F' was the word 'Mother', and a phone number whose code Katie recognised as the Torquay area. This must be Mrs Marshall's mother.

She smiled warmly at the little girl, who was standing twisting her scarf round one hand. 'Take your coat off, sweetie. It's hot in here. Look, I think this must be your Grandma's number. Your Grandma in Torquay? You know the one?'

But Hailey, extracting herself from her coat, shook her head.

'Well, we'll phone and see who answers,' said Katie, increasingly puzzled by the child's reactions. Was she suffering from shock? But they'd have noticed that at the hospital, surely.

She punched out the number, and listened as the call connected.

The voice answering the phone sounded brisk and efficient. 'Bea Felix.'

Katie hesitated, wishing she had taken a couple of seconds to plan what she was going to say to the woman.

'Hello, Mrs Felix, my name's Katie McLure. Are you Jennifer Marshall's mother?'

'Yes,' said the voice. 'Are you a friend of Jennifer's?'

'A - neighbour,' said Katie, wanting to keep things brief. 'I'm really sorry to tell you that Jennifer and Phillip were involved in a car accident today; they're in Newquay hospital. The social worker there has asked me to find someone to take care of the children in the meantime. Can you help at all with that?'

There was complete silence at the other end of the phone.

'Mrs Felix?' said Katie. 'I'm sorry I can't tell you exactly how Jennifer is, but the babies are fine and... '

'What babies?' said Mrs Felix, and Katie blinked.

'Daniel and Lara - your daughter's twins,' she said uncertainly.

'My daughter has *twins*? Dear heavens. I had no idea, Jennifer doesn't keep in touch... I'll come as soon as I can, of course. Where are they?'

'The twins are being looked after at the hospital, but I've got Hailey right here with me. I could... '

'You've got *who* with you? *Hailey?*'

'Yes,' said Katie, surprised. 'She's fine, completely unhurt, but... '

'Ms McLure,' said Mrs Felix, and Katie shivered suddenly at the horror-stricken tones in the other woman's voice. 'Something is very wrong there. My granddaughter Hailey drowned in Turkey over two years ago. Jennifer had a severe breakdown afterwards; that's when she broke off contact with the family. I don't know what child you have there with you, but Hailey Marshall is dead. Now if you give me some details and phone numbers I'll go and look after those babies. And you'd better do something about the other child.'

Katie felt as if she'd been dealt a physical blow. Her voice shaking, she reeled off the necessary information, then put the handset down with fingers that were cold and clammy. Jennifer Marshall's daughter Hailey was dead. So who was the Hailey Marshall she knew?

Hailey had gone through to the sitting room, where she was huddled in a corner of the sofa. Head whirling, Katie sat down beside her and took her hand, struggling to find the right words.

'Sweetheart, you told the ambulance man your name was Libby. What's your other name, Libby?'

Hailey began to cry. 'I'm going to die,' she whispered. 'She said if I told anyone at all, ever, she'd come and get me.'

'Who? Your mu - Jennifer Marshall?'

Hailey nodded, and Katie hugged her close, feeling the little girl's thin body tremble in her arms. Her stomach churning nervously, Katie leaned back until she could look into the child's face.

'Sweetheart, I can see how difficult this is for you. But I promise, I absolutely promise I won't let anyone hurt you. No-one at all. Mrs Marshall was very wrong to say that, because it's just not true. And now I know you aren't Hailey Marshall, it's very important you tell me your real name, because then I can help you. We can find out where you belong.'

Katie could hardly believe the calm words that were coming from her own mouth.

Hailey was shaking visibly now, her hands moving up towards her face.

'Before Hailey Marshall? She said never, ever tell. She hurt me.'

'I promise I'll keep you safe, darling.'

The child took a deep breath and looked up at Katie, and the anguish in her eyes made Katie want to weep.

Two tears rolled down Hailey's cheeks. 'My name was Olivia Granger.'

'Olivia? So you said 'Livvy' to the ambulance man this afternoon? Right, Livvy. Let's see if we can find out where you belong.'

A sudden bell jingled urgently and insistently in Katie's head, and for a second it was difficult to breathe.

Have you seen Olivia Granger?

She'd been driving past the bus stop... and seen a poster... a vibrant little girl whose name was... Olivia Granger. The child who disappeared... and they said she had drowned. Last summer.

Oh my God, thought Katie, as the full implication of Olivia's presence in the Marshall household hit her full force. The child hadn't drowned, she'd been taken, she must have been. Jennifer Marshall had lost her own child and she had taken this one, and Olivia's parents thought that their daughter was dead. Dear God, what should she do now? Phone the police? Livvy's parents?

It was difficult to keep her voice steady and reassuring, but she had to, for Hailey's - for Olivia's sake.

'Can you tell me your proper address, or your phone number, Livvy?'

But addresses and phone numbers were quite beyond Olivia. Katie sat on the sofa, rubbing the little girl's back, her mind racing. More than anything else now she wanted to talk to Mark, but he would still be high above the clouds, heading south. So she would deal with this alone.

'Okay, sweetheart. I think the best thing would be just to phone 999. The police'll come and they'll know where to find your mum and dad.'

The child stared at her, no expression at all on her face now.

This time Katie had to physically steady herself to dial the number. This was all beyond comprehension. Mrs Marshall was mad. And what about Phillip Marshall? He had seemed so much more normal than his wife. Why had he done this? What kind of person could do a thing like this to a little child?

It was a relief to give the emergency operator the details. Help was promised. Katie put the phone down and was sitting cuddling Olivia when the handset buzzed again. Trembling, she lifted it to her ear.

'My name's Howard Moir; I'm in charge of the investigation into Olivia Granger's disappearance. We're on our way now. Could you tell me what's been happening?'

Katie could hear her voice shaking. 'She's here. Olivia. She's been with a Marshall family in Polpayne, she… ' Still unsteady, Katie told the story again.

'Sit tight,' said Howard. 'We'll be right with you.'

Katie turned back to the child on the sofa. She was crying quietly, making no attempt to wipe her tears away.

'Oh Livvy sweetheart. Let's make you a nice hot drink. That was Mr Moir, he's the policeman who's been looking for you all this time, and he's on his way over. Come through to the kitchen, darling. Some hot chocolate or something'll do you good.'

Olivia allowed herself to be led through to the other room and watched as Katie prepared a mug of hot chocolate. Katie looked round the kitchen as she encouraged the child to drink. This room looked like any normal, family kitchen. Baby things here and there, a wooden bowl of fruit on the table. But what horrors had gone on inside this house? Katie's breath caught in her throat as she spoke.

'Livvy darling, did Mr and Mrs Marshall - did they hurt you at all?'

Olivia laid her head on the table, pushing the mug away.

'Sometimes she hit me,' she whispered. 'And she said she would hurt me if I told. But Da - he was nice. I liked him.'

Katie stroked the short brown hair. 'And did anyone do anything else that was - nasty?'

Olivia shook her head. 'She wouldn't buy me jeans,' she said, her lips trembling.

A faint sensation of relief made itself felt in Katie's middle, and she managed to smile at the little girl. It sounded as if Olivia had merely been a substitute for dead Hailey. And her job now was to help Olivia as well as she could until the child's mother could take over.

'Drink your chocolate, Livvy, and don't worry. Everything'll be alright soon.'

But she knew that her words would be of little comfort to Olivia. She must have heard so many empty words in this house.

Abruptly, the doorbell rang. Olivia leapt to her feet, sending the half-empty mug crashing to the floor.

'She's come to get me!'

'No, no, she's in hospital, remember? It'll be the police. Come on, come with me.'

Taking Olivia's hand firmly in her own, Katie went to the door. Two police cars were parked in the windy street, and three officers were waiting at the door, sheltering under umbrellas. The oldest, a tall man with a tired, lined face held out his police identification, looking hard at the child pressed against Katie's side. His face suddenly relaxed into a smile.

'Olivia,' he said. 'Your mum gave me a photo of you. Want to see it?'

Olivia looked up at him, then at the two female officers, and to Katie's horror she gave a loud scream and wrestled herself free before stumbling into the kitchen. Katie couldn't stop her own tears as she spoke.

'I'm sorry, she's very scared at the moment. She's very confused, you'll understand.'

Howard nodded, then handed his colleague a car key. 'Of course. Maybe having the three of us here is too much.' He turned to his fellow officer. 'See what information you can gather about the Marshalls, Amanda, and find out when you can speak to one of them.'

The woman turned back to the car, and Katie led Howard and his colleague through to the kitchen where Olivia was cowering in the corner. Silently, she lifted Olivia and sat at the table with the child on her lap.

'It's alright, baby. These are friendly policemen, you don't have to be frightened. Let's listen to Mr Moir, okay?'

Howard produced a photo and slid it across the table to

the little girl. Katie stared, realising that 'Hailey' had spoken about this.

'Your birthday cake with the marzipan waves. You told me about that, didn't you?'

Olivia nodded solemnly, staring at the photo.

'And you said you wanted a pink cake for your next birthday,' said Katie, remembering. 'But I thought you were Hailey. Oh God, Olivia, I'm so sorry - '

She covered her face with her free hand. Howard leaned forward.

'You didn't know. How could you have known? Livvy. Listen. Do you remember being at the beach with your mum and dad and Joe? That last day you were with them?'

Olivia nodded.

'You made a sandcastle with your mum and then you wanted to go to your dad and Joe at the rock pools, and Mum let you go. What happened then?'

Olivia stared at him silently.

'Was Jennifer Marshall there?'

A nod.

'On the beach? Up the path?'

Olivia started to cry. 'On the path. She said come and look because she had babies in the car, and she was so nice and pretty and I love babies so I went just for a minute. But she didn't.'

'And she drove away with you?'

Another nod. Katie choked back a sob.

Howard nodded too, then leaned back in his chair and smiled. It was as if a light had been switched on inside him.

'Good girl, Olivia. And now I think it's time we phoned your mum and dad, don't you?'

Chapter Ten

Joe, cross-legged on the floor watching cartoons, laughed loud and long, a happy child's laugh. Maggie smiled at the sound.

'Funny, is it?' she called through from the kitchen.

'Mm-hm.' Joe was still engrossed.

Maggie went to join him. She hadn't seen much of him today. She loved the time she spent with her son, and knew that sharing the laughter, the tears, the work and the play - that was what being a parent was all about. She sat watching as the cartoon cat chased the mouse round and round the garden. Suddenly a dog leapt out of nowhere and flattened the cat. Maggie and Joe both jumped, then laughed together.

Livvy would have laughed too, Maggie thought wistfully. Livvy had laughed a lot.

Colin came through from the hallway. 'Sounds like fun,' he said, flopping down on the sofa beside Maggie.

It was times like this that Maggie couldn't help but feel grateful for her family. In spite of everything, they were together.

The cartoon came to a close, and Colin stood up. 'I'll put the pizzas in the oven,' he said. 'Is there anything to go with them?'

The phone rang, and Joe went to answer it.

'Yes,' said Maggie. 'I bought some coleslaw and there's a

lettuce too, you could - '

'Mum? It's Inspector Moir.'

Maggie looked at Colin, watching his face turn white. They had spoken to Howard only yesterday. Maggie felt her legs go weak, and the knot, even now never far from her middle, twisted painfully. Colin put his arms round her as she reached for the phone.

This was it. The moment she had been waiting for, an end to all the uncertainty, the waiting, the hoping. Maggie swallowed hard. Goodbye, Livvy, oh God Livvy, I loved you so much.

'Howard?' It came out as a hoarse whisper.

'Maggie,' he said. 'We've got her, Maggie, she's alive, she's with me now. She's not hurt, Maggie, she's scared and bewildered but she's not hurt at all. Maggie? Do you understand? We've got you Olivia back.'

Chapter Eleven

Still dazed, Katie sat with Olivia on her knee, listening while Howard phoned the Grangers and then a colleague at police headquarters. Rain was coming down hard outside, the heavy clouds looming overhead and turning the afternoon dark. The policewoman had left, waving cheerfully to Olivia, and Howard was grinning too when he returned to the kitchen. Katie smiled back shakily, knowing that tears were a lot nearer the surface than smiles. Her heart was still pounding away, and she could only imagine what was going through Olivia's head right now.

'All sorted,' said Howard. 'Mum and Dad'll be here in an hour or so. A police helicopter's going to bring them to collect you, Livvy, and it'll take you all home again too, if you like. Or a police car. You and Mum and Dad can choose.'

Olivia's eyes were as round as saucers. She looked up at Katie. 'I've never been in a helicopter before,' she said confidingly.

Katie cuddled her close. 'Neither have I,' she said. 'See how important you are? Everyone wants you to be back home with your real mum and dad just as quick as possible.'

Olivia nodded thoughtfully, then heaved a great sigh. 'The daddy here was nice too,' she said.

'He helped you, didn't he?' said Katie. 'That was good. But he knew all the time that you weren't Hailey, so it was very wrong of him not to let you go home. And the mummy here was very bad to take you away in the first place. They were both wrong, but you didn't know that, did you?'

She couldn't bear thinking about how frightened Olivia must have been, especially in the days before Phillip Marshall arrived home. It didn't make her proud to think that a child in her class had been fighting such a terrible private battle all this time - and she hadn't realised.

Howard leaned towards Olivia.

'Livvy, why don't you have a look around and see if there's anything you want to take home with you? Some toys maybe?'

Olivia thought for a moment, then slid off Katie's knee and ran upstairs.

Katie covered her face with both hands. 'The more I think about it,' she said through parted fingers, 'the more I realise that she gave me so many hints, the whole time. In her family picture she drew her real family. And she got the shakes once when another girl called Olivia came in. And the lost teddy, and the cat… And that awful bruise, Howard, she was badly bruised, you know, twice at least. And those birthday photos… dear God, she's only four, isn't she?'

'Stop, stop,' said Howard. 'Look at it as being a hundred piece jigsaw. Olivia gave you maybe ten pieces, you couldn't possibly see the entire picture. And I can see she trusts you, otherwise I'd have called for police psychologists and doctors. We'd have bundled her into a chopper and flown her straight home if she hadn't had you. But this is much better. She can wait with someone she likes and trusts, and her folks will come and collect her. That way she'll have closure here and it'll be much less traumatic. Thanks to you.'

Katie reached for a tissue and blew her nose. 'Thanks,' she said. Maybe one day she would believe him.

They sat in the kitchen, Katie telling Howard all she could remember of the 'ten jigsaw pieces' that 'Hailey' had given her. It was all so obvious now.

Olivia came back downstairs, and Katie's stricken heart leapt.

The little girl was carrying everything she had made at school over the past months. Drawings, paintings, clay birthday cake - it was all there. And the Halloween mask, and the shell box…

'I can't get my gull down, I want him too,' she said. 'And my plant you gave me, it's up on the bathroom window ledge.'

Howard held out his hand. 'Come and show me. I'll help you,' he said. 'We'll just have time before Mum and Dad get here.'

'I'll make coffee when the Grangers arrive, shall I?' said Katie. 'They might be glad of it.'

Howard nodded and went off upstairs with Olivia. Katie examined the coffee machine then texted Mark, glad when the answering text came just seconds later. Mark would wait at home until she called. At least that was one less thing to worry about.

Howard and Olivia reappeared with the gull and the African Violet. There was a tension about the policeman's chin that hadn't been there before, and Katie raised her eyebrows.

'Livvy, I think I left my mobile by the washbasin,' he said steadily. 'Could you get it for me, please?'

The child ran off, and Howard turned towards Katie.

'There's blood on her pillow and on the bed sheet,' he said in a low voice. 'Ask her what happened, would you?'

Olivia returned with the mobile and Katie managed to ask the question, fighting to keep her voice steady.

'Livvy sweetheart, Mr Moir's a bit worried you might have been hurt - he saw some blood on your bed. What happened, darling?'

Olivia was silent for a moment, but her voice when she did speak was matter-of-fact.

'She hit me this morning and my nose bled.'

Katie examined the child's nose. Now she was looking for

it, it was slightly swollen, but nothing to indicate a serious injury.

'That was bad of her, Livvy,' Howard said. 'We'll get a nice doctor to have a proper look at you when you get home. Make sure you're not hurt at all.'

'I'm fine,' said Olivia. 'I want to put my stuff in a bag now.'

Katie rummaged around for plastic bags and helped Olivia pack everything up. She lifted the lid off the shell box to wrap it in kitchen paper and was startled to find a package of Diazepam inside.

'Livvy, what are these?'

'Those are the pills I had to take. But I don't take them now.'

Howard reached out and took the pills, his face tight. 'The doc'll see about this too.'

Eyes brimming with tears, Katie went back to her kitchen paper. Olivia probably hadn't had many of the pills recently, but that didn't mean they hadn't harmed her.

'Is that the lot now?' she asked, wrapping the last of the belongings.

Olivia stood still, then touched her shorn head, tears spilling from her eyes.

'I want my hair back,' she said.

Katie bent and kissed her. 'Oh sweetheart, it's such a pity but it'll grow again, don't worry. Listen! Can you hear that?'

A car had drawn up outside, and voices were shouting over the noise of the storm that had quickly gathered pace. Howard went to the door, and Olivia flung her arms round Katie's neck.

'Come on, darling,' said Katie, blinking furiously as two tears escaped and ran down her own cheeks. 'Let's go and meet your mum and dad.'

Chapter Twelve

The helicopter lurched sickeningly as it rose into the night sky. The heavy rain was no match for the sharp, quick blades. Maggie reached for Colin's hand and closed her eyes. She had always hated flying, and this throbbing machine seemed altogether too fragile to risk her life in. But she had to, because it was the quickest way to get to Livvy.

For the first time since Howard's phone call, Maggie found herself with time to think. Livvy was alive. She was coming home. They had told Joe and watched his eyes grow huge and his face white before a beaming smile burst out of him.

'Mummy! Livvy'll be home in time for Christmas!'

'She'll be home in time for bed,' Maggie told him, hardly realising it herself. She and Colin phoned their parents, then Maggie phoned Sue, who immediately offered to come and stay with Joe while Maggie and Colin were away. They would put Olivia's bedroom back in order, she promised.

After that there was only just time to pack a bag with Livvy's favourite blackcurrant drink, a packet of biscuits, and Old Bear, of course, cold to touch now after his long sojourn in the attic. A police car arrived to take them to the helicopter, and the driver had more news than Howard had given them.

'She's been staying in Polpayne, in a family, as their daughter. Then this afternoon the couple had some kind of accident, and the hospital contacted someone to look after the little girl. She got on to a relative, who said the child in the family had died a couple of years ago, and so it all came out.'

Maggie struggled to take in the words. Livvy was alive.

'And is she okay? You're sure she hasn't been hurt?'

'We're pretty sure,' said the policeman kindly. 'Bound to have been a bit muddling for her, though.'

And how, thought Maggie. But they could cope with muddles, if that was all that was wrong. She could hear her own heavy breathing and consciously made herself relax. The one thing she had never allowed herself to dream of was happening. She was on her way to fetch Olivia. To bring her home. They had arrived at the helipad beside the hospital at Plymouth, and she was ushered into this horrible, tiny helicopter. Everything was so loud, she could hardly hear herself think. But nothing mattered at all now except the fact that she was going to get her little girl.

'It's windy, but don't worry, we'll make it alright,' shouted the pilot, slamming the door shut behind him.

Maggie felt as if her stomach was on one of those ghastly rides at an adventure park, being twisted and turned and shaken upside down, and she found time to be glad that she hadn't eaten that evening yet. It *was* windy, but she concentrated all her energy into waiting, just waiting to be with her daughter.

Another police car arrived for them when they landed, and Amanda Donnelly, beaming from ear to ear, drove them through dark, wet streets, past a little harbour, then up a hill where they stopped in front of a large white house.

Maggie started to shake. She couldn't help herself. Colin supported her up the path, gusts of wind blowing her hair all over the place, and then the door opened and Howard was there, smiling broadly, and Maggie realised she had never seen him smile like that before. Behind him was a woman, younger than she was and smaller, and there in her arms was Olivia.

'Livvy!'

Maggie almost fell forward. Olivia was clutching the woman. The child was pale, her hair was so short and she was all eyes, but dressed in a beautiful blue and white dress, and she was looking at them. Not smiling, not speaking - just looking.

'Careful, Maggie. She's fine, but give her a minute,' said Howard, gripping her elbow.

'Let's go into the living room,' said the woman, turning towards a door. 'Then you can sit with your mum and dad on the sofa, Livvy, and let them see you're okay.'

It was all Maggie could do not to wrench Olivia away from this other woman. But Olivia obviously needed time, and thank God, now they *had* time.

'Livvy. Oh Livvy darling, here we are at last, they brought us as soon as you were found. Are you alright, sweetheart?' Maggie said, trying desperately to sound calm.

The woman sat Olivia down on the sofa and Maggie perched gingerly beside her. She almost didn't dare touch her child, but all at once Olivia turned and climbed up into her lap and began to cry. Maggie felt Colin's arms go round her too, and here she was at last, holding her Livvy safe. There was nothing else to do except be thankful.

'I'll make coffee,' said the woman. 'You need some time alone.'

Howard left them too, and Maggie sat there in Colin's arms and holding Olivia, comforting her sobbing child. She had got her world back.

'It's going to be okay, Livvy,' she said. 'You're coming home.'

Gradually, the sobs subsided until Olivia was silent, cuddled right up against Maggie.

'Alright?' said Maggie, forcing her own tears back. She kissed Olivia. 'You must have been so frightened, darling, but we've got you safe now.'

Olivia looked from her to Colin and gave a little smile.

Maggie blinked furiously.

'Who's the lady?' said Colin, and Olivia sat up straighter.

'And what about the people who kept you here?' said Maggie, pulling out a tissue and wiping her eyes.

'That's Miss McLure, she's my teacher,' said Olivia, and Maggie was simply thrilled to hear her daughter's voice. Olivia sounded *comfortable*. She might have been frightened and distressed, but she was able to be comfortable now. Another band slackened round Maggie's insides.

'A school teacher?' Colin gave an almost laugh. 'They sent you to school?'

Miss McLure came in with a coffee tray, and Maggie looked at her. This woman had discovered that Livvy was in the wrong place. She would never be able to thank her enough.

'Miss McLure, I don't know what to say. Thank you so much for helping Livvy.' She turned to Howard who had followed Katie back in the room. 'Can you please tell me what's been going on here?'

She wanted to know everything, every detail of her child's life over the past months. The very first part of the story almost defied belief, though.

'This woman took Livvy right up to the top of the cliff path and Colin and I *didn't notice?*'

'Maggie,' said Howard. 'One thing I've learned from police work over the years is that unbelievable things happen right under people's noses every day of the week, without anyone being any the wiser. And you know that most of the path isn't visible from the beach. My guess would be that Jennifer Marshall saw Olivia somewhere, in a shop or wherever, was struck by the resemblance to her own child, and followed you home. She may have been watching you for days, waiting for an opportunity to take Olivia.'

Maggie shuddered. Watching them for days.

'We haven't been able to question the Marshalls yet,' Howard said. 'But we're fairly sure Livvy was kept drugged at a different place. We don't know yet where that was. But then they moved here to Polpayne shortly afterwards, and Livvy became Hailey Marshall and started school. And Katie has more or less saved her sanity, I'm sure.'

'Mrs Marshall was alone here with Olivia at first,' said Katie McLure. 'She always struck me as being a very emotionless kind of person. Then when Mr Marshall came back from staying in America he looked after Hai - I mean Olivia more, and that was better for her. He was warmer, much more normal. It's unbelievable he went along with it all. I just wish I'd twigged to what was going on a whole lot sooner than I did.'

Olivia jerked upright on Maggie's knee. 'Am I going to school on Monday?'

'Sweetheart, I'm afraid we live much too far away for you to go to school here,' Maggie said. 'But don't worry. If you want to you can go to pre-school in Carlton Bridge after Christmas.'

She saw Olivia's face fall.

'Tell you what - we'll drive over one day next week and visit Miss McLure and your class, and you can say goodbye to the children. How's that?'

Olivia still looked doubtful, and Maggie felt hot tears pricking in her eyes.

'Great idea, we'll have a party,' said Katie McLure, crouching beside the sofa. 'We'll have a "Goodbye Hailey Hello Olivia" party.'

'With a cake,' said Maggie, warming to the idea. 'A birthday cake - you missed your birthday.'

'With pink and white candles!' cried Olivia, her whole face lighting up, and Maggie felt tears run down her face as she clutched her daughter to her heart.

Chapter Thirteen

He had no idea how long he had been unconscious. When he came round, Phillip was lying in a hospital bed and all he was aware of at first was a dull pain in his leg and a tightness round his chest. The van. There had been an accident. Where was Jennifer, and what had happened to Hailey? The events of the day crashed into his head and he moaned, then stopped because it hurt.

Carefully, Phillip moved his head and saw that he was in a room all by himself. He had a drip going into his left arm and there was a bank of monitors beside the bed but they didn't appear to be switched on.

The bed sheets were draped on a cage over his legs. His left foot was encased in something, and his head felt tight too. He raised a hand to touch it, and a nurse hurried in.

'Good, you're awake. Do you remember what happened?'

His throat hurt when he spoke. 'It was a van. We were hit by a van in the car park.'

'That's right. We gave you a short anaesthetic to get you sorted. You've got seven stitches in your head so don't touch it, and your leg's broken, it might need an op but it won't be today. You've got a couple of broken ribs too so lie still. Nothing dangerous, though, don't worry. This is the orthopaedic ward. You're in the side room at the moment but I expect they'll move you through to the main ward soon.'

'My wife and my - the children?'

'I'll go and find out for you.'

She patted his shoulder and left, and Phillip stared after her. She couldn't know about Hailey, or she wouldn't have been so kind. What a mess he was in. Would he be prosecuted? Charged? Of course he would. And Jennifer, what would happen to her? And Hailey?

The nurse would find out about that and there would be no more kindness or patted shoulders, because he had done an appalling thing. They would all despise him and they'd be right. He wouldn't blame them. What was he going to do? There was no-one he could turn to for help. Christ, he had assisted his mad wife to abduct and hold a child, who would help him? If only he could turn the clock back.

The nurse returned with an older woman a few minutes later. Both their faces were grave, and Phillip braced himself for contempt.

But the news wasn't what he was expecting.

'Mr Marshall, I'm Sarah Campbell, consultant orthopaedic surgeon. I've been overseeing your treatment since your arrival.'

As she spoke she was checking his pulse. The nurse stood silently to one side while the doctor sat down on the edge of the bed and looked at him. Phillip nodded, his mouth dry.

'I'm afraid I have some very bad news for you. Mr Marshall, your wife was brought in with some very severe injuries, and I'm afraid we were unable to save her. Jennifer died a little while ago in the A&E department, but I can assure you she didn't suffer. I'm very sorry.'

He stared, then nodded, aware that panic was making his heartrate increase. Jennifer was dead. He was alone now. No Gran, no wife, no child. Tears burned hotly in his eyes and spilled down his cheeks. The nurse wiped them away before giving him a tissue in his hand.

Sarah Campbell stood up. The kind expression was still there.

300

'We'll leave you alone for a while now. There's a police officer coming to see you about the girl who was with you, but that can wait a little.'

She squeezed his hand and left, the nurse following on.

Left alone, Phillip lay struggling to breathe calmly. Sobbing hurt his ribs. An image of his wife before Hailey had died, before the Black Patch, swam in front of his eyes. He had failed her. Her death was his fault too. If he'd got help as soon as he'd returned she would still be alive today. Hailey who was Livvy would have gone home and maybe he'd have been able to see her sometime.

It was about fifteen minutes later when they came back, and he knew by their faces what had happened. Now they knew; someone had told them all about the child who wasn't his daughter. The nurse didn't meet his eyes as she checked his foot from the bottom of the bed, and the doctor spoke briskly and coldly.

'The police officer's here and I think you can manage to speak to her for a few minutes. Ring if you feel it's too much for you.'

The nurse handed him the usual kind of hospital bell, and both she and the doctor left the room. There was a murmur outside the door before the police officer came in.

'I did it,' he blurted out, as soon as the woman entered the room. 'Jennifer was mad with grief when Hailey died, God help me I should never have left her alone so long but I didn't know. When I came home she'd taken the kid and I didn't even find out who she was. I hid her too, because if I hadn't we could have lost the twins, and then of course because I loved her, oh God I'm sorry, I'm sorry.'

Sobs jerked his chest and pain seared through his torso but he was glad because it was all he deserved. The policewoman stood motionless for a moment before speaking.

'Phillip Marshall, I'm arresting you on suspicion of child abduction. You do not have to say anything, but it may harm your defense, if you do not mention when questioned, something which you will later rely on in court. Anything you do say may be… '

The remainder of her words passed over him. When she had finished she stood silently for a moment.

'Is Hailey, I mean Livvy, is she alright?' Philip forced himself to ask.

She stared, and he saw that she was furious. 'What do you think? Do you have any idea what her family's been through? You've got a lot of explaining to do but as you're not going anywhere soon that can wait. I'm sorry about your wife.'

'Can I see her?'

'Your wife?'

'No, Hai - Livvy.'

'Mr Marshall, I should think that you are the last person on this earth that Olivia either wants or needs to see right now. I'll be back tomorrow.'

She left the room, and he shouted after her.

'Tell her I'm sorry! Please! Tell her I'm so sorry.'

The effort made him cough and the pain that reverberated through his ribcage made him dizzy. The nurse came back in and silently adjusted the drip in his arm. Phillip closed his eyes again. Everything was out in the open now. The whole story would be in the papers soon and he would be damned to hell and back in most of them. But he didn't care. There was nothing more he could do now.

Chapter Fourteen

Howard Moir's telephone buzzed, and he went through to the kitchen to answer it. Katie sat watching Olivia, cuddled on her mother's knee, and a huge lump came into her throat. I'll miss her, she thought. Hailey had needed her, but Olivia didn't. Olivia had a loving, caring family. How lucky they were.

Maggie Granger fished in her bag.

'Look, Livvy, here's Old Bear. And I think we'd better get going soon. I hope it's not so windy now.'

'You can tell us all about your helicopter ride when you come to visit,' Katie said to Olivia, who was holding her bear and looking round, her eyes huge and solemn again.

'Yes, give me your phone number, and I'll be in touch,' said Maggie. 'And please, I think I might want to have a long talk soon, about Livvy's life here, and you probably know more than anyone.'

Katie nodded. 'Of course. We can talk all you want.'

She wrote her mobile number on a post-it note from the kitchen and Maggie pushed it into her bag. Watching Olivia put her coat on, Katie realised how badly she wanted to stay in touch. She wanted to hear how Olivia settled in back at home, to know that the story really did have a happy ending.

'Can I say goodbye to the babies too?' said Olivia, looking from her mother to her father to Katie.

'What babies?' asked Colin.

'Jennifer Marshall had twins towards the end of October,' said Katie, watching as bitter resentment clouded Maggie face. 'They're at the hospital waiting for their grandmother to come for them.'

'She was expecting *twins* and she still took Livvy away,' said Maggie, and the anguish in her voice told Katie a little of what the other woman had gone through.

'She's obviously a very disturbed woman,' said Howard, appearing in the doorway.

'Has your colleague been able to talk to her yet?' Katie asked, but Howard shook his head.

'She was allowed to see Phillip Marshall, very briefly. He admitted concealing Olivia here. He said to tell you he's sorry. I gather he was trying to keep his family together.'

'Keep his family… I don't think I want to hear this,' said Maggie, and Katie put her hand on the other woman's shoulder.

'*Can* I say goodbye to the babies?' asked Olivia again, and Katie, seeing the pain in both Maggie and Colin's faces, bent down to the little girl.

'Sweetheart, it's too late tonight. Lara and Daniel will be fine, don't worry. Their Grandma will be here soon and I expect she'll take them back home with her for a while.'

She stood up again, and smiled when Maggie mouthed 'thanks'.

It was difficult to take in, but five minutes later, Olivia was gone. Katie stood on the pavement with Howard, waving as the car with the Granger family set off down the road. It won't be the same without her, thought Katie. Polpayne Castle Primary without Hailey. But how wonderful for Olivia. She would have to think very carefully about breaking the news to the other children. This was all going to be in the papers, maybe even tomorrow, and heaven knows what would be printed. It would be best to have the parents there too on Monday morning, and get psychological support for the first day or two as well. She would phone Jeanette McCallum when she got home, and start the organisation of what would undoubtedly be a very intensive time for the class.

She turned to Howard. 'What'll happen now?'

He grimaced. 'I'm not quite sure. Phillip Marshall will be charged, of course, but Jennifer was the real offender here and I'm afraid she's dead. I didn't want to say anything in front of Olivia; there'll be time enough for her to deal with that when she's back home. Phillip will recover eventually.'

He stared down the road where the car had disappeared. 'Will Livvy be okay, do you think? Will she be strong enough to get over this?'

The lump was back in Katie's throat. 'In one way I think she will. In a few years' time she might not even remember very much about it, but it'll have changed her, it must have. They'll all have to rebuild their lives.'

Howard nodded, pulling out his car key, and Katie turned towards her own vehicle.

'Thanks for everything, Howard. You'll come to our party at school, won't you?'

Howard looked round and grinned at her, and again she saw the deep satisfaction in his eyes. 'Try and stop me,' he said.

Chapter Fifteen
Two Years Later

Phillip leaned back in his seat as the train sped through the countryside. He'd been released the previous Friday and it was so good to be a free man again. His time in prison hadn't been easy; he hadn't been popular with the other inmates, some of whom had even nicknamed him 'the paedo'. He wasn't, of course, and he knew that they'd been perfectly aware of that fact or a lot more than mere name-calling and being ostracised would have happened to him.

It was horrible, knowing that the harrowing events that occurred after his return from LA had all been down to him. Even today the guilt was crushing. His actions had caused so much suffering, firstly to Hailey and her real family, and secondly to his own children, who had now lived the first two years of their lives with their grandmother rather than their father. And thirdly of course to Jennifer. She might be alive today if he'd got help for her straightaway.

Well, two years in prison had paid his debt to society, and now he could make a fresh start. He owed it to the twins. He would never forget the apprehensive expressions on their little faces when he walked into Bea's home last week. He was a stranger to them. Lara had made friends quickly, but it had taken all weekend before Phillip and his son had been 'Daddy' and 'Danny'. It sounded impossible, but now he had to put the past behind him and build up a good life for the three of them.

But before he could even begin to do that, he knew he had to see for himself that Hailey was alright. He couldn't move on with his life without knowing, seeing, just once, that she had survived the trauma and was happy again.

'Bad, bad idea, Phillip,' Bea, his mother-in-law had said, and she was right. Phillip knew there was no way he could just approach the Grangers and ask after their child.

The train pulled into Plymouth station and Phillip strode down the platform. Now to find the bus to Carlton Bridge. He didn't plan to go to the Granger home, he would just wait outside the primary school and watch for Hailey when she came out. He wouldn't speak to her, he would make sure she didn't even notice him - but if he saw with his own eyes that she was okay, it would be enough. The downside was, of course, that he couldn't be a hundred per cent sure that Hailey would be at school today; she might be off sick or at the dentist. But he would have to take a chance on that.

The bus deposited him round the corner from Carlton Bridge Primary, and he walked along to the newsagent's opposite the gates. This was perfect, he could stand here and pretend to be looking at the small ads in the window. Ten minutes should do it, and then he could go back to Bea and the twins with a lighter heart.

After a few moments, a bell rang shrilly in the school, and soon the first children appeared, running across the playground to a little crowd of adults waiting at the gates. Eagerly, Phillip scanned the girls' faces. He would know Hailey at once, he was sure. She'd have longer hair now, of course, and she was two years older, but she would still be the little girl he'd taken care of back then.

The stream of children grew larger, and Phillip watched anxiously. A lot of these little girls had brown hair, and were about the right size too. But none of them were Hailey. He stood watching one girl as an older boy led her along the road.

That could be her, he knew she had a brother - but wouldn't he recognise her straightaway? *Was* it her? He couldn't be sure. Or was she one of these slightly bigger girls over there? How big *would* she be, exactly?

The children were chattering excitedly, some to each other and others to their waiting mothers. Phillip shrank further into the doorway. He mustn't be seen here, and although he didn't see Maggie Granger, that didn't mean she wasn't here. The expression on her face when she'd looked at him on the last day of the trial would haunt him forever.

There weren't many children left now. A boy ran towards a woman waiting beside a car just along the street from Phillip.

'Jess! Why are you here? Where's Mum?'

'She had to take Slinky to the vet's. He got a thorn stuck in his mouth,' replied the woman, opening the passenger seat door for him. 'So you three are staying with me in the meantime. Where's your sister? Oh there she is, come on scally-wag! Your mum said you can give Tommy his bottle while she's at the vet's!'

A dark-haired child careered along the pavement and flung her schoolbag into the back beside a baby in a car seat.

'Why's Mum at the vet's? Hey, Tommy, that is *my* Old Bear! Stop dribbling on him! Jess, can I - '

She slammed the door shut and the car drove off. Phillip stared. The size was about right, and the hair was right too. And her face, it was delicate, like Hailey's. But there had been nothing at all in that child's body language or her manner that reminded him in the slightest of his quiet, shy, polite little Hailey.

'Phillip? Are you okay? Bea said you were coming here, you haven't done anything stupid, have you? Come on, get in the car.'

It was Thea. She'd been a tower of strength to Bea these past two years, supporting her when Jennifer died, and at the trial, then helping with the twins. She'd even visited him in prison.

He could hear the tears in his voice. 'She wasn't there, Thea. I didn't see her.'

She looked at him soberly. 'Phillip, the child you were looking for doesn't exist. She's only in your head now.'

He leaned back as she turned the car and took the road towards Torquay. Thea was right, he knew. His own Hailey was safe in his heart, and he would keep the second Hailey there too. He met Thea's eye and she grinned cheerfully.

Phillip took a deep, shaky breath. This was his second chance, and it was up to him to take it.

It was time to go back to his own children now, to Lara and Danny. It was time to start again.

If you enjoyed *The Cold Cold Sea*, here's an extract from
Linda Huber's debut novel,
The Paradise Trees.

Chapter One
Friday, 7th July

He had found exactly the right spot in the woods. A little clearing, green and dim, encircled by tall trees. A magical, mystery place. He would bring his lovely Helen here, and no-one would ever find them. No-one would hear her when she screamed and begged for mercy, and no-one would come running to rescue her, like they'd tried to with the first Helen. This time it was going to be perfect. A sacrament - something holy. He was looking forward to it so much.

He'd first noticed her in the village shop last weekend. She was buying bread and fruit, and he'd even helped her when she dropped an orange and it rolled down the aisle towards him. He'd picked it up and handed it back to her, and just for a second their eyes had met. In that brief moment he'd known. He had found another Helen. She had Helen's brown eyes, Helen's long dark hair; even the shape of her body was Helen. Slim, but with delicious curves in all the right places.

Of course he hadn't said anything then, just 'you're welcome' when she smiled a quick 'thank you'. Her eyes were dark and troubled, and a sudden rush of sweat prickled all over his body. He went and hung around behind the shelf with the soap powder until she'd paid and left, and then he asked old Mrs Mullen at the check-out who she was. Mrs Mullen was the biggest gossip in Lower Banford, and usually

311

he was very careful not to start her off. He didn't want to be seen chit-chatting about the village people in their local shop. Now, however, he listened gratefully as she prattled on.

'That's Alicia Bryson, Bob Logan's daughter. She's up for the day to see poor Bob after that last little stroke he had, his fifth one I hear and he's not doing so well. Margaret Cairns – his sister, you know, she looks after Bob but it's getting too much for her, she's nearly seventy herself after all – was saying yesterday that Alicia and her little girl were coming for the summer too. I suppose… '

He hadn't listened any more. Alicia Bryson? No, she was Helen… his Helen. And she'd be in Lower Banford all summer, that was all that mattered. He would find her and make her his own darling love. And there was a child, too, another Helen? Little Helen? How perfect.

And now it was Friday and the sun was setting behind his beautiful woods. Most schools had broken up today, so his Helens might be packing now, getting ready for their journey even as he was thinking about them. Mrs Mullen would know when they were due; he would go and find out first thing tomorrow. And then, whenever it was, he'd be waiting for them. Big Helen and little Helen, and very soon they'd be on their way to join his first Helen, in Paradise.

He would do it all in a beautiful ceremony at the holy place in the woods, and surely then he'd be able to lay the ghost of his own special darling to rest. Helen, haunting him from Paradise.

She wouldn't be alone for much longer.

Chapter Two
Sunday, 9th July
Alicia

Alicia Bryson eased her elderly VW back into fifth gear after what seemed like the hundredth lot of road works, and glanced across at her daughter. Eight-year-old Jenny was dozing in the passenger seat, dark hair already escaping from her precious pigtails – Pippi Longstocking was the latest craze – and a selection of soft toys on her lap. Poor kid. This wasn't the best start to the holidays for her, a long, boring drive up the motorway when she could have been out celebrating the start of the summer holidays with all of her friends in Bedford.

Alicia grimaced. This was so not what she wanted to be doing today. Just exactly how was she supposed to give her daughter a fun-filled summer holiday in a tiny Yorkshire village where they knew no-one except her father and Margaret and there wasn't as much as a swing park?

And now they were stuck behind a smelly white van, hell, even on Sunday everyone and his dog was travelling up the M1. Tight-lipped, Alicia pulled out to overtake. Lower Banford here we come.

You're going back to the bad place.

The thought came into her head as clearly as if her childhood self had spoken aloud, and Alicia winced. Other kids had had loving homes. She'd had 'the bad place', the house where her father still lived, and it was even coming back as a ghost in her head now.

It just hadn't seemed fair. How she'd longed for parents like her friends had: friendly, strict only when they had to be, and caring. Instead she'd had family prayers for hours every evening, listening to her father's rants about God and the good life and lectures about the devil and all his works. The devil's works included things like women wearing trousers, novels, all music except hymns and psalms… As a child Alicia had been afraid of her father, and when childhood gave way to puberty the accompanying hormones and tantrums had turned life into a nightmare. The climax came when she was fourteen and her punishment for sneaking off to the cinema with a boy was the loss of her hair, hacked off by her father in a sickening fit of self-righteousness.

Remembering her teenage angst brought tears to Alicia's eyes, and she blinked repeatedly. The fast lane of the M1 wasn't a good place to start bawling about something that had happened half a lifetime ago. How lonely she had been back then. Mum had been no help at all; she had prided herself on being obedient and submissive right up to her death. Alicia had been left to fight her own battles.

'Bo-ring. Are we nearly there?' said Jenny, sitting up and pouting out of the window.

'We are, and you're being very good,' said Alicia, patting Jenny's jeans-clad leg. It wasn't all doom and gloom, Jen was here too. Time to put stars into her daughter's eyes.

'You know what? Aunt Margaret's got a dog now. We kept it a secret to surprise you. His name's Conker and he's huge, he's a Newfoundlander. Chocolate-brown colour. You'll love him.'

Jenny stared, her face lit up like Christmas and Easter rolled into one, stuffed animals clutched to her chest. 'Did you hear *that*?' she whispered. 'A new friend. Conker.' Eyes shining, she gazed back out of the window, and Alicia smiled to herself. Oh, how very much she loved Jen. Her dreamer.

'Why did we never go to Grandpa's for the holidays before?' said Jenny, turning back so quickly Alicia jumped. 'Tam goes to her Grandma's all the time.'

'Just a sec,' said Alicia, thankful that a speeding motorcyclist halfway up her exhaust was giving her a couple of minutes' thinking time. What could she say to that? That 'Grandpa' had been a terrible father and she had run away to Margaret the day after her sixteenth birthday and could count on the fingers of one hand the number of times she'd been back in Lower Banford since?

Hardly. She didn't want to shatter Jen's illusions about her one remaining grandparent who was going to die soon anyway. And how awful did that sound?

'Well, Grandpa hasn't been well for a few years now,' she said. 'And before that you were just a baby.'

And the whole purpose of this 'holiday' was to find another solution for her father, she thought grimly. A care home was going to be the best option, and as his next of kin – as uncomfortable as that felt – Alicia knew that she was the person to organise it.

A road sign loomed above them and Alicia flipped on the indicator. At last, here was their exit. She swung off the motorway, her shoulders up to her ears with tension.

Here was Merton, first place on the road back home and nearest big town. The fateful cinema was still here. Alicia glared at it as they passed, then grinned. It had got her a free haircut, hadn't it? Better just practise the irony, she'd need it again before the summer was over, she could see that coming a mile off.

After Merton came the Banfords, a trio of villages along the River Ban. Her old secondary school was in Upper Banford, with memories of French homework done on the bus, and agonising over boys and spots. And always being the outsider, the only one who didn't have eyeliner or jangly bangles or whatever the latest fashion was. Then came tiny Middle

315

Banford whose one claim to fame was the ambiguously-named Ban Theatre Festival; four weekends each June when the South Yorkshire Drama Club performed whatever it was they'd spent the past several months rehearsing. This year it had been *A Midsummer Night's Dream*, and the press reviews for once had been favourable.

Two miles on was Lower Banford, nestling between the river and the wooded hillside, quiet and peaceful. *The bad place.*

'Lower Banford!' said Jenny, sitting up straight as they passed the road sign. 'Mummy, we've arrived!'

'We have indeed,' said Alicia. Her voice came out a hoarse whisper, and she cleared her throat a little too hard, aware that Jenny was still looking at her.

The village street was deserted. Apparently shops still closed on Sundays here. It was a yesterday kind of place, old houses with old people living in them. Her father's house was right at the back of the village, the garden bordering on the woods that crept round the hillside. A pretty place that held dark memories.

Alicia turned up the narrow lane, inching past the row of cars parked along one side, and then through the gateway to pull up under the Scotch pine in front of the house. Two storeys of crumbling red brick covered in green ivy, a weed-and-gravel driveway leading round to the long back garden. Home sweet home. Or something.

This is the bad place. You've come back to the bad place.

The young voice was tinged with fear now, a haunting little whisper in her head. Where were these thoughts coming from? Panic fluttering in her throat, Alicia stared up at her father's bedroom window. Was the voice her childhood self? A sudden wave of nausea made her gut spasm and her legs shake. Bile rose right into her mouth and she swallowed, desperately trying not to retch. This was the bad place and for the first time since the night of her sixteenth birthday she was actually going to sleep under this roof. For six long weeks there would be no escaping this house and the parent she had run from.

The nausea passed as suddenly as it had come. Knuckles still white on the steering wheel, Alicia took a deep breath, cold sweat on her forehead. She needed to get a grip. All that was left of her father was a frail, old man, and she was an adult now. She could do this. Jenny was staring at her, puzzlement all over her small face.

'Mummy?'

To Alicia's relief, Margaret opening the front door created the necessary diversion, for as soon as Jenny saw Conker prancing about the hallway she was off, soft toys forgotten for once.

Resignedly, Alicia turned and lifted her handbag from the back seat, knowing that all she wanted to do was grab her daughter and drive away and pretend that everything was all right. But grown-ups didn't do things like that. They faced reality.

She fixed a brave smile on her face and opened the car door.

The Stranger

His vigil started just after lunchtime. He had been quite unable to stop himself. The thought of Helen coming to Lower Banford, driving along the village street and then up Woodside Lane… He had to be there to see it. An early-morning visit to the shop yesterday and a casual remark about summer visitors had set Mrs Mullen off, he'd listened to a long monologue about tourists before she provided him with the only detail he was interested in: Alicia Bryson and her daughter were expected on Sunday afternoon.

At twelve on the dot he stationed his car near the bottom of Woodside Lane, and settled down to wait for Helen. He had an excuse ready, in case anyone saw him and tapped on the window. One of the houses further up the lane was empty, and he was going up to have a quick look round, wasn't he? After all, his own place was nothing special. Looking at property was a perfectly natural thing to be doing.

Nobody noticed him so he didn't need his excuse. There was nothing he could do except sit and wait, but the thought of Helen driving towards him, getting closer by the minute, nearer and nearer… How wonderfully exciting that was, an amazing feeling, almost orgasmic. It made his entire body tremble and the sweat, never far off, soaked through his shirt yet again. He was waiting for Helen… He didn't want it to end.

And then suddenly, they were here. Fortunately the lane was narrow, so you had to slow right down when you turned in from the main road. Helen's car crawled past him and there she was, and oh, she was just as perfect as he remembered, with such a beautiful worried expression on her face. If only he could hold her and kiss that frown away.

An instant later he saw the little girl and knew straightaway that here was another true love, an even greater love, if such a thing was possible. Little Helen, gazing out of the passenger seat window, and oh! – she'd seen him, she had looked straight at him – what had she thought? Did she realise that here was the man who was going to send her to Paradise? No, of course not.

But send her he would. And soon. What a wonderful time he would have, planning his ceremony, making sure that the road to Paradise was smooth.

His Helens had arrived.

Come and visit us at
www.legendpress.co.uk

Follow us
@legend_press

John E. Roueche   Lynn Sullivan Taber   Suanne D. Roueche

The Company We Keep

Collaboration

in the

Community

College

Published by the Community College Press, a division of the American Association of Community Colleges
One Dupont Circle, N.W.
Suite 410
Washington, D.C. 20036
(202) 728-0200

Coordinator of Publications: Ron Stanley
Manuscript Editor: Vicki Whitaker
Design: The Magazine Group, Inc.
Printing: Jarboe Printing

ISBN 0-87117-282-8

This book is dedicated to our friend and colleague
RUSSELL G. MAWBY
Chairman and Chief Executive Officer
W. K. Kellogg Foundation
Battle Creek, Michigan

whose extraordinary leadership and vision of community renewal and rediscovery have inspired American community colleges to become true community partners in improving the quality of life for all citizens.

Contents

ix PREFACE

1 INTRODUCTION
   Edmund J. Gleazer, Jr.
   President Emeritus
   American Association of Community Colleges

23 I. CHAPTER AND VERSE:
   How We Came to Be Where We Are
   Lynn Sullivan Taber
   The University of Texas at Austin

39 II. COMMUNITY COLLEGES AND COLLABORATION
   J. Richard Gilliland, President
   Metropolitan Community College
   Omaha, Nebraska

57 III. COMMUNITY IS OUR MIDDLE NAME
   Robert McCabe, President
   Miami-Dade Community College
   Miami, Florida

81 IV. COMMUNITY COLLEGES AS A NEXUS FOR
   COMMUNITY
   Byron N. McClenney, President
   Community College of Denver
   Denver, Colorado

93 V. COLLABORATION AT CHATTANOOGA STATE
   James Catanzaro, President
   Chattanooga State Technical Community College
   Chattanooga, Tennessee

105 VI. PARTNERSHIPS AT HUMBER COLLEGE:
   A Pathway to Institutional Success
   Robert A. Gordon, President
   Humber College of Applied Arts & Technology
   Ontario, Canada

129 VII.   PARTNERSHIPS:
            The Parlaying Principles
            Carl M. Kuttler, Jr., President
            St. Petersburg Junior College
            St. Petersburg, Florida

147 VIII.   COMMUNITY COLLEGE PARTNERSHIPS:
            A Door to the Future
            Norm Nielsen, President
            Kirkwood Community College
            Cedar Rapids, Iowa

163 IX.   BUILDING THE COMMUNITY COLLEGE OF THE
            FUTURE THROUGH PARTNERSHIPS
            Thomas E. Barton, Jr., President
            Greenville Technical College
            Greenville, South Carolina

183 X.   THE GREAT BALANCING ACT:
            Community Needs Versus Resources
            Jerry Sue Thornton, President
            Lois Baron, Lois Baron Communications
            Cuyahoga Community College
            Cleveland, Ohio

203 XI.   ACADEMIC RHETORIC VERSUS BUSINESS REALITY
            Paul C. Gianini, Jr., President
            Sandra Todd Sarantos, Vice President, Educational & Economic
                Development Services; and Provost, Central Campus
            Valencia Community College
            Orlando, Florida

227 XII.   THE DALLAS COMMITMENT:
            Partnerships in the Era of Collaboration
            J. William Wenrich, Chancellor
            Martha Hughes, Executive Director, Educational Partnerships
            Dallas County Community College District
            Dallas, Texas

243 XIII.   A STATE AND LOCAL INITIATIVE TO CREATE A
            WORKFORCE DEVELOPMENT PARTNERSHIP:
            Case Study of a Bellwether State
            Sally J. Andrade, Director, Center for Institutional Evaluation
                Research, and Planning, The University of Texas at El Paso
            Dale F. Campbell, Professor and Director, Institute of Higher
                Education, University of Florida

265 XIV.   REPOSITIONING THE COLLEGE AS AN ESSENTIAL
                COMMUNITY PARTNER
                James L. Hudgins, President
                Starnell K. Williams, Vice President for Advancement
                Midlands Technical College
                Columbia, South Carolina

285 XV.   INFORMATION TECHNOLOGY:
                Collaborating for Change
                David H. Ponitz, President
                Sinclair Community College
                Dayton, Ohio

297 XVI.   THE ROLE OF THE COMMUNITY COLLEGE IN BUILDING
                COMMUNITIES THROUGH COALITIONS
                Janet Beauchamp, Executive Director, Think Tank
                Maricopa County Community College District
                Tempe, Arizona

319 XVII. A MISSION OF LEADERSHIP
                Charles C. Spence, College President
                Carol Spalding Miner, Campus President
                Tracy A. Pierce, Senior Public Relations Coordinator
                Florida Community College at Jacksonville
                Jacksonville, Florida

345 XVIII. STRIKING A BALANCE:
                Creating The Collaborative Mosiac
                John E. Roueche
                Lynn Sullivan Taber
                Suanne D. Roueche
                Community College Leadership Program
                The University of Texas at Austin

APPENDICES
375 A.   Individuals to contact at each college/institution
381 B.   Resources

387 INDEX

405 ABOUT THE AUTHORS

Preface

With one collective foot firmly planted in one century and the other raised mid-air, in mid-stride, toward planting itself on the doorstep of another, community colleges may never have had a more challenging occasion to look at who we are and what we might become. This occasion demands that we look *inward* to make important discoveries about ourselves, to identify the strengths and weaknesses that support or threaten our institutional lives. Simultaneously, it warns that we must look *outward* to identify the continuing and emerging realities of this new time. The dual and serious nature of the continuing realities—pressing educational, economic, and societal needs—the emerging realities—increasing expectations and demands on education, accompanied by decreasing resources—and the blurring of some time-honored traditional boundaries between institutions and philosophies cannot be ignored. Clearly, we are well-advised to know ourselves better and reach out to know others. We must choose wisely the company we will keep.

In our desire to identify "the company" and to assess its potential value for community colleges, we invited the CEOs of 14 community colleges across North America, the director of a state agency, and the director of a national project to share their stories about partnerships, collaborations, and alliances—that is, about "the company they keep." We wanted to provide an update of information about the diversity of arrangements that are drawing serious national and international attention, and we wished to document any trends in college responses to the notions and the realities of being conveners, catalysts, connectors, and collaborators. While we regret being unable to include all the college partnerships and collaborations that have earned high marks in these arenas, those presented in the following chapters will provide solid documentation for ideas whose times have come.

We preface the book further with this note of explanation. The authors refer interchangeably to partnerships, collaborations, collaborative initiatives, and alliances. The vocabulary was evolving even as they wrote, and it continues to evolve. Perhaps at this juncture it is sufficient to say that the wide variety of terms serves to remind us of the breadth and depth of this developing community college role. The extraordinary variety of the arrangements described in the various chapters of this book attest to them, as well. We are pleased to include the following authors:

Edmund J. Gleazer, Jr., *President Emeritus, American Association of Community Colleges*

J. Richard Gilliland, *President, Metropolitan Community College (Omaha, Nebraska)*

Robert McCabe, *President, Miami-Dade Community College (Miami, Florida)*

Byron N. McClenney, *President, Community College of Denver (Denver, Colorado)*

James Catanzaro, *President, Chattanooga State Technical Community College (Chattanooga, Tennessee)*

Robert A. Gordon, *President, Humber College of Applied Arts and Technology (Ontario, Canada)*

Carl M. Kuttler, Jr., *President, St. Petersburg Junior College (St. Petersburg, Florida)*

Norm Nielsen, *President, Kirkwood Community College (Cedar Rapids, Iowa)*

Thomas E. Barton, Jr., *President, Greenville Technical College (Greenville, South Carolina)*

Jerry Sue Thornton, *President, Cuyahoga Community College*

Lois Baron, *Lois Baron Communications (Cleveland, Ohio)*

Paul C. Gianini, Jr., *President;* Sandra Todd Sarantos, *Vice President, Educational and Economic Development Services, and Provost, Central Campus, Valencia Community College (Orlando, Florida)*

J. William Wenrich, *Chancellor;* Martha Hughes, *Executive Director, Educational Partnerships, Dallas County Community College District (Dallas, Texas)*

Sally J. Andrade, *Director, Center for Institutional Evaluation, Research, and Planning, The University of Texas at El Paso (El Paso, Texas);* Dale F. Campbell, *Professor and Director, Institute of Higher Education, University of Florida (Gainesville, Florida)*

James L. Hudgins, *President;* Starnell K. Williams, *Vice President for Advancement, Midlands Technical College (Columbia, South Carolina)*

David H. Ponitz, *President, Sinclair Community College (Dayton, Ohio)*

Janet Beauchamp, *Executive Director, Think Tank, Maricopa County Community College District (Tempe, Arizona)*

Charles C. Spence, *President;* Carol Spalding Miner, *Campus President;* and Tracy A. Pierce, *Senior Public Relations Coordinator, Florida Community College at Jacksonville (Jacksonville, Florida)*

We owe a debt of gratitude to these authors who accepted our invitations to tell their stories and, thus, to contribute mightily to what we know about this developing new role and responsibility for community colleges. Their enthusiasm, candor, energy, and interest provided very special support during the entire process. Moreover, their stories of success and community development gave us great hope for the current phenomenon of collaboration, and their accomplishments inspired a serious sense of awe.

Finally, we offer our heartfelt thanks to those here at home—Bob Taber, Sheryl Fielder, Teri Rucker, Julie Leidig, and Vicki Whitaker, our on-site editor—who, on more than one occasion, made certain that the light at the end of the tunnel would not be an oncoming train! We came to rely on their attention to detail as they read and edited, time and again; they made this manuscript better than we possibly could have made it ourselves. Yet, in no way do we mean to suggest that the critical assistance, attention, and care that they provided to the publication process should be judged by how well the process was ultimately completed. We accept total responsibility for the final product.

Our experiences with all of these friends and colleagues will remain as very special recollections of this important adventure.

Austin, Texas   John E. Roueche
January, 1995   Lynn Sullivan Taber
                                                            Suanne D. Roueche

INTRODUCTION

Edmund J. Gleazer, Jr.

President Emeritus
American Association of Community Colleges

The approach of a new century has put many educational institutions into a planning mode. Among these is Harvard University, whose president recently declared:

The planning process has been much more than a matter of looking inward. We're very much a part of the larger world. We need to be open to it, and engaged with its fundamental problems in ways that a university can contribute most effectively.

The provost of the University added:

Harvard has enormous strengths...Today we are increasingly called to bring these to bear on our world problems, whether they be environmental pollution or violence in our streets (*Alumni Gazette*, 1994, p. 1).

Substitute the term "community college" for "Harvard" and "university," and "community" for "world," and the provost's statement is fitting and timely for the nation's community colleges. In fact, many community colleges that have made such commitments will be featured in this book. The League for Innovation in the Community College, in mid-1993, declared:

Community colleges, as yet largely untapped resources, are emerging as the nexus for the resolution of both local and national concerns...Serving as a frequent hub for local networks dealing with community problems, they are accustomed to working collaboratively with all types of community groups (League for Innovation, 1993, p. v).

What are these "community problems," these "local and national concerns" with which the community college can deal? Surely it is not necessary here to provide an extensive list, but several that have forced themselves into public view will be cited as illustrations.

COMMUNITY PROBLEMS AND LEARNING

The epidemic of violence in our communities, changes through "downsizing," required upgrading of skills, economic restructuring, a diverse population that can lead to conflict and fragmentation of communities, health care problems, changing family structures with accompanying implications for child care and financial support, increasing numbers of people living beneath the poverty level, severe shortages of adequate housing, citizen distrust of government, and low participation rates in civic life can all be included in any litany of community problems. This litany is not intended to depress or overwhelm the reader but rather to indicate areas in which there is a need for learning. These "problems" involve behavior, relationships, attitudes, skills, and values— all products of learning. Because the problems are here and now, adult learning is of highest priority. Adults are the present actors and, therefore, can have the most immediate effect on their circumstances. Certainly, childhood and youth learning are also of critical importance. Ideally, the two generations would be learning concurrently.

Community colleges are in place in most communities in this nation. Their primary focus is on adult learning. Through more than 30 years of experience, they have developed strengths to deal with community problems. In doing their work they have positioned themselves to become their communities' most valuable aids to learning. How did this come about? How did the college get pushed *out* into the community? What attributes did it acquire to deal with community problems? Is infusion with the community a diversion from the institution's primary mission or integral to that mission? The somewhat historical narrative that follows highlights institutional experiences that demonstrate the value of responding to present community needs.

COLLEGES PUSHED INTO COMMUNITIES

When I addressed the American Association of School Administrators (school superintendents) at their national meeting held in Cleveland, March 31, 1958, I responded to this question: "What shall we do about education at the 13th and 14th grade levels?" The educational administrators attending were concerned about how to accommodate the tidal wave of enrollment which would be sweeping through their schools, as well as what kinds of postsecondary opportunities would be open to high school graduates. They obviously perceived the junior college to consist of the 13th and 14th grades which were under their supervision, a common perception in those days. There was as yet no public community college in Cleveland, nor in Ohio.

In June 1971, I returned to Cleveland and spent several days at Cuyahoga Community College in connection with a national study of community colleges. By this time, CCC had been in business for eight years. The doors had opened on September 23, 1963, to some 3,000 full- and part-time students, the largest opening-day enrollment figure at that stage in the history of the flourishing community college movement. By 1971, the enrollment was approximately 17,000—the sixth largest of the colleges and universities of Ohio—and more than 30,000 were projected to be enrolled by 1980.

I interviewed people representing many of the sectors of the college and community. My questions dealt with the future of the institution, how it would be changing, how it needed to change. These were among the themes I heard:

- Can we function as a multiracial institution—a bridge between diverse ethnic and cultural groups?
- One of the primary functions of this institution is to help residents of the city to live...how does this change our focus as we look ahead?
- We have not really reached out...we don't know our students, where they are from and where they are going...but this is beginning to change.
- Maybe it's time for us to take a leadership role—to tie the area together, to be a catalyst for community development.
- We need to deal with the problems of our community in order to be a real community college.

Discussion of such issues apparently worked their magic, for in *The Urban Community Colleges Report*, September 1993, the caption for the lead article was "At Thirty-Something Cuyahoga CC Spurs City's Revival." The Metro Campus, it was stated, is linked to the area's business leadership, to a wide array of publicly funded training and retraining programs, to universities, public housing authorities, major hospitals, displaced homemaker programs, and musical and recreational organizations. The calls are being answered for the college to be a catalyst for community development, to deal with the problems of the community, to tie the area together, and to take a leadership role.

DOORS OPEN TO COMMUNITY ISSUES

Cuyahoga was one of more than 20 community colleges that opened in the big cities during the early 1960s. Before 1960, there were no public community colleges in Cleveland, Miami, Dallas, Fort Worth, Philadelphia, Pittsburgh, Denver, Seattle, Spokane, St. Louis, Portland, Birmingham, or a dozen other major cities. The colleges were formed, and they grew during the boom of the 1960s.

During the economic and social ferment in American cities during that decade, big-city community colleges experienced the turmoil directly. The concerns of the community were a wave that washed back and forth across and through the institutions. Colleges found that they had opened their doors not only to community students but to community issues. A better life was promised to those who came. By and large, that promise held in the face of unexpected challenges, among them that the population responding to the promise was one of unmatched diversity in race, styles of life, economic means, psychological and emotional needs, and educational preparation; moreover, many in that population had a profound distrust of the community's institutions.

The big-city community colleges were dealing with unconventional, nontraditional students. It was the impact of that highly diversified student population that forced the college to change. Faculty and administrators set themselves to discovering how to make learning effective for their new clientele. They found that it was necessary to design a curriculum to fit the level of educational development attained by the people and to adapt educational programs to meet their needs. To learn about the people with whom the institution was working, the college moved out into the community setting. Relationships were established with families, neighborhood centers, manpower agencies, social workers, recreation centers, and churches. The college began to cut across ethnic lines, socioeconomic classes, educational interests, and geographic boundaries. People found that the college provided a place and an opportunity to discuss community issues in an informed way.

In fact, the very process required to establish these colleges unexpectedly laid the groundwork for continuing relationships with community organizations and for a catalytic role. Old and often archaic political subdivisions and vastly different economic and racial neighborhoods were traversed in the sometimes agonizing struggle of shaping a new district. At the same time that cities were being split, pushed, squeezed, and ruptured by the pressures of beltways, urban renewal, and political and racial conflict, these new colleges brought often-contending groups together around a new and common interest. People and groups, who had no reason to before, were obliged to get along together. A new institution added to the tax bill promoted a great deal of discussion. Certain questions about the area were bound to be raised. The citizens found themselves discussing values—what they believed about community life, what was important, and what they were willing to pay for. They asked, "What is happening to our community?" "Is this a desirable place in which to live?" The goal and the process of establishing a community college had created a community forum. Not only was an institution built, but a means was inaugurated for continuing interaction among members of the community.

VIOLENCE IN THE CITIES

In 1963, concerned about fragmentation in the nation's cities and impressed by the positive ways in which some of the colleges were responding, I asked the delegates to the 43rd annual convention of the American Association of Junior Colleges[1] (AAJC):

> With the increasing fragmentation of community life and the growing complexity of social problems, in what ways will community colleges become cul-

[1] The AACC has experienced several name changes. The names which appear in this foreword are true to the organization's history, as the piece is a historical perspective.

tural and social centers for community life? Will they be cohesive forces among diverse elements in the population?

There was good reason to raise this question. At the same time that the pace of establishing new institutions was accelerating, violence was breaking out in our cities.

In 1963, serious disorders, involving both whites and Negroes, broke out in Birmingham, Savannah, Cambridge, Chicago, and Philadelphia...In August, 1965, there was Watts, the Los Angeles riot, worst in the United States since the Detroit riot of 1943. Events in 1966 in Chicago and Cleveland made it appear that domestic turmoil had become part of the American scene (National Advisory Commission on Civil Disorders, 1968, p. 19).

According to the National Advisory Commission on Civil Disorders, established by President Lyndon B. Johnson, "The summer of 1967 again brought racial disorders to American cities, and with them shock, fear, and bewilderment to the Nation" (National Advisory Commission on Civil Disorders, 1968, p. 1). The president directed the commission to answer three basic questions:

- What happened?
- Why did it happen?
- What can be done to prevent it from happening again?

The commission's basic conclusion in its report, submitted in 1968, was: "Our Nation is moving toward two societies, one black, one white—separate and unequal." The report could actually be summarized in the president's language calling for the establishment of the commission:

The only genuine, long-range solution for what has happened lies in an attack—mounted at every level—upon the conditions that breed despair and violence. All of us know what those conditions are: ignorance, discrimination, slums, poverty, disease, not enough jobs. We should attack these conditions— not because we are frightened by conflict, but because we are fired by conscience. We should attack them because there is simply no other way to achieve a decent and orderly society in America (Lyndon Baines Johnson, Address to the Nation, June 27, 1967, in National Advisory Commission on Civil Disorders, 1968 p. i).

CALL FOR CHANGE

The president's words provided needed assurance and encouragement to the leaders of the growing number of community colleges in the cities, even though much of the information was not new to them. Many of their colleges were in the "combat zones." What was particularly significant in the commission's report was the call for educational institutions to change how they related to their communities in order to step up the attack upon the conditions described by the president. For some community colleges, these recommendations were a validation of directions in which they

were already headed. For others, many of them in the first few years of establishment
and preoccupied with the building of new plants and related activities, the report was
a disturbing reminder of work yet to be done.

Some of the commission's findings and recommendations had particular relevance
to the evolving community college, such as the following:

In an atmosphere of hostility between the community and the schools, education cannot flourish. A basic problem stems from the isolation of the schools
from the other social forces influencing youth. Changes in society—mass
media, family structure, religion—have radically altered the role of the school.
New links must be built between the school and the communities they serve.
The schools must be related to the broader system which influences and edu-
cates ghetto youth (National Advisory Commission on Civil Disorders, 1968,
p. 244).

The commission emphasized the need for better connections between the institutions
and the community, as well as perceptions of the student and the institution in the context of a larger system. Apparently, community colleges had not become visible enough
on the urban scene to warrant special attention. However, the recommendations for the
schools had significance for community colleges not only at that time, but also as guiding principles for the future.

Another salient finding was that of poor communication between the educational
institutions and members of the community:

The lack of communication and the absence of regular contacts with ghetto residents prevent city leaders from learning about problems and grievances as they
develop. As a result, tensions, which could have been dissipated if responded to
promptly, mount unnecessarily, and the potential for explosion grows
inevitably. Once disorder erupts, public officials are frequently unable to fashion an effective response; they lack adequate information about the nature of
the trouble and its causes, and they lack rapport with local leaders who might
be able to influence the community (National Advisory Commission on Civil
Disorders, 1968, p. 148).

The word "ghetto," in the commission's report, may no longer be an apt de-
scriptor. Many of these problems have become diffused throughout a population
area. For community colleges the recommendations are most helpful when applied to
the entire district. And in this connection, no institution in the city has become more
useful in tracking change and in relating to community leaders than the community
college. As we shall see, through years of community college maturation, community assessment as a continuing process has been fundamental to program development
in these institutions.

In many ways, without mentioning the community college by name, the commission's report demanded attributes from the community educational sector of the kind
that would be influential in shaping the future profile of the community college.

CATALYSTS IN COMMUNITY DEVELOPMENT

As a result of what I was seeing in my visits to community colleges in 1967, I reported two findings to a University of Chicago workshop for administrators of university adult education:

- The campus is the length and breadth of the community college district, and
- community colleges are recognizing their responsibility to serve as a catalyst in community development and individual improvement (Gleazer, 1967).

By 1969, programs of the AAJC began to show keen interest in the problems of the cities. Projects were initiated with inner-city community colleges. Further, at the annual meeting in Atlanta, delegates heard Mayor Stokes of Cleveland describe rioting in the Hough section of that city, growth in the low-income population, and a worsening of housing conditions. Norvel Smith, a black president from Merritt Community College in Oakland, California, asked the convention whether community colleges could change to meet the changes in society. In introducing the dominant theme of the meeting, I announced:

We are centering this program around the real and inescapable issues in higher education and society: student protest, faculty concern for greater involvement in college affairs, needs of disadvantaged minority groups, and the general unrest that pervades many college campuses.

At this point, as I reflect upon that statement, I note concern about the issues of "society," but somewhat more concern for the issues on campus. That situation was to change rapidly over the ensuing several months. A harbinger of things to come in the association, as well as for its member institutions, was signaled by Charles Hurst, president of Malcolm X Community College in Chicago, who walked out of the first general session when an all-white choir sang "Dixie."

Subsequent to the Atlanta meeting, the board of directors of the association issued a policy statement with respect to the "disadvantaged" to serve as guidance in the development of association programs. An urban college project was initiated with support from the federal Office of Economic Opportunity and the Ford Foundation. In addition, a specialist for minority group programs was appointed to the association staff.

TO EXPERIENCE THE REALITY

At the AAJC 50th annual convention in 1970, the theme was "A Time of Change." Participants reviewed the remarkable growth in the number of new institutions (500 during the decade), new campuses all over the country, the mounting number of colleges accredited by regional associations, and supportive public interest. It was a time for celebration. However, the turbulence of the cities followed the delegates to their meetings and disturbed the usual routine of the sessions. Caucuses of racial interest groups were organized to promote their respective agendas both within the association and in their institutions and regions. As I addressed the opening session, I could not forget the background against which our congratulatory activities were taking place—there were problems existing in our social environment that pressed for attention:

> In winning the battle for public interest there are now other powerful social needs to be recognized—needs, incidentally, which can either be competitors or allies depending upon how we move into what I believe is a new arena of action. Public interest in our institutions during this next decade will not be captured by dramatic growth but by ways in which our institutions relate to man's most compelling problems. And if this is to be done, radical change is required in many of our present concepts, definitions, and structures.

> So I say—let us more frequently leave our offices and classrooms and laboratories and the warm and secure fellowship of those we know and understand, to experience the reality that surrounds those whom we would teach—to know their concerns, their anxieties, their environmental pressures. We may need to learn to listen more even if this means speaking less. We may need to place more reliance upon firsthand experience in community life rather than upon the abstractions of reports, memoranda, and critiques of society. We need to reduce the level of abstraction to primary involvement with the sights, the sounds, the smells, the touch of the environment as it bears upon the lives of the people with whom we would work. From this experience come the insights and clues to educational needs. Then the process is to derive suitable and fitting objectives, functions, form, and organization for educational services.

> There seems to be mounting evidence, in a time when society is faced with staggering problems caused by poverty, environmental pollution, stress, crime and delinquency, and even the problems of affluence, that these institutions which we represent may hold the potential for becoming a new kind of nexus for community approaches to solutions. If this be the case, a hard, thoughtful examination must be made of the implications which these opportunities and challenges suggest for new kinds of structures of governance, new administrative styles, new support patterns, new kinds of interdigitation with the community at the institutional level (Gleazer, 1970, p. 5).

The board of directors of the association, aware of the rising concerns of many of their constituents, authorized a "hard, thoughtful examination of the implications which these opportunities suggest" for both the association and its members. The study, "Project Focus," resulted in substantial change in the association's organizational structure and in a call to the colleges " 'to be there,' a kind of people's college, an educational resource center for the community, a liberating means for people in a society where opportunity for education means opportunity to live as a person" (Gleazer, 1973, p. 239).

COMMUNITY-BASED EDUCATION

In fall 1973, I presented to the association's board of directors a paper prepared as part of intensive planning efforts by the association staff. The paper, titled "After the Boom...What Now for the Community Colleges?" suggested that community colleges were entering a new era and that the future belonged to institutions that would be community-based—responsive to needs and wants in the community that the college would be able to serve. Among these needs would be career development; individual development; family development; institutional services, such as in programs to train and upgrade employees; and the provision of a focal point, a center for the community, a place and reason for coming together. The approach put the emphasis on the word "community" in the term *community college*.

A result of board consideration was adoption of a new mission statement for the association:

The mission of the American Association of Community and Junior Colleges is to provide an organization for national leadership of community-based, performance-oriented postsecondary education.

What is a "community-based, performance-oriented postsecondary institution"? Some of the characteristics were described:

Community facilities and resources will be used in the institution's services. Programs will be made available in industrial plants, churches, health facilities, neighborhood centers, business establishments, and in the schools. Facilities built specifically for college purposes, such as libraries, gymnasiums, and technical buildings will be opened up and utilized by the community as needs and interests justify.

Faculty, administration, and board will have interest in and knowledge about the community. College personnel will have responsibility to maintain a continuing inventory of data required to set college priorities. Pertinent information will be available not only about students but the environments from which they come.

The college will serve as broker in seeing to it that identified postsecondary educational needs are met either through its services or other appropriate institutions. It will accordingly exercise initiative in establishing working relationships with the public schools, vocational institutions, universities and colleges, and other community agencies.

The college will be perceived as part and parcel of the community rather than providing services for the community. In programming as well as facilities utilization there will be continual interchange between community and college within a specific geographical area. These relationships have been described as symbiotic rather than paternalistic.

The college will be aggressive in searching out community educational needs. It may make information available about the community to other community agencies for planning and program purposes. It may provide counseling services. It may contract to train people for specific purposes. It may provide library and recreational facilities. As broker it can encourage communication among those agencies which impinge upon the lives and circumstances of its students. It can offer programs, for example basic adult education, or see to it that other appropriate agencies provide such services. The college is committed to both the individual and social benefits of education and will merchandise that concept (Gleazer, 1974, p. 11). [For a discussion of the concept *performance-oriented*, see reference cited.]

AN INSTITUTIONAL FRAME OF MIND

Broad interest was evidenced in the aforementioned description. American Association of Community and Junior Colleges (AACJC) member institutions considered the implications in terms of their own institutional development. More precise descriptions of what it meant to be "community-based" were developed as the concepts were applied:

A community-based, performance-oriented college is one that draws its sense of mission from its community. It studies the community carefully to determine what its needs are. It does this in cooperation with other human service agencies in the community. It also studies the resources that are available to meet the needs identified. It works cooperatively with other agencies to develop services responsive to the identified needs. It assesses institutional responses and reports results to the community in terms citizens can understand and support. The whole process is continuous...Being 'community-based' means an institutional frame of mind as well as a set of skills (Yarrington, 1975, p. 9–11).

An example of this institutional "frame of mind" is found in the ways adopted by an Illinois community college in the mid-seventies to apply its capabilities to community problems and issues. The strategies described below are based upon a policy position of the Board of Trustees of Waubonsee Community College in Illinois:

- Maintain continuous and intimate involvement in the service area, so that the institution is immediately aware of community needs.
- Focus on community issues as they emerge and develop co-sponsored task forces or ad hoc committees in cooperation with other interested community institutions, groups, and individuals. The task force, or community advisory committee, is tailored to the particular issue.
- Initiate workshops, seminars, and conferences (e.g., community forums) to study the issue and to develop solutions.
- The college then designs and executes educational programs which satisfy the needs of the solution from an educational perspective. Other agencies, newly formed, if necessary, provide the needed non-educational components (Gleazer, 1980, p. 21).

COMMUNITY LEADERSHIP

Further emphasis was given to the community role for community colleges in the opening address to the association at its 1974 annual meeting by Alan Pifer, president of the Carnegie Corporation of New York. Asserting that many Americans are yearning for societal reconstruction during the next decade, he urged that educational objectives often perceived as secondary be given new priority:

> Other institutions will have a part to play, of course, but I see the community college as the essential leadership agency. Indeed I am going to make the outrageous suggestion that community colleges should start thinking of themselves from now on only secondarily as a sector of higher education and regard as their primary role community leadership...Not least, they can become the hub of a network of institutions and community agencies—the high schools, industry, the church, voluntary agencies, youth groups, even the prison system and the courts—utilizing their educational resources and in turn, becoming a resource for them (Pifer, 1974, p. 23).

Declaring itself eager to advance both the theory and practice of community-based education, Valencia Community College (Florida) described itself as an educational cooperative: "Members of the community are partners in an enterprise which they have created and which they support for their benefit" (Fischer and Gollattscheck, 1974, p. 15).

Nine additional institutions joined with Valencia to form a cooperative for community-based education which they named COMBASE to "promote activities which lead to development of resources to address problems and improve quality of community education."

ARRAY OF ADULTS USE COLLEGE

Another significant development in 1974 reflected the rising participation rates by adults in college programs and the consequent need for educational planners to change the ways they perceive the educational needs and interests of the community. The state of Florida, a leader in community college development, found that conventional ways of predicting community college enrollments—numbers of high school graduates, percentage expected to go on to college, etc.—just did not work any more. They grossly underestimated enrollments. The state, therefore, sought valid ways of projecting community college enrollments as a percentage of the total population. It was apparent that not only recent high school graduates but a much broader spectrum of the public was using the college. The enrollment increases were almost paralleling the percentage of increase in the state's population as a whole.

The fact that a much broader spectrum of the public was using the college revealed widespread acceptance of the institution and highlighted its potential for influencing the quality of community life. A further effect was the increase in the number of community organizations whose activities intersected those of the college.

Cooperative Arrangements

At the national level, new cooperative arrangements formed. Among these were relations with unions, community schools, vocational schools, and business and industry. In 1975, the association, the United Auto Workers Union, and the AFL-CIO formed a joint task force to tackle problems and issues of mutual concern.

Community schools and community colleges had many goals in common but few linkages. The advantages of cooperation seemed obvious. AACJC and the National Community Education Association initiated collaborative activities at both the national and local levels with the assistance of the Mott Foundation. Also invited into continuing relations were adult and continuing education associations, such as the Adult Education Association, the National University Extension Association, and the National Association for Public Continuing and Adult Education.

Concurrent with these efforts, AACJC affirmed:

Look for the most significant linkages in the next ten years to be among the secondary schools, vocational schools, community schools, and comprehensive high schools from which community college students come. The common meeting ground as well as the possible potential source of abrasion will be in the implementation of the concept of life-long learning and the continuing education of the adult learner (Gleazer, 1975).

By 1977, the president of AACJC would report to his board about successful regional conferences sponsored by the association and the American Vocational Association to reduce or eliminate the barriers to effective collaboration between vocational schools and community colleges. The conferences were based upon a yearlong study of successful articulation efforts among institutions offering vocational education at the secondary and postsecondary level.

A program was established with financial assistance from the U.S. Department of Labor, to "test the viability of community colleges as catalysts for establishment of Community Education-Work Councils to bring various elements of a given community together to assist in the transition from education to work" (Mahoney, 1979, p. 4).

Community Forums

Circumstances in the late 1970s led to the further development of activities that had been a part of community college evolution: community discussions of community issues. Stimulated by President Jimmy Carter's interest and success with town meetings, the National Endowment for the Humanities saw community forums as a way to have broad participation and informed discussion of issues of concern to local citizens.

NEH leaders had become aware of the experience of community colleges in conduct-ing community forums. A number had participated in the "American Issues Forums" during the Bicentennial. The Courses by Newspaper Project, supported by the Nation-al Endowment for the Humanities, involved community colleges across the country. Persons with experience in such programs were invited to a national meeting in 1977 for two days of discussion directed to the utilization of community colleges as the insti-tutional base for community forums.

Good forums, it was agreed, result in citizen education and action. They can assist in shaping public policy by:
• providing a disciplined approach to a statement of the questions,
• promoting informed discussion,
• involving many sectors of the community, and
• developing a sense of involvement.
The forum process was seen as integral to the ways in which community colleges oper-ate. Through forums, national issues could be translated into a local agenda for analy-sis, discussion, and action.

We believe the community college has a mission to engage itself in community-based research as well as citizen education. What better agenda than to tackle the actual problems that trouble our society and each of us as individuals? What better strategy than to involve as many citizens as possible in the local analysis, discussion, and in practical approaches to solutions?

This dynamic process is ideally a community enterprise. The community college, hopefully, is experienced in the identification of community needs and resources, in enlisting cooperation by a wide spectrum of community agencies, in using a variety of learning formats—including the mass media. The commu-nity college has subject area specialists and community education specialists. It has a mandate to serve its community (Gleazer and Yarrington, 1977, p. 5).

For the next several years, hundreds of community colleges sponsored forums deal-ing with a variety of issues from "Energy and the Way We Live" to "Death and Dying" and "Crime and Justice." I found most significant the large numbers of cooperating orga-nizations. In a visit to a Florida community, I observed more than 40 cosponsors of the Crime and Justice program. Sponsors ranged from TV stations to the county sheriff's department, other colleges and universities, the court system, the chamber of com-merce, the public library system, the League of Women Voters, etc. The discussions were lively, well-attended, and successful in every way. Beyond that, however, it became clear that one of the great contributions made by forums to that community was to shape a network of communication and interaction among a large number of organiza-tions that influenced the quality of community life. Both the relationships formed and the process used would continue to be assets of the community-based college.

Another glimpse of the extent to which the colleges were relating to other com-munity organizations and agencies was provided in a limited survey by the Policies for

Lifelong Education Project of AACJC. During the years 1977-1978, more than 1.5 million individuals were served through 10,000-plus cooperative agreements in effect on 173 campuses in 37 states.

A New Mission

Toward the end of the decade, new factors began to bear upon the evolving mission of the community college. Inflation was rampant. Voters in several populous states passed property tax limitation measures. The effects of these and other forces were to move funding—and consequently more policy determination—to state levels, and for searching questions to be asked at both state and local levels about the legitimate mission of these institutions. A result was the view by some policymakers that the college should return to the campus and limit its scope to programs and services more conventional and academic.

Another important factor was the perception by many policy makers that the projected decline in numbers of high school graduates meant that it was time to "wind down" the apparatus of postsecondary education. Few policymakers seemed aware of the adult learner phenomenon and society's need for continuing education. Even more troubling, in all my travels and conversations with legislators, governors, and state planners, seldom did I hear education acknowledged as a resource to be utilized in dealing with pressing societal needs such as mental health, corrections, unemployment, economic development, rising costs of health care, family disorganization, and energy conservation and development.

The mounting policy tensions were described in a Brookings Institution study of community college financing:

Shrinking resources may force the choice between remaining a part of traditional higher education or moving to become a community-based service organization. It may no longer be possible to have it both ways (Breneman and Nelson, 1981, p. 17).

It was in this context of issues and policy choices that the leadership of the AACJC and its institutional representatives spent more than two years in an attempt to conceive a statement that would embrace appropriate new directions for the association and its member institutions. The following was adopted as a guide for the 1980s:

The mission of the American Association of Community and Junior Colleges is to organize national leadership and services for individual and community development through lifelong education (American Association of Community and Junior Colleges, 1981, p. 17).

Among the continuing objectives cited of particular relevance to our discussions here were these:

• To encourage working relationships with and among other institutions and agencies, at local, state, national, and international levels, having similar concerns for individual and community development.

- To provide vigorous national leadership in education for employment and economic development.
- To provide leadership in making available education which enhances the quality of life for the individual and the community (American Association of Community and Junior Colleges, 1981, p. 17).

To many community college leaders, the new mission statement did not represent new concepts as much as validation at the national level of a road already taken. However, as just indicated, not everybody agreed. Broad-based discussion was called for, discussion similar to that which took place when many of the institutions were established. In effect, these were the questions—what kind of education do the citizens want and need, and what are they willing to pay for?

DISCUSSION OF THE MISSION

Citing previous experiences of its member institutions with community forums, AACJC called for 1,000 of its members to join with other community organizations in fall 1980 to discuss those questions. Each college was urged to begin its own analysis of local issues surrounding the mission of the college, to develop materials to create an informed discussion, and to build a network of cooperation. The goal was the broadest possible involvement of the community in thinking through the mission of the local community college.

The forums were conducted in hundreds of communities during October and November, 1980. Simultaneously, Courses by Newspaper published a mini-course on education for community development in some 500 newspapers. Kits of forum materials were sent to all participating colleges. Briefs were distributed dealing with the following topics:

- What is meant by education for community development?
- What is the nature and purpose of community education?
- Who provides community education?
- Whom does community education serve?
- Who will pay for and control community education?

To what extent the forums influenced public policy probably cannot be determined. However, it is unlikely that this book would have been written if the colleges had diverted markedly from the course laid out during the years that have been reviewed. This part of my story comes to a close at the year 1981, because I wanted my contribution here to be grounded in two decades of experience (the 1960s and 1970s) as a participant/observer in the process through which community colleges were shaping their mission.

WHAT WAS LEARNED? WHAT IS TO BE LEARNED?

Values in Cooperation. There are at least three compelling reasons for forging connections with other community-based institutions:

- Economies may be possible.
- Learning opportunities are opened up beyond the classroom.
- A coalition of effort in interpreting the high social value of education will be much more effective than individual, and perhaps self-serving, activities of any single kind of educational institution.

We need new and stronger coalitions of those who support education for improving the human condition. The views that unite us may be a good deal stronger than the turf problems that often divide us.

Collaboration Can Be Difficult. In 1976, the AACJC was awarded a contract by the U.S. Department of Labor to establish education-work councils in at least five local communities across the country. Local community colleges were to serve as council initiators. James Mahoney, director of the program, reported that the colleges were excellent resources for initiating and nurturing councils, but he identified interorganizational difficulties that must be dealt with. "Collaboration," according to Mahoney, "has a positive ring, but it caused no end of difficulty, confusion, and frustration." Problems included:

A missing sense of program ownership; an incapacity to overcome the initial nebulousness of the project's purposes and characteristics; reluctance on the part of members to relinquish 'territorial rights,' both in terms of professional worlds and geographic ones; membership turn-over caused by community politics, job changes, professional and family commitments; fatigue, and the dominance of a single organization (Gleazer, 1980, p. 50).

Is Education for Community and Individual Development "Collegiate"? The community and individual development orientation of the community college was stressed by the AACJC in a 1980 letter to James T. McIntyre, Jr., director of the U.S. Office of Management and Budget, urging that a community college official be placed at the highest possible level in the new Department of Education. It was stated as follows:

Community college missions and objectives are different from secondary schools, on the one hand, and four-year colleges and universities on the other. They work closely with secondary schools and four-year colleges and universities. But they have a distinctive community-based, postsecondary mission that has its own separate integrity. The community college no longer draws its definition of what it is and what it does from the secondary school (two additional years—grades 13 and 14—offered at the local high school, under the governance of the school board), nor does it draw its definition from higher education (first two years of college for students preparing to transfer to a baccalaureate institution). It draws its mission and priorities from its community. It is a community college because it assesses community educational needs and resources; it develops educational services in response to those needs; and it evaluates the results and shares its findings with the community in terms it can understand and support. The reference point is not the school or the university; it is the community (AACJC, 1980, p. 43).

Where Are the Big Decisions Made? What are the consequences for the community college as control moves toward the state level? What happens to the quality of responsiveness at the local level, citizen involvement, and local initiatives as the locus of significant decision making moves steadily toward the state capitol? What will be the implications for the community college in its community relationships? What could be done through legislative means to encourage local initiatives and responsiveness? What decisions should be made at what levels? And what of the trend toward larger districts? The presumed advantages of political power, economy, and efficiency, must be balanced carefully against the substantial values of significant local involvement.

Must It Be "Either-Or"? In the Brookings study of financing community colleges, it was asserted that "shrinking resources may force the choice between remaining a part of traditional higher education or moving to become a community-based service organization. It may no longer be possible to have it both ways" (Breneman and Nelson, 1981). Is this true? If so, why? It has been almost 15 years since the study was made. What do the chapters of this book reveal about the capacity of the community college to be broadly comprehensive? What have their communities decided and demanded?

What Is it Worth? How do we measure the benefits of the colleges' role as catalyst, collaborator, convener? The need for measures of performance in terms of institutional objectives has never been more important. Tight money has the effect of focusing the eyes of legislators on the more traditional community college functions, the "regular" college programs. They insist that the case has to be made for education that deals with community problems. "Value added" is a promising concept whose development is still before us.

Mission statements, appropriation formulas, and policy guidelines often do not provide for compensation to the college administrators or faculty who devote time and energy to arranging collaborative efforts and participating in them. Seldom is support provided by state funding formulas. AACJC's Policies for Lifelong Education project established this as one of the most evident areas of need and change identified in its study of cooperative agreements (Gilder, 1979).

Is There a Blind Spot? Now we will consider one of the most perplexing problems. I have indicated that in interviews with legislators and government leaders in several states I seldom heard education mentioned as a resource for dealing with pressing soci-

etal needs in areas such as mental health, corrections, unemployment, economic development, rising health care costs, family disorganization, or energy conservation and development. Few people in policy-making positions in either state or federal governments seemed to be aware of the many ways in which community colleges were relating to critical economic and social problems. Why? Is the picture different now? Are the possibilities becoming more evident?

EDUCATION NEEDS TO CONNECT

The situation does appear to be changing with respect to employment, but as far as I can see, the connections with other community needs are not often apparent. A few years ago I was in a "less-developed country" meeting with representatives from 20 other "less developed countries." The topic was poverty in those countries and what adult education could do to address it. I heard education described as indispensable for agricultural development, economic development, health maintenance, potable water supply, and stable family organization. And the thought came to my mind that we, in our "developed" country, had something to learn from all of this. Here education was being viewed as integral to a system of community development, not as a separate enclave. In fashioning our social policies, we can benefit from the approach described by Frederick Harbison. In addition to emphasizing the essential nature of goals, he touches upon the fundamental need to plan in comprehensive ways. He describes this as the "sector approach":

> The sector approach, moreover, goes far beyond the traditional boundaries of formal education; it encompasses training and human resource development in other sectors such as agriculture, health, nutrition and public service. Thus, unlike other sectors, education or the nation-wide learning system is not a relatively self-contained system. It has multiple intersections with almost every facet of national development. In reality, the sector approach involves a comprehensive analysis of national development from a human resources perspective (Harbison, 1973, pp. 7–8).

BE AWARE OF THE INTERSECTIONS

Add the word "community" to the above quotation, and the approach is timely and provocative. Education is perceived as having "multiple intersections" with almost every facet of (community) development. There are now reasons to suggest that there may be growing awareness of the intersections and consequent possibilities and costs. For example, a slogan, born in Africa, has gone mainstream and become a favorite of politicians and writers: "It takes a whole village to raise a child." Here there is recognition of the total educative influence of the village environment, and for us the question becomes how to assure that educational institutions play their facilitating role in a system of many forces.

Current studies of the "epidemic of violence" in our communities reveal the inadequacy of simplistic solutions (e.g., "three strikes and you're out," gun control) in the face of an intersecting, interlocking mosaic of such factors as schools, housing, jobs, family, drugs, poverty, diversity, and racial conflict.

I have mentioned "costs," as well as "possibilities," in the intersections of education with other social institutions. Perhaps nowhere is there a more powerful example than can be found today in California. The San Francisco-based Center on Juvenile and Criminal Justice reported that in 1994–95, California will spend as much on corrections as on the University of California and California State University systems. The amount is $3.8 billion, according to the private research group. At the same time, the California Postsecondary Education Commission reported that state support for corrections had increased by 172 percent over the last decade, while funds for higher education had grown by only 38 percent. The two California research organizations warned that public higher education is likely to suffer as the state scrambles to pay for a new and tougher crime bill ("Ways and Means," 1994). Surely any educator must be compelled to ask from the standpoint of self-interest, let alone social interest, whether it is not essential that education intervene in ways that will help change the direction of those trend lines. Obviously, the same thing could be asked about health costs and other expensive community problems.

To Facilitate Discussion

Developments like these may have been in the mind of Sheldon Hackney, chairman of the National Endowment for the Humanities, when he said that Americans needed to discuss serious questions affecting national life. He spoke of NEH's special initiative to promote "The National Conversation" and the positive response of people who were ready to talk:

Something is going on here. It is, I believe, that a critically important topic is being opened up. People's fascination with it is fueled by communal strife around the world and by racial and ethnic friction from South Central Los Angeles to Bensonhurst, from Libertyville to the World Trade Center Tower.

We hope to build creative partnerships throughout the country with churches, community centers, libraries, community colleges, museums, unions, and other organizations that serve segments of the population that are sometimes overlooked. These partnerships can help to stimulate and facilitate the discussion among citizens from all walks of life (Hackney, 1994, p. A56).

Hackney's call must have a familiar ring to those who work in the community college field for, as I have sought to report, "creative partnerships" and "citizen discussion" have become characteristic of their institutions. These are strengths whose value becomes increasingly evident. The chapters that follow attest to that.

REFERENCES

American Association of Community and Junior Colleges. "Annual report." *Community and Junior College Journal*, 1980, 50(5), 43.

American Association of Community and Junior Colleges. "Annual report." *Community and Junior College Journal*, 1981, 51(5), 17.

Breneman, D.W. and Nelson, S.C. Unpublished manuscript. (For elaboration see the authors' book, *Financing community colleges*.) Washington, DC: The Brookings Institution, 1981.

Fischer, O.R., Jr. and Gollattscheck, J.F. "Valencia Community College as an educational cooperative." *Community and Junior College Journal*, 1974, 45(3), 12–15.

Gilder, J. (Ed.). *Policies for lifelong education: Report of the 1979 assembly*. Washington, DC: American Association of Community Colleges, 1979.

Gleazer, E.J., Jr. "Community colleges—Catalyst for community development." Unpublished manuscript. Chicago: University Adult Education, University of Chicago, 1967.

Gleazer, E.J., Jr. "A time of change." *Junior College Journal*, 1970, 40(7), 3–5.

Gleazer, E.J., Jr. *Project Focus: A forecast study of community colleges*. New York: McGraw-Hill Book Company, 1973.

Gleazer, E.J., Jr. "After the boom…What now for the community colleges?" *Community and Junior College Journal*, 1974, 44(4), 6–11.

Gleazer, E.J., Jr. "AACJC approach—A significant linkage." *Community and Junior College Journal*, 1975, 45(5), 2.

Gleazer, E.J., Jr. *Values, vision, and vitality*. Washington, DC: American Association of Community and Junior Colleges, 1980.

Gleazer, E.J., Jr. and Yarrington, R. "Why community colleges should be the institutional base for community forums." 1977 Assembly Papers. Washington, DC: American Association of Community and Junior Colleges, 1977.

Hackney, S. "Organizing a national conversation." *The Chronicle of Higher Education*, April 20, 1994, A56.

Harbison, F. *Education sector planning for development of nation-wide learning systems*. (OOLC Paper No. 2) Washington, DC: American Council on Education, 1973.

Harvard University Office of News and Public Affairs. *Alumni Gazette*, Winter/Spring, 1994. Cambridge, MA: Harvard University Office of News and Public Affairs.

League for Innovation in the Community College. *Catalysts for community college change—Guidelines for community colleges to conduct community forums*. Mission Viejo, CA: League for Innovation in the Community College, July 1993.

Mahoney, J.R. *Community education work councils: The AACJC project, second year*. Summary and analysis. Washington, DC: American Association of Community Colleges, 1979.

National Advisory Commission on Civil Disorders. Report. (DHHS Publication No. 0-291-729) Washington, DC: U.S. Government Printing Office, March 1, 1968.

Pifer, A. "Community college and community leadership." *Community and Junior College Journal*, 1974, 44(8), 23–25.

"Ways and means." *The Chronicle of Higher Education*, May 11, 1994, A25.

Yarrington, R. "Assessing the community base." *Community and Junior College Journal*, 1975, 46(3), 9–11.

CHAPTER I

Take me to your leader.

–Anon

Lynn Sullivan Taber
Community College Leadership Program
The University of Texas at Austin
Austin, Texas

CHAPTER AND VERSE:

How We Came to Be Where We Are

Community is our middle name.

—President Bob McCabe,
Miami-Dade Community College

THE CHANGING FOCUS OF COMMUNITY COLLEGES

Never has the community college been more on center stage. And never in the history of the community college has there been the excitement we are seeing now as colleges partner with their communities to create productive linkages. Community college partnerships and collaborative efforts are expanding successfully into broad enterprises—with business and industry, other segments of the educational system, community-based organizations, and local and foreign governments—including nations such as Bangladesh, Japan, Nicaragua, Russia, and Thailand. Many colleges are also linking with the information highway via other kinds of partnerships. As a result, programs and services are provided to populations in formerly hard-to-reach places, and communities access worldwide information linkages.

It is increasingly apparent that community colleges are not only serving their communities in traditional ways such as providing continuing education or community services but also in pioneering ways. Many are participating in long-term partnerships with other community stakeholders, both public and private, to solve community problems. Others are taking an active role in their region's economic development.

Although a growing number of community colleges report informally that their partnerships and collaboration with their communities have been on the rise, there is not yet an inventory of such efforts. There is not a consistent vocabulary to use, a consensus about what this expanded involvement with the community means, or any way to clearly describe the community college's role. Nor is there a consensus among community college educators as to whether these partnerships and collaborative efforts are consistent with the community college mission, in spite of the recommendations of the American Association of Community and Junior Colleges' (AACJC) Commission on the Future report, *Building Communities* (1988), which has received national attention.

We recall that most American junior colleges have changed their names since the 1970s, adding the word *community* to emphasize mission focus, long before the publication of *Building Communities*. Today, virtually every one of those communities faces daunting challenges. In addition to the growing complexity of societal problems, resources have become scarce, and the escalating rate of change can be overwhelming. But, as Dr. Gleazer notes in the Foreword of this book, community colleges are well-positioned to become their community's most valuable resource in the processes required to solve these complex problems.

As we considered this apparent shift of focus, we reflected on the best way to probe its dimensions. There is room to explore; the questions are many. For example, what is the nature of these partnerships or collaborations? Are they different from the traditional continuing education or community education activities? Why do colleges involve themselves in these ways? What are their expectations? What results are realized? What are the costs? Who in the institution is responsible for these partnerships? What observations are made by community colleges regarding their participation in future partnerships? Are community colleges identifying particular roles to play—that is, should the college be a convener, catalyst, connector, collaborator, or play some other role?

These are the types of questions we sought to answer by writing this book. In our search for answers, we asked 14 community college CEOs, whose colleges were located in different kinds of communities and who were known to be actively partnering with those communities, to share their experiences. We also thought that the perspective of those providing leadership to a statewide effort (workforce training development, in this case) in which community colleges were partners would be of interest. Finally, we believed that the results of the Beacon Project on building communities would further enlighten us. After reviewing the reported partnership and collaboration activities, we now have the sense that what community colleges are doing today *is* different, worth exploring, and, indeed, part of a major transformation in the societal role of the community college. We think the reader will arrive at the same conclusion. Before revealing the variety of activities reported by these colleges, it is helpful to create a context. We do this by reviewing the platform of history upon which the work of today's community colleges rests. For as we shall see, since the time of the early junior colleges, this segment of the educational system has been evolving toward its emerging role as community convener, catalyst, connector, and collaborator.

The Mission of the Community College. Responsiveness and service to the community are central to the community college mission. Originally founded to provide the beginning two years of a university (or transfer) education, the nation's first junior colleges were private and formed in the period between 1835 and 1900. Public two-year colleges began to emerge around the turn of the century. Most agree that William Rainey Harper coined the term "junior college" and that he helped found Illinois's Joliet Junior College (in 1902), the oldest publicly supported two-year college in America. Frye's penetrating analysis, *The Vision of the Public Junior College, 1900–1940*, provides a candid view of the evolution of the modern community college, then called the junior college. He notes that early growth of junior colleges—between 1870 and 1920—occurred in areas growing in population by internal migration. "This internal migration of opportunity-seeking traditional European peoples appears to have created local small-town demands for access to higher education" (Frye, 1992, p. 11). These pioneering citizens especially valued freedom and upward mobility, both part of the appeal of public higher education.

The Commitment to Community. During this early period, leaders articulated a commitment to civic education. In 1915, Alexis Lange, a University of California advocate for junior colleges, argued that the curriculum in every junior college should be dominated by "civic education." This would be "training for the vocation of citizenship," creating "the will to participate vigorously, militantly…in advancing community welfare" (Lange, 1915, pp. 442–448). These early colleges were often governed by local boards of education and administrators whose vision had ramifications for junior college curricula. For example, in *Cardinal Principles of Secondary Education*, a 1918 publication of the United States Bureau of Education, leaders expressed their collective objectives: health, command of fundamental processes, worthy home-membership, vocation, civic education, healthy use of leisure, and ethical character. This early emphasis on civic education and responsiveness to community values was to be a theme continued through the years ahead. The expression of this emphasis became apparent in the more common use of the word *community*. Palinchak (1973) noted that the phrase *community education* began to be seen in a limited way as early as 1926, when the Pasadena California Board of Education described "fitting the commercial course of the high school and junior college to the needs of its *community*." Byron S. Hollinshead wrote about "The *Community* College Program" in 1936, and in 1939, Hayden authored "The Junior College as a *Community* Institution." However, as Palinchak notes, the phrase "community college" did not come into common use until the late 1950s and early 1960s.

Industrial America. Between 1900 and 1940, America was becoming industrialized. Occupations, and as a result, the country's social structure, changed dramatically. "Status competition was a familiar element in American society and [with] the changes occurring with industrialization...this status competition gave rise to demands for education as a form of occupational certification" (Frye, 1992, p. 16). Junior colleges were uniquely qualified to meet this social mobility objective. As a result, occupational or semiprofessional/professional training programs were added to the transfer programs already in place. This was especially true between 1920 and 1945.

The Junior College. The nation's public school systems originally governed most junior colleges. However, the emergence of the junior college as a segment of higher education with a unique mission required a collective professional voice. And so, the American Association of Junior Colleges (AAJC) was founded in 1920 and defined the junior college role to be the provision of the first two years of the baccalaureate sequence. The college was to be an institution offering two years of instruction of "strictly collegiate grade." However, in 1925, AAJC amended its official definition of the junior college to include:

> The junior college may, and is likely to, develop a different type of curriculum suited to the larger and ever-changing civic, social, religious and vocational needs of the entire community in which the college is located (Bogue, 1950, p. *xvii*).

This is a broader conceptualization of the former, more narrowly defined purview of the college. Myran described this evolution:

> By the 1930s the junior college had already established some of the basic building blocks of the community based college. It had inherited the utilitarian leanings of the land-grant university, and it was often controlled by a local board or advisory committee. It was becoming a positive force in the communities it served, and those people who led or taught were creating the 'open door' concept. The valuing of all students, regardless of background, and the nurturing of those who attended was to become a cornerstone of the community based college (Myran, 1978, p. 3).

Post–World War II. At this point in their development, the colleges began to recognize the appropriateness of fulfilling an emerging adult-oriented continuing education need. Technological and societal changes motivated communities to ensure widespread access to education and training through expansion of community or technical college offerings. This was especially true when, at the end of World War II, the GI Bill propelled thousands of young people into higher education, and in particular, into the community college. In 1947, the President's Commission on Higher Education recommended the development of a *community college* which would "become a center for learning for the entire community, with or without the restrictions that surround formal course work in traditional institutions of higher education. It gears its programs and services to the needs and wishes of the people it serves..." (Vol. I, p. 69). The commission also called for public education to be made widely available to all Americans regardless of their race, sex, creed, color, or economic status.

The first book featuring the term *community college* in its title was written by Jesse Bogue in 1950. In it, Bogue, then Executive Secretary of the American Association of Junior Colleges, described the mission of the community college as service primarily to the people of the community. Then, during the sixties and seventies, "problems related to race, poverty, urbanization, and rapidly changing employment patterns mandated a broadening of the college mission to provide a more comprehensive base for the development of human resources in the community" (Myran, 1978, p. 3). In 1978, Harrison Williams, then Chairman of the Senate's Human Resources Committee, sponsored the "Community Schools and Comprehensive Community Act of 1978" (Gleazer, 1978). This proposed legislation was typical in the mid- and late seventies, when there was a revival of exhortations for community colleges to practice what was then called community-based education. As Myran wrote:

> Community-based education is a phrase that symbolizes an institutional value system; it is not a series of courses, an approach to instruction, or a description of the location of services or activities. It is a phrase that can be grouped with terms such as lifelong learning, life-centered education, the knowledge revolution, the communications age, the postindustrial society, and the learning society (Myran, 1978, p. 1).

As a reflection of growing community emphasis, AAJC changed its name to the American Association of Community and Junior Colleges (AACJC) in 1972. No longer primarily a baccalaureate or occupationally-focused institution, by the seventies "the various [community college] curricular functions noted in each state's legislation usually include[d] academic transfer preparation, vocational-technical education, continuing education, remedial education, and community service" (Cohen and Brawer, 1982, p. 15). In 1992, the next organizational transition resulted in the taking of a third name—the American Association of Community Colleges (AACC). The community college was no longer to be junior to the universities; it had developed a separate identity—one with the community that it served precisely at its center.

COMMUNITY EXPECTATIONS

All community colleges offer programs in the five legislated curricular areas; however, the emphasis a particular program receives may vary. The menu of programs and services differs based not only on the vision of the college's leaders, but also on community needs and priorities. Not surprisingly, the more responsive to the community the college becomes, the greater, too, are the expectations. Ravitch noted (a bit tongue-in-cheek) that the role of the community college was to:

preserve democracy, eliminate poverty, lower the crime rate, enrich the common culture, reduce unemployment, ease the assimilation of immigrants to the nation, overcome differences between ethnic groups, advance scientific and technological progress, prevent traffic accidents, raise health standards, refine moral character, and guide young people into useful occupations (Ravitch, 1983, p. xii).

Between its commitment to open access and its responsiveness to the community, the community college had become known as the people's college.

Mission Issues. As this relationship with the community matured and deepened, dialogue and disagreement about the community college mission became more apparent in the professional literature. Opinions polarized. Community college leaders such as Bender, Brawer, Cohen, Eaton, and Richardson have all expressed the view that the transfer curriculum, not community education, should remain the college's central mission. Cohen, Birnbaum, Pfnister, and Geiger observed that remedial courses and community education "are detrimental to the perception of the college as a provider of grades 13 and 14" (Cohen, Birnbaum, Pfnister, and Geiger, 1985, p. 13). Richardson and Bender exhibited concern that the community college's:

> need to provide social services…with the need to prepare their clientele for immediate employment, leaves [them] with little energy and few resources to offer challenging transfer programs to those who enrolled with the ultimate intent of earning a baccalaureate degree (Richardson and Bender, 1987, p. 3).

Commenting on what they saw as the fractured mission of the community college, Cohen et al. observed that, given the structure of the community college and the administrator-dominated governance system, "there were no vociferous alumni who would object to an expanded mission for their alma mater, no entrenched faculty sufficiently powerful to deflect the drive for new students and new missions" (Cohen, Birnbaum, Pfnister, and Geiger, 1985, p. 3). As a result, some believe that the transfer curriculum—seen as the colleges' link to legitimacy—has been watered down and weakened. Cohen and Brawer add that "if the colleges are only to provide access, a stepping stone to a job or some other school, along with the illusory benefits of credits and degrees, then their status as schools is marginal" (Cohen and Brawer, 1982, p. 304). Eaton articulates her fear that "if [community colleges] do not plan now for major changes, they run the risk of gradually metamorphosing unintentionally—into something other than colleges, perhaps into experimental education centers or community and educational service centers" (Eaton, 1992, p. 5). In fact, this eventuality would support the belief of some—that the community college "has no reason for existence other than to serve its students and the business community" (Cohen and Brawer, 1982, p. 306). However, they argue that if the community college wants to maintain its position in higher education, it must return to a focus on the collegiate function. Cohen believes that "institutional legitimacy is compromised to the extent that colleges tend away from their basic educational functions...Notwithstanding all the calls for new missions, the colleges must be instructional enterprises" (Cohen, 1980, p. 42).

THE CASE FOR COMMITMENT

For every voice arguing against it, there is another advocating the responsibility community colleges have to be active community partners and to help solve community problems. After early calls for a focus on community in the 1920s, followed by second and third iterations in the 1950s and again in the 1970s, the late 1980s saw yet another wave of support for the community colleges' role as active community partners. Spokesperson Edmund Gleazer, Jr., president emeritus of the AACC, notes that "the community institution goes to the people who live and work where it is located, makes a careful study of the needs of these people for education not being offered by any other institution of learning, analyzes these needs, and builds its educational program in response" (Gleazer, 1992, p. 5). He observes that community colleges' formal and informal ties to the K–12 system and to the universities provide valuable access points. "Through its vertical connections in the education hierarchy and its horizontal relationships with other community agencies, the community college can literally be 'the middle man'" (Gleazer, 1984, p. 11). Gleazer contends that the emphasis of the community college should be community. With the perspective of one who has spent a lifetime providing leadership to America's community colleges, Gleazer asserts that "the mission of the community college today is to encourage and facilitate lifelong learning with community as process and product" (Gleazer, 1991, p. 11).

Others agree. When 19 distinguished Americans were appointed by the AACJC in 1988 to develop recommendations for the future of the community college, this was their conclusion:

The goal is not just outreach. Perhaps more than any other institution, the community college also can inspire partnerships based upon shared values and common goals. The building of community, in its broadest and best sense, encompasses a concern for the whole, for integration and collaboration, for openness and integrity, for inclusiveness and self-renewal (Commission on the Future, 1988, p. 7).

AACJC's policy statement on Community Services and Continuing Education reflects the Association's commitment to this orientation:

The major components of community services and continuing education are civic literacy, work force training and retraining, cultural enrichment, and community resource development...Implementation is achieved through experimentation and broad community collaboration involving constituencies both within and external to the institution (AACJC, 1989).

In support of this policy statement, the AACJC 1989 Public Policy Agenda, Goal 4 asserted that "community colleges can play a pivotal role in strengthening community

life" and pledged to help community colleges carry out that role (AACJC Board of
Directors, 1989, p. 1). AACJC offered to:

- help national and state governments recognize the powerful role community colleges can play in economic development;
- encourage student and staff service to the community;
- work with colleges to improve relations among community groups with varying interests and backgrounds; and
- promote the role of the college as the convener of community leaders and as a forum for discussion and mediation between diverse community groups.

Other leaders recognize the importance of including community colleges as partners in community problem solving. In May 1993, for example, the Colorado State
Board passed a resolution "encouraging the employees of the Colorado Community
College and Occupational Education System to become actively involved in discussions and policy-making in their local public schools as a means to strengthen the
State's overall education system" (Colorado State Board, 1993, p. 10).

Outlining the reasons why the Corporation for National and Community Service
wants community colleges to participate heavily in efforts to build community through
service, an official stated:

> You [community colleges] are setting a first-rate example of what it means to be
> an educational institution inspired by civic purpose. You are showing us how
> the mission, welfare, and fate of the college and community are integrated and
> unitary (Liu, 1994, p. 12).

This is not only a public sector perception. Foundations looking for entities which can
successfully collaborate with others to lead reform efforts, turn increasingly to the community college. The Hitachi Foundation recently sponsored a series of community forum
projects with the objective of increasing communities' capacity for problem-solving. Julie
Banzhaf, Director of Programs for the Hitachi Foundation, made this observation:

> We look for projects that represent integrative approaches to community problem
> solving and develop models for innovation transfer to other communities. Community colleges...are emerging as the nexus for the resolution of both local and
> national concerns. Why?...Community colleges reflect this country's democratic
> idealism and its commitment to universal access and equality of educational and
> economic opportunity. Not only are they highly accessible to the entire citizenry,
> but they represent the greatest diversity in higher education and have a long history of involvement in traditional forms of citizen education...community colleges
> play a leading role in their communities and regions. Serving as a frequent hub for
> local networks dealing with community problems, they are accustomed to working collaboratively with all types of community groups (Banzhaf, 1993, p. v).

In another example, the Ford Foundation, in supporting 17 American cities engaged
in education reform efforts (through the Urban Partnership Project), includes community colleges as members of nearly every team. Several cities' teams are convened

and/or coordinated by the local community college. The Ford Foundation plans long-term commitment to the most successful of these efforts in the form of substantial financial support. This involvement signals the foundation's confidence in community colleges as central members of the community and as organizations with significant contributions to make. Others agree. Nancy Armes LeCroy described it this way:

> As neutral territory with an established value base that honors different perspectives, community colleges are understood to be islands of refuge which promote community renewal above any particular special interest agenda. They are in close proximity to neighborhood problems and are within commuting distance of ninety-five percent of the nation's population. They are accustomed to working jointly with all manner of community groups—seeking in all of these relationships to provide an open and rational review of options. They are action oriented, constantly looking toward workable and fair outcomes. They are innovative, welcoming the discussion of true and fresh ideas and encouraging their implementation whenever possible (LeCroy, 1993, p. 6).

Community Colleges: Positioned to Serve. Responsive community colleges listen closely to their communities. As a result, they are aware of the communities' critical needs. Local business and industry representatives complain that workers are not adequately skilled. Community college personnel see their potential students experiencing difficulties while in the K–12 system. They read the same newspaper headlines that the community's citizens read every day; they confront problems the community faces. It makes sense that the local community college would want to help.

Beyond wanting to help, there are several reasons why community colleges are well-prepared to serve in this role. First, they are associated with education and learning—two important processes associated with successful community problem-solving. Next, they can build on community relationships developed over the years. Finally, in most cases, community colleges are tax-supported and should logically be expected to dedicate resources toward addressing community issues. Boone (1992) cites the following additional evidence that the community college is well-positioned to assume the role of leader and catalyst in bringing groups together:

- The college's mission, funding base and record of achievements "deeply imbed it in the fabric of the community" (Boone, 1992, p. 9).
- The college's multidisciplinary nature makes it more useful to addressing community problems than most community-based organizations, which are narrow in scope.
- The college is perceived positively by its community.
- The college understands the social, economic, and political environment surrounding the community.

Communities are increasingly comfortable with, and dependent on, the college's participation and supportive role. Community colleges have been building successful collaborations for workforce training for decades, as Cleveland Mayor Michael White noted in his address to the 1994 Leadership 2000 conference (Jackman, 1994). Company Town Shutdown (Turnage, 1994) describes the pivotal role Virginia Highlands Community College played in revitalizing Saltville, Virginia, after its largest and primary employer shut down in 1971. Theobald believes that community colleges are already in the forefront of providing lifelong learning opportunities, workforce training, and utilizing technology effectively. They "could play a more dramatic role," he writes, "if they saw themselves as leaders." He goes on to observe that community colleges are "natural conveners of the school systems in their areas" and that they "could play a major role in advancing discussion of [social] policies." He concludes, stating, "I believe that the community college should see itself as the heart and brain of its community" (Theobald, 1994, p. 21). At the 1994 AACC Convention, Secretary of Education Richard Riley commented: "I believe that the community college system of America is one of the great unknown strengths of our democracy...What [they] do matters a great deal to the life of this country" (Hendley, 1994, p. 35).

Role Issues. Colleges committed to participating in community enhancement or problem-solving efforts are considering what form this community assistance should take, as well as the extent to which the college's resources should be allocated to this purpose. Even if they are philosophically committed, not all community colleges feel they can dedicate substantial assets to underwriting extensive community problem-solving collaborations. Today's scarce resources have forced many community colleges to consider eliminating some programs and/or services, so the inclination to minimize support to these linkages should not be surprising. However, if a community college elected to minimize its prior commitment to community collaboration, the support which comes from outside organizations or agencies as a result of this community collaboration might be reduced. The college would risk being seen as an undependable partner, whose interest in the community wanes when the going gets tough—community expectations may be such that the community college cannot decline to collaborate with the community without losing significant support. Further, many grant agencies are now looking for evidence of substantial collaboration as a requirement for success in the funding sweepstakes. This sends a message that collaborative efforts will be actively supported and encouraged. Finally, scarce resources may in fact make engaging in many partnerships desirable, allowing colleges to extend their reach.

PRESENT COMMUNITY COLLEGE ROLES

In the profession, there has been discussion about whether participation in or leadership of community collaboration fits within the community college's mission. We note that, traditionally, community colleges have been flexible in adapting their services to better meet their communities' needs. Some colleges are more integrated into the everyday life of their communities than others. In general, community college programs and services tend to reflect the needs and characteristics of the community that they serve.

The extent to which a particular community college offers these programs or services is dependent upon a number of things, including its community's needs, the resources and talent available, and the vision of the college's leaders. It is true that all community colleges currently collaborate with their communities in some form, but the nature of the partnerships formed to provide programs and services varies mightily, as the reader will see.

WHAT'S AHEAD?

In this book, readers will find detailed descriptions of some of the most forward-looking initiatives in the community college universe. We hope that readers will uncover meaningful concepts, ideas, and possibilities. The colleges included here were selected because they have given the issue of community partnerships significant reflection and, subsequently, great commitment. The authors know that this small sample barely scratches the surface. We regret being unable to include the many other institutions that excel in community partnering.

We asked our sample colleges to share examples of the work they are doing with their communities and to comment on the nature and extent of the results of these associations. As the reader will discover, the variety of associations reported is noteworthy, as is the creativity the colleges bring to new combinations of organizations and resources. Each college handled their chapter-writing task differently. Some approached the topic broadly, giving examples of many types of partnerships. Others focused on a particular area—Sinclair Community College, for example, explained how they capitalized on their expertise in technology to organize resources and relationships for community support and enhancement.

The following chapters showcase the stories of many successful collaboration efforts. Some have been functioning for several years—others are still in the formative stages. Each is unique, tailored to meet the needs of the particular community. In most cases a collegewide vision undergirds the college's partnership promise. Supported by committed boards and eager community leaders, the colleges have expanded their capacity and productivity in ways not initially foreseen, acting as force multipliers. Here we explore the experiences of a few, which we believe will provide inspiration to many.

REFERENCES

American Association of Community and Junior Colleges, Board of Directors. *AACJC 1989 public policy agenda*. Unpublished report. Washington, DC: American Association of Community and Junior Colleges, 1989.

Banzhaf, J. "Preface." *Catalysts for community change: Guidelines for community colleges to conduct community forums*. Mission Viejo, CA: League for Innovation in the Community College, 1993.

Bogue, J.P. *The community college*. NY: McGraw-Hill, 1950.

Boone, E.J. "Community-based programming: An opportunity and imperative for the community college." *Community College Review*, 1992, 20(3), 8–19.

Cohen, A.M. "Dateline '79 revisited." In Vaughan, G.B. (Ed.), *New directions for community colleges: Questioning the community college role*, 8(4), 33–42. San Francisco, CA: Jossey-Bass, 1980.

Cohen, A.M., Birnbaum, R., Pfnister, A.O., and Geiger, R.L. *Contexts for learning: The major sectors of American higher education*. Washington, DC: The National Institute of Education, 1985.

Cohen, A.M. and Brawer, F.B. *The American community college*. San Francisco, CA: Jossey-Bass, 1982.

"Colorado state board encourages involvement with K–12 schools." *Advisor*, 1993, 23(4), 10.

Commission on the Future of Community Colleges. *Building communities: A vision for a new century*. Washington, DC: American Association of Community and Junior Colleges, 1988.

Eaton, J. "The coming transformation of community colleges." *Planning for Higher Education*, 1992, 21, 1–7.

Frye, J.H. *The vision of the public junior college, 1900–1940: Professional goals and popular aspirations*. New York, NY: Greenwood Press, 1992.

Gleazer, E.J., Jr. "Partnerships for learning." Speech to the National Conference on the Role of Community Colleges in the National Technology Transfer Program, University of Michigan, Ann Arbor, MI, May 22, 1978.

Gleazer, E.J., Jr. *The community college: Values, vision & vitality*. (3rd Printing). Washington, DC: American Association of Community and Junior Colleges, 1984.

Gleazer, E.J., Jr. "To improve the human condition." Paper presented at the Eighth Annual Tri-C Symposium, Cuyahoga Community College, Cleveland, OH, March 1991.

Gleazer, E.J., Jr. "Evolution of junior colleges into community colleges." Manuscript submitted for publication, 1992.

Hayden, S. "The junior college as a community institution." *Junior College Journal*, October, 1939, 10, 70–73.

Hendley, V. "Community college leaders meet federal education leaders in Washington." *Community College Journal*, 1994, 64(6), 35.

Hollinshead, B.S. "The community college program." *Junior College Journal*, 1936, 7, 111–116.

Jackman, M. "Cleveland's rebirth." *Community College Times*, 1994, 6(16), 8.

Lange, A. "A junior college department of civic education." *School and Society*, September 25, 1915, 2, 442–448.

LeCroy, N.A. "Building on natural strengths: The role of the community college in community development." In *Catalysts for community change: Guidelines for community colleges to conduct community forums*. Mission Viejo, CA: League for Innovation in the Community College, 1993, 1–6.

Liu, G. "Community colleges: Critical partners in national and community service." *Trustee Quarterly*, Spring 1994, 10–12.

Myran, G.A. "Antecedents: Evolution of the community-based college." In Harlacher, E.L. and Gollatscheck, J.F. (Eds.) *New Directions for Community Colleges: Implementing Community Based Education*, 1978, 6(1), 1–6. San Francisco, CA: Jossey-Bass.

Palinchak, R. *The evolution of the community college.* Metuchen, NJ: The Scarecrow Press, 1973.

President's Commission on Higher Education. *Higher education for American democracy, A report.* Vol. I. Washington, DC: Government Printing Office, 1947.

Ravitch, D. *The troubled crusade: American education, 1945–1980.* New York: Basic Books, 1983.

Richardson, R.C. and Bender, L. *Minority access and achievement in higher education.* San Francisco, CA: Jossey-Bass, 1987.

Theobald, R. "Changing success criteria for the 21st century: What can community colleges do?" *Community College Journal*, 1994, 65(1), 16–21.

Turnage, M.A. *Company town shutdown.* Annapolis, MD: Berwick Publishing, 1994.

United States Bureau of Education. *Cardinal principles of secondary education* (Bulletin No. 35). Department of the Interior. Washington, DC: Government Publishing Authority, 1918, 22.

CHAPTER II

In Chapter Two, Richard Gilliland, President of Metropolitan Community College in Nebraska, outlines the value of partnerships to the community college and the important issues that must be confronted. These include learning when to say no, which is especially critical in the face of increasing numbers of requests for external commitments. He points to the worth of nurturing internal partnerships and encouraging employees to use them to think and act creatively. Metropolitan's Experimental College—a think tank activity—draws on a cross-section of faculty and staff to explore ways to enhance the college's curriculum and instructional approaches. It pioneered the use of the Scandinavian Study Circle and explored possible applications of the Danish Folkhighschool movement methodologies to the college's instructional programs.

*Another innovative activity at Metropolitan is their partnership with sister institution Nebraska Indian Community College (NICC). NICC serves Santee Sioux Native American people, whose culture is significantly different than the predominately Euro-American culture at Metropolitan Community College. Joint projects include annual staff development activities, curriculum development, and cultural celebrations. Both institutions are committed to a long-term partnership. The reader will appreciate the special perspective represented in the chapter which follows—*Community Colleges and Collaboration.

* * *

J. Richard Gilliland

President
Metropolitan Community College
Omaha, Nebraska

COMMUNITY COLLEGE AND COLLABORATION

This country will not be a good place for any of us to live in unless we make it a good place for all of us to live in.

—Theodore Roosevelt

FROM DEPENDENCE TO INTERDEPENDENCE

Opportunities for collaboration by community, technical, and junior colleges have existed for years. Our institutions have long been known for their cooperative arrangements. A 1978 national survey, conducted by what was then AACJC, American Association of Community and Junior Colleges, indicated that among the 173 colleges responding to a survey there were more than 10,000 cooperative arrangements serving more than 1.5 million people. Each institution indicated an average of 59 cooperative arrangements serving 8,781 persons at each campus. Gilder and Rocha indicated: "Cooperative arrangements, it is clear, have enabled local community colleges to dramatically extend and broaden learning opportunities and services by sharing resources" (1980, p. 11). The authors stated that a typical college is a meaningful resource to other community providers and that the mission emerging at that time was seen as the nexus for a learning condition that appeared to be solidly established by activities and services.

Indeed, being the people's college has long implied that our institutions are community-based. We network and collaborate with a wide range of public and private organizations in our service areas. Over the years that networking has expanded to regional, national, and international scope. Opportunities for institutional collaborations that exist today go well beyond the relationships of our early years. Even in the early years, however, community colleges clamored for opportunities to collaborate and to build partnerships in their communities. Although good numbers of such arrangements ultimately resulted, those partnerships were almost always initiated by the community college. Today, that has changed.

Much more common today is that individuals, companies, service organizations, other educational institutions, and community organizations across the nation are soliciting community college involvement. We moved from an initial dependent condition through the establishment of our independence. Finally, we have begun to develop balanced, interdependent alliances wherein all the partners gain from each other's special strengths and talents. This creates a curious and, in many cases, new experience for community college decision makers. Having come from a background of trying to be all things to all people, we are now beginning the process of learning how to sift through the many opportunities and offers that are available to us.

Saying "no" to a potential partner is difficult, if not impossible; it certainly is a new experience for long-term community college leaders. It raises many important questions about when our institutions should say "yes" and when should they say "no." Ernst (1991) indicates that some of the questions we now must ask include: When do we overextend ourselves by offering programs and services that are not in concert with our basic mission? When do we indicate that we will not be involved in activities that are more appropriately provided by other agencies? How far can we extend increasingly limited resources to new partnerships? When should a community college simply say "no"?

There are conflicting philosophical positions regarding the proper role of community colleges. Some argue that they should focus on the academic transfer curriculum as their primary mission, with a secondary emphasis on career education, while others believe they should be community builders, appropriately having elaborate and extensive community partnerships. However, widespread attempts to do more for our communities with stable or declining resources when demands to be involved in partnerships are growing results in tough choices for decision makers. For a number of reasons, we no longer are in a position to accept all opportunities for linkages. Indeed, it is easy to withdraw from the initial commitment of many leaders in the past that suggested we should try to be all things to all people. Not only will continued acceptance of all opportunities water down our ability to place emphasis in specific areas, but it also stretches resources beyond their limits. There are many pitfalls in partnerships that must be considered concurrently with the exciting advantages.

WHY COLLABORATION?

Nielsen (1994) emphasizes that partnerships can be doors to the future for community colleges. When his institution, Kirkwood Community College, conducted an effectiveness study in 1990, they concluded that they needed to emphasize partnerships with public and private agencies. He makes a strong case for sharing resources among different partners, including money, expertise, personnel and facilities. Institutions, whether public or private, no longer have the information, the skills, the resources, or most of the other needed ingredients to independently function in the current era.

In this age of specialization, we need to team up with others who possess special talents, skills, or resources, while contributing our own set of capabilities and resources. When these ingredients are mixed in a carefully orchestrated and sensitive way, greater synergy can be accomplished than by any one organization operating independently. Among companies, institutions, and agencies in the United States, there is an increase in "teaming mentality." There seems to be an awakening of an understanding that everyone benefits when individuals and organizations come together in collaboration. In *The Seven Habits of Highly Effective People,* Covey (1989) describes the value of moving from initial dependence through independence and ultimately toward interdependence. Indeed, his work and that of a few others have focused on the many reasons that collaboration and interdependence are the way of the future.

Building partnerships calls for new skills if we are going to capitalize on the full range of potential opportunities. Perhaps we are talking about collaboration at a new, more complex and sophisticated level when compared with earlier arrangements our institutions have had. For example, it is common today to see collaborations on community college campuses with as many as six or eight different organizations that bring different resources to the equation of cooperation.

The identification of effective teaming skills is still being analyzed according to Kanter (1989), but it does appear that some of the most effective skills include the ability to gather information, understand how to resist preconceived notions and ideas, develop good listening skills, openly and honestly test assumptions, and achieve consensus. Traditional managers may find it difficult to adjust as their organizations move toward building alliances. When new strategic alliances are formed, not only must the new relationship between two or more partners be nurtured, but the expected changes within each of the partner organizations must be anticipated and addressed. Both require careful attention.

To fully realize the potential of partnerships, a number of vulnerabilities and challenges must be overcome. In some cases, partners collaborate with uneven levels of commitment. Obviously, this unevenness results in further uneven allocation of financial resources, time, and attention to detail. A problem many have experienced in community colleges relates to pairing with organizations whose resources are even more limited. If organizations are not careful, such relationships can fail because both enti-ties cannot contribute equally to the partnership. Self-respect in the relationship is damaged or lost when all parties do not feel they are sufficiently contributing to the relationship. Another potential problem relates to offering trust. Occasionally, one par-ty in an alliance will not readily extend trust before another partner enters into the same level of trust in the relationship.

Also related to trust is the problem of conflicting loyalties. Sometimes partners in a relationship have other partners with whom they are working, which creates a con-flict of interest for at least part of the partnership. While politics makes strange bed-fellows, partnerships ultimately have to transcend politics and enter into a true profes-sional and even personal trust relationship.

How Far Should the Community College Go as Partner?

The diverse options available to community colleges as partners in their communi-ties include functioning as convener, catalyst, connector, collaborator, change agent, conspirator, champion of the powerless, and even creator of controversy. We might then ask: What is our proper circle of influence and to what extent are we a causative factor in community change? The role for our institutions can range from being simply a physical space where different individuals and groups come together and combine energies to being an agent of social change. Referring to a democratic society characterized by interaction and sharing, Dewey indicated that one way of determining these relationships is to ask two questions: "How many and varied are the interests which are consciously shared? How full and free is the interplay with other forms of association?" (Dewey, 1916, p. 83).

As for the many issues relating to alliances and partnerships, each college must make up its own mind about its appropriate role in the community. Doubtless, with many different partnerships in existence, our institutions will engage in a variety of dif-ferent levels of intensity of partnerships ranging from passive to very active.

In *Building Communities: A Vision for a New Century* (Commission on the Future, 1988), the authors indicate that strengthening relationships beyond the community college—with schools, industry, business, social agencies and policy groups—is necessarily a key factor in the building of community. There are numerous opportunities for our institu-tions to be a forum or a catalyst for activities and programs. While this may appear to be a rather passive involvement for our community colleges, one needs only to look at the important need for safe and effective environments where community members can openly discuss and evaluate major problems and projects. For example, a number of institutions across the nation are serving as springboards for discussion and examina-tion of community problems. Communities are responding to the current national effort to improve the quality of elementary and secondary education supporting

GOALS 2000, the federal government's current response to school reform. Although this is not what might be considered a leadership role, it is an essential role—to bring together wide-ranging interests and opinions in a constructive environment with the ultimate goal of improving our elementary and secondary schools.

Related to the role of institution as public forum is the role of convener of resources. Most of our institutions are familiar with and are active in recruiting new businesses and industries to their communities. Community colleges play visible and often major roles in bringing together private business leaders, state government, chambers of commerce, and other key agencies in successful economic development projects.

A more active and assertive role is that of colleague and collaborator. In this role community colleges are full participants in the planning and implementation of projects, programs, and activities. Perhaps of all the different types of partnerships and alliances in which our institutions may become involved, this action-oriented role has the greatest potential for results. Of all types of community-based organizations, community colleges may be in the best position to bring about results.

Opinions vary on the extent to which community colleges should be partners, conveners, or leaders of community and social change. But, most community college leaders believe that no other organization in society is as well-positioned to deal with economic, social, cultural, and political issues as the community-based and locally focused community college. Such a role has risks—colleges that assume a leadership role, for example, may be accused of taking political or social engineering positions. A safer path is to avoid controversial positions. Such is the challenge of leadership.

For example, exploring the various meanings of Columbus Day, October 12, 1992, with other interested community partners could have been controversial and even problematic for a community college. However, in an attempt to turn something potentially quite negative into a constructive forum to improve community relationships and community partnerships, some institutions did take on this controversial subject (Gilliland, 1992).

Whatever the multiple roles decided on by each community college, there are remarkable and ever-increasing opportunities for alliances, partnerships, and collaborations. Institutions will enter the new century less than what they are capable of being if they do not pursue vigorously the incredible mosaic of opportunities that now exists for involvement while at the same time balancing what they do, where they commit resources, and what opportunities they must turn down.

TYPES OF COLLABORATIONS AND THEIR RESULTS

When we think of partnerships and collaborations, we usually think of other organizations working with us. An alternate approach would be to start with the idea of collaborating with ourselves. So often, especially at larger community colleges, multiple internal resources are unrecognized or insufficiently appreciated and used. Some of the very best teams are partnerships among our faculty and staff. We have multiple communities of interest and a wide range of capabilities within our community colleges.

Internal Partnerships. At Metropolitan Community College (MCC), we have become increasingly reliant on or own employees to provide the various aspects of personnel and staff development services. Interesting and effective teams have been created to provide services that are truly specific to our needs. Obviously, one of the advantages of this is that our own employees have immediate knowledge of our culture, in contrast to outside "experts" who may come in totally unaware of significant cultural qualities that will have a major impact on the success or failure of staff development programming.

Another example of working through the development of internal partnerships is the creation of a component of our college's governance system called the College Action Council (CAC). This group draws its membership from all college employment groups and diversifies its membership based on type of work, campus locations, gender, ethnicity, and other forms of diversity. The result is highly diversified governance teams that can share ideas and respond to issues from the broadest range of cultures and experience possible.

Experimental College. The Experimental College exists as a distinct unit within MCC. Consisting of a membership that is as diverse as the CAC, this multifaceted "think tank" draws talents, experiences, and background from every corner of the institution. The think tank group meets on a regular basis and has resources to explore new ways in which we might enhance and develop our college's curriculum and instructional approaches.

In its one and one-half year's existence, the Experimental College field-tested electronic mail, which was followed by full institutional implementation of this communication capability. It also pioneered the use of the Scandinavian Study Circle; now discussion groups use study circle techniques, which have become an added instructional methodology at the college. For example, instruction can be provided via the distance learning system to multiple college locations using a study circle approach. The study circle method is now being used in both credit and non-credit courses.

Other projects of the Experimental College "think tank" have been the college multi-media development centers; exploration of the Danish Folkhighschool movement and its applicability to Metropolitan Community College's instructional methodologies; the development of a multi-media presentation for use as a demonstration to faculty and staff to advance the use of multi-media in the classroom; and discussions such as those with Swedish distance learning practitioners and partners. In fall 1994, a political science class will be taught simultaneously through television to students at a Swedish Folkhighschool and students at MCC.

A current focus of the Experimental College is finding a nontraditional mechanism to enhance high quality and efficient communication among all staff, faculty and students in a multi-campus environment that is characterized by rapid enrollment growth. This will be a major project, but the nontraditional approaches characteristic of the Experimental College result in innovative recommendations.

College Foundation. Internal partnerships at Metropolitan Community College include the college foundation. Our college foundation has served to raise substantial amounts of money for student scholarships and other student needs, and has created valuable connections with community leaders and organizations through the appointment and energetic activity of foundation board members.

How do you partner with yourself? An organization cannot expect to successfully partner with others if the talents, experiences, and capabilities of its own diverse faculty and staff are not synergetic. Countless opportunities for teamwork and collaboration frequently go unrecognized or unappreciated within community colleges.

Alliances with Government and Community Organizations. *Omaha City Libraries.* Joint community projects have become an effective, worthwhile activity through which MCC has built vital alliances within its community. During 1993 and 1994, MCC held wide-ranging discussions with the City of Omaha Libraries to consider ways in which our institution can join forces with the libraries to provide major educational services through all of the larger branch libraries. The library system is short of funds, and MCC is pressed for instructional space. Together we are beginning to explore the possibilities of joining our two organizations so that we can provide those services that we are most capable of providing in cost-effective ways within the branch library settings. Both organizations will save money while concentrating on their areas of greatest strength and ability.

In the 1970s, a similar project was attempted with considerable success in Oklahoma City, called OASES, or Open Access Satellite Education Services (Gilliland and Little, 1977). This project joined the Oklahoma County Library System and South Oklahoma City Junior College to provide a number of services in branch libraries in South Oklahoma City. The experimental project resulted in the expansion of partnership activities between the two organizations. Patrons living near the branch libraries indicated a willingness to enroll in credit and non-credit courses at a convenient, familiar neighborhood facility. Those same patrons were initially unwilling to travel a much greater distance to the main campus of the community college. In short, the OASES project served as a springboard for unserved and underserved populations to begin their community college experience in a convenient, friendly, accessible neighborhood library and then move on to the main campus of South Oklahoma City Junior College (now Oklahoma City Community College). Involved in the development and implementation of the OASES Project, this writer has carried this idea to Omaha, and the concept of library/community college partnerships is being explored on several fronts in the Greater Omaha community.

For example, an agreement has been reached to construct a joint facility with the suburban LaVista, Nebraska, library system where a wide range of library and community college services will be provided. The facility is now under development and is expected to open in 1998. One special feature of this joint facility will be the use of the "wired city" concept. Each home in the community of LaVista will have fiber optic linkages with the joint library/community college center. This will enable the library system and the college to provide many services directly to all of the homes in LaVista. The implications for providing both credit and non-credit Metropolitan Community College courses through this fiber optic system are exciting. Discussions are also underway with other library systems in the college's four-county service area to provide similar services. This instructional approach combines convenient, high quality teaching in a way that should prove to be less expensive than current traditional instructional delivery approaches. Baker (1988) reports on a library system in the state of Washington that has combined services with Lower Columbia College's library. The same philosophy of cooperation and partnership described in Oklahoma City and Omaha has proven successful there.

Economic Development. Community colleges across the country can point to a variety of successful government and community alliances as strong, mutually beneficial connections between the institutions and the community. As financial resources become more scarce and the values of partnerships become more pronounced, relationships with governmental bodies and community organizations could be an area of growth of partnerships for our institutions.

Many community colleges over the past decade have played critical roles on economic development teams. Community colleges have helped to expand the workforce in their communities by providing the training necessary for growth of existing businesses or the recruiting of new ones. Possibly the greatest benefits are the close working relationships that are established between a college and businesses and corporations of all types.

When a community college becomes indispensable to a chamber of commerce or to businesses in its community, many other factors fit into place. For example, it helps colleges when chamber members or other community leaders testify in support of revenue increases for their community college before state legislatures. Being involved in community-building projects at the request of community leaders, the mayor, or the chamber of commerce, leverages the position of the community college and provides the recognition colleges have worked for over the years. We become mainstreamed— essential organizations in our community in the eyes of major community leadership.

For example, a focused, important partnership has been created between MCC, the Nebraska State Department of Economic Development, the Greater Omaha Chamber of Commerce, and the City of Omaha in industrial recruitment projects. Each of the partners has brought resources and skills to the equation so that our city has been remarkably competitive in recruiting major national and international businesses. During the past six-year period, the city of Omaha's unemployment rate has been one of the lowest in the nation. A principal reason for this low rate has been the addition of more than 20,000 new jobs in more than 300 companies during that period. Many jobs were created by new businesses opening in the city. Moreover, the tax base now has been increased, and secondary businesses and ancillary support services, which prime the motor of economic growth and development in our community, have been created.

Omaha Job Clearinghouse. The Omaha Job Clearinghouse (OJC), initially proposed in a community economic development study, finds ways to target young people who are nearing graduation from high schools but are either in jeopardy of failing to graduate or have no plans for further education upon receiving their high school diploma. The philosophy of the OJC has been to help individuals enter a career track and become productive, taxpaying citizens and to provide much-needed workers for a growing industrial and commercial base of employment. Since the OJC was initiated in 1990, nearly 2,000 students in area high schools have gone through counseling, assessment, and job-shadowing experiences. This, in many cases, has given them a much clearer picture of the world of work and has led to entry-level jobs in companies throughout our community. On the other hand, many have learned that, to have a reasonable chance at a successful career, they will need to attain some form of postsecondary education. Businesses have rallied to support this OJC project by committing jobs as well as time with job-shadowing experiences. As a result, they have gained not only valuable employees but, because nearly half of the enrollees in the OJC are persons of color, employers have also gained valuable diversity in their workforces. Minority students are being provided economic opportunities previously not available to them. The partnership has combined strong efforts on the part of the Greater Omaha Chamber of Commerce, the Omaha Public Schools, and the United Way of the Midlands Chapter, along with Metropolitan Community College; more than 300 businesses have participated in this project to date.

Business Partnerships. *US West.* An example of close partnering with business involves MCC's 10-year alliance with US West. Spanning only five states when it began in 1984, the project now covers 14. It is a partnership with the Communication Workers of America, US West Business Resources Incorporated, and Metropolitan Community College—referred to as the Career Bridge Project. MCC counselors and project managers have worked with colleges and universities, trade schools, and proprietary institutions to assess abilities and interests of current US West craft employees. Then, based on the development of a detailed learning plan resulting from the individual assessment, employees are able to enroll in courses to prepare themselves for major changes in job requirements at US West or for other meaningful employment outside the company in the event that their positions are eliminated. (Like many other major corporations, US West has downsized its workforce during the past decade.) US West pays all tuition and fees for employees who successfully complete counseling activities and instructional programs. Management has agreed with Communication Workers of America union representatives that it is in the best interest of both management and union members that employees have the very best skills possible for current and projected jobs with US West. It is also important to provide useful skill training to the employees should they have to leave.

This alliance is a cost-effective project for US West and an excellent opportunity for MCC to build bridges with individual employees and the management of US West, and with many institutions of higher education who act as sub-contractors, providing assessment and educational services across a 14-state region. To date, more than 6,000 US West employees have taken advantage of services provided through this three-way partnership.

Valmont Industries. Another successful business partnership involves Valmont Industries, a major producer of center pivot irrigation equipment for both national and international markets. This company has developed an alliance with MCC; the college is now conducting a detailed job analysis of all major classifications of Valmont Industries' employees. A systematic review of each employment category has resulted in a description of specific job characteristics for each employee. This list then provides management not only with the opportunity to hire individuals who best fit job requirements but with the ability to provide relevant training for current employees to help them become more productive and efficient in the workplace.

Every major job group at Valmont is being carefully analyzed. Once this project is completed, all employees will move through a carefully designed continuing education and retraining program. Benefits to Valmont include focusing on skill building within their workforce and helping management ask critical questions about assembly lines, procedures, and production techniques, which result in improvements in efficiency and effectiveness. Assessing worker capabilities at Valmont Industries enabled MCC to develop significant expertise that is now provided in a variety of settings as a profitable activity for the college and a useful service to the business community.

Applied Information Management Institute. At the local level, MCC is a partner along with several other area postsecondary institutions in the Applied Information Management (AIM) Institute. This private, non-profit organization was established through the cooperation and leadership of our chamber of commerce, nearby higher education institutions, and major information technology corporations in the Greater Omaha area. The AIM Institute provides an excellent forum for business and education to determine clearly what the consumer (business) needs and what the provider (education) is or should be offering. MCC's involvement in AIM has aided MCC's restructuring of its basic management information systems. This, in turn, has resulted in more relevant and rapid responses to business needs.

Together with AIM, MCC has submitted a proposal to the National Science Foundation to create a center for multimedia development. This collaboration has indirectly helped us to develop internal multimedia production capabilities, used by faculty to enhance and diversify their classroom presentations. Also, our work with the AIM Institute has resulted in a computer and information technology course guide that incorporates the offerings of all Omaha area postsecondary institutions. This guide is a ready reference for area businesses and industries, outlining existing courses and programs that their organizations may need.

Educational Partnerships. Some of MCC's strongest alliances have been in educational collaboration. Our successful work on the multi-party OJC arrangement resulted not only in strengthening the emerging relationships but in opening the door for discussions with secondary schools. The development of the Tech Prep curriculum and high-school-to-college 2+2 partnership agreements have been bolstered by the rapport established through our OJC work.

Bellevue University. In 1992, Bellevue University, located in a small community adjacent to Omaha, was the only institution to oppose openly MCC's proposal to the State Postsecondary Coordinating Commission to substantially expand the college's academic transfer program. Bellevue felt that MCC's continued growth, expansion, and diversification would cause the university economic problems and declines in enrollment. At that time, the relationship between MCC and Bellevue University officials was not positive. Shortly after the proposal was approved unanimously, MCC and its colleagues from Bellevue University hosted a workshop intended to put contentious experiences behind them and move forward in collaboration. One partnership that has resulted is a joint MCC-Bellevue instructional program at one of Bellevue University's suburban shopping center locations.

The two institutions are offering an advanced client-server training program which provides 36 semester hours of intensive training for experienced mainframe computer operators. The courses take advantage of the special strengths and abilities of both institutions in a cost-effective manner. The first classes we have offered are full, and a waiting list has been formed. Both institutions will do well financially on this project; moreover, it is a tangible partnership activity that has opened the door to additional areas of collaboration that are far more bold than this initial effort. Future plans include combining our student records systems so that transcript transmittal can take place seamlessly between the institutions. In addition, we have just signed a comprehensive articulation agreement that provides for easy integration of students between Bellevue and MCC.

We are not limiting our thinking to students attending MCC for two years and then Bellevue University for two more; our plans call for students to be simultaneously

enrolled at both institutions and able to move back and forth in an effective and efficient manner. Several potential areas for further collaboration are now being explored
due to this initial, successful effort.

North/South Video Link. Four other institutions have teamed with Metropolitan Community College to create a North/South (Nebraska) video link. Wayne State College,
Peru State College, Northeast Community College, and Nebraska Indian Community
College have joined, under MCC's leadership, in discussions to create a multi-institution audio and video link so that each institution can provide its very best services to
the other institutions. We have prepared jointly an external funding application that
will provide the seed money to establish the necessary mechanical and electrical connections among our campuses. In addition to providing course work on this system, we
also expect to enhance student transfer among our institutions and provide staff development workshops and other administrative communications.

Nebraska Indian Community College. Of all of MCC's partnerships, the crown jewel is
with Nebraska Indian Community College (NICC). Early in 1991, Metropolitan
Community College began discussions with NICC representatives about how we
might work together to the mutual benefit of all our students and staff. Over a number
of years, we had looked for opportunities to develop a sister institution partnership
with an institution from a different nation or different culture.

In pursuit of this goal, Metropolitan Community College organized and led delegation trips to Central America, the former Soviet Union, Sweden, and Denmark to
explore opportunities for international educational partnerships. Although some students and faculty have participated in beneficial exchange activities, distance and
expense have not allowed us to do as much as we would have wished. What we lacked
was an institution with which we could create a truly close and effective partnership
that involved many people, including students, faculty and staff, as well as a relationship that would not be overly expensive.

Our partnership with Nebraska Indian Community College was formalized on
Columbus Day, October 12, 1992. Both institutions agreed to adopt the other and to
create a true sharing collaboration where students, staff, and communities would be
served by and contribute to this relationship. We have worked diligently so that each
organization feels that it is not only receiving but also giving in relatively balanced
ways.

Although Nebraska Indian Community College serves Winnebago, Omaha, and
Santee Sioux Native American people who, in some cases, reside close to Omaha, the
reservations of these three tribes are considered by the U.S. Government to be sover-
eign nations. The cultural differences between the Native American people and our
predominantly European culture at Metropolitan Community College are significant
and consequential. For example, one experiences a greater cultural difference between

the Santee Sioux and individuals in metropolitan Omaha than between Omahans and people in Copenhagen or Helsinki. In our partnership with Nebraska Indian Community College, we believe we have found that personal and professional multicultural relationship that we have so long sought with a sister institution.

Projects resulting from the partnership include annual joint staff development activities that explore virtually all aspects of community college student service, instructional methodology, and management. We share instructional techniques. We share how we address the range of learning styles in the classroom. We talk about how we conduct ourselves as educational leaders. Virtually all subjects about community college services are covered. Discussion of the very different approaches that our institutions take to providing services has yielded unusually valuable insights about how two such different colleges can be successful. We have found these workshops to have been among the most valuable experienced in a long community college career.

Faculty members from both institutions have helped each other develop curriculum and instructional techniques in such diverse instructional areas as commercial photography, drug abuse and rehabilitation counseling, psychology, Native American history and culture, and microcomputer technology. Courses are being offered jointly on campuses at both institutions with students traveling between colleges; faculty co-teach courses from both institutions. Faculty, staff, students, and community members from the Native American reservations assist MCC in conducting a wide range of cultural celebration events, such as our folk music festival at the college's Fort Omaha Campus and an intertribal pow-wow. Without the involvement of Native American people, these events would not have been so successful. Representatives from both of our institutions have met continuously since fall of 1992 to explore new projects and additional ways in which we can be true partners; the list of activities and projects continues to grow. In reviewing the list of qualities that describe how and why partnerships work, it is gratifying to know that our relationship with Nebraska Indian Community College has achieved most of these qualities. Both institutions, the students they serve, and their respective communities clearly have been the beneficiaries.

Adopt-a-School Project. Another partnership that has proved to be very effective for MCC has been our involvement with the Omaha Public Schools through their Adopt-a-School Project. In 1984, MCC adopted Miller Park School, an inner-city elementary school with a multicultural student population. Since that time we have adopted a junior high school, another elementary school, and two high schools. We learned that adoption was not a one-way street. In fact, from the beginning we have received as much as we have given. Through these partnerships we learned the importance of a balanced sharing between organizations.

We frequently host events on our campuses for our Adopt-a-School partners. Students from our partnership schools provide artwork, musical performances, and other activities on an almost-weekly basis at the college. A writing partnership between elementary school students and students in our chemical dependency counseling program has been an especially valuable project. The college students write to elementary students about major substance abuse problems they are studying. The elementary school students respond to these letters; these exchanges occur throughout the school year. The elementary students are at a critical age in terms of decisions and actions that they may take in terms of alcohol and controlled substance use. They receive valuable information from their college writing partners, and the college students achieve major field experiences beneficial to their planned learning programs. Both student groups benefit.

MCC has been asked to share information about school and college partnerships with the Syracuse University Center for Research and Information on School/College Partnerships. The current edition of Linking America's Schools and Colleges (Wilbur and Lambert, 1991) provides a valuable guide to educational partnerships nationally. A second edition is being prepared under the sponsorship of the American Association for Higher Education and is an outstanding resource for ideas for expanding and improving existing partnerships and developing new ones.

Joint Community College Projects. Community colleges maintain perhaps their strongest partnerships with local community groups through economic development activities and educational partnerships. In addition, important opportunities exist for learning and sharing with institutions and organizations on a regional, national, and international basis. For example, COMBASE and the League for Innovation are excellent networking/cooperating institutions. Information provided by individual institutions is shared, and participating organizations learn and grow from this process. Accessing the numerous national consortia is an important activity for institutions that are serious about maximizing their partnership possibilities.

Recently, Metropolitan Community College participated as the lead institution in a Beacon College Project. MCC partnered with nine other community colleges throughout the middle United States to study developing and enhancing leadership diversity in American community colleges. Each of the institutions approached the subject differently; as a result, each had important ideas and projects to share with the others and all learned from the collaboration.

In 1985, MCC organized a delegation trip of 35 community college leaders to Denmark and Sweden to establish partnerships and linkages with the Folkhighschool movement in those countries (Gilliland, 1986). In 1989 and 1990, MCC organized similar trips to the former Soviet Union in which 43 persons participated. Each of these delegation trips served as a platform for sharing ideas among the institutions represented; each of us learned about the efforts, the successes, and the failures of our colleagues in terms of creating effective international and intercultural programming. As a result of these delegation activities, partnerships and exchanges with our higher education colleagues in Europe have continued to the present day.

On the state level, there is the potential for some rather severe competition among community colleges. Competition for scarce resources and for legislative support can create a divisive environment. We must realize that we are all in the same boat; and if there is a leak in one end, the whole boat will sink. Collaboration has proven to be a far more effective approach than mutually exclusive competition in promoting the mission and overall ideals of community colleges. Effective collaborations in several states have resulted in improved funding and have enhanced legislation governing educational opportunity.

CONCLUSIONS

Six points can be made about the potential values and benefits of partnerships. First, we, like so many others in both the public and private sectors, have to gather and shepherd scarce resources. We no longer can afford to go it alone. We must find cost-effective ways to provide ever more varied service in an environment of stabilized or declining resources. Second, we clearly have experienced many benefits by learning from other organizations and other people's areas of strength and experience.

Third, the building of trusting professional relationships has opened many doors for further collaboration and the provision of more extensive service to our community. Fourth, a "teaming" mentality has emerged in America. To be in concert with this interdependent approach to service, we need to join forces with others.

Fifth, the value of diversity is inherent in the mentality of sharing and teaming. Valuing diversity means sharing ideas, learning from each other, and being accepting of others. It is also good business in that it is cost effective. Most important of all, it is the right thing to do.

Finally, creating partnerships, collaborations, and alliances is a critically important way of extending community colleges into the community. Ideally, the boundary between the college and the community will disappear, and the college will become one with the community. The greatest benefits to our communities and our colleges can be achieved as unity is attained. As respect for the uniqueness of its members grows, and as unity emerges among its people, so grows the community.

REFERENCES

Baker, R.K. "Expanding small college LRC services through creative partnerships." *Community and Junior College Libraries,* 1988, 6(1) 89–93.

Commission on the Future of Community Colleges. *Building communities: A vision for a new century.* Washington, DC: American Association of Community and Junior Colleges, 1988.

Covey, S.R. *The seven habits of highly effective people.* New York: Simon and Schuster, 1989.

Dewey, J. *Democracy and education.* New York: The Macmillan Company, 1916.

Ernst, R.J. "Knowing when to just say no." *Community, Technical, and Junior College Journal*, 1991, 61(5), 41.

Gilder, J., and Rocha, J. "10,000 cooperative arrangements serve 1.5 million." *Community and Junior College Journal*, 1980, 51(3), 11–17.

Gilliland, J.R. "Leadership, diversity and Columbus: A manifesto for social change." *Community, Technical, and Junior College Journal*, 1992, 62(5), 19–22.

Gilliland, J.R. "Folkhighschools: Exchanging ideas with the people's colleges of Scandinavia." *Community, Technical, and Junior College Journal*, 1986, 56(5), 22–26.

Gilliland, J.R., and Little, P. "OASES public library community college partnership." *Community and Junior College Journal*, October 1977, 48(2), 14–15, 32.

Kanter, R.M. *When giants learn to dance*. New York: Simon and Schuster Trade, 1989.

Nielsen, N.R. "Partnerships: Doors to the future for community colleges." *Leadership Abstracts*, May 1994, 1–2.

Wilbur, F.P. and Labert, L.M. *Linking America's schools and colleges*. Washington, DC: American Association for Higher Education, 1991.

Chapter III

Miami-Dade Community College is living testimony to the exhortation by the AACC that "community colleges, through the building of educational and civic relationships, can help both their neighborhoods and the nation become self-renewing" (Commission on the Future, 1988, p. 6). Its Overtown Project is made up of a comprehensive set of relationships designed to redevelop a troubled neighborhood. Kanter (1994, p. 99) observed that "the risk of missing a rare opportunity also motivates leaders to enter into relationships with open-ended possibilities." Most of the Overtown Project's relationships have "open-ended possibilities," of necessity, because the partnerships' objectives are so broad. Miami-Dade clearly experiences the sense of interdependence and connectedness described by Lorenzo and LeCroy (1994) as important when today's community colleges plan for the future. "Institutions must come to view themselves as part of a much larger socioeconomic system, rather than as independent and semiautonomous-autonomous entities" (Lorenzo and LeCroy, 1994, p. 16). President Robert McCabe's belief that no American institution is better prepared to help solve the country's pressing social problems is reflected in the wide variety of ways this college reaches out to its community.

***

Commission on the Future of Community Colleges. *Building communities: A vision for a new century*. Washington, DC: American Association of Community and Junior Colleges, 1988.

Kanter, R. M. "Collaborative advantage: The art of alliances." *Harvard Business Review*, 1994, 72(4), 96–108.

Lorenzo, A. L. and LeCroy, N. A. "A framework for fundamental change in the community college." *Community College Journal*, 1994, 64(4), 14–19.

Robert McCabe
President
Miami-Dade Community College
Miami, Florida

COMMUNITY IS OUR MIDDLE NAME

The gums best understand the teeth's affairs.

—West African saying

GENESIS

In August 1963, I arrived at Miami-Dade Community College in the midst of great excitement. Furniture was being moved into the first permanent building of an institution that would bring a new concept and great hope to our community. In the spirit of the day, which Miami-Dade has steadfastly maintained, the college committed itself to open doors for all. It would admit any high school graduate and would design its educational programs specifically to prepare people for jobs in our community. Each person would have the opportunity to fully develop his or her talent as a basis for gaining a fair share of the good things this country had to offer. The emerging community colleges were, and still are, the most American of institutions.

The college grew rapidly, and the nearly perfect match between the growing economy and the education provided at the college generated great support from our community. In those early days, my predecessor, Peter Masiko, Jr., was asked why the college was so successful. He said, "We were there at the right time with at least some of the right answers."

Over the last three decades, there has been great change in American society. As we have entered the Information Age, the minimum information skills needed for employment have continued to rise. Among poor Americans, the great hopes of the 1960s have faded into despair and distrust of our institutions. The masses of Americans who are leaving high school with minimal academic skills are being joined by substantial numbers of unskilled immigrants. Thus, the gap—between the skills needed for employment and full participation in the society, and those of our population—continues to widen. Ever-increasing numbers of Americans are slipping into a growing underclass, and social service systems are in disarray and mostly ineffective.

The American community college may have more to contribute to the solution of these massive problems than any other institution. We are still in the right place, located in sites throughout our country that include virtually every one of the most needy neighborhoods. But if we are to be there with at least some of the right answers, a very different institution, with a very different perspective on service than that which powered the early growth of community colleges in the 1960s, will be required.

ALL THINGS TO ALL PEOPLE

In the 1960s, there was a high level of commitment to the purposes of community colleges, and there was excellent funding. In most places, community colleges were new and not well-defined. Thus, there was considerable latitude in developing services— the community colleges were defining themselves.

Things have changed. Legislators throughout the country are struggling with strong resistance to additional taxes and with priority needs beyond the available resources. As budgets tighten, there is an increasing review of programs and significant pressure to establish priorities that limit services. This would result in providing only the core programs that were developed in the 1960s—academic and occupational instruction for "qualified" students in traditional on-campus settings. The rallying cry of those who would restrict is, "You can't be all things to all people." While this pressure for constraint might come first from legislators and boards, there is also pressure from within institutions. With inadequate budgets and salaries that have not kept pace with inflation, pressure from within is very understandable. People say that we need to put a priority on raising salaries to competitive levels and that resources for basic programs are inadequate. Under these circumstances, they ask how we can involve ourselves in new services to reach out to our community. It will take strong leadership, persistence, and unrelenting conviction to help the college community, boards, and legislators understand that reaching out to improve our communities should be considered a core service for the effective community college of the 1990s.

COMPREHENSIVE COMMUNITY DEVELOPMENT IS ESSENTIAL

In a country with our wealth, it is unacceptable for large numbers of Americans to be living in intolerable conditions. In every city in America, however, there are neighborhoods where populations live in shameful circumstances considered dangerous by the rest of the community. There is an ever-growing number of people who are unable to care for themselves and who must be supported by the rest of society. To illustrate, in Florida over the past six years, the cost of Aid to Families with Dependent Children has risen by no less than 20 percent annually.

The growing underclass threatens the very well-being of our country. We are learning that it is essential to improve the quality of life and the quality of neighborhoods throughout our country. Children must have the opportunity to grow up in a healthy environment if they are to become contributing citizens, leading productive lives.

To be competitive in a world economy, American business and industry needs a well-prepared, stable, and productive work force. Business and industry need all of our people. Our people are our human capital and our greatest resource as a nation. We cannot afford to accept the great loss that occurs when the circumstances of life for so many Americans preclude their opportunity to fully participate in the society.

There are many things that have contributed to the breakdown of our social services. Without doubt, one is the rigid division of responsibilities. As agencies try to provide services that deal with a narrow element of people's lives, they fail. It is clear that effective programs deal with people holistically and that agencies need to work together and to view their services in a much broader way. For community colleges, this means a broader interpretation of the services that are considered to be our responsibility.

THE COMMUNITY COLLEGE AS A COMMUNITY RESOURCE

Community colleges have been situated where they are convenient for as many citizens as possible. They have facilities—for meetings, the performing arts, recreation, and physical education—that were built to serve their students. But those physical resources can be the basis for the development of healthy neighborhoods around the colleges as well.

Even more important are the human resources that these institutions represent. At Miami-Dade Community College, with over 2,500 full-time employees, the breadth of skills and talents is awesome. In addition, important skills have been developed in working effectively with people. These skills are based on a fundamental commitment to the value of all human beings. When our human resources are used to support community cultural events and services on our campuses and to reach out to provide services in our community, the positive impact on the community's quality of life can be virtually beyond measurement.

Miami-Dade Community College has 55,000 credit students. Consider what we could achieve if as few as one-fourth of our students provided some community service as part of their educational program. They would become an important human resource helping out in our communities while participating in life experiences that would foster understanding of our society's problems. They would have an orientation to public service that could continue throughout their lives. Too often, the community college campus has been isolated from the people of the community, particularly in our poorest neighborhoods, and has served only those who generated their own interest in the college and voluntarily entered its doors. A major goal for community colleges should be to convert the great resources that they represent into a massive service force that will help transform and improve their neighborhoods.

Reaching Out to Business and Industry. The 1990s have been a time of great change. Business leaders indicate that their personnel must be prepared for more than a lifetime in one occupation. They must have the skills, competencies, and attitudes that will permit them to reshape their careers, to learn new skills, and to shift into new jobs as change in the workplace continues. Thus, there is a need for dynamic and continuing education that is designed specifically for the time, place, and needs of business and industry.

Many community colleges are now reaching out with very flexible, custom-designed, custom-timed, and custom-located programs in support of their local businesses and industry. These are among the most important services that community colleges can provide, and because adaptability is one of their major strengths, they are uniquely prepared to provide such services.

MIAMI-DADE COMMUNITY COLLEGE IN OUR COMMUNITY

The Greater Miami community has changed dramatically and so has the college. The first integrated college or university in Florida, Miami-Dade Community College in the early 1960s had a student population that was 85 percent white non-Hispanic, 60 percent male. A majority were full-time students who were academically well-prepared. In 1994, 80 percent of the student population are in minority groups. Miami-Dade has the largest enrollment of Hispanics and the largest enrollment of African Americans of any college or university in America. Nearly 60 percent of the students are female, a majority of students are on part-time schedules, and 75 percent of all entering students' tests show that they are academically underprepared. The programs of the college have changed dramatically, and the college has continued to integrate itself into the community as a foundation for improving the quality of life for our residents. Reaching out, and inviting in, have come to be basic components of the college's operations. We have become a cultural center; a meeting ground; a source of expertise in solving community problems; a flexible training ground for government, business, and industry; and a center for activities for economic development.

Perhaps the most dramatic demonstration of how well our multiple roles are accepted occurred after Hurricane Andrew. Two weeks after the hurricane, 66 percent of Dade County voters approved a two-year property tax to establish a $100 million community endowment for the college. The measure passed in all but three of 405 precincts, including all of those that had been devastated by the hurricane.

GENERAL COMMUNITY OUTREACH

Miami-Dade Community College is developing a new phase of community support based on the concepts of service learning and neighborhood transformation. The college provides students with training in, among other things, law enforcement and fire fighting, public service, and the health care professions, while providing the community with vision and dental care, educational outreach, and small business development.

Professional Training Programs. In 1971, Miami-Dade Community College joined with federal, state, county, and local government agencies to establish the School of Justice and Safety Administration. This regional training school offers various degree programs through the Administration of Criminal Justice Department in addition to certification and licensing in different areas of law enforcement and public safety provided by six divisions: the Police Training Institute, Private Sector Security Training Program, Fire Academy, Corrections Training Institute, Assessment Center, and the Traffic Safety Training Institute.

The college trains police and firefighters for the county and for 26 municipalities, thus providing standard training for all the organizations which must work together. Miami-Dade takes great pride in knowing that over 18,000 police officers, firefighters, justice, and safety personnel have gone through the basic courses and another 23,000 have had advanced development training—that we have produced men and women who, in many ways, affect the daily lives of all South Floridians.

Meeting the Health Needs of the Community. In 1966, the Division of Medically Related Programs was formed to work with the medical community in planning a curriculum for health care workers. The Medical Center Campus was established in 1974 in the Medical Center Complex, which includes the University of Miami School of Medicine, Jackson Memorial Hospital, Veterans Administration Hospital, Dade County Public Health Service, and other private and public health facilities. The Medical Center Campus expanded its nursing, physical therapy, medical sonography, medical laboratory technology, and emergency medical technology programs to include community-based programs that reach out to those women and men who, perhaps, have never realized their potential for development.

Today the Medical Center Campus is the primary educator and trainer of health professionals below the M.D. level in Dade County. Over two-thirds of the registered nurses graduated annually in Dade County receive their degree from the Medical Center Campus. Over 200 students per year graduate from current allied health technology offerings, which include dental hygiene, diagnostic medical sonography, emergency medical services, health information management, health services management, medical laboratory technology, physical therapy assistant, radiation therapy technology, radiography, respiratory care, and vision care technology/opticianry.

The Health Careers Opportunity Program provides career/personal counseling, tutoring, test-taking skills, and motivational self-esteem workshops for students who are often facing insurmountable odds. Another of these programs, Project Independence, provides occupational training to single mothers who are recipients of public assistance. The program prepares students to enter employment and become self-sufficient; students receive bi-monthly individual counseling to assist in attaining success. Project Independence is also in operation at the Wolfson Campus (downtown) and the North Campus (northwest Dade County).

At the North Campus, two clinics were established—one for dental hygiene in 1968, and one for vision care in 1970—to provide professional settings in which students could gain well-supervised practical experience. The clinics were open to the public and provided free dental and vision care. Today, the Dental Clinic, now located at the Medical Center Campus, serves an average of 5,000 patients each year. The clinic has 30,000 patients of record, all of whom receive dental services free of charge, with no restrictions. In 1977, the Vision Clinic, along with several thousand patient records, moved to the Medical Center Campus. Over the last five years, it is estimated that almost 18,000 patients have had general optometric exams, contact lens exams, and general service visits.

Training in Other Professional Fields. There are also many specialized training courses that enhance the skills of people already in professional fields. The Center for Business and Industry and the Metro-Dade Transit Agency Partnership provide job-specific training in such areas as management and customer service. The Affordable Housing Management Education Program (A HOME) is the first of its kind in Florida. This intensive, 40-hour, week-long program is offered to community-based organizations and to government representatives to help alleviate the lack of affordable housing in Dade County. Workshops at the Wolfson Campus cover such topics as how to evaluate neighborhood conditions, housing needs, and political climate; legal issues in housing development; financing and funding sources; design and construction methods; and state, federal, and local housing resources.

The Wolfson Campus in downtown Miami is the location of two specialized programs. Working Solutions, funded by a grant from Florida's Health and Rehabilitative

Services, assists women over 30 years of age who are widowed, divorced, or separated and are suffering financial and personal difficulties as they seek to reenter the job market. The World History Institute for Secondary School Teachers, sponsored by the Woodrow Wilson Summer Institute, provides secondary schoolteachers from throughout Dade County the opportunity to explore innovative social history teaching techniques.

As Miami-Dade Community College serves the county's citizens in life, it also serves many of them at the end of their lives. Since 1964, the Funeral Services Program at Miami-Dade's North Campus has demonstrated a strong commitment to community involvement through a largely unheralded devotion to caring for the indigent dead. The Florida Funeral Directors' Association asked Miami-Dade to establish the mortuary science program—the first at an American public community college. Today, with over 1,000 graduates, Miami-Dade's program is the largest of 42 accredited programs in the United States with modern facilities for embalming, restorative arts, pathology, cosmetology, a funeral service chapel, and a casket room laboratory facility. When the program began, no one could have imagined that by 1994, over 7,000 people, now as many as 250 a year, would be prepared for burial and interred by students of the program—free of any charges to the taxpayers of Dade County. Nor would anyone have thought that, 30 years later, the program's students and faculty would be so dedicated that they would spend their free time renovating and cleaning up Dade County Cemetery, where indigent persons are buried. "Quietly, always with accorded dignity, often unnoticed, unspoken, the dead arrive, their bodies properly attended, provided caring attention, reverently, then removed to their final resting place," says the department chairman.

Programs that Assist the Economic Health of Dade County. As early as 1969, Miami-Dade Community College responded to the stated needs of the African American community through the formation of outreach centers in Coconut Grove and Homestead. The Kendall Campus opened a center for community development and developed an innovative grading system so that students could move at their own pace. The Miami program was the breeding ground for a National Council on Community Service for Community and Junior Colleges, which encouraged two-year colleges to be actively involved in the community, to address pressing social problems, and to work with other organizations committed to community service and education. Director Patrick J. Distasio said, "The community service dimension of the two-year college may be the single most important characteristic distinguishing it from other institutions of higher education."

The residents of troubled communities have basic needs, among which are affordable housing, adequate health care, and protection from violence. Another essential need, which creates community growth, is access to jobs. Liberty City—a predominantly African American neighborhood in northwest Miami—suffered through years of steady degeneration. In 1989, Miami-Dade Community College established the Liberty City Entrepreneurial Education Center (EEC). The EEC has several components. The Small Business Resource Center, for instance, offers training in small business management, provides expert assistance, and maintains the EEC Business Research Library, which houses a wide variety of business publications and other resource materials. The center has four objectives: to foster and promote entrepreneurship, business development, and economic revitalization in the African American community; to provide a broad-based community resource facility; to offer college credit and non-credit courses to degree- and non-degree-seeking students; and to provide educational outreach services.

Although it has an academic focus, the EEC has developed into a multi-purpose facility that serves the needs of the Liberty City community and various minority organizations throughout Dade County by providing meeting space, small business consultations, and program support for minority business and community-based projects. In 1992, the EEC opened the Liberty City Small Business Development Center, in conjunction with Florida International University, with funding from the Small Business Administration. This facility, which augments the existing centers at FIU's north and south campuses, provides a free counseling service to small business owners. Since its opening in January 1992, the Small Business Development Center has provided space for the Florida Department of Labor to operate a Job Service Center. This effort to assist employers and job seekers from within the community screens an average of 1500 job seekers each month.

The Homestead area, still recovering from the economic devastation caused by Hurricane Andrew, is benefiting from Miami-Dade's involvement with the small business community. In 1992–93, the Homestead Campus received a $100,000 grant to establish Merchant to Merchant, in conjunction with the Entrepreneurial Center, to offer assistance to small businesses recovering from the hurricane.

Also in 1992–93, grants totaling $2.8 million provided initial funding for the Business Incubator Center at the Homestead Campus. The center provides technical assistance to new businesses in the Homestead area, providing entrepreneurs with instruction in marketing, management, finance, and accounting. In October 1993, concerned leaders from the Homestead community met in an effort to establish a common agenda and well-planned approaches to solving community needs. Hurricane Andrew, which had struck Homestead on August 22, 1992, "dramatically compounded the historical impoverishment of this area, sending the poverty rate well above 50 percent today," stated Roy G. Phillips in the formal presentation outlining the proposed mission and programs of the Coalition of Homestead Neighborhood Groups. Phillips, president of the Miami-Dade/Homestead Campus and president of Tools for Change— a non-profit economic development technical assistance corporation—was asked to facilitate creation of the new organization.

Assisted by attorney Charles Elsessor of Legal Services of Greater Miami, architect Joseph Middlebrooks, and Nancy Allen of Tools for Change, Phillips outlined activities, responsibilities, and resource requirements for each area of interest identified by the coalition:

- education and training;
- family development and support;
- youth development;
- safe neighborhoods;
- adequate housing;
- infrastructure improvements; and
- community/economic development.

These college partnerships with Homestead community groups have already begun to show results in raised economic, educational, and social levels for the residents of Homestead and its environs.

At the Kendall Campus, members of a national entrepreneurial organization, Students in Free Enterprise, conceived a plan to teach elementary school children the basics of owning a business. Armed with cookies and lemonade, they launched The Great Cookie Project at two schools. They encouraged the children to develop marketing plans for their cookie businesses and, as one might expect, the "props" quickly disappeared. The students then went to the local Chamber of Commerce for "cookie money." The Chamber thoroughly approved of the project and agreed to underwrite the cookie cost of $12 to $15 per school which was probably the greatest return for the least investment in their experience. Today's cookie eaters may well be tomorrow's business owners.

Miami-Dade was one of the first community colleges in the United States to be designated as a serviceman's opportunity college by the U.S. Department of Defense and the American Association of Community and Junior Colleges. In the mid-1970s, through Project AHEAD, service personnel could pursue a continuous education while they were on duty at various locations. By the end of the 1993 fiscal year, the Veterans' Upward Bound program at the Kendall Campus had served 480 veterans through its federal grant. Program counselors also worked with hundreds of local veterans, a significant number of whom were homeless—whether eligible for the program or not—and also on federal, state, and local sources of aid for education and job training.

One 51-year-old Vietnam veteran, who had only completed the ninth grade, was totally blind and wore braces on his legs. The Department of Vocational Rehabilitation had refused him services, saying his disabilities were too severe for him to attend school. In 1990, with the help of the Veteran's Upward Bound program, he passed his college entrance exams and then earned his GED in 1991. He earned an Associate of Arts in social work, received several awards for academic achievement, and became a member of Phi Theta Kappa, a national honor society. He earned a Bachelor of Liberal Studies at Barry University in 1993, and he has been accepted at Nova University for graduate study. Before losing his sight six years ago, he was self-employed as a custom home improvement carpenter, using skills that he had learned from his father and grandfather. Today, he has a home office equipped with a voice synthesizing computer, and he works as a computer processor and a behavioral therapy counselor. The community has gained the skills of this man who otherwise would have been dependent on society for his most basic needs.

Opening the Doors to Independence. The Microcomputer Education for Employment of the Disabled (MEED) program, established at Miami-Dade in 1989, is a special and unique training program. The program creates job opportunities for unemployed, severely physically disabled adults through practical training in business PC software. With easy access to a PC, persons with hearing impairments, visual impairments, or upper body disabilities are as competitive in business as any able-bodied persons. Between 80 percent and 90 percent of MEED students graduate and become microcomputer specialists.

MEED has a strong, close partnership with the local business community through its Business Advisory Council. One hundred corporate executives participate in the council and are personally involved with student activities, financial and equipment contributions, field trips, evaluation of performance, internships, mentorships, employment opportunities, and classroom instruction. MEED has long been an exemplary model of partnership among the private sector, public agencies, and a community college. The MEED program at Miami-Dade has produced 120 graduates who have gained the opportunity to obtain satisfying jobs, financial independence, and upward mobility.

A Concern for Our World. In 1980, reflecting the worldwide effort to protect the environment, work was begun on the Environmental Demonstration Center, a project designed to prove that people could build their own homes and live comfortably without using large amounts of energy. Located on three acres of native pine land west of the Kendall Campus, overlooking a lake, the center was built over a two-year period by staff and volunteers who "held in common, in one way or another, a vision that the life-styles that human beings choose individually, directly effects the whole of humanity," according to the E.D.C. Newsletter. The experimental house had no air conditioning, but there were skylights and solar collectors overhead and two windmills on the roof—one generated electricity and the other pumped water from a well. It was the only building of its kind in Florida.

By 1985, the center had expanded to include the Owner Builder Center, boat building, the Nature Center program for children, health and fitness, food and nutrition, self-sufficiency, and environmental ethics. The centers offered classes, consulting, tours, a resource bank, and demonstrations of alternative systems. The Owner Builder Center offered Florida's first do-it-yourself building courses. In its first three years, over 2,000 men and women successfully completed courses on ways to build energy efficient homes and to remodel older ones. A number of the students went on to build their own homes.

As it did for miles around, Hurricane Andrew wreaked havoc with the center, completely ripping it apart. The centers are scheduled for rebuilding, the popular courses will be continued, and there will be increased emphasis on environmental ethics as an area of study.

Early Care and Education. At Miami-Dade, student success is our number one priority; it is the reason for our existence. We believe that the seeds of success should be strongly nurtured during early childhood, that children's determination to succeed should keep pace with their growth. Miami-Dade's commitment to this concept has resulted in an early childhood program that is nationally recognized for its excellence.

The Center for Early Care and Education had its beginning in the Pre-School Laboratory (PSL), which was established in 1965 to train education majors, child care providers, public school teachers, and early childhood professionals in the community. Today, the center has grown to include, in addition to the pre-school lab and the Children's Resource and Referral Center, a satellite learning center which, through contract with Dade County Public Schools, houses a public school serving kindergarten, first and second grades for children of students, staff, and faculty of the college. The PSL also provides a school-age child care program for the satellite center. In 1992–93, the program accepted 66 children (ages 3 to 5) of North Campus faculty, staff, and students, as well as community children.

The Center for Early Care and Education is fulfilling the promises of its purpose statement: to enhance children's education and care, to be an advocate for children, to increase the quality and quantity of early care, and to increase public awareness of how strongly the health of children and families impacts the economic and social growth of the community. The center also provides coordination for professional development programs for Department of Health and Rehabilitative Services employees; persons employed in commercial child care agencies, public and private schools; and early childhood program administrators. It provides resources and child care referrals for county government and corporate providers, as well as for parents.

In cooperation with the Child Care Resource and Referral program, Kiwanis of Dade County, Metro-Dade Child Development Services, the National Council of Jewish Women, the Mitchell Wolfson Sr. Foundation, and the Junior League of Miami, the college provides a mobile resource van for program support, a child care voucher system for Hurricane Andrew victims, child development centers in South Dade (to be established soon at all campuses), and a family development center within Rainbow Village (a public housing development).

In 1990, the AGAPE program was created by Professor Joe McNair, a member of the North Campus faculty. Out of his own love for education, he has ignited in the churches of Overtown, a community adjoining the campus, a passion for both teaching and learning. Professor McNair takes students who have declared teaching as a career goal into the Greater Bethel A.M.E. Church to serve as tutors and role models to the children of Overtown. Volunteers from other churches in the downtown area provide additional adult models. This program is expanding through an interfaith alliance of churches called Faith in the City. The alliance arranges to transport children from four elementary schools to the church for the afternoon programs.

Striving to Meet the Community's Need for Literate Citizens. In 1989, Miami-Dade established the Southeast Florida Training Center for Adult Literacy Educators with state funding through the Florida Adult Education Act. During the five years of the center's operation, over 9,000 persons have participated in specialized training for adult educators who would teach persons with limited English proficiency who were educationally disadvantaged, homeless, handicapped, already working, or at-risk. The center assists program managers in the development of community outreach and program promotion techniques. The center also helps local policy makers and government leaders understand the impact of illiteracy in Florida through workshops, seminars, and conferences. In 1991, the Bureau of Adult and Community Education directed that the center should take on the responsibility of providing these programs throughout the entire state. Thus, the center's name was changed to Florida Training Center for Adult Literacy Educators.

Sports Facilities—Sports/Health Programs. For 17 years, the North Campus and the Kendall Campus participated in the National Youth Sports program for disadvantaged children. Unfortunately, federal funding cuts in the late 1980s resulted in the loss of this program at both campuses. Each campus immediately took up the challenge to continue providing services to youth and adults in the community.

At the North Campus, the Youth Swimming Program was established and offers a wide variety of activities, from the early-age "waterproof" swimming lessons for infants to water safety and lessons for pre-schoolers, to water sports activities for adults. Since the early 1980s, year-round programs include Youth Gymnastics and Youth Judo, as well as a Wellness Program that is open to the entire community.

In 1970, a summertime Men's Basketball League was initiated for high school students and adults, and the Adult Baseball League is in its first year of operation. In all, some 5,000 children and adults are participants in programs, and another 400,000 to 500,000 residents use the campus sport facilities on a yearly basis.

For more than 20 years, the Kendall Campus has opened its facilities to the children of Dade County through summer sports camps. In summer 1994, approximately 1,000 children, aged seven to 16, will participate in these programs: Go All-Pro Basketball Camp, three week-long sessions; the Grant Long Basketball Camp, featuring the Miami Heat star; Jaguar Volleyball Camp for Girls, two week-long sessions; and four one-week baseball camps.

Each year, some 400,000 Dade County residents, children and adults, use the Kendall Campus sports facilities. In the year following Hurricane Andrew, the tennis courts, gym, ball fields, and track were restored to their pre-hurricane condition. The Olympic-sized swimming pool reopened in June 1994, much to the delight of hundreds of swimmers who enjoy the pool year-round. Sports teams from outside Dade County use the facilities at both campuses which, in turn, provides additional recreational activities for the community-at-large.

Service Learning Integrated into Miami-Dade's Curricula. The college always responds positively to local community needs. In fact, service-learning activities currently exist on all campuses. In early 1994, the college developed Partners in Action and Learning, a program to establish a collegewide service-learning infrastructure and to apply service-learning strategies via two pilot site projects and 10 mini-grants. Covering all four of the nationally identified community service areas—education, public safety, human needs, and environment—the Partners in Action program will harness and apply the extensive resources of the college's faculty and students to work shoulder-to-shoulder with local communities to meet their existing needs. Through the program, the learning experiences of Miami-Dade's students serving as volunteers will be enriched as will the communities in which they work.

The results of the program will be immediate and enduring. In the short term, student volunteers will assist in neighborhood transformation and in mentoring activities for at-risk youth. Miami-Dade students will develop increased analytical thinking and the ability to apply current course content to the real world; they will become involved in solving community problems; they will understand the root causes of poverty; they will begin to understand the congruence between talk and actions; and they will come to understand cultural, historical, political, and economic variables. The long-lasting effects of the program will be revealed as students remain involved in community service work long after their service-learning placement ends. The communities will reap the rewards.

COMPREHENSIVE PROGRAMS

Overtown Neighborhood Partnerships and The Wellness Center. For many years, the Medical Center Campus maintained its excellent reputation for preparing people to work in the health fields. However, the campus was insular and specialized. Each day students and faculty came to the campus from all over Dade County, and then returned to their homes. There was no relationship with the surrounding community.

Overtown has had a vibrant and tragic history. Developed as the African American center of a segregated city, the area grew to become a stable, family-centered community that was the center of African American business and cultural activity. In the 1940s and 1950s, Overtown was a Mecca for music buffs, both black and white. Ray Charles,

Lena Horne, Lou Rawls, Patty LaBelle, B.B. King, Johnny Mathis, and Aretha Franklin all performed at the still-segregated Miami Beach hotels such as the Fountainbleau, but they could not sleep in Miami Beach. They had to return to Overtown, and it became their own town.

In the 1960s, segregation ended, and Overtown was fragmented by an East-West expressway to the airport and the behemoth highway, I-95. As African American residents began to shop in the previously segregated business areas, and as more affluent African American families moved into newly accessible areas of Miami and Dade County, businesses lost their customers, closed up, and put neighborhood residents out of work. Most of the middle class left as the neighborhood deteriorated. The rioting and violence that occurred during the 1980s compounded the isolation of Overtown and its remaining, far less affluent residents.

Today, despite redevelopment initiatives by both city and county government, Overtown remains an example of the acute conditions of poverty. Underneath those expressways, daily life is pervaded by high crime, poor education, poor health, unemployment, a high rate of single parenting, and inadequate housing. According to the 1990 census, 70 percent of Overtown's families were single-parent, female-headed families with at least one child under the age of 18. Of these families, 64 percent lived in poverty. Only 7 percent of Overtown's 4,000 households were owner-occupied. The unemployment rate was 22 percent for females and 23 percent for males. Of all residents, 54 percent lived in poverty. The 12,000 residents had a median household income of $9,181. Statistical data for the 1980s were equally abysmal.

This led Tessa Martinez Pollack, president of the Medical Center Campus, to introduce, in 1987, the concept of a broader, community-based role for the campus. She believed that the innate capacity of Overtown residents could and should be nurtured and encouraged, that they had the power and ability to change not only themselves but their neighborhood as well. Pollack felt that Miami-Dade Community College had an obligation to reach out and use its assets to help the neighboring community of Overtown in its struggle to survive. Qualified staff and developing students committed themselves to the goal of making the neighborhood a better place to live.

From that beginning, the Overtown Neighborhood Partnerships project was introduced. In 1991 Miami-Dade established The Wellness Institute to provide linkages with residents of the neighborhoods surrounding the Medical Center Campus. The Wellness Institute, "an evolving dream," has five outreach activities underway: Medical School for Kids; Scientist-for-a-Day; We're Great Kids; A Laboratory Theatre; and Students in Service/Growing Up Healthy. Its primary initiative is The Overtown Neighborhood Partnerships project, a comprehensive program based on full involvement with the community. Since going into full operation in March 1992, the Partnerships project has engaged the residents in an educational process which, by their own work and with the support of many partners, leads toward systematic change for the social and physical transformation of their neighborhood. In 1993, a Community Forum was organized for the discussion of issues and solutions. A Merchant's Alliance was also formed to provide technical assistance in business development, marketing, and expansion. Miami-Dade's role has been to bring the forces together—with residents at the center of all arrangements—to determine a joint plan and carry it out for the benefit of all Miami.

The Wellness Institute's Medical School for Kids and Scientist-for-a-Day are collaborative projects between Dade County Public Schools and the Medical Center Campus. Medical School for Kids, now entering its fourth year, is a two-year program which has been completed by 57 middle school students. Scientist-for-a-Day involves 45 fourth grade students from Dunbar Elementary School. These youngsters come to the Medical Center Campus over a seven-week period and participate in educational experiences. These projects expose youngsters from the neighborhood to the atmosphere of learning and accomplishment. They perform easy, basic experiments and meet with the professional faculty. Of 24 students involved in the first Medical School for Kids, 23 remain in school, 22 are doing exceptionally well academically, and three are attending magnet schools.

We're Great Kids all started with dirty hands when a preschool teacher in the Allapattah YMCA daycare program realized that the children had no concept of personal cleanliness or good nutrition. The program coordinator contacted the nursing department at Miami-Dade's Medical Center Campus, asking for a nurse to come and tell the children about hygiene and good health habits. From that small beginning in 1992, We're Great Kids has grown to a comprehensive volunteer program involving service-learning experiences—for students, faculty, and staff—ranging from preschool daycare to after-school athletics to numerous family activities. Over 105 volunteers provided human service hours for 208 children. This preventive health care initiative represents a key means for breaking the cycle of health problems in this poverty-stricken neighborhood.

As part of The Wellness Institute outreach, Professor Alberto Meza, a faculty member who has been recognized nationally for innovation, designed A Laboratory Theatre: A Day in the Life of a Child. This project involves student service-learners in designing and implementing a variety of fine arts workshops for children in grades 4 through 8. The service learners aid children in producing a work of their own that depicts their personal view of life. There is also a fund-raising event showcasing the children's artwork. Meza has enriched both campus and community life. His play, "Las Casas," restored in the homeless men who were his actors a voice and the sense of contribution that comes only with connection to a purpose. Professor Meza has a second production underway, entitled "Affection/Infection," in which college students, students from Booker T. Washington Middle School, neighborhood residents, and AIDS-infected patients focus on the issues of AIDS.

Growing Up Healthy is another Medical Center Campus initiative that has a great impact upon the health problems caused by poverty. It is a service-learning project which benefits student development through important service to the community.

Working in cooperation with the Ann-Marie Adker Overtown Community Health Center, Overtown Neighborhood Partnerships, Dade County Public Schools, Phillis Wheatley Elementary School and their Parent-Teacher Association, Miami-Dade staff and volunteers are providing an initial physical examination and a personal health record for each child in the Overtown area public schools. From the time the program began in February 1993, to April 1994, over 260 volunteers had committed an average of five hours each to the program. This year, volunteers worked two to three hours each week assisting a program coordinator—who worked 20 hours a week on session preparation, including equipment and supply upkeep. Since November 1993, two medical transcript students and their faculty member have spent more than 150 hours entering the children's medical data into the Overtown Neighborhood Center database. Health screening sessions were held with almost 500 children and their parents.

Growing Up Healthy has expanded to include special Saturday clinics in the four public schools serving the area, five day care centers, and two Headstart programs. We believe that this program—providing personal health records, immunizations, routine checkup schedules, instruction on basic health care, and access by the Dade County health care system—is essential to the overall mission of the Medical Center Campus and affirms the importance of service to others and the community.

In summary, the Overtown Neighborhood Partnerships project has accomplished a great deal in three short years, and plans for the transformation of the neighborhood are going forward with enthusiasm. Early successes include:

- Growing Up Healthy has provided physical examinations for 400 children and immunizations for 350 children.
- A network for disseminating information among property owners and managers within Overtown has been established with the Overtown Neighborhood Enhancement Team (NET) office and the Overtown Apartment Association. The network coordinates programs and activities to enhance the Overtown Community.
- The Overtown Community Forum convened over 50 Overtown residents for a "grassroots" discussion of problems and proposed solutions for impacting the neighborhood.
- The Overtown Merchant's Alliance, Inc., convened Overtown's 40 "Mom and Pop" businesses and other public and private sector partners (such as Republic National Bank, Miami Capital, Barnett Bank, Costco, Miami-Dade Chamber of Commerce) for enhanced development.
- The Overtown Youth Leadership project has engaged 30 youngsters in leadership development and its application to community service projects to benefit Overtown.
- Five issues of Overtown Happenings, a quarterly newsletter publication, have been published, with some content written by Overtown residents.
- The Overtown Crime Prevention Project has developed a resident-driven plan to address crime-related issues which includes neighbors training other neighbors, youth and family recreational programs, and a block watch.

- Greater Miami Neighborhoods, Inc., and Miami-Dade Community College signed a Memorandum of Agreement with the Enterprise Foundation which designates Overtown as Enterprise's second site for technical assistance in neighborhood transformation.
- Overtown Neighborhood Partnerships convened the State Urban Partnerships Team in an all-day session with Overtown residents and agencies in October, 1993. It was the first time that all of Overtown's Community Development Corporations (CDC's) had ever gathered as a collective voice before state officials.
- As mentioned earlier faculty and students of the Medical Center Campus wrote and performed "Affection/Infection," an interactive drama mentioned earlier in this chapter, highlighting the AIDS crisis, shown to over 200 adults, teens, and children of Overtown at the Booker T. Washington Middle School. The Dade County Department of Health and Rehabilitation Services was so impressed that they have agreed to provide funding for additional performances.
- The AGAPE project, also mentioned earlier, has tutored 30 students in 1993 in math, reading, and language arts utilizing students who have declared teaching majors at the North Campus of Miami-Dade Community College.
- The Child Development Program of Miami-Dade's North Campus is providing technical assistance to Rainbow Village Housing Development (located in Overtown) in the establishment of a family service center. The center will provide family support systems within the housing development which will include day care, the training of child care workers, family conference space, and other family-based activities exclusively for the residents of Rainbow Village.

Grants and continuation commitments totaling $1,227,186 have been received for the Overtown Neighborhood Partnerships programs. This is only the beginning of what we believe is an easily replicable program wherein a community college becomes a working partner in ensuring its own neighborhood's future.

Cultural and Recreational Interaction with the Community. The college's cultural calendar encompasses music, dance, theater, workshops, conferences, and a variety of offerings; all are open to the public. In the earliest days of Miami-Dade's cultural effort, the college choir provided the sole entertainment. In 1965, the college offered weekend courses leading to a junior college degree, and, to keep the weekends lively, there were free lunchtime concerts. Fall 1972 brought concert pianist and noted music educator Ruth Greenfield to the Dade County Courthouse steps. There she performed for the first Lunchtime Lively Arts Series of open-air concerts. Greenfield said, "We wanted to keep people downtown and bring them back to the city, to enrich the cultural life of the community." Cultural offerings to the community in 1975 included art shows, events that offered folk, rock, jazz, and classical music, craft and photography workshops, dance presentations, movies, and concerts. In the Bicentennial Year, 1976, a jazz festival on the North Campus included Dizzy Gillespie, Wally Cirillo, Joe Diorio, Alvin Batiste, and the Mythril Quartet. By 1985, the Lunchtime Lively Arts Series had presented over 500 events featuring international and national talent in several downtown locations.

Today, it is estimated that close to half a million people have found their way to downtown Miami as a part of the many performances of the Lunchtime Lively Arts Series. Miami-Dade's reputation as a major cultural presenter has continued to grow. In 1993 alone, the Wolfson Campus cultural affairs department worked with 11 community groups, 11 local arts groups, eight national arts groups, and nine international arts groups. By the close of 1993, the cultural affairs department at the Wolfson Campus was recognized by the Association of Performing Arts Presenters as one of five exemplary programs in the country.

The Wolfson Campus's Cultura del Lobo, a three-year-old program, presents a series of provocative works by dancers and musicians, as well as media and performance artists from all parts of the world. The series features unique and unexpected forms of art, allowing participants to experience and benefit from the gathering. In 1993, the Miami-Dade Wolfson campus expanded its three-year-old program to 18 performing arts events, 15 gallery exhibitions (of four to six weeks each), 17 educational outreach programs, and two films series. Special projects included the Subtropics Music Festival, which featured 14 performances, two one-week artist residencies with strong community involvement, a visual arts exhibition, and a public radio series. The film festival educational component presented 13 panel discussions and a film screening. The International Hispanic Theatre Festival featured seven panel discussions and an acting workshop.

Heralded as the finest and largest literary event in the nation, the Miami Book Fair International is a literary extravaganza with a year-long schedule of events, lectures, seminars, and literary readings that stimulate and scintillate one's mind. More than 500,000 people from all over the world attend. The festivities culminate with the fair, an enchanting eight days that are free and open to the public, held annually each November on the campus grounds. Over 300 authors from around the globe and more than 500 national and international book vendors gather in the streets surrounding the Wolfson Campus. Former First Lady Barbara Bush, a keynote speaker at the Book Fair Gala, called the Fair "an embarrassment of riches." From the local community, the Fair touches the lives of more than 100,000 students and children who participate in events throughout the year.

Celebrating Ethnic and Racial Diversity. For almost two decades, the various Miami-Dade campuses have been presenting a variety of performances in celebration of the area's rich cultural diversity. Miami-Dade is proud to offer residents and visitors within its reach a rich and varied selection from which to choose their cultural enrichment. The events presented in the 1990s have become so numerous that they cannot all be mentioned here, but a brief review will highlight past events.

In 1974, the "Princess of Black Poetry," Nikki Giovanni, appeared at the North Campus, and the Pen Players presented "Ceremonies in Dark Old Men." Black Awareness Week in February included a three-day jazz festival with famous performers from around the world. Today, Black History Month is celebrated with art shows, performances of music and dance, and theater.

Each February, Miami-Dade hosts a celebration of Black Heritage with Igwebuike on the Kendall Campus, on the Wolfson Campus, and unnamed but enjoyable celebrations at Medical Center Campus, North Campus, and Homestead Campus. Kizomba, derived from a Swahili word for celebration, is a college/community program that encourages and promotes a greater understanding and appreciation of the various cultures that make up the Greater Miami area. Celebration of Black History Month enables a diverse, multiethnic population to share and experience the heritage of the African American people in this annual observance honoring African American history, culture, and tradition. Events range from a performance of the Alvin Ailey American Dance Theatre to lectures by celebrities such as Della Reese and Danny Glover and distinguished African American scholars to Miami-Dade students' creation of an African village.

In July 1992, Miami-Dade, The Alliance for Media Arts, and the Center for the Fine Arts co-sponsored a film series with an educational component, entitled "Interrogating Identity." This program complemented a Center for the Fine Arts exhibition with the same title, organized by the Gray Gallery of New York. The exhibition explored what it means to be "black" in American, British, and Canadian societies. The educational component included panel discussions conducted by artists and cultural leaders of color. The project received excellent press, created a high level of dialogue in the community, and formed a truly multicultural audience at the Alliance for the Media Arts, located in Miami Beach.

The Kendall Campus has celebrated Hispanic Heritage Week since 1974 through academic events, such as workshops on issues ranging from NAFTA to ecology, and cultural events such as concerts, dance presentations, and art exhibits. One special evening is eagerly anticipated by the entire community—Empanada Night. The empanada, a turnover with a flaky crust and a spicy or sweet filling, is made differently in each Latin American country. More than 12 countries are represented on Empanada Night with thousands of freshly made, and quickly devoured, empanadas.

In recognition of the contribution of Hispanic people to the theater, Miami-Dade co-sponsored the educational component of the VIII International Hispanic Theatre Festival. The festival brought world-renowned playwrights, directors, and artists to the Wolfson campus. The critics' series and an intensive acting and creativity workshop were held at El Carrusel Theatre in Coral Gables and at Ground Level Artists' Space in South Beach. All of these sessions were offered free to the public.

Most Asians living in the greater Miami area first settled in other parts of the hemisphere. Thus, the Chinese community in Miami has hyphenated ethnic roots: Chinese-Cuban, Chinese-Nicaraguan, Chinese-Jamaican, Chinese-Argentine, and many others.

At the urging of the Asian-Latino community, Miami-Dade's cultural affairs department developed the program, Chinese in the Americas, focusing upon Chinese contemporary arts—performing, visual, and media—from Canada to Argentina, to be woven through the 1994–1995 and 1995–1996 seasons. The two-year exploration of how Chinese artists have been influenced by the American host countries is expected to draw audiences from the various Chinese communities. In addition, the programs will be supplemented with educational and community outreach events coordinated with local, national, and international representatives from the numerous Chinese communities in the Americas.

Arts Education for Young Students. In 1984, the Florida legislature set aside $50,000 to begin plans for the South Florida School of the Arts (New World School of the Arts) to train future Performing and Visual Arts Center (PAVAC) students. Plans called for a school which would offer high school diplomas through baccalaureate degrees. Very little can match the sense of accomplishment and excitement the college experienced with the opening of the New World School of the Arts (NWSA). Opening its doors to nearly 400 carefully auditioned high school students in fall 1987, the New World School of the Arts enrolled its first college class in fall 1988.

Located in renovated space adjacent to the Wolfson Campus, the school provides quality arts training from the tenth grade to the bachelor's and master's degrees through unprecedented collaboration of the three separate educational segments: Dade County Public Schools, Miami-Dade Community College, and Florida International University. Under the leadership of Richard Klein, previously of New York's "Fame" High School of the Performing Arts, Miami's school became even more innovative and comprehensive. It provides gifted high school students a chance to get a realistic view of professional training in a carefully sequenced and accelerated dual-enrollment program.

The New World School of the Arts has had a major impact on the complexion of Miami-Dade's cultural offerings. These talented high school students (two of them 1994 Presidential Scholars) bring the vitality of youth to performances, but the sheer talent they display eclipses whatever other attributes they may have.

The Importance of Fine Arts in Community Relationships. In 1971, the Kendall Campus Gallery, the college's first gallery, opened in two adjoining classrooms. Today, the permanent collection at the Kendall Campus numbers over 600 pieces, is open for an average of 150 days per year, and has approximately 15,000 visitors annually.

The New World Center Art Gallery—renamed the Frances Wolfson Gallery in 1980—for contemporary and ethnographic art opened on the Wolfson Campus in 1976. In 1980, the new North Campus Art Gallery was dedicated to Mary Taylor, one of the school's first women administrators and now a gallery owner in California, who donated a 30-piece collection, including posters by Claes Oldenberg, Andy Warhol, Fred Eversley, and Roy Lichtenstein.

Following the Wolfson family tradition, the Mitchell Wolfson Jr. Gallery opened in 1984 with a collection of decorative and propaganda arts. Mr. Wolfson's private collection of more than 50,000 objects has provided shows of objects of the Art Deco period, ceramics and glass, and 20th century Italian design. In 1990, this gallery was reorganized and named the Centre Gallery, providing exhibits of contemporary art. There are three galleries at the Wolfson Campus today—the newest is the InterAmerican Gallery, established at the InterAmerican Center in the late 1980s.

Over the last 24 years, since the first gallery opened at the Kendall Campus, the college's art collections have been enjoyed by more than 375,000 residents—art in, by, and for the community.

COMMUNITY—OUR MIDDLE NAME

America faces tremendous social problems, and we at Miami-Dade believe that no institution is better prepared to help solve these problems than the community college. The fundamental tenet of the community college, the belief in the value of all human beings and the importance of providing opportunity for all, constitutes the fabric of the greatness of our country. Community colleges are the most American of institutions. At this difficult time in our history, we are in the right locations, we have great local credibility, and we represent an awesome resource that can be a significant instrument in the transformation of American neighborhoods. The Miami-Dade story, told in this chapter, is illustrative of the story of so many community colleges reaching for new levels of community participation, energizing the colossus represented by our faculties, staff, and students working to make our America of the 21st century one of hope and prosperity for all.

CHAPTER IV

Fordham University's *Index of Social Health*, which has tracked statistics on 16 major social problems such as the high school dropout rate and unemployment since 1970, "peaked in 1972 at 79 on a scale of 100. Since then it has been on a downward trend, falling to 42 for 1990, and to an all-time low of 36 for 1991" (Lorenzo and LeCroy, 1994, p. 14). The impact of these problems manifests itself most clearly in the nation's cities. Denver is no exception. "Disorienting to most people, this web of change is beginning to have an enormous impact on human behavior, affecting families, politics, and social institutions such as schools and colleges" (Gilley, 1991, p. 3). The faculty and staff of the Community College of Denver have recognized the challenging problems of their urban communities. Knowing that Denver's educational system could provide the vehicle for community recovery and renewal, Byron McClenney, president of the Community College of Denver, worked to convene a broad collaborative group of representatives from the city's public and private sectors. Called the Denver Network, the group is working to change the system to ensure success for students moving through the educational pipeline and into the workforce. The college's leadership role in this long-term effort is one example of the many ways today's community colleges are positioning themselves as America's problem solvers. As Wynne observed:

> American community colleges are at the threshold of an enormous opportunity to reposition themselves as the ultimate problem solvers in a nation struggling...While American...leaders at all levels are frantically searching for economic, educational, and social answers, current conditions are bringing the American community college to its moment in history (1994, p. 18).

There is much work to be done now. The following chapter, Community Colleges as a Nexus for Community, provides some excellent examples of ways to perform that work.

* * *

Gilley, J.W. *Thinking about American higher education*. New York: American Council on Education & Macmillan Publishing Company, 1991.

Lorenzo, A.L. and LeCroy, N.A. "A framework for fundamental change in the community college." *Community College Journal*, 1994, 64(4), 14–19.

Wynne, G.E. "Repositioning: A winning strategy for community colleges." *Community College Journal*, 1994, 64(3), 18–23.

Byron McClenney
President
Community College of Denver
Denver, Colorado

COMMUNITY COLLEGES AS A NEXUS FOR THE COMMUNITY

No matter what accomplishments you make,
somebody helps you.

—Althea Gibson Darben

DENVER'S CHANGING COMMUNITY

A careful comparison of 1990 and 1980 census data in most community college service areas would compel leaders to reassess their approach to community development. This comparison would be particularly telling for large cities, because in many ways it is there that quality of life has deteriorated most significantly. This deterioration has created challenging community-wide problems, such as those related to poverty and unemployment. Consider the following census information about Denver, Colorado:

- The population of Denver decreased five percent between 1980 and 1990.
- Denver's percent of state population fell from 17 percent to 14.2 percent.
- Minority residents of Denver increased from 33 percent to 39 percent.
- White families with children tended to either move out of Denver proper or to send their children to private schools. Sixty-six percent of public school students are now people of color.

- There is a trend for middle-income minorities to move to the suburbs.
- Denver family households headed by a female increased from 26 percent to 31 percent.
- One-third of all Colorado welfare recipients reside in Denver.

Census information tells us that (a) there are higher numbers of "at-risk" young people in Denver proper, (b) the population left behind has lower levels of income and educational attainment, and (c) this population is overrepresented in service and blue-collar jobs. Add to this mix the extremely high public school dropout rates for people of color (50 percent) and evidence of increasing gang and drug activity faced by this community. Like many American cities, during the 1980s Denver also had to deal with a recession and with turmoil in its school system. But efforts by single-focus agencies to address these problems have often failed. When contemplating solutions to these challenging problems, it is difficult to identify the community-based entities that could understand well enough the interactive issues, or gather enough courage and energy, to act in any significant way.

THE CASE FOR COLLABORATION

A look at almost any community in America will reveal public school reform efforts, advocacy for early childhood education, welfare reform initiatives, public campaigns about drug abuse, efforts to counteract the impact of gangs, programs to provide opportunities for people of color, special projects for dislocated workers, an emphasis on business involvement in the schools, authorities or entities created to foster economic development, and community-wide planning programs. These efforts proceed on a project-by-project basis. There is little recognition of the interdependence required to make fundamental changes. However, because communities are facing declining resources, and because the problems are far too complex for any one entity to solve, collaboration is now emerging as a vehicle to frame solutions to complex community problems and to prevent further erosion of quality of life. But what entity or organization possesses a broad enough or varied enough bundle of perspectives, skills, and resources to step forward as a convener or facilitator of collaborative efforts? Now more than ever before, community colleges have begun to ask whether they could and perhaps should be that entity.

A COLLEGE CONSIDERING ITS ROLE

Many would consider the effort to convene, facilitate, or link community problem-solving efforts as a step beyond the mission of a community college. The college's attempt to create this kind of nexus for community could be viewed by some as a desire to be a social service agency. Others might fear that the community college is competing with community-based organizations. On the other hand, it is difficult for colleges to back away when faculty and staff begin to understand what is at stake.

The faculty and staff of the Community College of Denver (CCD) began to discover what was at stake when they conducted an environmental scan of its service area during the 1986–87 academic year. Products of the scanning activity included background or issue papers that summarized population characteristics and trends, as well as community economic and social priorities. These carefully researched papers described an urban center facing serious challenges, many of which had implications for the future direction of the community college. Some troubling characteristics came to light:

- unemployment/underemployment/poverty,
- high illiteracy rates,
- economic underdevelopment,
- a lack of adequate job training,
- problems in the welfare system,
- insufficient minority access to education and employment,
- multiple demands on single heads of households,
- high public school dropout rates,
- inadequate levels of available child care,
- limited support for small businesses, and
- the many challenges faced by special populations, such as the disabled or those with limited English proficiency.

The results of this scan guided the creation of the institution's first strategic plan and affected a comprehensive city plan that was developed during the 1987–88 academic year. Ten action goals were identified in the city plan, and three of these had direct implications for CCD: (a) stimulate Denver's economy, (b) create excellent, integrated education at all levels, and (c) expand economic opportunities for the city's poor. The supporting narrative for these three goals addressed all of the troubling characteristics identified in the environmental scan conducted earlier by CCD. The need for collaboration was stressed as the only feasible way to generate solutions with a lasting impact.

The environmental scan and the comprehensive city plan were reviewed by (a) the CCD College Advisory Council (consisting of community leaders), (b) the internal college Planning Council, and (c) the entire faculty and staff of CCD, in a retreat setting. Planning documents from the first several planning cycles included mutually agreed-upon college philosophy and mission statements, college goals, strategies, and action priorities. These documents have been updated on an annual basis since 1987.

Operational plans and budgets at the college are driven by these planning documents as each unit of the institution attempts to link its activities to the directions outlined. The extent to which the thrusts and values of the early planning years have been sustained can be illustrated by two of the action priorities for the 1994–95 academic year:

- continue to develop and expand community-based learning opportunities and services; and
- continue the tradition of valuing, celebrating, and promoting diversity/multiculturalism in a humanistic, caring way.

During each fiscal year, the college chooses only five or six of these priorities to direct institutional activity. The importance of community interaction and collaboration has been a consistent theme during an eight-year effort to position CCD as a vital partner in community development.

AN EARLY COLLABORATION

Refined strategies to accomplish each priority have been developed every year since 1987 and have kept institutional leaders focused on a needy community and the underserved people who reside there. No group was in greater need than the Hispanic community, the largest minority group in Denver. Then, as now, Hispanics also made up the largest group within the public school system and had the highest dropout rates. Low family income levels, unemployment, and low levels of educational attainment added to the woes of this important sector of the local community. College leaders began to talk with community representatives and other educators in 1987 about ways to address these problems. What emerged was the Colorado Institute for Hispanic Education and Economic Development. The Institute was funded by CCD, Metropolitan State College, and the University of Colorado at Denver (the three institutions that share a campus known as the Auraria Higher Education Center located in downtown Denver), with CCD serving as host and fiscal agent.

Launched during the 1987–88 academic year, the program has been led by a community board and an executive director. The most successful of the Institute's projects has been a leadership development effort that now has several hundred alumni. The institution gained a significant boost from an $800,000 Kellogg Foundation grant. The working relationships formed between institutions and community leaders have influenced additional projects such as the creation of the Small Business Development Center (SBDC) and the Denver Network, each of which will be discussed in following sections.

EXTENDING THE MODEL

The collaborative model CCD pioneered in the development of the Hispanic Institute has been followed by other collaborative efforts. The most noteworthy of these have been the Colorado Campus Compact and the Denver Network. In each case, CCD serves as host and fiscal agent.

The Colorado Campus Compact is a coalition of 21 Colorado state, public, and private university and college presidents creating public service opportunities for students and encouraging the inclusion of service as an integral part of the undergraduate experience. Students, faculty, and staff are involved in programs that improve our communities, strengthen our nation, and offer learning experiences. In rural areas as well as cities, students volunteer for needed community projects. The Compact is part of the national Campus Compact that embraces over 400 postsecondary institutions.

The Denver Network's mission is to develop a collaborative partnership between K–12, higher education, business, and the community to ensure the kinds of changes necessary to enable significant numbers of underserved, urban students to prepare for and attain postsecondary degrees. More will be reported about the Network in the section of this chapter dealing with the college's relationships with the public schools.

The Hispanic Institute, the Colorado Campus Compact, and the Denver Network share these characteristics of note: (a) the use of a community board or steering committee to lead the effort, (b) employment of a full-time professional director, (c) multiple funding agents (each of the partners contributes some type of resources), and (d) the Community College of Denver is host institution to each effort.

COLLABORATION FOSTERING COMMUNITY DEVELOPMENT

From its 1987 involvement in comprehensive city planning and its early experience starting the Hispanic Institute, CCD has become an important partner in efforts to address community needs. None of the efforts has had greater community impact than a broad collaborative project called the Denver Family Opportunity Program (DFO). In 1988, the mayor of Denver asked the president of CCD to chair the DFO governing council as it attempted to reform Denver's welfare program and stimulate self-sufficiency among recipients of Aid to Families with Dependent Children. That involvement continues today. CCD has become the leading provider of education to hundreds of participants who intend to leave welfare support behind. More than 500 participants at any given time are pursuing certificate and degree programs leading to employment. The working relationships forged with the Denver Department of Social Services and the many community-based organizations involved in the welfare reform effort have created other avenues for partnerships beyond the DFO collaboration.

For example, CCD's Women's Resource Center and outreach centers called Technical Education Centers (TEC) have become partners with case managers from Denver Department of Social Services and human service workers in community organizations. Another link has been with the Job Training Partnership Act program in Denver, which has become a major source of funding for the DFO. These relationships have created expanded services for the poor people of Denver. It is now routine for community-based organizations to refer clients to one of the training programs of CCD, primarily to the Technical Education Centers.

EXPANDING COLLEGE SERVICES

In addition to new linkages that have arisen from partnerships such as those with the DFO, the college has made some decisions regarding service delivery that have expanded partnership opportunities. One example involved extending the TEC operation (open-entry, open-exit, self-paced vocational training) to the poor neighborhoods of Denver. A local operating foundation, hospital leaders, and college personnel came together to establish a center for allied health programs at TEC East. The Mayor's Office of Employment and Training and the Private Industry Council joined with CCD to obtain a Youth Fair Chance grant from the U.S. Department of Labor to establish another center—TEC West. This operation is overseen by a 65-member advisory group that represents all segments served by the center. CCD's capacity was extended from one TEC center to four, with one opening each year during the period 1991 through 1993. This provided the opportunity for additional working relationships. In each case, center staff members have created a communications network with community-based organizations, police, and recreation centers in a sector of the city.

In a second example, other funding agencies including foundations and private sector organizations stepped forward to help establish a teen-parent program at TEC North. (The project included development of a child care center that has since become a model for other TEC sites and involvement of numerous community leaders who have visited the center.)

The reputation earned through CCD's existing partnerships and collaborative relationships presented the institution with a third opportunity, which held great promise for the local small business community. Following the environmental scan and strategic plan, CCD, in cooperation with the Denver Metro and Minority Chamber of CommerceMinority Chambers of Commerce, entered into a working relationship with the Small Business Development Center (SBDC). The center guides small business owners and would-be entrepreneurs in planning and start-up functions. An emphasis on support for minority businesses was present from the outset, but over time an opportunity has emerged for synergy in support of small business owners. The resources of the large chamber and the continuing education division of CCD have been blended to deliver a wider range of services than would be found in a typical SBDC. An Advisory Committee, with members drawn primarily from a coalition of minority chambers of commerce, oversees the effort. The Advisory Committee members (including representatives from the college's division of continuing education) have been able to obtain resources for the SBDC that are well beyond anything imagined during the earlier days of this effort.

PARTNERING WITH THE PUBLIC SCHOOLS

Involvement with the business community, partnerships with social service entities, and wide-ranging discussion with community leaders heightened college awareness of the importance of the public schools. These discussions led to a focus on work with the public schools. During the environmental scan conducted by CCD, it had become apparent there was a serious problem with dropouts in the public schools. Further, it became clear that CCD did not have a productive relationship with school personnel. Two strategic choices over the next two years led to direct involvement of college personnel with people working at the elementary and high school level. These experiences paved the way for more important and extensive programs later.

The first strategic choice was to experiment with a pilot project in a small elementary school where the principal wanted more parents involved in the school. A request came for CCD to offer English as a second language and adult basic education courses in the evening to serve the high percentage of Spanish-speaking parents. Enrichment activities were planned for the children while their parents attended classes. The project flourished; similar courses and activities were introduced in a dozen elementary schools over the next several years.

A second strategic choice led to CCD's participation in the Colorado VIP Program, a private venture initiated by a Denver Public Schools board member. CCD was paired with different four-year colleges and universities in each of the public high schools. The intent was twofold: to convince ninth grade students and their parents of the importance of postsecondary study, and to help them pursue their goals. Information sessions were held in the public high schools, and the students made visits both to CCD and to the paired university. Each year the work was launched with the new ninth grade students and continued with the other students as they advanced through high school. Results for CCD have been dramatic—from only six recent high school graduates (from the previous May) enrolled at CCD in 1986 to more than 600 in 1993–94. These two initiatives, along with later cooperative tech prep efforts, helped CCD staff develop solid working relationships with counselors and faculty members in the public school system.

CREATING THE DENVER NETWORK

Based on the strength of working relationships in place, a more ambitious undertaking came together during 1992 when the college convened a broad collaborative group. The members of this group shared the view that more of Denver's disadvantaged center city youth must graduate from high school and successfully move to and through higher education. Members included representatives of the public school system, area public universities, the Denver Department of Social Services, private foundations, the JTPA network, and many community-based organizations. Discussions with the Ford Foundation about this objective led to an invitation to join their Urban Partnership Project. This decade-long commitment sponsors the efforts of 17 American cities that are organizing to ensure success as students move through the educational pipeline. The Denver collaborative group (known now as the Denver Network) decided to accept this invitation as well as a planning grant that provided start-up resources. CCD acts as fiscal agent for the project.

The members of the Denver Network believed it was important to conduct an inventory of the existing programs purporting to address the problems in the Denver Public Schools. The resulting summary was an extensive list of fragmented approaches being pursued by numerous groups, all of whom believed they were helping the schools. Although most of them were no doubt contributing to incremental improvement in small areas, the problem was that even with all of this assistance, critical indicators such as the dropout rate were not improving. With this information as a base, Denver Network members extensively discussed what could really make a difference for disadvantaged center city young people.

Led by CCD staff, the group engaged in some "break the mold" thinking to produce a plan. The plan called for the creation of student advocacy teams. These teams were to represent selected elementary, middle, and secondary schools that made up a feeder pattern—that is, schools that serve a group of students and their families from kindergarten through high school. There was also to be a higher education team that would support the advocacy teams in any way requested. Planners imagined that advocacy teams might ask for tutoring assistance, tours of local campuses, or other such instructional and planning support. Members of the higher education team would meet regularly with the student advocacy teams to heighten collaboration. The idea was to ask each student advocacy team to create systemic change in the neighborhoods and the schools that would encourage disadvantaged students and lead to their educational success.

Funding from the Ford Foundation for the second year, in addition to many in kind contributions, launched the action plan. Three clusters of schools responded to open invitations to become involved. These feeder-pattern advocacy teams were approved by the Denver Network steering committee to begin work during the 1993–94 year. By the end of the 1993–94 year, the higher education team was being developed. In addition, discussions continued about what structure would best support the work of the Denver Network. All agreed that a full-time director was needed to focus Network efforts and to facilitate the collaboration required for success; a person was hired to serve in this capacity in December 1993. Early work with the three feeder-pattern advocacy teams led to the reaffirmation of the advocacy team concept and led to the commitment to add at least one new feeder-pattern advocacy team in 1994–95. While the jury is still out on the effectiveness of this long-term effort, fundamental decisions made by the group, such as the establishment of cohort tracking, bode well for the future. A network of advocacy teams is currently covering the neighborhoods in which the poorest people in Denver live and attend school. Moreover, there is a city-wide commitment to increase the numbers of disadvantaged young people who gain entry to higher education.

BUILDING OTHER LINKAGES

The recognition of the importance of these links, along with a belief in collaboration, has led CCD to enter a host of additional relationships focused on the urban agenda. For example, understanding the problems created by adult illiteracy led to the expansion of college-based programs and fostered a responsiveness to a partnership with the Colorado Department of Social Services, the Employment First program. This program, which offers GED preparation for food stamp recipients, is conducted in collaboration with the Colorado Department of Social Services. Under the umbrella of this program, many local businesses and corporations have contributed to helping people earn a GED certificate and develop job skills.

A combination of college experiences (involvement in early childhood education, providing child care for students, and relationships between CCD's Office of Continuing Education and the Denver business community) led to creation of both the Work and Family Resource Center and the Parent's Helpline. Partnerships with the Office of the Governor and Channel 4 (an NBC affiliate) made it possible for more than 100 corporations to receive services from the Work and Family Resource Center. The center offers child care resource and referral services, as well as parent education and professional development opportunities for employees of child care providers. In addition, hundreds of parents get direct help from a cadre of trained volunteers who staff the center's Parent's Helpline, a component of the center.

Understanding workforce needs and the needs of welfare recipients who want to become self-sufficient led to yet another partnership, this one in job development, funded by the Governor's Job Training Office. The institution joined with a local operating foundation, with Denver Department of Social Services, and with the local business community to create job opportunities for welfare clients as they emerge from programs at CCD or from the services of one of the community-based organizations. Relationships with more than a dozen leading businesses and corporations enable CCD to operate a very successful computer training program for people with disabilities. Equipment donations, software, internships and many in-kind donations support the effort. As with many other collaborative ventures, other ways to serve disabled individuals and the business community emerge in the normal course of the relationship.

Additional opportunities arise every week in the life of CCD as it continues to focus on the community's needs. The college is open to and actively participating in the relationships described here and others. In all of this, the institution has flourished, doubling in size over a six-year period to an unduplicated head count enrollment of 11,915. CCD's student body is currently the most diverse of any institution of higher education in Colorado. This year, 50 percent of the student body belongs to an ethnic minority group. Further, CCD degree graduates transfer to baccalaureate colleges and universities at rates higher than the average of all Colorado community colleges. The Community College of Denver has become the leading point of entry to higher education for first-time college students who are residents of the city and county of Denver.

CONCLUSION

The assertion that a community college should see itself as providing a nexus for community may be seen by some as presumptuous or inappropriate. While few would deny that collaboration is needed to solve community problems, some might say that community colleges serving as a nexus are straying from their central mission. Most community college practitioners, however, would agree about the importance of understanding the needs of the institution's service area and the importance of engaging in community service activities. Most community colleges, particularly those with a comprehensive mission, will not be straying if they simply link their ongoing efforts to other community processes focused on the community's most significant issues and problems. If the experience of the CCD over a period of eight years is any indication, few if any other community entities can bring to the table the breadth of understanding and commitment to the disadvantaged found in most community colleges. The opportunity to be of service has never been greater.

The issues of workforce preparation, school reform, welfare reform, illiteracy, economic development, and access for minorities are on the agenda for cities, states, and the nation. Never before have community colleges been so well-positioned to contribute what they do best. That is not to say that it will be easy. Collaboration is hard work, and it is difficult to sustain. No community, however, can be as good as it might be without the direct involvement of the local community college. Because of their mission, tradition, and commitment, community colleges can provide a nexus for community.

CHAPTER V

Lorenzo and LeCroy (1994, p. 18) have noted that "America's pioneering, 'go it alone' philosophy must begin to give way to a more pluralistic, 'do it together' mentality," and the folks at Chattanooga State Technical Community College are doing just that. The faculty and staff of CSTCC recognize the value and importance of working closely with their community. Collaboration at Chattanooga State describes activities that range from participating in community visioning to the development of urban teaching and learning centers. President James Catanzaro and a number of college staff provided leadership to their city's community visioning process. In doing so, the college became intimately aware of the community's priorities and needs, ultimately enabling them to better serve the community.

Through Catanzaro's discussion of the nature and importance of alliances in his community, we sense his agreement with the observation that "we must move beyond the laissez faire character of educational partnerships that has so far dominated the landscape" (Johnstone, 1994, Part 4, p. 2). Aggressive pursuit of alliances to create effective urban teaching/learning centers, to enhance the community's cultural life, and to facilitate economic development through entities such as the Center for Environmental Technology, the Center for Advanced Technology, and the proposed $20 million Executive Training and Regional Conference Center, reflect this community college's commitment to collaboration. Addressing a concern of some, Catanzaro makes the noteworthy observation that "strategic alliances do not divert efforts and funds from central college operations and missions, because by definition they address strategic goals identified in the institution's planning activities."

* * *

Johnstone, D.B. "College at work: Partnerships and the rebuilding of American competence." *Journal of Higher Education*. [online], 1994, 65(2), 168ff. Available: e-mail: lbindx@utxdp.dp.utexas.edu

Lorenzo, A.L. and LeCroy, N.A. "A framework for fundamental change in the community college." *Community College Journal*, 1994, 64(4), 14-19.

James Catanzaro
President
Chattanooga State Technical Community College
Chattanooga, Tennessee

COLLABORATION AT CHATTANOOGA STATE

Sticks in a bundle are unbreakable.

—East African saying

FORMING STRATEGIC ALLIANCES

A revolution is under way in America in the management of for-profit and not-for-profit organizations. Right-sizing, re-engineering, out-sourcing, the forging of strategic alliances—today these are as critical to corporate success as management by objectives, return on investment calculations, and asset considerations have been since the 1970s. We recognize now that even a talent-rich organization with a strong resource base and a hefty, long-standing market share cannot thrive alone in an environment of global completion and accelerated change. Collaboration with others, with customers, even with competitors, is essential for many to heighten performance—for some it is a matter of survival. From Fortune 500 giants to incubating companies, partnering is proving to be a highly effective, cost-saving approach to meeting both internal and external challenges.

Community colleges, more than most entities, can benefit from strategic alliances. Outreach, program development, fund raising, community relations, capital project development, image enhance-

ment, and instruction can all be greatly advanced through strategically planned, negotiated, and executed affiliations. Strategic alliances or affiliations are more than the
opportunistic partnerships of the past. They are carefully identified and formally
secured relationships that address mainstream institutional requirements. Typically,
they are entered into because:

- they provide a level of service beyond the organization's capability (due to limited
  financial, physical, and human resources, or legal/policy constraints);
- they are mutually beneficial to the college and to the partners and thus lead to "natural" associations that support the missions of all partners;
- they can enhance the image of the college;
- they can often meet major college advancement needs in a tighter time frame than
  traditional means; and
- they can contribute to overcoming campus parochialism and enrich the culture of
  the institution by bringing together—on an extended and regular basis—faculty
  and staff with the employees and supporters of outside organizations.

The widespread practice of strategic planning, we argue, should now be followed
by strategic affiliating. Colleges are constantly recognizing environmental changes and
new challenges that result from these changes. The achieving of many of an institution's short- and long-range goals—which arise from recognizing these new challenges—can and often should be met via the construction of strategic alliances. Goals
thus met can be achieved without compromising the college's objectives or its efficiency. If properly structured, alliances can fulfill expectations even more effectively than
actions taken by the college alone.

Strategic alliances merge the resources of the college with those of partners,
expanding the college's resource base. Strategic alliances introduce college leaders
to new fields of play—or segments of society—and move advancement efforts forward in bold new ways. Contrary to the fears of some, strategic alliances do not
divert efforts and funds from central college operations and missions, because by
definition they address strategic goals identified in the institution's planning activities. (Curiously, alliances are often only a few phone calls and negotiating sessions
away from being achieved.) Perhaps most importantly, strategic alliances provide
powerful linkages with the community and thus fulfill a basic mandate of the community college.

At Chattanooga State Technical Community College (CSTCC), a Tennessee Board
of Regents institution, strategic alliances have fostered significant enrollment growth,
improved program quality, enhanced the school's image, and made the college an
impact player in community and economic development. They are the result of careful assessment of community and college advancement needs, and of an institutional
bias toward establishing partnerships. Partnerships are "front burner" because they can
assist in improving quality, they can ease the limitations and instability of traditional
funding sources, and they can reduce the costs and constraints associated with philan-

thropic solicitation. Following are descriptions of several alliances that have contributed dramatically to Chattanooga State—a college of contagious warmth and enthusiasm, a college which powerfully addresses community needs, a college whose faculty, staff, and administrators are respected as transforming leaders.

URBAN TEACHING/LEARNING CENTERS

One of the most significant challenges urban community colleges face is the recruitment and retention of inner-city residents, particularly those who live in government development centers, or housing projects. Residents are often reluctant to venture outside their neighborhoods even for schooling, especially if it means attending a suburban community college. Transportation, child care, financial considerations, and a host of other practical obstacles stand in the way. Frequently, inner-city students are also underprepared for college study. Yet it is in urban neighborhoods where the fabric of our society is experiencing the greatest strain and the opportunities for community colleges are the most significant.

After several years of intensive, but traditional, efforts to recruit inner-city students, Chattanooga State decided to go directly to the neighborhoods to help residents make the transition to college attendance. The projected costs of establishing "outposts" seemed prohibitive, despite the strong potential for college and community benefit. However, this goal could be achieved through alliances.

The Chattanooga Housing Authority, by agreement, provided double housing units to the college in two large urban neighborhoods. These spaces were joined internally, then remodeled and furnished to college specifications through a partnership with the area Private Industry Council (PIC). The PIC also joined the college, neighborhood associations, and the Urban League in staffing the sites and in marketing the new learning centers to local residents.

These collaborative efforts, begun in 1992, have provided neighborhood residents with adult basic education, remedial and introductory college courses, counseling, tutoring, mentoring, and a full array of on-site student support services. The results have been dramatic and wide-ranging. Already over 100 students have been admitted into regular college programs through these learning centers, and many are now working toward degrees on the main campus. Many people who would not have come to a campus previously have entered college, faculty and staff have developed relationships with neighborhood minority leaders, and together we have implemented new initiatives to address inner-city problems. The college's minority enrollment has increased (a high-profile strategic goal) and college relations with the minority community have improved (an important administration interest). Two teaching sites have been created with minimal college investment, and two neighborhood communities have been enhanced. These neighborhood centers have been so successful that the college is developing a third center, also through collaboration. It is projected that every inner-city sector will have a learning center before the year 2000.

A unique outcome of this effort has been the development of a business course for advanced students, where the class project is the planning and startup of a business. The first business now being developed is a neighborhood child care center to be owned and operated by class members. This new venture will provide work for unemployed students, and it has also led several students to enter the college's degree program in early childhood education. Without partnerships, the college could not have moved so expeditiously and effectively into urban centers.

COMMUNITY VISIONING

In the early 1990s, Chattanooga State became involved in the resurgence of the Chattanooga area. The community was undergoing rebirth, and while the college had long been a major supplier of training for area business and industry, it was not a prime contributor to community development. In order to honor its mission and to be positioned to take advantage of future opportunities, the college had to move to center stage in community affairs.

Chattanooga, like many cities across America in the 1980s and early 1990s, began to seek direct citizen input and consensus on strategies for area advancement. In 1984, a major community goal-setting effort, under the guidance of political and civic leaders, led to the raising of nearly $800 million to accomplish over 100 projects. These projects ranged from establishing a shelter for battered women to the opening of the nation's longest pedestrian bridge, which provides miles of uninterrupted walkways within the city.

When community leaders began to consider forging anew an areawide vision for the year 2000, Chattanooga State was there to assist. Public-private partnerships led to nine communitywide visioning meetings and hundreds of hours of sifting through 1,200 citizen suggestions for improvement. The college president chaired the visioning effort and the faculty and staff assisted first in group facilitation, and later, worked toward goal achievement. They identified 27 new goals and 120 projects. Citizens and college faculty and staff are now working toward goal realization and the completion of the projects.

Learning about emerging community needs and citizen attitudes directly from the 2,600 participants in the city visioning process enabled college leaders to initiate program changes that are and will continue to be the key to enrollment growth and continued institutional viability. Leadership of the city visioning process also brought Chattanooga State into the heart of community planning, far beyond what the college could have achieved alone. It prepared the college to enter the arena of community advancement. Establishing a political and civic institute and a world-class training and conference center were just two outcomes of college participation in the visioning enterprise.

EXECUTIVE TRAINING AND REGIONAL CONFERENCE CENTER

The community, corporate executives, the chamber of commerce, county and city governments, and local economic development practitioners recognized the need for a world-class executive training and conference center. The college, however, had neither the taxing authority to fund, nor the trainers to staff, such a center. Alliances made it a reality. Two types of alliances brought it about—one with potential funding sources and another with elite training organizations. Project costs are currently estimated to be $20 million, and expectations for program quality will require participation by the leading training organizations and business schools in the country.

Limited state and local government funding for such an enterprise called for the establishment of a steering committee that could explore these issues. Representatives of large area corporate entities and the Tennessee Valley Authority (one of the largest public utilities in America and the largest landholder in the region) joined together to assist in the effort. It is this alliance of public and private partners with CSTCC that is putting together the backing for the construction of a five-story attachment to the city's new trade and convention center, where the training center will be housed. The trade center will provide, again by partnership, clear-span exhibit space, a multi-story parking garage, food service, and extra breakout rooms. The conference center will feature an auditorium, research capability, telecommunications, video production facilities, and specially designed training spaces. The funding partners will be the primary users of the center's training, teleconferencing, information search and navigation operations, and video production capabilities. National training leaders such as the Center for Creative Leadership in North Carolina and NASA are early partners. They provide a level and scope of training well beyond the capability of most institutions in the U.S., let alone a mid-size community college serving an area with 350,000 people.

This exciting new CSTCC venture has advanced the college's role in corporate training. It has enabled the college to enter new markets and operate at all training levels of virtually any organization, offering training subjects ranging from basic skills to advanced management theory. The college has been able to raise the status of its training connections to that of contractual partner. Through the conference and training center, the college can be assured a key role in the development of Southeastern Tennessee's information superhighway. Improvement in market penetration for college corporate training and exceptional image enhancement are among the other significant results of this new partnership.

COLLEGE PROGRAM DEVELOPMENT

Among the most exciting and instructive affiliations have been the college's new relationships with the widely acclaimed Hunter Museum of Art and the Chattanooga Little Theater. By the late 1980s, Chattanooga State had overgrown its fine arts building and abandoned drama as an instructional program, despite a well-designed auditorium and excellent support facilities. Program demand, however, was strong in both disciplines. To meet this demand, it was clear the college had to increase facilities and staffing in art and reconstitute a theater department—both daunting tasks.

The cost of building additional labs for painting, sculpture, pottery, and the like, and limitations in staffing, both instructional and technical, blocked the way to expanding the art program. Yet, in a single year, partnerships made excellent teaching space available, made it possible to hire several of the region's finest artists as adjunct faculty, and enhanced the college's prestige. The CSTCC's high-level commitment to marketing this new joint venture increased enrollment for college courses and for the non-credit offerings of the museum. Previously constrained by lack of specialized space, the college now can provide a full spectrum of courses in the visual arts. In partnership with the museum, the college now offers art courses in stained glass, watercolor, cast silver, jewelry making, basic pearl and bead stringing, basket weaving, and bronze casting.

Partnership with a thriving community theater made it possible to leap from having virtually no theater program to providing a full-blown degree program in less than a year. This partnership came complete with opportunities to perform in and technically support eight major productions a year. Highly educated and experienced acting and technical directors from the Little Theater became adjunct members of the CSTCC faculty. They brought a level of expertise to the program that even those colleges with well-developed programs cannot obtain.

Mutual benefit is the key to successful alliances. In these examples, the museum and the theater benefit from high profile advertisements in the college's fall, spring, and summer schedules, which are mailed to over 200,000 households. The theater enjoys the use of a 400-seat alternative facility and the assistance provided by the college's music and drama faculty. The museum can now offer a wider array of classes and optimize the use of space.

The college is enhanced by marrying several of Chattanooga's outstanding cultural arts organizations to college credit and continuing education programs. They are the model for the future development of the remaining college arts programs—choral arts, instrumental music, graphic design, and advertising art.

SATELLITE CAMPUS DEVELOPMENT

Making educational opportunities available to residents in outlying areas is a significant challenge to many of America's community colleges. Until recently, people from sizeable communities in Chattanooga State Technical Community College's service area were served only after making long drives to the main campus or through distance learning, which was delivered primarily through instructional fixed television. Enhancement of services to these outlying communities and support of their economic development efforts were high priority goals of the college's 1991 strategic plan.

Chattanooga State Technical Community College has a large, six-county service area. The challenge of providing appropriate satellite campus space loomed large for both financial and practical reasons. By 1992, however, through joint planning with city, county, and state governments, the public schools and, most importantly, the Private Industry Council (PIC), two optimally located 15,000-square-foot sites were purchased and remodeled without the use of college funds. These satellites now function as "one-stop shops" for employment assistance, ABE/GED, library services, child care, vocational training, and college study. Through these operations, achieved in less than one year, CSTCC is serving rural populations effectively. A comprehensive set of college-level courses and corporate training and recruitment activities are also offered through these satellite centers.

Market penetration, as demonstrated by enrollment increases from these areas, is one major outcome of this partnership. A second is that new relationships with outlying communities, and their leaders and businesses have taken hold. CSTCC, previously distant and unconnected, is now a hometown operation in several local communities.

POLITICAL AND CIVIC INSTITUTE

A traditional role of America's postsecondary institutions is to prepare students for participation in the democratic process, and, by implication, for political and civic leadership roles. Another primary role, for community colleges specifically, is to prepare citizens for successful careers. During Chattanooga's 1992 visioning activity, the notion to create a political and civic institute to prepare people for careers in politics and community agencies took hold. This idea combined the two aforementioned goals of American higher education and, therefore, was a natural fit with the mission of Chattanooga State, but it required broad support to be successful. Therefore, Chattanooga State joined with the Chattanooga Area Chamber of Commerce to develop the Political and Civic Institute.

The Institute conducted a series of workshops, some of which were presented live on cable access television. The workshops culminated in a weekend retreat. At the retreat, participants engaged in leadership development exercises, and the faculty instructed them in the mechanics of campaigning. They covered the purposes and rewards of public office and agency leadership, grass roots candidate development, fund raising, media relations, and a review of public offices, agencies, and organizations. The final retreat exercise was a day-long competitive campaign simulation that brought together all of the program elements into a real-world challenge and specifically prepared students for the campaign trail. Participants described this simulation as especially useful. This venture, conducted in partnership with the chamber, has positioned the college as an important agent of community development. It has also been an effective vehicle for involving the leaders of our region and community in the college.

The college possessed the financial and administrative capability to launch such an institute alone; however, gaining the support of area businesses and the community-at-large was markedly improved by CSTCC's affiliation with the Chattanooga Area Chamber of Commerce. Alliances enhance existing institutional capabilities, and such was the case with the Political and Civic Institute.

ALLIANCES WITH BUSINESS AND INDUSTRY

Chattanooga State recently created two distinguished centers that offer credit instruction, corporate training, technology transfer, and, in the near future, business incubation. These centers—the Center for Environmental Technology and the Center for Advanced Technology—directly and specifically respond to area economic development needs.

The Center for Environmental Technology is based in the college's large environmental science and technology program. The program, which includes hazardous waste technology, industrial hygiene, environmental technology, and health physics, features a three-acre outdoor training lab that offers students challenges in full-scale inspection and toxic waste clean-up. Students confront problems in rail cars, storage tanks, on land, in swamps, and in wooded areas, encountering environmental challenges as they would on the job. The outdoor lab, nicknamed "The Environmental Playground," is the result of a joint venture between the college and several major chemical companies.

The center also participates in the region's International Congress of Environmental Commerce and Technology (ICONECT), a not-for-profit consortium of research institutions, manufacturers, and consulting and law firms, which is chaired by the college president. ICONECT holds international conferences on environmental technologies, facilitates technology transfer from higher education institutions and research labs in Europe and the United States to area businesses, and works with the U.S. Department of Commerce on corporate "matchmaking."

This partnership with corporations, the area university, national research labs, and private consulting and law firms not only enriches the college's instructional programs by keeping them at the cutting edge, it positions the college to play a key role in supporting economic development and providing proprietary training to regional firms. The college, standing alone, could not amass the resources or have the connections to operate at the world class level that ICONECT and the "Playground" allow.

The second center, the Center for Advanced Technology, developed as a collaborative effort between the college, IBM, and General Electric. This center now focuses on preparing employees of regional manufacturers for the transition to computer-integrated manufacturing primarily through the IBM AS400 computer system.

IBM and GE provided about 50 percent of the equipment and software used in the Center. The college has installed and maintained AS400s. It has also worked with IBM sales representatives in designing and implementing computer-integrated manufacturing processes, thus fulfilling its commitment to assist companies in the service area that are instituting advanced technologies.

These are two of several alliances with business and industry that have significantly improved college instructional programs. They have also brought the college to wider relationships with the manufacturing community, notably in technology transfer and training.

JOINT PROGRAMS WITH THE PUBLIC SCHOOLS

For a century, public elementary and secondary educational institutions have been isolated from the higher education community. Today, however, a number of initiatives to end that isolation are visible across America. In fact, collaboration is sweeping America with lightning speed. Tech prep programs abound, and the quest for the "seamless" student experience from pre-school to a terminal degree is now taken up throughout the land.

At Chattanooga State, these new associations have led to several unique and exciting partnerships. No alliance has been more promising for the college than one with the public school systems of the area, a partnership called Joint Enrollment. Supported by the state's department of education and the Tennessee Board of Regents, the program encourages high school juniors and seniors who have a 3.0 or better GPA and a score of at least 19 on the ACT to take college classes at the high school through Chattanooga State. College credit is earned simultaneously with units that apply to high school graduation.

The program introduces over 500 students each semester to college-level study, thereby facilitating the transition to postsecondary institutions. In fact, many students begin college with a full semester completed; others enter at the sophomore level. Students also develop faculty contacts at the college and are more likely, therefore, to select Chattanooga State upon graduation from high school. Also, the college, for the first time, has become an option for upper-quartile students.

Another alliance Chattanooga State has forged with the public schools focuses on improving high school calculus instruction through the use of new technologies. Partners in this alliance include the University of Tennessee at Chattanooga and a local private college. The effort is funded by the National Science Foundation.

The outcomes have been noteworthy. There is documented evidence of improvement in student performance, principally through the effective use of graphing calculators.

Better articulation from high school through Chattanooga State to university study has been achieved, leading to an integrated progression of study and to college course equivalencies. The course development process has also been quickened and enhanced by this partnership.

A second math consortium was developed with the University of Kentucky and five other Kentucky four-year colleges. This partnership is founded on the sharing of new teaching/learning strategies and materials, and on the professional development of math faculty. Consortium activities have led to optimal articulation agreements among the participating institutions and to improved teaching/learning strategies.

These consortia demonstrate that the alliance is a powerful way to advance college instructional capability—in these cases, to reform the teaching of mathematics. They also aid in the successful transition of students from high school to college-level work.

SUMMARY AND CONCLUSION

Community colleges are, by nature, connected institutions. They build empowered relationships with their communities. Their strength lies in the many ways they tie in to local business, government, and professional life. These "tie-ins" broaden the influence of the college and allow it to achieve far more than it could alone. Chattanooga State, through collaboration, has carried out many new initiatives. CSTCC has contributed to a city's quality of life by assisting government agencies and corporations in the development of wellness programs; developed the capability to access the college's library and the Internet by computer for a high school; provided vocational training for electrical workers, carpenters, and machinists unions; and held academic olympics for area middle and secondary schools.

Strategic alliances can be remarkably successful because they permit us to meet challenges as they come over the horizon, arm-in-arm with powerful allies. They can improve college life and service. They are a means of fund raising and, most importantly, of achieving key goals established through strategic planning.

Chapter VI

Catanzaro exemplifies the leadership described by Kanter (1994, p. 99), who observes that "collaborative relationships draw energy largely from the optimistic ambition of their creators." This is also true when it comes to Robert "Squee" Gordon, president of Humber College of Applied Arts and Technology, and the author of the next chapter. Gordon's energy and entrepreneurship have engendered a well-thought-out mission, symbolized in the components of a "value diamond" (illustrated in the chapter)—customer service, innovation, excellence, and staff development. Humber uses strategic partnerships to link its operational activities to meeting the needs of its constituencies.

Although there are many partnerships in which Humber is routinely involved, three types are discussed here: human resource collaboration (especially staff development), partnerships for programs and training services (including several extensive international collaborations), and partnerships for physical resources. A particularly notable physical resource partnership—with seven partners—led to Humber's moving into a renovated building (the exterior of which has been designated a historical site) more suitable for its purposes while turning over an existing campus site to the municipal and metropolitan government to be shared with a local school board to create parkland and playing fields.

The persistence and creativity exhibited by Humber are among the important characteristics of community colleges that construct successful partnerships. The value of the college faculty and staff conceptually thinking through the college's mission and strategies is also apparent in this interesting piece.

* * *

Kanter, R.M. "Collaborative advantage: The art of alliances." *Harvard Business Review*, 1994, 72(4), 96–108.

Robert A. Gordon

President

Humber College of Applied Arts and Technology

Toronto, Ontario, Canada

PARTNERSHIPS AT HUMBER COLLEGE:

A Pathway to Institutional Success

Don't overlook the importance of worldwide thinking. A company that keeps its eye on Tom, Mary, and Harry is going to miss Hans, Marie, and Yoshio.

—Al Ries

To ensure Canada's prosperity, Canadians must build effective partnerships, and working together, bring about change in a number of critical areas.
— Steering Group on Prosperity (1992)

Partnerships can be defined as cooperative relationships where parties have specified joint rights and responsibilities in common enterprises. When fully operational, these partnerships can become the catalysts for collaboration, providing the synergy for empowering people and creating new and entrepreneurial opportunities. At Humber College, short- and long-term partnerships have become part of Humber's organizational way of accomplishing and enhancing the college's mission. This chapter will demonstrate how partnerships formed by Humber College have become a fundamental strategy for excellence in operations, a cultural dimension of the institution, and a continuous learning process for the college, as it seeks to enhance its educational programs for its community.

By using three key operational elements of a college—staff, programs, and resources—and providing a description, analysis, and interpretation for each element, this chapter will demonstrate the effectiveness of partnerships for Humber College.

BACKGROUND

Humber in Ontario. Humber College of Applied Arts and Technology is a large public, urban, multi-campus institution located in the northwest sector of Toronto—Canada's largest city. Humber has more than 11,000 full-time students, 70,000 part-time students, scores of corporate training customers, and two- and three-year diploma programs, certificates, and post-diploma programs comprising more than 130 offerings. With an annual budget of $120 million (Canadian), Humber is one of the largest colleges in the province of Ontario and, indeed, in North America.

Education in Canada is under provincial jurisdiction. Ontario's system of 23 colleges, as established in 1965, is unique, as are the other nine provincial systems. In Ontario, the college and university systems are parallel but separate, and the colleges are not transfer institutions, as they are in several other provinces. A single provincial Ministry of Education and Training regulates elementary, secondary, postsecondary, apprenticeship, and all other formal, institutional education and training in the province, including private and commercial endeavors. The Minister of Education and Training receives college-related advice from an appointed, system-level Council of Regents. This Council, working through the Council of Presidents for the colleges, also conducts collective bargaining with the two college unions representing faculty and support staff.

The Purpose of the Colleges. The Colleges of Applied Arts and Technology, commonly known as CAATs, were mandated to fulfill three roles pertinent to the social and economic circumstances of the 1960s. They were to provide (a) career and occupational programs leading to a diploma in four broad areas—applied arts, business, health, and technology, (b) basic education and remedial programs so that all adults would have an opportunity to receive postsecondary training or education, and (c) adult education to the community, including contract training for business and industry.

A recent major focus study in Ontario, titled *Vision 2000* (1990), has reaffirmed the original mandate. However, the colleges have been directed to refocus their services and activities toward the following:
- career education embedded in personal, social, and employment skills;
- accessibility with opportunities to enable success at college;
- quality assurance through systemwide academic standards; and
- life-long learning to meet the diverse needs of students.

Most importantly, a focus has been placed upon the forging of partnerships and the development of collaborative decision-making processes.

The College Structure and Its Students. Humber, like all CAATs, is governed by an appointed 17-member community-representative Board of Governors, of whom four are internally elected members—one each from the student body, support staff, faculty, and administration. The board is responsible to the Minister of Education and Training. The college president is a voting member and responsible to the board. At Humber, there are four vice presidents and approximately 1200 full-time staff, half of whom are directly involved in instruction.

The student population, like the city of Toronto, is multicultural, multiracial, and multilingual. The general population is also aging; thus, one-third of the full-time student body is over the age of 21, with an increasing "graying" of what was a very youthful student constituency in the 1960s and 1970s. The current recession and double-digit unemployment percentages have had an inflationary impact on both student numbers and average age.

Humber's Environs and Resources. The official "community" of each college is a specific geographic territory or catchment area. Humber's catchment area consists of the westernmost metropolitan Toronto boroughs of Etobicoke and York. Both are cities in their own right, relatively small in area and, collectively, have a population of about 400,000. Of the 10,000 businesses, the vast majority are very small, with a few medium-sized industries. Potential students living within the catchment area are free to choose any college they wish; there are four colleges in Metro Toronto and three others within easy commuting distance. The CAATs operate primarily on government grants, based on the number of students, and have no taxation powers or out-of-district fees. Humber has relied on its human resources to build a quality institution capable of attracting students.

The significant physical resource of the college was, and is, land: approximately 250 acres situated near an international airport with easy access to the major arterial highways of southern Ontario. Coupled with this physical resource, the nurturing of talent, creativity, and innovation has resulted in one of the largest, most successful colleges in Canada.

HUMBER COLLEGE: MISSION, VALUES, AND PHILOSOPHY

Figure 1 provides a conceptual view of the relationships between Humber's mandate, mission, values, operations, and the strategic role of its partnerships with the external community. These partnerships allow the college to pursue opportunities for interaction with its clients and stakeholders, whether local, regional or provincial, national or international.

The Mission and Values. It was several years before Humber's three mandated roles were fully articulated. Humber's mission states that it is a comprehensive, accessible,

CONCEPTUAL VIEW
OF
HUMBER COLLEGE'S PARTNERSHIP STRATEGY

FIGURE 1.

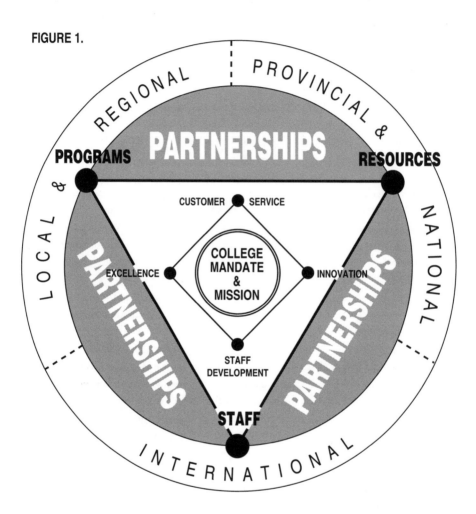

flexible, responsive, and accountable institution, characterized by a humanistic approach and a commitment to excellence. The common mandate for all CAATs, coupled with Humber's own mission, is symbolized in the components of the "value diamond"—customer service, innovation, excellence, and staff development.

Customer service is the primary cutting edge of the value diamond. Such service implies attention to the needs of the stakeholders, as well as response to and anticipation of such needs. A commitment to innovation evolved from the continuing, systemic contradiction of decreasing funds and increasing demands for services. The factors creating this paradox are well-known to educators: inflation and the growing deficit, coupled with technological change and unemployment, in a climate of increasing global competition. A focus on excellence complements both customer service and innovation, and implies an emphasis on meeting and exceeding the expectations of clients and stakeholders. Staff development is the essential basis of these values. In order to avoid stagnation, the college maintains qualified, fully competent, and committed staff, who are supported by a wide range of professional development opportunities and programs.

The Operational Triangle. At the most fundamental level, any educational institution must provide staff, programs, and resources to accomplish its mission and realize its values. The quantity/quality "mix," and the management of these three "internal" elements, constitute the basic operation of the college as it relates to clients and the community.

The word *Staff*, for the purposes of this conceptual view, includes all human resources of the college—support staff, faculty, and administrators. As symbolically represented in Figure 1, this element is the pivotal point of all operations. *Programs* refers to all aspects of curriculum and training services, and includes the broader notion of programming and all modes of delivery—full/part time, on/off campus, and so forth. *Resources* includes all finances and facilities including land, equipment, tools, and supplies.

Strategies are the methods by which these policies are put into action. Figure 1 illustrates the strategic role of partnerships that link Humber's operational triangle to its clients. The central circle, containing the mandate and mission, represents the core of the organization and goal-setting activities that are essential for strategic management. The core mandate and mission are set in an encompassing "value diamond," indicating that policy development is continuously influenced by these values and vice versa. This core is also reflective of, and helps shape, the culture of the college. Partnership, in the sense that each partner contributes and each gains within the relationship, therefore constitutes one manifestation of Humber's way of "being in the world." The circular configuration of the entire figure illustrates the notion of a dynamic, dialectical whole in which every partnership, directly or indirectly, affects every other partnership.

As a result of Humber's history, circumstances, mission, and goals, there is, within the conceptual framework presented in Figure 1, a multitude of bilateral and multilateral partnerships linking the institution to its clients and its internal and external stake-holders. Using the "operational triangle" to categorize partnering activities, three types of partnerships will be discussed as sub-themes. All three elements of the triangle are present in these sub-themes. However, the thrust of the partnership activity in each sub-theme falls within one of the general categories of human resources, programs and training services, or physical resources. Although the sub-themes are treated as individual or grouped illustrations, as stated above, they are interconnected and organic, forming a tapestry. The tapestry tells the story and articulates the meaning of Humber College.

PARTNERSHIPS FOR HUMAN RESOURCE DEVELOPMENT

Human resource development must be the primary focus in creating a culture in an institution. People are the key to delivering any mission that revolves around excellence in education. As has been said with more truth than jest, "the pathway to partnerships is paved with participating people."

Assessing Human Resource Development. Early on, the baccalaureate degree and several years of experience were the primary qualifications for a teaching post in the CAATs. All Ontario colleges have their own in-service teacher training program and a two-year probationary period. In a comprehensive assessment taken at Humber College in the early 1980s, it was determined that the staff had great talents, but lacked a dynamic professional development program. The central office for professional development at Humber had minimal impact on the institution. Many of the faculty were becoming cynical; there was an absence of core values, faculty were starved for involvement and recognition, and the best developmental practices and opportunities were bureaucratically controlled.

Staff attitudes could be described as a ratio of 20:60:20. That is, 20 percent of the staff were self-starters, eager to be empowered; 60 percent were observing leadership behavior to see how the self-starters were treated; and 20 percent needed to be challenged. If this kind of situation is not handled skillfully, an organization is soon dominated by the cynicism of its faculty and staff. The challenge to redesign the culture became obvious. Many programs had been conceptualized, but they were based upon a core value exercise that the senior staff undertook very early in the planning process for the college. Creating values and getting staff aligned were critical in the plan for transformation within Humber's culture.

Human Resource Collaborations. The first major undertaking for the college during reassessment was the mission review. Four values—care for customer, innovation, quality excellence, and professional development—became the foundation that would guide college operations, be the basis for all decisions, and be central to all orientation programs, whether for staff or students. Guided by these emerging values, the college community agreed on a mission statement that has been relevant now for more than a decade. Staff involvement, teamwork, and the concept of a shared vision were important human resource processes used during the mission review—this clearly expressed institutional commitment to employee development. Following the determination of the mission statement, all divisions in the college were required to develop consistent human resource plans, and faculty and staff were asked to develop three-year personal plans consistent both with the mission and with their divisional plan. Funds were allocated to sponsor activities that would empower staff. This mobilization of resources created a positive and energetic force in the culture. The resulting plans set the stage for several major program thrusts that would develop staff and create a high level of expertise.

Affiliations with professional associations became a major thrust. Faculty and staff were encouraged to actively participate in organizations such as the Association of Canadian Community Colleges (ACCC), the National Institute for Staff and Organizational Development (NISOD), and provincial associations. Today, for example, Humber College continues to send faculty to NISOD's annual meeting in groups of 10 to 15. These faculty are selected by previous participants, who provide an orientation and a follow-up meeting. This process might typically involve more than 20 people talking about innovative teaching strategies. In fact, several previous participants now offer programs themselves, and they continue to celebrate teamwork and collegiality, values that were deliberately fostered by these activities. Similar experiences occur as a result of ACCC and provincial teachers' conference meetings. College staff have also attended numerous training programs sponsored by the Michigan Consortium and the prestigious League for Innovation. There are many such examples, but the main ingredients for success are sponsored association involvement, selection by peers, celebration of teamwork, and the building of a sense of community. Humber staff who participate in international projects also develop a wide range of skills. International staff development opportunities are discussed in more detail later in this document.

The most pivotal human resource activity initiated at the college was a campus-based graduate master's program in community college leadership offered through a partnership with Central Michigan University. This three-year degree program comprises 10 courses, each offered in a weekend format on campus at Humber College. Cohorts of 30 candidates participate in each program cycle. The key to the success of the program has been the participation of national and international faculty, who are also able to use the college as a resource for research projects. The college president and vice presidents also have taught courses in this program. In addition to the collegiality that develops from such interaction, the program provided excellent opportunities for aligning staff development with organizational development. Eight cohorts have participated in the program during this decade, and there is a waiting list for future offerings. Many of Humber's part-time teachers are now expressing an interest in this type of developmental activity. The result of the master's program has been the development of a core of talented trainers throughout the college. There is now a cadre of teachers and staff to provide training to business and industry, to conduct international projects, and to serve as consultants or trainers internally and at provincial workshops. In order to capitalize on this talent, Humber hosts an annual campus showcase featuring as many as 30 workshops and keynote speakers. Again, the result is a sharing of skills and the building of a sense of community.

It is beyond the scope of this chapter to document all the staff development activities at Humber College. However, it should be noted that, building upon the enthusiasm generated by the master's graduates, Humber College has now developed a campus-based program of doctoral studies in conjunction with Michigan State University. This program was modeled largely on the Central Michigan University experience, and it has yielded similar, positive results.

These educational models motivated Humber's support staff, in turn. As a result, the college now offers baccalaureate courses in partnership with York University/Atkinson College>. Many of Humber's support staff have entered this program, and today several have earned their undergraduate degrees and advanced to the graduate level. All of these initiatives have created a critical mass of enthusiasm and energy serving to transform Humber's culture.

Results of Human Resource Collaborations. Many staff are now so motivated and skilled that there is an abundance of leaders at the college who can effectively plan and organize programs, and do research. Faculty are beginning to publish. Humber's next annual professional development report will contain 12 articles written by Humber faculty and staff. This marks the beginning of a new level of maturity and growth.

Another result of staff development programs, important to the development of a learning and empowering culture on campus, is Humber's recognition and awards program. This is a faculty- and staff-initiated program of peer nomination and selection. The staff awards program includes support staff awards, teaching awards, awards for innovation, leadership awards, and student appreciation awards. After a peer selection process, these awards are generally reviewed by the college's governing body—the Academic Council. In all, over 50 awards are presented at college celebrations throughout the year, culminating with an annual president's breakfast for all Humber faculty and staff.

This rather brief but representative sample of human resource development partnerships demonstrates the centrality of staff development to institutional success and performance. It is important that programs are designed at all levels—for students, support staff, faculty, administrators, and the board.

The predominant, essential ingredient for institutional success is people power. It is the talents of the staff that transform an organization, since these talents create a culture that enhances a sense of empowerment for its constituents. This empowerment leads staff to internalize the core mission and values, and the principles of partnership as a professional way of life.

PARTNERSHIPS FOR PROGRAMS AND TRAINING SERVICES

Two types of partnerships will be highlighted in this section—those with an international dimension and those with North American private sector organizations. First, international partnerships are considered. Humber's evolving internal dynamic has been reflected outwardly in a multitude of international relationships. These are seen as additional learning opportunities for faculty and staff, and are legitimized by the active support of senior management.

Assessing Humber's International Partnerships. Partnerships with out-of-country colleges, universities, technical institutes, non-governmental organizations, and other agencies and institutions have increased the strength of Humber College's human resources and programming. Increased overseas visibility for the college has acted as a beacon for attracting students and other resources from around the world.

Humber's current success in the international field has evolved over a 20-year period. Beginning in the early 1970s, with a small partnership involving St. Vincent Technical College in the Caribbean island country of St. Vincent, Humber now partners with consortia and individual institutions throughout the world. The following three examples provide some perspective on the diversity and benefits of these international activities.

Collaborations in International Programming. *African Continent.* Since the late 1980s, Humber College has been leading the development of a major cooperative venture involving several Canadian institutions and polytechnics in Botswana, Lesotho, and Swaziland. Humber made initial contact while managing a short-term project in the early 1980s on behalf of the Association of Canadian Community Colleges. Subsequently, the principal of the Swaziland College of Technology (SCOT) came to Canada and, speaking with federal government officials in Ottawa, reinforced the value of further institutional cooperation and development. It was suggested that partnerships between Swaziland and Canada could also possibly include the neighboring countries of Botswana and Lesotho.

Prior to this project, the southern African institutions in Botswana, Lesotho, and Swaziland had relied heavily on expatriates for curriculum development, faculty, and even polytechnic management. The purpose of this project was to train nationals, particularly women, to assume these roles. The human resource development basis of this project permeated virtually all of Humber's international project activities including curriculum development, institutional planning, developing industry/education relationships, educational management and support staff development, faculty updating, and the development and implementation of computer-based management. For many college staff, this was their first experience in a primarily non-white environment, and it resulted in a greater appreciation for the culture shock faced by the many Africans, Asians, and others who find their way to Humber's doors. Now entering its fifth year, this Canadian government-sponsored project has been expanded beyond Botswana, Lesotho, and Swaziland to include South Africa and Namibia.

Bangladesh. The second example of international partnerships is quite different. Bangladesh is one of the poorest places in the world and one of the most difficult in which to develop a sustainable partnership. Challenges include the distressingly low per capita income, frequent natural disasters, and immense cultural differences, not to mention the distance from North America and associated difficulties with communications. Within this context, Humber has cultivated a partnership with Micro Industries Development Assistance Society (MIDAS), a non-governmental organization delivering small business education and training, providing business and industry research capability, and furnishing equity-based loans to the micro-enterprise community. This overseas partnership is atypical in that it links Humber with a private sector training organization known throughout the region for its highly trained personnel.

This partnership involves the cooperative delivery of technical workshops in Bangladesh that focus on such diverse areas as promotion for small business, program design strategies for business and technical education, and the writing of culturally suitable case studies for business education. Humber personnel work with Bangladeshis as co-facilitators to develop and deliver the workshops. Expertise is transferred from Humber to MIDAS and from MIDAS to Humber. Specifically, MIDAS is developing an increased facility to deliver fee-based seminars and workshops to in-country clients, while Humber faculty and staff are polishing delivery skills, learning about international markets, and further increasing their cultural sensitivity and awareness.

The Humber-MIDAS linkage also enables Bangladeshi groups to spend up to one month in Canada, studying approaches to business education in the private and public sectors, and to have considerable interaction with Humber personnel. Funded by the Canadian International Development Agency (CIDA), the Humber-MIDAS linkage provides an opportunity for faculty and staff to work with the private sector overseas in an environment which, to put it mildly, is challenging.

Malaysia. The third international partnership example is also drawn from Asia. During the past three years, a partnership developed among Humber College, Malaysian Ministries, and MARA, one of Malaysia's largest training agencies. In terms of size, scope, and complexity, this is one of the most significant overseas partnerships in which Humber has been involved.

The Malaysian-Humber partnership began with several visits by Humber personnel to Malaysia and follow-up visits by senior Malaysian officials to Humber. When visiting Humber, officials from the Malaysian Ministry of Human Resources were particularly interested in the curriculum development capability of Humber's staff (using the DACUM technique), while MARA staff focused on engineering technology programs. Discussions and visits took place between Humber and Malaysian personnel over a period of several years before major activities were actualized.

The first partnership activity with the Ministry of Human Resources personnel was modest but important. Two officers from the Malaysian Ministry were assigned to work closely with a senior member of the college's Program Development Department for a three-week period. Following this, the Malaysian Ministry asked Humber to develop a customized program in Competency Based Education (CBE) for staff from eight different Malaysian ministries. This has expanded to include management training programs offered to groups of Malaysian officers who attend these programs at Humber throughout the year.

The Humber-MARA program has blossomed over the years. It now includes customized delivery of training up to program completion, the diploma level (four and six semesters), and industrial experience for students with an equivalent to Grade 12. Some students return to Malaysia to assume upgraded positions in Malaysian industry, while articulation agreements have been negotiated with various universities for the top graduates to go on for an engineering degree. To deal with the volume of students, Humber has developed partnerships with other Ontario colleges and now places many of the MARA students in these colleges. In effect, Humber has assumed a role of broker on behalf of MARA.

As with the other partnerships, Humber staff are challenged to upgrade their skills and develop their cultural sensitivity in order to provide the level of training required by Humber's Malaysian partners. However, unlike some of the other partnerships, the broad scope of the Malaysian partnerships has created points of contact and strong relationships between Humber and Malaysians in virtually every Malaysian province. These are contacts who consider themselves to be part of the Humber community, having studied and worked with our faculty and staff for as long as three years. At this stage, when Humber staff make one of their frequent trips to Malaysia, as required by the partnership, it is an opportunity to renew acquaintances with old friends.

Results of International Partnerships. International partnerships have provided Humber College faculty and staff with unique challenges and opportunities to upgrade their skills, develop new relationships, operate with a global perspective, and increase their personal sensitivity and awareness. As a result of the international partnerships described here, and the many others in which Humber has been involved, there is rarely a week that goes by when the college does not receive invitations to participate in new overseas ventures. These unanticipated results that provide additional international opportunities have had a major catalytic effect on Humber's global networking activities and on human resource development.

If the main advantages of international opportunities are in enhancing the intercultural skills of the staff and refining the curriculum to be congruent with the mission of a multicultural college, then it is important to avoid the pitfall of concentrating such experience in a few people. The more experience certain individuals acquire, the more they are in demand by the public and private sector international agencies. The posting and formal selection of people for overseas assignments, while pairing the inexperienced with the experienced, are important practices to be developed.

In terms of the infrastructure for international projects, a decentralized model has functioned effectively for nearly two decades. One part-time administrator and one part-time administrative assistant coordinate these activities throughout various academic offices within the college. To further strengthen these efforts and avoid embarrassing overlaps, a collegewide International Committee has been formed to provide a focal point for information, but not to centralize the activities. This decentralized approach is in itself an innovation and typical of the college philosophy for empowering staff to take advantage of new opportunities. With over 200 faculty and administrators involved in international projects and contracts over the last decade, the cultural awareness of the staff, their close associates, and those they mentor has been raised. In turn, these projects and contracts have enhanced the mission and curriculum of a multicultural, multiracial organization. The partnerships are a "win-win" proposition, and these off-shore activities complement local and national activities.

Assessing Private Sector Partnerships. In the past five years, over a dozen formal partnership relationships (alliances) with the private and public sectors have been developed. The local and national partnership outcomes described in this section can best be categorized as alliances. What distinguishes an alliance from a collaboration is the more formal nature of the agreement between the partners to work together toward mutually beneficial ends. Humber's entrepreneurial business entity is its Business and Industry Services (B&IS) unit. The college has a long history of working directly with the private sector, government, and labor through small, marginal departments and units scattered throughout the academic and service divisions of the college. These units and their talent, experience, customer bases, systems and procedures have been integrated and upgraded into a major revenue producing and customer service "one-stop-shop" business. In the past five years, over a dozen formal alliances with the private and public sectors have been developed.

Partnerships are publicly recognized through the display of an engraved plaque hung in the board room of the B&IS area (called the Business and Industry Services Centre or BISC). Each recognized partner has a duplicate plaque formally presented by the president of Humber. The general purpose of these alliances has been to provide mutual benefits by maximizing the use and development of human and physical resources, increasing access to markets, and continuous improvement. Although work-force training has been a primary focus, technology transfer and economic development have also ensued (as illustrated by Humber's exemplary partnership/alliance with Kodak Canada, described later).

Collaborative Alliances in Programming with Business and Industry. Three models of alliances with the private sector have emerged in Humber's experience—the sectorwide, the learning factory, and the company consortium. The sectorwide model is industry-specific. The focus is primarily human resource development with a competitiveness agenda. Since the late 1980s, the provincial and federal governments, using a cost-sharing approach, have encouraged industry sectors to form councils responsible for training and development. Typically, all stakeholders are involved in the individual councils—those from business, labor, government, and education. Humber has been active in the auto parts, electrical/electronics, and plastics sectoral councils, and has provided expertise and support in assessment of training needs, planning and coordination, curriculum and instructional development, as well as the delivery of high quality training in flexible formats.

Plastic Industry. In the case of the plastics industry, this sectorwide, multi-stakeholder alliance has led to Humber's full involvement with a unique training center—the Canadian Plastics Centre for Training (CPCT)—which serves the industry on a national basis. In partnership with the Society of the Plastics Industry of Canada (SPI), the Ontario Federation of Labour and the Canadian federal and Ontario provincial governments, Humber helped design, develop, equip, staff, and implement training at a location adjacent to the main college campus. Hands-on training in the four major plastics processing technologies (injection molding, blow molding, blown film, and extrusion) is offered nationally. Concomitantly, Humber's diploma programs in the Schools of Business, Manufacturing and Design, and Information Technology and Electronics provide management, supervisory, and accounting courses, such as plastics engineering technology, computer aided design (CAD), and robotics courses and programs.

The second model has been dubbed the learning factory. Human resource development aims primarily at filling the competency gap between the current and needed or desired levels of competencies in an organization. The effectiveness of such development is measured in competency gain and, secondarily, in terms of the effectiveness of the input of these "new" competencies toward achieving business targets such as productivity and competitiveness. The learning factory approach links learning directly to business requirements and manufacturing excellence strategies. Since competency acquisition is considered intangible, the only measure of success is in terms of business results. Typically, a single medium-to-large company works with the college to develop an integrated learning strategy for all employees. The learning plans include experiences that range from upgrading basic communications and interpersonal skills, to automated manufacturing and just-in-time supplying, to total quality management and continuous improvement. Close monitoring and measuring of business results are essential to the model. By way of illustration, one major client of Humber experienced the following in just over one year: 40 percent productivity improvement, 50 percent reduction in quoted lead time, 45 percent reduction in total waste, 20 percent reduction in floor space, and 80 percent reduction in stockroom inventory.

The third model, the company consortium, features collective alliances of either heterogeneous or homogeneous companies. Common learning needs among the companies are matched with Humber's learning services. The immediate effect is a reduction of training costs for all members of the consortium. The value-added benefit for each member, including Humber, is the inter-organizational networking and benchmarking that results from the interaction of "cohorts in training" at many levels and across many functions in several organizations. When similar, but non-competing or competing companies' personnel hear each other's stories and realize that there are no "greener pastures" in the business, they begin to share and find ways of helping each other with ideas and solutions to common problems.

Kodak Canada. Kodak Canada Inc., a subsidiary of Eastman Kodak based in Rochester, New York, is a member of one of the consortia described above. Kodak is located in York (part of Humber's catchment area) and, with a workforce of 2300, is that city's largest employer. The relationship with Kodak has been selected from among the scores of companies with whom Humber has close relationships as a model typifying the best of what is possible. This relationship dramatically illustrates the synergistic nature of Humber's partnership culture.

The first contact was a phone call by Kodak in 1987 to inquire about Humber's capability to provide advanced mathematics training/upgrading. Kodak was launching a quality leadership initiative, and statistical process control (SPC) training was central to that initiative. The success of this program led to further training in automatic equipment mechanic (AEM) skills. Humber assigned an account manager to work with the company to assess its growing needs for continuous improvement competencies.

To provide custom services more economically, Humber developed, with Kodak's interest and support, a consortium of several companies, each having a few staff people requiring specialized skills in the same fields. Kodak joined Facelle (a subsidiary of Proctor and Gamble), Labatt's Breweries, and Continental Can to test the concept in the spring of 1988. The consortium flourished, and training has expanded into many other areas. This initial service of assessing, upgrading, and retraining the technical workforce entailed teaching mathematics, blue-print reading, chemistry, AEM skills, and robotic maintenance. These services continued through the 1980's and into the 1990's, expanding into the multiple-skill development of production staff and supervisor training. All learning services for Kodak are conducted on an in-house, custom basis. Since 1989, the company has provided Humber with revenues of approximately $375,000 per year.

Results of the Kodak Alliance. The success of this partnership has exceeded all expectations in its impact on the culture and image of Humber. In 1989, Kodak's chief executive officer agreed to sit on Humber's first capital campaign cabinet, and he continues today as a member of Humber's Foundation Board. Kodak Canada also made a five-year capital contribution to Humber of $125,000. In 1990, Kodak produced a video with the college for presentation at a major training conference and, subsequently, to Humber's Board of Governors. Kodak owns an extensive tract of land in York, and discussions have been ongoing regarding a site for Humber to build a major campus in that city.

Kodak's chief executive officer, on his own initiative, began marketing Humber's services to his associates and in his business speeches. Kodak staff participate freely in many college activities, ranging from program advisory committees to focus groups. On the occasion of the 25th anniversary of the Ontario CAAT system, Humber and Kodak collaborated on a joint advertisement published in one of Canada's national newspapers.

In 1993, Kodak's chief executive officer was awarded an honorary diploma from Humber College for his outstanding contribution and long-standing advocacy of "Continuous Learning for Constant Improvement" (the trademark logo of Humber's B&IS). Humber has also dedicated an on-site training room (in the Business & Industry Service Centre) for Kodak's exclusive use. In addition, several Humber instructors, at various times, are fully resident at the Kodak plant.

The relationship continues to grow, now in terms of technology transfer. Canada's first full digital imaging teaching installation has been operational at Humber since June 1994. Kodak significantly discounted the price of the equipment, has committed to a technical advancement program (which will provide continuous updating of equipment), and is acting as a supplying coordinator for Humber, using its own funds so that the best discounts can be obtained. Humber will repay these cash outlays on its behalf over an extended period, as revenue is generated through the sale of training services offered by the digital imaging lab. A joint marketing plan including Apple Canada, Inc., will allow Humber to become Kodak's digital imaging training resource for its customers and suppliers, and, furthermore, to act as a technology transfer agent in the marketplace.

The growing seamlessness of this relationship is one of its outstanding characteristics. The full spectrum of stakeholders is involved, from the Board of Governors to the students, governments, labor, and related private sector industries. With respect to the latter, as Humber seeks relationships with other companies, this outstanding partner realizes the benefits of expanding the cooperation and has helped Humber access other business partners and suppliers. From the traditional customer-supplier relationship, this partnership has gone through a full transformation to a reciprocal supplier-customer relationship. Both organizations are becoming integrated and totally collaborative, not just for financial gain, but for the sake of the community and stakeholders. The most significant lesson from the Kodak experience is that it takes a great deal of commitment, energy, and effort to develop, foster, and maintain such rich relationships. Humber has been working on this collaborative alliance for over eight years, and both partners are still consciously diligent—more like family than business!

PARTNERSHIPS FOR PHYSICAL RESOURCES

Assessing Physical Facilities. During the 1980s, Humber College had established an excellent reputation for its programs but lacked facilities to accommodate the growing demands of business and industry. New programs in rapidly changing technologies required state-of-the-art facilities. The college needed enhanced library and resource centers. Suitable office space for faculty was at a premium because of the high demand for instructional space. More space was also required for a student center, bookstore, and swimming pool for the community. Since more than 80 percent of the Humber's students are drawn from outside the college's boundaries and all over the world, a student residence was envisioned. Both the college's off-campus housing and its off-campus 220-bed residence were feeling the pressure of a large metropolitan housing problem, where rental space was scarce and expensive.

The college's plant was well-scheduled and, in fact, overused. Space was not available for further expansion, and the government had few dollars to assist the college. Any expansion would depend on the development of partnerships. The assets of the college amounted to valuable land that could be marketed or traded, a solid reputation with all levels of government and the private sector, an emerging cadre of talented and innovative staff, and a keen entrepreneurial board and administration. Using these assets, partnerships were the key to creating a future for the college through risk-taking and joint ventures with government and the private sector.

Physical Resource Partnerships/Collaborations. Land, the one significant physical resource of the college, has become a focus for creating partnerships in order to realize the mission of the college. When revenues drop and there is a strong commitment to maintain or even expand services, the two major options are (a) to use existing resources innovatively, possibly raising revenue and/or (b) to cut costs. Humber's land use and building program provides an excellent example of how these two options may be used to make major changes in a period of reduced funding and retrenchment. Partnerships were the key to mobilizing plans for expansion, while leadership, risk-taking, and joint ventures with government supported that process. Many of the facility developments were intertwined—one opportunity often led to another as the partnerships evolved. Two examples will illustrate this aspect of partnerships—the college residences and the south campus.

College Residences. The CAATs were originally intended to be commuter colleges, at least in the populous sections of southern Ontario, and residences were never part of the facility plans for these colleges. Over time, however, it became evident that Humber, with its large "out-of-catchment" population, would have to solve its housing problem. The Ministry would not make capital funds available to Humber for a residence since the precedent would open the door to requests from other colleges. When the college system was first developed, nursing training had been transferred from teaching hospitals to the CAATs, and Humber inherited a 220-room nurses' residence adjacent to a hospital, which was in a prime location. Working in partnership with a developer, Humber negotiated a real estate transaction that traded the nurses' residence and three acres of college property to the developer in exchange for the construction of two 360-room residences on Humber's north campus. The Ministry approved the "no cost" residences to enhance the living accommodations at Humber, thus servicing 720 out-of-area students. Not only do the residences recover all costs, they also generate much-needed college revenue.

A whole new set of possibilities has opened as a result of the residences. A summer language program to teach English to exchange students and business people is flourishing. International fellows can now be housed on-site to take advantage of the full range of academic, social, and athletic services. At other times, when the residences are not filled with full-time students, they are used to house sports teams who use Humber's facilities for training and tournaments.

Humber's South Campus—Lakeshore. The second example is a tribute to persistence and patience. Since the late 1980s, it has been obvious that the college would have to consolidate some of its campuses to focus resources on specific sectors for better customer service and to cut overhead and reduce expenditures. A decision was made to concentrate Humber's operations on three major campuses—one each in the north and south of Etobicoke and one in York. The southern campus is known as Lakeshore. It stands on a prime piece of property, part of which is under the control of the Metropolitan Toronto Regional Conservation Authority, including the lakefront itself and public boating facilities. The existing building was originally a primary school teacher training institution; it had been renovated to accommodate postsecondary programs. It had gradually outgrown its usefulness and capacity for the type of programming required on this campus; a very different facility was needed to implement Humber's long-range three-campus strategy and to relieve some of the pressure at the north campus. No capital dollars were forthcoming from the Ministry of Education and Training for new, large-scale buildings, so Humber looked again for innovative ways to use its real estate resources to provide improved educational services.

Situated near the shore of Lake Ontario, the existing campus is also adjacent to a nineteenth-century psychiatric hospital, now closed and declared a historical site. Although it has taken several years, a seven-way partnership has been formed so that, simply explained, Humber will move into the renovated psychiatric hospital buildings as its new campus, while preserving the buildings' exteriors for historical purposes. The site of Humber's existing campus will be turned over to the municipal and metropolitan governments, and will be shared with a local school board to create parkland and playing fields. The Ontario Government Management Board Secretariat (overseer of public funds and the highest government authority involved) will provide some funding, supporting the creation of expansive green space and sports fields for public use, as well as the preservation of a heritage building to be used for public education. Parking will be shared by the partners. These arrangements, in turn, will give the conservation authority improved access to its lakefront property, and the seventh partner, the Ministry of Education and Training, will be able to oversee the refurbishing of a major college campus at no cost to itself. The whole area will be managed by a joint board of directors, with Humber having full jurisdiction over the use of the refurbished hospital buildings. In order to finance some these facility renovations, a tract of land owned by Humber, and adjacent to the north campus, will be sold for low-cost housing, thereby generating much-needed revenue.

Results of Physical Resource Partnerships. Creative partnerships—with provincial and municipal governments, the private sector, Humber's own students through the Council of Student Affairs—and the sale of disposable land, have enabled the college to double the space at the north campus and triple the space at the south campus over the last few years. These complex and creative entrepreneurial negotiations have resulted in the following new campus facilities:

- the finest college library in the province,
- a residence for more than 700 students,
- a second student center,
- a community swimming pool,
- a new campus store,
- a state-of-the-art technology building,
- a national plastics training center,
- a new faculty office building, and
- a business and industry center.

The college has also been able to acquire facilities with state-of-the-art space and equipment for the new Plastics Training Centre. All ventures were accomplished in addition to the ongoing/annual campus improvements and renovations.

These facilities are complements to the excellent programs that presently draw more than 50,000 applications for 6,000 freshman places. Humber has the highest rate of applications in the entire province, as measured by a central applications center for all the colleges.

These collaborative facility partnerships have created a campus synergy that has provided the framework for the college to advance its mission and goals in the present and the foreseeable future.

CONCLUSION

The Synergism of Partnerships. Each of the three sub-themes—human resources, programs and training services, and physical resources—has provided a brief glimpse of partnerships as a vehicle for the development of the character and culture at Humber College. Figure 2 attempts to capture the essence of the synergistic aspect of the partnership strategy. As the figure depicts, the professional development of staff is the pivotal point that must be nurtured and made available continuously at all levels in the organization. Once the mission of Humber was articulated and institutionalized with supportive staff programs and a recognition and award system, the evolving and growing talent base became an integral part of the entire organization.

Champions, leaders, and trainers have emerged to design and develop international projects, opening up many opportunities for realizing Humber's obligation as a global citizen. As a bonus, the college faculty and staff have been able to enhance their intercultural and teaching skills. Such ventures have also provided revenue for further research, proposal development, feasibility studies, infrastructure development, and equipment acquisition. The alliances with industry through Business and Industry Services and the more than 80 college program advisory committees have further enhanced Humber's capability to transfer skills to, and share experience with, international clients such as MARA in Malaysia and Micro Industries Development Assistance Society in Bangladesh. In addition, creative partnerships have established linkages necessary to bring about the physical facility development so critical for positioning Humber as a major supplier of educational and training services to the postsecondary marketplace, the community, industry, labor, and government.

The Canadian Plastics Centre for Training (CPCT), as indicated at the top of Figure 2, serves as a final exemplar of the synthesizing effect of partnerships at Humber. The establishment of this Centre could only have been realized in the Humber context through:

- the professionally-developed talent base for program planning and organizational development;
- the infrastructure, systems, and procedures developed by Business and Industry Services to create a viable business and marketing plan, and to obtain the necessary equipment donations;
- the participation of internationally, interculturally experienced staff to work with diverse groups at many levels to forge the necessary partnerships; and
- the experience, networks and links with local real estate developers and municipal authorities to develop the actual facility.

The significant economic development and technology transfer value of the CPCT is illustrative of how the partnership culture of Humber can have a local, national, and international impact. Therefore, not only is the college realizing its mission, but the faculty and staff are also challenged to listen to their customers and innovatively build

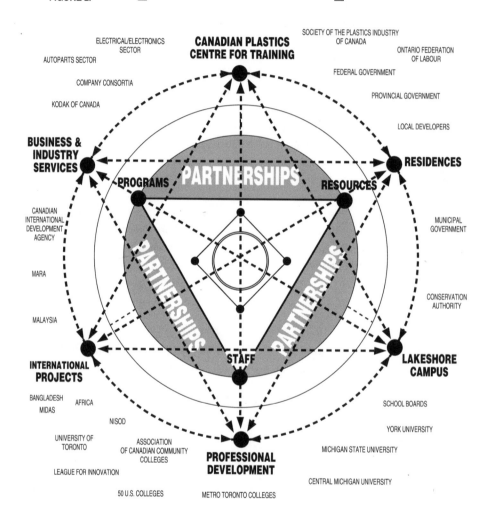

THE SYNERGISM OF HUMBER'S PARTNERSHIP STRATEGY

FIGURE 2.

THESE EXAMPLES REPRESENT ONLY A PORTION
OF THE ACTUAL PARTNERSHIPS AND LINKS

on the continuously emerging opportunities for providing quality learning services to stakeholders. Such an integrated, planned partnership program provides a pathway to achieving excellence.

The Continuing Challenges of Partnerships. As with team sports, there can never be too much talent, but the stars must also be team players. In private sector parlance, Humber has learned to both "make and buy" its talent. The selection process for staff (potential "stars") has, in conjunction with the unions and governing bodies of the college system, become more rigorous and exacting. At the same time, the provision of extensive support to new and existing staff is essential. Complementing the "buy" aspect of procuring highly qualified staff is an extensive "make" (team building) program as exemplified in the master's and doctoral activities. This organizational development and succession planning strategy is essential to the future of the college and critical for meeting its goals. The major caveat that has emerged is the need to simultaneously foster the development and enhancement of specific technical skills and knowledge to remain current in the marketplace. Industry linkages are, once again, the main conduits for secondments (temporary assignments), internships, visits, speakers and exchanges.

Putting energy, talent and liquid resources into facilities for the future may, in fact, leave the college "equipment poor." If financial resources are shifted into updating and expanding facilities, then equipment may soon be out-of-date and in poor condition. These priorities need to be balanced, and as either one, or both are pursued, there are fewer dollars for salaries. As a result, tensions with the unions could rise. These are continuing issues requiring a visionary board, senior management leadership, and innovative partnerships. A reasonable balance must be maintained among these elements while keeping the main mission in view.

Humber continues to be as affected by the economy as other organizations, and both "boom-proofing" and "recession-proofing" are constant challenges. In the present time of recession, it takes enormous energy and a sizable withdrawal of "good-will capital" to cope with closing down programs, layoffs, and restructuring. The ability to cope and to bounce back is directly related to the strength of the networks, collaborations and alliances built up over the years. Having established partnerships, maintaining them is critical.

Through Humber's persistence in pursuing and fostering relationships, trust levels have risen, and personal self-assurance has generated leadership and willingness by the faculty to take risks and pursue new opportunities. Staff perceptions of appreciation and empowerment have been, and continue to be, internalized and consolidated, moving the college closer to its mission and goals. With multiple opportunities for teamwork and collegiality, these partnerships, and the developments that have resulted, help build and maintain high morale and motivation. All these initiatives are a part of an integrated strategy to enhance the quality of staff and programs, and contribute to the central mission of the college for providing quality and excellence in education.

The author acknowledges, with thanks, the contributions made to this chapter by Humber College staff, and most especially those of William Sinnett

CHAPTER VII

Just as Humber College has been able to leverage its assets into viable, needed facilities, St. Petersburg Junior College (SPJC) has similar successes to report. SPJC leaders collaborated with the Allstate Insurance Company, state, and community leaders to acquire a gift from Allstate of a 131,344-square-foot facility and 20 acres of land. The site has become the headquarters for SPJC's Criminal Justice Institute, Corrections and Law Enforcement Academies, fire science programs, and other college initiatives. This contribution represented the largest corporate gift ever presented to a Florida college or university and the largest such gift to an American two-year college.

Other noteworthy activities at SPJC include four "summits" convened by the college to bring leaders together to consider important challenges, including the role of community colleges in shaping the nation and in preparing the workforce.

Internal partnerships and collaborations, which have been mentioned by several chapter authors, have worked well for St. Petersburg. In a special internal collaboration, personnel focused their attention on the importance of ethics in education with some important results. They produced a college textbook on ethics; the college assessed its own behavior and then put its ethical values into practice.

President Carl Kuttler notes that ethical behavior has been significant in SPJC's success and has nurtured friendships as well. "As the saying goes, success comes not just from what you know but from whom you know. Intercompany relationships are a key business asset, and knowing how to nurture them is an essential managerial skill" (Kanter, 1994, p. 108).

* * *

Kanter, R.M. "Collaborative advantage: The art of alliances." *Harvard Business Review*, 1994, 72(4), 96–108.

Carl M. Kuttler, Jr.
President
St. Petersburg Junior College
St. Petersburg, Florida

PARTNERSHIPS:

The Parlaying Principles

Even if you are on the right track,
you'll get run over if you just sit there.

—Will Rogers

STRATEGIES FOR SUCCESS

They said my mother never met a stranger. Mom may not always have known best, but she cared about people and met everyone with a recognition of their potential. That may aptly describe the operating style of any flourishing community college. Making friends molds our future, and each friend's potential expands our own.

With deep roots as Florida's first two-year institution, St. Petersburg Junior College knows one simple truth—no partners, no posterity. This college began in 1927 with five civic leaders and a loan, and we have made good on their investment in our future. SPJC is second in America in Associate in Arts degrees granted and 25th in Associate of Science degrees granted, although in terms of enrollment the college places 46th, according to *Community College Week*'s "Second Annual 100 Top Associate Degree Producers" (1994). The same report shows that in Florida SPJC is a leader in producing minority graduates.

We have no delusions about our success—it is the result of shared vision among hundreds of committed people—community leaders, generous business partners, trustees with acumen and an unflinching focus on excellence, and a progressive faculty interested in change but mature enough to recognize folly.

For seven decades now, our partners have been as close as a local school principal's office or as far away as the People's Republic of China. Our maturity has sharpened our vitality. We have learned to expect success, inspect performance, and suspect anything that seems second-rate. We may fail somewhere next week, but it will not be because we are aiming low or quaking at challenges. We will find new friends, forge new partnerships, and never forget our heritage as we enter what I hope will be known as the Education Century.

The College's Mission. A successful college continually updates its mission and the strategies for realizing that mission. In the late 1970s, SPJC conducted a mission revision process that included the input of college faculty, staff, selected students, and key community leaders. SPJC's commitment to an inclusive, partnering process has been a consistent theme. Collective perceptions were shaped into a strategic plan, which guides the institution's work.

One Institution's Framework. Successful strategies for realizing the mission, of course, vary from institution to institution and situation to situation. After much deliberation and many attempts to chart our path, SPJC has devised a formula that works for us. We resort to Greek-speak here to help define the components of our strategy—*pedagos, ethos, technos,* and *synergos*. Upon these four pillars, the college collaborates with an array of partners.

Pedagos (teaching and learning) is our mission first and foremost. The *ethos* (set of guiding principles) of an institution keeps it from straying off course or being blinded by merely fashionable trends. *Technos* (technology) is the empowering force of our era, as surely as other eras were transformed by fire or steam or nuclear power. Ultimately, *synergos* (synergy) capitalizes on interrelationships and brings together the strengths of the institution with those of other organizations, so that the total effect of this cooperation is greater than the actions of any single entity taken independently.

PEDAGOS—TEACHING AND LEARNING PARTNERSHIPS

The college's mission revolves around teaching and learning. It is "the first thing every morning and the last thing at night." We continue to refine this mission with faculty, staff, and our service community.

Dual Credit Program. For high school students who had the required discipline and study skills and were ready for college work, SPJC, in conjunction with area high schools, developed the Dual Credit Program. The initial program evolved from the credit bank concept, in which students took college courses early and the college saved or "banked" their credit until their high school graduation. Our approach was different in that these students completed the coursework at their high schools rather than coming to campus.

Then, in 1983, former Florida Governor Bob Graham took this concept even further. The governor felt that many high school students were ready for college and that these students should not have to wait to complete these courses if they were indeed ready. He also felt that students should not have to take the same courses in high school and college. The program originally designed by SPJC and its high school partners became state law.

Students selected for the state program took college courses and received both high school and college credit. Unlike Credit Bank Program students, these students had their fees paid and textbooks provided by the state. Upon graduation from high school, the student could either enter the community college or transfer the credits received to a university. The Dual Credit Program was initiated as one of five acceleration mechanisms that enable high school students to simultaneously earn college credit toward an associate's or bachelor's degree and high school units toward a diploma.

In 1988, having developed a model program for the public sector, SPJC, in partnership with area private schools, pioneered a private school dual credit program. Several years later the legislature officially included private schools in the dual credit program. In the 1994–95 academic year, the program will expand again to include tech prep students in the public school system.

Program participants are usually juniors and seniors with weighted 3.0 grade point averages (GPA). St. Petersburg Junior College hires instructors, most of whom are high school teachers who meet the requirements for college-level instructors set by the regional accreditation association (the Southern Association of Colleges and Schools). The dual credit instructors follow the college's course objectives for each dual credit course taught. These objectives, developed by SPJC faculty, outline minimum outcomes to be achieved, regardless of the mode or the location of the instruction. The instructors and their students use the same textbooks used on SPJC's campuses. Evaluations of instruction are regularly conducted by the students, by the high school's Dual Credit Liaison (a school staff member hired by the college), and by the Dual Credit Program Coordinator (the college's full-time staff specialist responsible for coordinating the program).

More than 13,400 students have participated since the program's inception in 1983. With the 1994 advent of the tech prep program—which will contain some dual credit courses—this number promises to increase significantly.

More recently, the college, the local school district, and the University of South Florida have developed a three-year baccalaureate degree program. High school students take one year of college-level work by enrolling in the dual credit program, the international baccalaureate program, or the advanced placement program. After receiving their high school diplomas, they may take one year at St. Petersburg Junior College and then transfer to the University of South Florida for their junior and senior years. All of this academic work may be completed within Pinellas County.

Serving Underprepared, At-Risk Students. *College Reachout Program.* The College Reachout Program is a state-funded program and partners resources with community colleges and universities. The goal is to strengthen the educational motivation and preparation of low income and educationally disadvantaged students who may benefit from postsecondary education. The program is designed for middle and high school students. The University of South Florida (USF), Hillsborough Community College (HCC), and SPJC are consortium members. Students receive tutoring and mentoring, and participate in educational field trips. Selected participants also join students from USF and HCC as residents on the USF campus for a special summer program.

The Summer Youth Employment Program. This program provides basic skills, work maturity, and job readiness training for 90 to 100 youths, ages 14 to 17. Students participate in activities designed to make them better students and employees. In addition to classroom work, they get experiences in the world of work. They also get to see how business operates by spending a day at Enterprise Village, a partnership which includes the Pinellas County Private Industry Council, the school board, and SPJC.

The Pathway Program. The Pathway Program is designed to increase diversity in the college's selected admission health programs. Recruitment for the program occurs districtwide, but all program activities are conducted at the college's Health Education Center. Students selected for the program matriculate in a specialized core of courses. Successful completion of these courses and other pre-arranged prescriptions guarantees admission in a selected admission health program. Partners for this program include approximately 26 area hospitals that provide mentors and internship opportunities.

The National Youth Sports Program. This is a special summer program for at-risk students that includes a math/science instructional component. Students also receive instruction on sports fundamentals, the importance of proper nutrition, and drug education. Partners for this program include the National Collegiate Athletic Association, which funds the effort, and the local school board.

PIC Support. In the 1994–95 academic year, 30 additional students will be funded by the Pinellas County Private Industry Council. The students will receive instruction on the world of work, including job readiness and work maturity skills, as a specific part of their support services rather than as an implied part of their college courses.

Career Connections Program. The Career Connections Program has been designed specifically for African American males and others who are underrepresented in the college population. These students also will be accorded the Project Success support network. The Florida Progress Corporation is a sponsor and various community organizations provide mentors. They will participate in job-shadowing and an "outward bound" experience designed to improve group communication, improve the trust level within the group, increase motivation and resourcefulness, improve problem-solving techniques, and teach conflict resolution techniques.

Partnerships with the Public and Private Sector. *Health Education Center.* In 1978, representatives of a regional hospital council came to the college to request an increase in the number of trained nurses and other allied health care graduates. When talks began, the college had no facility, no plan for expansion, and no budget. Working with partners such as the Bay Area Hospital Council, the Florida Legislature, the College Development Foundation, Exxon Oil Co., and leading businesses in the district, and taking advantage of provisions of the Florida Academic Improvement Trust Fund and the Florida Community Contribution Tax Incentive Act, the college purchased a $2.9 million property, acquired an adjacent property in a condemnation, received $3.5 million in appropriations from the Florida Legislature for renovations, and raised a matching amount from a communitywide fund-raising campaign in its district. The college also enjoyed matches from the state Academic Improvement Trust Fund.

Allstate/State/City/College. The concept of public/private partnership is always operative at St. Petersburg Junior College, and when the Allstate Insurance Company moved to its new facilities adjacent to the college's Carillon Training Center, SPJC once again embraced an opportunity for service by beginning the process of "free" site acquisition. The college approached community leaders who shared this vision. Together, they asked Allstate to invest in the college and the community. This effort blossomed when Allstate Insurance Company officials, Florida state officials, college trustees, and community and education leaders worked together to meet a community need. Allstate executives agreed to deed the facility to the college as a gift for educational use. The city of St. Petersburg and college officials worked with the state legislature to detail tax provisions that accelerated credits for Allstate. The state subsequently provided the college with $4.5 million for initial renovations and another $3 million for two special facilities—an indoor firing range and an emergency vehicle driving range. The gift from the Allstate Insurance Company to the college amounted to more than 20 acres of land, including a facility with 131,344 square feet, all valued in 1988 at $11.15 million. This contribution represented the largest corporate gift ever presented to a Florida college or university and the largest such gift to an American two-year college.

In addition to becoming the headquarters for SPJC's Criminal Justice Institute, Corrections and Law Enforcement Academies, and fire science programs, the Allstate Center became another site for the Open Campus Corporate Training Services program. The center assumed the role of host to community activities, including space for a special office on home financing for the disadvantaged, underscoring the college's commitment to service and community involvement. The college also continues to pursue the establishment of a college-administered public safety center that will provide federal, state, and local training.

The Allstate Center is testimony to the benefits of cooperation among state and local governments, private enterprise, and education working together to achieve common goals. The SPJC Allstate Center—once an attractive regional headquarters for the insurance company—now thrives as a training facility. Its impact is felt, not only in Pinellas County, but throughout the state, the southeast, and the nation.

National Guard. From August 1992 through March 1993, SPJC participated in a federally-funded military training partnership known as the Florida Teletraining Project. Its purpose was to evaluate the feasibility of using community colleges to provide occupational training to Florida armed services personnel. This training, which involved the use of a two-way, interactive satellite telecommunications network, forged an educational partnership between SPJC, Florida Community College at Jacksonville (FCCJ), Valencia Community College, the University of Central Florida's Institute for Simulation and Training, and the Florida National Guard.

Using distance-learning technology, the training met the same objectives as training received on local military bases. The courses, taught live via satellite, included five Military Occupational Specialist areas: Administrative Specialist, Supply Specialist, Military Police, Hazardous Materials, and Total Quality Management. A military instructional assistant served as a facilitator, with the actual instruction conducted via satellite by FCCJ faculty with the help of on-site SPJC faculty. According to student evaluations, one of the most effective elements of the video teletraining process was the presence of on-site faculty who facilitated the instructional process, provided course information, and administered tests.

Because they were earning college credit for some of the courses, a majority of the students rated the teletraining experience higher than conventional military training. Students indicated that they preferred training in a college setting. They expressed an appreciation of the subject knowledge of the college instructors. They also enjoyed participating with other college students in on-campus activities. Students in the Military Police course were particularly enthusiastic about SPJC's state-of-the-art training facility in the Allstate Center. The site offers a defensive tactics studio, a forensic lab, an apartment for crime scene simulations, and a mock jail and courtroom. It also enables students to use the latest computerized simulation equipment for firearms training.

Drug War Academy. Building on the relationship developed with the Florida National Guard (FNG) under the Florida Teletraining Project, SPJC received a contract with the FNG to develop and implement Multijurisdictional Counterdrug Task Force training (MTF), a program that combines classroom, scenario, and distance-learning instructional modes. The SPJC Criminal Justice Institute (CJI) had collaborated previously with the Pinellas County Sheriff's Office Narcotics Bureau in its drug interdiction training efforts. The bureau has served as a model of multiagency, multijurisdictional cooperation, a model the MTF program seeks to replicate throughout the Southeastern United States, Puerto Rico, and the Virgin Islands. A program whose mission is the promotion of multicounty, multiagency, multijurisdictional task force cooperation, the Multijurisdictional Counterdrug Task Force Training Program is staffed by representatives of local, state, federal, and military agencies, including the FBI, DEA, IRS, ATF, U.S. Customs, Coast Guard Intelligence, and the Florida National Guard.

CJI's Multijurisdictional Counterdrug Task Force staff has developed curricula and scenarios that are national in scope, regionally responsive, and operationally focused. MTF reveals the vast degree of military support available to local law enforcement as it delivers training to three target audiences—law enforcement managers and planners, drug enforcement personnel, and public administrators with authority to make decisions and commit resources for the development of counterdrug task force applications and military support capabilities.

MTF presents four schools or courses several times each year—Drug Task Force Investigations, Interdiction and Conspiracy Investigations, Intercept of Secure Communications, and Command and Control. The thread that binds the four schools together is a computer system on which officers enter their investigative accomplishments daily. This allows them to discover relationships that would not be apparent if they were working manually and/or separately in their own agencies. The computer training module provides students with the technology to establish a documented database for use by supervisory and prosecution personnel.

Cultural Diversity Training Institute. While CJI was pursuing its regional and national cooperative venture with the Florida National Guard, it received a request for help from a local law enforcement agency. Unfortunately, its in-house cultural sensitivity training was threatening to divide—rather than unite—the department. Stepping in to fill this training need, CJI gave birth to the Cultural Diversity Training Institute. During its first year it enrolled more than 3,000 participants.

The uniqueness of the program lies in a simple core idea: the belief that you cannot become sensitive to the culture of others until you have first endeavored to become sensitive to yourself. In short, cultural diversity training begins with understanding the self—its beliefs, values, traditions, fears, taboos. From this starting point participants are encouraged to reevaluate what they think about themselves and others within the context of their world view. The premise is: The way you view yourself is the way you view the world.

Through group and individual exercises, participants consider the nature (and danger) of stereotypes, personal and group power, and the enigmatic concept of "power-equality." They also discuss power distillates (such as constitutionality) as they pertain to officer rights, citizen rights, and civil rights in a country of diverse cultures. Affirmative action, women in the workplace, sexual harassment, police brutality, and aspects of various subcultures are among the topics considered.

International Partners. The International Center at the college administers three scholarship programs designed to provide skills that enable student participants to improve their personal economic futures and expose them to the societal rewards of a democracy. These three programs are the Cooperative Association for States for Scholarships Program (CASS), the Nicaraguan Peace Scholarship Program (NPSP), and the Afro-Caribbean Scholarship Program (ACSP). All operate under a consortium agreement with Georgetown University and the Florida Department of Education. In addition to coursework for these academically talented, economically disadvantaged students, the "experience America" program provides actual experiences in democratic living.

Other major international efforts include hosting international students from many nations, building (with Georgetown University) one of the largest training programs for Central American students, and assisting countries of the former Soviet Union to develop community college systems. Of special interest are the exchanges with the People's Republic of China and Russia.

People's Republic of China. SPJC is reaching across the globe into the heartland of the People's Republic of China, where educational initiatives have resulted in visits with high-level government officials, faculty and student exchanges, and unprecedented exposure to another culture for college students in each country. The college gained a partner when Central Florida Community College and its president, William Campion, joined in projects related to Central America and China.

The efforts began in 1991, when the Chinese Ministry of Education visited SPJC to develop formal linkages between U.S. community colleges and Chinese educational institutions. Forgoing opportunities with more urban colleges, SPJC reached out to Baoji Teachers College (now Baoji College of Arts and Science), a rural institution with little previous exposure to the West. A sister college relationship has led to significant initiatives on both sides of the Pacific and involved each president serving as the other institution's president for short periods of time.

An early manifestation of the agreement was the arrival of a Baoji faculty member who, since autumn of 1991, has taught English as a second language and has designed computerized ESL programs for SPJC. President Yang visited SPJC and served as its honorary president in March 1992. The next month, an 18-member delegation of national and provincial education officials visited SPJC and other American colleges and, in a separate visit, four faculty and administrators from Shaanxi Business Management Institute came to Florida.

During the 1992–93 academic year, two SPJC faculty members taught at Baoji. In China they applied American perspectives to the teaching of English. They brought valuable knowledge and experience back to SPJC. Baoji College returned the favor in the 1993–94 academic year, when a Baoji math instructor came to SPJC to work with SPJC students. The relationship was cemented further by a delegation of five people from Baoji College and the Shaanxi Provincial Education Committee who visited SPJC in September and October 1993; a reciprocal trip of SPJC delegates was scheduled for May 1994.

Meanwhile, student-to-student relations have flourished. SPJC's Zeta Tau Alpha chapter of the Phi Theta Kappa (PTK) honor fraternity has sponsored forums on U.S./China relations, led a book drive for Baoji College, and, perhaps most significantly, initiated a successful student exchange. In March and April 1993, the chapter hosted one administrator from the Beijing Municipal Bureau of Higher Education and two academically talented university students. This was the first student-to-student exchange for the People's Republic of China since the Tiananmen Square explosion of 1989. Two PTK advisors and two chapter officers visited Beijing in July and August 1993 and met with students and administrators from eleven different universities in Beijing, Xi'an, and Baoji.

The relationship with China and its people is priceless and productive. Through these ties, SPJC students, faculty, staff and administrators, and the college's service community have learned and will continue to learn more about China than any textbook or curriculum could teach.

Russia. In 1990, the college began a relationship with representatives of Russian higher education, while that nation was still a part of the old Soviet Union. A presidential exchange was undertaken with Leningrad State University (now the University of St. Petersburg). This culminated in a meeting of Russian University President S. A. Merkuriev and his economics law professor Anatoly Sobchak (mayor of St. Petersburg) with President George Bush and selected members of his Cabinet, under the auspices of SPJC.

Turmoil in the former Soviet Union has put many of the initiatives on hold. However, the mayor of St. Petersburg (Florida) and a private cultural organization are working to house selected treasures of the Kremlin Museum at a community museum in Florida.

ETHOS—A SET OF GUIDING PRINCIPLES

One key to being a good partner, of course, is establishing that we share common values and have a pattern of activities that reflects those values. How well do we "walk our talk"? This was stated clearly in October 1982, when Paul Ylvisaker, then dean of Harvard's School of Education, addressed a group of college and university trustees in Louisville, Kentucky. During his presentation he challenged schools and colleges to "become the starting place for reestablishing the importance of moral education and character building." Thomas Gregory, former SPJC Board Chairman and former Chairman of the Florida Commission on Ethics, attended that meeting and brought its challenge back to the college.

What ensued was a multi-year commitment with the college leadership in direct partnership with a pioneering faculty at our own institution. It has led to collaborations with many other colleges and universities and a modest movement promoting quality instruction in applied ethics in higher education. Dale Parnell, former president of the American Association of Community and Junior Colleges, and now professor at Oregon State University, has commended the SPJC initiatives in applied ethics.

However, the original spark came from Ylvisaker. Upon hearing his challenge, the college immediately conducted a study on the appropriateness of teaching ethics in higher education. The study concluded that a relationship existed between the decline of ethics in our society and the systematic deletion of ethics courses at every educational level—high schools, colleges, and universities.

Among the materials gathered during the research phase was a series of nine monographs from the Hastings Center on the ethical education of selected professionals, including lawyers, engineers, journalists, businessmen, social scientists, and policy makers. Some of these concepts were incorporated in a course SPJC approved in 1984 with the following learning goals:

- the student will understand the historical development of ethics;
- the student will demonstrate the nature of ethical issues when confronted with examples of situations containing such issues;
- the student will understand the relationship between the foundational values of a society and the quality and mode of life in that society; and
- the student will apply consistent and logical reasoning processes to resolve ethical issues.

Technology afforded the college the opportunity to practice its ethical values regarding the use of copyrighted software in its extensive microcomputer network. In the institution, software was being duplicated for use in computer classes. We sought to rectify this situation by obtaining site licenses from each of the affected vendors, which was unprecedented at this time for organizations such as ours. The total cost of this "correction process" was in excess of $200,000.

The college also prepared a brochure on the proper and legal use of software for all students, staff, and participants in computer workshops and in the ethics institutes conducted for public officials.

Our faculty soon felt that a suitable text for the required course did not exist. Marketplace ethics and a balanced treatment of various moral theories were not covered. The faculty wanted reader-friendly language and a better book design. In collaboration with 15 authors from across America, and McGraw-Hill publishers, the college produced its own text—Ethics Applied—which is in its second printing and in use at three universities, as well as at SPJC.

One of the purposes of education is the transmission of culture. SPJC feels very strongly that the study of ethics is an integral part of this educational purpose because morality is such an integral part of everyday life. Student evaluations of the course imply that students have acquired concepts and skills that will be invaluable to them as they confront personal and professional dilemmas, and as they consider the great moral issues of our times.

TECHNOS—TECHNOLOGY

Harnessing the power of technology to address institutional goals is everyone's objective. However, getting it done with limited resources is a challenge, and in this arena, especially, collaboration and partnering are crucial to success.

In 1988, the AACJC Commission on the Future of Community Colleges issued *Building Communities: A Vision for a New Century.* One recommendation was that community colleges should develop a campuswide plan for the use of computer technology. This plan should ensure that educational and administrative applications are integrated, developing incentive programs for faculty who wish to adapt educational technology to continue to extend the campus, and providing instruction to the workplace, to schools, and to other community organizations. As the report was being issued, SPJC was poised to embark on a continuous multimillion-dollar technology vision.

Project Flamingo. Project Flamingo is an SPJC initiative to create a collegewide, integrated computer network for the purposes of improving instruction, strengthening administration, and fostering communication. Through Project Flamingo, SPJC sought to take advantage of existing, emerging, and cutting-edge computer technology to address its goals, forge partnerships, and establish an integrated collegewide network. By developing relationships with such partners as Unisys, Apple, and Digital Equipment Corporation, the college gained gifts and discounts worth millions of dollars and leapt into the technology century at a pace ahead of most other institutions.

The project seeks to provide educational support to faculty. Technology should improve instructional delivery, through the use of multimedia, individualized instruction, distance-learning through shared files and programs, exploratory learning, and collaborative projects through the Internet. The electronic transfer of completed course assignments is contemplated as a future application.

Opportunity of a Lifetime. Perhaps the capstone of SPJC's use of technology to enhance teaching and learning, and the example that best demonstrates the creative value of partnerships, is the college's initiative to build a new "high-tech" campus in the city of Seminole. The college is currently receiving a three-year state appropriation of $6,450,000. Additional appropriations totaling $16,820,000 are anticipated in fiscal years 1996–97 through 1998–99.

We now are engaged in the planning phase for the Seminole Campus and, in the process, have asked visionaries from each of our vendor partners—Unisys, Apple, and Digital—to serve on a technical advisory subcommittee working with campus and community leaders on design and infrastructure possibilities. A number of exciting options and opportunities are available to us.

In addition to providing a limited AA program, the college probably will initiate new non-health-related "high-tech" academic programs such as biotechnology and environmental science. Many existing high-tech programs—such as engineering technology and telecommunications—may be relocated to that site to be part of a showcase for high-tech instructional delivery through electronic classrooms with learning consoles, monitors, two-way audio and video, high ceilings to accommodate theater-style lighting and projection technology, unobtrusive computer workstations built into desks, cameras, and projectors. The Seminole Campus also is slated to be the potential hub for the college's distance learning initiative—the source for uplink and downlink transmissions to the rest of the county and throughout the world. The "master teacher" concept has also been discussed in conjunction with the Seminole electronic classrooms. Outstanding instructors could come to the classroom studio to offer unique presentations to the entire district.

Related to the distance learning component of Seminole's future is the potential move of the college's television studios to that site and further integration of the traditional telecourse program with more widespread, networked transmission of video and voice through the use of fiber optics and other communications technologies.

The college has been involved with video and video transmissions as a part of instructional delivery since 1977, when SPJC, in partnership with both the state of Florida and Pinellas County Schools, developed a microwave distribution system that linked all of the college's sites to each other and to school system sites. Videotapes and other visual materials are now delivered to individual classrooms via a closed circuit system, negating the need to purchase expensive "stand alone" equipment. Seminars and lectures also can be delivered to off-campus sites via microwave, thereby eliminating the need to have everyone travel to one site, or to have potential participants miss activities or programming because of location.

The college acquired cable broadcast capabilities through public access, which has been granted by three of the district's four cable companies. The Florida Satellite Network Grant initiative also provided a satellite receiving station, and the college acquired several additional satellite downlinks that are linked to Instructional Television Fixed Services (ITFS) and therefore capable of distribution through the college network. This network has allowed the college to develop the state's largest telecourse program, serving more than 4,000 students annually during 105 weekly broadcast hours on a college cable channel and an additional seven broadcast hours on the local PBS affiliate. The PBS broadcasts are part of a consortia arrangement with six neighboring community colleges. Consortium members agree on the courses to be offered and share broadcast costs.

The college's cable broadcasts include 29 credit courses. Each semester, students whose schedules are restricted or different are able to enroll in the general education courses required for graduation. Orientations, reviews, and exams are all completed with a flexible campus schedule, but the actual coursework is taken via television.

The vision for Seminole includes the full gamut of high-tech services including the combining of computer and video in the distance learning equation, registration via telephone and home computer, and automated information machines (AIMs) that could provide access to a broad range of information from faculty and student schedules to a directory of campus events. Throughout the site, orientation, testing, advising, financial aid, and business office activities would be computerized so that students would be able to access all of these services and complete most of the related tasks electronically from their homes. The library would be less of a repository for books and periodicals and more the reception point for information from a variety of electronic sources—the access road to the Information Highway.

SYNERGOS—SYNERGY

SPJC's mission includes helping a "dynamic community meet a broad range of educational goals." Over the years, this commitment has been reflected in a variety of successful partnerships with government agencies, business and industry, the criminal justice system, and public and private schools. Although all of the college's outreach efforts attempt to achieve common goals of the community, the following collaborations illustrate specific benefits that have accrued as a result of some of SPJC's innovative partnerships.

Alternative Funding. During the early stages of the college's mission assessment process, we recognized that there were many institutional needs, including the replacement of old and/or obsolete equipment, rebuilding of old buildings with leaky roofs, and resurfacing parking lots with many potholes. As the oldest community college in the state, SPJC had many alumni and friends but hardly a dollar for renovation.

The college had to decide whether it deserved better and how it could capitalize on the perceived goodwill it enjoyed. The solution came when the legislature allowed college trustees to hold a referendum election to levy a small, one-time-only property tax that produced $4.2 million (including accrued interest). Support from local newspapers helped communicate college needs, including conditions the college wanted to correct and the reasons why the community should support the institution.

Twenty thousand people heard this message of need. Within 120 days, the referendum was conceived, communicated, and approved. The board of trustees wanted to ensure that as we spent these dollars, we would make certain to address student outcomes as well. The trustees' support of the referendum had been based on their desire to see nontraditional results for the money. They were not interested in a larger student population, or more buildings, or additions to college endowment funds. They wanted increases in student progress, including improved test scores, and other measures of academic achievement. With the tax dollars, we were able to meet several quality goals and to correct many of the facility problems.

Other strategies included creating an auxiliary endowment from the proceeds of the sale of the college bookstore and increasing the endowment with the receipts from contracted services such as cafeteria, vending, and bookstore operations. Currently this endowment stands at $3 million.

The College as Convener. The college then chose to draw on national resources. Designing a concept known as the Educational Roundtable, the college sought to measure the effectiveness of the changes that had been implemented previously. Having experienced success in local partnerships, the college began to see itself as a catalyst for forging alliances to give impetus to national initiatives. This thrust was encouraged by John Roueche, professor and director of the Community College Leadership Program at The University of Texas at Austin, who helped design its implementation.

Roundtable on Institutional Effectiveness. In January 1987, the first Roundtable on Institutional Effectiveness was convened at St. Petersburg Junior College. The chair, Terrel Bell, joined eight other participants, people with significant backgrounds and familiarity with community college education in America. They were challenged to offer a critique of SPJC. The college was candid in its desire to draw upon the expertise of the participants. It was a risk-taking venture for the college, of course. We asked: "How can we become one of America's best colleges?" In addition to being affirmed and energized, we received a new, nationalized agenda. The Roundtable on Institutional Effectiveness provided the impetus to make significant improvements in several areas of the college's operation. Special attention was given to the areas of strategic and long-range planning and assessing the effectiveness of college programs. As a result of the Roundtable, SPJC implemented several program enhancements and enlarged the total array of services to at-risk and minority students, including mentoring and basic skills programs.

Roundtable on Educational Partnerships. In February of 1988, SPJC convened a second Roundtable on Educational Partnerships. The focus of this Roundtable was to communicate information on the strengths of the community college movement to 19 educational leaders. Participants included CEOs or other leaders from the American Association of Community and Junior Colleges, the American Vocational Association, the

American College Testing Program, the College Board, the Southern Region, Educational Testing Service, U.S. Department of Education, the Association of Governing Boards of Universities and Colleges, the Council on Postsecondary Accreditation, the Institute of Educational Management, Harvard University, the Association of Community College Trustees, the American Association of School Administrators, the State Higher Education Executive Officers, the National Association for Equal Opportunity in Higher Education, the National Institute for Staff and Organizational Development (NISOD), the University of Texas at Austin, the American Council on Education, and the National Association of State Boards of Education. The college sought advice from this group on "leadership," both style and substance. They analyzed the college's teaching styles, its leadership culture, its view of its role in national policy development and implementation. They listened. They critiqued, cajoled, and sparked the college to accept responsibility for making changes that reflected national policies and initiatives. This had the effect of validating many college principles and programs, while confirming the need for others to be developed.

The college then commissioned a formal evaluation of the Roundtable concept, which identified refinements. The college sought to magnify its programming concepts for this group in an effort to ascertain how it might better accomplish its goals. The secret of the success of this (and any) Roundtable was the quality and experience of the participants. Again, we asked for counsel, and again we were enriched.

Presidential Library Summits. The college spearheaded two other initiatives—one at the Carter Library in Atlanta and the second at the Ford Library in Grand Rapids. The topic of the Carter Library initiative in October 1988, which was attended by approximately 300 college presidents, was "The Role of Community Colleges in Shaping the Nation." The Ford Presidential Museum initiative in October 1989 was entitled "Work-Force 2000" and was attended by more than 280 participants. This convocation dealt with the role of community colleges in preparing the workforce for the year 2000. As with most think-tank experiences, the tangible results would be found in each college's change in culture and programs as they began to see themselves as national policy partners. Major newspaper stories helped increase national awareness of the role of community colleges as change agents. The interaction among presidents created the climate for developing consortia and other partnerships. These presidential conferences included presentations from former U.S. Cabinet members, corporate leaders, and news media figures. Similar meetings are being planned with former Presidents Reagan and Bush and with representatives of the Nixon Library.

Transforming Government Seminar. In May 1994, the college convened a leadership seminar in partnership with the governor of Florida and the state Commission on Government Accountability to the People on "Engineering Government Transformation." One hundred seventy-five leaders of state government, representing virtually every agency, attended. They heard presentations from outstanding advocates of re-engineering, including a representative from Digital Consulting Services, the vice president of Chrysler Corporation, the chief finance officer of the Royal Canadian Mounted Police, and a re-engineering specialist who has guided American Airlines reformation, among others.

CONCLUSION

We face a new century that will be characterized by rapid change, but we do so with some unchanging goals—to reach and teach the unreached and the untaught, to press every step for academic excellence, to find the funds that enhance learning, to teach the way that changes lives, to prepare for tomorrow's choices, and to stand for quality, whatever the cost. To face such challenges alone would be unrealistic. But our history with partnerships and collaborations has taught us we can realize tomorrow's dreams if we harness the energies and expertise of our friends.

Author's Note: Grateful appreciation is expressed for the contributions to this work made by Calvin Harris, James Olliver, Esther Olliver, Michael L. Richardson, Patty Curtin Jones, and James Moorhead of the college staff.

REFERENCES

Commission on the Future of Community Colleges. *Building communities: A vision for a new century.* Washington, DC: American Association of Community and Junior Colleges, 1988.

"Second Annual 100 Top Associate Degree Producers." *Community College Week,* July 18, 1994, 8–23.

Chapter VIII

Johnstone wrote, *"Even when a visionary company and a nontraditional college establish a partnership, keeping the relationship healthy takes constant attention"* (1994, Part 4, p. 1). Norm Nielsen, president of Kirkwood Community College, could have authored these words, as well. The community relationships carefully nurtured over the years by Kirkwood personnel have resulted in many partnership opportunities in the private and public sectors. When it came time for the college to raise private funds, these relationships figured prominently. Balz (1987) found that community college donors have one or more of these reasons for giving: their employees' children are served by the community college, the college plays an integral part in community life, the college provides training to their current employees, and/or the college prepares individuals who then become company employees. Kirkwood's successful $6.5 million major gifts campaign several years ago was possible because of longstanding, mutually fulfilling liaisons and a significant presence in the community.

Another community contribution Kirkwood makes is through distance learning. Robert Atwell, president of the American Council on Education, has observed that distance education is *"clearly one of the more promising areas"* for collaboration (Desruisseaux, 1994, p. A36). Through partnerships, Kirkwood has developed an extensive network of distance communication services, including microwave telecommunications to eight communities, instructional television fixed service networks to area school districts, an educational cable channel that can be viewed in more than 64,000 area homes, and a satellite service that provides a wide range of programs and services.

Likewise, Kirkwood has a number of successful economic development partnerships with area business and industry. The Cedar River Paper Company called its collaboration with Kirkwood a *"dream relationship."* Community College Partnerships: A Door to the Future describes this relationship and the many other ways Kirkwood partners with its community.

* * *

Balz, F. *Donors to higher education.* Washington, DC: National Association of Independent Colleges and Universities, 1987.

Desruisseaux, P. "Promoting collaboration in North America." *The Chronicle of Higher Education,* 1994, 40(41), A36–A38.

Johnstone, D.B. "College at work: Partnerships and the rebuilding of American competence." *Journal of Higher Education.* [online], 1994, 65(2), 168ff. Available: e-mail: lbindx@utxdp.dp.utexas.edu

Norm Nielsen
President
Kirkwood Community College
Cedar Rapids, Iowa

COMMUNITY COLLEGE PARTNERSHIPS:

A Door to the Future

'Know thyself' is a good saying, but not in all situations. In many it is better to say 'know others.'

—Menander

Kirkwood Community College identifies community needs, provides accessible, quality education and training, and promotes opportunities for lifelong learning." Developed as a result of an institutional reassessment completed in 1992, this mission statement describes the core values that have been an integral part—the heart—of Kirkwood since its inception in 1966. From its beginning, Kirkwood's purpose was to be of service to the community. But the pursuit of partnerships has been a key element in its history. The formation of partnerships, integration into the community, and resource development have been essential for the growth of the college.

The evolution of a successful community college does not just happen. An organization has to have the commitment to deliver a quality product, to build trust, and to be willing to take risks. Only then can good things begin to happen. This chapter tells a story of building long-term partnerships that benefit the college, its students, its staff—and ultimately, the people of the community.

KIRKWOOD COMMUNITY COLLEGE

Kirkwood Community College is located in east central Iowa in the city of Cedar Rapids, 30 miles from Iowa City and the University of Iowa. The college serves a seven-county area with a population of 346,315. The cities of Cedar Rapids and Iowa City are economically healthy with a balanced mix of service, agriculture, and industry. The area has excellent public and private K–12 schools, comprehensive human services, and a relatively low unemployment rate. The surrounding counties are predominantly rural and have been more vulnerable to the ups and downs of the economy in recent years. In addition to Kirkwood and the University of Iowa, postsecondary opportunities in the area include three private four-year liberal arts colleges and one two-year proprietary college.

Kirkwood Community College began to take shape in January 1965, when area educators established a steering committee to discuss establishing a vocational school in the area. A 1964 survey discovered that only 43.71 percent of the high school graduates in the seven-county community were enrolled in post-high school education, far below the 58 percent state average. This figure was partially explained by the fact that what was then known as Area X was one of only four areas in the state that did not have a junior college or any postsecondary institution other than four-year colleges. It was apparent to many that the area was not meeting all of its citizens' educational needs.

In May 1965, the Iowa State Legislature passed enabling legislation to establish a statewide system of community colleges and vocational-technical schools to serve multicounty areas. The law gave the county boards of education the responsibility for forming a merged (multicounty) area in which a community college or a vocational-technical school could be established. The legislation allowed community colleges to provide comprehensive services, including the first two years of college work, vocational-technical training at the high school and postsecondary level, job training and retraining, vocational education for persons with physical and socioeconomic disabilities, high school completion programs, and community and continuing education opportunities.

The dream of the early planners was realized in fall 1966, when the college was launched with nine vocational-technical programs. Kirkwood Community College opened its doors to 199 students in a single building. The arts and sciences division was established in 1967, and ground was broken for the first permanent building on a 315-acre site on the south edge of Cedar Rapids. Three years later, the North Central Association granted full accreditation to the college.

Today, in its 28th year, Kirkwood has become the fifth largest institution of higher education in the state of Iowa, with learning centers in all seven counties and an enrollment of almost 10,000 in its credit programs. The college offers more than 100 applied science and technology programs, career options programs, and arts and sciences, plus an extensive community/continuing education curriculum. Adult basic education and high school completion courses are provided to nearly 5,000 area residents each year.

SUCCESS FACTORS

Several key factors contributed to Kirkwood's rapid growth. The first was a dedicated board of trustees and a visionary leader. The second factor was the recognized need, early on, to communicate the mission and purpose of the college to a variety of constituencies. Finally, the college worked to build relationships locally and at the state and national levels to facilitate growth and to build the credibility of the institution.

Role of the Trustees and Leaders. The first board of trustees of Kirkwood was elected in May 1966. Each trustee represented a geographic area roughly corresponding to each of the seven counties in the district. These first trustees were a group of individuals committed to the goal of building a quality community college from the ground up.

President Selby Ballantyne, the board, and the staff had a vision in the early years of a comprehensive community college that would serve all members of the community. The dream was to offer all residents of the seven county area—regardless of limitations of time, money or ability—the opportunity to change their lives. In order to achieve that rather lofty goal, both the board and the president recognized the need to gain acceptance and trust from the community. They also knew that, with limited funding from the state, they could not achieve the dream alone.

Building Relationships. The formation of the Area X district and the concept of a community college did not meet with universal acceptance in the seven counties. With much misunderstanding about what the college would offer and who would be served, some people were concerned that Kirkwood would be taking students away from the private and regents' institutions and questions arose regarding the revenue needed to build such a college.

The founders recognized early on that the various publics would need to be educated and informed about the activities of the college. The board began holding their meetings regularly in each of the seven counties—a practice that continues to this day. They invited community leaders to join them at dinner following board meetings. They toured businesses and industries, learning about their needs and gauging the economic climate. The president, the college staff, and the board became frequent speakers to community groups. The result was that over time the college became accepted as a vital ingredient in the educational mix of its service area.

These early efforts opened many doors in the surrounding communities. Advisory committees provided input and advice on community needs for program development.

Opportunities were sought for partnerships, both in the public and private sectors. Funding through local, state, and federal grants was essential. As a result, Kirkwood became aggressive and successful in grant acquisition.

FIVE EDUCATIONAL PARTNERSHIPS

Kirkwood faculty have initiated efforts to build programs based on quality. Today, working with 87 community advisory committees, Kirkwood's faculty continue to shape and redefine programs. Their initiatives have enhanced the reputation that has allowed Kirkwood to develop the relationships that have become integral to the institution.

Serving the Underserved. In 1968, a memorandum of agreement between Kirkwood and the Iowa State Men's Reformatory provided educational programs for inmates. Also, in 1968, the Kirkwood Skill Center was established to assist persons physically, emotionally, economically, and socially handicapped. Acting in collaboration with the Iowa Division of Vocational Rehabilitation, several exemplary initiatives were developed.

Alliance with Mount Mercy College. In 1969, Kirkwood entered into a collaboration with Mount Mercy College, a four-year liberal arts college in Cedar Rapids. Mount Mercy emphasizes career development, marketing its services to nontraditional and commuter students. Together the colleges administered the Career Opportunity Program (COP), a federally funded program provided to minorities, Vietnam veterans, and individuals below the national poverty line the opportunity to become teachers.

In 1971, Kirkwood signed an articulation agreement with Mount Mercy that the college would accept credits from Kirkwood graduates holding Associate of Arts (AA) and Associate of Science (AS) degrees. The long-standing bond between the two institutions culminated in 1993 with the Kirkwood/Mount Mercy Trust. The goal of the trust, seeded by funds from a private donor and supporters of both colleges, is to train and educate skilled, qualified employees through a broad educational experience. Funds from the trust will help Kirkwood students enrolled in specific career areas such as construction technology, industrial maintenance, and communication electronics who plan to transfer to Mount Mercy. After they transfer, students will be employed by Mount Mercy to supplement their financial assistance. The students will then be potentially employable as middle managers by local businesses. Development officers from both institutions are now working in tandem to raise the funds to build the corpus of the trust. This innovative long-term alliance continues its ripple effect. To date, Kirkwood's transfer students represent one-third of Mount Mercy's graduating class (approximately 280 students) each year.

Truck Driving Program Partnerships. In 1971, the college established a five-week program to train semi-trailer truck drivers. To get the program off the ground, several local industries and the Teamsters Union donated equipment, materials, and personnel to the college. In 1991, CRST, Inc., a national trucking firm with headquarters in Cedar Rapids, contributed $250,000 to build a new driving range for the program. Each year, Kirkwood has trained more than 1,000 drivers for CRST. The truck driving program now serves more than 1,200 students each year.

Education and Health Care. Early partnerships with health care providers helped get the health education programs off the ground. A respiratory therapy program was started, jointly sponsored with the Veteran's Administration Hospital in Iowa City. The Department of Neurology at the University of Iowa worked with Kirkwood to start an electroencephalographic assistant program. The nursing program used the facilities of Mercy Hospital in Cedar Rapids for clinical training.

In 1990, the college formed a partnership with St. Luke's Hospital in two rural Iowa communities, Monticello and Tipton. In both towns, the two entities share a building for joint delivery of education and health services. In Monticello, an earlier decision to close the local hospital was a devastating blow to the community's 3,200 residents. St. Luke's, in an effort to maintain and preserve their support of the community's medical needs, stepped in with Kirkwood to breathe new life into the facility. Each institution renovated a floor of the building, and today it is a viable learning center and a non-emergency medical facility. As a result of these partnerships with area hospitals, other cooperative ventures are being developed.

Environmental Training. The quest for partnerships has extended beyond the immediate community, fueled in part by the college's aggressive grant-seeking activity. For example, in 1970, Kirkwood received a grant from the Environmental Protection Agency to provide coursework in water and wastewater treatment training for military personnel stationed in Germany. At approximately the same time, Kirkwood began to offer on campus several Manpower Development and Training Act courses in water and wastewater treatment. In 1975, Kirkwood received $250,000 from the EPA to help fund the construction of a wastewater treatment training facility at the Kirkwood campus, the first such community college facility in the nation. An addition to the facility in 1980 nearly doubled its size. By 1993, the Environmental Training Center (as it is now called) was offering more than 30 courses in water and wastewater workshop programs statewide, with over 1,000 registrations. The novel programs of the Environmental Training Center met a need in the community, the state, and the nation. The center was responsive to the needs of industry and at the same time was a good steward of its grant moneys.

In 1987, Kirkwood and the Eastern Iowa Community College District formed the Hazardous Materials Training and Research Institute (HMTRI) to serve the environ-

mental health and safety training needs of industry. Both colleges had developed expertise in environmental training and recognized that combining their strengths was in
their best interests.

The institute is self-supporting, with additional grant funds from government and
contract training dollars from industry. The mission of the institute is to promote the
maintenance of a clean and safe environment through education and training. Its goals
include:

- preparing a certifiable environmental health and safety curriculum,
- securing grants and contracts to deliver training,
- establishing national networks of two-year colleges to deliver education and training, and
- marketing the training and curriculum prepared by HMTRI and its sponsor colleges.

In its seven years of operation, HMTRI has organized national and regional hazardous
materials training workshops for community colleges all over the country. As a result
of these workshops, more than 100 two-year colleges in the nation use HMTRI texts.
HMTRI is the designated Executive Office for the National Partnership for Environment Technical Education (PETE) serving colleges, industry, and government laboratories in a 10-state region for the U.S. Department of Energy.

On a national level, HMTRI coordinates the Community College Consortium for
Health and Safety Training (CCCHST) funded by the National Institute of Environmental Health Sciences (NIEHS). The consortium, comprising over 20 community
colleges from across the nation, provides NIEHS-model training in waste site operations and chemical emergency response to industrial workers. CCCHST has trained
more than 4,500 workers to date. In 1994, HMTRI responded to a first-time request
from the National Science Foundation (NSF) to support advanced technological centers at community colleges. HMTRI, partnering with PETE colleges nationally, began
official operation in October 1994 as NSF's first and only advanced environmental
technological center.

SERVING THE COMMUNITY THROUGH DISTANCE LEARNING
AND ECONOMIC DEVELOPMENT

M any college partnerships have evolved because of college participation within the
community. This visibility was built on the foundation of two programs intrinsic
to Kirkwood Community College—distance learning and economic development.

Distance Learning. The Kirkwood Telecommunications System (KTS) represents
the college's commitment to providing educational opportunities to all residents of the
seven-county area. The college recognized that providing expanded educational services to larger communities, such as Cedar Rapids and Iowa City, as well as to the res-

idents of the rural communities, would require innovative thinking and planning. Kirkwood first attempted a communications network that linked several outlying communities with the campus by telephone. College credit courses were offered by audio conferencing for several years.

Microwave Telecommunications to Eight Communities. In 1975, the college began plans for increasing its services through an interactive microwave telecommunications system, capable of sending and receiving audio and video programming to eight cities and towns in the district. In 1979, the National Telecommunication Information Administration (NTIA), under the U.S. Department of Commerce, awarded Kirkwood a grant for construction of an elaborate video and audio interactive instructional system. This project was begun in 1980 with a total construction cost of more than $3 million (the NTIA award provided funds for 40 percent of the total costs). President Bill Stewart and the Kirkwood trustees elected to divert capital funds from much-needed building expansion to help pay for the delivery system.

The Kirkwood Telecommunications System fulfilled a promise to make education and training easily accessible to all of the constituents of the Kirkwood service area. Students at eight learning centers in seven counties can now participate in live classes, seeing each other on color monitors and interacting with instructors and fellow students via microphone. The microwave offers more than 70 hours of credit classes a week. Faculty can hold their classes at any of the seven remote sites or on the main campus. The college continues to serve the Iowa State Men's Reformatory using the KTS system.

Telecommunications with Area School Districts. Another telecommunications delivery system under KTS is the Instructional Television Fixed Service Networks (ITFS). This system provides audio and video transmission to area school districts that have equipped their classrooms with ITFS reception and audio response hardware. Through this network, schools receive quality high school courses that their districts might not be able to offer otherwise due to costs, low enrollment, or other factors. Along with high school courses, Kirkwood offers "early bird" college credit in calculus, psychology, and sociology to high school students in their buildings. During non-school hours, college-level credit and non-credit programs are offered to all learners in rural communities.

In addition, ITFS allows school districts to share resources. Through these microwave links, Cedar Rapids Community Schools and the Grant Wood Area Education Agency offer a variety of staff and faculty development programs. Reception sites are located at several businesses in the Cedar Rapids area, allowing employees to take part in both credit and non-credit offerings.

Educational Cable Channel. An important component of the ITFS system is the Kirkwood educational cable channel, which can be viewed in more than 64,000 homes subscribing to cable television. The central objective of the cable TV network is to offer college credit telecourses both in semester and block formats. In fall 1993, Kirkwood began serving as a regional switching center for the Iowa Communications Network, a statewide multichannel fiber optics network. The system connects all community colleges of Iowa as well as the three regents' institutions. Additionally, it connects all 99 counties with two-way audio and video capability. This network serves as an additional delivery system for video-based live/interactive credit or non-credit classes as well as other educational telecommunications traffic. Implementation of the fiber optics network allowed the college to offer 15 additional credit classes at the distance learning centers. During spring semester 1994, the KTS system served 1,987 students, 72.8 percent of whom attended classes away from the Cedar Rapids campus. The Kirkwood Telecommunications System now allows any resident of the seven-county area to earn an AA degree at any of the county centers in a normal two-year cycle. No resident of the seven counties is farther than 22 miles from an attendance center—an unbelievable feat for a community college district covering 4,300 square miles.

Kirkwood Satellite Service provides uplink and downlink capabilities for selected college activities as well as for regional and community educational and economic development services, providing programming on a national and international basis. Programs received via satellite on the Cedar Rapids campus can be sent out over the microwave and ITFS systems either live or on a delayed basis.

From its inception, Kirkwood realized that barriers to education—time, money, and opportunity—needed to be lowered if a community college was going to serve its total community. People who, 25 years ago, would have been denied educational opportunities now have the chance to pursue their goals. In addition, the KTS system has presented the college with innumerable opportunities to provide a variety of programs and services to the communities it serves and has opened the door to new partnerships.

Economic Development. Kirkwood's Economic Development Services (EDS) is a full-service, regional delivery system for customized job training, retraining, and new or expanding business development services. The program originated in 1983, formalizing the coordination and delivery of economic development programs and services on a regional basis. Kirkwood has successfully partnered with local industry to improve competitiveness and productivity through workforce training and retraining.

New Jobs Training Program. With the passage of the Iowa Industrial New Jobs Training Program in 1983, businesses are now able to finance training for new employees by diverting funds from state withholding taxes and local property taxes. The law allows community colleges to enter into partnerships with expanding industries, as well as those needing to retrain an existing workforce. Kirkwood issues federally tax-exempt and taxable certificates on behalf of businesses. Repayment is achieved through a diversion of a portion of state withholding taxes that are directed to the college and a diversion of local property tax receipts from businesses' new capital investments through the creation of a tax increment financial (TIF) district. The outcome has been a more diverse and expansive industrial base. Kirkwood has provided $42 million in training assistance for 141 businesses, creating 7,830 new jobs in the area since 1983.

While the New Jobs Training Program has been an excellent tool for forging partnerships with industry, the Economic Development Services division is a key player in a much bolder team consisting of local and state economic development officials and area Chamber of Commerce organizations. As an example, Kirkwood has worked hand-in-hand with Priority One, the Cedar Rapids Area Chamber of Commerce economic development arm, to develop the Cedar Rapids-Iowa City Corridor into a fast-growing and diverse manufacturing sector. Priority One raises more than $600,000 annually from contributions to support economic development efforts to attract new business.

Kirkwood is a key player in the economic development of the region, and the college has played a major role in the attraction and start-up process of many new businesses, as well as the expansion of existing businesses. In each instance, Kirkwood has been at the table with state and local economic development professionals to mold a package that would entice the company and be economically viable for the region. Several examples follow.

Genencor International, a biotechnology firm using a fermentation process to produce industrial-strength enzymes, began operating its $85 million facility in 1988. Kirkwood played a leading role in assisting the company in linking employees and technology to optimize the potential of technology and the contributions of people. Genencor's facility has been through five expansions since construction began, and the company is planning an additional expansion.

Cedar River Paper Company, a $230 million corrugated medium recycling mill, is now under construction in Cedar Rapids, to open in July 1995. Within an 18-month time frame, Kirkwood EDS will assist with the employee hiring process, development of the company's work system design, the ISO 9000 certification process, and delivery of customized training to new employees. The company and its local construction partners have called the alliance with Kirkwood a "dream relationship," citing the college's anticipation and delivery of planning sequences and training needs.

American Profol, a German-owned company producing sheet plastic through a plastic extrusion process, located in Cedar Rapids in March 1993. Kirkwood designed the screening process for hiring and assisted in the process by writing employment advertisements, identifying appropriate assessment tools, conducting preliminary interviews, and scheduling employee physical and drug testing. After employees were hired, but before their departure to Germany for a five-month apprenticeship program, Kirkwood developed and delivered an intensive two-week training course.

The five-year program was designed to provide comprehensive academic support and guidance for area residents who would not otherwise have an opportunity to attend college. The program targeted those with deficiencies in basic skills; with substance abuse problems; and/or with critical needs for financial help with child care, transportation, tuition, and other costs related to college attendance. A staff member from the Hall Foundation has served on the committee that administers the program, and the project has assisted more than 700 "at-risk" students who are working to achieve their goals.

Rockwell International. Another major gift was made by Rockwell International, a large employer in the Cedar Rapids area with whom Kirkwood has had a close working relationship. In one year alone, Kirkwood provided training programs for almost 4,000 Rockwell employees. When approached during the campaign, the company pledged $200,000 to be used to purchase state-of-the-art instructional equipment and to provide scholarships for the unemployed, the underemployed, and single-parent students. According to the vice president for human resources at Rockwell, the $200,000 gift to the college is the largest donation ever made by the Rockwell International Corporation Trust to a community college.

AEGON's Gift. The major gifts campaign served to enhance Kirkwood's image among its constituencies. Many other partnerships have since been generated, including one partnership with AEGON USA, whose chief executive officer served as a co-chair of the campaign. During the campaign's celebration event, the CEO indicated that AEGON USA was planning to develop a national corporate data center in a facility that would include an educational component.

That disclosure led to further discussions and culminated in the building of a $10 million facility on the Kirkwood campus. More than one-fourth of the 55,000-square-foot building has been dedicated to an information technology center to be operated by the college. The center offers seven computer classrooms used for credit programs as well as for business and industry training. It also includes a computer lab with 75 computer terminals, open to students and the public. This state-of-the-art center was constructed at AEGON's expense and represents a gift to the college in excess of $1 million.

$1.3 Million Pork Education Center. Another major project for Kirkwood came about in response to a decline in the hog production industry in Iowa. Iowa's position as the nation's pork production leader has been challenged due to several factors: the aging Iowa farmer; the lack of young, skilled workers and managers; outdated production facilities; and environmental and health concerns. In 1993, the college responded to this situation and built a new swine confinement facility that now serves 60 to 80 Kirkwood students studying pork production. This facility incorporates the most

advanced technology in production and in the educational program. Thought to be one of the most advanced of its kind in the country, the $1.2 million facility features a breeding and gestation building, farrowing rooms, nurseries, classroom and computer lab, and a finishing building. Closed-circuit television enables students and Midwestern producers to view the procedures without entering the production facility. The connection to the state's fiber optic system will allow access to all 99 counties in the state of Iowa. Additionally, through Kirkwood's vast satellite uplink facilities, educational and training opportunities can be extended nationally and internationally.

This project would not have been possible without major financial support from Pioneer Hi-Bred, the Mansfield Foundation, Diamond V. Mills, Agri-King, Growmark, the Wallace Technology Transfer Foundation, Firstar Banks, Meyocks & Priebe Advertising Inc., and the Iowa Pork Producers Association. While Kirkwood allocated $300,000 to the facility, these investors contributed almost $1,000,000. In return, they are able to increase their own client exposure by participating in program delivery over the college's telecommunications system. Moreover, they participate on an advisory committee that determines the direction for curriculum, programming, and techniques that will have an effect on the industry over the next decade. Through their support for this teaching laboratory, these partners have helped to create a model for Iowa's pork producers as they plan expansions, equipment replacement, or new facilities.

FRIENDS AND PARTNERS CONTRIBUTE TO KIRKWOOD'S SUCCESS

Kirkwood's success over the past 28 years has not been an accident. The college's leaders recognized the need to build lasting relationships in the community. They accomplished that goal by seeking advice and expertise from individuals, businesses, governmental bodies, and community groups; hiring a dedicated faculty and staff; encouraging an entrepreneurial spirit; taking risks; and responding to the needs of the community. They developed innovative, quality programs. The result has been a relationship of trust between the college and its constituencies. When the college launched its major gifts campaign in 1990, its 25-year commitment to building relationships bore fruit. The individuals and corporations who had worked with and been served by the college contributed financially and joined in more partnerships with the college.

Resources for the community college are becoming more limited. Federal, state, and local governments are challenged to provide more and more services at a time when there is increased competition for tax dollars. As the demands of the workplace continue to change at a dizzying rate, business and industry require new programs to help workers keep pace with changes in technology. Companies, faced with their own revenue shortfalls, continue to lay off employees, displacing hundreds of thousands of people throughout the country. Community colleges are better positioned than any sector of education to respond to these challenges. It is essential that we take the initiative by reaching out to the regions we serve.

The key is to find some friends. Make those friends partners. Then find more friends. We must be willing to build key relationships to address the important needs of the community. Partnerships are the door to our future.

Chapter IX

President Tom Barton's chapter about Greenville Technical College's long-term community partnerships describes a cornucopia of college/community collaborations. For example, since 1968 a variety of partnership arrangements have evolved between General Electric and Greenville Tech. As technologies changed and the company's need for training increased, the college assigned a Greenville Tech faculty member full-time to the company's training needs. More recently, the college has delivered thousands of hours of team development training for work process improvements and partnerships among shifts, departments, vendors, and external customers.

Being a good citizen ranks high among Greenville's priorities. Examples range from giving assistance to Hurricane Hugo victims to providing a house and outdoor area to a program that trains assistance dogs. In this program, dogs are trained to help people who are wheelchair-bound with daily living tasks. Several people who were helped by the program have enrolled at Greenville.

In an example of a higher education partnership, eight four-year colleges and universities currently offer 26 undergraduate and graduate degree programs to 2,000 students each semester at the University Center at Greenville Tech. One of the few multi-institutional "minicampuses" in the nation, the University Center is the largest of such programs in the southeast. Public and private institutions are represented. The center is housed in a building purchased, renovated, and equipped by Greenville Tech and leased to the center. This collaborative effort provides accessibility and convenience to students and the community.

* * *

Thomas E. Barton, Jr.
President
Greenville Technical College
Greenville, South Carolina

BUILDING THE COMMUNITY COLLEGE OF THE FUTURE THROUGH PARTNERSHIPS

The impersonal hand of government can never replace the helping hand of a neighbor.

—Hubert H. Humphrey

THE FOUNDING OF GREENVILLE TECHNICAL COLLEGE

Greenville Technical college is located in Greenville, South Carolina, in the northwest section of the state. Situated almost equidistant from New York and Miami, it is the state's most populous and most metropolitan county. The county's population is greater than 330,000 and is predicted to increase to 350,000 by the year 2000. Greenville is situated along the I-85 corridor, which has been cited as one of the key business and industry cores in the nation. In the last 25 years, Greenville County has experienced a healthy industrial growth rate due to new industry moving to the area as well as expansion of existing facilities. More than 200 new industrial concerns have moved into the county, with a total capital investment of $4,735,954,000 and the creation of 47,000 new jobs.

This level of prosperity is a relatively recent achievement in Greenville and in the state. In 1961, South Carolina was faced with a slow economy based primarily on textiles and agriculture. This resulted in a serious lack of jobs, the out-migration of young people, and an inability to attract industry. In that year, the State General Assembly, encouraged by then-governor Ernest F. Hollings, passed one of the most significant pieces of legislation in the state's history. The new law established in strategic locations a statewide system of technical education centers that would become catalysts for economic and industrial development and improved living standards for South Carolinians. These centers were to be coordinated by the South Carolina State Board for Technical and Comprehensive Education, and each center would be governed by a local Area Commission for Higher Education.

The first to apply for a center under the new law was Greenville County, whose residents enthusiastically endorsed the concept. The application was approved in September 1961, and the institution opened its doors to students in September 1962 as the Greenville Technical Education Center. With an enrollment of 400 in the first year and only three departments of study, the new center consisted of one building on eight acres of land—a former landfill donated by the City of Greenville.

The establishment of the statewide system and the education center in Greenville had a positive impact almost immediately. It contributed to an influx of new and diversified business and industry never before experienced in upstate South Carolina. The Special Schools Division, the first part of the system to be activated at the center, attracted industry through its offerings of specialized recruiting and training of employees at no cost to the employer. This no-cost policy remains in force and continues to be a strong drawing card.

The name of the center was changed to Greenville Technical College in 1972 when state legislation granted approval for the institution to offer freshman and sophomore college transfer programs. Until that time, county residents had no local access to public postsecondary education other than the technical programs offered at the Greenville center. The main campus now covers 150 completely landscaped acres with 24 buildings on an architecturally modern campus. Student enrollment has grown to an annual headcount of more than 44,000. The institution continues to be funded by Greenville County for operations and maintenance, and by state funds and tuition for salaries and benefits.

The success of Greenville Technical College is attributable to the unsurpassed support and confidence of the community, as demonstrated by the formation of partnerships and collaborative initiatives. These partnerships have been the direct result of the college's quick response to the diverse needs of this highly industrialized region of South Carolina. Three major types of partnerships will be discussed:
- those with specific constituencies, such as members of the college's advisory boards, area business and industry, the health care professions and public agencies;
- those that focus on community problem solving; and
- those with the public schools and nearby institutions of higher education.

CONSTITUENCY PARTNERSHIPS

Advisory Boards. One of the first decisions at Greenville Tech was to charter advisory boards for each program of study. These boards included (and still include) professional people in the fields of study offered at Greenville Tech, and the boards were (and are) a vital link to the needs of business, industry, and the job market. A few years later, to make these advisory boards more viable, the position of Director of Advisory Boards was created. The director was charged with coordinating and overseeing the boards and their activities. This change resulted in such a sophisticated network that in 1980 Greenville Tech hosted a regional conference attended by hundreds of community/technical college personnel in the southeast who were interested in making similar changes in their advisory boards.

Under the Director of Advisory Boards, improvement in the advisory boards has been dramatic. In addition to advising each program, the boards act as strong liaisons that create close relationships, collaborations, and partnerships with the profession they represent. They conduct annual (more frequent, if necessary) evaluations of staff, curricula, equipment, and facilities. They keep the college informed of workforce needs, assist in faculty development, provide a steady flow of student scholarships, and advise program directors and prospective graduates on job placement. They conduct follow-up surveys of employers and employees, and make recommendations for improving the quality of all program facets.

An essential role of the advisory boards is to help the college acquire much-needed equipment. Advisory board members alone have been responsible for the donation of millions of dollars worth of state-of-the-art equipment from the companies they represent. They also have made possible faculty development through return-to-industry training programs of inestimable value.

Advisory board members now number more than 800. They have become so essential to college operations that they, along with the deans and department heads of the programs they represent, now report their evaluations, recommendations, and suggestions directly to the college administration. Suggestions are then submitted to the Program Review Subcommittee of the Greenville Tech Board for response and action.

Business and Industry Partnerships. Many partnerships with business and industry have grown along with the college and the community. They include cooperative operations with long-established firms that are expanding, as well as companies newly located in the area. These partnerships have proved to be mutually beneficial. A few of these will be described here in detail.

The Michelin Training Center. A close working relationship developed between Greenville Technical College and Michelin Tire Corporation beginning in 1973 when Michelin, an international firm, located manufacturing facilities and its U.S. corporate headquarters in Greenville. Access to high-level technical training for its personnel at Greenville Tech was a prime factor in the company's decision to move there. In a spirit of innovation, cooperation, and community advancement, the college and the corporation began joint construction of a 17,000 square foot training center on the college campus in 1986—the first time a public organization had built such a facility on a technical college campus in the state. Michelin contributed a large portion of the cost of the building and supplied the equipment and furnishings. The corporation uses this facility during the day, and the college uses it in the evening.

The Michelin Training Center, dedicated in 1987, received the prestigious "Keeping America Working" award from the American Association of Community and Junior Colleges (now AACC) and the Association of Community College Trustees. This unique industry/education partnership has had significant benefits for the community. The economic spin-offs of proximity to a corporation with more than 2,000 employees have touched every sector of the community.

General Motors Automotive Service Educational Program (ASEP). Another cooperative arrangement that deserves highlighting is the General Motors Automotive Service Educational Program (ASEP). Greenville Tech was chosen as a site for the ASEP, with the stipulation that the program would serve as the central automotive training resource center for four locations in the state. It is the only complete General Motors training program in South Carolina and one of 55 in the nation. With the advent of advanced technologies in the manufacture of automobiles, GM developed a two-year associate degree program to train entry level technicians for the workforce. Three elements continue to be necessary to make the program successful: the GM dealer, the college, and General Motors. GM provides equipment and new product technologies to the college. Educators can transfer this knowledge to students in the program, which is divided into classroom and lab sessions, along with work periods at GM dealerships. Moreover, faculty are required to attend professional development workshops and seminars throughout the year in order to meet standards set by General Motors.

Vehicles, books, equipment, and delivery materials given by General Motors to the program exceed $100,000 each year. In addition, the college has new GM vehicles, valued at $1 million, that are used for training purposes. This GM/Greenville Tech relationship has saved the college tens of thousands of dollars over the past 10 years through donations alone. In return, the continuing education division generates approximately 174 days of GM contract training yearly. Moreover, graduates of this program, almost without exception, have guaranteed careers awaiting them upon graduation—and the demand for ASEP graduates increases constantly.

Relationships with General Electric. One of the earliest partnerships established by the college was with General Electric's Gas Turbine Manufacturing Operation in 1968. GE's installation has become the world's largest producer of gas turbines. The special schools division provided specialized programs, and Greenville Tech assumed the responsibility of providing pre- and post-employment training for the company. As technologies changed and the need for retraining became more essential, a Greenville Tech instructor was assigned full-time to the company for computer training for entry-level employees, supervisors, and managers. Initially, there were more than 600 requests for training, covering all three work shifts. The number of trainees now exceeds 1,300. This computer training resulted in the development of a program called "Reasoning-Based Training Methodology," now a corporate standard for training.

More recently, the college's Management Center and the Continuous Improvement/Cycle Reduction Department of General Electric have delivered thousands of hours of team development training for work process improvements and partnerships among shifts, departments, vendors, and external customers. In return, the corporation has supplied advisory board members, faculty development opportunities, substantial donations, and consignments of materials and equipment to the college.

Advanced Machine Tool Technology. In the early 1980s, Greenville Tech was chosen as the site for the State Advanced Machine Tool Technology Center. The purpose of the center was fourfold: (1) to develop courses and offer advanced machine tool technology training to qualified students, (2) to develop and offer instructional programs in state-of-the-art technology to existing industries throughout the state of South Carolina, (3) to serve as a resource to attract new industries to the state, and (4) to provide specialized training and assistance to faculty from other state technical colleges. The center is closely interrelated with the college's computer-aided design and manufacturing (CAD/CAM) programs, which use the most current technology in the industry.

Out of the establishment of this center grew one of the strongest partnerships the college has yet developed. Cincinnati-Milacron, one of the area's largest users of machine tool technology, equipped the State Advanced Machine Tool Resource Center with millions of dollars' worth of CAD/CAM and Computer Numerical Control (CNC) equipment. Recently, the corporation has spent several million dollars to replace outdated equipment to ensure that the center has up-to-the-minute technology.

The Advanced Machine Tool Technology Center is an even more important factor in upgrading the workforce than was foreseen. In addition to the established curriculum, the college has held a number of continuing education courses, seminars, and workshops featuring nationally known speakers on subjects such as machine vision, geometric dimensioning, super abrasive tolerances, and global competition.

The center also serves as a resource for the technology transfer efforts of the Southeast Manufacturing Technology Center (SMTC), a federally funded program designed to assist small industries in remaining competitive in a global market. As more and more small businesses and industries approach the college for training programs, both credit and non-credit, SMTC continues to yield valuable returns for Greenville Tech. These small firms flourish as they take advantage of these offerings.

Cryovac. In 1988, one of the largest industries in the Greenville area—Cryovac, a division of W.R. Grace and Company—was experiencing a shortage of applicants and employees with the potential to advance through their training to the highest operator level. Faced with this shortage, Cryovac approached the Career Advancement Center at Greenville Tech to develop a General Manufacturing Certification Program to address the problem. Cryovac and Greenville Tech collaborated to identify men and women who could move successfully through Cryovac's program and adhere to the basic educational and technical requirements of the company. The program was so successful that it has been implemented in Cryovac plants in other parts of South Carolina and in Texas. Similar programs have been developed for a number of other companies, providing employment for hundreds of South Carolinians and meeting the staffing needs of large manufacturers.

The Southeastern Institute for Advanced Technologies. The Southeastern Institute for Advanced Technologies (SIAT), a comprehensive program linking facilities, professional expertise, and services for business and industry, uses an "umbrella" strategy that brings together many diverse partners to meet community needs. Through SIAT, Greenville Tech has become a "technology broker" for businesses, both large and small. One of the most important partnerships for SIAT has been the Computer Integrated Manufacturing Alliance. This alliance was originally sponsored by IBM, which has provided the college with hundreds of thousands of dollars in equipment and services over the last six years.

Other national partnerships through SIAT include the AutoDesk Education partnership, the Intergraph Education Center Alliance, and a partnership with Industrial Training Corporation (ITC) and COMSELL. Greenville Tech was the first institution to form partnerships with Intergraph, ITC, and COMSELL, and these relationships have become models for institutions across the country.

Other Constituency Partnerships. Other partnerships and collaborations include those with Mita and Hitachi, Japanese firms that have located in Greenville in recent years; BMW Manufacturing Company, a German automotive manufacturer; Sagem-Lucas, a French/English firm, supplier to the automotive industry; Ellcon National; Amoco; Dana Corporation; Reliance Electric; 3-M; Wangner Systems; Hoescht-Diafoil; Kemet Electronics; Lockheed-Aeromod; Stevens Aviation; and many more. Many of these longstanding partnerships are the result of Greenville Tech's continuing education division's initiatives with more than 300 different companies during any year.

Health Care Professions. Local hospitals have always supported the college professionally and financially. In 1971, the hospitals agreed that all nursing and other allied health fields personnel training would be provided by Greenville Tech. The result was the development of a nursing division, offering the associate degree in preparation for

R.N. certification, along with a large-scale continuing education program of courses in critical care and other specialties. A comprehensive allied health division, comprising 13 departments offering associate degree, diploma, and certificate programs, was also developed.

The college is currently expanding the allied health departments to meet the growing health care needs of an increasing population. To assist with this effort, local hospitals have made substantial monetary contributions for constructing and equipping a new 65,000-square-foot nursing/science building on the college's main campus. In cooperation with other hospitals in upstate South Carolina, they provide numerous clinical training sites for students and employ the vast majority of graduates of both divisions. The demand for graduates of these high-quality programs is substantial.

A recent allied health partnership developed when a Piedmont Healthcare Foundation grant was awarded to the dental hygiene department to provide services to patients of the Greenville Health Department. Students are gaining clinical enrichment by performing procedures away from the dental hygiene clinic through rotations to the Public Health Department Dental Clinic. This partnership enhances dental student training and, at the same time, provides an important public service to those people in the community who are economically disadvantaged.

The latest consequence of the college's history of hospital partnerships involves obtaining additional space for college programs. Because of the college's funding shortages, the Medical Center is providing 12,000 square feet of space for a Culinary Arts Campus. Partnerships with hospitals have been strengthened through the years by the fact that many at the college have served on various committees that studied health care expansions and services. In return, hospital administrators serve on advisory boards and ad hoc committees, providing valuable service to the college. In addition, the former director of medical education at the Greenville Hospital System has served several terms as a member of the college governing board, further strengthening this relationship.

Public Agencies. The criminal justice department at the college, which offers the associate degree and a wide array of seminars, workshops, and teleconferences, has developed an outstanding partnership with the Sheriff's Department of Greenville, the Police Department of the City of Greenville, and other similar agencies in upstate South Carolina. Most graduates of the programs are hired locally—often before graduation—or continue their education at a four-year college or university and return to the local community to enter the law enforcement profession.

The present sheriff of Greenville County is an alumnus of Greenville's criminal justice department. He is now president of the National Sheriff's Association and sometimes serves as an adjunct faculty member for the college. He is an outspoken supporter of the quality of the college's law-enforcement training. Having highly respected public officials involved in many Greenville Tech programs enhances the college's image and serves as an excellent recruiting tool.

The city of Greenville and the management center at Greenville Tech have teamed together to advance the careers of employees in the city police department and the Greenville fire department. Called Public Service, the program began in 1988 and has served more than 480 city employees. It is an intensive professional development program that has been a model for other governmental agencies. The city pays for the classroom instruction and the books for those accepted into the program. In addition, some employees of public service agencies have become outstanding adjunct professors at Greenville Tech, and many others serve on college advisory boards.

The South Carolina Workforce Initiative—a partnership among state government, business, local adult education programs, technical colleges, and literacy programs—coordinates the services of educators with the needs of employers and the community. It focuses on job-specific and basic skills training, ensuring a productive, adaptable, and competitive workforce. Since this initiative began in 1988, approximately 3,500 employees of 53 different companies have completed these skill programs either on campus or in-plant and many of them have continued as students at the college. Close to 1,000 employees in 66 different firms currently participate in the initiative.

COLLABORATIONS FOR COMMUNITY PROBLEM SOLVING

Community problem solving, in collaboration with an array of civic and service organizations, charitable agencies, and other nonprofit groups, is a high priority for Greenville Tech. For example, the Greenville Urban League, Inc., United Way of Greenville County, Legal Services of Western Carolina, Community Food Bank, United Ministries, the Department of Social Services, the Department of Housing and Development, the NAACP, and others work closely with the college to provide equal opportunity for high quality education on flexible schedules and at affordable costs. Many faculty and staff at the college hold membership or have leadership roles in these organizations. Members of the faculty and staff have formed a "Speaker's Team" and, along with a group of "Tech Ambassadors" made up of current students, readily accept invitations to tell the Greenville Tech story at meetings of these and other groups, including community centers and churches.

Walkathon. One of the most publicized charitable events of the year in Greenville, the March of Dimes Walkathon, begins and ends on Greenville Tech's main campus. Physical plant personnel are responsible for setup and many other aspects of this event, which receives national attention for its extraordinary success. This annual Walkathon is not only a public service; it also gives residents an opportunity to visit the campus and enhances the institution's position as a partner with the community.

Emergency Assistance. Other civic and service collaborations include those with public agencies to provide assistance during times of emergency. College, state, and local officials have devised a plan for coordinating efforts for the orderly handling of emergency situations. Greenville Tech is prepared to provide mental health counseling, truck drivers for distribution of needed equipment, volunteer construction workers from the student body, and other assistance. After Hurricane Hugo struck the coast of South Carolina in 1989, the college's truck driving training students and faculty made several trips to the coast to deliver rebuilding materials. Several crews of college employees went to the badly damaged coastal area to help with residential housing. These relief measures were provided free of charge.

Affordable Housing. Students in the carpentry program have worked with Habitat for Humanity volunteers to construct, free of charge, a number of houses and other facilities. This is a valuable public service that has provided hands-on training for students and is an excellent return on the investment of taxpayer's money.

School for the Arts. The South Carolina Governor's School for the Arts is a state-funded program for gifted children. Two years ago, when the program needed space for administrative offices, the Greenville Tech administration provided office space on the college's main campus for the Governor's School. This space will be available to the school until a permanent office location is established.

Child Care and Advocacy. When the need for child care personnel in pre-school agencies outgrew the supply, a child development program was incorporated into the allied health division. In 1988, a child development center was built on the main campus to provide urgently needed care for the children of students, faculty, and staff, along with clinical training for future employees of child development and early childhood agencies. This nationally accredited center has helped meet the needs of parents who have returned to college for job training. The center is also host to regional and national conferences focusing on child care.

The South Carolina Educational Resource Center for Missing and Exploited Children, also founded by Greenville Tech, addresses another highly publicized problem. Offering conferences, workshops, and seminars on child abuse, self-esteem, family violence, and any issue that may have a negative impact on children, the center presented more than 60,000 hours of child abuse prevention programs in 1992–1993. This center has been expanded to all the technical colleges in the state and is the only program of its kind in the nation that receives funding from a state legislature.

In addition, space has been allocated on campus for a Greenville branch of the state's Health and Human Services Finance Commission. This "outstation" deals with child care providers who work with parents receiving federal vouchers for child care. This partnership, which provides training for clients referred by agency personnel, has been another "plus" for the college.

Base Relocation. In the college's early years the Greenville community was faced with the closing of the Donaldson Air Force Base, resulting in the loss of jobs and population that had been an important economic asset for some 25 years. Greenville Tech immediately joined forces with city, county, and state agencies to turn this imminent loss into an opportunity by planning for the use of the thousands of acres of land (complete with runways and hangars) that became available, along with buildings suitable for offices and other uses.

College administrators served on numerous committees to develop the Donaldson Center Industrial Park at the former air force base. The park has steadily attracted new business and industry such as Lockheed-Aeromod, 3-M, Proctor and Gamble, the Autozone Distribution Center, Palmetto Helicopters, Donaldson Air Service, Advantage Aviation, and others—all partners of Greenville Tech. Because of the park's ideal location, the college also located its truck driving training and aircraft maintenance technology programs there, taking advantage of the layout and facilities. In this first experiment with off-campus location, both programs have experienced steady growth.

Space for Army and Air Force Reserve Units. Local air force and army reserve units are now using office space on the college's main campus to house two full-time personnel and a storage facility for records. Five army reserve units, with 60 reservists in each unit, meet on the campus one weekend each month. Allocating this space provides another community service and has also attracted new students to the college.

Services for Older Adults. Responding to a need for programs for retirees and elderly people in the community, Greenville Tech initiated a life enrichment center for older adults in 1989. Corporate sponsors, civic clubs, churches, and synagogues all contributed to this new venture, focusing on the unique educational and social needs of the mature adult (age 50 and over). Social concerns, travel, recreation, fitness and nutrition, fine arts, history, personality assessment, job referrals, and volunteer training are addressed by the center. Members and program leaders plan and implement frequent fund-raising activities. More than 1,000 people participate monthly in the various events sponsored by the program, and growth is likely to continue. A $10 annual fee allows members to attend all functions.

The public relations benefits of this center in the community cannot be exaggerated. The program has garnered attention and kudos from across the country. It attracts numerous visitors annually who research ways in which they can start similar programs for the 50 and older population. The center has reaped a number of prestigious awards, including the Governor's Health Promotion for Older South Carolinians Award and the National Outstanding Community Health Promotion Program Award.

Adult Education. Greenville Tech's adult education division, now among the largest in the state, was initially begun in response to several factors. Greenville County had a high illiteracy rate and a large percentage of residents who had not completed high school. At the same time, local industry was clamoring for employable high school graduates. The adult education division has been effective through its offering of developmental (remedial) studies and high school completion, and has been a valuable feeder to other programs at the college. However, many potential students, for family or job reasons, could not attend classes on a regular campus schedule. The college took education to these students—a common Greenville theme—by establishing 22 tutoring centers in churches and community centers, staffed by volunteer teachers and some college personnel.

In a related initiative called "Project Book Find," which originated in the southern part of the state, Greenville Tech cooperated with a number of institutions to obtain some 250,000 books from a major school book publisher. These new, free books have been placed in minority churches and community centers throughout Greenville County.

Services for Internationals. In response to the influx of multinational companies and their employees, who wanted to help their children retain their cultural identities and native languages, the college has offered children's language classes in Japanese and German. Special classes in Spanish at one local elementary school—a new outreach program for the college—are also underway. It was also part of a natural progression that a renewed emphasis was given to English as a second language. These activities will continue to grow as our partnerships with international industry expand, accelerating the internationalization of upstate South Carolina.

Assistance Dog Program. Several years ago, the Speech, Hearing, and Learning Center, along with local Rotary Clubs, approached the college in their search for a location for a Southeastern Assistance Dog Program. This involves training dogs to help people who are wheelchair-bound with such tasks as improving mobility, using elevators, and carrying books, packages, and other objects. Greenville Tech provided a house and an outdoor area for the program. An added benefit was that this program made it possible for several people who are physically challenged to enroll at the college.

WORKING WITH THE PUBLIC SCHOOLS AND HIGHER EDUCATION

Public School Partnerships. Greenville Tech's partnerships with the county's public schools are among its most important and productive. Legislation that established the state technical system required that the Superintendent of Schools and the Chairman of the Board of Trustees of the local schools serve as ex officio members of the Greenville Area Commission, creating an excellent working relationship that has made a variety of cooperative ventures possible.

Articulation. Several years ago, an articulation agreement—the first in the state—was reached between the college and the career (vocational) centers of the public schools, giving high school students the opportunity to take courses applicable to their careers at the college following high school graduation. This facilitates a smoother transition from high school to the college and, in many cases, shortens the completion time for a technical education program. The college has traditionally offered scholarships to the most deserving graduates of the career centers.

Tech Prep Consortium. A more recent partnership with the School District of Greenville County is the Greenville County Tech Prep Consortium, designed to improve educational programs in applied math, science, and communications, which prepare students for a technologically advanced society. High school tech prep teachers come to the college to spend a day with a faculty member in their respective academic disciplines. This cooperative endeavor will continue to transform students into employees who think critically, have skills in problem solving and the use of resources, have learned to work effectively with others, have learned to acquire and use information, and have good oral and written communication skills.

Public School Outreach. College counselors, recruiters, and community outreach personnel (including Tech Ambassadors selected from the college's student body) have open invitations to visit the public schools to describe programs available at Greenville Tech. These college representatives also encourage the use of the Advanced College Entrance (ACE) program for juniors and seniors, allowing them to take college level courses and put them in escrow for postsecondary education.

Science and Math Enrichment. Increasing awareness among public school students of the value of a strong background in mathematics and science is one of the college's top priorities. Action toward reaching this objective has included "Summer Enrichment in Math and Science," a four-week program designed to provide hands-on experiences in mathematics and science to economically disadvantaged eighth and ninth graders. The program was initially funded by the National Science Foundation and the U. S. Department of Energy and is now in its fifth year. The program is supported currently by the Job Training Partnership Act, and students are paid a small stipend for each hour they participate. Program participants use the latest computer hardware and software and perform various experiments in chemistry, engineering, physics, biology, and related fields. The program includes field trips to local industries, museums, and art centers. Participants also receive mentoring from Greenville Tech students and information on career opportunities in mathematics and science.

In addition to this local program, the institution is involved in a similar statewide project. A faculty member in the college's Arts and Sciences Division is a member of the South Carolina Math-Sciences Advisory Board, which is primarily charged with designing a plan for math and science education in grades K–12. One assignment of the Advisory Board is to identify needs in these two areas of study that are not currently being addressed.

Higher Education Partnerships. Although it is now the largest metropolitan area in the state, Greenville County has never had a public four-year college or university within its borders. Aware of this unmet challenge in the college's service area, an independent higher education consulting firm conducted surveys of Greenville residents, including Greenville Tech students and graduates, to assess the need for four-year and graduate degree programs.

The surveys verified that because Greenville lacked a public four-year university, thousands of working adults were essentially "place-bound" as a result of job, family, and financial obligations. Armed with this information, Greenville approached the major four-year colleges and universities in the state for assistance in providing further education within the county. These institutions readily recognized the opportunity for a presence in Greenville and for service to an area of such potential. As a result, the University Center was opened on the Greenville Tech campus in 1987.

Multi-Institutional Campus. The University Center at Greenville Tech is one of the only multi-institutional "minicampuses" in the nation. At present, eight four-year colleges and universities offer 26 undergraduate and graduate degree programs to some 2,000 students each semester, making the University Center at Greenville Tech the largest of such programs in the southeast, both in terms of enrollment and the number of member institutions.

Virtually all sectors of South Carolina public and private higher education are reflected in the center's roster of member institutions. In addition to South Carolina's three research universities (Clemson University, the Medical University of South Carolina, and the University of South Carolina-Columbia), the Center is served by two historically black institutions (South Carolina State University, a public land-grant institution, and Voorhees College, a private, church-related, liberal arts college); a private, independent undergraduate university (Furman University); and two regional public universities with primarily undergraduate missions (Lander University and the University of South Carolina-Spartanburg).

Each of the participating institutions confers its own degrees and furnishes its own professors. In 1992, the center's philosophy of team building led the state's two largest research universities, the University of South Carolina-Columbia and Clemson University, to begin co-teaching and co-awarding the master of public administration degree, a first between two long-standing rivals.

The University Center is governed by a board of directors, consisting of the presidents of the institutions, and an executive committee composed of the institutions' chief academic officers. The board, which also includes voting representation from

Greenville Tech, operates under the authority of the statewide Commission on Higher Education. Planning and development are supported by an advisory council of business, industrial, and civic leaders in Greenville County.

The center's entire operation is housed in a $3.5 million multi-story building—purchased, renovated, and equipped by Greenville Tech and leased to the consortium. An excellent connector to other higher education institutions, it provides accessibility and convenience to students, and is an excellent return on taxpayer investment. Because of its projected growth, the University Center will soon be housed in a larger facility adjacent to the campus that was donated to the college by a local philanthropist.

Partnerships with higher education institutions do not end with the University Center. Close cooperation naturally exists among the 17 technical colleges in the state. In addition, an exchange of ideas and information between several similar colleges across the nation and Greenville Tech emphasizes the "don't re-invent the wheel" philosophy that is typical of the thinking of the college's administration, faculty, and staff.

Promoting International Education. A critical part of Greenville Tech's role in collaboration with other higher education institutions is that the college has taken the lead in promoting international education among the technical colleges in South Carolina. Greenville Tech initiated the formation of the South Carolina International Education Consortium and secured a grant from the U.S. Department of Education Title VI-A program to revise existing courses and develop new ones that offer students education about other cultures. The goal of this consortium is to ensure that all students who receive associate degrees will be able to demonstrate cross-cultural awareness and understanding, particularly important in upstate South Carolina. More than any other area of the state, this region is intimately tied to the global economy, as home to both international investment on a grand scale and American firms active in worldwide exports. Preparing employees for the workforce of the future will require an openness toward other cultures on the employees' part. A multicultural education will make Greenville Tech graduates better citizens for the 21st century and more desirable candidates in a global job market.

The Role of Technology. All partnerships with educational institutions are being greatly enhanced by the college's distance learning capability in the new J. Verne Smith Library and Technical Resource Center. Teleclasses, telecourses, and teleconferences are in large-scale use, both on and off campus. Distance learning reception sites have been placed in the Greenville County Office Building and in the Piedmont Exposition Center (the site of some of the nation's largest exhibits and conferences). Reception sites are currently located in classrooms in temporary facilities at the two new campuses, made available by the public schools in the county for the college's use while construction of the new campuses is underway. More sites are being planned at a number of other locations. The college also has its own 24-hour cable television channel that offers courses, educational programs, and general college information.

ONGOING COMMUNITY SUPPORT

Due to the college's longstanding active commitment to meet community needs by partnering with all segments of the community, Greenville Tech enjoys significant support from its constituencies.

The Greenville Tech Foundation, Inc. Governed by a select board of community leaders, the Greenville Tech Foundation, Inc., is a nonprofit organization created to support the college exclusively by supplementing declining higher education allocations based on funding formulas. Equipment acquisition, student scholarships, faculty development, and other college needs that depend on increased funding have been targets of its supplemental efforts.

The foundation has begun a three-year, $5 million major gifts campaign for which substantial gifts have already been received or pledged. Some 50 successful local business leaders, along with representatives of civic and service organizations, have agreed to participate in this campaign. The donations and endowments generated by the campaign will make possible the college's future expansion, which will be described later in this chapter.

Community Volunteers. In 1992, in another effort to cope with state-funding shortages, Greenville Tech began a volunteer program and received immediate response from community residents. Volunteers do not replace paid faculty and staff, but they supplement and complement the activities of paid personnel.

Greenville Tech provides sufficient work space, equipment, and supplies so that the volunteers can perform their tasks. As of early 1994, the volunteers had contributed 8,400 hours of service for a dollar value of approximately $109,200 (based on evaluations by the Human Resources Department).

Professional Societies. The professional societies of dental, medical, engineering, legal, production and inventory control, purchasing, and other occupational groups have established student chapters on campus. Members of these organizations give freely of their time to enhance student awareness of the careers they represent. When space is available, the host societies hold their meetings in facilities on the college campus. As with civic and service organizations, college administrators, faculty, and staff have membership in these professional societies and serve as officers or members of their directing boards.

Economic Development Involvement. The college is closely affiliated with state and local development boards, planning commissions, the Greenville Chamber of Commerce, and chambers of commerce in other municipalities in the county. Greenville Tech is usually the first site that is visited by industrialists and business leaders seeking information on pre- and post-employment training (both specialties of the college) and evaluating the status of high-tech laboratories and instruction. When firms decide to locate in the area, they are candid about the role that Greenville Tech had in convincing them to settle in Greenville. The economic development organizations routinely refer industrialists who are considering relocating to the area to others who testify to the positive effect that the college's offerings have had on their "bottom line."

Political Support. Greenville Technical College's progress has been made possible by the uninterrupted confidence and support of political connections at every level— city, county, state, and federal. For example, the city donated the land for the main campus—a former landfill that is now a prime example of successful land reclamation, thanks largely to professional planning for full use of the acreage and a continual emphasis on landscaping and groundskeeping.

The college maintains personal contact with county government and members of the county legislative delegation, and a progress report is made annually to each of those bodies. There is similar contact with the governor of the state of South Carolina, with elected state constitutional officers, and with members of the general assembly from across the state who hold responsible committee positions. Those contacts extend to senators and representatives in the United States Congress, who were influential in bringing about the college's inception and continue to believe that the technical education system in the state is the major factor in the economic turnaround of the last 30 years.

Positive political connections are more important now than ever, as the college embarks on an extensive expansion program to prepare itself to provide a world class workforce for the future. This expansion includes two new campuses in the fastest-growing areas of the county, where both population and industrial growth have far exceeded early predictions. The land has already been purchased for the new campus. Greenville county government has approved a millage increase to fund construction of permanent facilities that will replace temporary quarters now in use at the new campuses. The approval of several state government agencies has been necessary every step of the way. Construction of the facilities is expected to begin in early 1995, with occupancy scheduled approximately one year later.

Public Relations Support. In 1986, the largest cable television station in the area offered to produce and televise, free-of-charge, a 30-minute weekly public affairs program for the college. This long-running series features interviews with business, industrial, community, and political leaders, as well as representatives of Greenville Tech on subjects of public interest, and has proved valuable to college public relations, marketing, and recruiting efforts.

The College Community. The role that college personnel have played in Greenville Technical College's development cannot be overlooked or overstated. The faculty and staff have exhibited outstanding leadership and professionalism at every level. Greenville Tech personnel are student-oriented, conscious of the importance of quality instruction in an environment designed for learning, and dedicated to preparing students for successful futures. College administrators, faculty, and support staff are prime partners in support of the philosophy of technical and community colleges.

CONCLUSION

Planning institutional changes, restructuring the organization as necessary, and putting vision for the future into practice as technologies advance and competition becomes more global have set the tone for an aggressive, progressive institution. Greenville Technical College's progress would not have been possible without the numerous partnerships described here; nor would the partnerships have been possible without the college's total commitment to being an active, contributing partner with the community. This is the firm foundation that will carry the institution forward with the ability to serve future generations.

CHAPTER X

Cuyahoga Community College President Jerry Sue Thornton and college leaders stress that a continuous focus on community, striving to be community-centered, and maintaining flexibility and adaptability are central to success in community partnerships. This commitment is practiced in their evolving women's programs, Unified Technical Center, Global Issues Resource Center, and the Quadrangle project.

Women's programs at Cuyahoga Community College (Tri-C) have evolved as changing needs have emerged. In 1966, Project Eve served adult women by assisting them in establishing or reestablishing themselves in the workplace. As women at Tri-C began to complete college programs and become established, they needed services for women in management and other leadership positions. Tri-C responded.

In another example of adaptability, the Nuclear Age Resource Center, established in the fall of 1985, evolved to become the Global Issues Resource Center. It now offers educational outreach, training for global responsibility, and specialized materials for teachers. Its library has extensive reference holdings.

Tri-C has also maintained a long-term partnership, called the Saint Vincent Quadrangle project, with a number of major Cleveland institutions and community organizations. The goal of the Quadrangle project is to renew the distressed neighborhood community that surrounds the campus. Since the project's inception in 1981, its board has overseen the reinvestment of $200 million by member institutions and businesses. A master plan calling for reconstruction of a distressed commercial street, area-wide transportation and parking, adequate security, and new housing has been developed.

Thornton notes that Tri-C's successful partnerships "have inherent flexibility and a sensitivity to societal changes," supporting Sherman's (1992, Part 2, p. 1) observation that "when alliances can't adapt, most fail."

* * *

Sherman, S. "Are strategic alliances working?" *Fortune*, 1992, 126(6), 77–79.

Jerry Sue Thornton
President
Cuyahoga Community College

Lois Baron
Lois Baron Communications
Cleveland, Ohio

THE GREAT BALANCING ACT:

Community Need Versus Resources

There is nothing constant except change.

—Heraclitus

TRI-C'S FOUNDING IN TURBULENT TIMES

The definition of community—"a unified body of individuals; people with common interests living in a particular area; or an interacting population of various kinds of individuals in a common location"—(Webster's New Collegiate Dictionary, 1981, p. 226) is not an accurate reflection of the group of citizens living in Cuyahoga County in 1964 when Cuyahoga Community College (Tri-C) opened its doors. The people in the community were not unified, nor did they hold common interests.

After all, it was the 1960s—a time of social and political upheavals for this country: the Vietnam War protests, the civil rights debate and unrest, inner-city riots, the demands of the women's movement, and the rapid growth of the suburbs. During these years, the city of Cleveland was rapidly losing population and its economic base as were other cities across the country that were founded on heavy industry.

Yet in the midst of all of this instability, Cuyahoga Community College emerged. People holding widely ranging views on all the important issues of the day made up its student population. The college immediately was challenged by the word "community" in its name. Since its control, financial support, services, and students were largely confined to the geographical limits of the county, it was necessary to understand the complex diversity of the people who resided within that area. The college conducted an analysis of the population that brought it into contact with existing institutions, businesses, and community resources. This opened the door for the college to form partnerships with the community to serve needs and effect change. It was through partnerships that an ability to create, to change, and to make a difference, gave special meaning to the word *community* in Cuyahoga Community College.

However, Tri-C's challenge has always been to balance the expectations and demands of a community-centered organization with the capabilities and resources at the institution's disposal. The college's planning priority for this decade is identifying needs and establishing standards by which community-centeredness can be defined and achieved.

A DIVERSITY OF PARTNERSHIPS

Reaching out to the community through a multitude of partnerships, Tri-C plays an important role in serving the area's educational needs, stimulating economic development, and enhancing the area's quality of life. The college serves business, industry, and labor through such entities as the Unified Technologies Center, the Manufacturing Learning Center, the Computer Automated Logistics System, the General Motors Automotive Service Educational Program, the Machine Trades Apprenticeship Program, and programs serving the unions.

Career training is an important aspect of the college's partnership programs. More than 850 professionals serve on 66 advisory committees that deal with career areas and special programs. Over 200 employers pay tuition for 4,000 employees annually, and on-the-job training is provided for about 400 students a year, in cooperation with more than 200 local public and private sector organizations. The college's allied health program places students at more than 100 sites to gain clinical experience. This program also brings the college into association with professional accreditation organizations in various fields. More than 1,600 students are enrolled annually in Tri-C's Public Service Institute which, through several partnerships, offers career certification and in-service programs for municipal police and fire personnel, National Park Service employees, and private security personnel.

Opening opportunities to those who are functionally illiterate, Tri-C provides adult basic education for more than 1,000 people in Cuyahoga County annually. In partnership with Cleveland Community Access Corporation, Tri-C offers telecourses, community forums, and live, interactive instruction through Tri-C's Cable College. With the Urban League of Greater Cleveland, the college provides education and training for minorities, offering off-campus credit and non-credit classes throughout the county at high schools and community centers.

Tri-C also participates in partnerships with other educational institutions. Articulation agreements exist with area high schools and four-year universities, and dual admissions programs are offered with Kent State University, Cleveland State University, and Dyke College. In addition, the college has a matriculation agreement with the Ohio College of Podiatric Medicine. The Tri-C/Kent State University Teaching Leadership Consortium works to prepare students from underrepresented groups for teaching careers in urban settings.

Tri-C-sponsored events include such programs as the Martin Luther King Day celebration and the Jesse Owens Youth Program, which brings young people to Tri-C campuses for pre-college enrichment. There are sports, career days, and theater productions, as well as community activities that bring diverse organizations to campus facilities. To bring cultural arts to a broad community, the Cleveland Philharmonic Orchestra makes its home at Tri-C, and the college will soon provide the educational component for the Rock and Roll Hall of Fame and Museum. Tri-C's Partnership Through Diversity series brings nearly a dozen speakers to the campuses each year to address topics related to global issues.

The partnerships described here reflect the college's range of involvement. But we now turn to several programs that are unique and illustrate the flexibility and sensitivity these joint ventures must have over time, if they are truly to serve community needs.

Women's Programs. In recent years, the collective consciousness of this country has become more sensitized to women's special needs. Cuyahoga Community College has listened. In 1966, Tri-C established Project Eve, an innovative program designed specifically for women. This was a bold step at the time, since the adult female population was not considered a major source of potential college students.

When the program started, it provided educational and counseling services to adult women. Its goals were to help them assess their talents, renew their skills, and to assist them in establishing or reestablishing themselves in the workplace. This group included female heads of households, older unemployed women, wives of disabled and unemployed husbands, single mothers, and untrained housewives seeking outside employment opportunities. The program offered group and individual counseling, career information, personal assessment, outside speakers, one-day institutes on work and career options, and tours of businesses and industries. Workshops and short-term, non-credit classes were held on sex discrimination issues and promotion barriers to women. By the early 1970s, these programs were reaching thousands of women and did much to help the disadvantaged and those without skills to become prepared to enter the workforce.

The Displaced Homemakers Program, another Tri-C effort, began in 1975 and is funded by the State of Ohio. Services are available for women who have lost their primary means of support and include counseling, personal development workshops, and non-credit courses. The goal of the program is to move women into degree programs that will allow them to be self-supporting. The program staff is aware of needs for personnel in the business community. This can quickly translate into training programs at the college that will provide participating women with good job opportunities. At the present time, the college serves 450 women annually through the Displaced Homemakers Program.

As with many other programs at the college that are concerned with disadvantaged adults, the first step is not enrollment in credit courses, but forming relationships with people who have great potential, but who presently do not seek a degree. It is often difficult to convince these women that opportunities exist and that they can successfully take advantage of those opportunities. Thus, counseling is important and continues while they are at the college, no matter what program they pursue. Women who have experienced loss, especially those who are widowed or divorced, need encouragement and understanding. The college provides special services for battered women and maintains excellent relations with the referral support agencies in the community.

As women at Tri-C began to complete college programs and opportunities emerged, they needed services meaningful to women in management and leadership positions; thus, Women Focus and the Women In Management series were born. When Project Eve began, its goal was to help women enter the workforce; now there is a need to serve those who have succeeded. Both needs are being met by the college through Tri-C's comprehensive women's program.

Moreover, many graduates of the women's program come back to teach at Tri-C or to enter into successful business partnerships with the college. They are some of the college's most vocal supporters. They give their time to mentor others, and they provide role models for those taking their first steps toward a new, more productive life.

The Center for Applied Gerontology. As the women's movement was a dominant force in the 1960s, the 1970s saw the underserved aging population in this country become a vocal, organized, and important political and economic force. People were living longer and healthier lives with more post-retirement years available for self-enrichment. More women worked, and fewer family members were located near their aging parents. Many of these parents needed special services to remain in their communities. However, the elderly were having difficulty finding those services or were not finding them at all. To address this need, the college instituted the Center for Applied Gerontology in 1974 to bring Tri-C and seniors into a mutually beneficial partnership.

The belief that education is a lifelong experience served as the basis for program development. The college offered seminars, workshops, and special events; courses in the humanities, social, behavioral, and biological science; and courses on special interest topics related to health and well-being in the later years. The Elder's Campus, a daylong program held once a week, has become the number one educational choice for many of the county's retired persons. Older adults, some of whom are members of the advisory team, play an integral part in the planning and implementation of the program. More than 60 emeriti faculty also bring a wealth of experience and expertise to the classroom. Interestingly, the advisory panel decided to shatter the myth that the elderly are always willing to volunteer—seniors who teach are paid, and younger faculty members must volunteer their time.

Bringing the college into contact with 10,000 elderly people in 40 different locations and with the major agencies that deal with senior issues gives the Tri-C staff tremendous insider information. This enables the college to develop programs that are meaningful, that speak to real problems, that serve a variety of populations and interests, and that can appropriately serve the needs of the elderly and their families as they move through various life phases.

Although we hear about the need for more quality nursing homes, that is not where the majority of frail elderly people receive their care. In fact, only about five percent of such people are in nursing homes—most others are cared for at home by family members. It became clear early in the program's history that, while seniors had their own set of needs and problems, family members also needed special attention, especially those who served as caregivers. While many of these family members were required to function much like personnel in the nursing homes, they had no resources for training and support. In response to this need, in 1978 the college began to offer family caregiver training.

In the course of working with caregivers, Tri-C staff uncovered another problem. Increasingly, there are frail elderly who do not have a family member to care for them; yet, as the entire health care delivery system changes, there is more focus on providing in-home treatment rather than on institutional care. These changes have created a tremendous demand for paraprofessionals. A report by the Ohio Department of Aging, "Who Will Deliver the Care?" (1989), agreed on the need for trained home health aides, homemakers, and nurses' aides. The Ohio Council for Home Health Agencies (1989) stated that the need for these workers across Ohio was twice the available number.

Cuyahoga Community College, because of its partnerships with the elderly at the Title III nutrition sites, community senior centers, the Office on Aging, and other agencies that serve the elderly, is in a position to develop training programs that fill the need for paraprofessionals who work with the elderly. The college is already offering a core curriculum for nurses' aides and will begin classes for home health care aides this year. The college has been instrumental in curriculum development and in upgrading the profession's standards and salary scale. After completing training, nurses' aides and home health care workers must be approved by the State of Ohio and earn continuing education credits each year. In addition, the college has agreements with nursing homes and some area hospitals for clinical training. The need for workers in this field offers opportunities for people in the Displaced Homemakers Program and other programs for the disadvantaged.

The Center for Applied Gerontology is an example of how any program may evolve. It continues to serve the needs for which it was founded, but in response to societal changes, it has expanded its vision and provided a new range of services and training.

Science, Engineering, Math and Aerospace Academy. In the late 1980s, some disturbing reports predicted a dire future for our nation's economic health, created by an undereducated and underskilled future population. Both the United States Bureau of Labor Statistics (1991) and the Ohio Bureau of Employment Services (1990) projected that in the year 2000 five-sixths of the new entrants into the work force would be minorities, women, and immigrants, with a preponderance of minorities. The fastest growing jobs are projected to be professional and technical jobs that require higher education and sophisticated skill levels. The employment situation is expected to be especially difficult for African American males and Hispanics of both sexes. This message was repeated in a report of the American Council on Education and the American Association of State Colleges and Universities titled Educating One Third of a Nation (1988). By the year 2000, one-third of all school-age children will be African American, Native American, or Asian American. Almost 42 percent of all public school students will be minority children, children in poverty, or both. The report stated that minority students complete their undergraduate degrees at a rate far lower than their non-minority counterparts. It challenged institutions of higher education to renew and strengthen efforts to increase minority recruitment, retention, and graduation.

In their Master Plan for Higher Education (1988), the Ohio Board of Regents concurred with the other reports, stating that "due to the fact that the nation, state, and Greater Cleveland region must increasingly rely on minority populations for their future science, engineering and math personnel, a plan must be developed and implemented to attract, retain and successfully educate greater numbers of minorities for careers in these professions" (p. 12). The plan challenged public colleges and universities to increase minority participation and success in postsecondary education, particularly in programs preparing them for careers requiring a strong math and science foundation.

On the local level, the results of Ohio Mathematics Proficiency Test indicated that a large percentage of ninth-grade students do not have the requisite skills to succeed in college preparatory courses. In addition, some teachers are not adequately prepared to interest students in math and science, nor do they have the expertise in instructional strategies to enhance learning and achievement. The combination of these factors has resulted in unacceptably low success rates of first year math, science, and engineering college students.

These challenges have not gone unheeded. Cuyahoga Community College's sensitivity to these problems, combined with the proximity of the NASA Lewis Research Center, spurred an innovative partnership that resulted in the creation of the Science, Engineering, Mathematics and Aerospace Academy (SEMAA). Totally funded by

NASA, the academy became operational in 1993. Its goals are to target students who have been historically underrepresented in math, science, and engineering; to provide a set of learning experiences that constitute a pipeline in science, mathematics, engineering, aerospace, and technology for these students; to improve participation and success in college preparatory courses; to maintain interest in careers in these areas; to improve participation and success in postsecondary undergraduate programs; to increase parental involvement; and to monitor short- and long-term progress.

The program serves students from kindergarten through twelfth grade and is divided into activities appropriate to all age levels. Parental involvement is mandatory for family math and science classes for kindergarten through fourth-grade students. Class times are scheduled for after school, early evening, or Saturday mornings for the convenience of all parents, including those who work. The program provides activities to supplement and support the elementary school curriculum. It gives parents information on how to help their children with homework, provide positive encouragement, and build self-esteem and confidence. Also included are family computing activities and field trips to the local Children's Museum, the Tri-C United Technologies Center, and the NASA Lewis Research Center. At the end, everyone participates in a wonderful awards program that reinforces the students' progress and encourages them to continue through the higher levels of the academy.

Program activities vary with the age of the students. Students in grades four through six receive hands-on enrichment activities in biology, environmental science, chemistry, physics, and math. Research scientists participate at field trip locations and as guest speakers. Activities for seventh and eighth graders are targeted at improving their science and math skills. During a five-week summer camp, students complete two experiments per week, and during the school year, two experiments per month. In conjunction with the experiments and assisted by visiting research scientists, students choose a research topic and are required to make presentations on their completed work. Discussion of ethics and the philosophy of scientific activities is an integral part of all student interaction with practicing research scientists.

The high school program meets once a week from 3:00 to 6:00 p.m. with monthly tours to industrial sites. The summer camp component encourages self-paced education and training programs in the Interactive Resource Center at the college's Unified Technologies Center. It operates five half-days each week for five weeks and includes field trips to science, engineering, and math-related industries.

As an added reinforcement to the academy, the Northeast Ohio Science and Math Club builds on the student experiences from all levels. Contests and recognition programs add excitement to the learning process. At the higher levels, the club assists student placement in mentorships and internships in Cleveland area businesses, industry, government, or colleges and universities. Outside organizations and institutions are involved in science/math club programs, and this provides ongoing career information and support.

As the academy developed, other institutions were brought into the project. Tri-C provides most of the instructional sites, the faculty, and the curriculum, while NASA opens its center for educational experiences and provides technical expertise and funding. In addition, Cleveland State University, Kent State University, and Case Western Reserve University provide research facilities and instruction not available through Tri-C or NASA. One thousand students are involved in the academy's programs, and there are waiting lists for new enrollees. The program is still relatively new; further down the line, its success will be measured in terms of scores and entry into mathematics, engineering, and technology fields at the college level.

The Unified Technologies Center. The role of education in stemming the nation's decline in industrial productivity and economic competitiveness in the world economy was one of the important national themes of the late 1970s. In response to changing business conditions, specifically in the Cleveland area, Cuyahoga Community College opened the Unified Technologies Center (UTC) in 1986. Located in a separate $8.5 million building on the Tri-C Metropolitan campus, it was funded by the State of Ohio and designed to provide customized training for local business and industry. Its purpose is to assist organizations in meeting employee training needs, to anticipate and adjust to rapidly changing customer demands and business conditions, and to meet the challenge by helping business capitalize on their greatest resource—their people.

Originally, in analyzing and responding to the changing technological needs of local businesses and industry, the UTC concentrated on the following areas: office automation, computer-aided design, total quality improvement, and pre-technology education. Its programs reflected the enormous impact of the computer age on American society, including education. When the UTC began operations, it was designed to provide worker skill upgrading and services that would assist companies in introducing new technology into the workplace. Virtually every resource a company needs to integrate modern technology into its operations is housed under one roof. In addition, it houses the Louis Stokes Telecommunications Center, a state-of-the-art teleconferencing facility for conducting meetings and holding training sessions locally and worldwide. UTC clients can have custom-designed training programs for new equipment and technologies, and there are more than 200 computer workstations where trainees learn new technical skills. The center also provides business development and consultation services to foster new technology and information exchange.

The UTC is a component of the Cleveland Advanced Manufacturing Program (CAMP) and one of Ohio's Edison Centers. It is the college's primary vehicle for participation in areawide economic revitalization, worker training, and technology transfer strategies. Under CAMP, the UTC embraced a cooperative strategy, partnering with Case Western Reserve University, Cleveland State University, and Cuyahoga Community College. Through this combined effort, Case Western provides original research and Cleveland State applies it to the manufacturing process. The UTC trains workers in these new processes and serves as a comprehensive resource for smaller and medium-sized businesses. The UTC established a Manufacturing Resource Facility (MRF) to enhance competitiveness in the manufacturing sector. This facility provides state-of-the-market, hands-on demonstrations designed to help Greater Cleveland businesses understand technology and develop a greater ability to train their employees in manufacturing-related technology. It also supports credit programs in engineering, quality improvement, and business management, as well as non-credit seminars, demonstrations, and programs. Since 1986, nearly 2,700 companies and 200,000 people have participated in UTC programs.

When business conditions change, so does the UTC. It is moving away from such a strong focus on technology and more into quality management issues. A quality revolution is underway; meeting and exceeding customer expectations must be the focus of everything business does. It is no longer enough to believe in organization-wide continuous improvement. Businesses must have a well-executed quality improvement plan. This requires knowledge, skill, and equipment. Initially, the UTC believed the key to competitive success was technology; today, it believes that performance improvement, not just technology, is the key to success.

As quality improvement initiatives moved away from relying on hardware and software and into the realm of ideas and people, the need for resources and cooperative efforts became clearer. Today, it is agreed that in order to be competitive, one needs expertise from many sources, and resources must come together in structured alliances. In 1993, Blue Cross of Northeast Ohio, East Ohio Gas, and Ameritech formed the Quality Resource Consortium for collaboration, resource exchange, and education development to support quality improvement in its member organizations. These are not competing corporations, but organizations that share resources and support each other. In addition to these corporate partners, four colleges—Cuyahoga Community College, Lakeland Community College, Lorain Community College, and Stark Technical College—have joined in a cooperative agreement to form Enterprise Ohio, which will provide the services needed by the Quality Resource Consortium. All have business programs and have inventoried their individual services so they can subcontract with each other to provide education and training.

Cuyahoga Community College's leadership position with government, business, industry, and other educational institutions provides the college with enormous partnership advantages. Through these alliances, Tri-C's image is enhanced during levy campaigns, the college is able to acquire financial resources not otherwise available, professional development opportunities are available to the Tri-C faculty, and the operation of the college is enhanced through a free flow of information and consulting among the partners.

Global Issues Resource Center. In the fall of 1985 a partnership arrangement established the Nuclear Age Resource Center at Cuyahoga Community College to provide the general population with current, balanced, and understandable information about complex and changing issues of national and global security. With the help of the director of the library and the head of computer technologies at Cuyahoga Community College, the founders developed a budget and secured initial funding from grants, with Tri-C serving as fiscal agent. These funds were designated to establish the library and begin outreach programming. In addition, the college provided physical space, general office services, and financial assistance.

To provide the public with resources, the center established and maintained a clearinghouse of materials and programs about global security. It was essential that the center remain non-political and offer up-to-the-minute information representing all points of view on current issues of public concern. This experiment in citizen education has won national recognition on the PBS *McNeil Lehrer News Hour* and in *Lear's* magazine for being on the cutting edge in higher education.

The center provides for educational outreach through presentations at professional meetings and conferences, informing participants about the resources and projects of the center. It offers customized programs for diverse community organizations, including the Northeast Ohio Science Teachers Association, the Consortium of Gifted and Talented Teachers Annual State Meeting, the Social Studies Teachers of Northeast Ohio, and approximately 20 other groups, ranging from religious organizations to Rotary Clubs and Chambers of Commerce. Currently, the center's library contains more than 1,200 books covering 17 subject areas, as well as audiovisual materials, periodicals, classroom curricula, and reference files. Forty percent of the current materials are not otherwise available locally. The Nuclear Age Resource Center has served approximately 20,000 people through its library and media resources and its educational outreach activities.

As the center has matured, its constituencies changed from the general public to a greater number of teachers and those concerned with higher education. While maintaining its highly successful public events, the center now offers special packages for teachers, including developmental bibliographies on special subjects, for particular age levels, and on themes that aid teachers in presenting complex issues. It also developed a national pilot project for college faculty, offering skills training in educating for global responsibility.

As the world has changed, so have the issues concerning the center. Emerging major concerns are dispute resolution, energy, and waste disposal. With its change in focus, the center decided to change its name (in 1994) to Global Issues Resource Center, which more accurately reflects its range of concerns. Because this partnership is unique, the Environmental Protection Agency, now in negotiations with Cuyahoga Community College on a comprehensive hazardous waste project, will use the Global Issues Resource Center for its public education program.

Saint Vincent Quadrangle. In 1981, the Cuyahoga Community College Board of Trustees initiated the Saint Vincent Quadrangle project to improve the area surrounding the Metropolitan Campus and to turn around the decline in the inner city. The original partners included several major institutions in the area—Cuyahoga Community College, Cleveland State University, and Saint Vincent Charity Hospital. The Cleveland Foundation and the Gund Foundation provided $122,500 for start-up money. The Quadrangle's purpose was:

- to create and implement cooperative programs to improve the quality of life and physical community in the Quadrangle area;
- to encourage participation by area institutions, corporate entities and individuals to take an active interest in revitalizing the area, overcoming urban blight; and
- to seek ways to effectively and immediately renovate the Quadrangle area.

The Quadrangle board includes greater Cleveland executives of member institutions and businesses as well as civic leaders. A 15-member executive committee meets regularly to guide the organization, and the Quadrangle staff is led by an executive director and an associate director, both planning professionals. After four years of operation, the Quadrangle partners learned from the foundations that the project must become self-sufficient. They expanded participation through various types of dues-paying memberships for non-profit entities located in the area. Today, more than 40 businesses and institutions have joined the effort.

Since its inception, the Quadrangle project has overseen the reinvestment of $200 million by member institutions and businesses. It has developed comprehensive streetscapes; implemented weekly clean-up and grounds maintenance of public areas; established guidelines for future improvements that will ensure an attractive, well-designed environment; and implemented signage and other urban design solutions. All of these activities have unified the area, enhanced its identity, and made it a recognizable, major district of Cleveland.

In addition to the physical improvement of the area, the group developed a Quadrangle Police Force staffed by off-duty Cleveland police with full police powers. Vehicles patrol seven days a week and coordinate their activities with all Quadrangle area law enforcement agencies. New attention directed to the area and the support of the Quadrangle Police Force has reduced serious crime by more than 50 percent.

In 1994, the Quadrangle adopted a master plan that will guide future development and improvement in the area. The plan calls for reconstruction and streetscaping of Prospect Avenue, a distressed commercial street; the construction of architecturally interesting headquarters for the Visiting Nurse Association; and planning for area-wide parking and transportation. In addition, the Quadrangle supports the area's important joint-accredited child care facility; new housing, including construction of 120 new homes; and work by a community outreach committee that coordinates available resources and programs to address the needs of area residents.

Based on the idea that the college is part of a neighborhood, Tri-C's leadership role in Quadrangle area redevelopment proves that much can be accomplished through cooperation and purposeful action. Not only are the results visible through colorful promotional banners, coordinated directional signage, and various publications, but the Quadrangle is now represented in important citywide and downtown planning efforts.

Cultural Arts. *Showtime at High Noon.* With the population's move to the suburbs after World War II and the subsequent flight of businesses, many of the country's downtown commercial and entertainment complexes fell on very hard times in the 1960s. Cleveland was no exception. Once a great entertainment center, the Playhouse Square theater complex, with beautiful architectural settings for movies and live entertainment, hid a slow and painful decay behind its locked doors. During this time, most redevelopment was based on demolition and rebuilding, and such plans included Playhouse Square. But developers underestimated the power of some articulate and determined citizens who banded together to save three great Playhouse Square National Landmark theaters. They wanted to renovate the theaters into an exciting performing and cultural arts center. In 1979, The Playhouse Square Foundation approached Cuyahoga Community College about entering into a joint venture to save the theaters. Tri-C became the Playhouse Square Foundation's partner, signing a formal agreement in 1983.

Cuyahoga Community College became the fiscal agent for funds allocated by the Ohio Board of Regents to provide for physical improvement of the theaters and to establish a living-learning arts laboratory for the college in the heart of Cleveland's central business district. It would link the two entities in the continued development of high quality education and training programs in the arts, housing programs in the Playhouse Square facility as an extension of the college's Metropolitan campus.

To effect the arts programming at Playhouse Square, the college received $250,000 for movable equipment that would serve to establish college-sponsored educational programs in the theater complex. In addition, the foundation:
- made space available to the college, at no cost, for an office to administer college operations;
- provided 25 free rental periods to the college for annually sponsored activities; and
- made space available in the Foundation complex to offer educational programs in the fine and professional arts on both a credit and non-credit basis.

Cuyahoga Community College's goal was to promote art as part of lifelong education.

Reconstruction of the first theater, The State, began in March, 1983, and the college's first series of innovative, free, noontime programs began in 1984. Intended to change people's lives by changing their perceptions through the arts, the Showtime at High Noon series has built important relationships with many community groups. As the community evolved and became home to new and diverse groups, that diversity became evident in the Showtime programming. The imaginative productions, designed to appeal to audiences with little background in the arts, make serious music and weighty ideas as accessible as a Broadway show.

The Showtime at High Noon series draws more than 13,000 people each year. Audience evaluations show that its popularity cannot be explained by its free admission and convenient time alone. The quality of the performances and the variety of programming, from Renaissance music to baseball history, is a factor as well. To enable open access to these fourteen programs annually, they are funded by Cuyahoga Community College, the Cleveland Foundation, the Gund Foundation, and the Ohio Arts Council. In response to the large African American population in the community and student body, college programming stresses important cultural issues through the arts. In addition, the college's relationships with the Hispanic community, the Indian community, and the Philippine American community have resulted in productions of tremendously successful programs. These groups have the opportunity to use the talent brought in for the noontime programs in evening fundraising events. Relationships between Tri-C and a variety of community groups will continue to be strengthened through these unique programs.

JazzFest. In 1991, the United States National Park Service issued a report stating: "Jazz is a significant and unique American art form. It is important for the youth of America to recognize and understand jazz as a significant part of their cultural and intellectual heritage" (p. 3). The U.S. National Park Service encouraged "Congress to designate jazz as a rare and valuable national American treasure to which we should devote our attention, support and resources to make certain it is preserved, understood and promulgated." Tri-C has recognized this significant art form via its JazzFest since 1980. Within 10 years of its founding, JazzFest became an outstanding program with a national reputation. The 1993 event drew nearly 30,000 people who attended 11 days of concerts, clinics, master classes, workshops, rehearsals, lectures, symposia, and community outreach events, with the country's top jazz musicians participating.

But problems attended this great success. Acclaimed as the country's premier educational jazz festival, the event began as a modest project to be used as a stepping stone to ongoing educational programming. Over the years, the festival grew larger and larger, garnering more and more attention, but year-round academic programs were not established. The excitement caused by the festival overshadowed the need for a substantive curriculum to give people the opportunity to study jazz, to perform, and to be exposed to career opportunities, including teaching.

Finally, in 1993, the educational component became a reality. With $93,200 from the Cleveland Foundation and the Gund Foundation, the Excellence in Music Project was established. Cleveland is fortunate to have a special magnet school—the School of the Arts—in the Cleveland School System. The Excellence in Music Project funnels students from the magnet school into the jazz industry to perform, teach, or both. In the past, music schools trained students to play their instruments and understand music. Today, students also must become articulate advocates for music; therefore, the project calls for development of a curriculum that will formalize jazz studies at Tri-C. It is hoped that a baccalaureate in jazz will become available at a local four-year college.

New Programs. *Environmental Issues.* In 1993, the Environmental Protection Agency (EPA) asked Cuyahoga Community College to develop a comprehensive program to educate the community on environmental issues and to train a workforce to alleviate the environmental problems in the Cleveland area. Since every city in America is grappling with environmental challenges, this program would serve as a model for the nation. In the past, the EPA's focus for environmental protection and clean-up was based on the three Rs—Reduce, Reuse, and Recycle. With Tri-C, this proposed program will now incorporate a fourth R: Reinvest in the community.

Reinvestment is essential for retrieving lost assets for redevelopment and for sustaining healthful environmental practices. Such reinvestment cannot take place without cooperation between the government, educational institutions, industry, labor, and most importantly, the community. In addition, the disadvantaged population must be included in the planning, which is usually left in the hands of more affluent and influential groups. Residents are often unaware that living conditions can be improved and that they not only can participate in the process of making improvements in their neighborhoods, but in fact, have a responsibility to do so. The unemployed and underemployed are resources for the work required to clean up the environment, but they often lack the skills to carry out the tasks.

Taking advantage of this opportunity to make an important difference in the quality of life in our community, the college developed a plan that has three major components. First, the college will establish an Environmental Equity Task Force that includes representatives and leaders from community organizations, industry, and labor. Second, it will secure grass roots community input into the process. The third component involves the college's development of a program to train employees in environmental issues and to prepare people for careers in environmental fields.

The proposed plan has potential risks that must be addressed early on. For example, the inclusiveness required for the task force can create immediate problems. Recruiting members for such a task force is much easier than making them into a working body. Some people may come to the table with narrowly-focused agendas that conflict with those of other task force members. But since no one can escape, or in good conscience ignore, the environmental issues, it is possible through clearly focused goals to create a productive entity.

This same problem applies to community input, but is magnified due to the number of people involved. A clear idea of the problem's extent, as well as some possible solutions, must precede any public discussion. For example, people living with environmental dangers cannot be informed of these dangers and then asked to ignore them. They must be presented with a plan that decreases their risk and eventually creates a safe environment. Moreover, it must be a plan in which everyone can participate.

Actually, training plans and course development are the least difficult parts of the project. The college already has programs that assist corporations and industry to comply with applicable federal, state, and local regulation. Under development are a two-year associate of applied science program in environmental science technology and a tech prep environmental science technician program. The tech prep program will create opportunities for students, especially minorities and the economically disadvantaged, to seek careers in the environmental field.

Cuyahoga Community College was the EPA's institution of choice because of the college's curriculum in hazardous waste management, its established relationships with community groups and schools systems, and its close ties with business and industry. Prior partnerships encourage dialogue in this new endeavor and allow the use of established systems for new programming. Already, the task force has been formed, the hazardous waste management curriculum has been expanded, and proposed course offerings for industrial compliance and the environmental technician program have been developed. The community education program will proceed when the EPA completes its study of the problem areas and projects the work force needed for clean-up and redevelopment.

The North Coast Tech Prep Consortium. Nationwide, there is an unacceptable number of young people who are underprepared for postsecondary education and, therefore, are not considering further educational programs or courses—the "neglected majority." Cuyahoga Community College has a significant number of underprepared students enrolling in its programs. Recent national and regional studies of at-risk, underprepared students delivered a clear message to Tri-C: upgrading the skills of Cuyahoga County's future workforce is imperative. Moreover, it will not be enough to bring students to the level of high school graduates of the past. According to the Ohio Bureau of Employment Services (1990), virtually all of the 100,000 new jobs available in the area by the year 2,000 will demand at least some postsecondary education and training.

Although there is optimism about the increase in new jobs, there is not an accompanying optimism about future workers. Under the present educational system, the majority of high school students pursue the general course of study and are leaving high school with neither the technical skills to get a job nor the academic skills to go on to higher education. A different approach is needed. This is what the tech prep program is all about. Tech prep targets this overlooked group and offers a new option designed to develop competencies to enter a technical field right out of high school or to go on to a two-year college.

Beginning in the fall of 1994, the neglected majority will find itself the center of attention at Tri-C. In cooperation with 11 school districts, other community colleges, four-year colleges, and business and industry, Cuyahoga Community College has developed three areas of curriculum: (1) automotive, (2) computer, and (3) electronics with a common core of required proficiencies in mathematics, science, communication, and technologies. Each program is designed to lead to an associate degree or certificate in a specific technical career area. In addition, the program offers summer internships and job placement for students who want to go directly into the workforce.

An active and diverse advisory committee was established for the tech prep program. Subcommittees are working on education, marketing, and resource development. Business representatives attend the monthly teacher inservices, providing vital input into the development of applications. Representatives of the United Auto Workers union are involved in the apprenticeship programs.

Eleventh and twelfth graders are targeted for the tech prep program, but counseling for entry into the program begins with eighth graders to ensure they have the academic background necessary for success. Area businesses have indicated that new employees must be technologically trained and highly literate. People entering the workforce with the proper skills will reduce the need for, and cost of, retraining and re-educating. Thus, proper training will give the tech prep graduates an advantage over others and will have an important, positive effect on the economic health of Cuyahoga County.

THE FUTURE

According to Chief Justice Earl Warren, in his eulogy of President Kennedy, "The only thing we learn from history is that we do not learn" (November 24, 1963). Cuyahoga Community College recognizes that it cannot afford that kind of ignorance. If we view our partnership projects from a historical perspective, we see that the successful programs have inherent flexibility and a sensitivity to societal changes. These are the same characteristics needed for the community college to succeed in its basic educational mission. It is also clear that we have finite resources and must do more with less. This reality impacts all of American society, including the nation's community colleges. It is obvious that the government alone cannot solve most of our problems. We must work together toward common goals and make a difference in our own neighborhoods.

If we face facts, if we learn from our history, it is obvious that we need increased cooperation, larger structured alliances, and more shared resources. We need more partnerships, not fewer, but we must exercise care in constructing them. It is also true that accountability has come to the college campus. It is no longer enough to say we are making a difference—now we must prove it! This applies to our partnership projects as well. No matter how wonderful an idea seems, we must be results-oriented; if something is not working, we must fix it or discard it. Our most successful programs have expanded their services through multiple partnering. Some have cultivated new resources. The level of cooperation and involvement from so many institutions, businesses, and community resources has been gratifying. The solution to problems is achieved, not in isolation, but through combined efforts.

Every community college today is engaged in a daily balancing act—juggling unmet needs and limited resources. But the shaking tightrope looks a lot less formidable with a good crew, helping hands, and experienced performers. Our task is to prove

Chief Justice Warren wrong and learn from the past—it will make a tremendous difference to our future.

REFERENCES

American Council on Education and the American Association of State Colleges and Universities. *Educating one-third of a nation.* Washington, DC: American Council on Education, 1988.

Ohio Board of Regents. *Master plan for higher education: Toward the year* 2000. Columbus, OH: Ohio Department of Education, 1988.

Ohio Bureau of Employment Services. *Labor market projections—Cleveland PMSA. 1988–2000.* (HD 5725.03) Columbus, OH: Labor Market Information Division, Ohio Bureau of Employment Services, 1990.

Ohio Council for Home Health Agencies. *Ohio certified home health agencies annual registration report* (RA 645.36.03 A 33x). Columbus, OH: Ohio Council of Home Health Agencies, 1989.

Ohio Department of Aging. *Who will deliver the care? A study of the availability of home care professionals in Ohio.* Columbus, OH: Ohio Department of Aging, 1989.

United States Bureau of Labor Statistics. *Selected occupations, 1990.* Washington, DC: United States Department of Labor, 1991.

United States National Park Service. *Jazz: Music preservation and interpretation.* (S 311-1, 3-5). Washington, DC: United States National Park Service, 1991.

Warren, E. *Eulogy of the late President Kennedy.* (88th Congress S. Doc. 46 12551). Washington, DC: U.S. Government Printing Office, November 24, 1963.

Webster's New Collegiate Dictionary. Springfield, MA: G. & C. Merriman Company, 1981.

CHAPTER XI

President Paul Gianini, Vice President Sandra Sarantos, and others at Valencia Community College share with Cuyahoga Community College a long-term sensitivity to their community. Lorenzo and LeCroy made an observation that underscores Valencia's realization of the need for a dramatic shift in the college's focus.

> Since systems continually interact with their external environment, ongoing viability depends on how well they can adjust to environmental changes. Systems thrive when they become critical to the success of the larger system. As a result, strategies for the Information Age should reflect an outside-in priority: what's best for the community; what's best for the college; what's best for the unit; and what's best for the staff (1994, p. 16).

Gianini and Sarantos are convinced that a revised national education agenda that focuses on preparing citizens to be successful in the workplace is now required. They believe that "the American workplace is in trouble, and so is American higher education" (Johnstone, 1994, Part 4, p. 1). Gilley (1991) found that state governors noted the growing role of higher education in economic development and closer relationships with business and industry.

The authors recount the process Valencia has used to infuse economic development into the college's culture and practices as well as the accomplishments that have resulted. These include the receipt of 12 grants totaling over $3.5 million for economic development and workforce education, and projected 1994-1995 revenue of $1 million for the Office of Corporate Services.

* * *

Gilley, J.W. Thinking about American higher education. New York: American Council on Education and Macmillan Publishing Company, 1991.

Johnstone, D.B. "College at work: Partnerships and the rebuilding of American competence." Journal of Higher Education. [online], 1994, 65(2), 168ff. Available: e-mail: lbindx@utxdp.dp.utexas.edu

Lorenzo, A.L. and LeCroy, N.A. "A framework for fundamental change in the community college." Community College Journal, 1994, 64(4), 14–19.

Paul C. Gianini, Jr., *President*
Sandra Todd Sarantos, *Vice President*
  Educational and Economic Development
  Services; and Provost, Central Campus
Valencia Community College
Orlando, Florida

ACADEMIC RHETORIC VERSUS BUSINESS REALITY

*Education today, more than ever before, must see
clearly the dual objectives: education for living
and education for making a living.*

  —James Mason Wood

CHANGES IN THE WORKPLACE AND WORKFORCE

The U.S. Census Bureau recently reported significant findings regarding rapid growth in the percentage of full-time workers who earn low wages, are mired in poverty, and struggle to care for their families ("Poverty Gaining," 1994). The number increased significantly between 1979 and 1992; younger and less educated Americans were most affected. Equally disturbing, about 18 percent of the nation's 81 million year-round, full-time workers earned less than $13,000 per year in 1992, a 50 percent increase over the 12 percent who had low earnings in 1979. Although these low-wage earners tended to be female, less educated, or both, the Census Bureau found that the percentage of persons earning low wages rose faster among men than women. The proportion of women with low earnings increased 16 percent over this period while the proportion of men with low earnings jumped 83 percent. Many factors, including education, play into this national dilemma.

Roueche and Johnson (1994) indicate that millions of jobs have been transformed or eliminated over the past decade and that investment in education has come to be increasingly at risk. New global competition and high technology industries have evolved, requiring new workforce skills, knowledge, and worker behavior in order for companies to remain competitive. These skills bear little resemblance to those required by the industrial world just a few years ago. To no one's surprise, this shift in labor market demands has delivered monumental challenges to educational institutions worldwide.

CHALLENGES, CHANGE, AND CHANGE AGENTS

Emphasizing the need for colleges to re-examine their missions as a prelude for change, Robert A. Gordon, president of Humber College in Ontario, made a presentation at the 1994 NISOD conference in Austin, Texas. He pointed out several trends that have influenced, and are continuing to influence, the community college environment. These include: demands from legislators, budget crises, the need to change to keep pace, international competition, the growing learning industry, the electronic highway, and lifelong learning. He noted, however, that although most of these issues are similar in scope to those dealt with in years past, presidents are dealing with them very differently today because of external influences affecting the college community. Gordon emphasized that colleges need to study themselves in order to make serious plans to solve tomorrow's problems. Colleges need a profound rethinking of what they have been doing rather than simply adapting to the environment and accepting the status quo. They must become client-driven and provide value-added service to the customer.

The realization that our world is changing is forcing all of us in higher education to examine our history, refocus on our present, and plan differently for our future. This process of re-examination ultimately could result in changing college philosophies and perhaps mission statements. Regardless, colleges must accept the fact that America's workforce has changed and that our educational institutions must change with it or they will cease to exist as we know them today.

However, change in and of itself is meaningless without direction. In Florida, one of the first and primary directives is given by the Florida Department of Commerce when it states that the department is established to be an effective force in improving the quality of life for all Floridians by building an economy characterized by higher personal income, better employment opportunities, and improved business access to domestic and international markets.

The instrument best suited to assist in pursuing the Department of Commerce's goals, these authors believe, is the community college, where thousands of students each year start their studies in higher education and where thousands more simply start over. Community colleges are finding as many "starting-over" students enrolled for retraining and education as first-time-in-college students on their campuses. Savvy community colleges are finally realizing that students, regardless of their ages, must be well-trained in addition to being well-educated. This philosophy is becoming a part of the fabric of these institutions as their student population grows older and more aware of external forces and competition in the workplace.

The changing student population gives us a solid directive to revisit how we run our institutions. Looking at the age of our students, we find that the largest growth is beginning to occur in the 21- to 45-year-old age bracket. While presidents of colleges and universities in this country recently were concerned about the decline in the population of high school graduates, this issue has seldom been a problem in terms of college admissions, because so many adults beyond the typical college age have enrolled or re-enrolled in our colleges. According to Aslanian:

> The portion of adult students has been rising steadily over the past two decades roughly from 30 percent in 1970 to 40 percent in 1980 and to 45 percent in 1987. That means that for every collegian under age 25, there is one over that age (1991, p. 59).

Recognizing that the personal needs and characteristics of adult learners have changed provides another directive for academic soul searching. These people no longer comprise just the group who come only at night to our campuses. They are students who take classes throughout the college day, usually beginning at 8:00 in the morning and ending close to 10:00, or later, at night. Most interesting, but not surprising, is the fact that four out of five of them are studying for degrees in specific career fields, not liberal arts. Many of them were in college at one time in their lives and now must learn again how to learn as they return to the classroom after years of absence. In numerous speeches, Dale Parnell, former president of the American Association of Community Colleges (AACC), has referred to this type of student who started college, dropped out for a period of time, then re-enrolled, as one who "stopped out" rather than "dropped out" of college. Stop-outs are becoming commonplace on our campuses, the rule rather than the exception.

Perhaps the most relevant reason for colleges to change is the recognition that workers as well as college students have grown older. The average age in today's workforce is 36; by the year 2000, the average age will be 39. The number of young workers will drop dramatically simply because they will constitute a smaller percentage of the population. This may prove to be an advantage to this group since they will have less competition for better-paying jobs as they mature.

Compounding the problems previously addressed are at least two other notable influences forcing change :

• The nuclear family in the United States, as it was once perceived, barely exists. The Ozzie and Harriett image is no longer relevant even as a replay. For example, fewer than half of all American families have children under age 18 living at home, and among those that do, nearly one in three has only one live-in parent ("Ozzie and Harriet," 1994).

- The Pacific Rim and emerging Latin American nations are challenging this country with a level of competition that it has never seen in its history. As a result, the domestic market is no longer an American monopoly, which is one of the factors forcing this nation into the largest trade deficit in modern history.

Unfortunately, academics are prisoners to tradition. Our 3,400 institutions of higher education in this country come in all shapes and sizes—some good, some bad—but they still operate in a collegial setting where much pontificating is heard and little is done.

As change agents, the present authors believe that the stakes are much higher now and that education is on the brink of a national disaster. It is only through the development of a revised national agenda for education, focusing on productivity and accountability, that we can avoid the inevitable consequences for our country of an ill-prepared workforce. Most of those currently in the workforce will still be there in the year 2000, and reliable demographics illustrate a dramatic shift in the complexity and diversity in the workplace (Riley and Reich, 1993). This leads the authors to believe that an equally dramatic shift toward economic development is required of our community colleges.

Florida State University professor Walter Manley (1994) states that the first step for success in developing a clear organizational vision is constancy of purpose. The more precise and focused the goal of the proposed change, the greater the power to direct the organization's actions and reap employee commitments. Understanding the purpose of the change is also important for employee commitment and successful implementation.

THE MIRACLE CURE: ECONOMIC DEVELOPMENT

Acknowledging that little has been done to change the face of education to match that of tomorrow's business demands has prompted the authors of this chapter to make three major recommendations regarding the infusion of the concepts of economic development into the daily operations of community college life. The recommendations are complex, time-consuming, and difficult to implement collegewide without the proper support mechanisms in place.

The concepts involved must mirror the president's vision and may require a commitment from the college to develop or revise the mission statement to include economic development. A collegewide commitment to the community should be embodied in an economic development component which involves connections between the total business community and all facets of the institution.

Flowing from this new commitment, a strategic goal of the college should be to integrate the philosophy of meeting workforce needs through the concept of economic development into the academic and student affairs cultures of the college. To move their institutions forward in the economic development arena, community college leaders should consider the following recommendations:

Recommendation One. The president's vision, emphasized verbally and in written form, must stress the importance of accepting workforce development and retraining goals as a shared responsibility of all college employees and departments, not just that of a continuing education office pigeonholed in an off-campus center referred to as "that other" (and less important) area of the college. The college community must accept that continuing education is not an end in itself, but is one of many delivery systems put in place at the college to meet customer (business and student) needs.

While some college CEOs come from occupational and continuing education backgrounds, they often lose sight of that "haven of flexibility" they once supported as soon as their responsibilities broaden, and they begin focusing on credit programs, degrees, FTEs, and finances. Most presidents have reacted warily in the economic development arena, often using the lack of funding as an excuse for not meeting business and community needs.

Waiting for funding to catch up with college growth causes much anguish and anxiety when there is pressure to respond to external business trends. Many non-credit business and industry departments have become cost centers requiring "cost-plus" programs to fund their area and to add to the college coffers in order for credit departments to hire more full-time faculty. CEOs who want to modify their college's economic development direction find themselves in a position similar to that of a dirigible commander: waiting an extremely long time for the aircraft to move after the wheel is turned in the right direction!

Encroachment, including funding and administrative mandates, on local control by state legislatures or other political bodies slows the movement of change even more. While the model of the empowered community college is held as a beacon to other institutions with respect to the ability to react, meet local needs, be accountable, and be cost-effective, most political groups, while publicly talking about local empowerment, tend to seize any opportunity to impose state control and add another requirement to an already difficult process at the college.

Smart presidents, however, always try to choose the set of problems they want to deal with and continuously make tough decisions between what should and should not be done to support the mission of the college. Smart CEOs also look toward tomorrow and decline to spend their professional lives putting out brush fires. Vision and leadership toward tomorrow, and the tomorrows after tomorrow, are of paramount importance to moving the institution forward.

Remaining patient with the processes that must occur in order to introduce or reinstate a comprehensive workforce concept, the president must clarify his or her vision statement so that the direction of the college becomes clear. When the mission statement is completed, employees should have at their fingertips a reminder of their purpose at the college—to carry out the mission of the college which reflects the president's vision to educate students and meet community needs.

Once all support mechanisms are in place, the president should hire, or reassign, a responsible administrator to a visible and high-level position in the organization, underscoring the importance of economic development within the institution in order to allow action to occur.

Recommendation Two. Involve faculty and staff members throughout the college to help develop a new and relevant college mission statement to include the new economic development thrust that many will not initially understand or support. In fact, as colleges go through the process, there will remain a veil of non-compliance throughout the institution until the proof that the enhanced mission of the college will not be a financial drain, but will, in fact, open doors to new funding opportunities.

Colleges do not have to struggle with the notion that they must be all things to all people; they simply have to help people become the "things" they want to become. The schizophrenia of community colleges, teaching both Shakespeare and sonography, is probably best explained by Anthony P. Carnevale, chief economist for the American Society for Training and Development:

There is a split personality in these institutions (community colleges) in that they are both educational and economic institutions. They try to give students an academic education, to teach them about our culture, to make them better citizens, but they have an economic mission as well, a mission to train workers for the economic success of the country as well as the individual. Colleges are tugged toward their cultural mission.

They come from a model where their model is Harvard University, but they are much more tied into peoples' lives. The challenge is to fulfill the economic mission. The challenge is to not feel less of an educator because they are preparing people for work, to feel comfortable with their dual purpose. One of the problems community colleges and vocational/technical institutions have had is a poor self-image. They need more status and standing in the education department. They need more status in the legislative process. I was shocked when the Higher Education Reauthorization came up. The two-year system was never talked about as the core of the education system. Two-year colleges and vocational/technical institutions are the core of the education system (Stanley, 1993, p. 7).

Commitment to economic development in the mission of the community college, in the strategic plan of the college, and as a significant budgetary entity of the college, is critical to success.

When expanding or changing the mission of an institution, it is necessary to take into account the effect on the total institution. In a community college, a large piece of the action is affected by the faculty. A desire to learn about economic development may be perceived from a recent memorandum from the president of the faculty association at Valencia Community College to the vice president of educational and economic development services. Seven questions were posed:

- How is economic development being defined in this initiative?
- How will this initiative increase enrollment at Valencia?
- Will this initiative restructure/eliminate any of the current programs at the college? If so, which ones?
- What impact will this initiative have on faculty employment?
- What plans have been made to identify skills currently being taught in the associate of arts degree programs which will be needed for future employment?
- What provisions have been made for including faculty in the planning/implementation phases of this initiative?
- What plans do you have for using the expertise of the economists on staff to aid in the development of this initiative?
- How will the success of this initiative be measured?

At times, faculty members have a difficult time accepting new concepts they perceive as threatening the integrity of the traditional classroom, let alone one that supports taking their syllabus into a company break room! They may have an even more difficult time accepting the statement that Willard Daggett, an international consultant known for his efforts to create schools for the 21st century, recently made at a Valencia gathering: "If most faculty lost their jobs, they would be functionally unemployable."

Few traditional faculty members have addressed what Carol Aslanian states should be so obvious: "The idea that education precedes work in the standard life pattern of an adult has been replaced by the realization that the two are interspersed throughout adult life" (1993, p. 98). Her point is that students who work must conform to traditional credit classes, most of which are scheduled during the day, during the regular academic year, and on the "main campuses" where full-time faculty members were originally assigned to teach when they were hired. Students who take classes at centers close to their homes, or at their workplaces, usually have adjunct professors throughout their tenure at the college and seldom, if ever, see senior administrators on site.

All of these factors surrounding adult students validate the contention that the rudiments of higher education have not changed in 300 years with regard to instructors, to content, to time schedules, to campuses, to methodology, to materials, to evaluations, to credit, and to degrees. For all of these reasons, establishing traditional credit classes for the business community at business locations will continue to remain a problem for the traditional college unwilling to take that quantum leap into education in the 21st century. Many traditional faculty members may argue that quality cannot be maintained in their department if classes are not held on the "main campuses" under their close watch.

Aslanian supports the notion that "business as usual will mean no business with business." She continues:

> But what about the loss of traditional controls over programs and faculty for colleges that adapt themselves to company needs? The solution lies in a shift of attention from controlling processes as a way of assuring quality, to controlling outcomes as a way of assuring quality (1993, p. 100).

Colleges must try to accept this attitude regarding quality in order to support distance education methods of instructional delivery which, after the concept really begins to take hold, may become the norm, rather than the exception, as to how students are served.

As an example of success in doing business with business, Roosevelt University, located in the heart of Chicago's business hub, for many years attracted a highly diverse student population, average age 29. During the past four years, the university initiated the Partners in Corporate Education Program to deliver credit courses and full services to employees at their corporate work sites in the metropolitan Chicago area. According to Hirsch, the program was a success, but a codicil was issued: an institution should take careful stock of itself before leaping into the delivery of credit courses to business:

> An institution must be flexible and creative as well as committed to maintaining the integrity and quality of its academic offerings and services. Institutional investment must be made in staffing, marketing, trend analysis, and program development; and expectations and goals must be realistic (1993, p. 28).

College leaders emphasize that there are no shortcuts to long-term productive relationships with the business community and that prospecting with new corporations requires patience and persistence. There must be a master plan, systems, and procedures, as well as marketing analysis and marketing strategies. The leaders of the Partners in Corporate Education Program found that traditional academic administrative procedures often inhibited corporations from approaching colleges and universities and that a fresh approach and streamlined procedures may be necessary to capture corporate clients. Several of the components that helped Partners in Corporate Education achieve success with the business community were:

- commitment from top leadership,
- customer service philosophy with corporations and their employees,
- faculty involvement,
- support of service units,
- programming flexibility, and
- entrepreneurial planning.

This successful model illustrates that despite the initial reluctance of traditional faculty members to support this unique program, after much planning and strategizing took place, faculty members supported the concept; and they were selected to participate in the program (Hirsch, 1993).

Recommendation Three. The CEO vision and mission must be supported by the Board of Trustees and enhanced by genuine business partnerships. These partnerships develop through trust and commitment over time as a result of responsive collegewide customer service, an up-to-date shared vision, and a relevant college mission. Such relationships provide the light on the horizon and are developed because local businesses and industries have realized that there needs to be a symbiotic relationship between their areas of concern and educational institutions that are preparing workers for them.

Forging a new middle class of technicians from this relationship is considered America's best bet for offsetting the enormous displacement of workers by global competition, automation, industrial shrinkage, and corporate downsizing, all issues presenting enormous challenges to the state of Florida. The citizens of Florida recognize these challenges and have responded in *Challenges, Realities, Strategies—The Master Plan for Florida Postsecondary Education for the 21st Century* (Postsecondary Education Planning Commission, 1993). In this document, business partnerships and economic development are viewed as primary solutions to economic woes. These elements of education must contribute to the enterprises that produce high-value services and products, and to the preparation of an appropriately trained workforce. By collaborating with business, industry, and government, education's challenge is to use the state's limited resources and restructure what is taught and how it is taught. Economic realities in Florida include:

- Dramatic changes are occurring that impact skills required for workers in the marketplace and the structure and function of organizations.
- Florida is not sufficiently competitive in high value-added services and products for the new world economy.
- Florida's strategic location creates advantages for international trade opportunities.
- Industry, government, and education collaboration benefits industry, education, citizens, and the state. Commitments to previous economic development initiatives have been neither consistent nor long-term.

To address these strategic issues, the state of Florida is recommending:

- promoting economic development;
- strengthening international education;
- improving training programs;
- enhancing faculty resources;
- promoting the exchange of personnel, especially scientists and engineers, among educational institutions, government, and industry;
- maximizing the use of part-time faculty from industry and government to concur with existing market conditions; and
- preparing teachers with the ability to communicate theory and practice in applied technology programs.

On a national scale, Secretary of Education Richard Riley and Labor Secretary Robert Reich spoke before the House Education and Labor Committee on September 29, 1993, and highlighted the outcomes desired from economic development, including a new system that is designed to be bottom-up and outcome-oriented through venture capital via the School-to-Work Opportunities Act (Riley and Reich, 1993). The act reflects the recommendations of a wide spectrum of business, education, labor, civil rights, and community-based organizations. In addition, state and local government organizations with a strong interest in how American students prepare for careers provided input. The act is premised on the belief that work-based learning, integrated with related academic training, can provide American youth with the knowledge and skills necessary to make a successful transition from school to a first job in a higher-skill, higher-wage career.

...AND THE BEAT GOES ON

At the same time that state and national governments are developing strategic goals to deal with mounting problems regarding the economy and the shortfalls of education, our college campuses are coping with local employers who are raising their educational and training requirements at an unprecedented rate. The reasons for these rapid changes involve such phenomena as the evolving information highway and increasing global economic pressures. As a result of these workplace changes, employers can afford to be selective and more demanding when it comes to hiring employees with superior qualifications. The reasons for this include the following:

- New jobs are often not just more complex, but also provide the company with the only avenue to increased production and profit. Higher-level degrees and skills are required as well as three to five years of experience in the field.
- Many people applying for jobs are well educated and have proved that they can learn at a fast pace because they have post-graduate degrees with years of experience and have been "right-sized" out of their companies.

Dow Chemical has publicly stated that it will be hiring people who possess specialized skills, such as Ph.D. chemists. Other manufacturers have indicated they are looking for people who are geometry and complex math experts. Most ominous is the fact that many businesses, because of the increased need to watch the bottom line, will continue to rely on employee overtime and temporary positions. This trend could force many individuals into part-time, closed-ended, meaningless, and benefitless "McJobs."

Can today's educational institutions meet the new demands of this elite business community at their pace? The sad truth is that our bureaucratic organizations have accepted the status quo for so long that students are quickly learning that they can attend proprietary schools which, although costly, provide instructors (many without college degrees, but with years of experience) with up-to-date technical skills required to teach relevant courses to help students get high-wage, high-skill jobs.

In contrast to this scenario, many college faculty members graduated in the 1950s and 1960s. Their skills in some technical areas may be surpassed by the high school graduates enrolling in their classes. Lifelong learning is not a new concept, particularly in community colleges, but it is one that has been largely ignored by hundreds of faculty members at even the most prestigious institutions either because remaining technically astute has not been required or a means to update their skills has not been available to them.

Thus, there is an obvious mismatch between what is being produced via American higher education and what is needed in the American workplace. In the Doonesbury cartoons during the 1994 college and university commencement period, higher education was taken to task for producing individuals who will have bachelor's degrees, earn minimum wages, carry heavy financial repayment schedules, and be destined for a $6- to $7-an-hour-job. By contrast, community college data support the fact that the associate of science degree graduate has a higher beginning salary than does a person who has just completed a bachelor's degree in the arts and sciences, at least during the early career stages (Pfeiffer, 1994).

Before blowing the horn too loudly and too quickly on the success of the generic A.S. degree, however, one must be aware that thousands of students start these career-oriented programs each year, take four or five courses in order to feel proficient, "stop out," then go directly into the workplace. The false assumption here is that the skills obtained from these courses will last for years to come and remain relevant to the skills needed by employers.

This myth only accentuates the real problem of educational institutions retaining an outdated system that is flexible enough to meet business and student demands only through non-credit continuing education departments. Curriculum flexibility must occur throughout the institution, and in all departments, to counteract the resistance to change which is clearly misunderstood by older students.

THE MANY FACES OF ECONOMIC DEVELOPMENT

Economic development has been defined in many ways. David Goetsch defined it as "the process of creating new jobs and retaining existing jobs by mobilizing resources to attract new businesses while helping existing ones prosper" (1988, p. 38). Carol Sanders (1988) portrayed economic development as organized, planned, and cooperative efforts between the public and private sectors designed to improve economic conditions in community and state.

Valencia Community College has defined economic development as those activities and processes undertaken by staff and faculty aimed at improving customer satisfaction. Customers are defined as business and industry, taxpayers, and the legislature (i.e., constituencies who pay education's bills). Students are defined as the college's major clients. In addition, economic development is the process directing the college's resources, programs, and services toward ensuring the existence of a skilled and knowledgeable workforce for strategic industries and businesses, supporting the creation of new jobs that result in Central Florida becoming a more globally competitive region.

This comprehensive definition simply means that through the economic develop-ment process the college will assist the community in attracting new high-wage, high-skilled industry jobs and support existing businesses by providing the required educa-tion and training necessary to enhance production. Regardless of definition, economic development must revolve around the principle of partnerships between the public and private sectors. There cannot be economic development without this ingredient.

How is economic development really different at Valencia? Rather than allowing internal constraints to dictate decisions affecting the general public and business com-munity, economic development at Valencia has forced staff members to administer their programs using an "outside-in" approach that focuses totally on customer needs and college resources to meet those needs. Valencia's economic development process includes offering to students and businesses packages of programs and services that include technical education, tech prep programs, general education, business assess-ments through account executives, technology transfer, international programs, con-ferencing services, continuing professional education, and others geared toward stu-dent success in the workforce.

Economic development is as much a political process within a community as it is a series of business decisions. Development depends as much on the political atti-tudes, aspirations, and visions of elected local and state officials as it does on busi-nessmen and women. The history of regions that have experienced long-term economic growth since World War II demonstrates that economic development flourishes and is sustained in areas where there is a partnership between business, government, and education. Leaders of these segments need to be committed to the task of fostering development in order for it to occur (Sarantos, 1993).

THINKING (AND RESPONDING) GLOBALLY

Economic development is not just a local phenomenon that occurred yesterday and is talked about today. Pursuing redevelopment of economies in all extremities, our world seems to be shrinking as technology ties remote corners of the world together. Due to global competition, many community colleges find themselves in the throes of internationalizing their curricula the better to prepare students for the world of work.

In Florida, for example, the current value of international exports and imports is outpacing tourism as the state's number one source of business revenue; 15 percent of all the new jobs in the Metro-Orlando area are in some way tied to international busi-ness. This external factor has heightened Valencia's awareness and prompted the addi-tion of a broader definition of economic development, including recognition of this growing global job market.

Understanding and accepting these types of alterations in the local economy occurs when we view ourselves as part of the global economy. Because of the appreciation for, and interest in, international issues, the college now finds itself in partnerships with educational institutions and businesses in Costa Rica, Brazil, Ecuador, and the Netherlands.

As a result of strengthening these relationships, 25 postsecondary education and business leaders from the Netherlands visited the college in February, 1994, to inquire about how the college works with business and industry, how we prepare students for industry service, and how we tie the economic development thrust into the mission of the college.

Through a Linkage Institute grant program, the college contracted with the government of Costa Rica to work with three para-universities ("hybrid" institutions) charged with teaching avocational and postsecondary education. They needed assistance in developing a mission statement and long-range plan to foster their development into American-style community colleges. Valencia worked primarily with the largest of these institutions, the Collegio Universitario de Allejuela (C.U.N.A.), and planned to use it as a model for the other two. Over a three-year period, including many work sessions, visits, consultant reports, and basic human efforts, the project has now been completed. C.U.N.A. is standing on its own, proud of the fact that they are signing contracts for training with businesses such as Motorola, which is located in San Jose, Costa Rica. (The country of Costa Rica suffers from a traditional U.S. model in that their universities are producing more than enough doctors, lawyers, and engineers, but too few technicians to serve the needs of business and industry. As such, they find that without a trained workforce the government is having a difficult time drawing new business and industry to locate to their country regardless of tax and/or foreign incentives. Lessons are to be learned from this small country.)

Community leaders, viewing Central Florida as a microcosm of the United States and the rest of the world, must, once again, choose among alternative sets of problems to deal with. According to the *Wall Street Journal*, an unemployed worker in Western Europe makes more money per week than some employed Americans who have limited skills and minimal education (Wessel and Benjamin, 1994, p. A-1). The United States tolerates having millions of people accurately classified as the working poor while some European countries, such as Germany, pay unemployed workers well enough that they do not seek to be underemployed. The article continues:

> The U.S. creates lots of jobs. But by weakening unions and failing to adjust the minimum wage for inflation, it has allowed the wages of those at the bottom to fall. The result is companies that are more globally competitive, but also a widening gap between rich and poor (Wessel and Benjamin, 1994, p. A-1).

To counteract this dilemma, U.S. Labor Secretary Robert Reich proposes to drop training programs that do not work and combine the kind of investment in education, training and apprenticeship programs found in Europe with the labor mobility and flexibility found in the United States. The creation of new programs could help thousands of workers displaced by industrial restructuring and new government policies, such as the North American Free Trade Agreement. Many of the programs Reich is considering for elimination, however, are politically sensitive.

According to Jeffery Cantor:

The linkage between job creation and economic growth initiative goes counter to the ways in which these initiatives have traditionally been organized at state and local levels. Typically, the public policies and services related to these two areas, as well as to those involving a critically important third area, education, have operated as parallel systems with:

- economic development policies being the province of local government and local economic development agencies;
- job training being administered by corporations as well as by job training operators, such as JTPA; and
- educational practices being governed by local school systems and postsecondary institutions such as community colleges (1989, pp. 4–5).

Understanding and responding to global influences, while supporting the theme that economic development begins at home, colleges must anticipate and monitor changes in their state and local economies, reduce administrative barriers to college services and programs, and enhance technology transfer to assist manufacturers to compete in the emerging markets outside the United States.

CONNECTING TO BUSINESS AND "DOING" ECONOMIC DEVELOPMENT

According to Mundhenk (1988), 85 percent of community colleges "dabble" in economic development. These colleges, however, must realize that simply committing themselves to do economic development is not enough. Rather, they must cause it to occur.

In an effort to meet the challenge of economic development, to cause it to occur and provide more value to Central Florida's business community, Valencia created a senior-level vice president position in 1990, soon after the economic development goal was added to Florida's overall community college mission. This decision influenced a total redesign of the college's structure.

As a result of adding the economic development component to the college, six Industry Quality Teams have now been formed with over 120 staff members from all disciplines and all college locations involved in the process of infusing economic development into the college culture. The individual teams were created to mirror those industries designated by Orange County and the Economic Development Commission of Mid-Florida as targeted growth industries most important to the economic well-being of Central Florida communities.

These industries included: international business, health care, tourism, high-tech, sports, film, and television. To fit with the college's program mix, Valencia deleted the sports area and added public service, changed the international business area to general business to be more comprehensive, and enhanced the film area by adding entertainment.

Each team is composed of four major groups of employees throughout the college: resources, marketing, counseling (career awareness), and instruction. Each team has a team leader, and each employee group has a group leader. These 10 staff members, plus three members-at-large, serve on the Economic Development Council which is chaired by the vice president of educational and economic development services. Recommendations from the teams are submitted to this council for action. Each team's purpose is to support student success and research efforts at the college by identifying and communicating to faculty, staff, and students that the skills, knowledge, and behavior required by Central Florida businesses validate the relevancy of Valencia's curriculum.

In addition to sharing the same purpose, each team is responsible for the following goals.

- Determine the process currently used to update credit and continuing professional education (CPE) curriculum to verify that course content is relevant to business and industry needs.
- Identify collegewide connections to the business community in order to centralize, organize, and maximize college resources and services.
- Design a collegewide system to communicate industry information to students, faculty, and staff, including current and anticipated jobs for the next three years in Central Florida. Information will include required skills, knowledge and behavior, expected entry-level salaries, and average salaries for each type of job.
- Determine measurable goals for each Advisory Committee that will assist in validating information gathered as to overall skills required in the workforce.
- Determine marketing strategies to reach the 18- to 35-year-old population searching for career tracks that require an associate degree or enhanced skills to attain or retain a high-wage, high-skill job.
- Identify strategies applicable to tech prep goals that convert high school graduates into college enrollees, focusing on career goals and retention.
- Provide recommendations to the Executive Council (college vice presidents) on program areas that need to be revised, eliminated, or enhanced during the forthcoming academic year in order to meet the changing needs of the business community and to increase the number of graduates and successful leavers.

As a result of these team goals being accomplished, a comprehensive collegewide effort will be organized to maximize the use of job-related data for advising and directing students toward college programs that will result in the attainment of a job, not merely a degree. In addition, the college will be able to formulate a Valencia legislative priorities packet for upcoming legislative sessions stating where the college's budgetary needs are in order to respond to industry growth areas in Central Florida.

In addition to these results, the involvement of staff members on teams has allowed the college to build stronger bridges between education and the business world, illustrating the direct connection and relevancy of classroom instruction to the real world of work. Faculty members are beginning to use specific examples in their classrooms and are asking of students: how can you use what you learned today in your future career? In addition, faculty members are being challenged to answer the question as to how they can integrate the economic development concept into the college curriculum.

The following comment was made by a Valencia student completing an algebra instructor's evaluation:

> I hate and despise math, always have. Having been out of school 20 years, my fear level of algebra was very high. I survived elementary [algebra] and found a truth I would have never believed. I always knew I would never find a use for algebra in the 'real world.' I am in middle management and responsible for budgeting and projecting figures for my departments. I was given an impossible project one day, finals week, and was panicked until I remembered a formula I had just learned. It worked and I completed my project with room to spare. I returned to this professor for college algebra and, although I thank God I'll never take more math, I would take it with this professor again.

Another method Valencia uses to accomplish economic development and to determine the value that needs to be added to college services is to host monthly president's luncheons with area CEOs. The thrust of these events has changed over their three-year history from a "show and tell" about the college to organized focus groups that allow the guests to talk about what the college is doing right and in what areas the college should improve. In addition, their training and education needs are discussed as are their companies' strategic plans for the future.

As a result of listening to the needs of these business leaders, Valencia has been able to identify more clearly the strategic goals to guide the future of the college. One of eight major tenets of the college's comprehensive strategic plan, the economic development goal has been structured to allow for integration into the academic and student affairs cultures of the college, in order to enhance workforce competitiveness in Central Florida. Inclusion of this goal in the college's major plans for the future called for a redesigning of the college structure.

Valencia's Office of Corporate Services is another result of listening more carefully and connecting the college's goals to those of the business community. This office sends sales teams to meet with area CEO's and personnel officers to identify their education and training needs. After those needs are determined, the team recommends appropriate college courses, seminars, conferences, etc. Then staff members with relevant expertise (program implementers and faculty) meet with the businesses to design the programs and courses. The Corporate Services account manager follows up by conducting an evaluation with the company after the activity is completed.

By supporting this outside-in approach to curriculum and program design and delivery, the administration at Valencia has developed a powerful culture with which to bring about change. Part of this change was caused by defining the client and customer.

For years, many institutions of higher education have felt that these terms—client and customer—were synonymous with students. Not so at Valencia. Students are seen as clients; business and industry, taxpayers, and legislators are seen as customers. This clarification has paved the way for the Corporate Services office to become successful.

This new way of defining the marketplace and of delivering services to the business world has come about as a result of Valencia looking at external demands rather than serving internal constituencies. Support for this concept comes from Kami.

The outside-in company is neither pessimistic nor optimistic; instead, it is realistic...A company needs neither Pollyannas nor prophets of doom. It needs managers with down-to-earth realism who understand the world as it is, not as they would like it to be...Employees are very savvy; they can quickly detect false optimism and unrealistic goals, even when couched in inspiring verbiage. A good manager must adopt a pragmatic philosophy about the outside factors not under his or her control. 'What is, is.' If one cannot change it or do something about it, one must accept it without likes or dislikes, emotions or tantrums. This attitude should apply to standing laws and regulations, minorities, religions, races, mores, habits, social behavior, politics, and weather...The world of the future will be neither better nor worse; it will be different. Past experience becomes less and less valid and valuable. One must look at the future from an eyes-open perspective (1992, p. 42).

Because the Office of Corporate Services concentrates on being demand-oriented for the future, Valencia rarely decides not to deliver instruction because of lack of resources. To meet business needs, repositioning resources is often more important than adding new ones. At other times, there are opportunities for identifying and obtaining external funding to support such activities as the advent of the motion picture industry in Central Florida, as well as support for the out-placement of thousands of Martin Marietta Aerospace workers due to defense conversion and downsizing from 14,000 employees to almost 9,000 in just two years.

Because funding often means the difference between high-quality and mediocre instruction, all colleges must seek new sources of revenue. As a result of Valencia's responsive work with business and industry, 23 endowed chairs have been established at the college with donations made to the Valencia Community College Foundation. The chairs are in both traditional and nontraditional areas, such as quality, entrepreneurship, and economic development.

Even if funding is not an issue in the delivery of educational services, not all businesses and industries know what they need to enhance their bottom line. Nationally, they are receiving help from community colleges in all locations in terms of business assessments, training, and educational programs. Cooperative ventures with the industrial world are cropping up in remote locations. These provide businesses with trained employees and give faculty a better understanding of business needs while providing them with low-cost research.

So what is the real reason that Valencia must remain the catalyst, connector and convener in Central Florida? And why is it important to continue striving toward excellence and pursuing the understanding of economic development? The answer is clear—there is no other choice.

AS A RESULT OF VALENCIA'S EFFORTS...SO WHAT?

Attempts to infuse the concepts of economic development into Valencia's culture have been successful. Requirements for students in all classes now include enhanced critical thinking and communication skills. Valencia has identified other competencies needed for high-wage, high-skill employment and has incorporated them into traditional liberal arts studies. Structural changes are taking place in current programs, as well as in auxiliary opportunities for students to experience the work-a-day world.

To garner input and support for plans to infuse an appreciation of economic development into Valencia's culture, the vice president of educational and economic development services met in open forums with over 200 staff members in strategic groups around the college. Very few attendees knew what needed to be supported, and there were always more questions than answers at the end of the sessions. The primary question was, "Why is it necessary to do this?" The answers to this question, which are addressed in this chapter, and all facets of the research were shared with the groups. Although time-consuming, activities such as these "sharing" meetings are all part of the planning process and are necessary to provide avenues for cooperation and support.

Strategic planning appears to be an adequate vehicle for achieving college community consensus on economic development issues, and it certainly is in vogue. However, strategic planning on a collegewide level depends heavily on the work of committees and multiple aspects of the institution to implement recommendations, a weakness of the process. While segments of the organization may support the implementation of a new process wholeheartedly, there are no guarantees that they will accept the responsibilities asked of them and provide follow-through. It is difficult to hold a committee accountable.

Elizabethtown Community College (Kentucky) educators faced these planning challenges as they worked to define their technical program customers and move their institution into accepting program changes similar to those Valencia has faced. Their conclusion also resembled Valencia's. They defined their customers as "...the businesses, industries, and service organizations for whom [they] would be supplying new or re-trained employees as well as the universities to whom [they] would be sending transfer students" (Williams, 1994, p. 1).

Administrators at Elizabethtown found that curriculum development took much longer than usual because of the decision to involve as many staff members as possible in the research and development stages. As expected, some of the academics were skeptical. These skeptics, however, were pleased that a competency skills assessment was the key component in the process. This component was developed by the curriculum design team and program advisory committees after gathering input from local businesses, industry, community organizations, and other educational institutions. Results of a thorough survey were critical of the curriculum design process that based the curriculum on outcomes.

The business and education communities generally forge alliances only in troubled times, but now we are seeing joint programming as a common process due to the changing nature of both industry and education. Based on the philosophy of leading to an institution's strengths, the bridge from boardroom to classroom has become a two-way street. Businesses' frequently vitriolic criticism of education, while still apparent, is lessening as they find that they are part of the problem and, indeed, part of the solution.

On November 29, 1993, a major article in the Orlando Sentinel, entitled "Companies Take Training Initiatives," reported on how Valencia Community College has worked with the Orlando Regional Healthcare System to develop programs and graduate students trained in radiology, sonography, nuclear medicine, cardiovascular technology, radiation therapy technology, and medical laboratory technology. As one might expect, the cost of these programs is high. When asked why the hospital simply did not recruit nationally for these positions in lieu of starting a two-year program, their answer was that such people do not exist and they must train a labor pool of their own.

Other major corporations have turned to Valencia for help now that a sharper vision exists at the college and in the community on how the college does business with business. As an example, AT&T has come to depend on the college's professionalism to assess their company's educational needs. In addition to taking advantage of college services on site, approximately 300 of their employees are in a specialized advancement program, taking college courses on company time.

As a result of a longtime partnership with Martin Marietta, the company and the college recently received a $1 million grant from the U.S. Department of Labor for assessment, training, and outplacement services for approximately 4,000 people who have been laid off as a result of defense downsizing. Because of the success of this program, the possibilities are excellent for more funding to continue the project.

Another Valencia success story is the college's Center for High Tech Training for the Disabled where there is a comprehensive effort by program staff and the Business Advisory Council members to develop and nurture each student's employability. Last year, with the guidance and support of this special advisory council, the center graduated 26 people who were severely disabled. However, placement—not graduation—is the center's primary goal. The center's programs provide short-term, intensive, high-quality training in the high-tech, high-demand fields of computer programming and computer-assisted design. These students are "mainstreamed" into a traditional educational setting, rather than isolated in a rehabilitation center. A hallmark of the center is the successful partnership among business, education, and rehabilitation, benefiting all involved.

The Business Advisory Council, composed of leaders from industries and representatives of collaborating agencies, directs programs offered by the Center for High Tech Training for the Disabled. The direct involvement of these partners in the center's operation ensures that the training is responsive to the employment needs of the Central Florida business community, as well as the training needs of the citizens who are disabled (Clark, 1993).

Because of Valencia's successes in partnering with the business world, the college is poised at the best time of its existence to take advantage of funding opportunities to support the president's vision and understanding of the needs of this changing world.

Washington is creating significant funding opportunities that place greater emphasis on jobs. Education and labor are two big winners in the administration's 1995 proposed budget. In order to increase funding for programs, such as school-to-work transition, the present administration in Washington plans to delete a number of education programs, such as the cooperative education and SSIG grants. Valencia recently won a $2 million grant for the integration of academic and vocational learning and is well-positioned to take advantage of funding opportunities that tie education to the workplace.

Moreover, the Re-Employment Act of 1994, a top priority of AACC and the Association of Community College Trustees (ACCT), aims to combine $1.5 billion from a number of federal funding sources for workforce training and unemployment, which will open up significant opportunities to community colleges. Funding is expected to grow to $3.4 billion over the next five years.

In addition, legislation will be introduced to support comprehensive one-stop career centers that combine training, job searches, and placement. The centers will focus on school-to-work, work-to-work, and employment-to-work programs. The centers' success will be gauged by customer satisfaction and measurable outcomes. A notable policy change is that the programs are intended to produce high-quality results; hence, the training will not be shortened or hastened to meet more people's needs. If quality is compromised and outcomes not achieved, the centers will lose customers. The administration will close the door when funds are exhausted and ask for more money in the coming year based on demand. The U.S. Department of Labor supports longer-term training that delivers a set of skills and critical thinking abilities enabling workers to adjust successfully to change and avoid future unemployment. Because of Valencia's proactive stance in the economic development arena, the college will serve as a major trainer and possibly as the one-stop career center for Central Florida.

A bill on worker preparedness sponsored by Senator George Kirkpatrick and recently passed by the Florida legislature is a reflection of the federal direction. It mirrors the federal strategy of combining funds, changing the rules, and encouraging the use of community college programs that produce measurable results and contribute to solving unemployment and economic development problems.

In addition, the college is taking advantage of the closing of the Orlando Naval Training Center facilities and working to acquire the deed to one of the buildings. Primary emphasis will be on economic development and the creation of new jobs to reflect the mission of the Base Closing Commission. This mission is to ensure the citizens of Orlando that these facilities, when vacated, will have new tenants to help replace the $550 million in lost income.

CONCLUSION

Economic development serves the college and the community well. Infusing the concepts of economic development into Valencia Community College's academic and student cultures has resulted in many positive outcomes including:

- the creation of the Office of Corporate Services;
- the receipt of 12 grants involving economic development and workforce education, totaling $3,542,063 in 1993–94;
- the establishment of cross-communication between and among collegewide faculty and staff;
- the endowment of 23 chairs with private sector funds;
- the addition of 179 letters of agreement with 127 area businesses through the Office of Corporate Services (revenue for the Corporate Services office for 1993–94 was $500,000 with a projection for 1994–95 of $1,000,000);
- the establishment of the Center for High Tech Training for the Disabled;
- the enhancement of critical thinking and communication skills requirements for students;
- the development of six Industry Quality Teams to enhance research capabilities;
- the redirection of marketing strategies to meet the needs of the 18- to 35-year-old population for positions in high-wage, high-skill jobs;
- the development of a collegewide "outside-in" approach that focuses totally on customer needs and college resources to meet those needs; and
- the cultivation of a relationship with Enterprise Florida (a public/private statewide initiative) to assist the community in attracting new high-wage, high-skill industry jobs, and to support existing businesses by providing education and training.

As Valencia Community College approaches the 21st century, it has discovered that a forward-thinking institution cannot follow a 17th-century educational model. According to U.S. Senator Mark Hatfield:

The world is prepared to pay high prices and high wages for quality, variety, and responsiveness to changing consumer tastes. If we are to continue as the world's economic leader, we must develop the best-educated and best-trained workforce in the world in order to command those high prices and afford those high wages (1994, p. 2).

In conclusion, Valencia Community College has accepted the premise that the inability to change is not stability, it is stagnation and that, more than ever before, what students earn will depend on what they learn.

REFERENCES

Aslanian, C.B. "The changing face of American campuses." *USA Today*, May 1991, 51, 57–59. Reprinted by The College Board, New York.

Aslanian, C.B. "Organizations as students—The challenge for education." *Industry and Higher Education*, June 1993. Reprinted by The College Board, New York.

Cantor, J.A. *Exemplary practices linking economic development and job training.* 1989. (ERIC Document Reproduction Service No. ED 302 715).

Clark, D.H. "A partnership that works." *Community College Times*, October 5, 1993, 5–6.

"Companies take training initiative." *Orlando Sentinel*, November 29, 1993, 12–13.

Goetsch, D. "How to get involved in economic development." *Vocational Education Journal*, 1988, 63(5), 38–48.

Gordon, R.A. "Institutional change: Colleges and the new economy." Speech presented at the NISOD Conference, Austin, Texas, May 1994.

Hatfield, M.O. "Why we need the School-to-Work Opportunities Act." *Community College Times*, January 11, 1994, 2, 4.

Hirsch, A.N. "Education and business: Partnerships that work." *College Board*, Spring 1993, 27–30.

Kami, M. *Trigger points: The nine critical factors for growth and profit.* New York: Berkley Books, 1992.

Manley, W. "Lead, change or die." *Florida Trend*, January 1994, 61–63.

Mundhenk, R. T. "Community colleges as catalysts in economic development." *Journal of Studies in Technical Careers*, 1988, X(2), 107–116.

"Ozzie and Harriet fade from family portrait." *Orlando Sentinel*, August 10, 1994, 1.

Pfeiffer, J.J. "Florida education and training placement information." *FLOIS News*, Spring 1994, 2.

Postsecondary Education Planning Commission. *Challenges, realities, strategies—The master plan for Florida postsecondary education for the 21st century.* Tallahassee, FL: Postsecondary Education Planning Commission, September 22, 1993.

"Poverty gaining on full-time workers, census bureau says." *Orlando Sentinel*, March 31, 1994, 1.

Riley, R. and Reich, R. "Preparing for the workplace." *Community College Times*, October 19, 1993, 2, 4.

Roueche, J.E. and Johnson, L. "A new view of the mission of American higher education." *Leadership Abstracts*, January 1994, 7(1).

Sanders, C. "Economic development: Commitment, communication, and coordination." *Journal of Studies in Technical Careers*, 1988, X, 117–124.

Sarantos, S.T. "Economic development in partnership with education." *On Track.* Tallahassee, FL: Florida Economic Development Council, February 1993.

Stanley, R. "Q and A: Anthony P. Carnevale, ASTD." *Community College Journal*, April/May 1993, 63(5), 6–8.

Wessel, D. and Benjamin, D. "Looking for work—In employment policy, America and Europe make a sharp contrast." *Wall Street Journal*, March 14, 1994, A-1.

Williams, D. "Tailoring a college curriculum to fit customer needs." *Innovation Abstracts*, XVI(5), 1994.

Chapter XII

Dallas County Community College District (DCCCD) personnel routinely travel across the country with a team from the city of Dallas and its economic development representatives to make presentations and to develop training opportunities for businesses considering relocation. One such presentation resulted in AT&T's decision to locate a customer service megacenter in Dallas, leading to an addition of up to 2,000 new jobs for the city. DCCCD also partners with other entities to bring up-to-date workforce training to its residents, to share the building and maintenance of facilities in cost-effective ways, to increase the literacy levels of its citizens, to attract and support young people in their pursuit of education, and to facilitate their current students' continuation of their educational programs.

DCCCD's recognition of the importance of "jointly developed programs and facilities, as well as shared revenue and economic-enhancement opportunities," has led them to create an Educational Partnerships Office. This office serves as a point of contact for entities interested in exploring partnership arrangements with the district. The staff provides assistance in formulating pilot programs and provides limited financial support for start-ups. The Educational Partnerships Office provides support teams made up of representatives from the appropriate college departments to new initiatives. That office also interacts with regulatory agencies regarding unique programs that may require solutions to "first-time" challenges. The Dallas commitment, as the reader will see, is to "establish a climate encouraging ever-widening circles of partnership activities."

* * *

J. William Wenrich, *Chancellor*
Martha Hughes, *Executive Director,*
    Educational Partnerships
Dallas County Community College District
Dallas, Texas

THE DALLAS COMMITMENT:

Partnerships in the Era of Collaboration

Leadership is action, not position.

—Donald H. McGannon

EMBARKING ON THE ERA OF COLLABORATION

No serious student of American higher education doubts that we are in a major era of restructuring. Enrollment pressures, financial limits, demand for greater accountability and measures of effectiveness, and a public outcry for demonstrated "value added" from every public institution will cause significant changes in all of higher education, but especially in community-based institutions governed by locally accountable boards.

The myriad challenges facing higher education remind us of a euphemism coined by the U.S. Department of Defense during the 1968 Tet offensive by the Viet Cong in the Vietnam war. As U.S. troops encountered wave after wave of enemy combat attacks, the Pentagon, in press briefings, referred to the combat zone as "a target-rich environment." American higher education is in a "target-rich environment" today.

Community colleges usually have been the innovators in higher education, and it is reasonable to expect that tradition to continue in response to new challenges. Today, most state legislatures are impacted by limited budget resources and committed expenditures that are required by constitutional, judicial, and federally enacted mandates. In many states, including Texas, community college support generally falls in the category of unrestricted funds and, therefore, is "at risk" in each legislative session. Local financial support usually comes from property taxes, which are often viewed as overly burdensome in states that have not had a California-style tax revolt. Traditionally low community college tuitions have risen to the point where further increases will cause enrollment declines and, thereby, reduce total income from tuition. The U.S. Department of Education and the U.S. Department of Labor have recognized the contributions made by community colleges. This recognition, plus changes in federal legislation, have increased federal financial support for community colleges, but this involves "soft," one-time, competitive funding. The consequence of these converging limitations on traditional funding sources is the necessity to seek new sources of revenue and new ways of extending the productivity of current funding levels through new partnerships and collective, collaborative relationships.

As a result of the pressures and challenges, the rest of this century will be categorized by community colleges as the "era of collaboration" with a "commitment to partnerships." What is required is a whole new set of "win-win" relationships with private businesses, public and civic organizations, and other educational institutions. This kind of collaboration includes jointly developed programs and facilities as well as shared revenue and economic-enhancement opportunities.

DCCCD EDUCATIONAL PARTNERSHIPS OFFICE

In the Dallas County Community College District (DCCCD), the partnership development approach is already well underway. In 1993, an Educational Partnerships Office was created to enhance and extend the creative collaboration already extant in the seven colleges, the Center for Educational Telecommunications, and the Institute for Economic Development.

DCCCD values decentralized management and allows colleges to respond to the unique needs of their service communities. With regard to the development and support of community partnerships, however, the central administration has assumed a specific, clearly defined role. This role is to develop partnership opportunities with external entities, to identify delivery partners within the colleges, and to assist in the implementation of pilot or model programs. The work of the central office in no way limits or precludes similar explorations by individual colleges; in fact, the idea is to establish a climate encouraging ever-widening circles of partnership activities. The presence of the central office in the mix serves as a valuable communication tool allowing replication—not duplication—of worthwhile programs, as well as economies of scale, where appropriate.

The Educational Partnerships Office is a division of the Office of the Vice Chancellor of Educational Affairs, and it offers a number of services to the colleges, the educational TV center, and the economic development institute:

- The office provides a point of contact for external entities. These potential partners may not know where to access an opportunity in the DCCCD; the Partnerships office will pursue the request or refer as appropriate.
- The office serves as an information clearinghouse for a wide variety of collaborative activities being implemented across the district; such a central information resource is essential for referral services.
- Partnerships office staff represent the district in externally based initiatives until appropriate internal partners can be identified.
- Partnerships office staff provide assistance in formulating unique, pilot, or model programs at one or more colleges in situations with potential for replication across the district or beyond.
- The office provides limited financial support for initiating these unique, pilot, or model programs at one or more of the colleges.
- Office staff convene support teams for initiatives that access other district services such as resource development, information systems expertise, and curriculum development support.
- Office staff interface with regulatory agencies such as the Texas Higher Education Coordinating Board regarding implementation of pilot programs that involve unique, nontraditional challenges.

The creation of the Educational Partnerships Office underscores the commitment of the Dallas County Community College District to the "era of collaboration." Its work reflects and builds on a tradition of partnerships long-valued in the DCCCD. The following brief summaries of partnership activities are intended to provide the reader with an overview of the breadth of opportunities available to community colleges as they have occurred for the Dallas County Community College District. The programs and projects included are in various stages of development or operation and are not intended in any sense to be an exhaustive list.

ECONOMIC DEVELOPMENT

The economic development arena offers perhaps the quickest and possibly the most significant opportunities for collaboration with business and industry. The Economic Development Office of the City of Dallas and the Economic Development Division of the Greater Dallas Chamber of Commerce are active partners with the Dallas community colleges. Recruitment efforts to attract new business and industry to relocate to Dallas include representatives from the colleges. College personnel travel across the country with a team from the city and the Chamber of Commerce to make presentations and to develop training packages for prospective businesses. With assistance from Job Training Partnership Act funding from the Private Industry Council (which combines city and county governance members), or the Smart Jobs Fund from the Texas Department of Commerce, college representatives put together a complete training program to prepare new employees to begin work the day the relocating firm opens its doors. Recent examples in Dallas include the Greyhound Corporation, AT&T, and a number of smaller companies.

Greyhound Corporation. The Bill J. Priest Institute for Economic Development of the DCCCD provided a computer-based scheduling program for 300 new employees when the Greyhound Corporation decided to relocate its national scheduling center in Dallas. Greyhound linked the terminals in the DCCCD's institute to its host scheduling computer in New York so that trainees would experience the same system and conditions they would subsequently face on the job. Greyhound management recognized the training program as making a significant contribution to a 20 percent increase in employee productivity.

AT&T. AT&T made a strategic decision to relocate its customer service function nationally to five megacenters. The telecommunications giant invited cities interested in competing for a megacenter site to send teams to Jacksonville, Florida, to observe the training approach and then to develop proposals on training packages, available sites, and tax incentives for AT&T. The Bill J. Priest Institute for Economic Development staff worked with the Chamber and city officials to assemble a comprehensive proposal that was ultimately accepted by AT&T. This partnership will result in the creation of up to 2,000 new jobs in Dallas for customer service representatives who will have the requisite computer, communication, and human relations skills to function at the megacenter. The college district, by being a partner in these economic development efforts, gained large training contracts, helped increase the college district's tax assessment base, and created goodwill with community groups trying to develop new job opportunities for Dallas residents.

Small Business Services. Across the country, many community colleges have been designated as Small Business Development Centers (SBDCs) in conjunction with state governments and the U.S. Small Business Administration. These centers offer consultant assistance and educational programs for small businesses in such diverse areas as finance plans, marketing plans, shop layout, bidding procedures for government contracts, international business opportunities (especially with the North American Free Trade Agreement now in place), patents, intellectual property rights, and scores of other subjects of interest to small business developers. Those colleges not designated as SBDCs may have an office or a function devoted to providing customized training for business and industry. The Greater Dallas Chamber of Commerce plus the Small Business Development

Center and the Business and Professional Training Program, two programs operated by the district's Bill J. Priest Institute for Economic Development, have formed a partnership. As a service and a source of income, the Chamber sponsors and markets all institute training programs created for and directed at business and industry. The college district pays a 10 percent commission for all enrollments but does not have to market or advertise the services—a win-win partnership with the Greater Dallas Chamber, one of the largest chambers of commerce in the world.

WORKFORCE TRAINING

Another area in which the community college makes an obvious contribution to economic development is workforce education and training. The Dallas community colleges have a wide range of technical-occupational programs developed in concert with business and industry advisory committees to address local workforce needs. These programs also have come to reflect an appreciation of the value of industry-based education.

GM Automotive Service Educational Program (ASEP). Brookhaven College of the DCCCD has participated in the General Motors Automotive Service Educational Program (ASEP) since 1980. In this program, the college teaches an automotive technology curriculum developed directly with General Motors. Students selected for the program are hired by a General Motors dealership and go through the program in alternating blocks of study at the college and at the dealership. A similar partnership, the Ford Automotive Student Service Educational Training program (ASSET) was added in 1985, and the Nissan Professional Cooperative Apprenticeship Program (PROCAP) was added in 1990.

Builders, Contractors, and Unions. North Lake College offers a number of programs incorporating industry-based curricula. In partnership with Associated Builders and Contractors, Inc., North Lake trains employees of association member firms in a curriculum using industry materials and leading to a completion document recognized by industry that attests to students' capabilities as multiskilled construction supervisors. A credit program with Associated General Contractors, Inc. is geared toward developing supervisory and management skills. North Lake also has agreements with local unions in the electrical and plumbing and pipe fitting industries. In these programs, industry employs all students as apprentices. Students follow an approved degree program based on materials developed through the union training program and validated and upgraded through the college curriculum-development procedures.

Telecommunications Industry. District colleges are working with a major telecommunications firm to establish a program in cellular telephony. This program is unique in that it is based directly on the company's own instructional curriculum, courses that reflect the newest techniques using the latest equipment in this major growth industry.

THE IMPORTANCE OF FLEXIBILITY

In the process of developing these partnerships, DCCCD staff discovered unique challenges. When industry-specific training is offered in the workplace, students are generally screened, selected, or approved by the employer. As employers are willing to invest time and resources only in employees who are likely to succeed, some of our traditional placement tests and other assessment requirements seem superfluous. Moreover, because students in the workplace are generally adults with clearly defined educational goals, some advising tools that are important for traditional students—such as proof of high school graduation, transcripts from all colleges attended, and student interest forms—become onerous in the business setting. Since business and industry often bring students together from various locations for intense learning experiences, semester-based rules concerning scheduling of classes may preclude offering college credit.

The staff of the DCCCD Educational Partnerships Office took these concerns to the Texas Higher Education Coordinating Board staff, and, at their request, conducted an informal survey among Texas community colleges and determined that the issues are widely recognized. The DCCCD submitted a request for a statewide Coordinating Board Task Force to address these issues and formulate procedures that will enable community colleges to better serve business and industry. The Texas Legislature, in recent years, demonstrated a keen interest in the role of community colleges in workforce education and training. The proposed task force is expected to be important in enabling colleges to do the job effectively.

FACILITIES SHARING

Another area for fruitful partnerships and collaboration is in the development and operation of physical facilities. Several Dallas community colleges have extended new opportunities to their communities by joint developments with city governments or other civic entities.

Aquatic Facility. North Lake College, working with the City of Irving and the Irving Independent School District, built and now operates a jointly-funded Olympic-quality swimming pool. The facility is operated and its schedule is set to provide college classes (swimming, scuba, water safety, etc.), high school swimming classes and competitive athletics, and community recreational swimming opportunities. It brings all elements of the community together in a positive collaboration.

YMCA. North Lake College recently entered into an agreement to lease some of its open land to the Irving YMCA for a new facility. When completed, the college will have access to YMCA physical education facilities and classrooms. Students from the college's physical fitness trainers program will have student teaching/clinical opportunities in the YMCA. YMCA participants will have the use of the outdoor physical education facilities of North Lake College (ball fields, parcourse, etc.). If all goes as planned, there will be joint participation in the development and management of a child development facility shared by students and YMCA participants.

Library. The City of Irving recently passed a bond issue election to construct and equip a new library jointly with North Lake College. The library will be the major library for the northern part of Irving and will serve as the new and expanded library facility for North Lake College. It will be located on the college campus in a building constructed by the college, but finished, equipped, and stocked by the city. They will jointly share operating costs. While this project is two or three years away from completion, it is an indicator of the kinds of partnerships that must be considered in the future.

Soccer Complex. Richland College in northern Dallas County entered into an agreement in 1992 to allow a community-based youth soccer association to construct six first-quality soccer fields adjacent to Richland's current physical education complex and parking lots. The soccer complex (including fields, drainage, lighting, stands, etc.) was funded totally by the community soccer association, and it is used by association teams principally in the late afternoon and on weekends. Richland College uses the complex at other times for college classes and intramural sports. The soccer association maintains the fields in quality condition, and the entire community benefits from a creative partnership.

Telecommunications Center. Richland College and the DCCCD entered into a partnership to build the R. Jan LeCroy Center for Educational Telecommunications, the district center located on the Richland campus. The commitment by the (RISD) to rent space at the center enabled the DCCCD to build the facility. The LeCroy Center and RISD have separate office and work spaces; however, they share conference rooms and technical facilities.

The shared use of the technical facilities—instructor studios, broadcast studios, and technical support operations—serves the students and other constituencies of both districts for the cost of one operation. The partnership also involves other specific arrangements: the DCCCD has purchased the high-tech equipment; however, RISD provides maintenance. RISD has television channels and transmitters that provide access for DCCCD programming to all local cable television companies. In fact, the combined resources of the RISD public school access and the LeCroy Center satellite network access provide almost unlimited opportunities for shared programming.

Proposed Regional Law Enforcement Academy. Several colleges in the Dallas district offer Criminal Justice/Law Enforcement training programs and reserve academies. Recently, Dallas County proposed to develop a new regional academy to train officers for the sheriff's department and for outlying municipalities in southern Dallas County. (The City of Dallas operates its own academy in the city in a partnership with El Centro College.) Cedar Valley College, located partly in the southern part of the City of Dallas and partly in the City of Lancaster, will provide land on its campus for the new facility and will operate it jointly with Dallas County. The U.S. Army Corps of Engineers will construct the facility at cost with funding from the county. The proposed facility will include classrooms, a firing range, and a defensive driving course with a skid pad and wet weather simulator. The academy may serve as many as a dozen police departments in the outlying municipalities in addition to the sheriff's department.

Communication Highway. Another recent partnership involves the development of a public service with a community organization committed to creating a Freenet system in Dallas. Freenet is a recognized national program of information services provided for public access via computer. The Dallas program was initiated by a local group of enthusiasts who obtained the Freenet charter for Dallas through the national organization. They were joined by other interested parties: a group of volunteers who rebuild computers and supply them to service agencies and neighborhood centers; KERA, the local Public Broadcasting System affiliate; the DCCCD; local libraries; and others.

North Lake College, of the DCCCD, houses the file server and has provided the initial telephone lines to make the Freenet operational. North Lake will use the service to allow students access to faculty through on-campus computers or through modems. The lines will also allow the Freenet organization to begin to develop its public service databases. As the system grows, the DCCCD will put class schedules, announcements of special events, and public-service information on-line for public access.

National Guard Armories. As the Dallas County community colleges seek to serve citizens throughout the county, off-campus locations for classes often provide access to new and underserved populations. Such is the case with a model program being developed with the Texas Army National Guard. The DCCCD is a Servicemember's Opportunity College and has traditionally worked with local units of the National Guard to provide educational opportunities for service members. Recently, the DCCCD joined the Guard's State Education Office in planning efforts to support a program called the Texas Army National Guard Higher Education Cooperative (HECOOP). The long-range plan of this program is to offer college degrees at armories throughout the state through on-site classes and through distance-learning technologies. This plan will encourage military personnel to upgrade their educational credentials, enabling them to advance in the Guard and in civilian workforce pursuits.

The Texas Army National Guard is also committed to opening these educational opportunities to members of the communities in which the armories are located. A model program is being developed in Dallas through the cooperation of the Red Bird Armory and Mountain View College. Red Bird Armory is a newly expanded and renovated facility with excellent classroom space, and it is located in a neighborhood where Mountain View College would like to expand its services. College and Guard personnel will cooperate in advertising the classes and in providing assessment and advising services at the Armory. College classes will be offered at times the Armory is generally unused for Guard programs, thus providing more efficient use of a government-funded facility. The initial classes offered through this partnership are scheduled for spring 1995.

LITERACY PROGRAMS

The basic literacy level of the general population is one of the major issues underlying economic development, workforce development, and public education. Since basic literacy in English is essential for success in the educational pathways that lead into the American workforce, efforts in this area are a priority for the Dallas County Community College District.

The DCCCD has traditionally been a provider of developmental skills classes and English as a second language classes. Several DCCCD colleges participate in a partnership to provide literacy training in concert with the Dallas Area Interfaith Council's efforts to provide citizenship training to local people. The district also is developing a partnership with the Dallas public schools to provide literacy training through Adult Basic Education funds.

Recently, the DCCCD has joined other literacy providers in planning a major collaborative to address this critical issue in Dallas County. The initiative was started by the Dallas Citizens Council, a major civic organization which has a strong commitment to improvement in education. The Citizens Council convened a team that organized as the Literacy and Life Skills Task Force. This group brought an established service agency, the Dallas Adult Literacy Council, into the discussion as well as representatives from the DCCCD. The team evaluated both need and service levels in the county through discussions with a variety of service providers.

A major program recommendation is being finalized through the Citizens Council. Essentially, the proposal calls for the establishment of an electronic network to provide three essential services. First, there will be a bulletin board to be used by all providers. Second, there will be a database listing all available services by agency, area of the county, special target populations, etc. Finally, there will be a client tracking and referral system.

Participation by agencies will be voluntary, but the program will be coordinated by the Adult Literacy Council and will use the eight DCCCD locations as "regional hubs" for communication and appropriate coordination of services. The DCCCD will also manage the technical aspects of the system.

It is anticipated that funding for the network and the coordination services will come through grants of various types. When the countywide program is in place, all providers, including the DCCCD, should benefit through coordinated planning and collaborative initiatives that will be attractive to funding agencies.

PARTNERSHIPS TO ATTRACT AND SUPPORT YOUNG PEOPLE

The Dallas County Community College District is also involved in developing partnerships to enhance opportunities for students in the more traditional programs on our college campuses. Some of these are directed at recruitment of students, particularly people from underserved segments of the community.

Several programs are aimed at young people with the specific goal of getting them into college. A unique program, styled "Do the Bright Thing," was initiated some years ago by a member of the DCCCD Board of Trustees. The DCCCD and partners, including the Greater Dallas Community of Churches, the Dallas Public Libraries, and local radio and television stations, convened this program. It maintains a year-round "stay-in-school" message with a major back-to-school campaign each summer.

DCCCD staff serve on the development team for the Dallas Mayor's Summer Youth Employment Program, an initiative funded by local corporations. The DCCCD Foundation awards DCCCD scholarships to outstanding young employees in the program.

Middle College High School, a high school under the authority of the Dallas Independent School District, is housed on the El Centro College campus. Students have the opportunity to adjust to the college campus and to earn college credit while completing the high school curriculum.

A new program, called "Better Kids...Better Dallas," is funded by a private donor in the community who has issued a challenge grant to the citizens of Dallas. The program targets young people who have had minor brushes with trouble and offers them scholarships to the DCCCD colleges to help them redirect their lives.

A program sponsored by the Dallas Independent School District (DISD) offers scholarships to DCCCD colleges for DISD students who transfer into and graduate from a high school with an ethnic majority different from their own. The DCCCD colleges actively recruit from this group of students.

The DCCCD is a partner in an organization called University Outreach; other partners include the University of Texas at Austin, Texas A&M University, and the University of North Texas. Program staff offer various academic support services such as tutoring, summer review and enrichment classes, and SAT-preparation classes with the goal of developing college readiness classes in minority junior high and senior high students in Dallas County. The DCCCD has taken the lead role in developing student interest and achievement in the areas of math and science.

These involvements represent the district's commitment to the idea that a community must work together to enable and encourage youth to seek educational opportunities. Whether DCCCD staff act as conveners or partners in development or whether the colleges are simply the recipients of the students, the district considers these efforts essential in fulfilling a role as a responsible member of the community.

EDUCATION PARTNERSHIPS

A final area of partnership development involves structuring opportunities by which community college students can continue their educational experiences. The Dallas County Community College District is firmly committed to the idea that in order for students to position themselves to reach the fullest potential in the present and future workforce, they should have the option of a clearly defined pathway to a baccalaureate degree.

To facilitate the development of these pathways, the DCCCD pursues partnerships with senior colleges and universities. There are two major initiatives: a transfer guarantee and an enhanced transfer program.

Transfer Guarantee. Under the transfer guarantee, the DCCCD guarantees students that, if they follow the guidelines of the program, all their DCCCD courses will be transferable and applicable to their chosen baccalaureate degree. In developing the program, the DCCCD vice chancellor of educational affairs and his staff visited major Texas senior colleges and universities. Once it was clear that the DCCCD was trying to determine what the universities wanted our students to take—not trying to talk the colleges and universities into accepting what we wanted students to take—they became willing partners.

Under the partnership, the senior colleges and universities supply their degree requirements and course equivalency guides for all majors. To activate the program, a student identifies his or her transfer institution and major; a counselor then works with the student to specify the exact courses which will fit the senior college or university requirements to be taken in the DCCCD degree plan. A written agreement is executed, including any additional requirements such as minimum grade-point average; and the agreement is signed by the student, the DCCCD college, and the senior college or university. In most cases, especially if the student is transferring to a state school, the plan can be developed to allow the student to earn an Associate of Arts and Sciences degree from the DCCCD; however, if the requirements of the receiving institution are such that the entire DCCCD program is not completed, the DCCCD has been authorized to confer an Associate of College/University Transfer degree.

While the transfer guarantee will most often appeal to the Associate of Arts and Sciences degree student, the enhanced transfer program is a benefit primarily for the Associate of Applied Sciences graduate.

Enhanced Transfer Program. It is the position of the Dallas County Community College District that the student with technical skills acquired while completing the Associate of Applied Science degree and the general credential of a baccalaureate degree is well-equipped for success in the workforce. Several specific and unique programs build on this concept.

One important premise is basic to these programs. While senior colleges have traditionally accepted only the equivalent of two years of credit in transfer from a community college, the baccalaureate degree plan generally includes more than 66–70 hours of lower-division course work. In the enhanced transfer model, the senior college accepts a larger number of hours of lower division courses from the DCCCD college.

Several institutional agreements in support of this concept have been developed recently. Paul Quinn College is a historically African American college located in Dallas. The college's staff, working with faculty from Eastfield College, have developed a Bachelor of Technology degree based on the DCCCD degrees in electronics technology. In addition to the course work in the Associate of Applied Science degree, Paul Quinn College will also accept further hours in specialized electronics courses and some additional general education courses. In fact, the degree was designed as a total program that would fulfill all requirements of both colleges and their governing and accrediting agencies while giving the student two credentials: first, the technical degree that would enable him or her to enter the workforce and, second, the baccalaureate degree that would enhance his or her future options.

DCCCD staff have worked with DeVry Institute in its development of a baccalaureate degree in technology management. The DeVry program requires a student to hold an Associate Degree in Applied Science; however, DeVry will accept in transfer 20 additional hours of lower division general education or introductory courses that correspond to the requirements of the Technology Management degree.

Northwood University has also developed a baccalaureate degree in Applied Science in mid-management, and they will accept 90 hours of lower division courses in transfer from the DCCCD colleges.

Faculty from Richland College and the Educational Partnerships Office have been working on agreements with area state universities concerning articulation between the DCCCD program in Educational Personnel and the university teacher training programs. They have reached tentative agreements that recognize certain Educational Personnel courses as the equivalent of certain teacher preparation courses at the universities. Currently, the universities are considering increasing the number of hours taken in transfer by that same number, creating an enhanced transfer opportunity.

The benefits of the enhanced transfer program to the student are clear: DCCCD courses are generally lower in cost compared to senior colleges; furthermore, travel time and cost are reduced if the student can take more hours at the community college. The DCCCD colleges will benefit from the enhanced enrollments. In developing these partnerships, the senior colleges have concluded that their potential loss of revenue on these courses will be compensated by the increased number of people who will be encouraged to seek the baccalaureate degree under the enhanced transfer option.

The Dallas Education Center. In another example of a facilities and program partnership, El Centro College offers lower division classes and six area universities offer upper division and graduate courses in one downtown Dallas building. The Dallas Education Center was originally proposed by city officials, the Chamber of Commerce, and the Central Dallas Association as one alternative use of a large downtown department store which had been vacant for six years. Unlike most large American cities, Dallas had no university located in the inner city—but it does have El Centro College, which has fulfilled its community college role admirably.

With a grant from the Exxon Foundation to the Alliance for Higher Education in North Texas (a voluntary regional coordinating group of 27 colleges and universities and dozens of major businesses in the Metroplex), development planning began in 1992. Six area universities initially indicated interest in joining El Centro College to offer classes in the downtown facility: East Texas State University, Texas Women's University, the University of Dallas, the University of North Texas, the University of Texas at Arlington, and the University of Texas at Dallas.

El Centro was about to undergo a total renovation to update its facilities. Ironically, El Centro had begun in a vacant department store nearly 30 years earlier. While its facilities, including the one-time department store, had been upgraded periodically, the DCCCD Board committed an additional $10 million for complete renovation, beginning in 1994. The result was that El Centro needed temporary space for a transitional location of classes and offices when the renovation began in summer 1994. This need coincided with the opportunity to develop the Dallas Education Center (DEC). With support from local industry and the formation of a non-profit corporation to run the facility, the former department store was renovated in the spring of 1994 to become a downtown higher education facility. A few classes were offered in the summer of 1994, and the Dallas Education Center fully opened its doors in August 1994. The majority of initial course offerings resulted from the El Centro transition. As El Centro College completes its own renovation during 1995 and 1996, it is anticipated that the classes and programs offered by the universities will expand at the DEC while El Centro reduces its offerings there.

The partnerships formed as a result of interest in the DEC on the part of the community and the availability of a facility have resulted in substantial organizational change for participants. Special approval was granted by the Texas Higher Education

Coordinating Board for all universities to enter this collaborative relationship. A unique self-financing funding formula was developed. The universities created a common application form and shared course offerings. A "lean" administrative structure was provided by the Alliance for Higher Education on a contract basis. Student recruiting was a joint effort supported by business and industry.

The success of the Dallas Education Center is still uncertain, in part due to the uncertainty of downtown redevelopment and public safety in inner-city Dallas. The positive effects of the collaborative relationship will continue, however, between and among the many institutions involved.

CONCLUSION

These examples represent some of the major partnership initiatives of the Dallas County Community College District. They are some of the most visible in the larger community, and they may be the initiatives that create opportunities for broadening and redefining the mission of the community college. They may also stimulate changes in the traditional procedures through which that mission is accomplished.

However, they are no more important than the innumerable ways in which the faculty and staff of the Dallas County community colleges reach out to the community. These ongoing efforts serve in many spheres to develop the relationships that bring students into the arena of educational opportunity and provide faculty with the professional experiences that enlighten them about innovations in their fields so that their classrooms will reflect the cutting edge of knowledge.

The critical element here is synergy. It is the combination of a district culture that promotes partnership development and a college leadership that encourages such development within the communities the colleges serve. In such a climate, the commitment of individual faculty and staff will enable the Dallas County community colleges to respond to the challenges of this era of restructuring responsibly, creatively, and productively.

CHAPTER XIII

| |

The state of Texas is also recognizing the crucial importance of effective workforce training. In the following chapter, Andrade and Campbell chronicle a unique tri-agency partnership that transformed Texas's approach to occupational education. The State Board of Education, the Texas Higher Education Coordinating Board, and the Texas Department of Commerce teamed up to implement planning for regional workforce training. This chapter tells the story of that collaboration, with special emphasis on the role community colleges played. Organizations "that are good at partnering take the time to learn about the differences early and take them into account as events unfold" (Kanter, 1994, p. 105). The participating entities in this case seem to have done just that. The chronicle that follows provides an interesting statewide perspective of the community colleges' role.

* * *

Kanter, R.M. "Collaborative advantage: The art of alliances." *Harvard Business Review*, 1994, 72(4), 96–108.

Sally J. Andrade, *Director*
Center for Institutional Evaluation,
Research, and Planning
The University of Texas at El Paso
El Paso, Texas

Dale F. Campbell, *Professor and*
Director
Institute of Higher Education
University of Florida
Gainesville, Florida

A STATE AND LOCAL INITIATIVE TO CREATE A WORKFORCE DEVELOPMENT PARTNERSHIP:

Case Study of a Bellwether State

A problem is a chance to do your best.

—Abraham Maslow

A REGIONAL APPROACH

In the growing national debate over occupational education, many business and industry leaders view community colleges as major contributors to fulfilling their need for a competitive workforce. This chapter illustrates the role that a state community college authority played in coordination with community college leaders to ensure that their concerns about vocational and technical education influenced policy development.

The economic slump that began in 1986 forced Texas parents, community leaders, business and industry managers, and public officials to acknowledge that the Texas educational pipeline was not producing the skilled and educated workforce[1] which the state required to compete in the global economy. State policy makers envisioned the solution emerging through a mechanism for regional planning to improve vocational and technical education and train-

[1] The state of Texas chose to name its process Quality *Work Force* Planning. The authors use the more standard national usage of workforce when not referring to the Texas initiative.

ing. To accomplish this, the state community college administration worked with the public education agency and the state job training authority to create a tri-agency partnership that transformed Texas's approach to occupational education. Representatives from education and training providers and from business, industry, and labor met in regional committees to analyze labor market information, to identify targeted occupations, and to promote the improvement of vocational and technical education in public schools and higher education institutions.

The U.S. Departments of Education, Labor, and Health and Human Services identified the resulting initiative as one of six model workforce coordination efforts in 1990 (Boyd, Butler, and Andrade, 1990). In 1993, the National Center on Education and the Economy selected Texas as one of four states in which to implement the recommendations of the report *America's Choice: High Skills or Low Wages!* (Commission on the Skills of the American Workforce, 1990). Community colleges[2] played an essential leadership role in designing and ensuring the conceptual balance of Texas's new Quality Work Force Planning system. The context, development, and outcomes of this unique approach are illustrated here.

BACKGROUND

National Concerns. The Hudson Institute's report *Workforce 2000* (Johnston, 1987) may have been the first major document to draw significant national attention to problems facing United States employers in the global economy and, in particular, to concerns about the skills and potential competitiveness of the U.S. workforce. Beginning in the 1980s, however, innumerable reports and studies targeted these issues. For example, the National Alliance of Business (1986) issued an analysis of employment policies, arguing that our society cannot afford to have large segments of the population chronically unemployed or underemployed. Nor can we permit worker displacement and dislocation due to a failure to anticipate future workforce needs. The report emphasized that we must develop a national capability to provide our workforce with new skills. The Alliance followed up this report by initiating a Corporate Action agenda with additional written products—for example, *Who Will Do the Work?* (National Alliance of Business, 1989), and a series of activities designed to foster collaboration, networking, and information dissemination. The goal of the alliance was to turn business leaders into effective advocates and action agents for educational improvement and reform.

The Business-Higher Education Forum (1988) established a new project, a Task Force on Human Capital. The resulting document laid out these priorities for the nation:

---

[2] The term "community college" is used throughout this chapter to include all of Texas's 50 community and junior colleges, the Texas State Technical College System campuses, and the Lamar University associate-degree granting campuses.

- We must adequately prepare all of our young people to enter adult life with the basic education and skills essential in the modern world.
- We must help American workers adapt to a changing world by making it possible for them to take advantage of continuous training and retraining opportunities.
- We must nurture the American people's latent talent for inventiveness and creativity by encouraging the search for and use of new knowledge.

In the public sector, the National Governors' Association (1988) undertook a "Making America Work" project to document state initiatives for enhancing jobs, growth, and competitiveness and, subsequently, an "Excellence at Work: State Action Agenda" (National Governors' Association, 1991). This agenda addressed the need to facilitate excellence in the workplace by making fundamental changes in organizational decision making and behaviors, as well as the need to ensure quality workforce preparation through a wide variety of public and private policy changes and educational reforms.

The U.S. Department of Labor, in a joint project with the American Society for Training and Development, analyzed basic workplace skills research and findings on the organization and structure of training in the United States. The resulting report highlighted employers' concerns about (a) employees' lack of competence in the "three R's" (reading, writing, and computation); (b) their ineffective skills in communication, problem solving, teamwork, and leadership; and (c) a concern that employees' lack of self-esteem and motivation hampered their ability to develop attitudes and skills supportive of the life-long learning necessary to survive in a technologically advanced society (Carnevale, Gainer, and Meltzer, 1989).

The U.S. Department of Labor followed the workplace basics project by creating the Secretary's Commission on Achieving Necessary Skills (1991), which undertook an analysis of the implications of these skill shortages for the United States in the 21st century. Their report identified the importance of "workplace know-how"—comprising these skills, qualities, and competencies:

Foundation Skills
- basic skills—reading, writing, computation, speaking, listening
- thinking skills—creative thinking, reasoning, problem solving
- personal qualities—responsibility, self-esteem, self-management, integrity

Competencies
- use of resources
- interpersonal skills
- use of information
- understanding of systems
- application of technology

Perhaps the most dramatic summary of these issues came in the 1990 report *America's Choice: High Skills or Low Wages!* (Commission on the Skills of the American Workforce, 1990). The commission's nationwide research on schools and colleges indicated a consistent lack of focus on student skill attainment, with no clear national standard of achievement, resulting in few students being motivated to work hard in high school. In addition, the United States, unlike many other developed countries, does not have a national system of technical education degrees and certificates for students who do not pursue a baccalaureate degree. The commission's research documented that most large manufacturers, financial service organizations, and communications companies still are not concerned about a skills shortage because they do not perceive a need to move toward becoming high productivity work organizations.

Furthermore, during this same period, business and education leaders were faced with the following significant demographic changes:

- The U.S. population is aging.
- More women are employed in the workforce than ever before.
- The capacity of U.S. families to meet the needs of their dependents (both young and elderly) is becoming increasingly strained.
- As young workers become scarce, employers will have to compete to obtain skilled, entry-level workers.
- By the year 2000, significantly more U.S. residents will be members of a minority group (i.e., Hispanics, African Americans, Asian Americans, and others), and several of these groups are both growing more rapidly and have a younger population than the current white majority.
- Therefore, regional changes and their implications will be dramatic, as some areas continue to experience rapid population growth with a resultant strain on infrastructure and social resources (schools, traffic, etc.), while other regions will experience significant decline and a loss of skilled workers (Brown and Clewell, 1991; Hayes-Bautista, Schink, and Chapa, 1988; Johnston, 1987; Morrison, 1991).

The Role of Community Colleges in Economic and Workforce Development. As part of their comprehensive mission, public community colleges support economic development through the education and training of skilled workers. This objective has assumed increasing urgency given the national debate outlined above.

For example, in its analysis of the role of the community college in the 21st century, the American Association of Community and Junior Colleges identified alliances with employers for workforce training and retraining as an important component of the continuing education program (Commission on the Future of Community Colleges, 1988), and subsequently issued a national policy paper on workforce development (American Association of Community Colleges, 1993). Community college administrators traditionally emphasize the special responsibility and strengths of their colleges in enhancing workforce productivity (National Council for Occupational Education, 1990). Both business leaders (Rand, 1989) and government officials (Davenport, 1989) recognize the innovation, adaptability, and responsiveness to societal needs that have characterized community colleges as leaders in meeting U.S. workforce needs in the new internationally competitive economy. As a result, community college administrators are increasingly addressing and documenting trends, problems, and innovations in workforce interventions at their institutions and in their regional or state collaborative efforts (Roe, 1989; Waddell, 1991).

Texas in the 1980s. If states were countries, Texas would have the 14th largest economy in the world, ranking ahead of all states except California and New York. Texas will continue to grow and may double in population over the next 50 years. The U.S. Bureau of the Census reported that in 1990 the state had almost 17 million inhabitants. The most dramatic demographic change in the next 25 years will be a shift in racial/ethnic distribution. In 1970, Hispanics (primarily people of Mexican origin) made up about 16.5 percent of the state's population; by 1985, they composed nearly 23 percent. By 2015, Texas is expected to contain no racial/ethnic majority. For example, given only moderate immigration rates, by the year 2000, whites will represent less than 46 percent of the Texas population (Marshall and Bouvier, 1986). Children and young people will increasingly be Hispanic and to a lesser extent African American and Asian American, with white children becoming a minority before the turn of the century. This trend was evident by 1990 when white children became a minority in Texas public schools. The concept of "minority groups" is thus changing, and policy decision makers are beginning to talk about the "emerging majority," particularly in areas where Hispanics or African Americans will soon represent the majority population (Center for Health Policy Development, 1991).

Because the population of school-aged children is projected to increase 25 to 30 percent in the 1990s and because Texas will then be a state with a large pool of new workers, it has a potential workforce advantage compared to other states or regions in the world. Many policy makers and business leaders believe, however, that the most serious problem facing the state is the dramatic loss of young people from Texas public schools. The first comprehensive study of high school dropout rates was conducted in 1986, and it documented that one out of every three Texas adolescents left school before obtaining a diploma (Robledo, 1986). Following extensive legislative and school district efforts to initiate reforms, subsequent research showed that Texas high school dropout rates diminished between 1985 and 1989, from a 33 percent loss of students to a 31 percent loss. Nevertheless, analyses of student attrition rates indicated that all of the improvement occurred among the white population (with a 26 percent increase in their retention rate), while emerging majority student dropout rates actually increased (for African American students by nine percent and Hispanic students by seven percent). The state's public education system, therefore, continues to lose one-third of its African American students and over half (55 percent) of its Hispanic students (Cardenas, 1990).

Texas Responds. Within this national context of growing debate over employer needs for a skilled workforce and Texas's concerns about public school achievement, particularly by minority groups, two state government reports in 1987 pointed the direction for the development of a statewide regional planning strategy to improve vocational and technical education, which would ultimately result in the Quality Work Force Planning initiative. Business leaders served as advisors to both, and they were shocked at the minimal state requirements for labor market analyses by public schools and higher educational institutions with respect to planning for occupational programs. The original Master Plan for Vocational Education (State Board of Education, 1987) was developed as one of a series of mandates from House Bill 72 to improve public and higher education in Texas. Leadership from the Texas Council on Vocational Education and support from the Texas State Occupational Information Coordinating Committee (SOICC) assisted the Master Plan Advisory Committee in focusing on the need for a structured labor market analysis process in Texas. Among other things, the Master Plan called for pilot projects to explore the feasibility of regional planning for vocational/ technical education.

In addition, the Report of the Select Committee for Higher Education (Select Committee for Higher Education, 1987) highlighted the role that community colleges and all higher educational institutions should play to support economic development in Texas. The Select Committee emphasized that vocational/technical education must be responsive to rapidly changing job markets, adaptable to new training techniques, and responsive to individual student needs. For those reasons, the report recommended educational partnerships with business for effective local and regional planning. The findings of these two key documents were further reinforced in 1988 by the work of a statewide commission predominantly made up of business and industry representatives. It reported to the Texas Legislature that the economic future of the state would depend on the development of a skilled and internationally competitive workforce (Strategic Economic Policy Commission, 1989).

IMPLEMENTATION OF QUALITY WORK FORCE PLANNING IN TEXAS

The Tri-Agency Partnership. The State Board of Education and the Texas Higher Education Coordinating Board were mandated to move forward by the Master Plan for Vocational Education (State Board of Education, 1987). In order to include the perspective of Texas employers, they invited the participation of the Texas Department of Commerce, which administers the state's Job Training Partnership Act (JTPA) system. As a result, officials of the Texas Education Agency (TEA), the Texas Higher Education Coordinating Board, and the Texas Department of Commerce (hereafter referred to as Commerce) met to develop a strategy for defining and implementing a regional approach to planning for the improvement of vocational/technical education and job training in the state. The state administrator for community colleges represented the higher education agency—workforce development concerns of community colleges were paramount in his negotiations. Early attempts to organize ended in stalemates, as the agencies argued over statewide goals, regional areas, planning cycles, and funding allocations. Several months of fruitless dialogues taught them that there were only three major barriers to effective functioning of regional planning: your turf, their turf, and, of course, my turf.

Seeking grassroots input on how to confront local turf issues and to implement regional planning effectively throughout the state became the goal. The negotiators decided to form a tri-agency administrative partnership which would combine federal funding sources to pilot the concept, and they renamed the initiative Quality Work Force Planning. Each agency would contribute an equitable amount to support the effort. Each would have a representative on the administrative team—which decided how much money would be allocated and how it would be spent—and each agency would have a representative on the management team responsible for implementation of the pilot project process. They agreed on a compromise that would permit local applicants to define their own regions until the state legislature acted to define regional planning boundaries.

Funding the Pilot Process. Over a four-year period (1987–1991), $2,425,000 was allocated from federal Carl Perkins Vocational Education funds. In addition, the state commerce agency provided additional JTPA funds to contract with an independent evaluator for process and formative evaluation findings throughout the pilot stage. This became one of the most valuable investments by the tri-agency partnership because the results were crucial in documenting the flexibility of the process and the results of the pilot projects. Commerce also used JTPA funds to support the development of an automated labor market analysis process by the Texas SOICC.

Recognizing Perspectives and Priorities. The three agencies brought different, valuable perspectives and philosophies to the new partnership. The elected State Board of Education, represented by TEA, tended to focus on governance and control of public schools to ensure uniform implementation for all students. The higher education agency, represented by state community college administrators, was clear about its commitment to a coordination and consensus-building role among institutions and the need for a pipeline that encouraged high school students to continue on to college for additional education and training. Commerce and the JTPA network insisted that advocacy for students took priority over all other mandates. In terms of outcomes, public education spokespersons focused on reducing program duplication and costs; the community college representatives focused on the direct relation of regional planning to economic development; and JTPA system representatives focused on ensuring student skill development and accountability of institutions to employer requirements. All three agencies shared a common focus on encouraging education and training providers to base program improvement decisions (i.e., initiation, redirection, revision, or deactivation) on targeted occupations within regional labor markets and on creating clear career paths to those occupations for all students.

Emphasis on Local Ownership. The tri-agency partnership saw that the labor market analysis could be done more efficiently by state government. But, they also recognized that the long-range success of the regional committees and of the statewide planning system depended on the critical element of local ownership—that is, perceived local ownership of the regional database, of the committee analyses, and of subsequent inter-pretations and applications of the findings. They committed their agencies to making the regional planning tools accessible and to creating the local expertise to use them effectively. Therefore, state resources (funds, time, and effort) focused on creating broad-based committees with members who represented diverse community con-stituencies and on developing user-friendly planning tools so that the committees could generate relevant information for local decision makers. The Texas SOICC agreed to assist the pilot projects in undertaking labor market analyses and assessing the regions' educational and training opportunities (McKee and Harrell, 1989). Commerce subse-quently contracted with SOICC to automate and enhance the process (resulting in the SOCRATES system), thus giving each committee a powerful planning tool and a unique status in its region, as well as an incentive to encourage cooperation among the diverse stakeholders.

Sharing and Sensitivity. As the tri-agency management team worked together over time and learned from the implementation process, it accepted the necessity of always having each of the three agencies represented in decision making and in public pre-sentations—the former to ensure that the priorities of each were not overlooked, and the latter to reinforce symbolically at the state level the coordination that they were demanding be accomplished at the local level. Each learned the other agencies' vocab-ulary, legislated mandates, and board priorities, as well as the writing styles and other idiosyncrasies of different administrative officials. Sensitivity gradually emerged about the complexity of their different local agencies' policies, relationships, staff, and com-munity resources. Key support came from the SOICC, and joint staff meetings about the development of materials and needs for technical assistance by the committees became routine. In effect, significant interagency cross-training occurred, although that had not been an original objective. A similar effect eventually occurred at the local level as administrators from community colleges, public schools, and private industry councils learned more about each state system's role and potential contributions to pro-gram improvement.

Establishing Regional Planning Committees. The first three projects began in December 1987, with three additional projects added in November 1988, and the final three pilots initiated in September 1989. Each successfully established a Quality Work Force

Planning committee with representation from business and industry and from education and training institutions, although some had difficulty defining their tasks and pulling together their resources. In each region, the committee:

- identified key regional industries with the greatest potential for future employment;
- developed a regional list of targeted occupations for education and training based upon regional industrial analysis;
- compiled regional inventories of education and training programs of schools, community colleges, and PICS and of economic development organizations for use in the planning process; and
- developed a regional service delivery plan based upon targeted occupations and related programs, services, and activities.

The Statewide Mandate and a First: Developing Joint Tri-Agency Rules. The 71st Legislature passed a bill in 1989 that required regional planning for vocational/ technical education and training. The Texas Education Code, Chapter 21, was amended by adding Section 21.115, to ensure that:

There would be 24 Quality Work Force Planning Regions with the same boundaries as the existing state planning regions delineated by the governor; the membership of the Quality Work Force Planning committees was to be established; priorities for vocational/technical education and training programs were to be established for each region; and regional service delivery plans were to be developed.

Significantly, however, there were no funds appropriated to assist with the implementation nor with the committees' operational costs.

Working together, the public education and community college agencies responded to this new legislation by updating the Master Plan for Vocational and Technical Education (State Board of Education, 1990), focusing on achieving an integrated education and training delivery system through regional planning for a quality workforce. The Texas Department of Commerce added this initiative to its overall Agency Strategic Plan as a critical element in meeting Texas's workforce requirements.

The next major step involved the development of joint tri-agency rules, something never before attempted in Texas, for implementation of Quality Work Force Planning. After extensive work and revision by staff from the agencies, an initial draft was circulated throughout the state to obtain input from local institutions via each agency's network. Perhaps more importantly, a special meeting was held with the project directors and committee chairs of each pilot project to review the draft rules. Their focused critiques and suggestions assisted in the preparation of a final draft of joint agency rules for submission to the governing board of each agency.

The State Job Training Coordinating Council recommended approval of the rules to the governor as state Job Training Partnership Act policy on May 31, 1990. The State Board of Education adopted the rules on June 9, 1990. The Texas Higher Education Coordinating Board adopted the rules on July 13, 1990. (For a copy of the rules, see Texas Education Agency, 1990.) Thus, by the fall of 1990, unprecedented state administrative history had been realized, and the tri-agency management team was instructed to proceed with organization of Quality Work Force Planning committees in the remaining 15 regions and to assist the pilots with transition activities to meet the new boundary and other rule requirements.

GETTING THE PLANNING COMMITTEES UP AND RUNNING

Beginning in the spring of 1990, the tri-agency management team undertook an intensive travel schedule throughout the state to assist in spreading the word about Quality Work Force Planning. Initial activity focused on identifying people from all three networks, as well as representatives from business, industry, labor, and other state agencies at the local level, who would be willing to participate in a preliminary work group in each of the 15 regions designated to form a committee.

Emphasis was placed on these basic rules of committee formation:
- a 50/50 split between the public education and training sector and the private employer and labor sector; and
- a requirement that "voting members shall reflect the population characteristics of the region with regard to race/ethnicity and gender" and the "geographic diversity of the region, including urban, suburban, and rural areas."

The tri-agency management team emphasized that the issue was not one of tokenistic number counting but rather of assuring that all bases in the region would be included and thus able to participate in the consensus development process essential for the success of a committee. Although the tri-agency partnership had anticipated potential problems in recruiting racially/ethnically diverse memberships (and indeed some regions struggled in this effort more than others), the more complex issue turned out to be convincing the work groups that women must participate in the improvement of vocational/technical education in each region.

By September 1990, almost 1,100 volunteers from secondary schools, institutions of higher education (primarily community and technical colleges), private industry councils, and other public agencies had joined representatives from business, industry, and labor to serve. The private sector representatives made up 49.2 percent of the committee members. The committee's recruitment efforts succeeded with respect to race/ethnicity and to geographic representation, (67 percent white, 10.2 percent African American, and 21.9 percent Hispanic), but the agencies finally compromised on gender, which resulted in a disappointing 36.3 percent of committee members throughout the state being women. Given the emphasis on services to special population students, including girls and women, in the new 1990 federal Perkins Vocational Education and Applied Technology Act, this issue will undoubtedly be revisited in each region.

Full committees were identified, if not already fully functioning, by the fall of 1990. Each agency continued to provide support and technical assistance to the statewide effort, but a slight change had developed in that the tri-agency partnership defined a specific coordination role for each agency, with support from the other two. First, the state education agency would provide technical assistance in coordinating Quality Work Force Planning committee functions and operations. Second, the state higher education agency's community college division would provide technical assistance in developing program articulation agreements, 2+2 programs, and tech prep associate degree programs. Third, the Texas Department of Commerce would provide technical assistance in establishing and using regional labor market information systems and in developing school-to-work transition efforts.

OBTAINING STATE FUNDING

In addition, the tri-agency partnership developed a joint 1992–93 legislative appropriations request (another first to the authors' knowledge) to fund the activities conducted by the 24 Quality Work Force Planning committees and technical assistance from the state agencies. In response to a recommendation by the pilot project evaluator, a proposed annual budget of $90,000 per region was requested to provide for staff services and administrative costs for each committee.

Against many political observers' predictions, in 1991, the 72nd Texas Legislature included general revenue funding in a special rider to the Appropriations Bill, which allocated a total of $1.8 million per year of the 1992–93 biennium (a total of $3.6 million for the period), or $75,000 for each of the 24 Quality Work Force Planning committees, to fund the staff and related operating costs. About $2.25 million (62.5 percent) would come from the state's allotment of general revenue funding to public school vocational education; $400,000 (11.1 percent) from the federal Perkins funds allocated to the higher education agency; and $950,000 (26.4 percent) from the federal JTPA funds allocated to the State Job Training Coordinating Council, administered by Commerce.

Obtaining general revenue funding—in one of the toughest budget sessions of Texas history—was an extraordinary accomplishment. The probable reason for this success was the educational effort mounted by the volunteer members of the nine pilot committees and their demonstration of actual accomplishments due to the regional planning process. For example, the private consulting firm that handled the external evaluation documented increased knowledge among program providers and employers about future occupations and skills demanded in their regions and the status of related training options; increased capability to conduct labor market analysis and skills inventories and to develop program articulation agreements; and increased communication among employers, educators, and training providers to expedite the process of program planning, development, and evaluation (Decision Information Resources, Inc., 1991). Pilot projects reported new 2+2 programs (curriculum linkages between high schools, community colleges, and in some regions proprietary schools), as well as school districts raising their graduation requirements at the urging of business leaders to include higher levels of mathematics and science courses. Other successes included the initiation of new courses and programs, resource sharing agreements, retraining programs, services for at-risk youth, and an adult literacy coordination effort.

In addition, it became clear that Quality Work Force Planning was the unifying strategy to implement an integrated education and training delivery system to improve occupational education in Texas. Efforts and support systems for the success of Quality Work Force Planning include the following statewide components:
- a decentralized labor market information database system;
- a career guidance system to complement the database;
- an electronic education and training clearinghouse with inventories of available programs and resources;
- an automated student follow-up system to determine their pursuit of additional higher education or their employment;
- a basic skills and literacy support system; and
- a Texas skills development program to allow business and industry to participate more effectively in setting skills standards for workers.

Thus, state decision makers acknowledged the ongoing need for other tri-agency support systems to assist community colleges, schools, and other local partners in their efforts to improve workforce education and training programs. Only through such coordinated initiatives could statewide resources be marshaled to serve educational providers at the local level.

THE LEADERSHIP ROLE OF COMMUNITY COLLEGES

This chapter does not specifically address the many contributions of administrators and leaders from the partners other than the community college: public school districts and education service centers, universities, private industry councils, other public agencies, economic development organizations, businesses, industries, and labor organizations. The successful implementation of Quality Work Force Planning in Texas required vision and commitment from all of them, and their active involvement continues to energize its development.

Understanding the historical development of Quality Work Force Planning in Texas is necessary to appreciate the role which Texas public community colleges have played in that process. Texas, like several other states, does not have a "system" of community colleges. There are 50 public community and junior college districts with locally elected boards of trustees, and there is a state-funded Texas State Technical College

System, which has a board of regents appointed by the governor, with four campuses and five extension centers. Following national trends, Texas provides state aid to the community and technical colleges to provide for academic education to promote transfer to baccalaureate degree programs; technical education to prepare the workforce; remediation services to ensure open access; and adult training/retraining services to facilitate occupational transition.

In fall 1993, public community and technical colleges in Texas enrolled 407,382 students, or almost 51 percent of all higher education students in the state. The enrollment in these institutions has grown by 43,500 (or almost 12 percent) since 1989. Almost three out of every four students enrolling in public higher education in Texas for the first time attend public community colleges. About 33 percent of community college students are Hispanic or African American, and 13 campuses have minority enrollments of more than 50 percent. Since approximately 64 percent of all Hispanic and African American students who entered higher education as freshmen in Fall 1993 began at community and technical colleges, the access role of these institutions for the state is particularly important.

Developing the Concept. Committed to institutional autonomy, the community colleges were understandably skeptical of any further centralization of authority with respect to decision making or reporting about their instructional programs. Serious concern about the scope and long-range impact of the Quality Work Force Planning rules began to be expressed. To deal with this potentially disruptive situation early in the process, a special statewide meeting was organized, and community college representatives from each of the proposed 24 regions participated. This group reviewed the proposed rules to analyze their intent and to offer suggestions to the management team. The private sector chair of one of the larger Quality Work Force Planning pilot projects, a manager at a statewide telecommunications corporation, worked with the group to express the commitment of business and industry to the new process. At the time, he was the co-chair of the Higher Education Task Force that updated the Master Plan for Vocational and Technical Education (State Board of Education, 1990) and thus demonstrated the willingness of the private sector to support community colleges on these issues.

Community colleges played a primary role in organizing and supporting committees, either as a fiscal agent and/or site for the project, in five of the nine pilot regions. One community college, located in a predominantly rural region, assumed dramatic leadership through the three rounds of pilot project funding. Its Quality Work Force Planning committee insisted on developing a five-year plan, well beyond the state requirements, and it was one of the first groups to hone in on adult literacy, English as a second language instruction, programs for at-risk youth, and job development initiatives as crucial to the region's economic development, and, therefore, to the committee's work.

Statewide Implementation and Resulting Curriculum Changes. Because the legislature did not initially provide funding to the other 15 regions, local institutions were concerned about which entity would be expected to absorb the operational costs of the newly forming committees. Community colleges assumed a leadership role, either as a fiscal agent and/or as a site for the project director, in seven of the 15 new regions, and played a key support role in the other nine regions. For example, one committee decided to implement a type of membership fee, with school districts asked to pay an adjusted average-daily attendance rate and the colleges a flat $10,000 support fee.

Beginning in 1987, the state public education agency and the community college authority jointly funded a major initiative in 2+2 curriculum development. Because several community colleges had been working on developing 2+2 curricula with public school districts, it was natural that program articulation agreements, including the expansion of 2+2 programs, were a major thrust in many regions, with the community colleges taking the lead to reach out to additional high schools. New curriculum linkages throughout the state occurred in fields such as electronics and computer technology, as well as medical technology and other health occupations, and marketing. In addition, a technical college campus provided access for high school students to its occupational education courses.

Improving secondary and adult education was a primary goal for almost all community colleges, since better-prepared students would mean less need for the colleges to provide remediation services. Committees also used coordinated planning and follow-up activities to encourage ongoing dialogues between educators and employers. As a result, at the urging of local employers, one school district raised its high school graduation requirements to include more science and math courses. Other districts added new courses in response to local labor market demands, as well as developed new internships and resource sharing agreements with employers. One committee facilitated new regional dialogue about initiation of adult literacy program coordination efforts among local community colleges, private universities, school districts, the regional literacy coalition, and the council of governments.

Beginning in 1990, the Texas public community and technical colleges assumed additional leadership with respect to accountability issues. For example, their representatives took the lead in reviewing the higher education section of the Master Plan for Vocational and Technical Education. The community college authority's advisory task force recommended that the plan be revised to identify, for each goal and objective, new annual performance indicators and biennial outcome measures to evaluate progress in implementation, both by the state's higher education agency and by higher education institutions (Texas Higher Education Coordinating Board, 1991).

Texas, like many other states, faces a staggering revenue shortfall. Given a continued "no new taxes" philosophy, the state legislature and elected officials, including the governor and the state comptroller, expect higher education institutions to reprioritize their activities and to anticipate and plan for funding cuts. Performance-based funding and incentive funding, expanded state monitoring and institutional self-assessments with respect to student outcomes, presidential initiatives, and congressional legislation are requiring new levels of accountability, and community colleges face particularly comprehensive evaluation criteria. In addition, generating basic levels of trust—between state agencies and community leaders, between educational institutions and employers, between employers and union representatives—continues to be a goal that requires constant attention.

The Role of the Community College in Workforce Development for Texas. As state government policy moves toward a much more proactive stance, both in advocating the needs of employers for a skilled workforce and the needs of students for more opportunity, Texas community colleges are superbly positioned to assume a primary role in adult training and retraining. Of all the public educational institutions, they can best create the new client-focused delivery system that can be flexible, responsive, and accountable for skills development. At the same time, they are fostering new avenues of access for youth through the tech prep high school and associate degree programs that will ensure expanded educational and occupational opportunities for many young people generally ignored in the past. Because upper-level colleges and universities are reacting to the revenue shortfall by focusing on student enrollment caps and tuition increases, both policymakers and employers look to community colleges to maintain access and to ensure quality. Thus, the challenge for community colleges is how to foster resource sharing, eliminate program duplication, manage effective program evaluation, and ensure that the public is aware of their significant role in workforce development—objectives directly related to the mission of Quality Work Force Planning.

WHAT MAKES AN INTERAGENCY PARTNERSHIP WORK?

In 1991, a major national coalition of private non-profit and business professional organizations reviewed the difficulties and benefits of fostering interagency partnerships for more effective education and human service delivery systems (Melaville and Blank, 1991). This Education and Human Services Consortium emphasized the importance of state-level leadership but also pointed out that past efforts have frequently had an uneven effect on local communities, primarily because such state efforts routinely took on the characteristics of top-down planning. Thus, those state initiatives that originated at upper administrative levels were close to funding decisions but far removed from the actual provision of services occurring at the local level. In addition, many such interventions "were limited by insufficient resources, members without sufficient authority or genuine commitment to make substantial contributions, and the tendency of broad-based groups to avoid hard questions in favor of easy answers" (Melaville and Blank, 1991, pp. 18–19). The crucial factor determining their lack of long-term impact, however, was that such earlier state efforts often imposed rather than facilitated local action; as a result, local leaders tended to perceive them as intrusive and counterproductive.

In some respects, despite good intentions, the Texas Quality Work Force Planning initiative started out in the same vein, that is, with a complex application process for the original pilots, a heavy monitoring flavor, and a state-imposed goal that was locally perceived as creating "one more planning system." Nonetheless, vigorous dialogues and exchanges of perspectives occurred and, indeed, were consciously nurtured by the tri-agency partnership staff. These exchanges emphasized the maintenance and clarification of the common vision of a quality workforce for Texas, and the meetings began the establishment of a common vocabulary and a commitment to develop common definitions for funding obligations, planning outcomes, and reporting terms. The tri-agency partnership recognized its responsibility to provide technical assistance (meetings for the directors, orientation to committee members, statewide conferences where committee officers could come together and learn from the pilot projects) and to explore ways to offer incentives to the committees (labor market information analysis capacity, state operational funding, tech prep involvement).

The National Education and Human Services Consortium further identified five variables that shape interagency partnerships:

- the climate in which such initiatives begin,
- the processes used to build trust and handle conflict,
- the people involved,
- the policies that support or inhibit partnership efforts, and
- the availability of resources to enable these efforts to continue (Melaville and Blank, 1991).

Using these factors to analyze the Texas process helps to understand why community colleges assumed key leadership in the initiative.

Climate. Quality Work Force Planning originated in Texas during a period of intense scrutiny and criticism of public education and of challenges to the higher education system to assume more responsibility for economic development. This provided a major impetus for tri-agency coordination but also generated regular defensive/aggressive interactions among business and industry critics and educational administrators, which needed to shift toward a more collaborative perspective.

Processes. The tri-agency partnership learned that regular communication could only be ensured through a tri-agency management team that met regularly, traveled extensively, and addressed hard questions and sometimes unpleasant realities in order to establish statewide goals and objectives that made sense at the local level. They quickly recognized that all three members had to be present at all public meetings as a symbol of each agency's commitment to the partnership. In addition, they had to clarify agency roles, to resolve conflict, to make decisions, and, above all, to support the local volunteers from community colleges, high schools, private industry councils, community-based organizations, businesses, and industry who were charged with making Quality Work Force Planning happen.

People. The persistence and coalition-building skills of the pilot project staff, committee members, and management team helped to frame the statewide vision and operations of Quality Work Force Planning. A key objective was to involve local leaders and to identify or generate new leaders, particularly from Hispanic and African American communities and from women in education and business.

Policies. Because each agency brought a different set of governing policies (as well as philosophies, vocabularies, and mandates) to the bargaining table, an early decision by the tri-agency partnership was to target the passage of joint rules by the three boards. To accomplish this, staff had to engage and compromise over many issues, and the opportunity for review by local institutional representatives both improved the rules and provided significant information dissemination opportunities. The successful accomplishment of joint rules for Quality Work Force Planning thus had tremendous symbolic and implementation value.

Resources. The effective use of federal funds by the tri-agency partnership supported four years of pilot demonstration projects and the "bottom-up" development of state rules with direct input from community colleges, schools, private industry councils and other local institutions, as well as clarification of the planning process and regional outcomes. Results from the independent evaluation were crucial in obtaining state general revenue support for the statewide expansion. Quality Work Force Planning committees could reasonably assume that they would have the minimum resources available to assure them an organizational and informational base for advocacy and leadership to improve occupational education in Texas.

CONCLUSION

An analysis of these five leadership factors suggests that community colleges need to consider the dynamic elements of such interagency partnerships so that they can step forward in a more united fashion to assume a catalytic leadership role in impacting state and federal workforce development policy. Such a role requires a coordinated, proactive group effort by community college representatives to convey their potential education and training contributions to policymakers in contrast to the functions of public schools, the JTPA system, or business and industry.

From a statewide perspective, the Texas Quality Work Force Planning process demonstrated the importance and vitality of a checks-and-balances procedure. When any two of the agencies deadlocked on an issue, the third partner invariably facilitated clarification, exploration of needs and resources, compromise, and creative resolution to keep the process moving. Support from other state agencies, such as the employment commission and the SOICC, was critical. "Reaffirm the vision" (i.e., agency and institutional cooperation to ensure employers' ability to compete and students' ability to take advantage of educational and occupational opportunities) became the management team's rallying point. When Texas educational leaders focused on their mutually desired outcomes, they could usually find a way around state administrative roadblocks.

Quality Work Force Planning in Texas illustrates the critical leadership role that community college administrators and faculty must play in influencing state and federal policy. Without the strong higher "education" perspective provided by community college administrators to balance the "training" orientation of the private industry councils, Quality Work Force Planning would not have had its long-term focus on human development and opportunity, nor would it have been perceived as effective by business and industry leaders.

Supporting a similar development at local and regional levels continues to be the major challenge for the Texas tri-agency partnership. Solutions will not be developed in the state capitol or in Washington, D.C.—they have to be homegrown to ensure genuine local buy-in and long-term commitment to change. That is where authentic, long-lasting change takes place—in community colleges, schools, JTPA training programs, and among local employers, labor organizations, and economic development agencies across the state.

Realistically, however, the financial resources to initiate such local changes frequently come from the state or federal government. Allocations are often made by politicians who may not understand or fully appreciate the important contributions of community colleges. As can be seen from this case study of Quality Work Force Planning, community colleges can be major catalysts in the design, implementation, and evaluation of local and state solutions.

Sally J. Andrade is Director of the Center for Institutional Evaluation, Research and Planning at the University of Texas at El Paso. Dale F. Campbell is Professor and Director of the Institute of Higher Education at the University of Florida, Gainesville. Both served at the Texas Higher Education Coordinating Board in the Community and Technical Colleges Division during the period described in this chapter—Campbell as the Assistant Commissioner and Andrade as the Director of Research and Program Planning. The authors appreciate the assistance of Mark Butler, at the Texas Education Agency, Jim Boyd at the Texas Department of Commerce, and Richard Froeschle at the Texas State Occupational Information Coordinating Committee in the preparation of an earlier draft of this chapter.

REFERENCES

American Association of Community Colleges. *The workforce training imperative: Meeting the training needs of the nation.* Washington, DC: American Association of Community Colleges, 1993. (ERIC Document Reproduction Service No. ED 358 878)

Boyd, J., Butler, M., and Andrade, S.J. "Texas quality work force planning: Preparing Texas for the 21st century through a skilled and educated work force." In *Training the American workforce: Mark of excellence.* Washington, DC: National Governors' Association, 1990, 125–131.

Brown, S.V., and Clewell, B.C. *Building the nation's work force from the inside out: Educating minorities for the twenty-first century.* Norman, OK: University of Oklahoma, Center for Research on Multi-Ethnic Education, 1991.

Business-Higher Education Forum. *American potential: The human dimension.* Washington, DC: American Council on Education, 1988.

Cardenas, J.A. "Texas School Dropouts: 1986 to 1989." *IDRA Newsletter, XVII*(3), 1–5. San Antonio: Intercultural Development Research Association, 1990.

Carnevale, A.P., Gainer, L.J., and Meltzer, A.S. *Workplace basics: The skills employers want.* Washington, DC: American Society for Training and Development, 1989.

Center for Health Policy Development, Inc. *The Texas health promotion initiative: A strategic plan responding to diversity.* San Antonio, TX: Center for Health Policy Development, Inc., 1991.

Commission on the Future of Community Colleges. *Building communities: A vision for a new century.* Washington, DC: American Association of Community and Junior Colleges, 1988.

Commission on the Skills of the American Workforce. *America's choice: High skills or low wages!* Rochester, NY: National Center on Education and the Economy, 1990.

Davenport, L.F. "The role of the community college in meeting America's future labor force needs." *AACJC Journal,* 1989, 59(4), 23–27.

Decision Information Resources, Inc. *Quality work force planning in Texas: Evaluation of statewide implementation of a tri-agency initiative—Final evaluation report.* Houston: Decision Information Resources, Inc., 1991.

Hayes-Bautista, D., Schink W., and Chapa, J. *The burden of support: Young Latinos in an aging society.* Stanford, CA: Stanford University Press, 1988.

Johnston, W.B. *Workforce 2000: Work and workers for the 21st century.* Indianapolis: Hudson Institute, 1987.

Marshall, R.R., and Bouvier, L.F. *Population change and the future of Texas.* Washington, DC: Population Reference Bureau, Inc., 1986.

Melaville, A.A., and Blank, M.J. *What it takes: Structuring interagency partnerships to connect children and families with comprehensive services.* Education and Human Services Consortium, Washington, DC: Institute for Educational Leadership, 1991.

McKee, W.L., and Harrell, N.L. *Targeting your labor market: Using labor market information in regional planning for Texas jobs.* Austin: Texas State Occupational Information Coordinating Committee, 1989.

Morrison, P.A. *Congress and the Year 2000: A demographic perspective on future issues.* Santa Monica, CA: RAND for the Congressional Research Service of the Library of Congress, 1991.

National Alliance of Business. *Employment policies: Looking to the year 2000.* Washington, DC: National Alliance of Business, 1986.

National Alliance of Business. *Who will do the work? A business guide for preparing tomorrow's workforce.* Washington, DC: National Alliance of Business, 1989.

National Council for Occupational Education and the American Association of Community and Junior Colleges. *Productive America: Two-year colleges unite to improve productivity in the nation's workforce.* Chicago: City College of Chicago, 1990.

National Governors' Association. *Making America work: Productive people, productive policies—Follow-up report.* Washington, DC: National Governors' Association, 1988.

National Governors' Association. *Excellence at work: A state action agenda.* Washington, DC: National Governors' Association, 1991.

Rand, G. "Shared resources: Working both ways with business and industry." *AACJC Journal,* 1989, 59(4), 34–36.

Robledo, M. del R. *The Texas school dropout survey project: Executive summary.* San Antonio: Intercultural Development Research Association, 1986.

Roe, M.A. *Education and U.S. competitiveness: The community college role.* Austin, TX: University of Texas at Austin, IC2, 1989.

Secretary's Commission on Achieving Necessary Skills. *What work requires of schools: A SCANS report for American 2000.* Washington, DC: U.S. Department of Labor, 1991.

Select Committee for Higher Education. *Report of the select committee for higher education.* 70th Session of the Texas Legislature. Austin: State of Texas, 1987.

State Board of Education. *Career opportunities in Texas: A master plan for vocational education.* Austin: Texas Education Agency, 1987.

State Board of Education and Texas Higher Education Coordinating Board. *Career opportunities in Texas: A master plan for vocational and technical education (1989 update).* Austin: Texas Education Agency, 1990.

Strategic Economic Policy Commission. *A strategic economic plan for Texas.* Austin: Texas Department of Commerce, 1989.

Texas Education Agency. *Texas quality work force planning: Preparing Texas for the 21st century through a skilled and educated work force.* Austin: Texas Education Agency, 1990.

Texas Higher Education Coordinating Board. *A master plan for vocational and technical education, Part II: Master plan for higher education.* Austin: Texas Higher Education Coordinating Board, 1991.

Waddell, G. (Ed.). "Economic and work force development." In *New Directions for Community Colleges, No. 75.* San Francisco: Jossey-Bass, 1991.

CHAPTER XIV

Collaborations involving many and varied partners, such as the Texas Work Force Development effort discussed in the previous chapter, are complex and challenging. Midlands Technical College personnel are involved in several such collaborative efforts. One is of particular interest—Midlands's participation in the central South Carolina Council on Education. The Greater Columbia Chamber of Commerce created the council with the goal of developing a closer relationship between business/industry and education. The council's mission is to foster partnerships that lead to the development of a well-trained, competitive work-force. Midlands president Jim Hudgins was elected president of the 82-member group, and, as a result, the college's involvement is visible. The council is an effective force for improving education, and it also supports the developing tech prep initiatives in the area.

In another example of a multi-partnered team, Alliance 2020 is an initiative led by Clemson University in partnership with South Carolina State University (both land grant institutions), Midlands Technical College, and the 17 other two-year colleges in South Carolina. Funded by the W. K. Kellogg Foundation, the project "is designed to create a model for an interconnected network of constituent-based educational services and lifelong learning with various entry points and delivery systems...more than 3500 FTE faculty on 18 campuses and 173 sites across South Carolina will ultimately be involved in this long-term commitment to developing new ways of bringing programs and services to the people who can benefit from them." For more about these and other interesting partnerships, read Repositioning the College As An Essential Community Partner.

* * *

James L. Hudgins, *President*
Starnell K. Williams, *Vice President for Advancement*
Midlands Technical College
Columbia, South Carolina

REPOSITIONING THE COLLEGE AS AN ESSENTIAL COMMUNITY PARTNER

There is nothing like a dream to create the future.

—Victor Hugo

VISION FOR EXCELLENCE

The best partnerships, it seems, flourish when alliances are based on shared concerns and common goals. More by participation than decree, two-year colleges have become increasingly productive community partners, and their reputation as beneficial collaborators and team players is gaining strength. Since President Truman's declaration that a two-year college would be established in every major population center as a strategy for access to higher education and regional development, community colleges have been vitally linked to their communities. While technology has expanded community boundaries, colleges' commitments to regionally relevant service have remained unchanged.

Community colleges have evolved within their environments and, therefore, are bonded to them in unique relationships. In the early years, communities went to their colleges for the programs these institutions offered. Over time, colleges began to seek information from their communities to determine their particular needs that could be addressed with education, training, and participation in common projects.

Building Communities: A Vision for a New Century (Commission on the Future of Community Colleges, 1988) was the landmark document that captured the essence of community commitment and focused attention within the institutions on the importance of their relationships with the regions they serve. The report cited the need for college leaders to become coalition builders within their communities. Almost as if the term *community* in community colleges was suddenly translated into an imperative, colleges and their supporting populations found new ways to vigorously link their efforts in productive, purposeful initiatives, to play an integral part in community progress.

College leaders seeking to reposition their institutions as active partners in community development have adopted a proactive, flexible policy that whatever contribution *can* be made, *will* be made. Concepts and opportunities for new levels of arrangements with the community are only possible if all participants are open to experimenting with new perspectives on old problems. Change, as expressed in terms of America's ability to compete in world markets, is so fast-paced that teamwork and partnerships between education and communities are no longer just good ideas, they are vital.

Paralleling this pattern of increasing community involvement, the development of Midlands Technical College (MTC) in Columbia, South Carolina, is representative of the dynamic relationship that can form between a college and its community. MTC faced a challenge to evolve from an institution with a purely technical focus to a comprehensive college. The college sought to alter the community's perception of the institution. The college's commitment to community remained unchanged; however, the institution was evolving to support its rapidly changing external environment.

Founded as a single-purpose technical institute in the early 1960s, MTC began its life with a limited focus on quick technical training of area workers for specific job-related skills. The concept of community service and partnership belonged exclusively to a major research university located in the same city. As the community developed a more sophisticated strategy for its future, the college added programs and services that were responsive to the requirements of area employers. Without neglecting the urgent need for technical training, Midlands began offering a broad range of programs designed to provide a balanced, progressive curriculum.

As the college's mission evolved to a more comprehensive level, MTC began developing partnerships with multiple community agencies. The college found that it had to examine the college's relationship to its community and to reposition the institution, if necessary, for maximum contribution. In 1987, Midlands Technical College, by that time best described as a comprehensive community college, adopted a strategy to proactively reposition the college in the community. This deliberate choice involved a survey of its perceived position in the region and the development of the college's first vision statement. Articulated as the Vision for Excellence, the statement presented a concept of the college that included a renewed emphasis on education and business partnerships. A collateral set of value statements, which were adopted at the same time *Vision for Excellence* was published, established contribution to community as a key value of the institution.

A sequence of defining events followed the *Vision for Excellence*. A strategic planning process was established that described the kind of college the faculty and staff desired the institution to be. Through the planning process, the college realized that its image in the community was a barrier to its ability to fully reach its potential as an essential community partner (Hudgins, 1993).

Strategies for achieving the vision included establishing a marketing plan to increase the college's interaction with the community. A major goal of this plan was restructuring the college's image, thereby forming a new basis for enhanced community relationships. This approach proved to be an essential step in multi-level community involvement as it expanded the college's reputation and accountability with leaders from civic, business, and governmental areas, as well as the general public. Image enhancement, through targeted corporate marketing techniques, provided the college's leadership team with a basic platform for introducing MTC as a viable partner in community planning efforts (Williams, 1994). College personnel were encouraged to become more active on community task forces and committees as another way to raise MTC's visibility in the area. A continuing priority was to inform the entire community about the accomplishments and effectiveness of the college. A series of on-campus breakfasts for leaders promoted interaction.

The desire to be accountable to the community resulted in the development and implementation of an institutional effectiveness process at MTC. The resulting institutional effectiveness program grew from an expanded self-study and has become nationally recognized as a model strategy for making institutional effectiveness operational. Key elements of this assessment and renewal strategy stemmed from the college's vision statement and mission, and included an outcome-based evaluation component.

By projecting institutional strengths and addressing accountability to the public, the business community, and funding agencies, the college's significant contributions to community progress were recognized. Outcomes became enhanced opportunities to serve students and contribute to the success of the community. Because the college was able to position itself as a viable first choice in higher education, MTC has had an enrollment growth of more than 81 percent since 1987. Its orientation to student success has produced a comprehensive assessment model that helps students reach their full potential and personal educational goals.

LAY ADVISORY COMMITTEES

Extended outreach, accountability, and active involvement by the college and its leadership team cannot be overrated as key ingredients in establishing the institution's education and training as a vital factor in the community's development plan. Certainly, the active involvement of members of the college family in the community was important to the concept of forming partnerships, but the reverse situation was equally beneficial. In several key collaborations, community leaders entered the college arena.

An active partnership at Midlands Technical College was formed, linking the college's curriculum with the needs of the community through lay Advisory Committees. These sets of professionals from within the business or industry field most closely related to the specific curriculum area under study helped the college make informed decisions about what is taught within the curriculum and what exit competencies are most required by employers. More than 39 advisory committees meet periodically at Midlands Technical College to advise and review corresponding programs. Advisory committees are an integral part of the MTC process known as academic program review, which systematically evaluates each program.

Midlands Technical College established a two-way conversation with its customers and listened to their requests for alternate scheduling. The college now offers a variety of course delivery methods and times, including Weekend College, mini-semesters (short, intensive terms within traditional semesters), evening classes, and distance learning telecourses. All of these demonstrate the institution's intent to be accessible to members of the community on their own timetable.

Community alliances are both traditional, because they focus on service to the community, and innovative, because they spring from opportunities that are evolving with the progressive needs of the community. Reinvigorated and repositioned in the community, Midlands Technical College has assumed a meaningful role in numerous community partnerships. During the past several years MTC has collaborated in multiple concurrent partnerships and initiatives with civic organizations, public schools, senior colleges, and business and industry. Each partnership, unique in its purpose, has contributed incrementally to college and community goals.

CIVIC PARTNERSHIPS

A community college has the inherent responsibility to be involved in civic initiatives and contribute whenever possible to the synergy of purpose that should exist between college and community. Communities, like businesses, have formed teams to meet competitive challenges and maximize community strengths.

Workforce Literacy. Literacy is a common concern to the educational and civic leaders of a community. In South Carolina, the Governor's Initiative for Workforce Excellence, based in the South Carolina Employment Security Commission, addresses the problems related to an undereducated workforce. The program offers employers a range of options for basic skills training that can be tailored for workplace delivery. Basic skills training in this context may mean learning algebra, developing computer skills, or learning to read technical manuals. Programs are customized for each company. MTC, as well as the other 17 colleges in the state's two-year system, has within its continuing education division a workforce specialist to facilitate the linkage between education providers and employers. Workforce specialists serve as training consultants and are experienced in the development and evaluation of program objectives.

Enterprise Zone Designation. The city of Columbia, South Carolina, has applied to the U.S. Department of Housing and Urban Development to be designated as an Enterprise Zone. If approved, the designation will open the way for other grant-funded opportunities. The proposal, which was coordinated by the Columbia mayor's office, includes one of MTC's campuses and the Columbia campus of the University of South Carolina within the proposed Enterprise Zone. In this particular area of the city, low educational attainment is a key concern. The grant will help develop comprehensive education delivery systems such as technical job training, small business development, leadership training, child care for working parents, and transportation to adult education classes. One of MTC's vice presidents and the college's department chair for transitional studies are participating on the Enterprise Zone task force and are designing strategies for delivery of alternative education programs.

Central South Carolina Council on Education. In central South Carolina, the Greater Columbia Chamber of Commerce pioneered the Council on Education, created to foster a closer relationship between industry and education to ensure a more competitive workforce. The mission of the organization charges it with fostering partnerships that will contribute to developing and maintaining a premier workforce in the region.

The Council called together area secondary school superintendents and briefed them on the chamber's intent. After a very positive response from that group, the Council sent letters to key people representing business, industry, education, and government in central South Carolina, inviting them to become active in this innovative partnership. Eighty-two leaders responded with great enthusiasm, and the Council on Education was established. The council elected the president of its local community college as the chair of the organization.

The charge of the chair is to lead the 82-member council and to serve as a catalyst, convener, and resource developer. The decision to create the council was based on a need for communitywide commitment to a quality workforce enhanced by business, industry, and education working together on tough problems with elusive solutions. Council members shared a common belief that education was a basic ingredient for a prosperous community.

Historically, education and industry in this region could not agree on the root causes of some of the area's economic challenges. Education and businesses too often worked in different paradigms, frequently criticizing and analyzing each other, each unable to communicate its attitudes and values to the other.

By promoting dialogue within the Council on Education, business and education began to find fewer faults in each other's operations and to come together to address the problem of the undereducated worker. The Council provides each with opportunities to collaborate on changing existing policies that are detrimental to community progress. The Columbia Chamber's Council on Education also supports the tech prep initiative by asking business and industry to provide support and expertise in informing school boards and district superintendents about the value of tech prep.

Chamber Marketing Efforts. The Unified Marketing Task Force, a project of the Greater Columbia Chamber of Commerce, was created as a partnership designed to define and represent the Central Midlands of South Carolina to a broad audience. The task force drew its membership from economic development agencies, business, cultural groups, government, and education. Midlands Technical College was an active co-partner in this process and was represented on the task force by a senior institutional officer.

The task force sought to create a readily accessible computerized database that described the region in terms important to its various users. The database could be used as a decision-making tool by incoming businesses and people. Before the database was established, however, a lengthy series of focus groups and information-sharing sessions was conducted to gain agreement on the fundamental defining characteristics of the community. The process itself was therapeutic for the participating partners, and the result helped clarify the character and direction of the region for the potential clients of the database and for the partners themselves.

Because community colleges accomplish their mission on a variety of levels, MTC became a focal point in task force discussions and an integral part of the resulting description of the community. For example, families who access the chamber's database in the future will find that there are lifelong opportunities for education and career preparation; businesses will find the basis for a well-educated and skilled workforce in the area.

Armed Forces Personnel Relocation. An unusual opportunity for an active partnership evolved from the U.S. Department of Defense's consolidation/closing of numerous armed forces programs and facilities across the country. When several professional schools located at Fort Benjamin Harrison near Indianapolis, Indiana, received word they would be relocating to Fort Jackson in Columbia, South Carolina, the more than 500 families involved were concerned about moving to an unfamiliar part of the country.

In a partnership with Fort Jackson, a national financial institution, and the South Carolina and Greater Columbia Chambers of Commerce, Midlands Technical College became part of a mission to provide information and assistance to the affected families. Partners in this collaborative effort included the commanding generals of both forts, plus business and civic leaders.

One of MTC's vice presidents flew with four other officials to Indiana to address a gathering of approximately 650 people about the Central Midlands of South Carolina. The trip to Fort Benjamin Harrison followed many weeks of careful research on the concerns and needs of relocating personnel. The group established contacts that produced positive results and significantly lessened the anxiety of many military families.

International Development. MTC became a partner with several civic leaders who traveled abroad on an economic development mission to promote the community as a site for international development. In addition, the college's president, through his role as chair of the Council on Education (previously discussed), also conducted a series of meetings and site visits to gain an increased understanding of Germany's dual educational systems, credited with much of that nation's success in technical education. Partnerships between business and education contributed greatly to the success of the German system. In America, on the other hand, the private sector has traditionally expected the public school system to produce competent, employable graduates, more or less in isolation from the businesses that will employ them. Only rarely do students visit business and industry to observe the application of theory to the world of work. Business leaders just as rarely visit students and teachers in their schools. Site visits to Germany have encouraged new perspectives among MTC and its partners that should help to increase the effectiveness of future collaborations.

College Ambassadors. Midlands Technical College founded a College Ambassador program in 1992, designed to create core groups of outstanding students who would become advocates for the college in the community. The selection process for the Ambassadors included a personal interview to assess the students' desire to serve other students, as well as a minimum GPA.

Each year the process has become more competitive as students seek ways to contribute to their college. The Ambassadors have expanded their original duties of recruiting and registration assistance to include a number of community projects with various agencies and associations, such as working with the Greater Columbia Literacy Council to tutor adults in basic reading skills.

One of the most successful Ambassador projects was a recent campaign to collect school supplies to benefit an area organization that helps homeless and disadvantaged children. The Ambassadors, aware of the current corporate trend of downsizing and restructuring, contacted area offices and arranged to pick up unneeded notebooks, old files, and other such items to distribute to homeless school children. More than 2000 young students received notebooks through this cooperative effort.

Telecommunications. Other Midlands Technical College civic partnerships have generated intra-city visits with the local chamber of commerce, and gifts, such as a satellite reception dish. The U.S. Chamber has given a satellite dish to each of the 50 state chambers of commerce to place in their communities to facilitate the community's participation in national town meetings. MTC will be the local site for this important activity.

Public School Partnerships

A number of partnerships have developed naturally between Midlands Technical College and the area's public school system. Successes of this partnering relationship include federally funded outreach programs, such as Talent Search and Upward Bound, and an increasing market share of area college-bound high school graduates enrolling at MTC. In fall 1992, Midlands Technical College enrolled more than 30 percent of all area high school seniors who went to college, compared to 15 percent in 1987.

In addition, MTC recruiters visited area high schools and encouraged students to consider higher education's benefits and to attend MTC. Beginning in 1987, a few teachers, and within a three-year period, all area principles and district superintendents, invited MTC recruiters to offer the college's admission/placement test in the high schools during school hours. This unprecedented partnership became a positive way to introduce the possibilities of a brighter future to many students who were intimidated by formal admissions processes and their own uncertain academic abilities. The college became the only agency outside of the state's department of education to test for basic skill development in all area high schools. After the initial success of testing in the high schools, the college began offering additional services, such as post-assessment counseling, financial aid information, and on-the-spot admissions in the schools.

Tech Prep Initiatives. MTC was an early activist in the region's response to the national Preparation for the Technologies (tech prep) concept and a partner in the Central Midlands Tech Prep Consortium that links MTC with eight public school districts. The consortium emphasizes strategies in teaching and learning that reach beyond traditional methods of instruction and delivery systems, and encourages cooperation between secondary and postsecondary educational systems. As community commitment to tech prep developed, MTC authored the first federal grant proposal on behalf of the consortium. Members of the MTC staff involved themselves at various levels of the tech prep effort. Contributions ranged from serving on the tech prep consortium board to working on the marketing committee for creating explanatory literature and an identity program for tech prep in the high schools.

Cities-in-Schools Partnership. While much has been accomplished with traditional schools, MTC has also worked with nontraditional educational delivery systems, such as the innovative Cities-in-Schools program. Cities-in-Schools is an alternative high school program designed to increase enrollment and retention of at-risk students in postsecondary institutions. It is often a last chance opportunity for students who have not benefited from the usual educational process. MTC and Cities-in-Schools have a partnership that includes curriculum collaboration, tracking the academic progress of graduates of Cities-in-Schools who enroll at Midlands, providing college faculty mentors to students, and linking Cities-in-School graduates to others who have been successful at MTC. The department chair of developmental studies at the college also serves on the board of directors of Cities-in-Schools.

Elementary School Math Meet. Midlands Technical College is the originator and annual host for the Midlands Math Meet, a day of multifaceted competition for area fifth and sixth graders. Because business and industry stress working in teams, the competition is designed to stimulate and improve problem-solving skills in a collaborative setting. Teams of students from different schools compete in all categories.

The Math Meet is designed for students of all abilities. Students work on practice problems for months in their classrooms, and schoolwide competitions are held to identify contestants. Students from the college's three-county service area participate in the Saturday on-campus event at MTC.

Math Meet questions are presented in four categories: Individual Effort, Jeopardy, Hands-on, and Math at Work. In the Math at Work category, students work problems in the college's Technologies Applications Center, such as calculating the amount of raw materials its robots need to produce a specified number of plastic products. Through the Math Meet, students see firsthand how math plays a role in everyday life and in the workplace.

South Carolina Hall of Technology. Other forms of public school partnerships are important to developing future scientists and technologists. Providing positive role models for area students is one benefit of the South Carolina Hall of Science and Technology on the campus of Midlands Technical College. Recently, Colonel Charles F. Bolden, Jr., astronaut and space shuttle commander, was inducted into the hall in a ceremony conducted in partnership with the South Carolina Science Council, the South Carolina State Museum, and MTC. The full day's activities included morning and afternoon workshops for earth science teachers and students from middle schools throughout the state. Workshops were planned and facilitated by the MTC science department head and the curator of the state museum.

In the afternoon, Colonel Bolden spoke to the students, college faculty and staff, and community guests. He delivered a very provocative speech outlining the choices facing today's students and the opportunities available in the sciences. After his presentation, a permanent research and display room was dedicated as a resource for the community to learn more about the applications of science and technology.

Counselors Conference. MTC is the site of an annual Counselors Conference held on campus for area guidance counselors. The Counselors Conference is jointly planned, sponsored, and funded by MTC and the South Carolina Department of Education to provide professional development and collaboration of counseling personnel from middle schools, high schools, local agencies, and two- and four-year colleges. Themes and topics focus on specific issues requiring joint efforts by these constituencies. The conference provides a forum for discourse on such topics as cultural pluralism, legal and ethical issues in education, facilitating the success rate of at-risk populations, and preparing youth for career and college. Counselors frequently convey their renewed sense of the importance of the partnership between the community college and the high schools, after attending the conference.

Adopt-a-School Partnership. Midlands Technical College has three active Adopt-a-School partnerships with area elementary schools. The college and public school faculties together plan and implement yearlong programs in which core groups of 20 to 30 elementary school students spend several hours each month in a structured, experimental teaching and learning experience on the MTC campus. The program seeks to introduce fifth and sixth grade students to career options and innovative learning in the sciences and mathematics. MTC faculty collaborate with elementary teachers to develop, demonstrate, and perpetuate practical hands-on learning in math and science. In one example, MTC commercial graphics faculty have worked with young students on techniques for producing their school newspaper.

HIGHER EDUCATION PARTNERSHIPS

Midlands Technical College is the largest source of transfer students to the University of South Carolina, outside of schools in the university system, and is a partner with USC in many efforts designed to enhance the ability of the two institutions to serve the community. MTC has also formed partnerships with Clemson University, the Medical University of South Carolina, South Carolina State University, and other four-year institutions, creating expanded opportunities for area students.

Bachelor's Degrees Available. A bachelor of science in health science degree is offered by the Medical University of South Carolina (MUSC), which uses classroom space at MTC. MUSC teaches a full 40-hour curriculum and offers as many as three courses at MTC each semester. Students taking these courses are enrolled at the medical university, and all faculty are MUSC instructors. Students may complete the entire program on the MTC campus. MTC is also working in partnership with South Carolina State University (SCSU) to renew a project that would allow MTC students holding an associate degree in electronics engineering technology to earn a bachelor's degree from SCSU with courses taught by SCSU faculty on the MTC campus.

Partnerships with the University of South Carolina. MTC/USC Connections, an annual program, provides an opportunity for MTC students to tour the main campus of the University of South Carolina and speak with university admissions counselors. This program was first conceived to introduce the concept of transfer to a four-year college to the many first-generation college students who had entered higher education through the local community college. By removing this initial barrier, the program bridged a gap in continuing education plans.

MTC and USC have many other co-programs, including strong articulation agreements and professional development opportunities. One program cluster that is proving to be a stepping stone for women and minorities in the engineering fields is MTC's pre-engineering curriculum—a curriculum that enables qualifying students to enroll at USC as juniors in the college of engineering after completing two years at MTC.

Minority Participation in Science and Math. A grant funded by the National Science Foundation has made possible a partnership called the South Carolina Alliance for Minority Participation in Science and Mathematics (SCAMP), an alliance between MTC and six South Carolina colleges and universities to enhance the success of minority students in technical career paths. The alliance is an initiative to increase the number of minority students participating in the fields of science, engineering, and math and, ultimately, to increase the number of minorities holding doctoral degrees in these areas. Midlands Technical College is partnering in this alliance with two research institutions and four historically African American colleges. MTC is the only two-year college partner in the alliance and is developing the community college model for the region.

The alliance's approach to student success is based on the three R's: recruiting, retention, and research. It promotes interest in the sciences through pre-college programs for high school students and helps these younger students build a stronger learning foundation. As part of the recruiting program, teams of college students and faculty visit high schools throughout South Carolina to identify students interested in technical careers. Once identified, students are given guidance on the programs available through the alliance, which include summer bridge programs, scholarships and scholars programs, math excellence workshops, and direct research internships. Much of the alliance's success is based on helping students do well in identified gatekeeper subjects that lead to understanding advanced subject matter. Other potential partnerships include the possibility of MTC's providing instruction in developmental mathematics for students enrolling in senior institutions that do not offer remedial studies. These courses could be taught on either institution's campus and would be an important link in serving students and contributing to their success.

Educators in Industry Program. Each year MTC, the University of South Carolina, eight public school districts, and businesses and industry in the Central Midlands of South Carolina co-sponsor the Educators in Industry program that combines lectures with tours of area corporations. This collaborative effort exposes educators to current and emerging technologies, labor market trends, and the realities of the workplace. The program provides an increased awareness of the impact of technology on business and education, and a deeper appreciation of the need for their cooperative efforts.

Field tours of businesses and industries provide a window on the roles participating students will fill as future employees. MTC and USC have had very positive feedback on the course from participants, who earn graduate credit for the experience through the University of South Carolina and certification credit from the South Carolina Department of Education.

Alliance 2020. In 1994, Clemson University, in partnership with South Carolina State University (both land grant institutions) and the 17 two-year colleges in South Carolina, led an initiative to develop a new paradigm redefining the role of land grant colleges in the U.S. The multi-year project, funded by a grant from the W.K. Kellogg Foundation, is designed to create a model for an interconnected network of constituent-based educational services and lifelong learning, having various entry points and delivery systems. In essence, the project will examine the ways different institutions with diverse missions relate to each other as education providers. The resulting model will center on eliminating barriers to multidiscipline, multi-institution work. More than 3500 FTE faculty on 18 campuses and 173 sites across South Carolina will ultimately be involved in this long-term commitment to developing new ways of bringing programs and services to the people who can benefit from them.

One of Midlands Technical College's vice presidents represents the college as part of the partnership's core leadership group, Alliance 2020, which is charged with facilitating and piloting this venture. The group will target methods to involve many participants from all areas of the state and serve as a catalyst for fundamental change. Members will travel across South Carolina to interview constituencies and blend capabilities to increase the potential capacity for interaction. Closer collaboration between the grant's partners will broaden the possibility of all of the institutions working more closely on problems and needs of the region.

It is hoped that Alliance 2020 will stimulate an extraordinary level of dialogue and planning policy changes among educational institutions, public and private agencies, businesses and industries, and many populations throughout the state.

Institutional Effectiveness Leadership. In addition to collaborations with senior colleges, MTC has been a leader within its own statewide system of 17 two-year colleges in South Carolina in forming beneficial partnerships. In 1990, MTC was named a Beacon College by the American Association of Community Colleges and the W.K. Kellogg Foundation. The designation was based on the college's leadership role in developing institutional effectiveness initiatives appropriate for two-year community colleges. In partnership with the other two-year institutions in South Carolina, MTC piloted an institutional effectiveness model for the state and led a peer group of effectiveness coordinators through its first two years of formative planning.

At a breakfast meeting with MTC administrators and faculty chairs, the president of the state's flagship university commented that he had been told by the CEO of a local Fortune 500 company that specializes in writing software programs that the company liked to hire music majors from the university that have returned to MTC to earn degrees in a technical field. This, he explained, gave the company a very creative employee with the ability to be successful in the technical arena.

BUSINESS AND INDUSTRY PARTNERSHIPS

The increasingly urgent national goal of economic competitiveness has enhanced appreciation of two-year community-based institutions whose founding principles focus on enabling citizens to be productive, well-educated members of society. Community colleges were proactive in economic development before its current and growing popularity as a national priority.

One of the most powerful reasons for college and community partnerships is the concept of higher education as a gateway to enhanced quality of life and increased productivity for the American workforce. An educated citizenry frequently has been characterized as the most important ingredient for making the transition from a poor to a prosperous economy. For example, much of the success of the Japanese economy stems from a high school graduation rate that tops 94 percent and from the fact that most Japanese workers can interpret advanced mathematics, read complex engineering blueprints, and perform sophisticated critical thinking on the factory floor better than their American counterparts (Thurow, 1992).

Communities are interested in assuring a steady supply of skilled workers and providing on-going retraining opportunities. With low-skill jobs migrating out of the country, and mass production of technology-based products likewise finding a haven off-shore, assuring America's economic strength has become problematic. MIT economist Lester Thurow captured the essence of national concern in his book, *Head to Head*, where he writes that the quality of the workforce will be the key competitive advantage of the 21st century (Thurow, 1992).

One of Thurow's major theories posits that the U.S. has but two choices to offer—low wages or high skills. Unfortunately, the American paradox is that billions are spent annually on an education system designed to educate a workforce for an economic structure that no longer exists. For example, in 1900, 85 percent of the population worked in agriculture; in 1990, three percent worked in this field. In 1950, 73 percent of the population worked in manufacturing; in 1990, the number is 20 percent and declining. The reasons for these dramatic shifts can be traced directly to new technology and automation. These factors, in combination with the willingness of developing nations to provide unskilled labor at very low wages, have shifted the balance of world economics. These changes point to the need to refocus American education.

The retooling of the American workforce is perhaps the most economically critical mission in education today. In both the agricultural and manufacturing economies, only 15 to 20 percent of the nation's workforce needed to be well-educated, with the remainder requiring only minimum skills and the willingness to do hard work. However, the educational demands of the 1990s and beyond require that all American workers be reasonably well-educated in basic skills and have the ability to think, solve problems, and work in teams. Municipalities are looking to their community college partners for education, training, and retraining of local workers. City, county, and state economic development agencies are also turning to two-year colleges for a variety of services (Nielsen, 1994).

South Carolina has developed a comprehensive approach to economic development by offering cost-free training to workers in industries relocating to the state. Such partnerships are aimed at creating a critical mass of skilled technicians that will not only serve existing business, but will attract other high technology industries. With the dire warning that either high skills or low wages are America's only options, the need for full collaboration between business, education, and state and local government is clear.

According to U.S. Secretary of Labor Robert Reich (1993), working partnerships do not automatically occur. Rather, higher education leaders have a responsibility to collaborate with employers and workers to develop an understanding of the skills employers require and the jobs that are most desirable in the labor market. It is essential that all partners take time to develop a clear and shared vision of mutual goals. By working more closely, walls between classroom and workplace settings, academic and vocational instruction, postsecondary and secondary education, and younger and older students are coming down and being replaced with the concept of lifelong learning.

Workplace Literacy. MTC proposes to contribute to the success of community business by implementing a three-tiered system of workplace literacy and pre-employment training. An outgrowth of the college's participation in the Council on Education, this concept is being developed with representatives of the area's major industries to meet their needs. Discussions with corporate leaders made the college aware of their concerns about the education and skill level of people already employed as well as new applicants for skilled positions.

In response to this needs assessment, MTC has proposed a three-part program that will include employment skills training, pre-applicant training, and workplace literacy training. These areas of need reflect the fact that many of the area's unemployed are functionally illiterate. The public school drop-out rate is unacceptably high. The community does not have a critical mass of trained workers that will attract additional companies for technical jobs. The first part, the MTC employment skills program, will train underprepared workers for entry-level positions through intensive sessions incorporating basic literacy and employment skills necessary to obtain employment. It will also include job-specific skills. The second segment, a pre-applicant program, will provide a pool of qualified applicants for specific area job openings. This will be accomplished through pre-screening tests and assessment instruments, as well as general and specific training that provides basic employment skills.

The third program cluster will be workplace literacy training, designed to provide employees with the competencies needed for further job-related training. The instruction will increase the ability of workers to more readily adapt to change, understand and apply technological advances in the workplace, and respond to employer and customer needs more effectively. A Workforce Readiness Task Force is now in place to review and maximize opportunities for collaboration in this critical area of community-wide importance.

The college is active in business partnerships that seek grant funding for providing this workforce literacy assistance and training. Recently, MTC collaborated with five area companies to pursue federal funding of a workplace literacy model. This grant approach underscores MTC's commitment to fulfill industry's needs.

Advanced Technology Partnerships. Midlands Technical College, with an eye to establishing more advanced technology partnerships, has created a teaching factory on one of its campuses to introduce students to the hands-on applications of computer-integrated manufacturing. The teaching factory contains a working plastic cell injection molding process for which raw materials are supplied by area businesses as a demonstration of their support for this innovative enterprise.

The factory itself was made possible in part by a grant from IBM and Digital Equipment Corporation, which provided much of the equipment on the factory floor and in the computerized briefing center. Areas of the college were then made available for tours of business prospects who were considering locating in the area.

MTC is a partner in the Southeast Manufacturing Technology Center (SMTC), a component of a federally funded program that aids businesses in implementing advanced technology. The community college's role in this partnership is to facilitate the transfer of technology to small businesses in the area. Working with the University of South Carolina and several state government agencies, MTC is able to translate the latest in manufacturing technology to suit the needs of companies already in operation by demonstrating how older equipment and practices can be modified to be more competitive. This partnership is aimed at helping industry focus on continuous quality improvements.

Meeting Specific Needs. The college has collaborated with area business to provide pre-employment training to applicants for high-skilled positions. As a major plant was gearing up for expansion, MTC offered an intense three-week session focusing on economic awareness, employee involvement, and quality improvement for prospective employees. Completion of the program did not guarantee students a position; however, they were more likely to be well-prepared for the needs of the company and therefore more employable.

Several large corporations offered MTC courses on the businesses' sites during the noon hour and after work as an incentive for employees to upgrade their job skills. One very successful partnership is called Colonial College, arranged between MTC and Colonial Life Insurance. This Columbia-based headquarters identified more than 400 employees as potential students. Assessment, admissions, registration, advisement, and book delivery were all completed at the company site. Employees have enjoyed the convenience of the experience, and the company is proactively upgrading its workforce.

Another example of a direct partnership with an area business is MTC's participation with the Toyota Corporation's Toyota Technical Education Network (T-Ten). T-Ten is an automotive training program designed to upgrade the technical and professional level of incoming Toyota dealership technicians. Students attend classes at MTC and receive experience for pay at the sponsoring Toyota dealership. Upon completion, students receive an associate's degree.

Toyota Corporation awards the college $500 for each student enrolled in the program, which MTC uses to offset the student's tuition costs. Upon student graduation, Toyota awards tool stipends, professional exam fees, and uniform vouchers. Students receive credit toward master technical status that would have otherwise required several years of field employment.

Economic Development. MTC frequently hosts industrial prospects on its campuses in cooperation with the South Carolina Department of Commerce and the State Board for Technical and Comprehensive Education. Recruiting new industry to the state and existing industry expansion are often contingent on the company's level of comfort with the education and training of the workforce. The college is an active partner in this process. The president of MTC serves on the board of the Economic Development Alliance, which is aggressive in recruiting business to the college's service area.

CONCLUSION

Midlands Technical College's partnerships expand the possibilities of cooperation with civic groups and regional governments, other branches of education, and business. The college often has been the bridge between diverse collaborators—a role that is the heart of the community college's mission. The cornerstone of all activity is the philosophy that community colleges have an essential and unique role in the life, growth, and well-being of the communities they serve.

With enthusiasm, inventiveness, and energy, Midlands Technical College is realizing its vision to make a difference in the life of the community as an essential community partner. The vitality of the work that is being accomplished through active collaborations empowers the entire community to be prepared and competitive for future challenges.

REFERENCES

Commission of the Future of Community Colleges. *Building communities: A vision for a new century.* Washington, DC: American Association of Community and Junior Colleges, 1988.

Hudgins, J.L. "Presidential perspective." *Shaping the community college image.* Washington, DC: American Association of Community College Trustees and the National Council for Marketing and Public Relations, 1993.

Nielsen, N.R. "Partnerships: Doors to the future of community colleges." *Leadership Abstracts,* 1994, 7(5).

Reich, R.B. "Strategies for a changing workforce." *Educational Record,* Fall 1993.

Thurow, L.C. *Head to head.* New York: William Morrow and Company, 1992.

Williams, S.K. "Marketing the vision: A structured approach to marketing higher education." In Baker, G., *Handbook on the Community College in America.* Westport, CT: Greenwood Press, 1994.

CHAPTER XV

<hr>

Internal collaboration among members of the college faculty and staff is another aspect that draws our attention. In the following chapter, Information Technology: Collaborating for Change, Sinclair Community College *relates some experiences of the faculty and staff as they collaboratively constructed a strategic vision to transform their college using information technology. In addition to learning how to work well together, using the products of that collaboration to develop an institutional focus on technology has been the goal of Sinclair Community College. Sinclair's leaders would no doubt agree with Gilley that "the challenge for colleges and universities is to learn to maximize technology before new institutions and forms emerge to meet the educational needs of the twenty-first century and learning flees the academy" (1991, p. 174). Sinclair's idea of "positioning itself as the repository for technological expertise in the community" is underscored by Johnstone's observation that "economic resources will simply not be available to fuel higher education as we have known it...the only road through this minefield is in the direction of alternative modes of delivery, pursued to a large and coordinated scale in alliance with new technologies and new partners for learning" (1994, Part 1, p. 2).*

* * *

Gilley, J.W. *Thinking about American higher education.* New York: American Council on Education and Macmillan Publishing Company, 1991.

Johnstone, D.B. "College at work: Partnerships and the rebuilding of American competence." *Journal of Higher Education.* [online], 1994, 65(2), 168ff. Available: e-mail: lbindx@utxdp.dp.utexas.edu

David H. Ponitz
President
Sinclair Community College
Dayton, Ohio

INFORMATION TECHNOLOGY:
Collaborating for Change

There is one thing stronger than all of the armies
of the world: an idea whose time has come.

—Victor Hugo

Sinclair Community College today bears little resemblance to the original institution founded in 1887 as the YMCA College of Dayton. Sweeping, dramatic changes have marked its growth, especially in recent years. This is perhaps nowhere more evident than in the institution's relationship with the community it serves. Sinclair became the Public Community College of Montgomery County in 1966. The past 25 years have been particularly important in the development of what Sinclair is today—an institution with an enrollment of nearly 21,000, which makes it the largest single-campus community college in the state of Ohio and one of the largest in the United States.

Twenty-five years ago Sinclair began focusing significant energy on what are essentially startup issues—construction of facilities, curriculum development, and faculty development. Operating in an environment of semi-isolation from community issues has changed by necessity. If the Sinclair of 25 years ago was "in" the community but not "of" it, there has been a dramatic shift. The mission of the college has evolved, and the institution now plays an integral role in fulfilling the hopes, dreams, and aspirations of the people that it serves.

SINCLAIR'S MISSION: FINDING COMMUNITY NEEDS AND MEETING THEM

Sinclair's evolving social contract is reflected vividly in the college's newly adopted vision statement, which emphasizes "giving open access to opportunity, intellectual challenge, and self-discovery for students with diverse needs," "commitment to responsible citizenship within our community," and renewed commitment to the Sinclair credo—"find the need and endeavor to meet it." This is the essence of what community colleges should be addressing in their collaborative overtures to their communities.

Citizens have eagerly embraced Sinclair as a vast repository of resources that can solve problems or serve as an agent for change. As the number of the college's graduates grows in a community, so too does the recognition of the institution as a vital resource. The community college's role has grown into one of community problem solving. This has occurred in large part because of new technologies, especially when they have been effectively embraced and used.

USING TECHNOLOGY AS A VEHICLE TO MEET COMMUNITY NEEDS

Community colleges can serve their communities through information technology. To use information technology, college administrators, faculty, and staff first need to work together to identify and thoroughly explore many issues. Early in 1994, Sinclair launched an internal collaborative process that began by identifying what a college president should know about information technology to provide effective leadership for the transformation. Sinclair's key administrators held a series of meetings, and the discussions yielded valuable information. The questions and issues raised had broad applicability—to productivity, to access to learning, and to what a community college needs to do about its investment in information technology.

The final report, describing the outcomes of these sessions, was organized around seven questions.

- How does the institution shape its strategic vision for information technology?
- What are the key considerations?
- What are the ways of looking at information technology issues?
- What is the leader's role in information technology investment?
- What are the issues involving "payoff"?
- What technologies should be adopted?
- What are the transforming issues?
- What are the issues involving measurement of "payoff"?

How Does the Institution Shape Its Strategic Vision for Information Technology?

Establishing an information technology vision that is aligned with and supports the institution's strategic vision and its relationship to the community is critical. Community college faculty and administrators must work collaboratively to establish a vision of a redesigned or re-engineered approach to teaching and learning, using information technology. The investment in information technology can be a strategy for attaining the vision, while at the same time satisfying the spiraling demand for attaining strategic business objectives and collaborative efforts in the community.

What Are the Key Considerations?

Colleges that are making decisions about designing technological approaches to teaching and learning must consider many issues. These include:

- Determining the payoffs, short- or long-term. Who will benefit? (e.g. students, community, etc.).
- Determining the optimum ways of moving the institution toward the vision and infusing technology into the fabric of the college.
- Establishing how the information technology will be supported and how the college will react to global changes.
- Identifying the target beyond the vision: Should the college be a leader or a follower? Should the college be a leader in the community? Is the field changing so rapidly that the college cannot afford to be the leader, or, if it waits, does the college lose strategic position? In either case, the full capabilities of technology should be tapped to access the global community.
- Determining the ideal way of creating strategic opportunities. This includes determining what processes should be adopted to alter and enhance the teaching/learning environment.
- Determining how information technology can be used to accommodate potential new constituencies in the community.
- Developing a checklist of assumptions that will direct how to proceed. College mission and business decisions drive the implementation and use of technology. Strategies and goals, not the technology, must come first. It is important for people to determine what is possible before developing strategies and goals.
- Investing in the training of college personnel. Colleges are becoming market-based. There is no longer a monopoly on learning, and colleges must be concerned with competition, costs, and productivity. There must be a concomitant investment in people. Also, work value is enhanced when the workforce is trained to assume higher work functions.

WHAT ARE THE WAYS OF LOOKING AT INFORMATION TECHNOLOGY INVESTMENT ISSUES?

Geographic Issues
- What communities are being served?
- Where are students physically located in the community?
- How does the college provide access to all segments of the community?
- Who are the teachers (availability of community and global resources)?

Finance Issues
- How does the college ensure efficiency and accountability, and make a clear case that the benefits outweigh the costs?
- As more technology is adopted, different kinds of services can be provided. What costs will be incurred, and what pricing structure will be required as a result?
- How can affordability to community residents be ensured?
- How can efficiency and measurements be built into information technology expenditures?
- How can the college provide access given the limited financial resources of many two-year students?
- How can the college best facilitate networking and integration?
- How can the college leverage partners and alliances to pool resources to promote creativity, learning, and productivity?
- Can the college afford to continue giving students a wide variety of program options?
- After defining the desired level of access, what is the optimum way to align resources to achieve this level and to build in flexibility for growth in access?

Logistical Issues
- Who will have access to information (e.g., students, faculty, community, etc.)?
- What infrastructure is required to support internal access?
- How does the college facilitate anytime/anywhere access for faculty, staff, and students?
- How does the college best provide access (e.g., through distance-learning or just-in-time learning) as a marketing strategy?

Psychological Issues
- How can the college best foster the belief that students "belong" in college?
- When the investment is made, how does the college redesign instructional delivery so that minimal disruption occurs?
- What is the best way to redirect faculty and facilitate fundamental change?

Cultural Issues
- How can information technology be used to remove barriers within the community?
- What is the best way to provide access for the neglected majority?

- Can information technology be used to foster cultural diversity in the college and the community?
- How can information technology be used to empower groups within the community?

WHAT IS THE LEADER'S ROLE IN INFORMATION TECHNOLOGY INVESTMENT?

The college must strike a balance between macro and micro considerations in investment decisions. Change must be driven by vision and strategic opportunity. At some point, the blueprint for building a boat to cross the river of doubt must be tossed. Take a "leap of faith" and use continuous improvement methods to move through obstacles. Transformation becomes easier, and risk is minimized, if focus is maintained on the college's vision.

Quality innovations are the hallmark of a prospering institution—anything less equates with mere survival. However, reaching the jumping-off point requires research and asking appropriate questions in light of the college's unique position in the community. That position involves:

- dealing with multiple constituencies;
- knowing and supporting key players in the college and community;
- being a scholar of the process to create the vision, and articulating and promoting it;
- insisting that the proper issues are studied;
- educating the college's board of trustees;
- reevaluating the mission of the institution based on community needs;
- providing a seedbed for creative faculty and staff to function within the mission of the college;
- influencing national, state, and community external forces to support the college's vision;
- encouraging external decision makers to be supportive of the institution's mission and discouraging them from erecting obstacles;
- positioning the college as the repository for information technology in the community in order to leverage partners and new opportunities; and
- ensuring effective community partnerships with committed vendors. Institutions need more than internal information technology resources to respond to market-based issues.

WHAT ARE THE ISSUES INVOLVING "PAYOFF"?

Payoff to the college and community will come in different forms. By instituting appropriate strategies, the college can address questions of accountability and affirm its role as a major player in the community, foster more revenue streams, engender support for needed tax levies, provide opportunities for financial aid for additional students, and attract state and federal grants. Payoff to the community comes as economic development, increased access to learning, and the opportunity to rely on a proven performer.

WHAT TECHNOLOGIES SHOULD BE ADOPTED?

The college must ask the appropriate questions and have in place the proper strategies to evaluate information. It must differentiate between "leading edge" and "bleeding edge." The college must have a process by which it can tell the difference between "tech wizards" (who tout bells and whistles) and those whose information supports the strategic plan of learning. Seek out those who possess profound knowledge.

WHAT ARE THE TRANSFORMING ISSUES?

The college needs to define the transforming issues. It must prepare itself and its various constituencies to accept the results of transformation—the inevitable fallout of change. To attract support to bring about transformations, the college must help the community understand the issues. Incentives must be provided for the college and the community to embrace change. Promoting information technology as a tool of transformation, as opposed to a mere add-on, engenders outside support. Information technology is a vehicle for change (e.g., facilitating workforce preparedness and economic development) and a means of providing greater efficiency and opportunities for the college.

WHAT ARE THE ISSUES INVOLVING MEASUREMENT OF "PAYOFF"?

How does the college measure the attainment of information technology investment goals? How does it assess or measure productivity? How does the college install a measurement process? While the measurement strategy varies by type of investment (e.g., infrastructure versus specific projects), the assessment provides key decision makers with data for making decisions regarding business/organizational objectives.

Can the college measure the payoff? It is difficult to measure real benefits, and it makes a difference whether one is examining global issues or individual processes. Assessment of most innovations involves measuring something for the first time or in a way that differs from the past. There is a need to combine traditional and nontraditional systems of measurement.

It is important to establish a limited number of critical indicators of performance to determine if the mission is being met. Each institution must develop its own set of key indicators to assess payoff. A variety of indicators can be tailored to function as gauges for individual information technology investments.

Some examples of indicators that may be used are outputs (e.g., FTEs, penetration rate, long-term retention) and inputs (e.g., faculty hourly pay/FTE; class size; state, local, and student revenues). Other key indicators include cost structure, providing access for more people, payoff by cost reductions, and timetable for obtaining returns. Does the investment result in efficiency, effectiveness, or quality? Is value created, or is value lost? The college could also measure expanded or additional services versus the number of staff as a productivity indicator.

USING TECHNOLOGY TO PLAY A KEY ROLE WITHIN THE COMMUNITY

Careful attention to these considerations has helped position Sinclair as a techno-logical resource for the community. Technology plays a key role in Sinclair's collaborative efforts with the community and other institutions. Several examples follow.

Miami Valley Research Park. Sinclair is a member of the governing foundation of representatives from area colleges and universities, as well as the Air Force Material Command and the Aeronautical Systems Center at nearby Wright-Patterson Air Force Base. Miami Valley Research Park is a master-planned development aimed at supporting advanced technology and businesses of the future. Its relationship with major university research programs in the area has earned it the designation "Ohio's Applied Technology Center."

Advanced Integrated Manufacturing (AIM) Center. The Advanced Integrated Manufacturing Center is a partnership between Sinclair, the University of Dayton, and business and industry. It is a state-of-the-art teaching facility for the research and development of advanced manufacturing systems. The center consists of a model factory, applications laboratory, business and engineering support areas, corporate research facility, corporate seminar room, and computer room. Area manufacturers conduct research and development projects with Sinclair and the University of Dayton faculty. A range of education and training programs are offered at the AIM Center—from short-term, customized training, through associate, baccalaureate, master's, and doctoral degree programs.

Dayton Free-Net. Sinclair has cooperated with the University of Dayton, Wright State University, and the Dayton Business Committee to create the Dayton Free-Net. The Free-Net links citizens with the arts, business, education, government, and human services segments of Dayton and provides access to the burgeoning information super-highway. Through dial access to a computer, citizens connect to electronic bulletin board services, electronic databases, and the Internet. Sinclair provides the leadership for and offers a number of courses over the Dayton Free-Net.

Edison Materials Technology Center (EMTEC). EMTEC, a consortium of academic, government, and manufacturing members, develops and improves industrial materials (composites and metals) and manufacturing processes, identifies alternative materials, and improves the quality of processed materials. Sinclair is represented on the board of governors and the technical steering committee; faculty have participated in several applied research and development projects.

Instructional Television Fixed Service (ITFS). Sinclair, Wright State University, and Greater Dayton Public Television have been granted a Federal Communications Commission license to operate an ITFS facility that provides distance learning pro-gramming via wireless cable television. Workforce training programs are broadcast to companies and agencies within a 50-mile radius of downtown Dayton.

Information Technology Applications Center (INTAC). INTAC provides funds for Sinclair faculty and staff to develop artificial intelligence courses, create on-campus applications for artificial intelligence software, and assist businesses in developing artificial intelligence applications. Interactive touch-screen information kiosks have been developed by Sinclair faculty to assist students in selecting majors, scheduling courses, and obtaining information about the college.

Intelligence Systems Application Center (ISAC). ISAC supports applied research in artificial intelligence for the United States Air Force Aeronautical Systems Division located at Wright-Patterson Air Force Base. Sinclair faculty have participated in evaluation screenings of artificial intelligence application projects proposed by the Air Force.

Miami Valley Tech Prep Consortium. Sinclair serves as the host and fiscal agent for the Miami Valley Tech Prep Consortium, which consists of Sinclair, the University of Dayton, 57 area high schools, and numerous businesses in a six-county area. Through curriculum development, faculty development, and articulation agreements, seamless curricula from high school grade eleven through the associate of applied science degree have been created in allied health and engineering technology.

TV Sinclair. Students take independent study courses as alternatives to traditional classroom offerings through audiocassette, correspondence, broadcast and cable television, and videocassette. Students earn college credit toward associate degrees or take classes for personal enrichment on TV Sinclair.

Wright Technology Network. Sinclair Community College was a major participant in forming this consortium of technical organizations in Dayton, Columbus, and Cincinnati. The consortium supports research at Wright-Patterson Air Force Base and deploys commercial products and processes based on Air Force technology. The mission of the Wright Technology Network is to position Ohio as a world leader in advanced technology with emphasis on aerospace by supporting and using the economic, technological, research, and academic resources of Wright-Patterson.

CONCLUSION

Thanks to these and many other collaborations (many of which involve economic development programs), Sinclair and other community colleges have become centers for addressing major community problem-solving challenges in large part because of the role of technology. Technology is a key problem-solving tool. The community believes community colleges have well-managed, high-quality faculty and staff who understand technology, deal with the community in a non-political manner, and are eager to provide assistance.

The rising level of expectations for community colleges comes at a time of competing needs and dwindling resources. Community colleges have been caught in a fiscal squeeze between two ever-tightening pinchers. Certainly, the challenge for community colleges has become one of how to meet increased expectations in a cost-effective, efficient manner. Community colleges have more projects than time and funds will allow them to undertake. Each college needs a process by which it can decide whether to proceed with an outreach project. Several key questions and issues need active policy review.

- Is this a unique need that only the college can meet?
- Does the college need this project to tell its story to the community so the college can become stronger?
- Does the project fit the college's mission statement?
- Does the project have the potential of an additional revenue stream, or will it deplete funds?

As a natural byproduct of the instructional process, community colleges will often find themselves as the leaders of technology in their communities. In addition, because they are adopting more and more technology to solve problems, the demand for services is on the rise, as are expectations and calls for accountability. How does one balance information technology investment with other competing needs?

An institution must balance internal and external considerations. The college must ask: How can we use technology to shape the future that needs to happen, rather than sitting back and letting the future unfold before our eyes? It takes more than retrofitting existing facilities to accommodate the changing nature of instructional space.

Community colleges should seek to apply technology creatively, using it in new ways, including ways for which it was not originally intended. New technological tools will allow the community college to do things that it did not even know it wanted to do. The tools of the future are here today; we must be research-oriented and must re-engineer not only how we do things, but also how we think.

Certainly, to meet increased community expectations and provide greater access, community colleges must promote greater efficiency and accountability. They must link with other resources in the community. Partnerships and collaborations are being based increasingly around technology. By positioning itself as the local repository for technological expertise, the community college is better able to leverage partners and new opportunities in the community.

CHAPTER XVI

> *The best intercompany relationships are frequently messy and*
> *emotional, involving feelings like chemistry or trust. And they should*
> *not be entered into lightly. Only relationships with full commitment*
> *on all sides endure long enough to create value for the partners.*
> —Rosabeth Moss Kanter

Enjoying success in collaborative relationships requires a different kind of leadership and "membership" than that required in traditional, hierarchical organizational relationships. The "how," or process of collaborative efforts, is considered in the next chapter, The Role of the Community College in Building Communities Through Coalitions, *which summarizes the experiences of community college coalition participants. Community college personnel must understand the new kinds of relationships required of them in this age of collaboration. Writers in the field are beginning to offer their observations. Kanter (1994) sees collaborative relationships as going through stages analogous to courtship and marriage. And Gomes-Casseres believes that these are among the lessons learned by pioneers initiating alliances:*

- *Groups are only as strong as the alliances within them: manage individual relationships carefully.*
- *Effective groups are worth much more than the sum of the alliances within them: manage the group as a whole (1994, p. 74).*

The experiences of the community college leaders recounted in the following chapter are stimulating and thought-provoking. Additionally, they help us see that being a good partner is at least as important as developing collaborative leadership skills.

* * *

Gomes-Casseres, B. "Group versus group: How alliance networks compete." *Harvard Business Review*, 1994, 72(4), 62–74.
Kanter, R.M. "Collaborative advantage: The art of alliances." *Harvard Business Review*, 1994, 72(4), 96–108. (Above quote on page 100.)

Janet Beauchamp
Executive Director
Think Tank
Maricopa Community College District
Tempe, Arizona

THE ROLE OF THE COMMUNITY COLLEGE IN BUILDING COMMUNITIES THROUGH COALITIONS

The way to get things done is not to mind who gets the credit of doing them.

—Benjamin Jowett

BUILDING EDUCATION COALITIONS

Communities are changing. The way in which community colleges react to those changes, by leading changes or instigating collaboration, is a major topic on college agendas throughout the nation. "To thrive in the new millennium," says Paul Elsner, Chancellor of the Maricopa Community College District, "a new sense of connectedness and collaboration must be cultivated and, eventually, subsume the old separatist strategies." And, "community colleges have traditionally maintained strong ties with their communities and are thus better positioned than many educational institutions to understand the need for connection" (Elsner, 1993). There is a growing interest in how community and social needs affect learning and the learning environment.

In response to this growing interest, the American Association of Community Colleges selected the Maricopa Community College District to participate in the Beacon College Project. The project called upon its 26 college participants to form consortia with associate colleges to develop exemplary programs or services related to recommendations in the 1988 report of the AACC Commission on the Future of Community Colleges, *Building Communities: A Vision for a New Century*. Each Beacon College selected a different theme to demonstrate building community. Maricopa's theme was Building Education Coalitions. An education coalition is defined in the report to AACC, *Building Communities Through Education Coalitions* (Beauchamp, 1995), as a "structured organization of people representing any combination of schools, community colleges, universities, businesses, government, and community organizations who develop and implement a long-term plan of action to continually address the issues and problems of students, education and community."

During 1993–1994, the Building Education Coalitions project offered regional workshops, coordinated by the Think Tank and the Maricopa Community College District, for community college leaders and their community team members. The purpose of the workshops was to determine how community colleges have successfully developed processes for building education coalitions, how people's attitudes may have been altered by participation in these joint ventures, and what satisfactory outcomes have been achieved and measured. The coalition-building experiences of workshop participants tell a story of successes and valuable lessons in their efforts to serve the community through innovations in the community college.

Representatives from 22 community colleges participated in the interactive workshops with members of their "community team." Teams were combinations of college presidents, deans, faculty, and administrators along with school superintendents, government representatives, business managers, program directors, teachers, and counselors. Several teams included parents, community-based organization members, and university personnel. The workshops experimented with a variety of formats, ranging from keynote speakers, to open-group discussions, facilitated sessions, and small-group activities. The goals were to determine the process for building and enhancing education coalitions, and to determine which workshop format and length was the most effective to help participants understand fully the role of the community colleges in building community coalitions.

This chapter relates what we learned through various means about coalition building in 120 community colleges, slightly less than 10 percent of the community colleges in the nation. In addition to the information gathered from workshop discussions, we collected data from an evaluation and needs survey of the participants of each workshop, from follow-up interviews with workshop participants conducted three months after each workshop, and from interviews with coalition directors to determine to what extent they were leading or actively participating in a coalition.

The results show that projects of the coalitions are geographically widespread and contextually diverse. Their lengths of operation range from one month to 23 years, the average just under five years. The most common focus is secondary system educators. Top program areas are in staff development, retention and at-risk programs, workforce skills, articulation, and systematic change. Community leadership projects include student advocacy in Los Angeles, California; community forums in Phoenix, Arizona; citizen leadership in Beaufort, North Carolina; teacher seminars in Chicago, Illinois; and a principals' academy in Bronx, New York. Many community colleges have formed coalitions to support tech prep, a federally supported program for workforce development.

However, rather than focus here on projects and programs, this review of the Beacon College Project aims to provide a sense of the human interactions and group processes that occur in college-school-community partnerships. It offers the impressions of people in American community colleges as they work to build a sense of community through the development of education coalitions. College representatives relate how they are defining their roles and the developmental processes they are experiencing as they work to build communities beyond college walls. Their experiences tell of valuable lessons learned.

BACKGROUND

School-college partnerships have existed for more than a century. Jennifer Wallace, in her report, *Building Bridges* (1993), for the Education Commission of the States, says that one the earliest partnerships was initiated in 1892 at Harvard University. The goals then were similar to those of many partnerships today—improvement of teacher preparation, better articulation between secondary and postsecondary sectors, sharing of resources. Concerns expressed at the time were also similar to today's considerations:

* fear of lack of recognition,
* fear of losing control over territory,
* fear of domination by coalition partners,
* distrust, and
* lack of long-term commitment (Wallace, 1993).

Wallace (1993) says, "In the 1930s, the Progressive Education Association explored strategies for better school-college relationships. The post–World War II years saw an increase in the need for cooperation in training new teachers." Government policy, in response to Soviet superiority in satellite technology in the late 1950s, encouraged partnerships between business and schools through incentive grants from the National Science Foundation. In the late 1960s, a series of reports from the Commission on Higher Education of the Carnegie Foundation for the Advancement of Teaching (1984) raised new issues in school-college partnerships, such as increasing the number of students who aspire to higher education. The career education movement in the 1970s and interest in free enterprise education in the 1980s brought formative training on building relationships, not only between schools and colleges, but also with businesses and communities. Today, all of these driving forces are still present, with the additional need to address issues of diversity and a multitude of social problems.

THE ROLE OF THE COMMUNITY COLLEGE

Community colleges are being called upon to expand their roles. While school-college cooperation and other types of partnerships have been widely practiced for over a century in this country, the pressures placed on today's community colleges to help solve community problems via coalitions have increased dramatically. One consequence of these pressures is that issues regarding the community college mission come to life.

Community colleges, more than at any other time in their history, must now define, with greater clarity and sophistication, their distinctive mission as they reaffirm their determination to render service to their communities and the nation (Commission on the Future of Community Colleges, 1988, p. 6).

A majority of Beacon College Project participants believed that community colleges should be active in the development of an education-community coalition. While no one indicated that his or her college had a specific policy addressing this issue, each agreed that the community college is in a good position to lead community response to student needs. It was suggested that if community colleges expect to be heard, they should, at a minimum, be a part of the core group that organizes an education coalition.

Many argued that the role of the community college in building and enhancing education coalitions should be that of the proactive leader who convenes the initial meeting, articulates the issue(s), states the expected outcomes, and projects a clear vision of what the coalition can accomplish. Others felt that the role of the community college should be one of neutrality, acting without a preconceived vision, but recognizing the need to work in harmony with the schools and community.

Two community college representatives saw their role in coalition development as dependent upon certain circumstances:

- The community college should be the convener of education coalitions when "it is their issue."
- The community college should be part of the core group that creates a coalition when the college is a primary contributor.
- The community college should wait to evaluate the match between its mission and the coalition's mission when there is no consensus regarding the desired outcome.

There was a minority opinion that the role of the community college is solely to provide students with an academically excellent institution in which to prepare for life and work. No workshop participant indicated that the social needs of students should be ignored, but some felt that the community college can best serve the community on its "home court" and that to offer outreach would mean "watering down" services, especially when no additional resources are given specifically to support coalition activities. These people felt that when colleges extend services, efforts should be extended through an "appendage" of the institution, not through an integral part of it. Such a structure would allow severing relationships and services without harm to either the image of the institution or the students.

For those colleges that decide to become actively involved:

Building community must...begin at home. If the college itself is not held together by a larger vision...inspired by purposes that go beyond credits and credentials, the community college will be unable to build effective networks... beyond the campus. If the college itself is not a model community, it cannot advocate community to others (Commission on the Future of Community Colleges, 1988, p. 7).

On the other hand, is it not possible that the college may learn more about being a community within itself by inviting its staff to participate in community coalitions? The task of self-renewal is not easy and often is stimulated by another experience not so close to home. For example, within a national group called Renewal and Change for the Year 2000 (RC-2000), community college presidents and chancellors of large urban districts share information about how their colleges are building communities. Their extensive community engagements are rich learning experiences that help to change the structure of their institutions into "boundaryless" living systems—systems that have the inherent ability to grow with the needs of their communities and to help gently place the coalition into a position of entrusted power.

THE NATURE OF WORKING IN A COALITION

The process of building a sense of community is one in which members are bound together by a common vision, sharing a commitment to improve the quality of living and learning. Community building through working coalitions creates a new kind of entity, different in structure and process.

We have not been able to solve our problems within existing institutions, so it seems appropriate that we draw out the best ideas and innovations to create a new institution that represents the self interests of the rest. In doing this we will have represented the best thinking and resources, as well as the greatest problems and issues, to solve problems collectively. [It is] through community conversations that we can shift our focus from turf isolation to community building. This is not only possible, but it is happening—in small, but significant, ways throughout our nation (Elsner, 1994).

In a coalition, members of different organizations work together, united in a mission, sharing experiences and decision-making responsibilities. This creates a new arena where all members have an equal stake and new power sources are identified collaboratively. Because this is a new entity, participants are not always certain what the rules are and what their role is.

The role of the community college in building a sense of community was described by project participants as exciting, frustrating, rewarding, confusing, complicated, productive, and extremely tiring. Most Beacon College Project participants were leaders, members, and/or followers involved in one or more coalition attempts to solve community problems. While participants reported beginning their collaborative journey with an enthusiasm for the potential impact that working together can bring, most were unaware of the time, resources, and challenges this type of effort required before desired outcomes were achieved. In fact, an Arizona study demonstrated that most collaborative teams dissolve—or a majority of members leave—before goals are achieved (Beauchamp, 1989). For some, the venture is fulfilling a dream; for others, the journey is fearsome and frustrating.

DETERMINING THE VISION

Successful coalitions have a vision that all members share. "We must struggle through the process of defining a common purpose that engages everyone in the coalition. Otherwise, individuals return to their own agendas," said a Phoenix educator. This new approach to consensus building, as compared to previous forms of democratic voting, means that diverse thinking is channeled in the same direction. The previous "majority rules" scenario meant that the "minority lost," and losers frequently would undermine the team effort—no matter how meaningful. Most participants seemed comfortable, even appreciative, with the attention to understanding people's values and priorities. This works best when aligned with an atmosphere of wanting to share and support each other. Workshop participants understood the need to work within various cultures and had a sensitivity to diverse needs.

Business partners are likely to be less patient with the process and to be more task-oriented. Some noted that using systems thinking and a prioritization process, such as the tools in TQM (Total Quality Management), can hasten the consensus process. Education, community, and business participants all recognized that reaching consensus on a vision takes time in the beginning, but doing so results in more effective outcomes and keeps relationships intact for future joint actions, thereby saving time over the long run.

The importance of unified purpose cannot be overstated. As Elsner observed, entities "lose vitality when there is no vision widely shared." Unifying around a common vision was the single most cited reason for success—for both colleges and coalitions—mentioned in workshop discussions. One participant stated: "Once you agree together, you can go [forward] together."

STAGES OF COALITION DEVELOPMENT

There are four progressive stages, or levels, in the development of a team. The progression starts with an agreement, which may progress to a partnership, then become a collaboration, and finally, evolve to an operational coalition. The time required for this progression varies. Some coalitions pass very quickly through the first three levels, but not all groups progress to the advanced levels.

Building a coalition often starts with an idea for a program or activity involving representatives from more than one organization. The first level—agreement—is reached when representatives from more than one organization agree to a mutual purpose and come to a consensus on the goals of a program. As more resources are added to the successful program, the second level, partnership, may be attained. Levels one and two are characterized by the need to acquire and use finite community resources, such as money, time, materials, or equipment, efficiently. The third level, collaboration, is realized as the partnership commits more resources, assumes more responsibilities, and broadens its membership. A group at the collaboration level is distinguished by the need to sustain or enhance agreement and partnership activities through the infusion of new ideas and networking. The members of an operational coalition—the fourth level—share a long-term commitment to work collectively on selected community issues, some of which may not be defined. Operational coalitions are energized through long-range visions and a facilitation process that brings broad community ownership.

It is interesting to note that most Beacon College Project participants, after discussion, decided that the majority of their coalitions were operating at levels one, two, and three with a greater focus on programs. They observed, however, that the social aspects of "networking" are prominent in sustaining levels three and four. There was clearly a felt need to learn how to manage and observe the process of team development.

Because of the uniqueness of each situation, a step-by-step cookbook for developing a coalition would be difficult to write, and the exact replication of a functional coalition in one community may not be possible in another. Sharing "lessons learned" is believed to be more beneficial than attempting to replicate structures or other program components. This chapter, therefore, will summarize some lessons learned by community college personnel working in education-business-community coalitions, quoting workshop and survey participants when possible.

LEADERSHIP IN COALITIONS

Leadership in coalitions comes in two distinct forms: personal leadership and coalition leadership in the community. Although the two are interdependent, the first developmental priority is to recognize, recruit, and exercise personal leadership. This requires an understanding of what constitutes effective leadership. Participants felt that the term leader is used too frequently, with vague and varied meanings. Leadership, whether referring to personal or coalition leadership, connotes that there are followers. Workshop participants agreed that the term "leader" should not be used to describe position. A term such as "manager" might better describe position, they felt.

Workshop participants described their favorite leaders as visionaries, listeners, cheerleaders, coaches, consensus builders, promoters, action-oriented, and willing to follow through. Most approached the subject of leadership with personal humility. When asked, "Who of you considers yourself to be a leader?" few hands were raised. At the conclusion of the workshop, however, when asked the same question, most participants felt that they were leaders. When asked how the leadership characteristics above compare with the characteristics of a coalition acting as a community leader, they responded with the same list, but with one addition—unifier. Edgar Boone, Director of ACCLAIM at North Carolina State University, offers another perspective when he states:

> A number of approaches may be used to identify leaders...Which approach one uses in identifying leaders of a target public for a specific issue varies. The goal is to identify those leaders who reflect the beliefs and values of the target public and who wield influence among its members (1992, p. 6).

Personal Leader. Participants listed the components of leadership as role identification, implementation, measurement, communication, risk-taking, and celebration. Personal leaders of a collaborative team first must understand the issues, then be able to articulate them effectively, thus projecting a clear vision of the coalition's goals. The ability of a leader to accomplish this will determine the extent to which community leaders and team members believe in and commit to the goals, and sustain the coalition. Leadership "from the top" is a must, but it should not stop there. As groups develop meaningful mission statements and agree upon a course of action, it becomes easier to lead the effort at all levels. Sustained leadership of coalitions is difficult to maintain due to a lack of rewards and incentives, change in personnel, and limited resources. Wheatley observed that:

> Discussions of existing partnerships tend to focus on current leaders as the key to sustaining commitment and fail to consider the need for leaders to create a culture that will outlive them, to have strong leadership at all levels, or to seek broad systemic support (1993, p. 7).

Participants observed also that the role of leadership is to articulate the vision and clarify the mission of the coalition and that "consensus leads to empowerment [which] leads to leadership." In order to assume the responsibility of leadership, one needs first to build the confidence and self-recognition of that ability. Others empower by bestowing the right on a leader to lead; however, "inpowerment," or internal permission to act as a leader, has to come from confidence. That confidence can be gained through group discussions and consensus on the issues. Leadership is a learned and demonstrated skill. It should only be recognized and rewarded when it works. The participants in the Beacon workshops felt that an empowered state of leadership is present when leader and followers reach agreement. An empowered state of leadership requires broader commitment from policy makers, community leaders, faculty, and other agency workers serving students to keep the coalition movement alive.

Because coalitions are created and led by a volunteer effort, the responsibilities are often short-term. A broad and deep commitment is essential to share the burden of work and accountability in coalitions. While institutions gain stability through job descriptions, reporting traditions, and payrolls, new coalitions require a whole new scheme of organizational design and management. When left to chance, or to people with "time on their hands," coalitions die an early death. They are not for the faint-of-heart, nor for curiosity-seekers; they should be treated as though the success of their individual missions are directly dependent on the success of the coalition.

Shared leadership, which is found in effective coalitions, requires a transition from control by the leader to empowerment of others in the team. The unanswered question for many is: "How do you give away control, but maintain order and authority?" This is an especially significant challenge to those who have been trained and rewarded in a more traditional, hierarchical management style. It is often difficult for the "person in charge" to let go of old, comfortable ways and begin to work with the group to solve problems in new ways. Wheatley notes:

The habit of solutions that once worked…are now totally inappropriate…having rug after rug pulled from beneath us, whether by a corporate merger, reorganizations, downsizing, or a level of personal disorientation. I believe that we have only just begun the process of discovering and inventing the new organizational forms that will inhabit the twenty-first century. To be responsible inventors and discoverers, though, we need the courage to let go of the old world, to relinquish most of what we have cherished, to abandon our interpretations about what does and doesn't work. As Einstein is often quoted as saying: 'No problem can be solved from the same consciousness that created it.' We must learn to see the world anew (1993, p. 5).

The leader's responsibility is to lead the coalition team to an agreement on the issues, needs, and opportunities, and then to work with the group to create solutions and to find resources for effective implementation. Many interviewees recognized that the tools and techniques of TQM effectively support this role. Another of the leader's responsibilities is to devise strategies that guide the process from the beginning stage, in which coalition members are getting to know one another and are engaged in a social agenda, to a focus on the mission and the development of a program that will achieve that mission.

The Coalition as Leader. Many of the of characteristics of good personal leadership also apply to the leadership that the coalition provides to the community. Participants agreed that education coalitions must provide strong leadership in their communities, for several reasons. The coalition represents varied and divergent interests derived from a broad cross-section of the community. When this thinking blends into a consensus, it demonstrates how a whole community can think and act together. Coalition leaders recognize that often an organization cannot solve its own problems, much less the problems of an entire neighborhood. When the coalition truly represents the stakeholders on any issue, it can speak for the community. For example, a school-business council can make recommendations for academic changes based on industry needs. Other issues may include strategies to impress on the legislature the need for increased funding or to collectively portray the "best practices" in education to combat negative publicity. An issue that may be perceived as one group's self-interest, if heard only from that group, may be perceived as fact when stated with a communitywide voice.

LESSONS LEARNED

Collaboration Equals Relationships. Workshop participants agreed that, when it comes to creating a highly functioning coalition team, collaboration is about relationships! Relationships take time and awareness to develop and will always be the backbone of the coalition. Conversely, the deterioration of participant relationships was reported as the number one reason for the dissolution of a coalition. Change takes place, therefore, within relationships, not programs. Wheatley summarizes this concept: "With relationships, we give up predictability for potentials. If nothing exists independent of its relationship with something else, we can move away from our need to think of things as polar opposites" (1993, p. 144).

Working together as a community requires learning how to change the way we do business for the long term; for example, developing new, non-confrontational ways to manage decision-making tensions. An outgrowth of this professional development is learning how to manage community assets and resources for the benefit of both individuals and communities. What is being sought in the 1990s is honest caring and sharing. As a result of relating in this new way, a new sense of freedom is gained. There is a growing welcome for shared responsibility and shared risk-taking. In an address to the 1994 Leadership 2000 conference, Mike White, Mayor of Cleveland, recently quoted Andrew Young as saying, "We all came here in different ships, but we are in the same boat now." A fully functioning community coalition acts like one boat, with oars working harmoniously for progress.

When building coalitions, participants are forced to consider the consequences of the process of making connections between people and institutions. These connections do not simply happen. Rather, a complex mix of experiences, values, cultures, perceptions, and assumptions must be dealt with first—even before a plan of action is designed. It is important to be sensitive to diverse needs. Wheatley quotes Donella Meadows, who describes an ancient Sufi teaching: "You think because you understand one you must understand two, because one and one makes two. But you must also understand and" (1993, p. 9). When we view coalitions in this way, it changes the way we form opinions and how we act on those opinions. We are forced to consider the consequences of the process of making connections between people and institutions.

Another way to look at a new concept of leadership is holistically, that is, viewing the parts as a single entity that was created by the various experiences of participants. Wheatley summarized the phenomenon of a new institution in this way:

Scientists in many different disciplines are questioning whether we can adequately explain how the world works by using the machine imagery created in the seventeenth century, most notably by Sir Isaac Newton. In the machine model, one must understand parts. Things can be taken apart...and put back together, without a significant loss. The assumption is that by comprehending the workings of each piece, the whole can be understood. The Newtonian model of the world is characterized by materialism and reductionism—a focus on things rather than relationships and a search in physics, for the basic building blocks of matter (1993, p. 9).

People's values and priorities must be understood in a supportive environment. The goal of this new institution, some would say, is to get the neighborhood to work for itself—politically and economically empowered—with a common vision that includes calling on one's neighbors when needed.

It is important that members of a coalition become a team, working with a constancy of purpose. Some interviewees noted that teams develop, much like coalition structure evolves, in a series of stages. The stages of team development are much like the stages of courtship and marriage. The first stage is getting acquainted. One interviewee described this as the "mating dance"—the ritual of getting to know and accepting one another. The timing and style of this dance varies with the personalities involved and their level of commitment to action. The second stage is positioning. At this stage people state their positions and stake out control points. The third stage is achievement, when the members become adept at working together productively. The fourth stage is maturity, the natural state of making decisions together and moving more rapidly to desired output. Coalition members at this stage may say that their relationship "clicks."

As new team members are added to the coalition, the group experiences various degrees of each stage all over again. Coalition directors, for this reason, attempt to have "seasons" for new membership, so that special attention may be allotted to assimilating new people into the process, rather than assuming that the process will take place without assistance.

Beacon workshop participants, who felt that their coalition had reached the mature stage, referred to a state of effectiveness, but not always efficiency, in terms of allotment of time to group process. They felt that this was an acceptable tradeoff, given the importance of maintaining relationships in the group.

"Attitude Is Everything!" The necessity to begin with a positive attitude was cited consistently as a major factor in determining success or failure. American higher education, as American society in general, suffers from a growing climate of mistrust, sometimes hostility, and frequently fear, between races, generations, and public and private sectors. Ours is a system of constant change, self-renewal, and individuality. As responsive community colleges, we must support individual growth and build trust. Beacon participants generally agree that a sense of wholeness and an appreciation of interdependence are needed and that these can develop when a community comes together to solve common problems. Collaboration is about relationships, and the success of relationships depends on attitude.

Some coalitions begin with an "attitude adjustment" session to encourage more positive thinking and optimism about the abilities of young people and adults. It is emphasized that all different personalities and cultures can make positive contributions to a whole community. Experiences in alliances between classrooms, campuses, and communities can evoke kindred values and needs, and remind the participants that they are more similar than different. Young people and adults alike are encouraged to discover their roots and talents and to use them, in concert with others, to enhance the community and achieve coalition goals.

"The Experts Are Among Us." The question of who should be speaking with expertise opened the discussions about who were the most knowledgeable on the content and process of community building. Beacon College Project participants' opinions varied considerably, but a majority felt that "leadership comes at all levels." The belief that there are just a few knowledgeable people in any group gave way to the idea that everyone has something to contribute. Working together, a group can design a plan of action that is better than a plan developed by one person working alone. Coalition directors understand that they cannot know everything necessary to solve problems in a community. They are also learning that within their midst there is great knowledge, waiting to be invited to the planning table.

"To Be Successful, You Have to Love the Process." The most frequent reasons given for coalition ineffectiveness were "impatience" and "conflicting opinions." In the workshops, patience was described as a process having four elements—listening, understanding, learning, and committing time. Overall, as groups worked together for longer periods, members reported becoming more aware of the need to focus on the process of forming a structure and a plan, rather than devoting full time to the product as the total goal. Participants who had succeeded in team development in their coalitions felt that efforts to build trust and consensus were worth the time invested. Many believe that trust does not come overnight.

Conflicting opinions or disturbances were once viewed as a sign of trouble. The prevailing thought today, however, is that chaos can lead to creative order. The magic ingredient in the process is time—along with willingness to learn and to grow into a new way of thinking and acting. As evidence of this understanding, one workshop participant noted, "the old way of acting hasn't worked very well, so it seems right to try something new." At times, discussions in Beacon workshops seemed chaotic and loud because participants were in an obvious state of disagreement. However, as views were heard, a broader understanding resulted and a new sense of order emerged. Again, Wheatley can shed some light on this process:

Disorder can play a critical role in giving birth to new, higher forms of order. As we leave behind our machine models and look more deeply into the dynamics of living systems, we begin to glimpse entirely new ways of understanding fluctuations, disorder, and change. In motivation theory, our attention is shifting from the enticement of external rewards to the intrinsic motivators that spring from the work itself. Or, in other words, it helps to love the process of coalition team building (1993).

Another comment that brought smiles and sighs of recognition was: "My reason for giving in to consensus planning is laziness—it is simply easier to work with the group, sharing the burdens. I end up with more free time, more energy, and—surprisingly—more power." This was experienced in the speaker's third-grade class, where the students took responsibility for their daily schedule by creating a flow chart of activities.

As people begin to understand each other—their values, experiences, priorities, and styles of thinking—they also begin to understand that there can be a natural order to the change process. People want to be heard; they want to be effective; they want to be recognized. However, these needs cannot always be addressed in a two-hour meeting where expectations for action are high.

Business and Education: Partners with Different Approaches. Several interviewees observed that business people and educators approach the process of decision making differently. Educators tend to discuss and recommend at the committee level, review and confirm at the administrative level, review and approve at the board level, delegate within the administrative level, and finally assign for implementation to the staff level. This is a time-consuming process in which no one person "owns" the recommendation or decision. Educators in the coalition tend to follow this time-consuming process for making decisions about day-to-day operations or larger decisions that may affect systemic change.

People in business, on the other hand, tend to have a more streamlined approach to decision making. Their process often consists of discussion and recommendation at the committee level, review and approval at the executive level, and delegation of implementation to the staff level. This process is designed for time efficiency, because in business the timely claiming of a niche in the marketplace has a direct impact on profitability and organizational viability. While quick decision making is efficient, it may not always be as effective in terms of group "buy-in" and loyalty to the process. Merging two companies, for example, may happen quickly in an attempt to avoid trauma and complaints, but unexplained decisions may draw rebellion when it comes time to reposition the employees.

Coalition business partners are often frustrated by this process disparity. There is a difficulty with the time differential, and business people often do not understand issues from the educators' viewpoint, nor can they comprehend educators' limited resources (primarily of staff time) that are available to take action once the decision is made and responsibility is delegated. Business people are most often accustomed to implementing their decisions immediately, and the delays inherent in the educational system frustrate many to the point that they lose interest and leave the coalition. Conversely, it was noted that because the process of change is slower in education, the vision acquires ownership throughout the organization, team members are more bonded, and the implementation is more methodical. One participant noted, "If we jumped to implement every suggested change immediately, we would spend more time fixing the system than teaching. Our students cannot afford that."

Training Is Important. Assuming responsibility, like any new role, requires training and practice. Beacon participants give a high priority to training programs that bring together leaders at all levels and from diverse organizations. By bringing together a mixture of talents and positions, and providing an opportunity for people to discuss their experiences during training, those who are in charge of the daily operation of coalitions will find their jobs easier and more rewarding. Many stressed that such training could be a primary source of networking and could provide the information exchange needed to avoid "reinventing the wheel." The creation of cross-functional teams, representing all aspects of the coalition, should be the target of such training sessions. Team members should have opportunities to practice new techniques in non-threatening settings before using these techniques in real-life situations.

"A Crucial Task of Leadership Is Evaluation." Evaluation is the linking of past activity to future efforts. Students, parents, taxpayers, business persons, and college faculty and staff all want to know that their time has been well-spent and that the coalition's vision is achievable. Historically, society has rewarded leaders who could speak with emotional conviction and, while those with loud voices are still heard today, their followers will evaporate if hard, convincing evidence is lacking. In our current world of numbers and science, we seek truth through proof. One coalition member offered this observation: "In God we trust—all others bring data." The proper use of data is to evaluate continuously for improvement...not just reaching standards, but to go beyond standards to goals that are mutually set by the stakeholders in the community coalition. Stakeholders operating from different paradigms—they may be policy makers, frontline practitioners, sideline spectators, or bean counters—look for different kinds of data.

Research data can also engender understanding of and commitment to the coalition mission. For example, convincing faculty of the value of adding service learning to the curriculum may be facilitated by sharing quantitative and qualitative data attesting to the value of such experiences and learning. We need for the faculty to be convinced that the community has something of value to offer in the process—but we must be able to prove it, or the tactic will become just another trend.

Coalitions can benefit by using data enriched beyond numbers and statistics to include real-life stories portraying feelings, experiences, dreams, and failures. The charts that confirm large percentages of dropouts, for example, can come alive when supplemented with stories of the children and adults who struggle to succeed in school and in life. The most powerful leaders in the 1990s learn how to tell factual, but visual, stories that compel action. Some coalition directors are considering the benefits of inviting members from the disciplines of theater, psychology, and literature to help the group enhance this type of communication.

Many coalitions are designing change strategies based on research results, but data do not become information until they are interpreted. Interpreted data are learning tools, supports for rational decision making, and useful in gaining commitment. When using data for decision making, change agents can use constant feedback on how things are going to plot their courses of action. Also, those who will determine the fate of the coalition activities want to determine if the investment has been worthwhile. Research data can be used effectively for continuous improvement. For example, elementary and secondary schools can benefit from feedback from postsecondary institutions on how their former students are doing, so that they know which methods are working.

Change agents, like students, need constant feedback on how things are going. Otherwise, they are unmotivated to continue to change and learn. Just as evaluation results can inspire, inform, and assist with achieving institutional change, coalitions that demonstrate successful and continual evaluation processes stand the best chance of receiving sustained support. Community college coalition members, therefore, could benefit from training in evaluation processes.

"The Plan Is the Script, Which Can Be Rewritten Daily." Many participants believed that every coalition must create a long-range plan. Included in this plan should be a clear statement of vision, a strong mission statement, realistic goals with an attendant commitment of resources, and specific roles and responsibilities for coalition members committed to their successful implementation. The difficulty of operating a coalition without a plan is exemplified by one coalition's experience. Its representative noted that implementation of decisions was uncoordinated, resulting in wasted efforts and materials.

Participants in the Beacon workshops were encouraged, however, to learn that plans could be fluid and flexible to allow for adaptability. Indeed, some agreed with Karl Weick's contention that:

> Acting should precede planning, because it is only through action and implementation that we create the environment. Until we put the environment in place, how can we formulate our thoughts and plans? Strategies should be 'just

in time'...supported by more investment in general knowledge, a large skill repertoire, the ability to do a quick study, trust in intuitions, and sophistication in cutting losses (1979, pp. 223, 229).

" 'How-To' Cookbooks Probably Wouldn't Help Much." The pressure of time and the desire not to "reinvent the wheel" has led many to seek a manual or set of guidelines that would provide a model for organizing a new coalition, with checkpoints for identifying appropriate activities at different developmental stages. Because of local variations, however, a step-by-step cookbook for developing a coalition would be difficult to write and the exact replication of one functional coalition in another community may not be possible. One coalition member reported a need to reorganize during the first year of operation because members initially tried to replicate another coalition's structure. What was not accounted for in the replication process was that the assumptions and community environment in the "model" were different from the needs in another community. Inevitable operational difficulties arose and were accompanied by the frustration of lost time and effort. Applying "lessons learnèd" as basic guidelines is felt to be more beneficial than structure, or program, replication.

Much information is available through directories and databases on model programs.

These directories and databases provide a valuable network of people and ideas. What they don't do, however, is provide guidance in how to assess one's current situation—what human and other resources are available, in what type of culture will the partnership operate, [or] how to decide what elements of various partnerships are right and how to measure progress (Wallace, 1993, p. 4).

In Wheatley's words:

I no longer believe that organizations can be changed by imposing a model developed elsewhere. So little transfers to, or even inspires, those trying to work at change in their own organizations. There are no recipes or formulae, no checklists or advice that describe "reality." There is only what we create through our engagement with others and with events. Nothing really transfers; everything is always new and different and unique to each of us (1993, p. 4).

Lessons learned from other examples bring new questions to ask and new levels to try to reach.

"The Benefits Must Be Consistently for the Students." Participants reported that the coalitions which maintained a consistent focus on students and the forces that impact their ability to be successful were more likely to stay the course until satisfactory outcomes were realized. For this reason, if for none other, it is important to include college faculty and school teachers in the planning and implementation of collaborative activities. Coalitions that were formed because it "was the 'in' thing to do" or whose members were coerced into membership through guilt or political force, rather than with a focus on student success, were less likely to be successful. Such groups were more likely to disband before coalition goals were reached. Benefits of coalitions usually fall into one or more categories of direct benefit to students or indirect benefit to students through teacher/faculty enhancement, improved relations with community, or new resources. A somewhat new trend, brought about by the quality movement, is to deploy all educational resources against student needs. This brings more attention to how time and funds are being spent in relation to a plan for successful student recruitment, retention, and achievement.

Enhancing Teaching and Learning. Coalitions provide a rich training ground for teachers to learn about cooperation and later to encourage cooperation among their students as well. Other benefits of the connectedness that comes through membership in coalitions include sharing of teaching approaches and techniques, an increased sense of civic responsibility and commitment, and valuable insights on a host of social and community issues. Faculty and staff who benefit in these ways often pass along the benefits to students by way of improved teaching.

Other Benefits. The recent attention to community service (or service learning) has added benefits for community coalitions. By using the classroom as a community, students, faculty, and community "teachers" become equal partners in the learning process. Goodwin Liu cautions that "we should not use the community as a laboratory for that is seeking what we want rather than seeking what students and community want. We need to be responsive to and preemptive to the issues of the day" (Liu, 1994). If the role of the community college is to become that of a facilitator for resource sharing, then the faculty, staff, and administration must be experienced in this role through their own community collaboration effort. The interactions in the Beacon workshops demonstrated that those involved in coalition building have a deep commitment to open, candid communication and problem solving—once the environment is provided and the risk is shared. The community colleges appear to be readying themselves to take on the role of comprehensive, cohesive, and creative institutions that accept challenges far beyond previous expectations.

Establishing linkages between community colleges and universities is equally beneficial. New knowledge coming from a research institution can keep faculty abreast of current trends in the profession. In a national survey, 63 percent of community college faculty rated their intellectual environment as "fair" or "poor" (Carnegie Foundation for the Advancement of Teaching, 1984). The value of coalitions in reducing the isolation among community college teaching staff is being widely recognized. To four-year institutions, community college faculty can offer innovations such as new teaching strategies for disadvantaged students.

Faculty-community alliances can reduce the fragmentation of curriculum and increase relevance for students. In America, we have prided ourselves on our individuality and our ability to live and work independently. As our nation becomes more inter-dependent on other countries, our students need to understand the value of interdependence within the community. Community colleges have an obligation to teach tolerance of people and different cultures. There are benefits for students. In a world that they often mistrust, our youth seek release from their fears in an unnatural isolation that they hope will protect them from having their failures exposed. The alternative to sharing may be drugs, violence, or dropping out of school before goals are set or met. Faculty members need to help students learn to trust in themselves and their surroundings, and to understand that reaching out is a natural, healthy part of development. Participation in education coalitions can provide role models for students in a way that demonstrates cooperation is productive and that isolation should have its limits.

Other benefits of education coalitions reported by Beacon participants included:
- improved career information for students,
- a demonstrated need for lifelong learning,
- opportunities to explore solutions to common problems,
- leadership training,
- the strengthening of general education courses,
- attracting additional resources, and
- reallocation of current resources.

BARRIERS AND CONSTRAINTS

Many barriers to forming coalitions were related by Beacon College Project participants. They agreed that the following were the major barriers of concern:
- lack of perceived need for change and/or resistance to change;
- lack of time to plan, to think, and to practice new activities;
- difficulty of gaining stakeholder understanding and involvement in the coalition;
- inability to secure the resources necessary to support formation of the coalition;
- lack of data or poor access to data to support desirable changes; and
- lack of support and encouragement for risk-taking.

The process of identifying and discussing the barriers common to all participants was a team-building experience; it gave a starting point for the next planning step.

Participants also identified these stumbling blocks that arise once the coalition is formed:
- lack of a common vision;
- lack of appropriate training for coalition members;
- conflict between the identified desired outcomes of the coalition and the personal mission or agenda of individual members;
- power struggles within the ranks and territorial disputes among coalition participants;
- lack of commitment and follow through from the members;

- "union mentality" of some of the members;
- inadequate staff;
- lack of support from high level executives in member organizations;
- inadequate funding and the inability to shift from "soft" funding to "hard" funding or to be included in budgets of partner organizations; and
- insufficient time to implement the decisions developed by the coalition.

Workshop participants ranked the "lack of time" as the number one barrier to developing effective, broad-based coalitions and implementing systematic change in communities. "Poor attitude" came in a close second. Most participants agreed that if they had sufficient time, all other barriers could eventually be overcome. Some participants related that the amount of work involved in a successful coalition effort is often a deterrent to member commitment. Some suggest, however, that a burdensome work load comes from assuming a heavy load of responsibility alone rather than sharing it with others. For many Beacon participant teams, addressing time restrictions became a starting point for local planning.

One workshop held a lengthy discussion on the barrier of focusing on "at-risk students" rather than a conscious attempt to change the system to reduce the number of students at risk. The issues of diversity were discussed in several categories of successes, challenges, and barriers. There was no shortage of ideas on how to address the issue, but most participants were satisfied that the problems inherent in the issue could be solved without new and expanded resources.

CONCLUSIONS

A majority of the community college representatives interviewed and surveyed for the Beacon College Project had taken preliminary steps to form agreements and partnerships, but few had reached the productive stages of collaborative planning or full coalition structures. Some explained that they were waiting for someone else to take the lead and give directions, indicating that it might not be their right or responsibility to plan other people's agendas for community action. Some who assumed responsibility for community coalition development had decided that limited time called for restraint. These people elected to do a few projects well rather than taking on larger projects that would require more effort or riskier projects that might fail. Still others involved themselves deeply in the development of education coalitions.

Some community colleges are preparing to be comprehensive, cohesive, and creative institutions that accept the challenge of more extensive and long-range coalition work than was previously attempted. Successful coalition partners need to have a deep commitment to open, candid communication and problem solving. In order for this commitment to be realized, partners must share risk and create an acceptable environment.

To sustain community, the capacity to engage in common discourse is crucial. But literacy, at the highest level, means not just clarity of expression, it means integrity as well. In a world that concentrates more on symbols than on substance, both honesty in the shaping of ideas and courtesy in listening are crucial. Integrity in communications holds communities together" (Commission on the Future, 1988, p. 16).

Many believe that community colleges not only have the right to convene a coalition, but the responsibility to do so—taking initiative beyond that of catalyst, connector, or collaborator. In so doing they become a committed partner investing energy into a community coalition that builds natural, trusting relationships, and they exist to intervene in today's problems and to prevent future problems.

Pulling ourselves together is not a simple task. We need to learn how to place the community college in a central convening spot for community conversations. This means changing the way we view ourselves and our community, and the way we do business with each other (Pierce, 1994).

REFERENCES

Beauchamp, J.F. *Building communities through education coalitions: Beacon College Project recommendations.* Tempe, AZ: The Phoenix Think Tank, 1995.

Beauchamp, J.F. and Berkeland, H.B. *A partnership study of business and education.* (An informal study with which the author was associated.) Tempe, AZ: Phoenix Think Tank, 1989.

Boone, E.J. *Community-based programming: An opportunity and imperative for the community college.* ACCLAIM Project. Raleigh, NC: College of Education and Psychology, North Carolina State University, 1992.

Carnegie Foundation for the Advancement of Teaching. *National survey of faculty.* Princeton, NJ: Carnegie Foundation for the Advancement of Teaching, 1984.

Commission on the Future of Community Colleges. *Building communities: A vision for a new century.* Washington, DC: American Association of Community and Junior Colleges, 1988.

Elsner, P.A. *Encyclical III, on effective teaching and learning at Maricopa. Approaching the millennium—The impending revolution in higher education.* Tempe, AZ: Maricopa Community College District, 1993.

Elsner, P.A. Statement made as a member of the Steering Committee of the Think Tank Coalition. Phoenix, AZ, 1994.

Liu, G. Speech at the Campus Compacts in Community Colleges Conference in Scottsdale, AZ, 1994.

Pierce, D.R. Address to the final meeting of the Beacon College Project directors in Vail, CO, 1994.

Wallace, J. *Building bridges: A review of the school-college partnership literature.* Denver, CO: Education Commission of the States, 1993.

Weick, K. *The social psychology of organization.* New York: Random House, 1979.

Wheatley, M.J. *Leadership and the new science.* San Francisco: Berrett-Koehler Publications, Inc., 1993.

Chapter XVII

The next chapter, by Spence, Miner, and Pierce of Florida Community College at Jacksonville (FCCJ), considers community partnerships an important opportunity for community college leadership. After presenting examples of a wide variety of successful partnerships, the authors suggest considerations for the future, including the need to choose partners carefully, to consider declining invitations to partner under certain circumstances, to consider the value of providing behind-the-scenes leadership at times, and "to acknowledge that the complexity of partnerships will require longer-term relationships of a more complicated nature."

Observations regarding the role of the college's board of trustees and managers in successful partnerships are presented, underscoring the idea that partnering is a new way of doing business and requires the development of different skills and perspectives. Read A Mission of Leadership for a thought-provoking overview of the community college and its emerging, changing roles.

* * *

Charles C. Spence, *College President*
Carol Spalding Miner, *Campus President, Open Campus*
Tracy A. Pierce, *Senior Public Relations Coordinator*
Florida Community College at Jacksonville
Jacksonville, Florida

A MISSION OF LEADERSHIP

Let us not go over the old ground, let us rather prepare for what is to come.

—Marcus Tallius Cicero

LEADING THE COMMUNITY

Community college administrators and trustees are often asked where they think their college will be in the next five or 10 years. The response also should be a question: Where and how will our communities need us? Just as a corporation must shape its vision according to the best interests of its stockholders and the desires of its customers, a community college must craft its vision in the best interests of students, taxpayers, and the community the college serves. This free market analogy to community college management may rankle those with a narrow and traditional view of higher education, but as long as colleges rely on public tax dollars for funding, colleges cannot ignore the needs and demands of individual and corporate taxpayers.

Education has lost face in America. Community colleges, especially those that operate from a market perspective, can get it back. Where public schools fail, community colleges succeed. Students that universities pass over, community colleges propel. Community needs that no other organization can meet are ripe for community college intervention. Community colleges are not comic strip super-heroes that can simply fly into frame three and save the day in frame four. However, when education is part of the solution, community colleges are equipped to respond quickly and deliver quality better than any other educational entity.

It takes a special type of courage to ask a community, "What do you need?" and then meet that need either alone or with partners. Doing so requires that you assume a certain level of risk. You may fail. You may succeed and not get credit. You may open yourself up for criticism. Driving a car every day also requires that you assume risk, but you drive anyway because you need to get from point "a" to point "b." You can probably make a list right now of five community needs pointing to a certain direction, and you can probably identify at least three ways your college can assume leadership in each area. The question is, "Are you comfortable pulling into traffic?"

America's business and civic leaders now recognize that one of our country's greatest resources for solving problems—for getting from point "a" to point "b"—is the community college. U.S. Secretary of Labor Robert Reich has emphasized this message: "People in Washington, people on the President's cabinet, and the President himself cannot make things happen," Reich wrote. "Things have got to happen because people want them to happen. There have to be people out there who say now is the time to make this happen. Community college administrators are in a position of leadership, every one of you" (1994, p. 2).

As community colleges earn more local and national credibility, administrators and trustees of individual institutions will be confronted with program opportunities outside the comfortable realm of traditional education. These opportunities may be educational, cultural, social, political, or economic. They may come to the college as problems that need to be solved. Some colleges will decline to become involved. Others will accept the community's invitation to participate and follow their civic leaders to an appropriate conclusion. A few brave colleges will not only accept when asked, but also will provide leadership.

Florida Community College at Jacksonville (FCCJ) is a leadership college. *The Florida Times-Union*, Jacksonville's major daily newspaper, recently described FCCJ as a "vital cog" in the city's educational machine. In an editorial entitled "FCCJ: Leading the Way, Quietly," the college was recognized as filling a "niche of great significance to First Coast [Jacksonville area] residents" (1993, p. A14). The college was lauded for its leadership in education, in providing economic and educational access for minorities, and in the redevelopment of the central city.

FCCJ's broad community role did not develop by chance or administrative decree. It came from the college's employee-authored mission statement:

> We are dedicated to meaningful learning and excellent teaching, enabling individuals to achieve their hopes, dreams, and full potential, and to being a leading partner in creating a dynamic, prosperous community of enlightened leaders and thoughtful, effective, global citizens.

This mission statement is FCCJ's vehicle for community leadership. It is the battery that keeps the college going, the engine that moves it forward, and the body that encompasses everything the college does.

This chapter will discuss how FCCJ developed its mission. It will explore the community issues with which the college is involved and the college's response to those issues. It will also address the dynamics of creating partnerships and the risks involved. This is a chapter for those who choose to lead. This is a chapter for those who feel deeply that community colleges can inspire the advancement of the human condition in almost any circumstance.

How and Why FCCJ Became a Leading Partner

FCCJ's decision to change its name from "junior" to "community" college in 1986 was strategic. Area residents did not understand or appreciate the scope of FCCJ's mission or its impact on the community. College leaders were working to broaden the focus of the internal organization beyond service to the traditional, full-time, college credit student. In the mid-1980s, non-credit enrollments exceeded credit enrollments. The college operated the largest high school in the city and was training a growing portion of Jacksonville's workforce for both new and existing businesses. However, the full-time-equivalent (FTE) student funding these programs generated, and the programs themselves, were virtually invisible to the external community and unrecognized within the college.

In addition, before 1986, the college's partnerships developed only when an outside person or agency could breach college bureaucracy and find the rare administrator willing to adapt programs to meet a special need or offer programs at off-campus sites. The college culture treated special requests as intrusions rather than as mutually beneficial activities. FCCJ's four campuses were more likely to compete than to cooperate.

The college's name change triggered an alarm that FCCJ—the slumbering giant of Jacksonville—was waking up. But while the giant was stretching, enrollment was declining, and state revenues were beginning to deteriorate. The declining enrollment forced FCCJ to pay back $1 million of state funds, and the state's revenue shortfall soon took a further toll on the college's budget. As FCCJ's new marketing efforts began to show positive results, money to fund new growth was evaporating.

Even though the college's workload was increasing, its total budget allocation remained flat and the FTE decreased. While this may be a taxpayer's dream, it was a nightmare for employees serving more students with less resources. FCCJ needed a renewed vision and mission to carry itself through the immediate financial crisis, to consolidate its programs, and to prepare for the difficult fiscal years ahead.

The process of renewing the college's vision began with a diverse group of 50 staff, faculty, administrators, students, and alumni who gathered for two days to learn about the college's history and to ground themselves in the work of envisioning FCCJ's future. The group used a process called the community trusteeship visioning process, which was developed by the Lilly Foundation, Inc., for the National Association of Community Leadership. FCCJ administrators selected the community trusteeship process because it exhibited the same democratic values that are at the heart of the community college philosophy, and because the provost of the college's Open Campus (being one of three writers who adapted it for the National Association of Community Leadership) was well-versed in the process.

By launching the process with an intense study of its history, FCCJ was implementing the thoughts expressed by Warren Bennis (1989) in *On Becoming a Leader*: "Like the oarsmen, we generally move forward while looking backward, but not until we truly see the past—truly understand it—can we truly move forward and backward." Group leaders translated the participants' shared memories into a drawing by sketching pictures and symbols on a 20-foot mural. By using pictures and symbols, "one could see things whole," as Robert Greenleaf (1991) stated in his work on servant-leadership. The resulting timeline represented a historical progression of college politics, buildings, board members, administrators, and organizational changes. The group experienced the power that results from participating in the development of the timeline when, after more than an hour of discussion, someone exclaimed, "There are no students in our history!" In FCCJ's final vision, grievous omissions such as that were eliminated, and the concepts of "student" and "community" were elevated to their proper place as primary symbols of FCCJ's new direction. At the center of the final vision, a 15' x 6' drawing, a student is embraced in a heart supported by symbols of the community. Surrounding the student are representations of the community partnerships college stakeholders believe are vital to the college's future.

Groups of employees on each of FCCJ's campuses then reviewed the vision drawing in preparation for the drafting of a new college mission statement. The task of transforming the vision into the words of a mission statement was approached as a poet might set about his task. Authors of the final mission statement hoped that its language, though lacking rhyme and meter, would inject emotion into the work of the college and gain the acceptance of even the most jaded employee.

The new mission marked change in the college's emphasis in two important areas. First, where FCCJ was once centered around the traditional 18-year-old college-credit student, the new mission included all people within its service area. Second, the college carved out its role as a "leading partner in creating a dynamic and prosperous community...". While recognizing its role as a partner was a significant step, the key word in this phrase was (and is) *leading*. By choosing that word, FCCJ administrators, staff, and faculty embraced an organizational assertiveness that would be more than just responsive to external forces.

The college's personality was shifting from one of almost neutral stagnation to that of a dynamic member of the city of Jacksonville's leadership team. This culture shift required changes in services, classroom space, budget allocation, student services, and employee attitudes. The shift was an impetus to augment resources for FCCJ's high school, GED, and English as a second language programs. It also supported FCCJ's need for an open campus to serve the non-traditional credit student, the workforce, and those desiring professional development. The new mission inspired a change from a program-oriented approach to an entrepreneurial emphasis on students as customers. Both the process of developing the new mission and the mission itself created a collegiate energy which ensured that "student" and "community" would from that time forward be at the heart of Florida Community College at Jacksonville.

THE URBAN COMMUNITY COLLEGE

Challenges facing urban community colleges such as FCCJ reflect the changing face of America's cities. The mission and direction of urban community colleges are constantly impacted by societal forces common to almost every urban environment in America. These forces include:

- the weakening of urban schools at all levels, caused in part by corporate and residential flight to the suburbs, and the resulting diminished tax base;
- the significant increase of immigrants in urban areas, many with limited English and job skills;
- an increasing number of adults on welfare and urban families with a three-generation history of public dependence;
- the proliferation of illegal drugs and the decreasing age at which young people first participate in the drug economy, either as consumers or producers;
- the plight of the young African American male—young African American males are now more involved with the criminal justice system than they are with the higher education system;
- the continuing demise of the traditional family in low income urban communities;
- the high school dropout rate and pregnancy rate;
- the increase in new jobs coming from the lower-paying service sector, the decrease of higher-paying manufacturing jobs, and in many areas, the increasing number of government-sector jobs;
- ineffective public transportation and expanding traffic congestion; and
- a growing elderly population with fixed incomes.

Moreover, students enrolling in urban community colleges today are vastly different from those who enrolled 20 years ago. Twenty years ago that environment was middle class and university-oriented. Today, it is often poor and failure-oriented.

To serve today's students, leading colleges must unite their efforts with other positive community change agents. Community colleges throughout the country have merged their resources with partners in such creative ways as housing public agencies on campus; developing student and faculty volunteer programs; teaching in prisons, churches, and businesses; supporting economic development; hosting public forums on community issues such as crime, AIDS, and public transportation; initiating dropout prevention programs in schools; and cooperating with private agencies to help immigrants build a healthy quality of life. Without college leadership in the community, many of these programs would never have been realized. With colleges acting as leaders, conveners, and catalysts, much has been accomplished in improving the economies of urban America and the lives of urban Americans.

Florida Community College at Jacksonville considers itself to be among those institutions that take a leadership position within their communities. Annually serving more than 90,000 students on five campuses and four centers, FCCJ's academic programs support residents from every socioeconomic stratum in Jacksonville, which, with its one million residents, is the 15th largest city in the country.

FCCJ's academic programs include adult basic education, adult high school, postsecondary vocational training, college credit technical training, continuing education, tailored workforce education, and university parallel. A longstanding joke in Jacksonville is that wherever a dozen people are gathered, FCCJ will hold a class. The sentiment is a bit glib, but it illustrates FCCJ's entrepreneurial willingness to deliver instruction whenever and wherever the community needs it. FCCJ's dynamic approach to meeting student needs has led to average annual enrollment growth of about five percent and total growth of more than 30 percent in the last six years.

Unfortunately, enrollment growth and financial growth have had an inverse relationship during those six years. Funding per student has declined almost $500 since 1989. The primary reason for the drop has been the Florida Legislature's shifting of financial responsibility from the state to the student. FCCJ used to derive about 80 percent of its funding from the legislature and 20 percent from students. Now the split is 70–30, and the state has failed to adjust funding for growth, the increased cost of employee benefits, or inflation. The college has no taxing authority and receives no funding from the city. Despite Jacksonville's poor history of philanthropic giving, FCCJ has initiated a $10 million capital campaign to enhance state appropriations and counteract the decreased funding trend. With momentum from a highly successful employee effort, the college is now, for the first time, turning to its community for long-term, significant support.

Jacksonville's economy is largely service-based with a strong military influence, several major employers in the financial services industry, and a small but healthy manufacturing component. With its port, railways, and interstate highway system, Jacksonville is also a national transportation hub. Home to 23 hospitals, including an extension of the Mayo Clinic, Jacksonville has a growing national and international reputation as a health service center.

Jacksonville is experiencing population trends similar to those of other metropolitan areas. The largest minority group in Jacksonville, which comprises about 22 percent of the total population, is African American; Asian (mostly Filipino) and Hispanic populations in the city are small but increasing. Racial tensions have been evident in local politics, within the private sector, and within the city's criminal justice system.

Like many major cities throughout the country, the urban core of Jacksonville has been on the decline for a quarter century. Jacksonville's local government is "consolidated," meaning that the city council also serves as the county commission. While the consolidated form of government has many benefits, it has fostered an ongoing political battle between neighborhood areas for city services and infrastructure resources. The core city, low income neighborhoods, and the suburbs all struggle for a share of the same dollar.

Recent improvements to the core city have come in the form of both economic and neighborhood redevelopment. Jacksonville was recently awarded a National Football League expansion team. The team will play in the downtown area and its location there is expected to lead to new business development. The city recently committed to a $238 million bond issue to upgrade community facilities and infrastructure. Many of these upgrading projects, collectively known as "River City Renaissance," are targeted to take place in the inner-city area.

American cities, like the American people, are diverse and individualistic. Every township and metropolis exhibits a unique blend of social, political, economic, and cultural characteristics. Although many communities, especially urban communities, are affected by common forces, each community's response may be different because the personality and the operating environment of each community is unique.

Florida Community College at Jacksonville has assumed leadership and established partnerships within the Jacksonville area. Community forces common to many areas of the country motivated the college to act, but FCCJ's actions and results have been targeted to the specific needs of its service area. Through leadership in identifying forces affecting their cities, targeted actions, and positive results, community colleges like FCCJ demonstrate their fundamental value to the communities they serve.

FORCES SHAPING FCCJ'S LEADERSHIP AND COLLEGE PARTNERSHIPS

Diversity, Minority Population Growth, and Racial Tension. The 1960s American social movement toward desegregation has slowly but progressively shifted to a new movement of integration. From a time when one culture dominated and other cultures were viewed as non-conformists, America and Americans are beginning to adopt a collective mind-set that allows for the acceptance of multiple cultures without judgment as to either the dominance or the perceived quality of any one.

The trend of integration has been trumpeted throughout the workplace under the flag of cultural diversity. Acceptance of diversity throughout the corporate world is somewhat attributable to shifting demographics. The number of white Americans as a percentage of the country's total population is declining while the number of African

American, Hispanic, Asian, and other Americans as a percentage of total population is increasing. A growing minority segment translates to growing economic power for members of that segment through both consumption and production. This economic reality has eased the private sector into acceptance of diversity as a matter of good business—minority groups are now too large and too powerful to be ignored as consumers, employees, shareholders, or directors.

Florida Community College at Jacksonville began assuming a leadership role in the trend from desegregation to diversity and integration in the mid-1980s. Jacksonville has had the stereotypical history of a Southern city when it comes to coping with race-related issues; even today, racial harmony can still be tenuous. When FCCJ began building its minority student and diversity training programs, the college's first task was to bolster its own position, especially with respect to minority enrollment. Through several partnerships with the Duval County School Board, FCCJ has been able to extend its reach into the middle school level to begin preparing minority public school students for postsecondary education.

The college created a Black Student Success Office to manage these programs, to cultivate the relationship with schools, and to implement resource programs for minority students enrolled at FCCJ. Through this office, with the support of the FCCJ Foundation and private sector partnerships, the college holds an annual banquet to raise scholarship money for minority students. About 1,000 people from the college, the business community, and local government attend the banquet each year, which raises thousands of dollars. The strength of the college's Black Student Success Office enabled FCCJ to take leadership of the community's annual February celebration of Black History Month. In addition to numerous public events sponsored by the college's campuses, FCCJ entered into partnership with a local television station and the area phone company to publish a calendar that runs from February (Black History Month) through January. Each calendar month chronicles the contributions and life of a prominent African American leader of the past or present.

FCCJ recognized a need in 1992 to expand the Jacksonville area's access to diversity education. Several partners—including the Duval County School Board, the University of North Florida, the city of Jacksonville, and major area employers—joined with the college in 1993 to host the city's first national conference on cultural diversity. Now an annual event, the conference serves educators, employers, and employees (including top managers from Jacksonville's largest employers) by helping them understand the impact of diversity and the best ways to manage diversity within the organizational or civic environment.

FCCJ has taken two other direct steps to support economic growth for minorities. The first was the successful implementation of self-imposed affirmative action hiring procedures to balance employment at all levels of the college with community population race and gender ratios. The second was to increase minority business access to the college's purchasing dollars.

In partnership with minority-owned businesses, chambers of commerce, and local agencies, the college increased communication with minority businesses on every college bid. By increasing opportunity, FCCJ increased the likelihood of minority-owned or women-owned firms winning the bid. The results have been dramatic. While other agencies struggled with policy wording to set aside a percentage of dollars for minority businesses, FCCJ accomplished superior results just by integrating these businesses into the competitive process.

The overall results of FCCJ's leadership and partnerships within the racial relationships of the community are measurable. Black student enrollment in college programs has risen 52.5 percent between 1988 and 1993. African American students now represent 25.7 percent of the college's student body even though African American people comprise only 20.7 percent of the college's service area. Furthermore, their program completion in FCCJ's associate in arts increased 56 percent from 1991 to 1993. Attendance at and the scope of the college's diversity conference and African American History Scholarship Banquet continue to grow, as does the total dollar value of college contracts that minority-owned and women-owned businesses win through FCCJ's purchasing process. For all of their efforts, the FCCJ District Board of Trustees and college president Charles Spence won the 1993 Charles Kennedy Equity Award, given by the Association of Community College Trustees.

FCCJ's effective leadership in minority and racial issues has created other benefits for the college that are more difficult to measure. The strong relationship between the college and minority groups places FCCJ in a better position to anticipate and meet the needs of minority students. FCCJ has become a positive forum for discussion of diversity and other racial issues in the community. Should racial relations become troubled, FCCJ is positioned to provide further leadership and support for the community the college serves.

A Community's Quest for Prosperity. Another important opportunity for community college leadership is the rapidly growing need for education and training within America's workforce. Jacksonville, like almost every urban community in the country, faces the economic paradox of rapidly advancing workplace technology, in the face of a public education system that has yet to find answers to its social and educational challenges. The gap is growing between what traditional education provides and what people need in order to be productive citizens, and community colleges must find it within their resources to fill that gap.

Fifty-two percent of today's jobs require postsecondary education. By the year 2000, that figure will rise to 80 percent. The Jacksonville Community Council, Inc. (JCCI), a non-profit group concerned with improving Jacksonville's quality of life, reported in its 1990 Future Workforce Needs Study that among the greatest workforce problems for FCCJ's service area is "extremely high unemployment among youth and minorities worsened by insufficient work training and education opportunities" (1990). That same report listed among its conclusions:

Working partnerships between education institutions and the business community are needed now to develop the kinds of educational offerings and career-development opportunities required to prepare the future work force...Educational institutions may not be planning sufficiently or far enough ahead for the changing needs of the work force (1990, p. 18).

Recommendations from the report included: "Florida Community College at Jacksonville should be encouraged to continue and expand its efforts as a major local provider of workforce-related education and training." Even as JCCI was in the process of developing that report, Florida Community College at Jacksonville was developing its strategy to lead one of the largest workforce training partnerships in the country—the Urban Resource Center.

If an FCCJ venture ever embodied the full spirit of FCCJ's mission, it would be the Donald D. Zell Urban Resource Center. Through the use of technology and progressive, active instructional methods, the center is:

- helping students expand their potential and their value in the workplace,
- improving the quality of the northeast Florida workforce, and
- contributing to the community's economic development and prosperity.

The Donald D. Zell Urban Resource Center (named for a man who is a former member of the college's District Board of Trustees and a long-standing supporter of FCCJ) is not just a building or a program. The Urban Resource Center is an educational organism—a living entity—that will breathe, grow, and change according to the specific needs of its cerebral command center: a partnership between the business and civic community of northeast Florida and FCCJ.

This partnership emerged early in the center's creation when it was one of only three educational initiatives that the Jacksonville Chamber of Commerce Workforce Preparation Task Force endorsed for chamber and business involvement. The Chamber of Commerce Board of Governors also passed a resolution supporting the center.

The partnership was solidified when the college formed an Urban Resource Center advisory council of leaders from business, industry, community organizations, and government agencies. The council's purpose was to provide input on training and employment needs, to create partnerships, and to act as a liaison to the community. An executive committee, composed of members from the advisory council, was formed to manage the council's objectives, activities, and agenda.

Once the council approved the initial concept of the Urban Resource Center, the partnership grew exponentially, and market demand began driving the center's development. FCCJ representatives conducted extensive personal interviews with more than 100 northeast Florida business and civic leaders representing more than 70 organizations. The interviews were used to assess training needs and workforce problems and to exchange information about the Urban Resource Center concept. This intense, interactive process between FCCJ, the Urban Resource Center advisory council, and the northeast Florida economic community led to the development of the Urban Resource Center's 11 educational program initiatives.

With those initiatives defined, questionnaires were sent to more than 250 business, civic, and government agency representatives to determine their interest in each initiative, their willingness to support them, and their desire to participate on task forces being formed to address those initiatives.

Each task force was co-chaired by a representative from the business/civic community and an appropriate college leader. Even though the task forces completed most of their work prior to the opening of the center in 1993, many of these committees remain active. Now, they provide feedback and recommend program changes to ensure that the Urban Resource Center's educational product remains in lock-step with the needs of business and industry.

The extensive involvement of the community in every level of planning and implementation of the Urban Resource Center enabled FCCJ to identify immediate, high-priority training needs. The visibility of this partnership forced college employees involved with the project to meet private sector demands for quality and performance. The college's continuing relationship with its private sector partners strengthens FCCJ's leadership as a comprehensive institution for workforce training and education. The Urban Resource Center has positioned FCCJ as an institution that can and will adapt to the needs of a diverse student body, and it has helped position northeast Florida as a community that can meet the workforce training needs of new and relocating businesses.

While the Urban Resource Center is truly a monument to FCCJ's ability to simultaneously lead and serve the community, it was by no means the college's first experience with the private sector. References to FCCJ's potential as a workforce training center for northeast Florida appear in documents dating back to the early years of the college's existence. Through its history, FCCJ has worked with many of the area's business citizens.

FCCJ's potential began to develop into leadership in the early 1980s, when the college's newly created Center for Economic Development began working closely with the Jacksonville Chamber of Commerce and AT&T American Transtech. FCCJ committed itself to American Transtech's training, and American Transtech committed itself to Jacksonville. The college assisted the company with the recruitment, screening, and training of the initial 500-member workforce for the company in 1983. Since then, FCCJ has remained as American Transtech's training partner for a company workforce that has expanded and diversified to more than 5,000 people.

Since that training partnership with AT&T American Transtech, FCCJ's business and industry training partners began to read like a Who's Who of Jacksonville commerce: AT&T Universal Card, American Express Travel Related Services, Vistakon, Barnett Bank, Blue Cross and Blue Shield, Xomed-Trease, Goodyear Tire and Rubber Company, Seminole-Kraft, Maxwell House Coffee, Merrill Lynch, and many others.

The success of FCCJ's market-driven process for workforce training is easily measured in terms of workload. The college's workforce training hours exploded from

109,000 hours in 1987 to more than 1 million hours in 1990. The Urban Resource Center served more than 7,000 students in 1993, its first year of operation. It has also received two national business/education partnership awards since it opened.

The partnerships FCCJ has built by responding to this market have led to more than just growth in training FTE. The private sector's willingness to open its doors to the college has provided FCCJ with a new medium for marketing and delivering its programs to the undereducated and to those who need to update their skills. Finally, the college's market-driven process has helped FCCJ establish stronger and more personal relationships with leaders in the private sector. This outcome has strengthened FCCJ's platform for development efforts and diversified the college's community support network. While this result is difficult to quantify, in the long run it could prove to be the most valuable outcome of all.

Dealing with Urban Challenges. While workforce education and training may be the greatest leadership opportunity for community colleges, providing educational and social leadership for America's poor and illiterate may be community colleges' highest priority and greatest challenge. A national adult literacy survey, conducted by the Educational Testing Service for the National Center for Education Statistics, revealed that of the people who function at the lowest levels of literacy, approximately 30 million are in poverty. Without the skills necessary to function in a democratic, free-enterprise society, this disenfranchised population must capture the attention of not only community colleges, but also government agencies and the private sector. Many community colleges battle illiteracy, but leading community colleges are coordinating public and private sector allies in a holistic attack against the causes and effects of the problem.

FCCJ began building a united front against illiteracy in the Jacksonville area in 1986 by creating the Jacksonville Literacy Coalition. Comprising the Jacksonville Public Libraries, the *Florida Times-Union*, the Prudential Insurance Company, Learn to Read, and several community agencies, this umbrella organization's purpose is to unify the voice of literacy providers, build greater awareness of illiteracy, lead literacy advocacy locally and statewide, and initiate private sector partnerships to support literacy efforts.

FCCJ fully funded the first two years of the coalition by providing office space, a project coordinator, and operational funds. During the next six years, the coalition slowly weaned itself from the college. Today, the Jacksonville Literacy Coalition supports its own executive director, program coordinator, and two part-time clerical staff with state and private sector grants, membership dollars, and fund-raising activities. The college still provides office space, but the coalition is currently seeking its own location. Through the Literacy Coalition, FCCJ transformed a fragmented collection of programs into a community-centered team with a single mission.

FCCJ's adult studies department strives to impact broadly the college's service area by providing adult basic education courses, GED preparation and testing programs, adult high school classes, and English as a second language training in all areas of Duval County, especially in areas where educational needs are the most severe. Classes are conducted five days per week at four FCCJ campuses, at two FCCJ centers, at 22 community schools, and at more than 110 other community locations. Achieving such an intense saturation of the community was accomplished by initiating myriad partnerships with churches, libraries, community centers, facilities assisting disabled adults, homeless centers, correctional institutions, rehabilitation centers, senior citizen centers, and employers.

FCCJ received recognition from the National Alliance of Business in 1992 for the community partnership the college built to provide a family literacy program for residents of four Housing and Urban Development facilities. The "New Beginnings" program, which provided adult basic education, GED instruction, child care, and parent-child activities, received the alliance's Excellence in Community Partnerships award. FCCJ also established a partnership with the Duval County School Board (funded by a federal Even-Start grant) to operate a family literacy program for mothers and their children at four elementary schools. The college's literacy program for the homeless operates in 10 area homeless shelters and serves 400 people every year.

Literacy partnerships are often linked directly to workforce partnerships. Working with several business partners, FCCJ secured two national workplace literacy grants to develop 12 literacy skills programs based in the context of specific work environments. These programs were implemented for employees of 16 businesses as a company educational benefit. The business partners provided release time for their employees to attend the classes, space for the classes, and other resources. Additionally, FCCJ, Penn State University, and AT&T shared expertise to develop 40 hours of computer-based basic skills instruction for customer service employees. FCCJ also linked with Florida State University and the State Department of Transportation to teach contextual basic skills to transportation employees.

FCCJ views every work site in Jacksonville as a potential classroom, and for those work sites that do not have room for the college, FCCJ offers a computer and multimedia lab in the Urban Resource Center where businesses can send their employees for computer-assisted contextual instruction. The same type of computer-assisted instruction is used in a partnership with the state Department of Labor and Employment Security to provide GED preparation and work context basic skills instruction to welfare recipients.

FCCJ's leadership and the willingness of the college's neighbors to join forces have seeded successful literacy programs in some of the most challenging environments. Honest communication, clear definition of roles and responsibilities, and teamwork between FCCJ and the Jacksonville Sheriff's Office nourishes successful programs for incarcerated adults in Jacksonville's correctional facilities. In one year, GED classes in these facilities almost doubled in size from 554 participants to more than 1,000. With a new three-year federal grant, the college has expanded its offerings in correctional

facilities to include adult basic education courses and life transition skills. The college
has initiated partnerships with other community agencies to provide English as a second language training to more than 3,000 students every year and to expand its educational services for people with disabilities.

Program growth and student success is, once again, a simple measure of the success
of FCCJ's literacy partnerships. Adult high school enrollment is up, and graduation
numbers have increased at an average annual rate of almost 10 percent. The number of
GED graduates from FCCJ has increased at an average annual rate of more than 17 percent. The college's positive impact on the thousands of people whose educational lives
were once characterized by failure is also of profound importance, even though it is not
a measurable indicator of success. The quality of life in any community is related to the
educational level of the people who live in that community. By bringing educationally
disenfranchised people into the intellectual mainstream of the population, FCCJ and its
partners vastly enhance the economic, social, and cultural potential of the entire Jacksonville area.

THE GROWING COMPLEXITY IN AMERICAN LIFE

Lifelong learning has gone from slogan to reality. The growing number of adults who
are returning to college to upgrade skills and pursue new careers requires new educational delivery systems, as an alternative to the traditional 16-week on-campus term.
FCCJ addresses these needs through partnerships that provide distance education, military education, vocational training, and courses in a shopping mall.

FCCJ's partnership with Jacksonville's cable television company, Continental
Cablevision, began when Continental received its first charter from the Jacksonville
City Council. The charter specified that Continental would provide educational access
programming. The cable company and the college's initial attempt at a consortium with
the community's four educational institutions was unsuccessful. Only FCCJ was ready
to commit the resources necessary to program the channel.

In lieu of a consortium, a partnership with Continental Cablevision gave the college responsibility for programming an educational channel 24 hours a day. Though
neither the college nor the cable company pay each other for services or programming,
there are many mutual benefits of working together. The cable company treats the college as one of its vendors and allows it to send out promotional literature (at a cost)
with the cable bills. Also as a promotion, Continental offered free installation of cable
service with a course registration for several years.

The college employs a staff to schedule and transmit its programming to the cable
company. FCCJ also produces some of its own programs including Read, Write,
Research, which is now distributed by the Public Broadcasting Service. The cable company is responsible for transmitting the signal to more than 200,000 subscribers.

The partnership arrangement was duplicated with the other three cable providers in the two county area. Though different channel numbers are used for each cable company, the college programming is the same.

The cable telecourse program grew from eight course offerings in 1986 to 29 course offerings in 1993. During the same period, enrollment grew from 350 telecourse students to more than 6,000 with only the additional expense of instructors. The next negotiation in the partnership will be to propose programming additional channels as the college and the cable company expand their offerings.

FCCJ is also a leading partner in SUNSTAR, Florida's satellite transmission service which provides teleconferences throughout the state. This partnership allows the college to earn revenue as a teleconference site and gives it the opportunity to communicate with other receiving sites about important issues. Past teleconferences have included statewide training for Department of Health and Rehabilitative Services case workers and feedback on the progress of a legislative session. FCCJ has also served as an uplink for a teleconference on disabled student services.

The college combined distance learning and military education with a recent grant from the U.S. Department of Defense in which FCCJ, two other Florida community colleges, and a state university provided live, two-way audio and two-way video training to military personnel. The $1 million grant demonstrated the feasibility of community colleges as training centers for the military and provided FCCJ faculty with new skills in interactive distance learning.

Jacksonville's three navy bases have been partners with FCCJ in providing on-base educational programs for more than 20 years. The navy provides offices, classrooms, and furniture, and the college provides full-time staff advisers, full-time and part-time instructors, computer labs, and learning resources. Recently, accommodations have been made through a negotiated memorandum of understanding. In three memorandums, one for each Jacksonville base, the FCCJ has agreed to exempt the bases from the college's "less than 12" class-cancellation policy. With this agreement, the college cancels far fewer classes, and enrollments have grown from 627 students in 1986 to 3,698 students in 1993. The college also accommodates the military through a year-long schedule of six-week terms in addition to offering three traditional semesters every year.

For many years, FCCJ has convened community forums in public meeting formats and on television. When the television forums outgrew the college's in-house studio, FCCJ initiated a partnership with PBS affiliate WJCT Channel 7 to provide this service. Building on the research and resources of the National Issues Forums of the Kettering Foundation, the college and Channel 7 brought the community together to deliberate on issues such as AIDS, crime, and the national debt.

FCCJ co-produces six prime-time televised forums a year. The college picks the topic, designs and mails the brochure, and invites the resource people and the audience. WJCT dedicates the staff, studio facilities, editing, on-air marketing, and air time for the program. More than 41,000 people see each program, either as participants in the studio or as television viewers. The partnership has enhanced the station's mission of offering community programs and has given FCCJ great exposure. In addition to those who would normally attend the forum, residents can view the "reruns" on the college's educational access channel later in the year.

As American society continues to evolve, community colleges must behave as though their survival is dependent on their ability to adapt to their changing environment. A college's willingness to twist and bend to meet a specific community need is a tremendous asset for the people the college serves. This flexibility not only gains the respect of community members, but it helps separate community colleges from the expectation of mediocrity normally associated with public sector agencies.

THE RELATIONSHIP BETWEEN CULTURE AND QUALITY OF LIFE

Many communities rely on local educational institutions to provide and enhance cultural offerings for area residents. In Jacksonville, however, presentations of serious artistic significance are left almost completely to the area's educational community. Since 1967, the Florida Community College at Jacksonville Artist Series has been an unrivaled source of world-class cultural entertainment for the entire community.

A subscription program of professional Broadway productions, dance, opera, jazz, family-oriented programs, and other artistic forms, the FCCJ Artist Series doubled its offerings in 1993 to more than 50 performances a year. *Les Miserables, Cats,* and *The Will Rogers Follies* are examples of some of the performances. From 85,000 to 100,000 people attend these performances every year, and local media outlets help to promote each event. The FCCJ Artist Series budget of $2 million is almost double the city's $1.3 million appropriation for its entire arts program. Recently, non-profit groups, such as the Visiting Nurse Association, have sponsored first night performances of FCCJ Artist Series events as fund raisers. The non-profit organization has the responsibility to sell the house at benefit prices on the first night. The group keeps the fund-raising revenue, and the college benefits from additional advertising exposure, potentially reaching new markets.

Although Jacksonville has a long history of amateur theater and nearly 20 amateur companies, its community education programs for the arts have been minimal. FCCJ will open a $20 million complex in 1995 to vastly enhance art education for area residents. In preparation for that event, the college initiated a partnership with the University of Florida's fine arts department. FCCJ wanted the faculty expertise of the university, and the university wanted a larger presence in the Jacksonville area. The university's department of continuing education and FCCJ's Open Campus co-sponsored a workshop series featuring University of Florida faculty and promoted by FCCJ. The expenses and income were shared by the two institutions.

Jacksonville Community Council, Inc. and FCCJ worked to assimilate new residents more quickly into Jacksonville's culture and to promote volunteerism by educating area residents about Jacksonville's history. In the JCCI tradition, a citizen's committee was formed to develop the scope of the historical study. FCCJ then developed scripts for five videos that were broadcast on the local PBS affiliate and on the educational access channel. Videotapes were also available for sale. Production of this series, particularly the episode detailing Jacksonville's consolidated government, tied in with the city's celebration of the 25th anniversary of its consolidation.

Partnerships can be formed with individuals as well as organizations. The college formed a valuable partnership with local author and futurist Hazel Henderson. Henderson shares her wealth of prominent friends and acquaintances with FCCJ through her participation in the college's *Worth Quoting* television series. Her past guests have included Peter Russell, author of *Whole Brain Thinking*, and Alan Kay, president of Americans Talk Politics. Henderson's partnership with the college has produced an impressive collection of support materials and enlightening programs for FCCJ's educational access channel. The college recently made these tapes available internationally through a distribution contract.

Almost every day our society learns more about the value of artistic education and the importance of cultural opportunities to the overall quality of life in a city. Community colleges are better-positioned than any other educational institution (and most civic institutions) to be a leading provider of cultural opportunities for their communities.

Leadership to Create the Preferred Future. "Leadership with vision" and "community consensus to pull this city together" were the themes of Jacksonville's 1991 mayoral election. In a letter written shortly after the election, FCCJ President Charles Spence encouraged newly elected Mayor Ed Austin to create a vision for the Mayor's new team that would bring the city to consensus on community priorities. This communication eventually led to a unique partnership among the city, the Jacksonville Chamber of Commerce, Leadership Jacksonville, the National Association of Community Leadership, and Florida Community College at Jacksonville.

Mayor Austin formed a task force of 13 community leaders, including Spence, and appointed the president of the chamber of commerce as the committee's chairman. The group's charge was to plan a way to unite a metropolis of almost 800,000 people behind a shared vision and common goals.

Represented by FCCJ Open Campus President Carol Spalding Miner, the college and Leadership Jacksonville (a leadership development organization) suggested that the committee adopt the community trusteeship process that had been so successful at the college. The two organizations successfully proposed inviting all citizens to participate in the community trusteeship process in one gathering at the city's convention center, using Leadership Jacksonville alumni as facilitators.

Implementing the community trusteeship process required contributions of massive resources from all the partners. The *Florida Times-Union* donated advertising, and the television stations broadcast public service announcements. The college developed a database for keeping track of the process and taught the city and the chamber how to use it. The college and Leadership Jacksonville formed a team to recruit facilitators, many of whom were employees of FCCJ. FCCJ adapted the trusteeship training to fit a one-day format and trained 65 facilitators, a group that included FCCJ's president, board chairman and other college representatives. FCCJ's television production staff videotaped the history lecture for facilitators to study. FCCJ staff people also created and reproduced the history of Jacksonville timeline. The chamber provided staff support for the logistics of the process, mailings, and phone coverage. The city requested and administered the budget, generated letters from the mayor, and served as liaison to the city council communicating the citizens' views.

On February 1, 1992, more than 800 citizens participated in 37 groups to help create a vision for Jacksonville. For the next four months, the planning partnership orchestrated even more citizen participation. Neighborhood meetings were held, an hourlong television program was aired, and a 12-page illustrated report was produced. For the next year, the city, FCCJ, and WJCT continued to work together as Jacksonville's new citywide vision was implemented. Using the vision as his support, the mayor proposed and passed the $238 million "River City Renaissance" bond issue implementing many of the citizen's recommendations.

The college's role as a leading partner in this highly visible citywide venture increased the college's profile considerably. The city's, the chamber's, and the public's appreciation of FCCJ's contribution was a noteworthy testament to the value of the college's mission of community leadership. FCCJ was the constant, neutral convener of a citizen's group that exemplified the finest characteristics of the democratic form of government.

Residents in almost every town, county, or municipality in the country clamor to be heard. Because of the college's leadership, Jacksonville residents received the opportunity not only to speak, but to create Jacksonville's preferred future. Through civic leadership, FCCJ helped Jacksonville realize what other cities only dream about—a consensus of citizens supportive of their government.

DEVELOPING QUALITY PARTNERSHIPS

The major forces impacting American cities today and in the foreseeable future will only increase the need for community colleges to seek outside partners in search of solutions. The continuing crisis in funding for public schools and declining student performance will intensify the demand that community colleges work more closely with their major suppliers of students. The cost of the underprepared student is now borne fully by community colleges and employers. The burden for achieving academic competency must be shifted back to the public schools. Community college presidents and large city public school superintendents should develop a state-by-state plan for increasing competence of high school graduates. The development of tech prep and dual enrollment programs are only partially sufficient partnership models.

The speed of technological change in the workplace will continue to accelerate. Community colleges should be learning how to configure their programs and services to meet the needs of local employers. Corporations and businesses are looking for measurable competencies. Are colleges willing to guarantee courses, guarantee competency, or guarantee student satisfaction?

On the other side of the partnership, colleges cannot afford to maintain state-of-the-art technology. Data processing budgets are doubling at many colleges every five years. Current equipment for teaching will be available only through cooperation among institutions, businesses, and agencies. Shared-use models will create complicated technology consortiums. As these changes continue and accelerate, community colleges will have to:

- choose partners even more carefully, perhaps declining many external requests;
- acknowledge that the complexity of partnerships will require longer-term relationships of a more complicated nature;
- be prepared to create effective work groups aimed at a specific task that may require people working together via television or computer terminals and then dissolve the partnership once the task is done (for example, FCCJ was asked to lead a statewide consortium to create a tracking system for adult education students);
- plan for highly visible leadership roles requiring finesse with the media and the general public; and
- plan for major leadership roles which will only work if the role is behind the scene and low-key.

Much can be accomplished when no one cares who gets the credit. Many times, however, it is the credit that is the most valuable benefit to the partner. Knowing this from the beginning is critical to a successful working relationship. Giving and receiving credit is one of the thornier (and thus often ignored) issues in a partnership.

The city's Literacy Coalition is an example of FCCJ being a leading partner while maintaining a low profile. The college reached out to the public library and Learn to Read to join forces for a citywide effort to recruit volunteers and promote literacy education. The other agencies were able to get publicity, and all benefited through their different roles. The college was able to find volunteers to work with students who needed additional tutoring. In another example, the partnership between the FCCJ Artist Series and the Visiting Nurse Association nearly broke down when the VNA's brochures were published without the appropriate recognition of the college's participation. With this as a learning experience, expectations are now spelled out in advance when partnering to present these special events.

Seldom is a partnership equally matched. In fact, if the partners are too similar, the benefits of working together may be less than in situations in which each partner brings different attributes to the table. As a leading partner, a college needs to find a match in an organization with a similar mission or complimentary activity that brings different attributes to the partnership.

Many community colleges carry a sense of inferiority into their search for partnerships. Many have expectations that are too low. Community colleges can work with any foundation, large business, or governmental agency. The more successful the college is in its track record with smaller partners, the more confident it will be when it approaches the powerful community leaders and the community's leading institutions. Though the college may not be on the potential partner's agenda, most organizations value working together on worthwhile projects. The extraordinary participation of major employers with FCCJ's Urban Resource Center and the high visibility of FCCJ's partnership with Jacksonville's community consensus and vision process demonstrate the long-lasting and enriching relationships that can develop when a community college assumes community leadership.

It is important to choose partners wisely. Many well-known partners need all the credit and do little of the work. In a past partnership, FCCJ discovered that a business co-sponsoring a museum art exhibit wanted a comparable dollar amount of its donation in free tickets. The "sponsorship" and underwriting became a publicity event for the company with no financial benefit to the museum. The museum finally felt that it should not have chosen that partner, after all. Based on this experience, the college was very clear about its expectations when subsequently working with this partner.

More partners mean more opportunities for problems with control and communication. The more bureaucratic the organizations, the slower the progress toward the goal; but most importantly, the people who are representing the organization are critical to a partnership's success. A college should try to work with people who believe in the effort and can find ways to make things work. It is helpful if they are high enough in the organization to get things done and can either commit for the organization or have a clear and simple path to the person who can commit.

Be aware of the politics of all partner organizations. It is very helpful if all parties express their expectations and contribute fully. If the partnership does not foster a win-win situation, the partnership may accomplish its task, but chances are that future collaborations will not develop. If the partnership can be a win-win situation, chances are good that it will succeed and potentially lead to bigger, more meaningful joint projects in the future.

Establishing Community Leadership

The Trustees. Almost all successful community colleges share two characteristics. The first is a philosophical belief that adults should have free access to college at any age. The second characteristic, slightly more tangible, is a governing board that is unencumbered by politics, represents the broad range of local citizens, and serves as a beacon for the institution. Most community colleges possess the first characteristic at some level, but building and maintaining an effective board is a time-consuming, difficult, and continuous process. In some cases, the process may even be outside of the institution's control. An effective board, however, contributes significantly to a college's leadership potential.

FCCJ's District Board of Trustees has done so in a variety of ways. It approved the mission statement that boldly asserts FCCJ's desire to be a leading partner, and it selected "partnerships" as one of the 26 indicators used to evaluate the college's effectiveness. Individually, board members seek and solidify partnership opportunities. One trustee, a vice president of a major credit card company, is creating a partnership with her company, the federal government, FCCJ, and the Association of Community College Trustees to establish a credit education program for college students who are on financial aid. Another (now former) trustee has worked with several environmental groups to foster a green campus environment. In the process, this trustee forged partnerships with student groups, a local prison farm, city planners, and financial backers. In order for trustees to facilitate partnerships they must:

- create a free enterprise environment for the college by encouraging and giving careful consideration to new ideas;
- tolerate failures when partnerships do not work and focus on how to improve performance rather than punishing those involved;
- serve as facilitators for discussions of sensitive topics with external community groups and serve as liaisons when the institution is experiencing difficulty with a partner;
- risk seed money for new ventures while seeking primary funding (FCCJ has a successful record of securing grant funding for partnerships; and in many cases, the college funded a single position to initiate a program so that grant money could be pursued.);
- celebrate successes (board meetings can be a positive environment for thanking partners and for board members to be thanked for their support of community projects); and
- praise the college and its partners publicly for sharing resources and avoiding duplicate programs, thus, more effectively using taxpayer dollars.

The President and College Managers. It's much like the chicken or the egg question: Do leading community colleges weave themselves into the fabric of the community, or do colleges that are woven into the fabric of the community emerge as leaders? Whichever way it occurs, the internal culture of the most progressive colleges in America is one in which faculty, staff, and administrators are highly active and visible participants in the affairs of the community. College presidents and top managers stimulate and nurture that internal culture by:

- finding or creating opportunities (including board meetings) to discuss community issues and ways the college can help address those issues;
- encouraging and ensuring that staff members serve on boards and in volunteer positions in agencies and organizations in the community (the presidents of FCCJ's five campuses have selected this as one of five objectives they will use to measure their effectiveness as a team);
- encouraging teaching staff to have higher expectations, to dream bigger dreams;
- publicly praising staff members for their efforts on behalf of the college and its partners; and
- installing a planning process that involves input from appropriate community groups (which can be accomplished through direct participation, through a survey of needs, and through "key informant" interviews).

College administrators may never possess complete control over their organization's culture, but they will always influence the culture in a strong way. In conveying a theme of community involvement and civic leadership to other employees, a college's officials send a much stronger message through their actions than through their words. In attempting to encourage a college to move into community leadership, community college administrators should demonstrate exactly the behavior they hope other employees will emulate.

BROADENING THE SCOPE OF THE AMERICAN COMMUNITY COLLEGE

As the world's economies become more interdependent; as former Eastern bloc and underdeveloped countries become immersed in concepts like capitalism, free enterprise, and democracy; and as the collective knowledge base of humankind expands at an ever-increasing rate, the role of educational institutions in local and national leadership becomes more and more critical. The inherent attributes of community colleges may prove to make these institutions the most critical within education. The urban community college has become what Ernest Boyer calls the new American college—"a connected institution...committed to improving, in a very intentional way, the human condition" (1994, p. A48).

Through targeted local leadership, community colleges can improve the human condition within their communities in hundreds of creative ways. Administrators and board members of every community college in the nation must define the scope of their mission. Those bold enough to accept local, national, and, perhaps, international leadership within their province will rise as partners in a national coalition working for the advancement of society at every level. As individual community colleges gain membership in local leadership circles, this nation's collective community college system will emerge as a leading partner in meeting the domestic challenges of the United States.

REFERENCES

Bennis, W. *On becoming a leader.* Reading, MA: Addison-Wesley Publishing Company, 1989.

Boyer, E. "Point of view." *Chronicle of Higher Education*, March 9, 1994, A48.

"FCCJ: Leading the way, quietly." *The Florida Times-Union.* October 23, 1993, A14.

Greenleaf, R. *The servant leader.* Indianapolis: The Robert K. Greenleaf Center, 1991.

Jacksonville Community Council, Inc. *Future workforce needs study.* Jacksonville, FL: Jacksonville Community Council, Inc., 1990.

Reich, R. "The way things should work." *The Community College Times*, May 3, 1994, 2.

Chapter XVIII

*In today's uncertain world,
it is best not to go it alone.*

–K. Ohmae

John E. Roueche
Lynn Sullivan Taber
Suanne D. Roueche
Community College Leadership Program
The University of Texas at Austin
Austin, Texas

STRIKING A BALANCE:

Creating a Collaborative Mosaic

Perhaps the notion that private and public lives are at odds is incorrect. Perhaps they are so deeply involved with each other that the impoverishment of one entails the impoverishment of the other. Parker Palmer is probably right when he says that 'in a healthy society the private and the public are not mutually exclusive, not in competition with each other. They are, instead, two halves of a whole, two poles of a paradox. They work together dialectically, helping to create and nurture one another.'

—Bellah and Associates, 1985

STUDENTS: THE HEART OF THE MISSION

As this manuscript began to take on a life of its own, drawn from the personalities and experiences of the authors and their institutions, we were struck continually by the enormous diversity of the collaborations our authors were describing; by the amazing continuum along which their experiences could be plotted, from the serendipitous to the calculated; by the accommodations that companies of strangers and friends make to create and sustain relationships. In addition, we were struck by the successes of these experiences—a curious confession in light of our interest in collecting important information about collaboration in American community colleges and our obvious trust that there would be important findings to disseminate. While we believe that collaboration is one of the sleeping giants of our collective educational futures and while that belief influenced mightily our decision to author this collection, we were relatively unprepared for the depth and breadth of what we read; the complexities and the successes exceeded the expectations we had when we invited these authors to tell their stories. The solid reputations of these people and their institutions for extraordinary achievements in the collaboration arena led us to them, but we were nonetheless surprised at what we read. As we prepared the chapters for publication, we examined our curious reaction. We discussed what it was about community colleges that would fuel such energy toward their various collaborative efforts and make them so confident that their activities were appropriate and justified—even beyond the historical antecedents and the current realities that were described in Chapter 1.

We turned to community college mission statements—statements that have driven so many antagonists and protagonists to argue about the depth and breadth of the college's collaboration agenda—where we identified the student, as have many before us, as the *raison d'être* for the college's existence. We agreed that if students really are at the heart of the mission, then any college's collaborative efforts must be tied to a tradition of acting in the best interest and for the well-being of its students.

Celebrating Community

We found in Ernest Boyer's *College: The Undergraduate Experience* the poignant perspective that provides a foundation for creating a collaborative mosaic.

...[W]e have talked about the two great traditions of individuality and community in higher education. Colleges, we have said, should help students become independent, self-reliant human beings, yet also they should give priority to community. In implementing these two priorities, a balance must be struck.

But here we insert an important word of caution. To draw the line too sharply between these two traditions may, in fact, mask a more fundamental truth: To serve private priorities while neglecting social obligations is, ultimately, to undermine self-interest. And, it is more than mere sentiment to suggest that altruism richly benefits the self as well.

This point, properly understood, brings us to our vision of the undergraduate experience. It warns against making too great a distinction between careerism and the liberal arts, between self-benefit and service. We more comfortably embrace the notion that the aim of the undergraduate experience is not only to prepare the young for productive careers, but also to enable them to live lives of dignity and purpose; not only to generate new knowledge, but to channel that knowledge to humane ends; not merely to study government, but to help shape a citizenry that can promote the public good.

The undergraduate college in America has never been a static institution. For 350 years, it has shaped its program in response to the changing social and economic context. As we look to a world whose contours remain obscure, we conclude the time has come to reaffirm the undergraduate experience and, in so doing, help students move from competence to commitment and be of service to their neighborhoods, the nation, and the world (1987, pp. 296-297).

Colleges, as teachers, must model the behaviors that they strive to develop in their students—"...students must...begin to understand that, while we're all alone, we do share many things in common. And, while we celebrate individualism in education, I'm convinced it's immensely important that we celebrate community as well..." (Boyer, 1992, p. 1).

We also saw in college mission statements a commitment to providing the highest quality education at reasonable cost. The goal of strengthening the ties between self and community is worthy of extraordinary effort because such a goal leads to an informed and productive citizenry—the foundation of our social, economic, and educational systems. In the face of escalating costs, increasing demands and expectations, and decreasing revenues, colleges must adjust their thinking and their behavior away from old models designed during times when they more likely could afford what they needed and wanted, to designing new "models of entrepreneurship and flexibility" (Lorenzo and Banach, 1994, p. 5) that will allow them to better adapt to more "turbulent fields" (Emery and Trist, 1965, p. 21).

Turbulent fields are environments characterized by complexity, rapid change, and clustering. In this type of environment, conditions are so complex that it is difficult to understand the combination of forces that create the constant changes. Multiple factors experience dramatic change and the changes are linked. The turbulent field can have overwhelmingly negative consequences for the organization; in fact, the environment may change so drastically that the survival of the organization is threatened. A distinctive feature of the turbulent field is the interdependence among environmental factors. By shifting together and influencing each other, the effects are magnified. True turbulent fields are rare, but when they occur, planning is of little value because the changes are so dramatic and rapid. Individual organizations cannot adapt successfully through their own actions. Rather, survival depends on the emergence of values that have overriding significance for all members of the field (Emery and Trist, 1965, p. 21).

POSITIONED TO COLLABORATE

Community colleges are adaptable, capable of change in response to new conditions and demands or circumstances, operate with a continuing awareness of their communities, and have a nexus (defined as *a means of connection*) function in their communities' learning systems (Gleazer, 1984). They have the ability to be "close to the customer" (Peters and Waterman, 1982), with extraordinary linkages and networks between and among other colleges and with community organizations and institutions. The college's interactions with a wide array of community interests and students puts it in the unique position to embrace, connect, and convene. Because colleges are human enterprises in the teaching and learning business, they are positioned to take part in what some observers of important change in this country have described as "a fascinating convergence in the effective means used to change" U.S. institutions for the better (Chrislip and Larson, 1994, p. 5).

> They are working together because they have to; nothing else works to solve problems or to improve performance. Phoenix businessman Frank Fiore puts it this way: 'I like to say that the sixties was the 'we' decade, the seventies was the 'me' decade, the eighties [was] the 'gimme' decade, and the nineties will be the 'community' decade. We've tried everything else. I think people are beginning to realize that the other stuff doesn't work. Now we have to try something new.' When nothing else works, people begin to collaborate (Chrislip and Larson, 1994, p. 5).

> Current thinking about teaching and learning issues has identified collaborative learning as a valuable strategy for improving student performance; in business, current thinking is that no matter how long an alliance has existed or what its objectives might be, "being a good partner has become a key corporate asset...a company's *collaborative advantage*" (Kanter, 1994, p. 96). Successful alliances share some common characteristics.

- They must yield benefits for the partners, but they are more than just the deal. They are living systems that evolve progressively in their possibilities. Beyond the immediate reasons they have for entering into a relationship, the connection offers the parties an option on the future, opening new doors and unforeseen opportunities.
- Alliances that both partners ultimately deem successful involve *collaboration* (creating new value together) rather than mere *exchange* (getting something back for what you put in). Partners value the skills each brings to the alliance.
- They cannot be 'controlled' by formal systems but require a dense web of interpersonal connections and internal infrastructures that enhance learning (Kanter, 1994, pp. 96–97).

VARIATIONS AND DIMENSIONS OF THE PARTNERSHIPS

The chapters in this book reflect the aforementioned common characteristics, the creativity and resourcefulness that multiple observers have long identified with community colleges, and the enormous number of variations of and dimensions to community college/community partnerships. Moreover, the chapters report on different requirements, describe a variety of stakeholders, and articulate a myriad of commitments. In this final chapter, we wanted to close by organizing the extraordinary amount and diversity of information offered by our authors. As we looked for some useful, conceptual organizers, we discovered that tidy categories were not apparent. However, we finally decided that categorizing by *purpose* of the activity would be most helpful to the reader; it (1) would provide a way of thinking about the collaboration process, (2) would create a working shorthand that could convey and promote mutual understanding, (3) would facilitate the development of knowledge about this subject, and, most important here, (4) would provide a useful organizational framework for this broad-brush discussion. (Yet, we recognized that some of the activities described in this book represented two or more combinations of these categories, and we would have to make some arbitrary decisions about where they should be mentioned.) In bringing *The Company We Keep* to a close, we chose information from the foregoing chapters to create a living mosaic from the stories our authors told.

CATEGORIES BY PURPOSE

Economic Development
- participate in economic development activities
- provide workforce training
- facilitate technology transfer

Community Development
- participate in community development activities
- work with others to address community problems or issues
- provide for or convene forums
- enhance the community by being a good citizen

People Development
- provide a wide range of higher education options
- help people successfully complete education or training programs
- encourage interest in particular occupational areas, often by special populations
- increase diversity in an organization or an activity
- enhance the international or cultural experience

Organizational Development
- organize or structure the organization in ways to better accomplish work
- provide staff development opportunities

Resource Development
- raise money or secure donations for the college
- use, build, or acquire facilities for community college programs and services

ECONOMIC DEVELOPMENT

Participating in Economic Development. There have been at least six decades of arguments and counter arguments about the role of community colleges in economic development. The vocationalism issue has clouded these discussions—for example, what are the repercussions for students tracked into terminal nontransfer degrees? Are they shortchanged by a system that restricts their mobility and terminates their higher education experiences (Brint and Karabel, 1989)? Moreover, the discussions have been greatly affected by the people who write the economic development strategies that drive political theory and policy, people who typically have never attended or worked at community colleges—and, who, furthermore, do not understand the diversity of college missions or the enormous variety of their legal, state-assigned missions (Katsinas, 1994).

In spite of this, community colleges are playing an increasingly central role in the economic development activities of their regions. In recent years, their involvement with the private sector has mushroomed, particularly in the suburbs where perhaps the most prominent role they play may be providing continuing education and upgrading for currently employed workers (Katsinas, 1994). Doucette (1993) discovered that of the 1,042 community colleges he surveyed about customized workforce training programs, nearly all of the responding institutions (96 percent) were providing workforce training programs, and nearly two-thirds were providing training for the fastest growing entity in the manufacturing sector—companies with fewer than 500 employees. This latter finding is particularly important when one considers that this entity is described as "having great difficulty keeping up with the pace of technological change on their own" (Ross, 1993, p. 75) and that many mainstream economists believe that "an important key to building wealth in the 1990s will be the relative success or failure of small to medium manufacturers" (Katsinas, 1994, p. 74).

However, after describing the activities of 10 urban community college districts and campuses in community partnerships with governmental agencies, outreach programs for minorities, partnerships with public schools and universities, and partnerships with business and industry, the author of *Who Cares About the Inner City? The Community College Response to Urban America* concluded:

> The emerging mission and role of central city campuses continues to be misunderstood in their own communities. There is a sense of frustration concerning public understanding and acceptance of the social and educational roles of these colleges. Indeed, negative image and perception consistently plague central city campuses...

There appears to be no national consensus on the multiple mission and roles of the central city campus and its special programs that reach out to the community. It appears that each campus and each district is keeping up with urban issues in its own fashion (Weidenthal, 1989, p. 28).

It is clear that community colleges, by type and location, have taken a wide variety of positions about the appropriateness of the roles they have chosen to play and the range of activities in which they wish to participate. But when the economic development coalitions are successful, they help build impressive and effective relationships (Tucker, 1992). *Cuyahoga Community College*, for example, as a member of the Quality Resource Consortium, engages in collaboration, resource exchange, and education development that supports quality improvement in member organizations which include Blue Cross of Northeast Ohio, East Ohio Gas, and Ameritech. *Kirkwood Community College's* full-service, regional delivery system, Economic Development Services, provides customized job training, retraining, and new or expanding business development services. *Valencia Community College* has refocused its entire operation to ensure that every function is tuned in to the economic development needs of its region.

Workforce Training. "Up to 75 percent of the existing workforce will require significant retraining in the next decade and up to 80 percent of the new jobs created during that time will require at least two years of postsecondary education" (Roueche, 1993, pp. 4–5). The real problem of our time has become *unemployability*, not unemployment (Avishai, 1994). By the year 2000, America will be "out of qualified workers" (Kearns and Flanigan, 1990, p. 46).

It has been estimated that 20 to 30 percent of U.S. workers lack the skills they need to do their current job well, use some of the new technologies, or participate in training programs (Stone, 1991). Since the 1970s and 1980s, businesses have recognized the need to participate in fine-tuning the nation's schooling processes. However, as Clark has noted:

Business participation in the schools during the '80s can be characterized as 'tinkering at the margin'—low levels of investment with limited objectives, and was conducted on a fragmented, unstructured, duplicative and *ad hoc* basis. Today, for the most part, 'partnership' projects continue to be brief, episodic and student oriented...but the entire system needs help...a formal broad-based delivery system—infrastructure—needs to be established for substantive long-term joint efforts between the two sectors (1990, p. 15).

Florida Community College at Jacksonville has developed just such a substantive effort. Designated one of the Jacksonville Chamber of Commerce's workforce preparation priorities, a cross-section of college and business people met weekly for two years to develop tailored services and programs. The college's Urban Resource Center now offers 11 educational programs, assessment services, and workforce training for new and relocating businesses. Employees may use computer and multimedia labs on site. *Miami-Dade Community College's* School of Justice and Safety Administration provides certification and licensing in police training, private sector security, fire fighting, corrections, and traffic safety. *Chattanooga State Technical Community College's* Center for Advanced Technology prepares employees of a regional manufacturer for the transition to computer-integrated manufacturing. In an arrangement that crosses state lines, US West and Communication Workers of America subcontract with institutions of higher education in 14 states, including *Metropolitan Community College*, to assess the abilities and interests of current US West employees. After assessment, employees enroll in appropriate courses or training; US West pays the tuition and fees.

Humber College of Applied Arts and Technology designs, develops, equips, staffs, and implements hands-on training in injection molding, blow molding, blown film, and extrusion for a sector-wide, multi-stakeholder alliance of the Canadian plastics industry. Greenville Technical College's State Advanced Machine Tool Technology Center partners with the state of South Carolina and Cincinnati-Milacron, one of the area's largest users of machine tool technology, to develop courses and offer advanced machine tool technology training in state-of-the-art technology, and to provide assistance to faculty from other state technical colleges. The center also serves as a resource in attracting new industry to the state. The Hazardous Materials Training and Research Institute (HMTRI) at *Kirkwood Community College*, a self-supporting entity that receives grant funds and contract training dollars to provide environmental health and safety training, is designated as the Executive Office for the National Partnership for Environment Technical Education (PETE), and coordinates the Community College Consortium for Health and Safety Training.

St. Petersburg Junior College partners with the Florida National Guard to sponsor the Drug War Academy-Multijurisdictional Counterdrug Task Force. Classroom, scenario, and distance-learning instructional modes are used. *Midlands Technical College* is linked with the other 15 colleges in the state's two-year system through the Governor's Workforce Initiative, offering a range of options for basic skills training that can be tailored for workplace delivery. Their workplace literacy program has three parts—preapplicant training, employment skills training, and workplace literacy training. Like many colleges, Midlands Technical College is knee-deep in tech prep initiatives. The Central Midlands Tech Prep Consortium links the college and eight public school districts, encouraging cooperation and striving for better ways to train young people for transition to the workplace. *Valencia Community College's* Office of Corporate Services provides a sales team which meets with area CEOs and human resources managers to determine companies' training needs, to discuss potential customized training programs, and to validate the relevancy of Valencia's curriculum.

Technology Transfer. The movement of real technology, the ideas and methodology from scientists and engineers, into the commercial sector is referred to as technology transfer and, increasingly, as technology commercialization. It is often broadly defined as the movement of technical information and/or materials, used for producing a product or process, from one sector to another (Office of Technology Assessment, 1984, p. 596). Bloch suggests effective transfer requires:

- adequate support for basic research that generates new knowledge;
- people capable of performing research that generates technology and ultimately products that are viable in the marketplace; and
- communication, collaboration, and cooperation among people and institutions that generate new technology and those that have a need for it (1988, pp. 9–14).

Cooperation between people and institutions is necessary to address capital investment, feasibility studies for manufacturing, strategic planning for marketing, a positive regulatory atmosphere, and a trained workforce—components of the technology transfer and commercialization process...technology is not hardware, but rather is the application of knowledge (Roe, 1989, p. 43).

Sinclair Community College is actively involved in facilitating technology commercialization transfer. Its Ohio Applied Technology Center—a consortium of technical organizations in Dayton, Columbus, and Cincinnati, Ohio—supports research at Wright-Patterson Air Force Base and the development of technology transfer initiatives from the base to industries in at least 10 states. The Edison Materials Technology Center (EMTEC) at Sinclair is funded by a $3 million grant from the Ohio Department of Development and partners the college with other area colleges. Faculty are involved in research and development of new manufacturing and machining methods using technology transfer from educational and governmental institutions. In addition, Sinclair is co-recipient of special state appropriations with Wright State University to fund its Information Technology Applications Center (INTAC), which applies current information technologies to existing programs and serves as a conduit for technology between research and application.

The Southeast Manufacturing Technology Center (SMTC) at *Midlands Technical College* joins MTC with the University of South Carolina and several state government agencies. The center's goal is to aid businesses in implementing advanced technology. The community college's role is to facilitate transfer of technology to small businesses in the area and help industry focus on continuous quality improvements.

COMMUNITY DEVELOPMENT

Participating in Community Development. Community development is the focus of the second category of partnerships or collaborations, although activities may take various forms—community development, community problem-solving, convening forums, and good citizenship. Community development activities are designed to reinvigorate and restore entire communities. Community problem-solving brings together multiple stakeholders to address concerns in one segment—such as education. Forums provide opportunities to discuss important community issues, and citizenship entails activities that do not fall into the three previous categories but contribute to the well-being of the community.

Miami-Dade Community College's Medical Center campus, in partnership with local, state, and national entities, and with private foundation support, is working to help neighborhood residents reclaim and revitalize their community. Some of the college's goals are to develop the skills of residents, provide an encouraging environment, support system change in the delivery of public services, organize service learning, and provide educational opportunities. There are numerous community development partners involved in this project, including the Overtown Apartment Association, the Allapattah YMCA daycare program, and many community development corporations. The college has helped to organize groups of citizens; provided technical assistance in neighborhood transformation; worked with family, child care, and health issues; and offered a myriad of special programs and courses. Chrislip and Larson have made some observations that describe the beliefs and feelings of those committed to the project.

> Collaborative leaders are sustained by their deeply democratic belief that people have the capacity to create their own visions and solve their own problems. If you can bring the appropriate people together (being broadly inclusive) in constructive ways (creating a credible, open process) with good information (bringing about a shared understanding of problems and concerns), they will create authentic visions and strategies for addressing the shared concerns of the organizations or community. The leadership role is to convene, energize, facilitate, and sustain this process. As we have said, *the only consensus that really matters is that of the people who live there* (1994, p. 146).

Although it is too soon to determine the long-term impact of these efforts, Miami-Dade's involvement is an example of the modern American community college's ability to make vital contributions to its community.

Cuyahoga Community College's Saint Vincent Quadrangle Project partners with Cleveland State University, Saint Vincent Charity Hospital, the Cleveland Foundation, the Gund Foundation, and more than 40 businesses and institutions. The project's goal is to improve the inner-city area which surrounds the campus, improve the quality of life of the neighborhood's residents, and seek ways to renovate; and it has overseen the reinvestment of $200 million by member institutions and businesses to date. Results include implementation of weekly clean-up and grounds maintenance of public areas and the development of the Quadrangle Police Force which is staffed by off-duty Cleveland police with full police powers.

The Community College of Denver worked with community representatives and educators to create the Colorado Institute for Hispanic Education and Economic Development. Working toward community development through improving the literacy rate of its citizens, Florida Community College at Jacksonville sponsors a creative array of literacy programs for the homeless, for residents of several housing projects, and for mothers and their children at four elementary schools.

Community Problem Solving. Activities in this category represent comprehensive, multi-partnered efforts to address problems that require long-term, systematic interventions. For example, aware of the increasingly alarming signs that the city's educational system was not successfully moving students through the educational pipeline, the *Community College of Denver* worked with a cross-section of community leaders—representatives from the public school system, area universities, the local department of social services, private foundations, business leaders, and community-based organizations—to establish the Denver Network and increase student success.

In another example of a community problem-solving effort, *Midlands Technical College* is involved in a multi-year, Kellogg-funded effort—Alliance 2020—to create a model for an interconnected network of constituent-based educational services and lifelong learning with various entry points and delivery systems. Partners include Clemson University (the lead institution), South Carolina State University, South Carolina's 17 two-year technical colleges, public and private agencies, business and industry, and others. One goal the alliance has established is to redefine the role of land grant colleges in the U.S.

Convening Forums. Community colleges have a history of creating forums that bring citizens together to discuss important community issues. *Miami-Dade Community College* provided opportunities for the residents of the Overtown neighborhood to have grassroots discussions of problems and proposed solutions. *Chattanooga State Technical Community College* and *Florida Community College at Jacksonville* participated in the leadership of community visioning activities where citizens talked and worked together to identify mutual priorities and values.

Forum participants have not been limited to the immediate geographical area. *Midlands Technical College* convened the state's community colleges to develop, test, and disseminate campus-wide assessment models for rural and urban settings. *St. Petersburg Junior College* has designed and conducted statewide and national forums. The college's Roundtable on Educational Partnerships convened 19 educational leaders from organizations such as the American Vocational Association, American College Testing, the College Board, Educational Testing Systems, and the American Association of Community Colleges to discuss the contributions of the community college. St. Petersburg has also hosted two Presidential Library Summits—one at the Carter Library to consider the role of the community college in shaping the nation, and another at the Ford Library to discuss the role of the community college in the training of America's workforce.

Convening sometimes involves coalition-building—bringing together leaders representing various interests in a particular issue to work toward a common ground, toward understanding the larger picture, or toward changing the path of an issue of mutual concern (Tucker, 1992). *Midlands Technical College*, for example, was an active co-partner in forming the Unified Marketing Task Force—a project of the Greater Columbia Chamber of Commerce (South Carolina). Economic development agencies, business, cultural groups, and government and education representatives were among the participating sectors. Working to present the community's best side to any business or industry considering relocating to or establishing a new enterprise in the area, this diverse group identified what the community had to offer, put that data in an easily accessible, computerized database, and organized marketing efforts. The "big picture" goal of the task force was economic development, but the process built a coalition as well as community pride.

Community Citizenship. Activities that involve contributing to the well-being of the community—for example, taking personal responsibility for making the community a better place and helping those in need—are included in this category. Community colleges contribute people power and resources every day in this country. It is widely recognized that "citizens can and do develop a different kind of civic culture that makes their communities and regions stronger and more effective" (Chrislip and Larson, 1994, p. 11). Sometimes citizenship efforts are short-term, volunteer efforts—for example, when college faculty and staff volunteer to participate in a fund-raising walk, and/or to host the activities that precede and conclude the walk, as did *Greenville Technical College*, or when the colleges become active respondents to community disasters—such as hurricanes or floods—as did *Miami-Dade Community College* and *Greenville Technical College* when they were designated as emergency shelter sites and providers of transportation, equipment, supplies, and food. *Midlands Technical College's* College Ambassadors assist with community projects, work as reading tutors to community adults, and get involved in projects such as collecting and distributing old notebooks and office supplies to poor children.

The Community College of Denver serves as host and fiscal agent for the Colorado Campus Compact—a coalition of 21 Colorado state, public, and private university and college presidents meeting to formulate ways to create public service opportunities for students and to encourage the inclusion of service as an integral part of the undergraduate experience. The Compact is part of the national Campus Compact which involves more than 400 postsecondary institutions.

PEOPLE DEVELOPMENT

Chapter authors reported a wide variety of community college partnerships and collaborations designed to develop all categories of people—students, faculty, staff, employees, citizens, national guard and military personnel, at-risk youth, and disabled people. Colleges are providing development opportunities by providing a convenient and wide range of higher education options, helping people successfully complete education or training programs, encouraging interest in particular occupational areas (often by special populations), increasing diversity, and/or enhancing international or cultural experiences.

Providing a Wide Range of Higher Education Options. Flexibility is the byword in today's world. The 18- to 22-year-old full-time college student is a historical artifact in the community college. Today's college students need alternative delivery systems and convenient times and locations that will allow them to incorporate continuous learning experiences with their work and family lives. At the same time, more institutions must do more with less. Community colleges have collaborated with others to provide a wide range of these opportunities.

Particularly in metropolitan settings where the higher education needs of the populace are so diverse, cooperative enterprises created by multiple institutions are especially critical (Gilley, 1991). The Dallas Education Center, housed at El Centro College, partners the *Dallas County Community College District* with East Texas State University, Texas Women's University, the University of Dallas, the University of North Texas, the University of Texas at Arlington, and the University of Texas at Dallas. Plans include articulation agreements providing common student application forms, shared course offerings, and joint student recruitment efforts. The University Center at *Greenville Technical College*, is a partnership of eight four-year colleges and universities that offers 26 undergraduate and graduate degree programs. Currently, each confers its own degrees and provides its own professors. Moreover, the philosophy of team building that has been established in this center led to another collaborative effort—two long-standing rivals, the University of South Carolina and Clemson University, now co-teach and co-award the MPA (master of public administration).

Chattanooga State Technical Community College—working with the Chattanooga Housing Authority to establish neighborhood "outposts" (the Authority provided two double-wide housing units), the Private Industry Council (the Council helped remodel and staff the sites), and the Urban League (the League staffs the sites and markets the program)—provides counseling, adult basic education, remedial, and introductory college courses, tutoring, and mentoring in urban, outlying teaching/ learning centers. The centers are created in partnership with city, county, and state governments, the public schools, and the Private Industry Council; they are one-stop shops for employment assistance, ABE/GED education, library services, child care, vocational training, college courses, and corporate training and recruitment.

Humber College places a high priority on faculty and staff development. Recognizing that more of their employees would participate in further formal education opportunities if there were built-in incentives and more convenient times and locations, Humber offers a campus-based master's program in community college education (in conjunction with Central Michigan University), a campus-based doctoral program in higher education (with Michigan State University), and baccalaureate courses (with York University and Atkinson College).

Metropolitan Community College, in conjunction with the city of La Vista, Nebraska, plans to open a joint library/community college center. Each home in the town will be wired to fiber optic linkages connected to the center, making possible the delivery of credit- and non-credit courses. This option makes George Gilder's suggestion that "the age of broadcast has given way to *narrowcast*" [our emphasis] (Avishai, 1994, p. 47) a reality—that two-way computers will place events, books, teachers, and so on in homes and within everyone's reach.

Community colleges, in conjunction with partners such as cable companies, local public television channels, the National Telecommunication Information Administration (NTIA, in the U.S. Department of Commerce), public school districts, and other colleges and universities, are serving their constituents via microwave, Instructional Television Fixed Services (ITFS), cable, and satellites. *Kirkwood Community College* has a commitment to developing telecommunications capability and uses each of these vehicles. More than 70 hours of classes each week are conducted and sent to eight communities using microwave telecommunications. ITFS allows Kirkwood to provide audio and video transmission of selected high school courses to area public schools and early-bird college credit courses in calculus, psychology, and sociology. Faculty/staff development programs and some corporate employee training also reach populations via the ITFS Network. *Kirkwood Community College* indicated that their educational cable channel makes it possible for residents to earn an AA degree from attendance centers or in their homes. Satellite services allow these colleges uplink and downlink capabilities— permitting access to national and international programming. *St. Petersburg Junior College*, *Florida Community College at Jacksonville*, and *Valencia Community College* participated with the Florida National Guard and the University of Central Florida's Institute for Simulation and Training to provide two-way interactive satellite telecommunications network training to Florida's armed services personnel.

Dallas County Community College District is working with the Texas Army National Guard as a member of the Texas Army National Guard Higher Education Cooperative (HECOOP). HECOOP's long-range plan is to offer college degrees (first to the military, then to the public) at the armories in the state, using on-site and distance learning. *Florida Community College at Jacksonville* offers advising, computer labs, learning resources, and instruction on three Jacksonville Navy bases. The courses are offered on a yearlong schedule of six week courses—a format which meets the needs of Navy schedules.

A group of Nebraska colleges—*Metropolitan Community College*, Wayne State College, Peru State College, Northeast Community College, and Nebraska Indian Community College—are discussing the creation of a multi-institution audio and video link. Each institution could then provide its very best services to the other locations—e.g., offering courses, providing staff development, and facilitating student transfer among the institutions.

Helping People Successfully Complete Education and Training Programs. Value-chain partnerships link suppliers and customers (Kanter, 1994). Such partnerships in education make it possible for community colleges to connect with universities and K–12 systems to facilitate and encourage student success. In the first of several examples, the Pathway Program at *St. Petersburg Junior College* guarantees admission into a health care program to students who complete a specialized core of courses. SPJC also allows students in public and private high schools to earn college credit if they successfully complete prescribed dual-credit courses. Student fees and textbook costs are paid by the state for students selected for this program. *Metropolitan Community College* students may move directly into an advanced client-server training program, at nearby Bellevue University, which offers 36 hours of training for experienced mainframe computer operators. Future plans include combining their student records systems and allowing students to move back and forth between the two institutions.

Many colleges have articulation agreements with state universities. In the *Dallas County Community College District's* Enhanced Transfer Program, the senior colleges accept more than the traditional equivalent of two years of transfer credit toward baccalaureate degrees. DCCCD will benefit from enhanced enrollments, and the senior colleges have concluded that their potential loss of revenue on these courses will be compensated by the increased number of students who will be encouraged to seek the baccalaureate degree under the enhanced transfer option. To ease student transfers, *Midlands Technical College* offers annual tours, strong articulation agreements, and professional development opportunities for MTC students at the University of South Carolina.

Other community college programs work to mentor, tutor, and build skills in elementary and secondary school students, encouraging them to choose and complete postsecondary education and/or training. *Miami-Dade Community College's* AGAPE program, the brainchild of a faculty member, pairs college volunteers with representatives of an interfaith alliance of churches to provide tutoring and role models to neighborhood youth. *Midlands Technical College* and *Metropolitan Community College* participate in an Adopt-a-School program. At MTC, elementary students spend several hours each month in experimental teaching and learning experiences on campus. *Miami-Dade Community College*, the Dade County Public Schools, and Florida International University worked together to develop the New World School of the Arts—a high school and college program in which gifted high school students get a realistic view of professional training in a carefully sequenced and accelerated dual-enrollment program. *Midlands Technical College's* Cities in Schools partnership provides an alternative high school program designed to increase enrollment and retention of at-risk students in postsecondary institutions.

Other programs target adults. The *Community College of Denver* works with the Colorado Department of Social Services and many local businesses and corporations to help food stamp recipients earn a GED and develop job skills in their Employment First program. Project Eve, at *Cuyahoga Community College*, offers educational and counseling services, including career information, personal assessment, academic advisement, and workshops to returning adult women. The Mayor's Office of Employment and Training, Private Industry Council, Denver Metro Chamber of Commerce and the Minority Chamber of Commerce, hospital leaders, local foundations, and others worked with the *Community College of Denver* to create several Technical Education Centers (TEC) to offer open-entry, open-exit, self-paced vocational training in city neighborhoods. The Black Student Success Office at *Florida Community College at Jacksonville* coordinates with private and public entities to provide resources for scholarships (for black students attending college), for Black History Month activities, and for a popular annual calendar featuring black community leaders.

Encouraging Interest in Particular Occupational Areas. High school students take advanced calculus courses and learn the effective use of graphing calculators in a program developed by *Chattanooga State Technical Community College*, the University of Tennessee, and a local private college. The Miami Chamber of Commerce and *Miami-Dade Community College* co-sponsor The Great Cookie Project, which teaches young children the basics of owning a business. The Dade County Public Schools and Miami-Dade's Medical Center campus co-sponsor a two-year program that exposes children to an atmosphere of learning and accomplishment; they perform experiments and meet with faculty. The Overtown Scientist-for-a-Day project brings young people to the Medical Center campus over a seven-week period during which they participate in educational experiences. *Greenville Technical College's* Summer Enrichment in Math and Science program, originally funded by National Science Foundation and the U.S. Department of Energy and currently supported by JTPA, pays students a small stipend for each hour they participate. Students receive mentoring from GTC students, use the latest computer hardware and software, perform experiments, and learn about career opportunities in math and science.

Six South Carolina colleges and universities and *Midlands Technical College* make up the South Carolina Alliance for Minority Participation in Science and Mathematics, established to enhance the success of minority students in technical career paths. Funded by an initiative grant from the National Science Foundation, the project promotes interest in the sciences through recruiting, retention, and research activities. The Science, Engineering, Mathematics, and Aerospace Academy (SEMAA), funded by NASA, at *Cuyahoga Community College*, provides after-school, early evening and Saturday classes, and emphasizes parent involvement. It targets students who historically have been underrepresented in math, science, and engineering. Activities vary with the age groups and include summer camps and field trips. At higher levels, students are placed in mentorships and internships in Cleveland area businesses, industry, government, or colleges and universities. *St. Petersburg Junior College's* National Youth Sports Program, a special summer program for at-risk students, includes a math/science instructional component, along with instruction on sports fundamentals, nutrition, and drug education.

The National Collegiate Athletic Association, which funds the effort, and the local school board partner with St. Petersburg in this program.

The *Kirkwood Community College* Skill Center works with the Iowa Division of Vocational Rehabilitation to assist people who are physically, emotionally, economically, and/or socially handicapped. *Dallas County Community College District's* El Centro College operates a Middle College High School in downtown Dallas, attracting city youth who, it is hoped, will have a higher incidence of postsecondary enrollment as a result of their exposure to the college campus. Dental, medical, engineering, legal, production, and inventory control societies sponsor student chapters on the *Greenville Technical College* campus. Society members work with students and provide professional development opportunities. *Florida Community College at Jacksonville* provides ABE, GED, and life-transition skills to adults in Jacksonville's correctional facilities.

Increasing Diversity. The *Dallas County Community College District* offers scholarships to students who attend and graduate from a high school that has an ethnic majority different from their own. The University of Texas at Austin, Texas A&M, and the University of North Texas work with DCCCD to provide summer review and enrichment classes, SAT preparation, and tutoring for minority junior high and senior high students in Dallas County, with the goal of developing college readiness classes. DCCCD has taken the lead role in this effort to develop student interests and achievement in the areas of math and science. *St. Petersburg Junior College's* Career Connections Program provides a support network, job shadowing, and outward bound experiences specifically for African American males and others who are underrepresented in the college population. College Reachout, a state-funded project which partners resources between community colleges and universities, provides tutoring, mentoring, field trips, and summer programs on the University of South Florida campus for low income and educationally disadvantaged students who may benefit from postsecondary education. *Florida Community College at Jacksonville* has taken a direct step to support economic growth for minorities by increasing minority business access to the college's purchasing dollars. In partnership with minority-owned businesses, chambers of commerce, and local agencies, the college increased communication with minority businesses on every college bid, integrating them into the competitive process. *Greenville Technical College* learned that some employees of multinational companies located in the area wanted an educational institution to provide ESL and children's language classes in Japanese, German, and Spanish; the college provided these classes.

Enhancing the International or Cultural Experience. *Metropolitan Community College* hosted 35 U.S. community college leaders on a trip to Denmark and Sweden to establish partnerships and linkages with their Folkhighschool movement. *Midlands Technical College* organized a tour of Germany during which local civic leaders met with German educational system representatives to promote the community as a potential site for international economic development and to help local leaders understand the German dual-education system. *St. Petersburg Junior College's* International Center, which operates in conjunction with Georgetown University and the Florida Department of Education, offers college students experiences in coursework and in democratic living. SPJC developed the Cultural Diversity Training Institute in partnership with a local law enforcement agency, offering cultural diversity training and workshops on such topics as affirmative action, women in the workplace, sexual harassment, and police brutality. In the belief that the workforce of the future must have a knowledge of and openness to other cultures, *Greenville Technical College* initiated the South Carolina International Education Consortium. The Consortium's goal is to revise existing courses and develop others to educate students about other cultures.

Miami-Dade Community College's Cultura del Lobo is a series of works by dancers, musicians, media, and performance artists from all over the world. Eleven community groups, 11 local arts groups, eight national arts groups, and nine international arts groups participated in the 1993 event, designed to enhance citizens' international cultural experience. Another large-scale event, the Miami Book Fair International, is a yearlong literary extravaganza that culminates with a free eight-day fair, featuring 300 authors and more than 500 national and international book vendors. A two-year series of educational and community outreach events—titled Chinese in the Americas—explored how Chinese artists have been influenced by the American host countries. Hispanic Heritage Week presents workshops and cultural events including concerts, dance presentations, and art exhibits. Empanada Night, which represents 12 or more different countries, is a crowd favorite. Miami-Dade's Lunchtime Lively Arts Series sponsors events featuring international and national talent in several downtown locations.

Some community colleges have developed partnerships with others to enhance college offerings and/or the community's cultural experience. *Chattanooga State Technical Community College* is associated with the local Hunter Museum of Art and the Chattanooga Little Theater. As a result, teaching space has been made available, and some of the region's finest artists and technical and acting directors have been hired as adjunct faculty. A full spectrum of courses in the visual arts is now provided, and a full-blown degree program in theater is offered. The University of Florida's fine arts department and *Florida Community College at Jacksonville* have begun to offer arts workshops in anticipation of the opening of FCCJ's new $20 million complex which will house the college's art education program. FCCJ's Artists Series has 50 performances a year of professional Broadway productions for the community and students. JazzFest, held in Cleveland, Ohio, and considered to be the country's premier educational jazz festival, features 11 days of concerts, workshops, and other community outreach activities. Interest in the festival, now more than 10 years old, encouraged the establishment of the Excellence in Music Project at *Cuyahoga Community College*, with gifts from the Cleveland and Gund Foundations; the college is now working toward a formalized jazz studies curriculum.

ORGANIZATIONAL DEVELOPMENT

Restructure the Organization. Some collaborative activities involve changing the way colleges conduct their work. One of Metropolitan Community College's longest, most in-depth partnerships is its official sister-college relationship with Nebraska Indian Community College. Both institutions have agreed to adopt the other and create sharing activities in which all students, staff, and faculty can participate. Annual joint staff development activities are held, instructional technologies are shared, and discussions continue about improving both colleges' services. MCC is also working with internal collaboration. A diverse group of college staff and faculty meet regularly in a think-tank setting to explore new ways the college might enhance its work, including its curriculum and instructional approaches. Named the Experimental College, the group has overseen the implementation of electronic mail and pilot projects with concepts learned from the Scandinavian Study Circle and the Danish Folkhighschool movement.

St. Petersburg Junior College's Project Flamingo partners include faculty and staff, and representatives from Unisys, Apple, and Digital Equipment Corporation. The original project goal was to create a collegewide, integrated computer network to improve instruction and administration, and foster communication. One outcome is the planned construction of a new high-tech campus which may institute new academic programs such as biotechnology and environmental science. The facility will serve as a distance learning hub and feature electronic classrooms.

Valencia Community College has formed six Industry Quality Teams with more than 120 staff and faculty. The six teams mirror the six industries that are considered the keys to the mid-Florida economy; the teams plan to communicate current industry needs to all faculty and students in the college and to prospective students, and the college intends to make appropriate modifications to all programs affected by these needs. Various assumptions underlie these different ways of approaching work.

There is a belief that if you bring the appropriate people together in constructive ways with good information, they will create authentic visions and strategies for addressing the shared concerns of the organization or the community…This is a profound shift in our conception about how change is created and requires an equally profound shift in our conception of leadership (Chrislip and Larson, 1994, p. 14).

In recognition of this shift, *Dallas County Community College District* created an Office of Educational Partnerships which serves as a single point of contact for external entities wanting information about possible partnerships with the college, and the office budget includes limited support for selected new efforts.

Providing Staff Development Opportunities. The commitment at *Humber College* to staff development is best exemplified in its collegewide recognition and awards program. Faculty and staff worked together to initiate and conduct a program of peer nomination and selection. More than 50 awards are presented annually for activities that exemplify the institution's values and objectives.

Unfortunately, not all colleges implement such recognition programs. As some observers of the college scene have noted:

> It is somewhat ironic that the colleges that have brought the opportunity for lifelong learning to the masses have traditionally done so little to facilitate continuous learning within their own organizations...the organization committed to holistic thinking is, of necessity, the organization dedicated to continual learning (Lorenzo and LeCroy, 1994, p. 19).

RESOURCE DEVELOPMENT

> The growing consensus is that constraints on traditional revenue sources will remain through the balance of this decade, if not beyond. There is also a growing sense that 'doing more with less' is not a viable long term strategy. Sooner or later, the only thing that comes from less is less (Lorenzo and LeCroy, 1994, p. 17).

Others agree that "as much as this nation is beginning to accept...the need for an infusion of funds for education and training, the economic resources...will simply not be available to fuel higher education as we have known it" (Johnstone, 1994, Part 1, p. 2).

Raising Money for the College. Clearly, fund raising is totally dependent upon relationships, generally those which have been nurtured for years. Self-interest provides strong motivation. For example, employer donors want a labor pool of graduates with appropriate skills and strong work ethics; they have compelling reasons to strengthen their communities economically.

Valencia Community College's work with the business and industry community has led to donations that presently support 23 endowed faculty chairs, in areas such as quality, entrepreneurship, and economic development. *Kirkwood Community College* recently formed a trust—the Career Opportunity Program—with Mount Mercy College. Development officers from both schools raise funds to help Kirkwood students in technical programs, especially minorities, Vietnam veterans and economically disadvantaged students who wish to become teachers. AA or AS graduates transfer smoothly to Mount Mercy to complete a baccalaureate program. KCC is a member of the Cedar Rapids Area Chamber of Commerce economic development team, Priority One. The goal of Priority One is to develop the Cedar Rapids-Iowa City corridor into a fast-growing and diverse manufacturing area.

Kirkwood Community College, St. Petersburg Junior College, Greenville Technical College, Miami-Dade Community College, Valencia Community College, and *Metropolitan Community College* all have established college foundations. Successful fundraising supports student scholarships, faculty development activities, equipment, and facilities. For example, *Greenville*

Technical College has partnered with the local health care community to construct a new classroom building and underwrite health career programs. The college has also developed a successful volunteer program in which community residents provided 8,400 hours of service to the college last year, acting as tutors or assisting in other ways.

Facilities for Community College Programs and Services. Increasingly, community colleges are turning to partnerships, collaborations, and alliances to build or acquire facilities and share fixed costs. *Chattanooga State Technical Community College* is negotiating with the Tennessee Valley Authority to develop a facility for training, teleconferencing, and information search and navigation operations. The college is working with NASA and the Center for Creative Leadership in North Carolina to develop training programs that will be housed in the new facility. When representatives of a regional hospital council came to *St. Petersburg Junior College* and expressed the need for more trained nurses and other allied health care graduates, talks began. SPJC, in partnership with, among others, the Bay Area Hospital Council, the Florida Legislature, the College Development Foundation, and Exxon Oil Co., purchased some land, received legislative appropriations for renovations, and raised matching funds from a community-wide fund-raising activity to build its Health Education Center. Allstate Insurance Company gave SPJC a sizable campus and facility which has become a law enforcement academy, the home of a fire science program, and a corporate training services program. When *Kirkwood Community College* learned that a hospital in a rural community in their district was about to close, it negotiated a partnership where the building, on a shared basis with the medical community, became both a learning center and a non-emergency medical facility. Due to this creative partnership, two rural Iowa communities have a shared facility for joint delivery of education and health services. *Metropolitan Community College* is exploring a partnership between the college and the local library to provide more cost-effective services— the library needs funds and the college needs space. North Lake College in the *Dallas County Community College District* is constructing a library that will be finished, equipped, and stocked by the city of Irving. The new library will be located on campus and will serve as both the college and community library, with operational costs being shared jointly. After several years, seven entities partnered with Humber College to move one of the campuses to facilities more suitable for current and future needs; the existing campus will be turned over to the municipal and metropolitan governments and shared with a local school board to create parkland and play fields. In public education, there is a "single, clear direction: toward the forging of alliances to share fixed costs" (Ohmae, 1989, p. 147).

CONCLUSIONS

Anyone who tries to draw the future in hard lines and vivid hues is a fool. The future will never sit still for a portrait. It will come around a corner we never noticed and take us by surprise (Leonard, 1968, p. 139).

Perhaps at no time in the history of community colleges has the drawing of their collective futures been a more unsettling task. Traditional boundaries of familiar images are being blurred or wiped away on the artist's canvas. Community colleges' unspoken, informal agreements about turf issues are even now being renegotiated in diverse ways. Their more traditional, hard-edged geographic service regions are being redrawn—most seriously and obviously by technology, and then by their unique needs to specialize in programming (perhaps with "centers of excellence"), to provide customized programming to clients perhaps even far beyond their drawn service areas, and to become more international in scope (Lorenzo and Banach, 1994, pp. 23–24). The future will take colleges around corners they "never noticed," encouraging them to rethink their own boundaries in light of the reality that other entities important to the colleges' well-being are rethinking theirs. It will require that colleges seriously consider the nature of and appropriate limits on the company they will keep in their new ventures.

> The potential value of the relationship must be weighed against the value of all...other activities, which also make demands on its resources...Even when relationships have high value, an organization can handle only so many before demands begin to conflict and investment requirements...outweigh perceived benefits (Kanter, 1994, p. 108).

Woven in a visible and compelling way throughout these chapters are extraordinary responses to the critical realities of the current community college experience—i.e., increasing demands for and expectations of community college services occurring simultaneously with declining revenues. Moreover, there are responses to a rather common argument against establishing collaborative initiatives—i.e., colleges already have too much on their plates, and responding to new demands will jeopardize the quality of established services and programs.

There are increasing demands for and expectations of community college services occurring simultaneously with reduced and declining revenues.

Community colleges must look to the future in terms of their assumptions about their life support systems. These are some of the realities.

- Thirty-one states began 1993 with an operating deficit, resulting in zero or minimal state aid reimbursements to more than half of our nation's community colleges.
- The debate over K–12 school finance—compounded by discussions on choice and vouchers—has produced an unstable foundation for all educational funding and made community college planning more difficult.
- Increased hesitancy of the electorate to provide tax revenue for community college bonds and operation have limited educational options for students and career options for community college employees (Lorenzo and Banach, 1994, p. 5).

In light of these realities and others described throughout this book, we asked—and answered based on what we have learned—the following questions:

- Is it likely that community colleges can look to increased state financial support in the decade ahead? *We think not.*
- Is there an absolute limit on the amount of tuition and fees that community colleges can charge without adversely affecting the student market they serve? *We believe the answer is yes.*
- Is it likely that we can substantially increase class sizes to improve efficiency and generate a broader base of financial support? *This would be difficult to do given the collective power of faculty unions and the like.*
- Can we increase faculty workload, i.e., increasing from five organized classes to six? Again, this increased productivity could be accomplished only after years of negotiations and struggle. *We think it is unlikely.*
- Can we employ more part-time faculty? *We already are delivering 50 percent of our total hours of instruction with part-timers, and there is probably some limit to this as a strategy for financial solvency in the future.*
- Can technology help us become more efficient and productive? *Probably so, but the emphasis is more likely to be on the efficiencies—not necessarily on the effectiveness.*

Community colleges must identify what they can and will do well, but they must not assume that taking on new roles and obligations in one dimension will threaten or automatically diminish the quality of their service in another.

Community colleges' successes have established their reputations as "competent players in their communities" (Lorenzo and Banach, 1994, p. 11).

One consequence of this enviable position is that community colleges are now being asked by almost everyone to be a partner in almost everything. Even the leading thinkers in today's community college movement are advocates for new directions. We've heard calls to get more involved in workforce development, customized education, economic development, civic improvement, and, most recently, community leadership.

The result is that the agenda for community colleges is no longer clearly defined. And, it's likely their purpose will continue to blur as the waves of radical change get closer and come faster (Lorenzo and Banach, 1994, p. 11).

Perhaps we could take some lessons from the traditional values and mission of the land grant universities. Early on, these institutions had powerful missions to provide service to statewide constituencies, resulting in programs such as agricultural extension agents, home demonstration agents, and the like. They have a rich history of more than 130 years of quality in teaching, research, and service to the larger community. In fact, the University of Minnesota describes its campus as everything within the borders of the state. This history should be recalled by those who would argue against forming collaborations, warning that we may dilute teaching quality and/or our focus upon transfer education, for example, by taking on too many other activities and programs. This critical argument suggests that institutions can do only one or two things well without losing focus and/or direction. Just because a college assumes a new program, it does not follow that the quality of any other will be diluted. Quality is a matter of priority, focus, and leadership.

Truly, it is not each community and organizational partnership or collaborative on a stand-alone basis to which critics necessarily object; rather, it is the conglomerate, the mass of activities that can accrue, that has received the attention of critics of community colleges and begs for further examination and serious contemplation. However, the realities of increased demands, rising expectations, and declining resources leave community colleges no choice but "to look at what we do and to be honest about whether we should keep doing it" (Lorenzo and Banach, 1994, p. 28)—perhaps to break free of responsibilities and activities that are no longer of benefit and turn attention to others that are more likely to be so. These realities further encourage colleges to identify relationships that they want to establish, those that they are capable of establishing, and those that they are willing to sustain. Moreover, these realities seriously challenge, even threaten, colleges that choose to maintain their status quo and their traditional comfort level, or that put their faith in Rudyard Kipling's notion that "he travels the fastest who travels alone."

This leaves us with two realities: (1) there is a world shift toward realizing our interconnections and our interdependencies, and community colleges are inextricably locked in that shift; and (2) there is a critical need to establish new community partners, to look for new bases of support and collaborative funding. It is likely that as community colleges respond to community needs and to the needs of their constituencies for services, their constituencies will respond with support for programs and services that benefit them directly. In our local and global economy, we as individuals, as colleges, and as community entities (no matter the size) cannot function in isolation; we are all inextricably interlocked in the human enterprise. Observers of the complexities and the varieties of this enterprise agree that "success comes not just from *what* you know but from *who* [our emphasis] you know" (Kanter, 1994, p. 108). Indeed, we are now and will always be known by the company we keep.

REFERENCES

Avishai, B. "What is business's social compact?" *Harvard Business Review*, 1994, 72(1), 38-48.

Bellah, R.N. and Associates. *Habits of the heart: Individualism and commitment in American life.* Berkeley, CA: University of California Press, 1985. (The opening quote is found on p. 163.)

Bloch, E. "Technology transfer and the National Science Foundation." In Bopp, G.R. (Ed.), *Federal Lab Technology Transfer.* New York: Praeger, 1988.

Boyer, E.L. "Curriculum, culture, and social cohesion." *Celebrations.* Austin, TX: The National Institute for Staff and Organizational Development, July 1992.

Boyer, E.L. *College: The undergraduate experience in America.* New York: Harper and Row, Publishers, 1987.

Brint, S. and Karabel, J. *The diverted dream: Community colleges and the promise of educational opportunity in America, 1900–1985.* New York: Oxford University Press, 1989.

Chrislip, D.D. and Larson, C.E. *Collaborative leadership: How citizens and civic leaders can make a difference.* San Francisco, CA: Jossey-Bass, 1994.

Clark, D. "Business-education partnerships in the last decade: Rhetoric over substance." *Metro Connection,* 1990, 5(1), 15–18.

Doucette, D. *Community college workforce training programs for employees of business, industry, labor, and government: A status report.* Mission Viejo, CA: League for Innovation in the Community College, 1993.

Emery, R.E. and Trist, E.L. "The causal texture of organization environments." *Human Relations,* 1965, 18, 21–23.

Gilley, J.W. *Thinking about American higher education.* New York: American Council on Education & Macmillan Publishing Company, 1991.

Gleazer, E.J., Jr. *The community college: Values, vision and vitality.* Washington, DC: American Association of Community and Junior Colleges, 1984.

Johnstone, D.B. "College at work: Partnerships and the rebuilding of American competence." *Journal of Higher Education.* [online], 1994, 65(2), 168ff. Available: e-mail: lbindx@utxdp.dp.utexas.edu

Kanter, R.M. "Collaborative advantage: The art of alliances." *Harvard Business Review,* July–August 1994, 72(4), 96–108.

Katsinas, S.G. "A review of the literature related to economic development and community colleges." *Community College Review,* 1994, 21(4), 67–80.

Kearns, D.T. and Flanigan, F. "Why I got involved." *Fortune,* Spring 1990, 46–47.

Leonard, G.B. *Education and ecstasy.* New York: Delacorte Press, 1968.

Lorenzo, A.L., and Banach, W.J. *Critical issues facing America's community colleges (1994–1995).* Warren, MI: Macomb Press, 1994.

Lorenzo, A.L. and LeCroy, N.A. "A framework for fundamental change in the community college." *Community College Journal,* 1994, 64(4), 14–19.

Office of Technology Assessment. *Commercial biotechnology: An international analysis.* Washington, DC: United States Congress Office of Technology Assessment, 1984.

Ohmae, K. "The global logic of strategic alliances." *Harvard Business Review,* 1989, 67(2), 143–154.

Peters, T.J. and Waterman, R.H. *In search of excellence.* New York: Warner, 1982.

Roe, M.A. *Education and U.S. competitiveness: The community college role.* Texas: IC2 Institute, The University of Texas at Austin, 1989.

Ross, D. "Enterprise economics on the front lines." In Schram, M. and Marshall, W. (Eds.), *Mandate for Change.* New York: Berkley Books, 1993, 51-80.

Roueche, J.E. "Meeting the challenge: What does society need from higher education?" Essay prepared for the Wingspread Group on Higher Education. Racine, WI: Wingspread Group on Higher Education, December 1993.

Stone, N. "Does business have any business in education?" *Harvard Business Review,* 1991, 69(2), 46–55.

Tucker, K. "Building coalitions to initiate change." *Public Relations Journal,* 1992, 48(1), 28–31.

Weidenthal, M.D. *Who cares about the inner city? The community college response to urban America.* (Report for the Commission on Urban Community Colleges). Washington, DC: American Association of Community and Junior Colleges, 1989.

APPENDIX A

For more information, contact these individuals.

CHAPTER AND CONTACT PERSON	PHONE NUMBER	FAX
Chapter 1: Chapter and Verse: How We Came to Be Where We Are *Lynn Sullivan Taber* *CCLP, The University of Texas at Austin*	(512) 471-7545	(512) 471-9426
Chapter 2: Metropolitan Community College *Richard Gilliland* *President*	(402) 449-8415	(402) 449-8332
Chapter 3: Miami-Dade Community College *Clynne Morgan* *District President's Office*	(305) 237-7574	(305) 237-3761
Chapter 4: Community College of Denver *Byron McClenney* *President*	(303) 556-2411	(303) 556-3586
Chapter 5: Chattanooga State Technical Community College *James L. Catanzaro* *President*	(615) 697-4455	(615) 697-4796
Chapter 6: Humber College of Applied Arts & Technology *Robert A. Gordon* *President*	(416) 675-2284	(416) 675-3154
Chapter 7: St. Petersburg Junior College *Michael Richardson* *Executive Assistant to the President*	(813) 341-3243	(813) 341-3318
Chapter 8: Kirkwood Community College *Norm Nielsen* *President*	(319) 398-5501	(319) 398-5502

Chapter and Contact Person	Phone Number	Fax
Chapter 9: Greenville Technical College *Thomas E. Barton, Jr.* *President*	(803) 250-8175	(803) 250-8507
Chapter 10: Cuyahoga Community College *Michael C. Taggart* *Executive Director, Unified Technologies Center*	(216) 987-3061	(216) 987-3038
Chapter 11: Valencia Community College *Sandra Todd Sarantos* *Vice President*	(407) 299-5000, x3421	(407) 426-8970
Chapter 12: Dallas County Community College District *Martha Hughes* *Executive Director* *Educational Partnerships*	(214) 746-2446	(214) 746-2039
Chapter 13: Texas Workforce Development Partnership *Sally Andrade* *Director, CIERP, University of* *Texas at El Paso*	(915) 747-5117	(915) 747-5415
Chapter 14: Midlands Technical College *James L. Hudgins* *President*	(803) 738-2994	(803) 738-7821
Chapter 15: Sinclair Community College *Stephen Jonas* *Vice President of Administration*	(513) 226-3050	(513) 226-3080

CHAPTER AND CONTACT PERSON	PHONE NUMBER	FAX
Chapter 16: The Role of the Community College in Building Communities Through Coalitions		
Janet Beauchamp	(602) 731-8028	(602) 731-8111
Executive Director		
Phoenix Think Tank		
Maricopa County Community College District		
Chapter 17: Florida Community College at Jacksonville		
Carol Spalding Miner	(904) 633-8322	(904) 633-8435
Campus President		
Chapter 18: Striking a Balance: Creating the Collaborative Mosaic		
John E. Roueche,	(512) 471-7545	(512) 471-9426
Lynn Sullivan Taber, or		
Suanne D. Roueche,		
The University of Texas at Austin		

APPENDIX B

RESOURCES

1,001 EXEMPLARY PRACTICES IN AMERICA'S TWO-YEAR COLLEGES

Edited by John E. Roueche, Dale Parnell, and Carl M. Kuttler, Jr., with Patty Curtin Jones. Published in 1994 by McGraw-Hill, Inc., as part of the College Custom Series.

This volume reports exemplary practices in the nation's community, junior, and technical colleges. It offers a nationally representative sample of good ideas and model practices, and includes information about whom to contact to find out more.

COLLABORATIVE LEADERSHIP: HOW CITIZENS AND CIVIC LEADERS CAN MAKE A DIFFERENCE

Written by David D. Chrislip and Carl E. Larson, this book was published by Jossey-Bass Publishers in 1994.

"Collaborative Leadership is about how citizens and civic leaders can make a difference in addressing the most pressing public challenges in their communities." Part one of the book considers the reasons for growth in collaboration. In the second part, the authors look at collaboration in action and explore how citizens and civic leaders can be successful in these endeavors. The third part presents the principles of collaborative leadership that emerged from the authors' research.

THE COLLABORATION HANDBOOK: CREATING, SUSTAINING, AND ENJOYING THE JOURNEY

This book was authored by Michael Winer and Karen Ray. The Amherst H. Wilder Foundation in Saint Paul, Minnesota published it in 1994. 1-800-274-6024.

The book has four parts. Part I introduces a story that serves as a metaphor for participating in a collaborative process, and that metaphor is a connecting thread throughout the book. Part II presents a definition of collaboration and applies the metaphor of journey to the process of collaboration. Part III frames four stages of collaboration and guidelines for how to proceed. Part IV contains helpful appendices, including a resource list of books and articles, and forms for documenting the collaborative process.

SYNTHESIS OF EXISTING KNOWLEDGE AND PRACTICE IN THE FIELD OF
EDUCATIONAL PARTNERSHIPS

This commissioned report of the U.S. Department of Education's Office of Educational
Research and Improvement (OERI) is a synthesis of "the history, context, and types of
educational partnerships." The following elements of successful partnerships are
reviewed: top level leadership; grounding in community needs; effective public relations; clear roles and responsibilities; racial-ethnic involvement; strategic planning;
effective management and staffing structure; shared decision making and interagency
ownership; shared credit and recognition; appropriate, well-timed resources; technical
assistance; formal agreements; action and frequent success; patience, vigilance, and
increased involvement; and local ownership. The evaluation of partnerships, including
various outcome measures, is also considered. Authors are T. Grobe, S.P. Curnan, and A.
Melchior (December, 1990). The publication is available through ERIC (ED325535).

A GUIDE TO DEVELOPING EDUCATIONAL PARTNERSHIPS

Questions considered in this guide include:
What are the steps to developing a successful educational partnership?
How does a successful partnership begin?
How do successful partnerships begin implementation?
What is the role of evaluation and planning?
What happens when things go wrong?
Will the effort be worthwhile?
    The guide was written by N.C. Tushnet of the Southwest Regional Laboratory
(SRL). It was published by the U.S. Department of Education's OERI in October, 1993.
Copies of this book are available from the U.S. Government Printing Office. Call (202)
783-3238.

NATIONAL ASSOCIATION OF PARTNERS IN EDUCATION, INC. (NAPE)

209 Madison Street, Suite 401
Alexandria, VA 22314
(703) 836-4880
(703) 836-6941 (fax)

As described in their brochure, NAPE "is the only national membership organization
devoted solely to the mission of providing leadership in the formation and growth of
effective partnerships that ensure success for all students. NAPE defines partnership in

education as a collaborative effort between a school(s) or school district(s) and one or more community organizations with the purpose of improving the academic and personal growth of America's youth. Joining in the partnership effort are: parent organizations, businesses, universities, media, health care agencies, labor organizations, community clubs and organizations, foundations and government."

NAPE goals include increasing the number, quality, and scope of effective partnerships; promoting the need for and benefits of effectiveness partnerships to policy makers in government, business, education and other groups; increasing resources for the formation and support of partnerships nationwide; increasing local, state and national awareness of the importance of partnerships in the success of students; and providing improved services to an expanded and diversified membership.

NAPE was formed in 1988 as a result of the merger between the National School Volunteer Program (NSVP) and the National Symposium on Partnerships in Education. A national symposium (started in 1984 by the White House Office on Private Sector Initiatives) brings together 1,500 partnership directors, corporate decision makers, educators, volunteers, and public policy makers from around the world to explore and determine new roles for partnerships in education and community reforms. NAPE has a database of partnership initiatives of conferences, sponsors a national awards program, publishes a newsletter and leading texts in the field of partnerships, conducts campaigns to improve government relations and public awareness, and conducts national surveys and research projects.

NATIONAL ASSOCIATION FOR INDUSTRY-EDUCATION COOPERATION (NAIEC)

235 Hendricks Boulevard
Buffalo, New York 14226-3304
(716) 834-7047

NAIEC's stated goal is "to facilitate the school-to-work process for youth and adults and to provide industry with a skilled, technical and professional workforce.... The schools need industry's volunteer resources—personnel, facilities, materials and equipment—to help plan, organize and implement a comprehensive career education system. Industry depends on education—the primary human resource delivery system to the workplace—as a long term source of prospective employees with appropriate basic, employability, and marketable/transferable skills. Industry/education collaboration is essential in reducing the mismatch between jobs and job seekers and the gap between workforce requirements and student preparation for work, particularly among special needs groups. Education is also playing a key role in the training and retraining of employees, preparing individuals for self employment, and providing technical assistance to entrepreneurs."

NAIEC's programs are based on the following fundamental convictions:

1. A formal system-wide structure such as an industry-education council provides the most cost effective mechanism through which industry can channel its voluntary resources into the total academic and vocational program.

2. The primary areas for industry-education joint efforts directed at school improvement/reform are: cooperative planning, curriculum revision, in-service training of school staff, upgrading instructional materials and equipment, and improving educational management.

3. An industry-education coordination function at the state level is essential in helping unify the interaction between education and the employment community in the areas of school improvement and economic development. (All of the above is from the NAIEC descriptive brochure.)

NAIEC establishes Industry Education Councils and provides assistance by conducting workshops on leadership and collaboration; serving as a national clearinghouse for industry sponsored education materials; promoting innovative career education, entrepreneurship, and school-based job placement programs and materials; producing a newsletter featuring new developments; and making connections with other organizations involved in industry/school collaborations including the:

- U.S. Chamber of Commerce,
- American Association of School Administrators,
- National Association of Manufacturers,
- American Vocational Association,
- American Society for Training and Development, and the
- American Association of Community Colleges.

INDEX

INDEX

A

AACJC Public Policy Agenda, 31

Academic Council, 114

Adopt-a-School Project, 53, 276, 361

Adult Education Association, 14

Advanced College Entrance, 176

Advanced Integrated Manufacturing
Center, 293

Advanced Machine Tool Resource
Center, 169

Advanced Machine Tool Technology
Center, 169

Advantage Aviation, 174

AEGON USA, 158, 160

Affordable Housing Management
Education Program, 64

AFL-CIO, 14

Afro-Caribbean Scholarship Program,
138

AGAPE, 69, 75, 361

Agency Strategic Plan, 253

Agri-King, 161

Aid to Families with Dependent
Children, 61, 87

Allapattah YMCA, 73, 356

Alliance 2020, 278, 357

Alliance for Higher Education, 242

Alliance for Higher Education in North
Texas, 241

Alliance for Media Arts, 77

Allstate Insurance Company, 129, 135, 367

Alumni Gazette, 3

America's Choice: High Skills or Low
Wages!, 246, 247

American Association for Higher
Education, 54

American Association of Community
Colleges, 6, 9, 11–12, 14, 16–19, 26,
28–29, 31–32, 41, 67, 140, 145, 168,
207, 224, 248, 278, 299, 357

American Association of School
Administrators, 4, 145
American Association of State Colleges
and Universities, 190
American College Testing Program, 145,
357
American Council on Education, 145,
147, 190
American Express Travel Related
Services, 331
American Issues Forums, 15
American Profol, 157
American Society for Training and
Development, 210, 247
American Vocational Association, 14,
145, 357
Ameritech, 193, 353
Amoco, 170
Andrade, S.J., 245–246
Apple, 141–142, 365
Apple Canada, Inc., 121
Area Commission for Higher Education,
166
Artist Series, 336, 339, 364
Aslanian, C.B., 207, 211
Assistance Dog Program, 175
Associated Builders and Contractors,
Inc., 233
Associated General Contractors, Inc., 233
Association of Canadian Community
Colleges, 113, 115
Association of Community College
Trustees, 145, 168, 224, 329, 341
Association of Governing Boards of
Universities and Colleges, 145
AT&T, 223, 227, 232, 331, 333
Atkinson College, 114, 359
Auraria Higher Education Center, 86
AutoDesk Education, 170
Autozone Distribution Center, 174
Avishai, B., 353, 359

B
Baker, R.K., 48
Balz, F., 147
Banach, W.J., 349, 368–370
Banzhaf, J., 32
Baoji College, 138–139
Barnett Bank, 331
Baron, L., 185
Barton, T.E., 163, 165
Base Closing Commission, 225
Bay Area Hospital Council, 135, 367
Beacon College Project, 26, 54, 278,
299, 301–303, 305–306, 309–313,
315–317
Beauchamp, J.F., 299, 300, 304
Beijing Municipal Bureau of Higher
Education, 139
Bell, Terrell, 144
Bellah, R.N., 347
Bellevue University, 51, 361
Bender, L., 30
Benjamin, D., 217
Bennis, W., 324
Better Kids...Better Dallas, 238
Bill J. Priest Institute for Economic
Development, 232–233
Birnbaum, R., 30
Black Awareness Week, 77
Black Heritage, 77
Black History Month, 77, 328, 362
Black Student Success Office, 328, 362
Blank, M.J., 259–260
Bloch, E., 355
Blue Cross and Blue Shield, 331
Blue Cross of Northeast Ohio, 193, 353
BMW Manufacturing Company, 170
Bogue, J.P., 28
Boone, E.J., 33, 306
Bouvier, L.F., 249
Boyd, J., 246
Boyer, E.L., 342, 348–349

Brawer, F.B., 29–30
Breneman, D.W., 16, 19
Brint, S., 352
Brookhaven College, 233
Brown, S.V., 248
Building Communities: A Vision for a New Century, 26, 44, 141, 268, 300
Building Education Coalitions, 300
Bush, George, 139, 145
Business Advisory Council, 68, 223–224
Business and Industry Services, 118, 126
Business and Professional Training Program, 233
Business Incubator Center, 66
Business Research Library, 66
Business-Higher Education Forum, 246
Butler, M., 246

C
Cable College, 186
California Postsecondary Education Commission, 21
California State University, 21
Campbell, D.F., 245
Campion, W., 138
Canadian International Development Agency, 116
Canadian Plastics Centre for Training, 119, 124, 126
Cantor, J.A., 218
Cardenas, J.A., 249
Cardinal Principles of Secondary Education, 27
Career Advancement Center, 170
Career Bridge Project, 49
Career Connections Program, 135, 363
Career Opportunity Program, 152, 366
Carnegie Corporation, 13
Carnegie Foundation for the Advancement of Teaching, 301, 315

Carnevale, A.P., 247
Case Western Reserve University, 192
Catanzaro, J., 93, 105
Cedar Rapids Area Chamber of Commerce, 366
Cedar Rapids Community Schools, 155
Cedar River Paper Company, 147, 157
Cedar Valley College, 236
Center for Advanced Technology, 93, 102, 354
Center for Applied Gerontology, 188
Center for Business and Industry, 64
Center for Creative Leadership, 99, 367
Center for Early Care and Education, 69
Center for Economic Development, 331
Center for Educational Telecommunications, 230
Center for Environmental Technology, 93, 102
Center for Health Policy Development, 249
Center for High Tech Training for the Disabled, 223–225
Center for Research and Information on School/College Partnerships, 54
Center for the Fine Arts, 77
Center on Juvenile and Criminal Justice, 21
Central Florida Community College, 138
Central Michigan University, 113–114, 359
Central Midlands of South Carolina, 278
Central Midlands Tech Prep Consortium, 274, 354
Centre Gallery, 79
Challenges, Realities, Strategies—The Master Plan for Florida Postsecondary Education for the 21st Century, 213
Chamber of Commerce, 49
Chapa, J., 248
Chattanooga Area Chamber of Commerce, 101

Chattanooga Housing Authority, 97, 359
Chattanooga Little Theater, 99, 364
Chattanooga State Technical
    Community College, 93, 354, 357,
    359, 362, 364, 367
Child Care Resource and Referral, 69
Child Development Program, 75
Children's Resource and Referral Center,
    69
Chinese in the Americas, 78
Chinese Ministry of Education, 138
Chrislip, D.D., 350, 356, 358, 365
Chronicle of Higher Education, 21
Chrysler Corporation, 146
Cincinnati-Milacron, 169, 354
Cities in Schools, 275, 361
City of Irving, 234
City of Omaha, 48
Clark, D.H., 224, 353
Clemson University, 177, 276, 278, 357,
    359
Cleveland Advanced Manufacturing
    Program, 192
Cleveland Community Access
    Corporation, 186
Cleveland Foundation, 195, 197, 356,
    364
Cleveland Philharmonic Orchestra, 187
Cleveland State University, 187, 192,
    195, 356
Clevell, B.C., 248
Coalition of Homestead Neighborhood
    Groups, 66
Cohen, A.M., 29–31
College Action Council, 46
College Advisory Council, 85
College Ambassador, 273, 358
College Board, 145, 357
College Development Foundation, 135,
    367
College Reachout, 134, 363

College: The Undergraduate Experience,
    348
Colleges of Applied Arts and
    Technology, 108
Collegio Universitario de Allejuela, 217
Colonial College, 282
Colonial Life Insurance, 282
Colorado Campus Compact, 86–87, 358
Colorado Community College and
    Occupational Education System, 32
Colorado Department of Social Services,
    91, 361
Colorado Institute for Hispanic
    Education and Economic
    Development, 86, 356
Colorado State Board, 32
Colorado VIP Program, 89
COMBASE, 13, 54
Commission on Government
    Accountability to the People, 146
Commission on the Future of
    Community Colleges, 31, 44, 57, 141,
    248, 268, 300, 302–303, 314, 318
Commission on the Skills of the
    American Workforce, 246–247
Communication Workers of America,
    49–50, 354
Community College Consortium for
    Health and Safety Training, 154, 354
Community College of Denver, 81,
    356–358, 361
Community College Program, 27
Community College Week, 131
Community Development Corporations,
    75
Community Food Bank, 172
Community Partners in Progress, 159
Community Schools and Comprehensive
    Community Act of 1978, 29
Company Town Shutdown, 34
Competency Based Education, 117

Computer Automated Logistics System, 186
Computer Integrated Manufacturing Alliance, 170
COMSELL, 170
Consortium of Gifted and Talented Teachers, 194
Continental Cablevision, 334
Continental Can, 120
Continuous Improvement/Cycle Reduction Department, 169
Cooperative Association for States for Scholarships Program, 138
Coordinating Board Task Force, 234
Corporation for National and Community Service, 32
Corrections and Law Enforcement Academies, 129, 136
Council of Presidents, 108
Council of Regents, 108
Council on Education, 265, 271, 273, 280
Council on Postsecondary Accreditation, 145
Council on Vocational Education, 250
Counselors Conference, 276
Courses by Newspaper, 15
Covey, S.R., 43
Criminal Justice Institute, 129, 136–137
CRST, Inc., 153
Cryovac, 170
Culinary Arts Campus, 171
Cultura del Lobo, 76, 364
Cultural Diversity Training Institute, 137, 363
Cuyahoga Community College, 4, 183, 185, 353, 356, 361–362, 364

D
DACUM, 117
Dade County Department of Health and Rehabilitation Services, 75

Dade County Public Health Service, 63
Dade County Public Schools, 69, 73–74, 78; 361–362
Dallas Adult Literacy Council, 237
Dallas Area Interfaith Council, 237
Dallas Citizens Council, 237
Dallas County Community College District, 227, 229, 359–363, 365, 367
Dallas Education Center, 241–242, 359
Dallas Independent School District, 238
Dallas Public Libraries, 238
Dana Corporation, 170
Davenport, L.F., 248
Dayton Business Committee, 293
Dayton Free-Net, 293
Decision Information Resources, Inc., 256
Denver Department of Social Services, 87, 89, 91
Denver Family Opportunity Program, 87
Denver Metro Chamber of Commerce, 88, 361
Denver Network, 81, 86–87, 89–90, 357
Denver Public Schools, 89–90
Department of Housing and Development-South Carolina, 172
Department of Social Services-South Carolina, 172
Desruisseaux, P., 147
DeVry Institute, 240
Dewey, J., 44
Diamond V. Mills, 161
Digital Consulting Services, 146
Digital Corporation, 281
Digital Equipment Corporation, 141–142, 365
Displaced Homemakers Program, 187
Division of Medically Related Programs, 63
Do the Bright Thing, 238
Donaldson Air Service, 174

Donaldson Center Industrial Park, 174
Doucette, D., 352
Dow Chemical, 214
Drug War Academy, 137, 354
Dual Credit Program, 133
Duval County School Board, 328, 333
Dyke College, 187

E
East Ohio Gas, 193, 353
East Texas State University, 241, 359
Eastern Iowa Community College
    District, 153
Eastfield College, 240
Eaton, J., 30
Economic Development Alliance, 282
Economic Development Commission of
    Mid-Florida, 218
Economic Development Council, 219
Economic Development Division of the
    Greater Dallas Chamber of
    Commerce, 231
Economic Development Office of the
    City of Dallas, 231
Economic Development Services,
    156–158, 353
Edison Center, 192
Edison Materials Technology Center,
    294, 355
Educating One Third of a Nation, 190
Education and Human Services
    Consortium, 259
Education Commission of the States, 301
Educational Partnerships Office, 227,
    230–231, 234, 240
Educational Roundtable, 144
Educational Testing Service, 145, 332
Educational Testing Systems, 357
Educators in Industry, 278
El Centro College, 236, 238, 241, 359,
    362

Elder's Campus, 188
Elizabethtown Community College, 222
Ellcon National, 170
Elsner, P.A., 299, 303–304
Emery, R.E., 349
Empanada Night, 77, 364
Employment First, 91, 361
Engineering Government
    Transformation, 146
Enhanced Transfer Program, 240, 361
Enterprise Florida, 225
Enterprise Ohio, 193
Enterprise Zone, 271
Entrepreneurial Center, 66
Entrepreneurial Education Center, 66
Environmental Demonstration Center, 68
Environmental Equity Task Force, 198
Environmental Playground, 102
Environmental Protection Agency, 153,
    194, 197, 199
Environmental Training Center, 153
Ernst, R.J., 42
Ethics Applied, 141
Even-Start, 333
Excellence at Work: State Action
    Agenda, 247
Excellence in Community Partnerships,
    333
Excellence in Music Project, 197, 364
Executive Office for the National
    Partnership for Environment
    Technical Education, 154, 354
Executive Training and Regional
    Conference Center, 93, 99
Experimental College, 46, 365
Exxon, 135, 241, 367

F
Facelle, 120
Facilities Foundation, 159
Faith in the City, 70

Firstar Banks, 161
Fischer, O.R., 13
Flanigan, F., 353
Florida Academic Improvement Trust
    Fund, 135
Florida Adult Education Act, 70
Florida Commission on Ethics, 140
Florida Community College at
    Jacksonville, 136, 319, 321, 353,
    356–357, 360, 362–364
Florida Community Contribution Tax
    Incentive Act, 135
Florida Department of Commerce, 206
Florida Department of Education, 138,
    363
Florida Department of Health and
    Rehabilitative Services, 69, 335
Florida Department of Labor, 66, 333
Florida Department of Transportation,
    333
Florida Department of Vocational
    Rehabilitation, 67
Florida Employment Security, 333
Florida Funeral Directors' Association, 65
Florida International University, 66, 78,
    361
Florida Legislature, 135, 326
Florida National Guard, 136–137, 354,
    360
Florida Progress Corporation, 135
Florida Satellite Network Grant, 143
Florida School of the Arts, 78
Florida State University, 333
Florida Teletraining Project, 136–137
Florida Times-Union, 322, 332, 338
Florida Training Center for Adult
    Literacy Educators, 70
Folkhighschool, 39, 46, 54, 363, 365
Ford Automotive Student Service
    Educational Training, 233
Ford Foundation, 9, 32, 90

Frances Wolfson Gallery, 78
Freenet, 236
Frye, J.H., 27–28
Funeral Services Program, 65
Furman University, 177
Future Workforce Needs Study, 329

G
Gainer, L.J., 247
Geiger, R.L., 30
Genencor International, 157
General Electric, 102, 163, 168
General Manufacturing Certification
    Program, 170
General Mills, 158
General Motors Automotive Service
    Educational Program, 168, 186, 233
Georgetown University, 138, 363
Gianini, P.C., 203, 205
Gilder, J., 19, 41
Gilley, J.W., 81, 203, 285, 359
Gilliland, J.R., 39, 45, 47, 54
Gleazer, E.J., 9–10, 12, 14–15, 18, 26,
    29, 31, 350
Global Issues Resource Center, 183, 194
GOALS 2000, 45
Goetsch, D., 215
Gollattscheck, J.F., 13
Gomes-Casseres, B., 297
Goodyear Tire and Rubber Company, 331
Gordon, R.A., 105, 206
Governor's Initiative for Workforce
    Excellence, 270
Governor's School for the Arts, 173
Governor's Workforce Initiative, 354
Grant Wood Area Education Agency,
    155
Gray Gallery of New York, 77
Great Cookie Project, 67, 362
Greater Columbia Chamber of
    Commerce, 265, 271–272, 357

Greater Columbia Literacy Council, 273

Greater Dallas Chamber of Commerce, 232

Greater Dallas Community of Churches, 238

Greater Dayton Public Television, 294

Greater Miami Neighborhoods, Inc., 75

Greater Omaha Chamber of Commerce, 48

Greenleaf, R., 324

Greenville Area Commission, 175

Greenville Chamber of Commerce, 179

Greenville County Tech Prep Consortium, 176

Greenville Health Department, 171

Greenville Hospital System, 171

Greenville Tech Foundation, Inc., 179

Greenville Technical College, 163, 165, 354, 358–359, 362–364, 366

Greenville Technical Education Center, 166

Greenville Urban League, Inc., 172

Greyhound Corporation, 232

Growing Up Healthy, 73–74

Growmark, 161

Gund Foundation, 195, 197, 356, 364

H

Habitat for Humanity, 173

Hackney, S., 21

Hall Foundation, 159

Hall of Science and Technology, 275

Harbison, F., 20

Harper, William Rainey, 27

Harrell, N.L., 252

Harvard, 140, 145

Hastings Center, 140

Hatfield, M.O., 225

Hayden, S., 27

Hayes-Bautista, D., 248

Hazardous Materials Training and Research Institute, 153, 354

Head to Head, 279

Headstart, 74

Health and Rehabilitative Services, 64

Health Careers Opportunity Program, 64

Health Education Center, 134–135, 367

Henderson, Hazel, 337

Hendley, V., 34

Hillsborough Community College, 134

Hirsch, A.N., 212

Hispanic Heritage Week, 77, 364

Hispanic Institute, 87

Hitachi, 32, 170

Hoescht-Diafoil, 170

Hollinshead, B.S., 27

House Education and Labor Committee, 213

Hudgins, J.L., 265, 267, 269

Hudson Institute, 246

Hughes, M., 229

Humber College of Applied Arts and Technology, 105, 206, 354, 359, 365, 367

Hunter Museum of Art, 99, 364

I

IBM, 102, , 281

IES Industries, Inc., 158

Industrial Training Corporation, 170

Industry Quality Teams, 218, 225, 365

Information Management Institute, 50

Information Technology Applications Center, 294, 355

Institute for Economic Development, 230

Institute for Simulation and Training, 136, 360

Institute of Educational Management, 145

Instructional Television Fixed Services, 143, 155, 294, 360

Intelligence Systems Applications
    Center, 294
InterAmerican Center, 79
Intergraph Education Center Alliance,
    170
International Center, 138, 363
International Committee, 118
International Congress of Environmental
    Commerce and Technology, 102
International Hispanic Theatre Festival,
    76–77
Iowa Communications Network, 156
Iowa Division of Vocational
    Rehabilitation, 152, 362
Iowa Industrial New Jobs Training
    Program, 156, 158
Iowa Pork Producers Association, 161
Iowa State Legislature, 150
Iowa State Men's Reformatory, 152, 155
Irving Independent School District, 234

J
Jackman, M., 34
Jackson Memorial Hospital, 63
Jacksonville Chamber of Commerce,
    331, 337
Jacksonville Chamber of Commerce
    Workforce Preparation Task Force,
    330
Jacksonville Community Council, Inc.,
    329, 337
Jacksonville Literacy Coalition, 332
Jacksonville Sheriff's Office, 333
JazzFest, 197, 364
Jesse Owens Youth Program, 187
Job Service Center, 66
Job Training Office, 91
Job Training Partnership Act, 87, 176,
    232, 250–251, 253, 255, 362
Johnson, L.A., 205
Johnson, Lyndon B., 7

Johnston, W.B., 246, 248
Johnstone, D.B., 93, 147, 203, 285, 366
Joint Enrollment, 103
Joliet Junior College, 27

K
Kami, M., 221
Kanter, R.M., 43, 57, 105, 129, 243, 285,
    297, 350, 360, 368, 370
Karabel, S., 352
Katsinas, S.G., 352
Kearns, D.T., 353
Kellogg Foundation, 86, 265, 278, 357
Kemet Electronics, 170
Kendall Campus Gallery, 78
Kent State University, 187, 192
Kettering Foundation, 335
Kirkwood Community College, 43, 147,
    149, 353–354, 360, 362, 366–367
Kirkwood Foundation, 159
Kirkwood Industrial Modernization
    Service/Technology Transfer, 158
Kirkwood Satellite Service, 156
Kirkwood Skill Center, 152
Kirkwood Telecommunications System,
    154–156
Kirkwood/Mount Mercy Trust, 152
Kiwanis of Dade County, 69
Kodak Canada, 119–121
Kremlin Museum, 139
Kuttler, C.M., 129

L
Labatt's Breweries, 120
Laboratory Theatre, 72–73
Lakeland Community College, 193
Lambert, L.M., 54
Lander University, 177
Lange, Alexis, 27
Larson, C.E., 350, 356, 358, 365
Leadership Jacksonville, 337

League for Innovation, 3, 54, 113
League of Women Voters, 15
Learn to Read, 332, 339
LeCroy Center for Educational Telecommunications, 235
LeCroy, N.A., 33, 57, 81, 203, 366
Legal Services of Greater Miami, 66
Legal Services of Western Carolina, 172
Leonard, G.B., 367
Liberty City Small Business Development Center, 66
Lilly Foundation, Inc., 324
Linkage Institute, 217
Linking America's Schools and Colleges, 54
Literacy and Life Skills Task Force, 237
Literacy Coalition, 339
Little, P., 47
Liu, G., 32, 315
Lockheed-Aeromod, 170, 174
Lorain Community College, 193
Lorenzo, A.L., 57, 81, 93, 203, 349, 366, 368–370
Lower Columbia College, 48
Lunchtime Lively Arts Series, 75–76, 364

M
Machine Trades Apprenticeship Program, 186
Mahoney, J.R., 14
Making America Work, 247
Malaysian Ministries, 116–117
Malcolm X Community College, 9
Management Center, 169
Manley, W., 208
Manpower Development and Training Act, 153
Mansfield Foundation, 161
Manufacturing Learning Center, 186
Manufacturing Resource Facility, 192
MARA, 116–117, 126

March of Dimes Walkathon, 172
Maricopa Community College District, 299
Marshall, R.R., 249
Martin Luther King Day, 187
Martin Marietta Aerospace, 221, 223
Master Plan Advisory Committee, 250
Master Plan for Higher Education, 190
Master Plan for Vocational and Technical Education, 250, 253, 257–258
Math Meet, 275
Maxwell House Coffee, 331
Mayo Clinic, 326
Mayor's Office of Employment and Training, 88, 361
Mayor's Summer Youth Employment Program, 238
McCabe, R.H., 57
McClenney, B.N., 81
McGraw-Hill, 141
McKee, W.L., 252
Medical School for Kids, 72–73
Medical University of South Carolina, 177, 276
Melaville, A.A., 259–260
Meltzer, A.S., 247
Merchant to Merchant, 66
Mercy Hospital, 153
Merrill Lynch, 331
Merritt Community College, 9
Metro-Dade Child Development Services, 69
Metro-Dade Transit Agency Partnership, 64
Metropolitan Community College, 39, 354, 359–361, 363, 366–367
Metropolitan State College, 86
Metropolitan Toronto Regional Conservation Authority, 123
Meyocks & Priebe Advertising Inc., 161
Miami Book Fair International, 76, 364

Miami Chamber of Commerce, 362
Miami-Dade Community College, 57,
    353, 356–358, 361–362, 364, 366
Miami Valley Research Park, 293
Miami Valley Tech Prep Consortium,
    294
Michelin Tire Corporation, 167
Michigan Consortium, 113
Michigan State University, 114, 359
Micro Industries Development Assistance
    Society, 116, 126
Microcomputer Education for
    Employment of the Disabled, 68
Middle College High School, 238, 363
Midlands Technical College, 267,
    354–355, 357–358, 361–363
Miner, C.S., 321
Ministry of Education and Training, 108,
    123
Minority Chamber of Commerce, 88,
    361
Mita, 170
Mitchell Wolfson Jr. Gallery, 79
Mitchell Wolfson Sr. Foundation, 69
Morrison, P.A., 248
Motorola, 217
Mott Foundation, 14
Mount Mercy College, 152, 366
Mountain View College, 237
MTC/USC Connections, 277
Multijurisdictional Counterdrug Task
    Force, 137, 354
Mundhenk, R.T., 218
Myran, G.A., 28–29

N
NAACP, 172
NASA, 99, 190, 362, 367
National Advisory Commission on Civil
    Disorders, 7–8
National Alliance of Business, 246, 333

National Association for Equal
    Opportunity in Higher Education,
    145
National Association for Public
    Continuing and Adult Education, 14
National Association of Community
    Leadership, 324, 337
National Association of State Boards of
    Education, 145
National Center for Education Statistics,
    332
National Center on Education and the
    Economy, 246
National Collegiate Athletic Association,
    134, 362
National Community Education
    Association, 14
National Council for Occupational
    Education, 248
National Council of Jewish Women, 69
National Council on Community Service
    for Community and Junior Colleges,
    65
National Education and Human Services
    Consortium, 260
National Endowment for the
    Humanities, 14–15, 21
National Governors' Association, 247
National Institute for Staff and
    Organizational Development, 113,
    145, 206
National Institute of Environmental
    Health Sciences, 154
National Issues Forums, 335
National Park Service, 186, 197
National Science Foundation, 51, 103,
    154, 176, 277, 362
National Telecommunication
    Information Administration, 155, 360
National University Extension
    Association, 14

National Youth Sports Program, 70, 134, 362
Nature Center, 68
Nebraska Indian Community College, 39, 52–53, 360, 364
Nebraska State Department of Economic Development, 48
Neighborhood Enhancement Team, 74
Nelson, S.C., 16, 19
New Beginnings, 333
New Business Center, 158
New World School of the Arts, 78, 361
Nicaraguan Peace Scholarship Program, 138
Nielsen, N.R., 43, 147, 149, 280
Nissan Professional Cooperative Apprenticeship Program, 233
North American Free Trade Agreement, 218, 232
North Campus Art Gallery, 78
North Coast Tech Prep Consortium, 199
Northeast Community College, 52, 360
Northeast Ohio Science and Math Club, 191
Northeast Ohio Science Teachers Association, 194
North Lake College, 233–236, 367
North/South Video Link, 52
Northwood University, 240
Nuclear Age Resource Center, 183, 193–194

O
Office of Continuing Education, 91
Office of Corporate Services, 203, 220–221, 225, 354
Office of Economic Opportunity, 9
Office of Educational Partnerships, 365
Office of Technology Assessment, 355
Office on Aging, 189
Ohio Applied Technology Center, 355

Ohio Arts Council, 197
Ohio Board of Regents, 190, 196
Ohio Bureau of Employment Services, 190, 199
Ohio College of Podiatric Medicine, 187
Ohio Council for Home Health Agencies, 189
Ohio Department of Aging, 189
Ohio Department of Development, 355
Ohio Mathematics Proficiency Test, 190
Ohmae, K., 367
Oklahoma City Community College, 47
Oklahoma County Library System, 47
Omaha City Libraries, 47
Omaha Job Clearinghouse, 49
Omaha Public Schools, 49, 53
On Becoming a Leader, 324
Ontario Federation of Labour, 119
Ontario Government Management Board Secretariat, 124
Open Access Satellite Education Services (OASES), 47
Open Campus Corporate Training Services, 136
Orlando Naval Training Center, 225
Orlando Regional Healthcare System, 223
Orlando Sentinel, 205, 207, 223
Overtown Apartment Association, 74, 356
Overtown Community Forum, 74
Overtown Community Health Center, 74
Overtown Crime Prevention Project, 74
Overtown Happenings, 74
Overtown Merchant's Alliance, Inc., 73–74
Overtown Neighborhood Partnerships, 57, 71–72, 74–75
Overtown Youth Leadership, 74
Owner Builder Center, 68

P

Palinchak, R., 27

Palmetto Helicopters, 174

Parent's Helpline, 91

Parent-Teacher Association, 74

Parnell, D., 140, 207

Partners in Action and Learning, 71

Partners in Corporate Education
     Program, 212

Partnership Through Diversity, 187

Pasadena California Board of Education, 27

Pathway Program, 134, 360

Paul Quinn College, 240

Penn State University, 333

People's Republic of China, 138

Performing and Visual Arts Center, 78

Perkins Vocational Education and
     Applied Technology Act, 251, 254,
     255

Peru State College, 52, 360

Peters, T.J., 350

Pfeiffer, J.J., 215

Pfnister, A.O., 30

Piedmont Healthcare Foundation, 171

Pierce, D.R., 318

Pierce, T.A., 321

Pifer, A., 13

Pinellas County Private Industry
     Council, 134

Pinellas County Schools, 142

Pinellas County Sheriff's Office
     Narcotics Bureau, 137

Pioneer Hi-Bred, 161

Planning Council, 85

Playhouse Square Foundation, 196

PMX Industries, 158

Police Department of the City of
     Greenville, 171

Policies for Lifelong Education Project,
     15, 19

Political and Civic Institute, 101

Ponitz, D.H., 287

Pork Education Center, 160

Postsecondary Education Planning
     Commission, 213

Pre-School Laboratory, 69

Preparation for the Technologies, 274

President's Commission on Higher
     Education, 28

Priority One, 157–158, 366

Private Industry Council, 88, 97, 101,
     232, 359, 361

Proctor and Gamble, 174

Project AHEAD, 67

Project Book Find, 175

Project Eve, 183, 187, 361

Project Flamingo, 141

Project Independence, 64

Project S.T.A.R.T., 159

Project Success, 135

Prudential Insurance Company, 332

Public Broadcasting System, 143, 194,
     334–335, 337

Public Health Department Dental Clinic,
     171

Public Service Institute, 186

Q

Quaker Oats, 158

Quality Resource Consortium, 193, 353

Quality Work Force Planning, 246,
     250–257, 260–262

R

Rainbow Village, 69, 75

Rand, G., 248

Ravitch, D., 30

Read, Write, Research, 334

Reagan, Ronald, 145

Red Bird Armory, 237

Re-Employment Act of 1994, 224

Reich, R., 208, 214, 217, 280, 322

Reliance Electric, 170

Renewal and Change for the Year 2000, 303

Report of the Select Committee for Higher Education, 250

Richardson, R.C., 30

Richland College, 235, 240

Riley, R., 34, 208, 214

River City Renaissance, 327, 338

Robledo, M.delR., 249

Rocha, J., 41

Rock and Roll Hall of Fame and Museum, 187

Rockwell International, 160

Rockwell International's Air Transport Division, 158

Roe, M.A., 249, 355

Roosevelt University, 212

Ross, D., 352

Rotary Clubs, 175, 194

Roueche, J.E., 144, 205, 347, 353

Roueche, S.D., 347

Roundtable on Educational Partnerships, 145, 357

Roundtable on Institutional Effectiveness, 144

Royal Canadian Mounted Police, 146

Russia, 139

S

Sagem-Lucas, 170

Saint Vincent Charity Hospital, 195, 356

Saint Vincent Quadrangle Project, 183, 194, 356

Sanders, C., 215

Sarantos, S.T., 203, 205, 216

Scandinavian Study Circle, 46, 365

Schink, W., 248

School of Justice and Safety Administration, 63, 353

School of the Arts, 197

School-to-Work Opportunities Act, 214

Science, Engineering, Mathematics, and Aerospace Academy, 190, 362

Scientist-for-a-Day, 72–73, 362

Second Annual 100 Top Associate Degree Producers, 131

Secretary's Commission on Achieving Necessary Skills, 247

Select Committee for Higher Education, 250

Seminole-Kraft, 331

Servicemember's Opportunity College, 236

Seven Habits of Highly Effective People, 43

Shaanxi Business Management Institute, 139

Sheriff's Department of Greenville, 171

Sherman, S., 183

Showtime at High Noon, 196

Sinclair Community College, 35, 285, 287, 355

Skill Center, 362

Small Business Administration, 66

Small Business Development Center, 66, 86, 88, 232

Small Business Resource Center, 66

Smart Jobs Fund, 232

Smith Library and Technical Resource Center, 178

Social Studies Teachers of Northeast Ohio, 194

Society of the Plastics Industry of Canada, 119

South Carolina Alliance for Minority Participation in Science and Mathematics, 277, 362

South Carolina Chamber of Commerce, 272

South Carolina Department of Commerce, 282

South Carolina Department of Education, 278

South Carolina Educational Resource Center for Missing and Exploited Children, 173

South Carolina Employment Security Commission, 270

South Carolina Health and Human Services Finance Commission, 173

South Carolina International Education Consortium, 178, 364

South Carolina Math-Sciences Advisory Board, 176

South Carolina Science Council, 275

South Carolina State Board for Technical and Comprehensive Education, 166

South Carolina State General Assembly, 166

South Carolina State Museum, 275

South Carolina State University, 177, 265, 276, 278, 357

South Carolina Workforce Initiative, 172

South Oklahoma City Junior College, 47

Southeast Manufacturing Technology Center, 169, 281, 355

Southeastern Institute for Advanced Technologies, 170

Southern Association of Colleges and Schools, 133

Special Schools Division, 166

Speech, Hearing, and Learning Center, 175

Spence, C.C., 321, 329

St. Luke's Hospital, 153

St. Petersburg Junior College, 129, 354, 357, 360, 362–363, 365–367

St. Vincent Technical College, 115

Stanley, R., 210

Stark Technical College, 193

State Advanced Machine Tool Technology Center, 354

State Board for Technical and Comprehensive Education, 282

State Board of Education, 250–251, 253, 257

State Higher Education Executive Officers, 145

State Job Training Coordinating Council, 253, 255

State of Ohio, 192

State Postsecondary Coordinating Commission, 51

State Urban Partnerships Team, 75

Steering Group on Prosperity, 107

Stevens Aviation, 170

Stokes Telecommunications Center, 192

Stone, N., 353

Strategic Economic Policy Commission, 250

Students in Free Enterprise, 67

Students in Service/Growing Up Healthy, 72

Subtropics Music Festival, 76

Summer Enrichment in Math and Science, 176, 362

Summer Youth Employment Program, 134

SUNSTAR, 335

Swaziland College of Technology, 115

Syracuse University, 54

T

Taber, L.S., 347

Talent Search, 274

Task Force on Human Capital, 246

Teamsters Union, 153

Technical Education Centers, 87–88, 361

Technologies Applications Center, 275

Tennessee Valley Authority, 99, 367

Texas A&M University, 238, 363

Texas Army National Guard Higher Education Cooperative, 236, 360

Texas Department of Commerce, 232,
243, 250, 253, 255
Texas Education Agency, 250–251, 254
Texas Education Code, 253
Texas Higher Education Coordinating
Board, 231, 234, 241, 243, 250, 253,
258
Texas Legislature, 234, 250, 255
Texas Quality Work Force Planning, 260
Texas State Occupational Information
Coordinating Committee, 250–252,
262
Texas State Technical College System,
256
Texas Women's University, 241, 359
The Junior College as a Community
Institution, 27
Theobald, R., 34
Think Tank, 299
Thornton, J.S., 183, 185
3-M, 170, 174
Thurow, L.C., 279
Title VI-A, 178
Tools for Change, 66
Toyota Technical Education Network,
282
Training Center for Adult Literacy
Educators, 70
Tri-C/Kent State University Teaching
Leadership Consortium, 187
Trist, E.L., 349
Truman, Harry S., 267
Tucker, K., 353, 357
Turnage, M.A., 34
TV Sinclair, 294

U
U.S. Army Corps of Engineers, 236
U.S. Bureau of Education, 27
U.S. Bureau of Labor Statistics, 190
U.S. Census Bureau, 205, 249

U.S. Chamber of Commerce, 274
U.S. Department of Commerce, 102,
155, 360
U.S. Department of Defense, 67, 229,
272, 335
U.S. Department of Education, 18, 145,
178, 230, 246
U.S. Department of Energy, 154, 176,
362
U.S. Department of Health and Human
Services, 246
U.S. Department of Housing and Urban
Development, 271, 333
U.S. Department of Labor, 14, 18, 88,
223–224, 230, 246–247
U.S. Office of Management and Budget,
18
U.S. Senate Human Resources
Committee, 29
U.S. Small Business Administration, 232
Unified Marketing Task Force, 272, 357
Unified Technical Center, 183
Unified Technologies Center, 186,
191–192
Unisys, 141–142, 365
United Auto Workers, 14, 200
United Ministries, 172
United Way, 49
United Way of Greenville County, 172
University Center at Greenville Tech,
163, 177
University of California, 21, 27
University of Central Florida, 136, 360
University of Colorado at Denver, 86
University of Dallas, 241, 359
University of Dayton, 293–294
University of Florida, 245, 336, 364
University of Iowa, 153
University of Kentucky, 104
University of Miami, 63
University of Minnesota, 369

University of North Florida, 328
University of North Texas, 238, 241, 359, 363
University of South Carolina, 271, 276–278, 281, 355, 359, 361
University of South Carolina-Columbia, 177
University of South Carolina-Spartanburg, 177
University of South Florida, 133–134, 363
University of St. Petersburg, 139
University of Tennessee, 103, 362
University of Texas at Arlington, 241, 359
University of Texas at Austin, 145, 238, 347, 363
University of Texas at Dallas, 241, 359
University of Texas at El Paso, 245
University Outreach, 238
Upward Bound, 274
Urban Community Colleges Report, 5
Urban League, 97, 359
Urban League of Greater Cleveland, 186
Urban Partnership Project, 32, 90
Urban Resource Center, 330–333, 340, 353
US West, 49–50, 354

V
Valencia Community College, 13, 136, 203, 205, 353–354, 360, 365–366
Valmont Industries, 50
Veterans Administration Hospital, 63, 153
Veterans' Upward Bound, 67
Virginia Highlands Community College, 34
Vision 2000, 108
Vision for Excellence, 269
Vision of the Public Junior College, 1900–1940, 27

Visiting Nurse Association, 195, 336, 339
Vistakon, 331
Voorhees College, 177

W
Waddell, G., 249
Wall Street Journal, 217
Wallace Technology Transfer Foundation, 158, 161
Wallace, J., 301
Wangner Systems, 170
Warren, Earl, 200
Waterman, R.H., 350
Waubonsee Community College, 12
Wayne State College, 52, 360
Webster's New Collegiate Dictionary, 185
Weekend College, 270
Weick, K., 313
Weidenthal, M.D., 353
Wellness Center, 71
Wellness Institute, 72–73
Wenrich, J.W., 229
We're Great Kids, 72–73
Wessel, D., 217
Wheatley Elementary School, 74
Wheatley, M.J., 306–309, 314
Who Cares About the Inner City? The Community College Response to Urban America, 352
Who Will Deliver the Care?, 189
Who Will Do the Work?, 246
Wilbur, F.P., 54
Williams, D., 222
Williams, S.K., 267, 269
Women Focus, 188
Women In Management, 188
Women's Resource Center, 87
Woodrow Wilson Summer Institute, 65
Work and Family Resource Center, 91

Workforce 2000, 145, 246
Workforce Readiness Task Force, 281
Working Solutions, 64
World History Institute for Secondary
    School Teachers, 65
Worth Quoting, 337
Wright-Patterson Air Force Base,
    293–294
Wright State University, 293–294, 355
Wright Technology Network, 295
Wynne, G.E., 81, 285

X
Xomed-Trease, 331

Y
Yarrington, R., 12, 15
Ylvisaker, Paul, 140
YMCA, 235
York University, 114, 359
Youth Fair Chance, 88
Youth Swimming Program, 70

About the Authors

John E. Roueche is professor and director of the Community College Leadership Program at the University of Texas at Austin, where he holds the Sid W. Richardson Regents Chair in Community College Leadership. He has served as director of the program since 1971. He is the author of 33 books and more than 150 articles and monographs on the topics of educational leadership and teaching effectiveness. He is the recipient of numerous national awards for his research, teaching, service, and overall leadership, including the 1986 National Distinguished Leadership Award from the American Association of Community Colleges; the 1988 B. Lamar Johnson Leadership in Innovation Award from the League for Innovation in the Community College; and the Distinguished Research Publication Award from the National Association of Developmental Education. He received the 1994 Distinguished Faculty Award at the University of Texas at Austin.

Lynn Sullivan Taber is Senior Kellogg Research Associate and a Ph.D. candidate in Community College Leadership at the University of Texas at Austin. Lynn holds a B.A. in experimental psychology from Kent State University, an M.A. in college student personnel from the University of Colorado at Boulder, and a Master's of Management in marketing from Northwestern University. Employed as faculty member and administrator in community college education for 20 years, she has served at Laramie County Community College (WY); Triton College (IL); Florida Community College at Jacksonville; and the Community College of Denver (CO), where she completed a doctoral internship as assistant to the president. Her dissertation topic is the Denver Network, a community college/community collaboration. She has been a volunteer in numerous community services working with developmentally disabled adults, helping people learn to read, and participating in various community development activities.

Suanne D. Roueche is the director of the National Institute for Staff and Organizational Development (NISOD); editor of *Innovation Abstracts*, NISOD's weekly teaching tips publication; editor of *Linkages*, NISOD's quarterly newsletter; and lecturer in the Department of Educational Administration, College of Education, the University of

Texas at Austin. Author or co-author of more than 10 books and more than 30 articles and chapters, she was presented with the 1988 Distinguished Research and Writing Award by the National Council for Staff, Program, and Organizational Development. Suanne and John Roueche received the Distinguished Senior Scholar Award from AACC's Council of Colleges and Universities for *Between a Rock and a Hard Place: The At-Risk Student in the Open-Door College*. She is the recipient of numerous state and national awards in recognition for her leadership and service, including the Great Seal of Florida and the University of Texas at Austin's College of Education Distinguished Service Award. She has been named an Arkansas Traveler, a Kentucky Colonel, and a Yellow Rose of Texas.